# A Nursing Life:

## From Midleton to the Mater

# A NURSING LIFE:

## From Midleton to the Mater

**Aubrey Malone**

PENNILESS PRESS PUBLICATIONS

www.pennilesspress.co.uk

Published by

*Penniless Press Publications* 2019

© Aubrey Malone

ISBN 978-1-913144-00-5

Printed by Sprint Print, Rathcoole

# CONTENTS

## Early Years

My maiden name is Tuohy. I was born in Midleton in 1944. I'm told I come from a long line of blue-eyed brunettes who know what they want and will move heaven and earth to get it. I'm not sure about the last bit but I've always made up my mind quickly about things. I suppose that makes me boring, unlike the complicated children growing up these days who see so many sides to a situation and have that much more to weigh up as a result.

We grew up on McSweeney Terrace near the train station. There was always lots of activity around us. Sometimes Daddy used to bring us to the Clonmult monument and we played Blind Man's Buff there. It was built to commemorate fourteen men who died at an ambush in that village by the British Forces in 1921. Clonmult was just a few miles from us. In later years a slab was erected in front of it to commemorate a carpenter called John Walsh who was accused of making weapons for the United Irishmen during the 1798 Rising. He was flogged to death when he refused to give any of their names.

There were three in my family, all girls. That was regarded as a small number of children to have at the time. I'm the eldest. Maureen came along a year later. Then, after a gap of four years, May arrived. She was the pet, the 'bar of gold' as they say in Midleton.

I had a happy childhood but I don't think I appreciated it at the time. Do we ever? It's only now, reading stories of all the abuses that took place behind closed doors in the old days that I realise how lucky I was. We were surrounded by love all day and went to bed by the light of the silvery moon.

Most nights we said the rosary. We knelt on the floor with our elbows on the kitchen chairs. Daddy used to start it by saying, 'Thou, O Lord will open my lips.' We'd answer 'And my tongue shall announce thy praise.' We gave out one decade each when May was old enough to do that. Before she was, Daddy said two, the first and the last. Mammy gave out the second, I did the third and Maureen the fourth. I almost always lost count of the ten Hail Marys unless I looked at Daddy with his fingers on the beads. He usually knelt in front of me. When it was over we recited prayers for what seemed like the whole human race. These almost took longer than the rosary itself. Or maybe I was so tired it just felt like that.

Mammy came from better stock than Daddy. Her father was one of the biggest businessmen in the area. He had his hand in a lot of pies. Her uncle ran a pub in Cork. He spent most of his time upstairs doing the books, leaving his wife to pull the pints downstairs. When he died she sold it for a pittance. Afterwards she moved to Youghal.

Daddy grew up on a small farm outside the town. Mammy's father didn't approve of her going out with him. He did his best to turn her against him. 'A common labourer,' he was supposed to have said in disgust after she started to go steady with him, 'How could she sink so low?'

She met Daddy when he was doing some work at Grandad's house. They had a sofa that was in bits. They wanted it refurbished and Daddy offered to do it. He took it apart and re-built it from the ground up. Mammy said he made a lovely job of it. She used to make him cups of tea whenever he took a break from the work. That's how they got to know one another. Mammy knew Daddy was the man for her from the word go. She wasn't put off by Grandad.

After they married she said she was grateful to the sofa for bringing them together. Daddy said, 'Don't be too sure it was that. I'd been watching you go in and out of your house for a long time before the sofa job came up. Why do you think I was so quick to take it?' She was never sure if he was making that up or not. Either way it was a very romantic story.

Mammy had a sister called Bernie. She was a few years younger than her. She also had a brother, Seamus. He was always getting into trouble. He set fire to a pub once after being refused entry to it. He skipped off to America when the police started chasing him. Nobody ever heard from him afterwards. Mammy rarely talked about him. There was a rumour he died in a fight with a sailor in Pittsburgh one night. We were never sure if there was any truth in that. According to Mammy it could have happened. 'He'd pick an argument in a phone box,' she used to say.

Mammy's parents lived in a big house on Riverside Way on the banks of the Owenacurra River. It was only a few streets away from us. A lot of rich people lived there. We knew we had to be on our best behaviour when we were visiting them. There was a privet hedge in the garden and a tree-lined avenue up to the house. It had two bay windows at the front.

Her father, our 'Town Grandad', had a handlebar moustache. He always looked very severe. I thought he gave Granny a hard time. She was probably afraid of him. She didn't talk much. Every time she opened her mouth he shouted her down.

The house was huge but very cold – in all senses. It was also very dark. We were always brought into the 'good' room. All that meant to us was that we couldn't play in it. We just sat there while the adults had serious discussions about things that bored us rigid. It was long and rectangular with high ceilings. It had a piano and a big clock at the end of it – a grandfather one, suitably enough. The floors were wooden apart from the living-room one. That had a very luxurious carpet with lots of designs on it. I used to get dizzy looking at it.

We didn't enjoy the visits to our 'Town' grandparents much. We were too tense to. If you wanted something, even a drink of water, you had to ask for it. You were made to feel you were almost getting into heaven as the glass was taken down from the cabinet. It would be polished and polished before the water was put into it.

They owned one of the first televisions in the town but it was rarely turned on. They kept it inside a cupboard. You wouldn't have known it was there unless you opened it. We only had a wireless ourselves. It was bigger than their television. I loved looking at it in the dark. All the lights would be flashing. Daddy used to listen to boxing matches on it, especially the ones that came from America. Because of the time difference he often stayed up half the night waiting to hear how they turned out. If anyone asked him about a boxing match he'd say, 'I watched it on the radio.' It was almost like that to him.

Maureen and myself preferred music. We listened to Radio Luxembourg if we were allowed stay up late. I spent hours twiddling the knobs. I loved the funny noise it made when you were between stations. Maureen would be on the floor jigging around to songs like Bill Haley's 'Rock Around the Clock.' That was everyone's favourite song when it came out. I loved The Everly Brothers too, and Tommy Sands and Chubby Checker and Brenda Lee, Little Miss Dynamite.

The nuns in the convent hated us coming under these kinds of influences. They felt we'd be corrupted by them but that only made us want them more. Daddy told us 'Rock Around the Clock' was in a film and that some of the people who went to it got so excited they ripped up the cinema seats.

His parents, our 'Country' Granny and Grandad, were more welcoming than Mammy's. Their farmhouse had lots of nooks and crannies in it. It was covered with ivy on the outside. Even that made you feel welcome. I loved going out to see them. I used to feel a flutter of excitement going up the driveway and knocking on the door. Sometimes we were let stay the night. The next morning you'd hear cows and sheep in the surrounding fields.

The house was called Tara. It was named after the mansion in *Gone with the Wind*, Grandad's favourite film. The 'T' was missing so it just said 'Ara.' That must have confused the postman. Grandad never bothered replacing it. 'It sounds more Irish now,' he said. He had a mug with 'Tara' written on it. It was his mug and his alone. Nobody else was allowed drink from it.

Grandad had a big beard. Mammy said he could grow bees in it. I loved running my fingers through it. I had to stand on my tiptoes to do that.

He used to give us all big hugs when he saw us. He wore a woolly jumper that was full of holes. When we got inside the house there'd be a fire roaring in the hearth. You'd get the smell of meat and onions sizzling in the frying pan.

As we sat around the fireplace throwing sods of turf onto it he'd always say the same thing to me: 'Tell me everything that happened to you since the day you were born.' How could you answer a question like that? I used to look at him as if he was mad. Then he'd roar laughing.

Afterwards he'd take out his mouth organ. He was really good. Most of the songs he played were ones I didn't know but that didn't matter. I was fascinated by how fast his fingers moved. He got all sorts of notes, especially when he changed scales. He used to tap his foot as he played. Granny said to us, 'He won't be happy till he bores a hole in the floorboards.'

He often offered me a try at it but I was useless. Maureen couldn't get the hang of it either. I wondered how he got to be so good at it. He told me he taught himself. If he couldn't find it he used a comb with cigarette paper on it instead. That was harder. When I tried it, no sound came out. It was as if I was just blowing air.

Granny was quieter than Grandad. She spent most of her time in the kitchen. She used to whistle to herself to herself as she cooked. If you were near the pan she'd take something out of it and give it to you for a taste. She often smelt of garlic. I didn't like kissing her for that reason.

They had a dog, Mutty, that was a ball of energy. He didn't do any harm to anyone but he was very excitable. He used to nip at May's ankles until she cried. Grandad egged him on and that made her cry even more. Granny usually had to give her sweets to stop her. They had a supply of bullseyes in a cupboard that they kept specially for her because May was a big crier. After she'd had her fill of them she'd be fine again, at least until the next time Mutty started pulling at her. In time she got hysterical if he was anywhere near her, even if he was quiet and just wanted to be patted. But then one year Mutty was knocked down by a car and died. We all cried our eyes out when we heard the news. It was as if a human being had been taken from us.

Grandad gave us all the time in the world. He played games with us until the cows came home – literally. (Actually he didn't have many cows by the time we were growing up because he was in semi-retirement). My favourite one was Pin the Tail on the Donkey. We had great fun at that. Maureen nearly always won. She seemed to be able to see things even through a blindfold.

The games went on till all hours. We never wanted them to end. If we were staying the night we were put in the box room. It had a pitched roof on it. I banged my head off the beams any time I forgot to stoop. Maureen would go kinks laughing at me. 'Why can't we be put in one of the other rooms?' I kept asking. There were loads of unused ones.

They had a big garden out the back. It was like a jungle. That made it ideal for games of hide-and-seek. 'Don't get lost,' Grandad used to joke, 'People have ventured down there and never been heard of again.' There was a big tree in the garden with a rope tied to it. We swung around on it for hours, pushing each other around the bark until it knotted up and we had to start again. I often fell off and grazed myself. When I did, Grandad would treat it as a major accident, even for the tiniest cut. He'd take great care putting a plaster over the cut. He used to give me a sweet as a reward if I was brave and didn't cry. 'You'll be better before you're married,' he'd say after he put the plaster on.

Sometimes Maureen swung me too hard and I fell into a clump of nettles that were beside it. They stung like anything. I often howled as a result. It was worse than the pain you felt when you got slapped by the nuns in school. If it was bad enough, Grandad used to put ointment on it for me. He was very gentle applying it. He was so soft he hated hurting me even a little bit.

He loved hugging us. That was a novelty for us because neither Mammy or Daddy were showy. Not many people were in those days. They didn't throw their arms round one another like people do with their children now. In fact they didn't even hug one another. I can't ever remember seeing them kissing one another either. And of course they didn't tell us the facts of life. We were expected to pick those up in our own way. Or maybe by some sort of divine inspiration.

I got them from a girl I used to pal around with called Tess Meehan. She took great delight relating all the gory details to me one day in the schoolyard. Not that I believed a word of it. She was famous for making things up. She was such a notice box I thought she was just looking for attention. When she was finished I said, 'Tess Meehan, you're the worst liar I ever met.'

Tess was the girl who told me I wasn't dying when I got my first visit from 'Auntie Jane.' That was how we referred to our monthlies. Other people called it 'The Curse.' That was a more suitable name for it in my opinion. Why did Mammy not warn me about things like that? Maybe she assumed I'd be informed about it from someone like Tess. I was, but only after it happened. When you think you're bleeding to death it's a bit late to hear the words, 'It's just your period, you idiot.'

I walked to school every day with Maureen but I usually came home with Tess. The reason for that was because Maureen's classes didn't end until later than mine. A lot of the girls walked all the way in from the country. That meant miles in some cases. I felt sorry for them having to come so far. Now and then they'd fall asleep at their desks. The nuns we had in Babies and Low First felt sorry for them but Sister Serafina, our teacher from First Class on, used to rap them on the knuckles to wake them up. I wasn't spared either if I ever looked sleepy. The pain was very severe. It felt like pins and needles. I always sat on my hands to try and make it go away. If she saw you doing that she made you put them on the desk.

If Imelda Garvey told her father she'd been slapped in school she got another skelp from him at home for being bold. Daddy wasn't like that. He used to reward me for my pain. I usually got something like a Flash bar. I loved Flash bars. They cost twopence. I still remember the green wrapping they had on them.

You got slapped if you were late for school too. If we thought we were going to be late I used to climb over the wall at the back of our house. It was better than going the long way round by the lane that was at the front of it. I often scratched my coat on the briars if I tried to go too fast. Mammy gave out to me for that. She was always stitching it for me so the nuns wouldn't notice.

'If you got up in time we wouldn't have to go through this,' she said.

It was either that or something else. We couldn't be punctual if we tried and we suffered the consequences.

I never felt comfortable at school. Maybe that was because we weren't well off. Some of our clothes weren't as respectable as those of the other girls in the class. When we started wearing uniforms in our second year we all looked the same. That took the stigma away but I hated my one. It was far too long and it had a dark colour that depressed me. We were given a coat to wear over the uniform.

I hated that even more. I was always trying to think of ways of getting rid of it. It wasn't easy because our names were sewn into a label on the inside of the sleeve. One day there was a fierce downpour of rain and I seized my chance, turning it inside out so the rain would cause the ink to run. I threw it in a bush but the next day it was produced in front of the class.

13

Sister Serafina held it up before everyone. She said, 'Cé leis é?' That was Irish for 'Who owns it?' as I suppose you know. I felt like saying, 'Mind your own business, it's horrible anyway,' but obviously I kept my trap shut. I tried to act innocent by gazing blankly into space as she fastened her beady eyes on me. I looked out the window as if I I had nothing to do with it but when I didn't have one to wear home that day they put two and two together. They said I'd have to take it despite my protests that I'd never seen it before in my life. My name was sewn back in, this time in typescript instead of ink to stop any showers washing it away.

Cheeky escapades like that weren't in character for me. Most of the time I behaved myself. More often than not I was painfully shy. I never put my hand up in class, for instance, even if I knew the answer to a question. I hated being the centre of attention. I often felt that if I was absent from school I'd hardly have been missed. Not that I'd be bothered about such a thing. Being anonymous was a lot better than a teacher having a set on you.

That happened to Rosaleen Buttimer, one of my friends. She was usually in the wars for one thing or another. She brought a lot of it on herself. One day she tried to set her uniform on fire in the chemistry lab. She must have had a bit of Uncle Seamus in her.

School was boring most of the time. We sat like robots in woodwormed benches, half afraid to move in case we got a slap. We were never taught to like anything. It just had to be learned by heart. I was taught poetry the same way I was taught prayers. A lot of them meant nothing to me until years later. They were nothing more than words you parroted. Now and again you might get a flash and go, 'Oh so that's what they mean!' but it was rare.

We were taught most subjects through Irish. That made us hate them more. 'The English beat the Irish language out of us,' Daddy used to say, 'and then our teachers beat it back into us again.' Most of the emphasis was on grammar. That meant you never got a feel for the music of it. It just became drudgery.

Some of the girls were swots. The telitale sign was if they covered their copies in gelatine paper. One of them, Maura Dockery, covered hers in wallpaper. Talk about dedication.

Most of mine were falling apart. I kept tearing out pages anytime I got something wrong so Mammy and Daddy wouldn't see it. If you tore out a page at the front you had to tear one out of the back as well or it would hang out.

When I think of school now I find it hard to believe the things we put up with. You weren't allowed go to the toilet even if you were bursting. You'd put your hand up (the one that wasn't holding yourself 'down there') and wave frantically to get attention. When Sister Serafina finally decided to look at you she'd say something like, 'You can, but you may not.'

She had to be a bit more lenient after the day Imelda Garvey wet her knickers during the Irish class. I always felt grateful to Imelda for what came to be known as her 'little accident' that day. She saved a lot of us bladder problems in later years.

At the end of each day we burst through the gates like prisoners released from jail. Half three on Friday was like heaven. It meant two whole days without Sister Serafina, or 'Sore Fingers' as we nicknamed her. That was because of all the punishments she dished out with her ruler. Saturdays were for playing all our games, or visiting Grandad and Granny if we were good. Sunday was good too but as the day went on we'd get cramps in our stomachs thinking about having to face 'Sore Fingers' again the next morning.

On Sunday nights we were miserable. As we lay in bed trying to sleep, Maureen and myself used to say, 'Saturday night is my delight and so is Sunday morning but Sunday night gives me a fright to think of Monday morning.'

There was no joy in learning in those days. It wasn't the nuns' fault. It was the system. It was a system that said, 'You're here to suffer.' If you got a teacher who was soft you felt blessed.

There was a distance between us and the nuns that was never broached. If we saw them on the street we kept our heads down. They were like gods in habits to us. Our respect for them was tinged with fear. Some of the older ones looked saintly but they didn't teach. They seemed to be praying all the time. It was as if the tougher ones were reserved for us.

I didn't mind being hit for misbehaving but it was so wrong to have to suffer it for not knowing your lessons. God help you if you suffered from something like ADHD at that time. This condition hadn't been identified then, of course. The word 'hyperactive' wasn't in use either. If you were jigging about the place you were just seen as 'bold' and given six of the best – at least until the day Imelda Cawley had her 'accident.'

Imelda was the boldest girl in our class. She didn't know what fear meant. She was so bold she even knew what a French kiss was – the epitome of decadence for us.

There was a Retreat one year where we had to go without speaking for two hours. Imelda had verbal diarrhoea. For her not to be able to talk for two minutes was mental torture. She almost broke out in a cold sweat from the effort.

She loved making fun of things. She was so giddy you only had to look at her to want to go into hysterics. I thought she must have been born with a smile on her face. One day she put chewing gum on Sister Serafina's chair. She couldn't get up after she sat on it. You should have seen the look on her face. We all got detention for that. She suspected it was Imelda that did it but she couldn't prove it.

We all suffered when something like that happened. We were told we'd get off if we identified the culprit but that was the last thing any of us would have done. It would have been the ultimate betrayal. Some of the girls held it in for Imelda if they had to stay in after school if it was a nice day out but I didn't. To me it was worth it to see Sore Fingers' face as she tried to dislodge her bum from the seat without success.

Another day we were rhyming off our answers to the questions from our catechism book when Imelda got up to her tricks again. When Sister Serafina said 'Who made the world?' we all chorused 'God made the world.' That was the answer in the Catechism but Imelda wasn't happy with it. She put up her hand instead.

'What is it, child?' Sister Serafina asked.

'If God made the world,' she said, 'Who made God?'

Sister Serafina looked perplexed.

'What kind of a question is that?' she said, 'God made himself.'

Imelda couldn't contain herself when she heard that. She burst out laughing.

'What are you laughing at, you stupid girl,' Sister Serafina said.

'At somebody making themselves,' Imelda said, in between her giggles.

She was put sitting in a corner for the rest of the day for her insolence. She had to wear a dunce's cap on her head.

'Imelda Garvey,' Sister Serafina said as she stood there making funny faces at the rest of us when her back was turned, 'You're a disgrace to yourself and to the town of Midleton.'

Imelda didn't mind. After school that day I saw her at the convent gate with her gymfrock hoisted up to her waist. A group of boys were looking at her, their eyes popping out of their heads. A few minutes later she was playing 'kiss chase' with them. That was a game where you ran after boys to kiss them. I didn't know why Imelda did that because there were loads of boys interested in her. Maybe she just enjoyed it for the crack.

The nuns had their hands full with her. From the moment she woke up in the morning she was probably contemplating some mischief or other. Maybe Sister Serafina had to be tough with her. Very little work was done when she up to her tricks.

One day we got a composition to write called 'A Picnic I Enjoyed.' Imelda wrote, 'I didn't go on the picnic because the day was too wet.' That was the extent of her composition. When Sister Serafina saw it she threw Imelda's copy back at her with such force I thought she was going to break something. The pages fell out all over the room. Imelda was given a hundred lines for trying to be smart. I'd never have had the courage to do anything like that. I was far too nervous. Maybe that's why I enjoyed Imelda so much. She was my opposite.

Another day Sister Serafina gave me a note to bring around to all the other classes about an outbreak of head lice in the school. I got lost on my way back to our room and went in another door instead. A strange nun was standing there with a stick of chalk in your hand. 'What do you want?' she asked in a stern voice. I ran out the door. I started crying in the corridor because I didn't know where to go.

The caretaker came along after what seemed like an eternity. He asked me what class I was from. When I told him he led me back. As I opened the door Sister Serafina said, 'Where did you go to –

China?' Everyone went into convulsions laughing at me. I felt about six inches tall.

When I told Mammy what happened that evening she said not to worry about it, that it was only a small thing. Unfortunately I couldn't see it like that. I thought I'd made a total fool of myself. I felt so bad I told her I didn't want to go in the next day. She said I'd have to, that it would draw much more attention to me if I stayed out. In the end I gave in but my legs were like jelly as I went into the classroom the next morning. Nobody mentioned anything but I felt everyone was looking at me all day.

My life at school was a total contrast to home. I knew I could be myself there without thinking of anyone looking at me or passing judgment on me. That freed me up to be the cheery young girl I wanted to be, cavorting about the place like a wild animal if I felt like it.

Mammy and Daddy had a kind of 'open house.' There was always someone either coming or going. Most of them didn't need an invitation. They liked the fact that everything was so casual with us. We had a fridge with a door that didn't close properly and a formica table that didn't balance. You had to put bits of newspaper under one of the legs to stop it shaking. There was another table we played draughts on. It was circular. The draught board was embedded into it. We played games for pennies and argued tooth and nail about them. The next morning Mammy would find the pennies under the table. 'I think you enjoyed the arguments more than the draughts,' she said. There were chess pieces in a drawer on it but that was too hard for us so we didn't bother with them.

We had a big range in the kitchen. There was a pot of tea on it almost permanently. It started off weak enough but by the end of the day, after re-filling it for the umpteenth time and putting more tea leaves into it each time, you could almost run the proverbial mouse across it.

The Buckleys lived next door to us. Mr Buckley was a carpenter. You'd hear him hammering at all hours of the day and night. He never talked to us if he passed us on the street. It was as if we didn't exist. He didn't go to Mass either. People said he was a lapsed

Catholic. I didn't know what that meant. It sounded like some kind of disease. I wondered if there was a cure for it.

His wife was the opposite. She was an eccentric woman who spent a lot of her time kissing crucifixes. She never said anything to us but 'Nice day, thank God,' when she saw us. If you asked her a question she didn't answer you. She just screwed up her eyes.

The Buckleys didn't have any children. Instead they had two bulldogs. They terrified us. Any time I passed them on the street they growled at me.

'That's because they can sense your fear,' Daddy told me. 'Don't be afraid. The ones that growl don't normally bite. It's the same with people.'

There was a lot of wisdom in the things Daddy said. He didn't get much formal education but he had a lot of knowledge. I took his advice and found them quieter after that.

The man two doors up sold turnips. We used to think he looked like one as well. We called him Turnip Head. Daddy believed the way people lived affected the way they looked. He said people who owned dogs often started to walk like them. I didn't know about that but I used to go into stitches anytime I saw Turnip Head – at least when he wasn't looking at me. He had a terrible temper. You never knew what he'd do if he caught you laughing at him.

We got on much better with his wife than we did with Mrs Buckley. She had polio. She wore a lift in one of her shoes because one of her feet was shorter than the other. It was like a Cuban heel. It caused her to walk with a limp. I felt very sorry for her. She used to ask us to go down to the shops for her sometimes. It was always the same order: 'Two sausages, two Woodbines and a quarter pound of broken biscuits.' She'd give us a half crown and tell us to keep the change.

The people on the other side of us, the Dineens, had a big family. Mr Dineen worked in the creamery. His wife was a teacher. They had three sons and two daughters. The daughters were twins. They didn't play with us much, maybe because they were told not to. Mrs Dineen thought we weren't good enough for them. They didn't look like happy children to me. As soon as they were out of the cradle you got

19

the impression Mrs Dineen was already thinking about what they were going to do in life.

It can't have been much fun growing up in that kind of environment. Maureen and myself tried to take them out of themselves but if she was watching us it was difficult. They'd be whisked back inside the door as if we were bad influences. I'd hear her saying to them, 'Don't have anything to do with those girls if you know what's good for you. They're as common as muck.'

## Aunt Bernie's Mistake

The main visitor to our house was Aunt Bernie, Mammy's sister. She was my godmother. She lived about fifteen minutes away from us. A lot of the people in the town felt distant from her because she was so quiet. She also dressed strangely, walking around in high collars and gloves even in good weather.

Because she was our aunt, and because we liked her, we didn't judge her on her appearance. We took her as we found her. As we got to know her better, we hardly noticed what she was wearing or if it was out of season. We were just glad to see her.

She never bothered knocking at the door. She walked in as if she lived with us. A lot of the time it seemed as if she did. She had an easy manner with people she knew but if she wasn't comfortable with you it was impossible to get a word out of her.

She worked in the post office. We used to go in there sometimes just to see her. She was always very nice to us when we had something to post. She usually gave me something extra for myself as well as the change. When she did that she told me not to tell Mammy or Daddy.

She didn't marry. That surprised us all because she was beautiful to look at. She had lovely blue-green eyes and a heart-shaped face. I often asked Mammy why she never married. She always said something like, 'I don't know any more than you do. Sometimes that's just the way life works out.'

We grew up believing she'd had a child by a man called Dan Toibin, a farmer who lived out in the country. This was hushed up. It was referred to as 'Aunt Bernie's mistake.'

Dan was very good-looking and he knew it. There was always some woman or other hanging out of him. Mammy told Aunt Bernie she didn't think he was suitable for her but she didn't listen. How can you when you're infatuated with someone? Mammy felt she'd be hurt by Dan. She thought it was only a matter of time before he threw his eye on someone else.

They'd been going out together for a while when Dan met Una Conroy, the local beauty. He broke it off with Aunt Bernie soon afterwards. She made out as if it didn't bother her but everyone knew she was on the point of a breakdown. She hid it well but you could tell what she was going through from her face. I used to see her down in the church a lot. She always looked sad. She'd be doing the stations or maybe she'd be at Tenebrae or at Mass on The First Fridays, all on her own in a pew.

Other times I'd see her walking down by the river with her hands dug deep in her pockets. She'd always be lost in her thoughts, so much so that when you waved to her it would take her a few seconds to realise who you were.

Dan and Una married quickly. Aunt Bernie went to England soon after that. We never knew if she was pregnant or not with her 'mistake.' There was no way she could bring a child home with her if she was. Granny and Grandad wouldn't have stood for it. She'd have been seen to have committed an unpardonable sin. It wouldn't have mattered that she loved Dan.

That would have been almost irrelevant. Neither would Dan have been seen to have done anything wrong. The woman was always the guilty one in those days. It was her job to stop a man when he had too much to drink or went too far physically. The women had the babies and the men just waltzed back to their lives.

Granny went down to Dan's house one night before he married Una and asked him what his intentions were as regards Aunt Bernie. She wanted him to have a 'shotgun' marriage with her and to drop Una. There was no way Dan could have entertained such a notion. He was too smitten with Una.

Granny said, 'You put her in the family way; you have obligations,' but Dan said he'd heard Aunt Bernie had been with other men as well as himself. That was a big lie as she'd never looked at another man before Dan. It was a line men used to get themselves off the hook. Granny knew he was making it up but what could she do? It was long before DNA tests or anything like that. Not that it would have made a difference anyway. Dan had his mind made up. A million DNA tests wouldn't have changed it. Granny went home that night in a much worse state than she went out.

She felt sorry for Aunt Bernie, sorrier than Grandad anyway, but she couldn't have her in the house in her condition. She'd have been the shame of the town, a scarlet woman.

Some people believed Dan offered Aunt Bernie money to have 'something done' with the child in England. That was their way of saying he wanted it aborted. We all knew she would have totally gone against that idea. It would have broken her heart to give it up for adoption but in those days it was the only option if you wanted to keep your good name. She disappeared before any bump became visible. Nobody was ever sure if she had a baby or what she might have done with it. She was given leave of absence from the Post Office on health grounds but tongues wagged.

She went back to her job after she came home. She seemed to be a different person. The glow returned to her cheeks. It was as if she'd finally got Dan out of her system. Granny and Grandad were relieved that they could go on with their lives now like they'd always done, as pillars of the community, but they kept a closer eye on Aunt Bernie than ever before. She wasn't allowed any freedom at all now.

Some of the people on her street got wind of what happened. The narrow-minded ones cut her dead any time they passed her on the street. It was just as gossipy as McSweeney Terrace even though it was more upmarket. Behind the lace curtains everyone still wanted to know everyone else's business.

I always thought Aunt Bernie was more relaxed in our house than in her own one. She was quiet with her parents but chatty with Mammy and Daddy. She was always bringing us presents. One year she brought me a teddy bear that had a key at the back of it. It played 'Tulips from Amsterdam' when you wound it up.

A lot of people in Midleton regarded her as a sad case because she didn't marry. She seemed to give up on men after Dan, or maybe she thought men gave up on her. We never knew. She was usually deep in conversation with Mammy any time she called to us after she came back from England. I often wondered what they were talking about.

Any time I asked Mammy she'd just say it was 'boring adult talk' or something like that. If it was that boring, I'd think, why were they whispering or looking so intense? Aunt Bernie was quick to stop talking if I ever came into the room when they were having their heart-to-hearts. She'd jump up from her seat as if there was a bomb under it. Then she'd change the conversation onto me. She'd pull something from her pocket that she'd picked up for me on the way to the house, a gift, maybe, or a toy.

That was the year I made my First Communion. I was meant to feel holy but I didn't, or at least not as holy as I was expected to. There was too much happening. I got a lovely dress to wear and there was a photo taken of me in it. We put it in an album. Daddy had copies made. He showed it to people with great pride. Aunt Bernie gave me a ten shilling note and I treasured it. I promised myself I'd never spend it but of course I did, probably on something stupid. I can't even remember what I used it for now.

We made our First Confession shortly before that. I tried to make up false sins to confess because I couldn't think of any real ones.

Later on I had many. I used to go to Fr McCarthy to tell them. They said he was half deaf and could hardly hear you. There'd be a big queue outside his box for that reason. We convinced ourselves we could tell him we'd murdered someone and he'd still just give us three Hail Marys for our penance. But then one day we heard him shouting 'You what?' to someone in the confession box, his voice roaring down through the church. It was as if he suddenly got his hearing back. After that the queues trailed off.

Maureen made her First Communion the year after me. She was given a ten shilling note by Aunt Bernie too.

'I hope you won't be jealous,' she said to me as she was giving it to her.

'How could I be?' I said, 'You've given me so much over the years.'

She was glad to hear that. I read in a book once that the eldest child in a family can feel threatened when another one arrives and takes the attention away from them. I'm happy to say that was never the case between Maureen and me. In some ways I felt like her twin. We thought the same way about things. Sometimes we even started to say the same sentence when we were talking to one another. We walked to school together every day.

If Daddy was working on a building site our route he'd wave to us if he saw us passing. If it was sunny weather he'd be stripped to the waist, his skin glistening with sweat. Sometimes Mammy gave us sandwiches to bring to him. They were always the same: bacon with a slice of lettuce on them.

I loved roaming around the buildings he worked in if we had time to do that. A lot of them didn't even have floors in them so you had to be careful not to fall through the beams. He was usually drilling at something. The drill was so noisy it almost broke the sound barrier.

We used to put our hands in our ears if we were near him. We screamed to drown out the sound, or maybe just because we were excited. He wore ear plugs himself. If we said something to him he usually didn't hear us. Sparks of electricity used to fly off his drill when he was using it. They reminded me of fireworks. He wore a mask over his eyes to protect them. It was made of fibre glass or something like that. Maureen and myself could have stayed there all day but he'd rush us off to school, telling us 'Sore Fingers' would be out at the gate waiting for us with her ruler. Often he was right.

When Daddy came home in the evenings the first thing he did was put his drill in the garage with all his other things. We were never allowed go in there. It was like his sacred place. If ever something was broken in the house he'd go out to the garage for the necessary tools to fix it. He worked with such concentration, Mammy had to tell him to slow down sometimes. I remember her saying to him once, 'Rome wasn't built in a day.' Daddy said back to her, 'I wasn't on that job.'

He was very conscientious at his work but he found it hard to relate to the other people with him. They were rougher than he was. They talked about things he wasn't interested in, like sports and politics. A lot of them passed smart comments about women as well and that upset him.

If a woman walked by in a short skirt she'd get whistled at. When I started to develop breasts I got a few whistles from the people who worked with him. Daddy didn't like that but I didn't mind. It made me blush a bit but I was still flattered.

'I only work with these people because I have to,' he told us, 'Some of them would turn the air blue with their language.' A lot of them were in bad marriages, he said, and were cynical about women as a result. Daddy couldn't be cynical if you paid him.

As soon as their shift ended they all went down to the pub. Daddy joined them more often than not so he wouldn't be called a stick-in-the-mud but he didn't enjoy these evenings. They were all about sounding more impressive than the next fellow, he said, or drinking yourself silly. A lot of the time the ones who overdid it would be late for work the next morning as they slept off their hangovers. Daddy would have to cover for them.

One day the foreman who was working with him couldn't make it in. When Daddy met him the next day he asked him what was wrong with him. The man said, 'I got a bad pint in the pub. I don't know if it was the thirteenth or fourteenth.' Daddy wasn't amused at jokes like that.

He was often jeered for being too much of a family man. It was as if that was something to be ashamed of. He was also jeered for having daughters instead of sons too. Some of the people he worked with thought you weren't a real man unless you had sons. The foreman with the drink problem once accused him of being 'henpecked' by Mammy. Nothing was further from the truth. He never wanted a longer leash than she gave him.

'If I had a few affairs,' he said to her one night, 'they'd probably like me more on the site.' Mammy threatened to hit him with the frying pan if he came out with any more stuff like that. Daddy was amused.

'Maybe it's true that I'm henpecked after all,' he concluded.

He worked so hard it took a toll on his health. He had asthma and he was always getting viruses. He wouldn't spend the money to see a doctor so they took ages to go away. It would have been cheaper to pay the medical fee and get back to work but he didn't see it that way. He thought anything you gave to a doctor was money down the drain.

'Bugs go away in their own time,' he claimed, 'A doctor just charges you to watch nature take its course. He hated taking pills. He wouldn't take a sleeping pill to save his life. I often heard him tossing and turning in his bed when he couldn't sleep. Now and again he'd go down to the kitchen in the middle of the night and make himself a cup of tea.

If he was bad with the asthma he had to get the doctor and take to the bed. He hated doing that but Mammy insisted. Sometimes I did my homework in his bedroom. He'd coach me through it in his hoarse tones, struggling to get the words out. He was usually in the same pyjamas, the wine ones with the flower pattern and the white cord. It was painful watching him being forced away from work he loved. He'd look out the window at people drilling holes in the street and I'd see the sadness in his eyes.

When he was well he made up for all the lost time. He worked double shifts at whatever job he was on to try and make up for any wages he'd missed out on when he was laid up. Anytime he got a few pounds together he spoiled us rotten. He was always bringing home treats to the 'two best girls in Ireland.' (After May arrived that became the best three).

He was so relieved to be back at work he'd get almost high. Sometimes he went to the pub with his friends at times like that. He had no tolerance for drink because he took it so seldom. A small amount had an effect on him. When he was tipsy he'd sing sloppy songs and become sentimental. Most of them were old Irish airs.

The only English song he seemed to know was Lonnie Donegan's 'My Old Man's A Dustman' and he even got the words of that wrong. Whenever he started singing it we found it almost impossible to get him to stop. He'd do the same verses over and over again until we were fit to scream.

When he was in good form he unloaded his supply of riddles on us. One of them was, 'What noise annoys a noisy oyster?' The answer was, 'Any noise annoys a noisy oyster.' Another one went, 'Supposin' supposin' three men were frozen. Two died. How many were left? Answer: None, because it was only supposing.'

He had a big supply of corny jokes. I still remember some of them. 'What's the difference between a duck?' Answer: 'One of its legs is the same.' His favourite one was, 'Did you hear the one about the three eggs? Too bad.' (In other words, 'Two bad').

Mammy used to groan and say, 'The first time I heard that one I fell out of the cradle laughing.' We mainly enjoyed his jokes because he enjoyed them so much himself. We laughed at his laughter more than the jokes.

As we were lying in bed at night he'd say, 'Will I tell you a story about Johnny McGory? Will I begin it? That's all that's in it.' Then

27

he'd tickle us. When Daddy tickled you, you knew you were tickled. May used to scream with excitement when he tickled her. You could nearly mistake this for hysteria. Mammy thought he was more childish than us. She told him once that she was thinking of getting a soother for him.

If there was a good film on in the local cinema he'd bring us to it. We saw a lot of Ealing Studio films with actors like Alec Guinness and Stanley Holloway. If he had sons he'd probably have brought us to adventure films. Maybe he'd have preferred these but he was never selfish like that. Most of the ones we saw were romances. Now and then we saw a cowboy film. Jack Elam was usually the baddie. We thought his name was Jack Flam.

I remember being entranced with a film called *Now, Voyager*. That was the one where Paul Henreid put two cigarettes into his mouth and lit them, one for himself and one for Bette Davis, his co-star. In those days you were allowed to smoke in the audience too. It made it more like being at home. People didn't know too much about the dangers of passive smoking then. I used to love watching Marlene Dietrich with a cigarette in her mouth. She seemed to smoke them down to her toes. We heard a rumour that she had her back teeth removed to give her cheeks a sunken look. You'd hear crazy stories about Hollywood in those days. We were even crazier to believe them.

Another film Daddy brought us to was one called *Random Harvest*. It was showing in a cinema in Cork that specialised in old classics. I cried all the way through it. Daddy felt so sorry for me he put me on his lap to comfort me. May cried for a different reason – she wasn't tall enough to see the screen. All through the film she kept asking Daddy what was happening. It drove him crazy when she did that.

Every few minutes she'd jump up and say something like, 'What are they saying?' or 'Is the film any good? I can't see it.' Sometimes he had to bribe her to be quiet with sweets. Maybe she couldn't accept the fact that I was the one on his lap when she was younger than me.

'I'm never going to a film again,' she said on the way out of *Random Harvest*, 'Never again in my whole entire life.' The following week she was begging Daddy to take her to another one.

I remember the night the cinema closed down. It was after we were at a film called *Mrs Miniver* with Greer Garson. 'She's Irish,' Daddy said, 'Not too many Irish people made it big in Hollywood.' By now audiences had trailed off so much the cinema was practically empty. Most people wanted to see the new films. The manager was heartbroken. He'd have kept it going forever but he was practically bankrupt.

His bank manager forced him to sell it. The new owner turned it into a shop selling sporting goods. The manager was never the same again. He didn't know what to do with his time. He'd grown up on the old movies and now his passion was taken away from him. I heard he could never bear to pass by the building afterwards.

If we weren't able to get to the cinema we watched television. There were lots of cowboy programmes – Tom Mix out on the prairie, The Lone Ranger jumping from balconies onto his horse, William Boyd grey before his time as Hopalong Cassidy, the mysterious hero Zorro (we always called him Zo-Ro) dressed all in black and carving 'Z' onto his victims after he defeated them.

There were lots of comedies as well. We watched Terry Thomas with the gap in his teeth and Satch from the Bowery Boys with his baseball cap back to front and Charlie Chaplin eating his shoe and The Three Stooges bopping one another on the head or pulling each others noses. I liked Bob Hope with his ski slope nose and his corny jokes. Maureen used to laugh at Jack Benny being mean and trying to play the violin and calling out 'Rochester!' in that droning voice he had.

My favourite cartoon was Sylvester the Cat. He had a funny way of pronouncing words. He used to say things like 'I tawt I taw a puddydat. I did, I did see a puddydat!' There was a bear in it that couldn't say 'Sylvester' properly. He kept calling him George. 'Don't call me George,' Sylvester said to him one day, 'Call me Sylvester.' The bear replied, 'Okay George, I'll call you Sylvester.'

There was a bird in it too. He was called Tweety. He had a song that went, 'I'm a tweet little birdie and I'm in my cage, Tweety's my name but I don't know my age.'

When the weather was fine we didn't bother with films or television. Instead Daddy drove us to Shangarry in his Ford Anglia. We usually played 'I Spy' on the way. We amused ourselves by adding up the figures on the number plates on the cars ahead of us. Maureen was always first with the answer.

From Shangarry we went to the beaches of Ardnahinch and Ballynamona. I used to get a flutter in my stomach when we were going down the hills. We brought Aunt Bernie with us whenever we could. I always sat on her knee in the back seat. She'd dandle me up and down and sing songs to me. I remember one time we hit a pothole and I banged my head off the ceiling of the car. She went into a panic about that even though I was hardly hurt at all.

The sight of the beach was like magic to us. We'd spot it as we rounded the last bend for Shangarry. Daddy used to screech to a halt as we got to it. Sand would fly up over the windscreen. We'd take our buckets and spades from the boot to make sand castles.

If there was an ice cream van there we'd shout, 'I scream, you scream, we all scream for ice cream.' We used to hear it before we saw it. It played a song.

Daddy bought us cones if he could afford it. I always bit the bottom off my one. I sucked the ice cream down when I had the top part of it eaten. That was the quickest way to get at it. 'Greedy glutton,' May would say, gawking at me, but she was really the greediest of us. She always insisted on a 99. Maureen didn't like cones. She usually had a Golly Bar instead.

The car often broke down on the way to the beach. We all had to get out and push it if it did, including Daddy. He'd run along the side of it with the door open. He'd jump in as it began to gain speed. I was always afraid he'd leave it too late and it'd run away on him but he never did. As he sat in he'd pump the accelerator to keep the engine ticking over. When he got it going he'd rev it up high. Then he'd beep at us to get in. We usually cheered when we did that. He took off so fast you could smell the rubber of the tyres burning off the tarmac on the road.

We didn't have enough money to take a proper holiday but we enjoyed these day trips just as much, especially if Mammy packed a picnic for us. She'd usually have jam sandwiches and orange squash for us. Maureen and myself went swimming almost as soon as we got there, or at least flapping about in the water. Daddy tried his best to teach me but I resisted. When we came out of the water Mammy would have the sandwiches out. May used to get really upset if there was eany sand in them.

'Is that why they're called sandwiches?' she said one day. We laughed about that for years afterwards. It became a family joke. If we wanted to get a rise out of her we'd say, 'Would you like some *sand*wiches, May? We could have them on the *sand*.' She went mad when we did that. She ran after us and kicked us on the ankles if she caught us.

We played a lot of games on the beach. Rounders was our favourite. We used rulers for the wicket and a hurley stick for the bat. We dragged it along the sand to make the markings of the area we were going to be playing in. Maureen was like a ferret as she raced around the place. I kept trying to hit her with a tennis ball but I rarely got her. She'd slide home like a professional into the markings.

Some games we played just to get May worked up. I'd call her over to me and start talking to her about something. Meanwhile, Siobhan would crouch down behind her. Then I'd push her and she'd fall over her. Or else we'd make a hole in the sand and cover it with a page of newspaper, sprinkling sand over it so she wouldn't see it. If she fell in she'd get livid. Mammy didn't like it when we played games like that. She said they were dangerous.

We also played hide-and-seek. It was a bit different to the version we played in the house. We drew a square on the sand where the seekers had their base. There were two of these. One stayed at the base and the other went searching for the hiders in the dunes. The hiders tried to escape the first seeker and then run around the second one to get into the square. If you did that you won the game but it didn't happen much. Usually the seekers won unless the square was very big and you could run around it until they were too tired to catch you.

If the weather wasn't good enough to go to the beach we played on the street. We had no end of games – Queenie, hopscotch, skipping, leapfrog, marbles, tig – or tag as they call it nowadays. Sometimes we recited nursery rhymes as we were playing. Things like 'Jump, jump, sugary lump, the more you eat the more you jump, shake the blankets, shake the blankets turn the blankets over.'

There was an orchard at the end of our street. It was owned by a man who had a pellet gun. We used to rob apples from it by climbing as high as we could on the trees. If the apples were too high up we knocked them down with sticks. We reached the orchard through a hole in the wall. After a while he got wise to us and packed it up with brambles.

When he did that we had to climb the wall. I wasn't much good at climbing so Maureen helped me. She used to cup her hands for me. I'd put my foot into them and get a grip on it that way. Then I'd do the same for May. One day the man lost his temper with us and started firing bullets at us from his gun. One of them whizzed past so close to my ear I felt the wind of it. When Daddy heard about that he freaked out. He told me I could have lost an eye. That was the end of my apple-robbing.

We played in the house when the weather was wet. Musical Chairs was one of our favourite indoor games. May nearly always won. That was because she pushed everyone else out of the way when she wanted to sit down on one of the chairs. If we accused her of cheating she'd threaten never to speak to any of us again. Either that or she'd give us one of her 'I'll kill you,' looks.

Cards was another great favourite with us. We played Sevens and 25 and Rummy and Banker and Switch. When we got older we got in on poker. I was told I had a good poker face. I wasn't sure if that was good or bad. Maureen said, 'It means you're sly,' 'Thanks for the compliment,' I said. She was easier to read. If she had a good hand she blushed. If she was bluffing she blushed as well but in a different way.

Over the years I learned to distinguish between the two types. I got to know whether it was a good idea to 'see' her or throw in my hand when she put her money on the table. We only gambled for pennies but we got very worked up about them. The next morning

Mammy would find the pennies under the table. 'Look,' she'd say, 'That's what you were nearly losing your reason about.'

She was usually too busy bustling about the house to join us in the games. Sometimes she got migraine as well. If she got an attack of it we had to stop playing. The noise made it worse for her. She used to go into the bedroom and lie there in the darkness until it went away. She got lights in front of her eyes with it.

If she was bad we had to get Doctor O'Reilly to come to the house. I remember one day asking Daddy how she was. He said, 'She's in bed with the doctor.' He didn't realise what he said until we all started laughing. It became a family joke in time like the one about May's sandwiches.

One year Mammy had to get Dr. O'Reilly to the house three times in a month. Not long afterwards Daddy had him up to treat him for his asthma. The rest of us were always running temperatures. We had a lot of doctor bills. They depressed Daddy if he was struggling with money. I often saw him biting his nails as he sat by the phone. He'd be waiting for it to ring with some job offer he was waiting to come through. He'd have dug the roads to earn a few pounds to make our lives more comfortable.

When he was on a job he gave it everything. His bosses praised him for that. Mammy worried about the way he took so much out of himself to get things finished fast. He worked his fingers to the bone.

One day he came home as black as the ace of spades, as she put it. He'd just been demolishing a house and was fit to drop.

'You look as if a building fell on you,' she said to him.

'It did!' he said. I didn't know if he was joking or not. You never knew with Daddy.

The best times for him were when he was doing contract work. Some of these jobs lasted months. They saved him having to look up the papers for nixers. He got paid what he called 'wet time' on them. That basically meant you were still earning money even if you were only sitting around waiting for the rain to stop. That was the usual scenario but one company he worked for was so stingy they sent him home on these days so he ended up with nothing at all. He never complained about things like that. He just said, 'That's the way.'

He was often laid off in winter when the bad weather made work impossible. He wasn't in any kind of union so he had nothing to fall back on. There was no social security then. Even if there was he wouldn't have qualified for it because he was self-employed. Mammy thought it might be an idea for him to go to England but he didn't go for that. He had a Republican background. His uncle had been in the IRA and his politics were influenced by him. Negative feelings against the English were ingrained in him. 'I'd prefer to starve here than be rich over there,' he said. One of his heroes was Terence MacSwiney, the Cork republican who died on hunger strike in 1920. And of course Michael Collins.

When he was out of work for any kind of a long stretch, Mammy brought a few pounds in by doing sewing for some of the people who lived in the area. He appreciated her doing that but it was never going to be enough to feed five mouths even if she worked from dawn till dusk. When we were really badly off we got help from the Vincent de Paul.

I know how much it hurt Daddy to go down that road but sometimes he had to. He'd be in the back room when the volunteers called with their little envelopes containing cash or vouchers for fuel. Mammy always dealt with them. He was too ashamed to. He was terrified the neighbours would find out, in particular the Dineens. The only reason he agreed was because we were so much in debt to the shops for groceries and things.

One year the electricity was cut off. That was an eye-opener for all of us about how bad things were. I did a lot of my homework by candle-light around that time. In a way it was romantic, at least until the night I bumped my knee off a steel bar in the pantry. It bucketed blood. That caused all sorts of alarm bells to ring for Mammy and Daddy.

I remember looking at Daddy biting his nails one night in the dark as he tried to figure a way out of the problem. Eventually we had to pawn Mammy's wedding ring to get the supply put back on again.

Afterwards we had to be careful about everything. Daddy said, 'I'm afraid there'll be no treats from now on.' I knew it broke his heart to say that. Maureen and myself accepted it but May used to get so hysterical Mammy often had to give her a smack to bring her to her senses. Daddy told us we'd be in the Poor House if we weren't conscious of everything we spent. I didn't know what the Poor House was but from the sound of it I didn't want to end up there.

For the next few years Mammy and Daddy were put to the pin of their collars to take care of us. The idea of going to England came up again at that time. Mammy said he'd have to forget about his politics if it was the only place that offered him work. She didn't want him to go there unless it was absolutely necessary. She was afraid he'd get into a drinking scene over there like so many other emigrants in the building trade.

Things improved a bit when he was put working on a house in Kenmare. It needed a total overhaul. He got a lot of money from that contract. It meant we crawled out of the bottom of the barrel.

It was a long time since we'd bought anything new for the house. Now we started to think that way. We went shopping for things that didn't cost an arm and a leg. Second hand furniture was cheap. We bought end-of-the-line carpets for half nothing. Daddy was great at matching them up if they had patterns. He loved challenges like that. He'd be hours looking them up and down trying to get them to fit. We also bought things on Hire Purchase. Daddy referred to it as the Never Never.

'Why is it called the Never Never?' May asked him.

'Because you never get out of it,' he told her.

We were always topping up our loans instead of paying them off in full. It was a trap Daddy fell into, especially around Christmas when he didn't want to fall into the hands of the moneylenders.

One day he came home with a television set that looked the worse for wear. 'I got a good deal on it,' he told Mammy. 'I hope you did,' she replied, 'It looks like it's going to fall apart.' When she asked him if it worked he said, 'It does if you kick it.' It had one of those rabbit's ears aerials at the top of it.

When we got interference (or 'snow' as we called it) we took the ears off it and tilted them sideways to get it to work better. Sometimes we put them on a chair to get rid of the snow. We all became very good at that – and at kicking it when nothing else worked. We watched it every night for hours even if there was nothing good on it. It was like a toy that kept us going for hours. Maybe that was because we couldn't afford any other kind of toy.

Our circumstances got better after Daddy landed a week's contract to do up a house in Sneem. The man originally commissioned for the job had a drink problem. He fell out of his truck one night when he'd drunk too much and broke his leg. He was lucky not to get trapped under the wheels. The owner of the company knew Daddy slightly. He had his number in a book so he gave him a ring. Daddy was always great to jump at a minute's notice if something like that came up. He told him he'd be on the next bus. He threw his spirit level and a few tools into a bag and off out the door with him in his boiler suit. He'd have been sleeping in it if Mammy hadn't run down the street after him with his pyjamas.

It was a huge job, a total overhaul of the house. Daddy was doing the carpentry. Some other men were handling the electrical work and the plumbing. It was too far away for him to come home at night so he was put up in a house his boss owned. It was near the one he was renovating.

He rang home every night if he got a chance. Often he'd be out of breath. Mammy was run off her feet that week. I had the flu and Maureen was having trouble at school. She had a bad teacher that year. Nothing was going into her head at all. Mammy went through her homework with her every night in between bringing me meals up to bed. May was acting up as well. She always did when she wasn't the centre of attention. Normally she'd be Daddy's little darling at times like that but there was no Daddy. I could hear her screaming for attention from my bed. Whenever she did that, Mammy gave her a list of jobs she had for her to do around the house. That got rid of her quick enough. Anytime you mentioned anything about housework to May you wouldn't see her heels for the dust.

When Daddy came home he flopped into a chair. His boiler suit stank to high heaven. There was cement in his hair. I hardly recognised him at first. His face was all grease. 'They nearly threw me off the bus,' he chortled. He was almost high. There were wads of notes sticking out of his pocket. He threw them in the air and asked us to collect them. 'Finders keepers,' he said.

36

I couldn't believe you'd get that much money for a week's work. He said he was at it from the second he woke up to the second he went to bed. Mammy couldn't wait to get his suit off him to put in the washing machine. She had a big feed in the oven for him. He tucked into it as if he hadn't eaten for a month. 'I should go away more often,' he said as he munched away.

We lived like lords for a while but then there was a lull. Mammy would have loved him to have steady work but it was always a feast or a famine with him.

The closest he came to a regular job was one time when a builder came down from Dublin and took him on. He was a cute shot. He'd bought up a lot of abandoned houses around Midleton at dirt cheap prices. Daddy and a few other men made them ready for him to re-sell at a profit. Some of them had been with him on the Sneem job.

We didn't want for anything for the next good while. We'd have been better off if the money was consistent but it wasn't. That was because the builder didn't pay Daddy until whatever house he was working on was finished. Mammy thought there was something fishy about that. It meant the money used to come all at once. At the end of a job he'd be flush, just like after Sneem, except this time there was even more money.

The treats of old started to re-appear now. We got loads of goodies and Mammy was never short of shopping money. The icing on the cake was when he drove us into Cork for shopping sprees.

They didn't last too long. Within a year the market went bad. The builder scooted off and left a string of debts behind him. For his last job he gave Daddy a 'rubber' cheque instead of cash. It was the oldest trick in the book but Daddy fell for it. He was too trusting like that and he paid the price. 'There's one born every minute,' Mammy said, 'and two to take him.'

I remember the day the cheque bounced. Daddy had been on cloud nine going to the bank to cash it but he was only a few minutes at the counter when he was given the bad news. Afterwards he got roaring drunk. When he came home he started cursing, something I'd never heard him do before.

The materials the builder put into the houses was useless as well. It's a wonder they didn't all fall down. 'They're like paper houses,'

37

Daddy told us when the people he worked for came up to us complaining. 'If you sneezed,' he said, 'A wall would probably cave in.' It wasn't his fault. He was more involved in the carpentry end than the building but he was still blamed for it.

He wasn't the only one out of pocket. So were a lot of electricians and plumbers who were working with the builder. They tried to chase him through the courts but he was using a false name so they got nowhere. He'd met Daddy in a pub and employed him by what Daddy called 'a gentleman's agreement.' That meant he spat on his hand and then shook it. His phone number was written on the top of a discarded packet of Woodbines cigarettes. Whenever Daddy rang it he didn't get any answer. Eventually he went to a solicitor to see if there was anything he could do but he got the same answer as the plumber and the electrician.

'I'd forget about him if I were you,' the solicitor advised Daddy, 'He's probably skipped the country long ago. He could be in Ethiopia by now.' Daddy said, 'Where's that?' The solicitor just laughed at him. 'What does it matter?' he said, 'You're not thinking of going out there, are you? If you do, I'm afraid all you'll get is a sun tan.'

After that it was back to lean rations again for all of us. Mammy took it the worst of all.

'How did you let that chancer hoodwink you?' she said.

'Because I happen to take people at face value. Is that a crime?'

'I knew he was a bad egg from day one. It was as plain as the nose on his face.'

Daddy's work from then on was inconsistent. Some jobs only paid buttons. I was sad for him but he accepted it.

'It's better than a kick in the behind,' he'd say, even if he was only getting a fraction of what he was worth. He always looked on the bright side but when there was no work he got very down in himself. Mammy was still furious about the developer. 'Make sure you get money in the hand from now on,' she told Daddy, 'It's the only thing you can count on.'

They rarely talked about money to us but you could tell from their faces when things were bad. Daddy hid it more but the spectre of the Poor House haunted him - or the fear that the Local Council might take our house.

The sadder he was, the happier he acted with us. 'Who wants to hear a funny story?' he'd say if he got bad news. That shifted his attention away from it.

We loved his stories whether he was telling them because he liked to or to get his mind off his troubles. He never read them to us from books. He had difficulty reading because he left school at 15 but that didn't matter. He had much better ones in his head. With his imagination he could have been a great dramatist in today's world. Nobody thought like that then. If you couldn't read you were classed as illiterate and that was that.

When Mammy and Daddy were locked in their world of money problems we were left to grow up worry-free. If something was wrong we weren't told about it. 'Childhood is precious,' Mammy used to say to us, 'Enjoy it while it lasts.'

She always claimed a mother's best years were when children were very young. She said the happiest day of her life was the day she was told she was pregnant with me. I almost felt like crying when she said that. She was just as happy when she heard she was going to have Maureen and May. She never made any distinction between us but I thought I was her favourite even if she didn't say it. I was supposed to be the mature one because I was the eldest. Maureen was more emotional than me. May was more vulnerable.

I spent most of my time with Maureen because of the closeness of our ages. We slept in the same room. We often stayed awake half the night talking. We used to go through everything that happened that day. It was mostly talk about school when we were young. In later years it was boys.

They showed more of an interest in me than Maureen at first. I was believed to be better-looking than her but I didn't think I was. After a while they tended to get bored by me. When they got to know Maureen they became more fascinated by her over time. I think that was because she had more sides to her than me. With me what you saw was what you got, for better or worse. In other words I was a typical Cork lass. Maureen was different. She had a mystery about her. It intrigued anyone she ever went out with.

The nuns were always warning us about the dangers of men. We were advised to fold our arms so our chests would be covered. They must have thought men spent all day looking at women's breasts. I didn't get that impression. Or maybe it was that they just weren't interested in my ones.

They said if you sat on a boy's lap you should put some paper between you and him in case he got bad thoughts. Maureen told me one of her friends was warned not to wear patent leather shoes because a man could see your knickers if he used the shoes as a mirror. That sounded a bit elaborate to me. The boys I knew had more direct ways of trying to see my knickers. Tim O'Neill tried it one day by pulling up my skirt. I reacted by whacking him in the face. Older fellows stood at street corners in their drainpipe trousers making smart comments at us as we passed.

'Nice tits,' they'd say, or something equally childish. After a while we learned to ignore them. I thought boys who made comments like that were awkward with girls. They didn't make a very good job of hiding it. Other ones said nothing but they looked like they could rape you if they got you on their own. That was more of a danger if you were wearing something revealing like a low top or a mini-skirt. The nuns would have gone mad if they saw us like that. Maureen said I should have worn shorter dresses because I had good legs but I was too embarrassed to. I was happier when they were down below the knee. 'I'd kill to have legs like yours,' she'd say to me, 'I couldn't go near a mini with my cricket sticks.'

I spent hours talking about clothes with Maureen. That's something men can never understand about women. Maybe I didn't understand it myself either but we still did it. 'Does that go with my blue dress?' I'd ask her, twirling myself around in a blouse I'd just bought. Or, 'Do you think Sean Coughlan would like me in this coat? Or Peter Cronin?'

Sean Coughlan and Peter Cronin were the two 'pin-ups' from the boy's school. I imagined them going to Hollywood to be movie stars when they grew up. One day I saw the two of them in a chipper and we fell into conversation. Sean told me he liked a pinafore dress I had. That put me into seventh heaven. I couldn't wait to get home to try it on. If he'd said he liked me in a binliner I'd have worn it.

I went on a date with him once but it didn't go well. I felt he was trying his best to like me but couldn't. A few months later he asked

Maureen to go to a film with him. He even kissed her at it. She felt she had to confess that as a sin in confession because she didn't resist him. The priest asked her if she'd been 'intimate' with him. She didn't know what the word meant at the time. 'He only put ideas in my head,' she said afterwards.

Sean was amused by her attitude. He told her he'd been to confession to the same priest and that he'd confessed having bad thoughts to him. The priest asked him if he entertained the bad thoughts. 'No,' he said, 'but they sure entertained me.' I didn't know if that story was true or not. Maybe he heard itt somewhere else. You wouldn't say that kind of thing to a priest in those days and expect to get away with it. He'd nearly have sent you to the next parish for absolution.

I asked Maureen once why she thought boys tended to like me more than her at first but then went off me. She said she hadn't a clue but maybe I should let my hair down more.

'But my hair *is* down,' I said. I didn't know that was an expression meaning you should let yourself go. She laughed about that afterwards as much as she did about May and her sandwiches.

Maureen thought May was too indulged by Mammy and Daddy. She said that usually happened with the youngest child in a family. She was probably right. Everything changed for Maureen and me when May was born. Daddy was fascinated by her and Mammy over-protective. She got the best of everything, even during the bad years when Daddy was out of work. Whenever there was a money crisis an exception had to be made for 'Lady May,' as we called her.

It was incredible the things she got - and got away with. For one thing, she objected to wearing my hand-me-downs, conveniently forgetting that Maureen had to do this as well.

She complained about not having luxuries like some of the other girls in her class. She used to say to us, 'Why don't we go on overseas holidays like the Conlons?' The Conlons were as rich as Nelson Rockerfeller. They had a yacht in Kinsale. Their house was so big, Daddy said you could raise elephants in the living-room.

May refused her food sometimes. That wasn't fair to Mammy. I knew how hard she worked to rustle something up without breaking the bank. When things were bad she wouldn't put out a meal for herself, making do on our leftovers. That was in contrast to May. She was often unhappy even with the main course.

She was different to Maureen and me in almost every way. She had different friends from us because of her age and different tastes in books and music as well.

She adored Elvis Presley. Elvis was a bit wild for me but I understood his animal appeal. He was gorgeous but listening to him wore me out. He seemed to be from another planet.

She was much more of an exhibitionist than me. She'd stand at the mirror with a hairbrush in her hand using it as a microphone. She'd pretend to be Brenda Lee or whoever else was in the charts at the time. At parties she loved playing Charades. I had to be dragged onto the floor to do a partypiece but she was a natural performer. I was always amused by the way she never had to be asked twice to do anything in public. If she *wasn't* asked, on the contrary, she'd go into a decline.

Despite being younger than Maureen and me she felt she had a divine right to take over anything that belonged to us. We used to be shocked watching her putting on make-up that she'd 'borrowed' from us - without us being informed about it.

She was hardly into her teens when she started putting lipstick on. 'That girl has been around before,' Daddy said, scratching his chin in awe. He gave in to her on things he'd never have let us away with. Mammy was the same anytime we complained to her about May taking our things.

'The two of you are pains in the neck,' she'd say to us as she went off to play with her friends. Most of them were as cocky as herself. They pranced around the house as if they owned it. 'Like must attract like,' Maureen said.

My best friend outside the family was Davina Mulcahy. I went everywhere with her. We'd link hands going down the road laughing about nothing and heading nowhere in particular. When I was going off to play with her, Mammy used to say, 'I suppose we'll be lucky if we see you for supper.'

My best times were spent gallivanting around the place with her. Homework was often forgotten about. I'd do it like Speedy Gonzales, to get it over with. Or maybe I wouldn't do it at all. The excuse I usually gave was the old faithful one that I forgot my copy. Sister Serafina said if my head wasn't stuck on to me I'd probably have forgotten that too.

Despite everything I managed to make it through school without disgracing myself. I had multiple panic attacks leading up to the Leaving Cert but I scraped through it. I got a bare Pass in everything. My pages were full of learned-off facts. I knew the dates of battles in history but I didn't know why they'd been fought. I rattled off mathematical theorums without having the faintest idea what they meant. I could name most of the towns in Ireland but for the life of me I couldn't say what they were famous for.

'School should be outlawed,' I said to Daddy, 'It has nothing to do with life.' I knew he thought the same way but he couldn't admit it, at least not if May was listening. She'd have looked on it as an excuse to mitch.

Mammy didn't agree. She had the idea that if you didn't have the Leaving Cert you'd never get a good job. Maybe she was right but after I walked out the door of the convent for the last time I didn't seem to care one way or the other.

'It's like getting out of a concentration camp,' I said to Daddy – except I didn't do much concentrating there. Anyone in the same class as Imelda Garvey deserved a medal if they could achieve that.

## A New Decade

The sixties came in with a bang. I didn't go as far as burning my bra – it would have been a very small flame, I'm afraid – but I went on a march for women's rights one day. Sadly, that was about as far as my militancy went.

A lot of the girls I knew started talking about feminism around now. They complained about how wrong it was that women were chained to the kitchen sink. They picked up their ideas either from the papers or television programmes that were bought in from America. They dressed in mini-skirts and revealing tops. They said things like 'Cool!' if you showed them a photograph of a rock star or a football player.

Christine Keeler almost brought down the British government down when she had an affair with the Minister for War, John Profumo. For Daddy it was an endorsement of everything he felt about pagan England.

'Didn't I tell you all those politicians were corrupt?' he said. She was a call girl and Profumo a married man.

Political unrest was in the air in America too. We all thought we were going to die in a nuclear war after the Russians crammed the Bay of Pigs with a load of war ships in 1961 after getting together with the Cubans. I'd never heard of the Bay of Pigs before but for a few days that year it was all anyone talked about. We really thought our number was up.

John F. Kennedy was President of America at the time. 'If he spent less time carousing with women,' Daddy said, 'Maybe we wouldn't be all in danger of going up in a mushroom cloud.' He had that reputation but I still thought he was great, especially with his Irish ancestry. I was glad when he got tough with Khruschev, the Russian Premier. He had to back down when Kennedy threatened to open fire on his ships. Even Daddy admired him for that.

Afterwards he bought a picture of him. It had the Pope in it as well. You couldn't get higher praise in our house than that. There was a mirror between them. That got more attention from May than either of them.

After the Bay of Pigs incident passed, the big question around the house was what I was going to do with the rest of my life. The nuns were hoping I'd join them in the convent but it was the last thing in the world I wanted to do. I couldn't have lived in that environment. I don't know how they had that impression of me. Maybe it was because I was so quiet.

I'd got first place in a Catechism exam one year. I was given a certificate from the bishop for it. To the nuns it suggested I was pious. That view of me was reinforced when I went through a period of going to Confession almost non-stop. There were so many sermons about all the sins you could commit I had the fear of God put into me. I even got scruples for a while. Sister Serafina was kind to me at that time. She told me I needed to see God as a friend rather than someone who was judging me.

Mammy was disappointed when I told her I didn't want to be a nun.

'So what do you want to be?' she said.

'A nurse,' I replied.

I don't know where the words came from. I didn't know I was going to say them until I had them said.

'That's fantastic!' she said.

She was so quick to say it I started to wonder if I really meant them. Was I being too hasty in my choice of profession? I'd thought about it off and on over the years but I wasn't sure if I'd be suitable for it. Did I say it because I couldn't think of anything else? Because it sounded close to being a nun?

Sister Serafina came over to me before I left the convent. She was dressed in her long black habit. Her rosary beads trailed down the side of it. There was a big crucifix at the end of them. The beads rattled as she walked. Her veil was as tight on her head as it ever was. You never saw a strand of hair. She might have been bald for all I knew.

'So you're off to Dublin,' she said.

'Yes, Sister.'

I was leaving her world of catechisms and novenas and retreats and plenary indulgences and missions and miraculous medals and getting souls out of purgatory and purging the sins of the flesh and embracing the Holy Ghost.

For what? God only knew.

'I'll say a prayer for you,' she said.

'Was I that bad?'

'It's just my way of saying I'll be thinking of you.' She could never understand jokes.

She put on a serious expression.

'God bless you and keep you safe,' she said, 'I'm sorry you've decided not to take the veil but I'm sure you'll make a success of nursing.'

She smiled at me as she spoke. No longer was she the threatening figure she'd been to me for so many years. I saw a sadness coming into her. She seemed to be looking at me now not as a pupil but as an adult, someone like herself. That made me feel sad.

'I'm sorry I don't have a vocation,' I said. I always loved that word even though I didn't really know what it meant. Was it an actual voice you heard or just a sensation inside you?

'Don't be. It's not your fault. God wouldn't want you to choose a life that wasn't suitable for you.'

'Thanks, Sister.'

'But don't forget your prayers,' she said.

'I won't.'

'You're going out into the big wide world. 'There are a lot of dangers out there but you're a strong girl. I think you'll overcome the pitfalls.'

I saw a tear coming into her eye.

'I'll miss you,' she said.

At that moment I felt as close to her as I did to Mammy and Daddy, to Maureen and May, to Aunt Bernie. She wasn't a figure of authority any more. She was a person with just as many emotions as the rest of us.

'I'll come up and see you anytime I'm home,' I said.

'I hope you do,' she said, clutching my hand. I wanted to hug her but I couldn't bring myself to. In another world we could have been friends, people who talked about the things everyone talked about, not pitted against each other by a system designed to divide us.

For a lot of my childhood I resented the nuns. I thought of them like my jailers. That might sound dramatic but it was the way I saw school, right from the first day when I walked inside the railings of the convent. These seemed to me like prison bars too. That feeling was gone now.

I expected her to go into the convent but she lingered beside me. She had a poignant expression on her face. I wished I could have known what was going on in her mind. The obvious thing to think was that she was disappointed I wasn't joining her world but maybe that wasn't all of it. Maybe she envied me going off to another one. Was there a part of her that was unfulfilled by being a nun? That wanted to break free of it?

As she walked away from me into the convent I felt a lump in my throat - for both of us.

'Nursing is a fine profession,' were her parting words to me.

I wasn't sure why I was so drawn towards it. Maybe it was due to all the times I spent watching Daddy suffering with his viruses, or our neighbour with the polio. Daddy told me he remembered me playing with a nurse's kit I had as a child. It was a Christmas present I got one year. He said I was always poking stethoscopes into May, testing her for mysterious ailments.

Granny wasn't too pleased with my decision. 'Why couldn't she become a doctor?' she said to Mammy. 'If I threw a coin out the window I'd probably hit a nurse. They're ten a penny.' When she talked like that we just let her spin herself out. There was no point arguing with her. Her views were too entrenched.

There were no training facilities in Midleton so I decided to go to Dublin instead. I knew that would be a wrench for me and for everyone else as well but it was something I felt would be good for me in the long term, the first part of me leaving the nest.

I applied to the Mater Hospital on the north side of the city for my training. I wrote to the registrar not long after getting my Leaving results and they sent me on some literature about what the training entailed. After I submitted my application I wasn't sure if I should be excited or terrified. I watched the postman over the next few weeks with mixed feelings.

One wet Monday morning a letter came saying I'd been accepted. I had to read it three times before I believed it. The money became the big problem now. There was a fee that had to be paid accommodation to be considered as well. I knew there'd be extra costs for my uniform and books and all the other things I'd need.

'Can you afford it?' I asked Daddy.

'Of course, chicken,' he said, but I wasn't sure. We were only going to be earning a small amount each month during training so I hadn't a clue when I'd be able to pay him back, if ever.

I was a ball of nerves in the weeks coming up to going away. I didn't just have butterflies in my stomach, I had hornets' nests. Mammy was sick with loneliness and I wasn't even gone yet.

Maureen said she'd miss me like crazy. I said I'd miss her even more. I felt the same about May, bold and all as she was, and Imelda Garvey. Behind all her antics Imelda was as soft as putty. She gave me a pendant before I left that I treasure to this day.

Mammy booked a place for me in a B&B on the North Circular Road for two nights before I was due to report into the hospital. Mammy heard about it from one of the women she did the sewing for.

The landlord took in a lot of nurses. There were two other trainees due to be staying there the same night as me.

I cried for the whole week before I left home.

'I can't believe your attitude,' May propounded, 'I'd give anything to get out of this dump.' I had to laugh when she said that. We all knew if she had to go two miles up the road for a night she'd be a bag of nerves. She was still sucking her thumb at eleven years of age.

Aunt Bernie came around to say goodbye to me a few days before I left. She gave me a scissors as a present. It was blunt at the end. That meant you could put it in your pocket and it wouldn't make a hole in it. She took the day off work to say goodbye to me.

It took me ages to pack my things the night before I left. It didn't hit me that I was actually going away until I took my case out of the wardrobe. As soon as I set eyes on it I collapsed on the bed in a ball of tears. I was crying so much, Mammy heard me and came up to comfort me. 'We'll be up to see you before you know it,' she kept saying. If it wasn't for her consoling me I don't think I could have gone through with it.

'It's not like you're going to Africa,' she said.

The case was a crumpled old one. When I put everything in it I felt it was fit to burst. I had to sit on it to get it to close. The buttons kept popping open until I did that.

'That should be in the bin,' May said as she watched me, 'I bet it's older than I am.' She was probably right. I remember Granny having it at one stage.

I hardly slept a wink that night. All sorts of thoughts started coming into my head, making me wonder if I'd made the right decision.

Would I be able for the study? Would people be nice to me? Would I pass out at the first sight of blood? I was like someone on Death Row in a prison, getting ready to walk to the execution chamber the following morning.

My stomach felt like cement when the alarm went off the next morning. Mammy was too upset to see me off so she stayed in bed.

I was glad of that. I knew I'd have broken down saying goodbye to her. There'd have been a pair of us in it.

I decided to skip breakfast. I probably wouldn't have been able to keep it down anyway. I gave Maureen and May a hug but I was out the door before they could say anything to me. I wouldn't have been able to deal with that.

Daddy drove me to the train station. We didn't talk on the way. Both of us were too upset to.

The sun was shining but it only seemed to make things worse. It would have suited my mood better if it was raining. It usually was in Midleton, especially this early in the morning.

The train was late and I was almost glad about that. The delay helped me to get my thoughts together. I didn't think I'd have the courage to step on it when the time came. I was trying to build myself up for it. We sat drinking tea without talking. He knew the state I was in.

'Don't worry about a thing,' he said when the train finally pulled in, 'We're only a phone call away if you need anything. We'll be thinking of you every minute.'

Before I got on I asked him how Mammy was.

'Bearing up,' he said, 'She'll be fine. This is the worst bit.'

'Take care of her, won't you?' I said. He promised he would. I asked him how he thought she'd be.

'Up and down, I'd say. She's afraid that once you're gone, Maureen will be next.'

'Do you believe that too?'

'No.'

'What did you say to her?'

'I told her she might be right but that we'd still have three wonderful years with May.' I couldn't imagine they would be that wonderful knowing May but I didn't say anything. I just gave Daddy the biggest hug in the world.

'Get on now,' he said, pulling himself away.

I climbed on, throwing my case onto the seat with such force it nearly jumped off it again.

The buttons popped open. One of my blouses hung out. I was annoyed with myself, with everything.

The train started to move. Daddy pressed his face against the window the way children did, making his lips look funny. I was laughing and crying at the same time.

I was going to tell him to grow up but I knew I never wanted him to grow up. He waved at me and I waved back. We kept waving until the tracks swerved. Suddenly I couldn't see him anymore.

He was gone. Midleton was gone. I was headed towards somewhere I knew nothing about.

My mind was in a daze the whole way to Dublin. There was a man opposite me who looked like a farmer. He started to talk in a Kerry accent. I let him rant on.

He talked non-stop. I couldn't take in a word of what he was saying because of his accent so I wasn't able to talk back to him. He must have thought I was very rude. In some ways I was relieved I couldn't understand him. I didn't feel like talking anyway. I just kept drinking cups of black coffee. If I had any more of them, I thought, they'd start coming out my ears.

We passed town after town. The fields looked lovely but we only saw the backs of the houses so they weren't quite as nice. When we got to Connolly Station

I took a deep breath. This is it, sister, I said to myself, the Big Time. I'd never been to Dublin before. I couldn't believe the size of it. People were milling everywhere around me. I looked at the tall buildings and felt like a midget under them.

The sun beat down on me. I hadn't a clue how to get to North Circular Road. I tried to fight my way through the crowds. A porter told me where the exit from the station was. I couldn't find it for ages but then I did.

Out on the street I didn't know which way to go. There were signposts for places that meant nothing to me. With my terrible sense of direction I thought if I started walking I'd probably end up back down in Cork – or maybe in Kerry with my farmer friend from the train. I remembered the day when I got lost in the convent bringing the note about the head lice around to the other classes.

I walked up Talbot Street lugging my crumpled case. Every step I took, the buttons popped open and my blouse stuck out. I kept pushing it back but it was no good. It was determined to be seen.

Eventually I realised there was only one thing for it. I'd have to sit on the case to get it to close properly. I'm sure the people passing by thought I was a nutcase – a nut with a case.

I got a few funny looks from some of them. I decided I'd have to take something out to get it to stop it opening. Otherwise the whole population of Dublin would know what I was going to be wearing for the next few months.

I chose an old jumper to dump. I'd had it for donkey's years. I always hated it anyway.

God knows why I packed it in the first place. I stuffed it into a bin saying, 'Good riddance to bad rubbish.'

I thought I was going to be able to walk faster now but I wasn't. I was wearing a pair of shoes that were a size too small for me and they were pinching my feet. I stopped every few minutes to rest them, feeling the eyes of people on me. Were they aware of the fact that I was a culchie who hadn't a clue where she was going? I was sure I was a dead giveaway with my frightened face. And my sore feet.

I kept walking until I got to O'Connell Street. Suddenly everything started to look familiar. I remembered landmarks from photographs I'd seen in books and magazines – Nelson's Pillar, Liberty Hall, the statue of Daniel O'Connell. He was one of Daddy's heroes.

There was a woman standing on O'Connell Bridge with some shopping bags in her hands. I asked her if she knew where the bus stop was for North Circular Road. She walked me right up to it. It was opposite the Carlton cinema.

I stopped the first bus that came along. Luckily it turned out to be the right one. It was a 22A.

We started to move. In fact we started to race. I thought the driver must have been on drugs because he was driving so fast.

We wobbled so much I felt I was at the bumpers. Every time he came to a yellow light he went through it instead of slowing down. At one stage he took a corner so sharply I bumped my head off the window. A young man who was sitting opposite me saw me rubbing it.

'You could have a claim for that,' he said in a thick Dublin accent. He looked like a rough diamond.

'Where are you going?' he asked me. I thought he might have been trying to chat me up so I didn't answer for a few seconds.

'Dorset Street,' I said then.

'Dorset Street? Well you better get your skates on because we're at it.'

'Jesus!' I said. I realised he was right. The bus was stopped but the driver was getting ready to start moving again.

'Wait!' I shouted at him.

He stopped revving the engine.

'Where's the fire?' he said. He looked like another smart alec. He was chewing gum. There was a picture of a Page Three girl beside him from one of the English papers, the 'pagan' ones as Daddy called them.

I grabbed my case and leaped out the door. I'd hardly touched the ground before he was zooming off again.

I walked up to the North Circular Road. Daddy had written, 'Joe Carmody, Number 42' on a piece of paper he'd given me. He told me to memorise it in case I lost it. I couldn't understand why he said that. How could someone forget a two figure number?

After a few minutes I arrived at the address. I walked up the steps and knocked at a big brown door. It was such a relief to finally be there. My hand was almost falling off me from carrying the case.

I rang the bell. A tall man with glasses came out. He gave me a big smile.

'Are you Mr Carmody?' I asked him.

'The very man,' he said. He seemed to know who I was. 'Your parents have been on the line,' he said, 'They were worried that you hadn't arrived.'

'I'm always late for everything,' I said.

'Me too,' he laughed.

I walked into a sitting-room with him. He told me to take the weight off my feet. I sat down and looked around me. There were loads of pictures on the wall. Most of them were of young people with mortarboards on their heads.

All the furniture was gleaming. It was so different to our own house where everything was just thrown together. The table was made of glass so you could see your face in it. There was a lampshade in the corner beside a chiffonier.

'You look like you could do with a cuppa,' he said.

'I'd love one,' I said, 'I'm parched.'

He went off whistling and I continued admiring the room. Everything looked as if it had just been bought yesterday, including the carpet. It was a gorgeous beige one with a diamond pattern repeated diagonally every few inches. Daddy would have had his work cut out for him trying to match it up if he was doing one of the patch-up jobs he was reduced to during our poor times.

He appeared with the tea a few minutes later. My hand was so weak from carrying the case I could hardly lift the cup. I was afraid I'd spill it on his carpet.

He had some biscuits with him as well. I was so hungry I made short work of them.

He watched me amusedly as I munched into what seemed like a full packet of custard creams. He must have thought I hadn't eaten for a month. I was so stressed on the train I didn't have anything to eat there.

'Sorry for being such a glutton,' I said.

'That's what they're there for.'

For the first time in the day I was able to catch my breath.

'The other girls are here already,' he said.

'I'm looking forward to meeting them.'

He asked me about myself. He seemed to know a good bit already. I told him I hated leaving home but he said not to worry, that I'd be over my loneliness in no time.

'Midleton is only down the road,' he said.

We sat chatting for a while. Then he said he was going to ring Mammy to let her know I'd arrived.

After speaking to her for a minute or two he handed the phone to me.

The second I heard her voice I started to break down but somehow I held myself together – probably because he was in the room.

'How was the journey?' she said. She sounded relaxed but I suspected she was putting on an act too.

'Not too bad. I got here in one piece anyway.'

'How do you like Dublin?'

'It's a bit chaotic so far.'

'You should have been expecting that. How did the case hold up?'

'Not very well, I'm afraid. It kept popping open so I had to dump something.'

'I bet I know what.'

She often seemed to be able to read my mind.

'Go on.'

'Was it the woolly jumper?'

'How did you guess?'

'I knew you always hated it.'

'I hope you don't mind.'

'To be honest I was never gone on it. It owed you nothing. God knows how long it goes back. If the weather gets bad you can buy another one. There are so many bargains in Dublin.'

'It was one of the dreaded hand-me-downs. Maybe I should have posted it down to May.'

'Don't say things like that. She's bad enough as it is.'

'How is she? I suppose she forgot about me five minutes after I left.'

'She's doing cartwheels in the back yard as I'm talking to you. Looking for attention as usual.'

'That sounds like May all right. How is Maureen?'

'She's sitting here beside me. She sends you her love. So does Daddy. I won't put them on because I don't want to be running up Mr Carmody's bill. Tell him I appreciate him calling.'

'I will. Love to everyone.'

After I put down the phone I thanked him.

'Don't mention it,' he said, 'Your mother sounds very nice.'

'I'll miss her like anything.'

'All the girls here go through that. The first few days are the worst. You'll get over it once you get into the hospital. There'll be so much happening you won't have time to think.'

'I hope so.'

He started to talk about himself then. He said one of his daughters was a nurse too. She was in New Zealand. That sounded so exotic to me. I never knew anyone who'd been outside Ireland before. I'd heard about a girl from Midleton who went to Russia once. That sounded even stranger. I always thought that if you chanced going to Russia you'd be lucky to get back. I found myself worrying she wouldn't come back, that she'd be murdered by the kind of people who had the war ships lined up on the Bay of Pigs.

Mr Carmody laughed when I said that.

'There are some good communists too,' he said.

'I suppose,' I said.

I asked him about his wife. I was surprised it wasn't her who brought in the tea.

He went quiet for a few seconds. Then he said, 'She died a few years ago.' I told him I was sorry to hear that. I was going to ask him more about her but I could see by his face that he didn't want to go into it. Maybe the wounds were still raw. Behind his head on the mantelpiece there was a photograph of the two of them on their wedding day. She looked like a lovely woman.

Why was it that it was nearly always the nicest people who had the worst things befalling them in life? It tested my faith when I heard something like that. Why did God allow it? I knew what Sister Serafina would have said: 'She went to her reward.'

Maybe he saw me looking distressed because he got up from his seat.

'Let me show you your room,' he said.

I saw him looking at my case. It embarrassed me with its shabbiness.

'It's seen better days,' I said.

'Don't worry,' he laughed, 'I've seen worse. In fact some people have arrived here with nothing but what they were wearing. These walls could tell some stories.'

He brought me upstairs. The room was large. There was an oak dressing table beside the window. It had a bathroom off it. There were three single beds lined up in a row and three little wardrobes in front of them. They all smelt of mothballs.

'You must specialise in threes,' I said.

'I have lots of rooms,' he explained, 'Singles, doubles and threesomes. I thought you might like the company of the other girls to take your mind off yourself.'

'That's exactly what I'd like.'

'I'll leave you to get settled in for the moment. Anytime you feel like coming down for a cuppa, you'd be more than welcome.'

'Thanks for making me feel so good.'

'Not at all. I left home around your age too. I know what it's like.'

'I've probably been too sheltered growing up.'

'Maybe country girls are. Have you any plans for the rest of the evening?'

'Right now I just want to do nothing.'

'Good idea.'

After he went out I opened the case. I took out a can of Coca-Cola that I'd packed. It splashed all over my dress when I opened it. That was clumsy me all over. I should have known it would after all the pushing around. At least it hadn't burst.

I was too tired to unpack anything except my alarm clock. I went over to the window and looked out at the street. People were coming home from work. They seemed to have very serious looks on their faces as they brushed by one another. It was so different to Midleton where you'd only see the odd straggler. There were trucks and buses driving by too. I wondered how long that would go on, or if they'd stop me sleeping. Not that I expected to get much sleep anyway.

The hospital was across the street. A man hobbled into the out-patients department on crutches. I'd just seen my first patient. The nurses' home was a bit further back. It was strange to think I was going to be there for a long time. Maureen said if it was her she'd prefer to live out but I was too insecure for that. I couldn't have afforded it anyway.

When I finished my Coca-Cola it was starting to get dark. I closed the window and pulled the curtains over. I turned on the light. Suddenly the room looked smaller.

There was a mirror on the dressing table. When I looked at myself in it I realised how exhausted I was.

I decided to go straight to bed. I washed my teeth and undressed. Then I set the alarm. I lay down thinking about all that had happened in the day. I wondered what the two girls would be like.

I couldn't sleep for a while because of all the lights on the street. The honking of the trucks didn't help either but I eventually drifted off. I slept right through the night. That surprised me because I'd been having a lot of insomnia in the previous weeks.

I didn't wake up until the alarm went off. I was so worn out from all the worry I'd probably have slept till noon if it didn't wake me.

The other two beds had been slept in. There were clothes scattered all over the place as well so obviously the other two girls had come and gone without waking me. I must have put Rip Van Winkle in the shade.

I dressed quickly. I could hear Mr Carmody whistling in the kitchen. He seemed to be cooking something. I smelt rashers.

When I went into the dining-room I saw the two other girls already ensconced at the breakfast table. One of them had red hair. The other one was a brunette. They were giggling about something.

'So you're the one from Midleton,' the red-haired girl said.

They introduced themselves as Bridget and Cáit. Bridget was the brunette. She had a blue dress on her with a flower pattern. Cáit was dressed in an Aran jumper. Her jeans were scuffed at the bottom. She had poppy eyes and a round face.

Bridget looked a bit like the actress Claire Bloom. She came from Curracloe. Cáit was from Birr. They knew each other from Bridget's brother. He lived in Birr too. They'd come up on the train together.

They were much more relaxed with Mr Carmody than I was. I envied the way they were able to joke with him.

After breakfast we all went up to the room. No sooner were we in the door than Cáit started smoking a cigarette.

'Close it quick,' she said to me, 'in case he smells the smoke. There's a sign in the hall saying "No Smoking." I don't want to get kicked out of a boarding house on my first night in the Big Smoke – if you'll excuse the expression.' Already I knew she was going to be a laugh.

A few minutes later Bridget lit up. Then I joined in. I wasn't a smoker but I didn't want to be the odd one out.

I pretended I was used to it but as soon as I inhaled I gave the game away. I started coughing uncontrollably.

'Are you all right?' Cáit said, 'Maybe we should get a nurse. I believe there are a few around.'

'The smoke went up my nose.'

'Up your nose? That defies the law of gravity. Most things go down.'

'Not with me they don't.'

'You've obviously never had a ciggie before,' Bridget said.

I had to admit it. I nodded my head instead of saying anything for fear of the coughing getting worse.

We spent the rest of the morning swapping stories. Cáit reminded me of May. She often went off on tangents as she was telling her stories. Sometimes she'd be laughing so much as she told them she'd forget what the point of them was until we reminded her. I could see she'd lived a lot of life even at her age. She'd also had her share of boyfriends.

Bridget was from a family of five. She'd grown up on a farm. Her manner was reserved. She was more like me.

There was a kettle in the room so we were able to make tea without going down to the kitchen. Cáit had about ten Kit-Kats with her. We devoured them in between the cigarettes.

By the third or fourth one Cáit managed to teach me how to get the smoke to go down instead of up. Despite that I didn't enjoy them very much.

'Lucky you,' she said consolingly, 'It's an expensive habit.'

Both of them smoked Sweet Afton. Bridget told me I'd get a bad name if I kept smoking O.P.s' (Other People's) so I'd have to start buying my own. I knew there was no way I could tell Mammy or Daddy I'd got in on the habit. They'd both have gone mad, especially Daddy with his breathing problems. He said bronchitis ran in the family. But I needed them to ease my tension. I was going into a new world and I was low on self-confidence.

In the afternoon we had lunch in a little café in Phibsboro. As we were getting to the end of it, Cáit said, 'Let's have a gander at the Mater.' I thought that was a good idea.

We went up there without announcing ourselves. We just wanted to get the feel of the place.

'This is our secret field mission,' Bridget said, 'It's the last time we can come in here and misbehave if we want.'

'Let's drag one of the patients out of his bed,' Cáit suggested, 'and pull him across the floor. Then we can stamp on him to our heart's content until he's begging for mercy.'

'Er, I don't think s in the handbook,' Bridget said.

We rambled around for a while and then went for coffee. Bridget asked me if I got my registration forms. I had but I hadn't read them yet. Being such a pessimist I thought I'd see something in them that would send me straight back to Midleton.

We went back to the B&B for tea. Mr Carmody put on a fry for us. It was as good as any I'd ever had in my life.

'How are you getting your bearings?' he asked us. Cáit said she felt she'd been in Dublin all her life.

The three of us went up to our room afterwards for another chat. I told them all about myself and they did likewise. Girls get to know each other much quicker than boys because they talk more personally.

So it was with us. We held nothing back. I knew I was going to really like both of them. I was looking forward to working with them.

'Friends forever,' Bridget said at one stage, bringing us together for a group hug after what seemed like our hundredth cup of tea.

'I never made a lifetime friend in 24 hours before,' I said, 'but I'll make an exception for you two.'

Our lectures were due to start the following week. I was a ball of nerves thinking about what was in store for me. 'Don't worry about it,' Mr Carmody said to me as I was going to bed that night.

'Anticipation is much worse than realisation. I've seen so many girls come and go like you. They all get on fine. Just take a deep breath and say a Hail Mary.'

I knew what he meant about the anticipation. I always hated waiting for anything. The way my personality was I had to be getting on with things.

I tried to turn my mind off completely but I couldn't. Cáit and Bridget were much calmer as we got ready for bed. Five minutes after they lay down I heard Cáit snoring. Bridget and I stayed awake talking for a while.

Her stories of life on the farm reminded me of Grandad. I started to tell her about him but after a few minutes I heard her snoring too. I envied them both their ability to tune out so easily. I could never be like that.

I couldn't get to sleep for hours. Weird thoughts came into my mind. I had to take a sleeping pill in the end. Mammy packed a few for me. She must have known I'd be needing them. She probably knew me better than I knew myself.

Bridget and Cáit were gone when I woke up the next morning, just like the morning before. What was their secret that they could wake so early?

My body clock must have been wired backwards. It believed in staying awake at night and falling asleep during the day. I'd obviously be an ideal candidate for night duty if I ever qualified.

The room was in a mess. Neither of them had bothered to make their beds. There were teacups all over the place. And discarded Kit-Kat wrappers.

The smell of smoke was so strong I could hardly breathe. I opened the window wide to try and get rid of it.

Mr Carmody had tea and toast on the table when I got down to the dining room but I told him I doubted I'd be able for it. My stomach was in a knot.

'The condemned man always heats a hearty breakfast,' he said.

'Maybe, but not the condemned woman. Not this one anyway.'

I hated refusing it because he'd gone to the trouble of making it but I felt I'd throw up anything I tried to digest.

Apart from everything else I was sick from the cigarettes. It was all very well to play tough at night but you paid for it on the double the next day.

'Have it for yourself,' I said.

'I had mine already but Tiddy will be delighted with it.'

'Tiddy?'

'That's my dog.'

I paid him what I owed him and went upstairs for my case. I stuffed my nightdress into it and tried to freshen up. I put my head under the tap in the bathroom sink. The water was so cold I felt I was going to faint. I knew I had to wake myself up somehow.

I grabbed my case and belted down the stairs. When I got down to the hallway Mr Carmody was standing there. He was smiling sympathetically.

'Say a prayer for me, won't you?' I said.

'Go away out of that. You'd think you were going to Sing Sing.'

'The way I'm feeling, you could send me there with a heart and a half .I'd thank you if it saved me from that place across the road.'

'Try and be like the other two,' he said, 'They went off like they hadn't a care in the world.'

'I wish I could.'

'All your nerves will disappear once you get in there. It's like riding a bike. You need to get into the saddle.'

'Thanks,' I said, making for the door, 'That's all good advice. Sorry for leaving the room in such a mess. You'll probably be all day trying to tidy it.'

'Don't worry about it,' he said waving me off, 'That's what I get paid for.'

I ran across the road as fast as I could. I was anxious to be away before he got the smell of the smoke. My legs felt as if they were going to go from under me as the early morning cars sped by me. One angry motorist almost knocked me down. He only missed me by inches as I tried to weave in and out around him. I had visions of myself lying on the road with a crowd around me and an ambulance siren blaring. He gave me a filthy look as he passed me. It would have been a nice how-do-you- do if I passed my first day in the Mater as a patient instead of a trainee nurse.

I walked up the driveway towards the hospital. Don't think of anything, I kept saying to myself, just keep moving.

I reached the nurse's home. I walked up twelve steps to a large door. When I opened it I saw a room across the way with 'Admissions' written on it.

I knocked gently. A voice said 'Come in.'

When I got inside I saw a severe-looking sister writing something on a ledger. She gestured me to sit down with a vague wave of her pen. I put down my case. The chair was very hard. I looked around me at pictures of nurses from the past, all lined up in group photographs. At least they looked happy, I thought. Or were they just putting on smiles for the camera?

'Yes,' she said finally, 'You're the girl from Cork, aren't you?'

I nodded.

'I'm Sister Agnes. You'll be working under me when you get on the wards.'

I quivered at the prospect. I'd heard about her. She was supposed to be something of a harridan, someone you crossed at your peril.

I tried to think of something to say to her but I couldn't. Her eyes were peering at me, rendering me totally mute.

'Well?' she said, 'Have you got a tongue in your head?'

'Yes,' I muttered.

She stuck her head out expectantly.

'Yes, *what*?'

'Yes, sister.'

She told me what would be expected of me. I was given a list of things I needed to buy – a uniform, text books, copies, a folder, pens and so on. 'Don't forget a good strong pair of shoes,' she said, 'Nursing is hard on the feet.'

'Where will I get my uniform?' I asked her.

'In Boyers or Arnotts,' she said.

'What about my laundry?'

'You're to strip your bed every morning. Put the sheets in your pillow-case. Leave them outside your door and they'll be seen to. As regards your personal laundry, you can wash your garments in the sink in your rooms and dry them on the radiator.'

I wasn't sure I was taking all this in. I must have looked blank because she gave me a stern look.

'I hope you're taking all this in,' she said, 'I'm not talking to you for the good of my health.'

'I think I heard everything.'

'You think?' Her eyes got more stern.

'I'm pretty sure.'

She closed her ledger.

'We'll go upstairs now,' she commanded.

She locked her door. We went up a winding staircase. When we got to the top I looked down a long corridor. There was a statue of Our Lady in the middle of it.

Beside it was a stained glass window that looked out onto a quadrangle. There were twenty rooms in the corridor in all. Mine was second from the end. It was Room 19.

She took out a key and opened the door. After she went in she ushered me in after her. It was a large room with three beds in it. There were three wardrobes and a dressing table.

The wardrobes had shelves at the top and drawers at the bottom. They were all made of pine. There was a radiator beside one of the beds. It was the only thing that seemed warm.

'This is where you'll be staying with the other two young ladies,' she informed me.

'Yes,' I said, 'Bridget and Cáit.'

She gave a start.

'Oh. So you know them.'

'I met them a few days ago.'

'Very good. Anyway, I have to go now. Have you any questions?'

'What time are the lectures at?'

'Nine o'clock. The night sister will knock on your door at 7.a.m. Mass is at 7.30. We'll expect to see you there. Breakfast is served afterwards in the dining-room. Your name will be called out. If you're not there you don't eat. No exceptions.'

'Do we ever get a sleep-in?' I enquired. She sighed when I said that. Obviously I was giving off the wrong signals.

'If you have a morning off, put a note on your door so you won't be called.'

'What do we do if we want to go out?'

'You go out, girl,' she snapped, 'If you want to go out, you go out. Isn't that what people usually do when they want to go out?'

From the way she barked the words out you'd think I'd asked the most outrageous thing imaginable. I felt like saying, 'Shut up, you old cow,' but I held my tongue.

'Always sign out if you're leaving the premises,' she went on, 'and I mean *always*. The doors are locked every night at ten. The lights go out at 10.30. You'll get a late pass once a week. When you get back, go into the main hospital. Whoever is on the switch will contact the porter and he'll let you in. Please do so quietly. Don't on any account use the lift if it's after ten or you'll wake everyone up. And don't bring any men in. I mean, *ever*. Unless they're dying on the street and need emergency treatment. Have you got that?'

I tried to say yes but the word wouldn't come out. I nodded.

'You're expected to leave your door open until eleven,' she continued, 'for the home supervisor to clarify that you're on the premises. If you want to stay out for a night you have to have a letter from your parents. My advice is that you turn in early each night so you'll be able for the following day's labours. Nursing is a hard life. Many don't make it. Some people think all you need to make a go of it is a big heart. Be assured that much, much more is required. Do I make myself clear?'

I stared at her with my mouth open. It was like being back in school. Or even worse, boarding school.

Sister Serafina suddenly seemed like a softie.

'Do I make myself clear?' she repeated.

'Very,' I grunted.

A group of students clattered up the stairs as she finished. They were all talking animatedly. I presumed they were on their way from some lecture or other. They'd almost passed by me when I noticed Bridget and Cáit were among them. Cáit was telling some story or other. They were all breaking their sides laughing at it.

'Keep a lid on it, please!' Sister Agnes roared, 'I can't hear myself think.'

She stepped out onto the corridor. I followed her out. The talking stopped as the group passed by us. I watched them filtering into their rooms in ones and twos. A few of them gave me giggly waves behind her back, including Cáit.

I wondered how many of them I'd get to know. Bridget said there were over twenty girls in our set. There were 78 in the nurse's home altogether.

'I think that's everything for the moment,' Sister Agnes said, 'If you have any more questions I'll be glad to answer them.'

'Thank you Sister,' I said, doing a kind of curtsey.

She gave me a half-smile as she turned to leave. I watched her drifting off down the corridor. She stopped at the statue of Our Lady to kneel and bless herself.

I walked into Room 19. I tried to like it as much as I could, knowing I'd be stuck there for a long time. It seemed a bit institutional to me. I wondered if there was any way we could jolly it up – or if we'd be allowed to. The way Sister Agnes talked, you felt if you touched anything an alarm would go off.

I looked out the window. The group that were there a few minutes ago were crossing the quadrangle. As they did so a sudden wind came up. A few of them put their hands on their skirts to stop them blowing above their waists. A few others held their hats to stop them blowing off. Then they all started running.

I sat down on my bed. I wondered what the future held. Would I be good enough to stick the pace? As good as Sister Agnes demanded? There was no way I could know. All I knew for sure was that we were going to be treated like children. It was as if we were in some kind of unofficial boarding school.

I looked around me at the walls. They were all painted in a dour purple. Were we allowed even change that? I'd have to ask.

As I sat there thinking, Bridget and Cáit came in. Both of them had broad grins on their faces. They'd obviously been listening to Sister Agnes' speech.

'How did you put up with that batty oul' one giving you the third degree?' Cáit said.

'We got the same stuff,' Bridget added, 'I bet there wasn't a word different. She's like a robot.'

'I think I've made a terrible mistake,' I said, 'All we're missing is the manacles and chains. I wonder if they give you time off for good behaviour?'

Cáit laughed.

'She needs her head examined,' she said, 'if she thinks we're going to listen to that guff for the rest of the year.'

'It's like the Gestapo,' Bridget said.

We decided the only way to beat her was to bond together. That way we could have some kind of life.

I unpacked my clothes. The wardrobe was small but I managed to hang them in it. I took out everything. At last my battered old case was empty. I kicked it under the bed. I wanted it out of sight.

A little folder fell out of it after I kicked it. There were photos of Mammy and Daddy in it. I'd brought them with me to make me feel less lonely.

I showed them to the girls.

'They look like a lovely couple,' Bridget said. There was one of Maureen and May as well. May was sticking out her tongue.

'I'd say she's good fun,' Cáit said.

'She's just like you,' I said, 'A trouble-maker.'

'Where did you get that idea? You hardly know me.'

Bridget took a bottle of lemonade out of her bag.

'Anyone like a drink?' she said. We both nodded. She poured it into some plastic cups that were on a dressing table. We shared more stories of our past as we drank.

The pair of them went out to meet some of their friends afterwards. I was too tired to join them so I just lay down on the bed. I kept looking at the photographs of Mammy and Daddy. I wasn't sure if they made me feel more at home or not.

My emotions started to get at me again now that things were quiet. I knew Mr Carmody was right. I needed to do something to get my mind off myself. Otherwise I was going to be miserable about all the regulations.

I remembered packing a diary. I took it out of the case. I reached into my pocket for a pen and wrote: 'Day One. Met two lovely girls and a horrible nun. Want to go home already. Am trying hard not to give in to myself.'

As I was writing I heard a knock on the door. It was Sister Agnes. She didn't wait for me to answer it, walking straight in instead.

'Settling in?' she said.

'Kind of.'

'Good.'

She handed me a piece of paper. It had a list of books on it.

'These are the texts you'll need to start you off,' she said. 'Make sure you like them because you'll be seeing a lot of them. Like me.' I wasn't sure if that was an attempt at a joke or not.

'Don't buy all of them,' she advised, 'They can be very expensive. You might only need to know a few pages of some of them. It's cheaper to photocopy them in the library if that's the case.'

She handed me another sheet of paper that had the times of our lectures on it.

'You'll be at them for two months,' she said. 'Then you'll have six months on the wards. After that it's two more months of lectures. I think that's everything.' Before leaving she said we'd have continuous assessment for some of the exams. For other ones, inspections would happen 'on the day.'

She went on talking about other things but my mind trailed off. There was too much information about subjects that held no interest for me yet. I tried to sound like I was interested but doubted I made a very good job of it.

Finally she finished. She went off. After she was gone I started to feel cold so I pulled my bed over towards the radiator. I lay down on it in my clothes and pulled the covers over me.

I must have fallen asleep then because the next thing I knew it was morning. For the second time in a row I'd slept from teatime right through the night.

Bridget was standing above me laughing.

'Look at her,' she said to Cáit, 'enjoying the luxury of our hotel with the heat at full blast. It's been on all night. I bet that's going to cost a few bob.'

Sun streamed in the windows. She pulled the covers off me. It was only then I realised I was still in my clothes.

'Wake up, sleepy head,' she said, 'It's time for our lecture. If you're not down there in five minutes flat there'll be hell to pay.'

# My Career Begins

For the next two months we were on Block. That was short for Block Studying. At this stage I didn't know any more about my body than the man in the moon. We were up at the crack of dawn for Mass. Cáit dodged this as much as she could. She said it was hard to concentrate on your prayers when you were half-asleep.

It was even more difficult to take in complicated facts at the lectures if you were tired. The first few were about basic anatomy. Afterwards they got more complicated. I hated it when they were long-winded. A lot of them were. I'll never forget the ex-ward sister with the squeaky voice who yammered on for the best part of an hour one day on the art of crepe bandaging.

'She deserves a special prize for being boring,' Cáit said, 'Is there such a thing?'

We weren't allowed within whistling distance of a ward. I felt I was suffering from an overdose of theory. If I was faced with a patient who had an actual condition, I thought, I'd be the last person in the world that could help them.

'Why don't they just let us loose on the wards?' I said to Bridget one day, 'I'm sure we'd learn things as we went along.' One of the lecturers overheard me. She shook her head amusedly.

'If only it was that simple,' she said.

We got a set of assignments to hand in to our tutors. We were graded on these. I was always amazed mine weren't thrown back in my face. They were done in my inimitable spider crawl, the one that used to give the nuns in the convent minor coronaries.

I often found myself picking the brains of people wiser than myself for these assignments instead of giving my own views. That was especially the case if I was short of time handing them in to the tutor. I lived in terror that my sources would be tracked down and I'd be up for plagiarism.

The secret was learning to cover your tracks and not quote too directly from other people. Cáit did this much more than me. Sometimes she copied articles word for word from journals. I wouldn't have chanced that but she got away with it.

Some of the articles had nothing more in them than common sense but as Mammy used to say, 'There's nothing less common in life than that.' Other ones were so dense as to be unreadable. We were bombarded with facts and figures about every ailment known to man, usually with unpronounceable Latin names.

'How am I going to learn them all?' I asked Bridget, throwing my hands in the air, 'How am I even going to know the difference between minor and major ones?'

'If a condition sounds complicated,' she said, 'You can bet your bottom dollar it's one you don't want to have. The more syllables a disease has, the worse it is.'

Cáit said, 'I don't even want one with one syllable.'

It was a relief to have Practicals to get us away from the books. I made a fool of myself at some of them but nobody made me feel bad about that. Other students made mistakes too. We were all in the same boat.

I got to know most of them fairly well. We often had to do demonstrations on each other. That was a great way of breaking the ice. Two ward sisters from The Meath, what we called 'externs', were recruited to examine us for some of the Practicals.

One of them used to bring a skeleton with her. She dressed it in a uniform. They were both very pernickety about everything. We had to scrub up extra carefully for these sessions.

Some of the lectures were mixed in with demonstrations. One of these had us sticking syringes into a dummy to teach us how to give injections. The problem was that the dummies didn't scream if you did it the wrong way. I felt I was being lulled into a false sense of security.

'You worry too much,' Cáit told me. She was having a great time jabbing the dummy with repeated thrusts as if it was a dagger. It looked like a pin cushion when she was finished with it. 'Hold on there,' the lecturer said, 'You're meant to be a nurse, not an executioner.'

I found it difficult to concentrate on the lectures if I hadn't slept well the night before. A lot of them dealt with conditions I doubted I'd ever come up against.

'Jesus,' Cáit gasped after a graphic one on blocked arteries, 'You'd think we were training to be cardiac surgeons.'

She had no time for the lecturers. 'They like the sound of their own voices too much,' she complained. Bridget agreed with her and so did I. We knew we'd get most of the same stuff in any book. Cáit looked up the 'Sources Consulted' section at the end of the print-outs we got and photocopied the pages for us. Often we found the material was directly transcribed.

In theory we could all have had sleep-outs instead of trudging into lecture-halls to hear someone droning on about facts he'd slavishly copied from someone else. The problem was that we had to sign in for each lecture. You'd get into trouble if your name wasn't found on the sheet.

Cáit suggested we attend in shifts of two and forge the name of the missing person. I was nervous about doing that. There was always the danger the missing one would get called out to do some 'demo' - or that there'd be a random check of attenders from the branch examiner. If you weren't there for it you'd be in big trouble.

I rang home one night and told Mammy I was miserable. I said it was all getting too much for me. She became very upset. Then she put Daddy on. When I said the same thing to him he told me to come home on the spot. Mammy didn't think that was a good idea. I could hear the two of them having it out as I bucketed tears on the other end of the phone. Maureen even got involved. I heard her saying, 'What's going on?'

May came on then.

'You lucky thing,' she said, 'Up there where all the action is. Can I come up and see you?'

It was like a comedy. Suddenly my tears went away. I told Mammy I'd stick it out for a while more anyway.

A few days later I got a letter in the post. I recognised the handwriting immediately: it was from Aunt Bernie. There were just three words in it: 'Follow your dream.' Those three words said more to me than 300 could from anyone else.

I plugged on. Cáit and Bridget were great standbys for me. Seeing their struggles gave me the strength to fight my own ones. The main problem for me was the whole idea of studying. I thought I'd left it behind me after the Leaving Cert. Little did I know what I had in store for me. This was twenty times worse. A lot of nights I burned the midnight oil. I could have done with having matchsticks over my eyes to keep them open.

I still kept wondering why we couldn't go onto the wards except for menial chores.

'I'm afraid that's not the way it works,' Dr. Ford, our senior lecturer, said when I put the question to him.

'Imagine yourself on a motorway,' he said, 'without having studied the rules of the road. How would you cope?'

That kind of thinking bored me. I just wanted to get out on the motorway, licence or no licence.

The lectures went on interminably. They drained the three of us of our enthusiasm. We tried to get in a walk between the morning and afternoon ones to keep our energy levels up. Tucking into a nice dinner helped too, at least for a while.

Some days I 'comfort ate' to keep myself going. This wasn't too consistent with the things we were being lectured about. I'd listen to someone ranting on about the wonders of yoghurt or yalacta cheese and a half hour later I'd be stuffing myself with a hamburger for a treat.

One day a button popped on a pair of jeans I was wearing. That gave me a fright. It was a reality check. No more Kit-Kats from Cáit, no matter how much I craved them. The energy they gave you only lasted a short while anyway. After a half hour or so you'd get even more exhausted.

We got our first experience of ward duty after the first two month of Block were was up. Much as I'd looked forward to this, I was nervous thinking about how it would go. The way I felt reminded me of my first night in Dublin with Mr Carmody. In some ways this was worse. I'd have to face loads of people, to sound as if I knew what I was doing.

'Nonsense,' Bridget said, 'You'll be tailing the staff nurse.' She seemed to know a lot about it.

'What does "tailing" mean?'

'Don't ask so many questions. Just dive in.'

I knew she was right. I was over-thinking everything. That's what the lectures did to me. They turned me into a Thinking Machine.

On the night before I was due to have my first ward experience I made a promise to myself to take each day as it came from now on without putting the mockers on everything. If I wasn't good enough I knew Sister Agnes would be quick enough to tell me.

Bridget cut my hair so it wouldn't be falling into the collar of the uniform. She made me try it on before the mirror in the room. I thought I looked okay in it. She sewed my name into the lining. I knew there'd be murder if it got mixed up in the laundry.

She pinned a little upside-down watch onto my chest area. The last thing I put on me was Aunt Bernie's blunt-ended scissors. I was now, quote unquote, The Full Package.

I set the alarm for 6 a.m. but forgot to turn it on. The first thing I felt the next morning was Bridget digging me in the ribs saying, 'We slept it out.' She threw on her uniform.

'Look at herself,' she said, pointing at Cáit. She was out for the count.

She munched on a biscuit she'd left on the tallboy the night before.

'Here,' she said, 'Have some.'

I took a bite of it but it felt stale. I spat it out. She tugged at Cáit.

'Get up,' she said.

She almost had to pull her onto the floor. The two of us helped dress her. We barrelled down the stairs a few minutes later with our uniforms hanging off us.

Sister Agnes was standing at the front door with her mouth open. We raced past her across the courtyard to the hospital.

'Why do people always sleep it out on the most important mornings of their lives?' I said to no one in particular as I tried to straighten the veil on my head.

'It helps if you turn the clock on after you set it,' Cáit said.

'Cáit,' I replied, 'You're an absolute scientific genius to know things like that.' It was the only way to deal with her.

We were sweating like pigs by the time we reached the hospital. As soon as we got in the door we scattered to our separate wards. I was still running like the clappers. An old man on crutches was coming out the main door as I got to it. I almost knocked him down.

'Hey there!' he roared, 'I'm just after an operation, I don't want another one.'

I muttered an apology and raced on. I had a stitch in my side when I got to St. Ignatius Ward, the one I'd been assigned to. It was my first day and I was over half an hour late.

I'd been preparing for this for two months and already it was a disaster. What else could go wrong?

The matron was approaching. I didn't want to run into her so I ducked into a toilet. When I heard her footsteps receding into the distance I came out.

The floor was shiny. I walked very slowly in case I slipped. That was the last thing I needed. I could just imagine the bulletin headline: 'Nurse Enters First Ward On All Fours.'

All the patients seemed to be looking at me. I wondered if my hair was mussed. Maybe the seams on my stocking were crimped. Maybe I was wearing a bit of Bridget's biscuit on my face.

Sister Agnes was sitting behind a desk filling in a report sheet. I hadn't seen her since the day she admitted me. She was about to end her shift.

'Sorry I'm late,' I stuttered, 'The alarm didn't go off.'

She looked at me from behind a pair of glasses that were half way down her nose.

'Failed to go off? Why? Is it an old clock?'

'No. I'm afraid I forgot to turn it on.'

'Oh. That might explain it all right.'

She wasn't taking it as badly as I thought even if her sarcasm reminded me of Cáit.

'It won't happen again,' I said.

'I hope not.'

She gave me a calculating stare.

'You don't look well,' she said, 'Is there something wrong with you?'

My stomach lurched. There was no point pretending.

'I think I might be coming down with something.'

'Really? So you came in here to infect the patients with it.'

'Maybe it's tension. I wanted to make a good impression considering it's my first day.'

Her expression changed. For the first time I saw kindness on her face.

'Relax,' she said, 'We won't be asking you to do any quadruple bypasses just yet.'

I tried to smile. She told me to sit down. My knees were shaking so much they were sending out an S.O.S. in Morse Code to the rest of my body to panic.

I had a folder with me. I rested it on them so she wouldn't see.

'The best way to start is to get right down to business,' she said.

'I'd be glad of that.'

'Okay. Let me give you a run-through on the patients.'

She took a deep breath.

'The woman in the bed at the end is Mrs Coffey. She has a urinary tract infection. She kept most of the patients awake all night with her groaning. She thinks nurses were put on this planet solely to cater for her needs. There was a window open about a tenth of an inch last night and she never shut up about the draught. But the biggest draught Mrs Coffey needs to worry about is the one between her ears.' (She said this loud enough for her to hear).

'Oh.'

'The lady beside her, Mrs Cadogan, has nothing wrong with her but she won't rest until we find something so we have her on various medications. If you're giving her a glass of water with her pills make sure you hold the glass to her lips as she tends to dribble. She usually ends up getting more water on the sheets than in her mouth so she's one to watch too. We don't want her getting pneumonia from wet sheets, do we?'

'No,' I said with as much conviction as I could muster.

I looked over at Mrs Cadogan. She seemed bewildered. Sister Agnes gazed at me, pulling her glasses up a bit as she went on.

'Beside her is Bríd Finney. She's just passed a gallstone. It's in a little bottle beside her bed so don't mix it up with her sleeping pills. She's treating it with the same reverence one might give to a piece of rock from Jupiter. She has an oozing wound. If it becomes infected there will be serious consequences for all concerned.'

She looked across the ward.

'Right, Mrs Finney?' she bellowed.

Mrs Finney was reading a newspaper. She didn't seem to be too concerned one way or another.

'Further down from her is Ginny Conroy,' Sister Agnes continued, 'She's recovering from an appendectomy. Further down again is Charlie Thornton. He has a strangulated hernia. And, yes, it's just as painful as it sounds. But of course you know that already, don't you? Because you've spent the past few months swotting up on all sorts of hernias, not just strangulated ones. You could probably educate me on them rather than vice versa.'

I tried to smile but it came out more as a grimace.

'The boy at the end of the ward is Oisín Casey, our youngest patient. He's seventeen going on two. He twisted his ankle after falling down a stairs.'

'God love him,' I said.

'He must. He got off light. The boy could have been killed, or at least paralysed. It's a mystery the people God chooses to spare.'

She went quiet.

'Is that everyone?' I hazarded.

'No. The woman nearest to him is going down for surgery tomorrow. She's fasting so there's a sign above her bed. Across from Mrs Cadogan is Julie Grogan. She has bad burns all over her. She let a pot of boiling water fall on her. There's no end to the kind of damage people can inflict on themselves once they put their mind to it.'

I tried to take it all in. How could I even remember these people's names, never mind anything else about them? She was throwing me in at the deep end. I wasn't sure if she was trying to give me information or frighten the life out of me.

One thing I knew for sure was that she wasn't interested in easing me in gently. Maybe that was good for me. For some reason I always found myself more tense with gentle people because I was so afraid of letting them down. Rough ones made me act rough too. When they tried to bully me my Tuohy dynamism came into play.

'It's all here in the notes,' she said finally, 'You'll be with Irene today. I'm off now.'

With that she was gone. I looked around. Irene was coming towards me. She came up to the desk.

'Hello, partner,' she said, giving me a big smile. I started to relax.

'Phew,' I said, 'That was some speech. Did you hear it?

'That's mild coming from Aggie. Wait till she gets into her stride.'

'What's she like to work with?'

'When you get past her horrific manner she's as right as rain. Like a lot of people with brusque personalities she has a big heart. If I was in trouble she'd be the first person in the world I'd go to.'

'Really?'

'On my word. Her bark is worse than her bite.'

'That's good to hear. Are the patients are as bad as she said?'

'They don't bite either.'

At that a young man in a bed nearby shouted out, 'I do!'

I wanted to laugh but didn't. I felt it would have given out the wrong signal.

'That's Oisín,' Irene said. 'He's wired to the moon.'

The morning passed in a haze. Irene started to chat more freely to me after the night sister went off.

She told me she was from Palmerstown. She was in her final year. She loved the job but she was going to have to leave it soon. Her husband worked in a bank. He'd just been transferred to Donegal. She thought she'd be leaving Dublin at the end of the year.

'That'll be hard for you,' I said.

'God is good. We'll see how it goes.'

She went off about her business and I was left with my tasks. I took Mrs. Cadogan's temperature and made her bed.

A few minutes later Mrs Coffey started clamouring for attention. I knew what Sister Agnes meant. She was like a child throwing her toys out of the pram.

I went over to her when I got a minute. She told me she was waiting on the result of a blood test. She was none too pleased that it was delayed.

'You're not the only one,' I said, 'There's a big backlog.' I'd have known that even if I wasn't working in the hospital.

'I've been hearing it for the past two months. It's all backlogs, backlogs, backlogs. When are you lot going to get your act together? This hospital is radically under-staffed.'

'That's nothing to do with me.'

'Did I say it was?'

I didn't want to get into an argument with her. I knew there could only be one winner in such a scenario.

'How are you feeling?' I asked her to change the subject.

'Terrible, if you must know. I have a pain in my back that feels like a JCB just fell on it. The bed is making it worse. What do you use for mattresses here – rocks?'

'How bad is it on a scale of one to ten?' I asked her. That was the standard question we were advised to ask all the patients.

'Eleven,' she replied tartly.

I jotted down a few notes about her and got away as fast as I could. With people like that, I knew you could spend the whole morning trying to placate them and you'd still end up back at square one.

The man with the torn ligaments hobbled around the ward on a crutch. Mrs Cadogan spent most of the morning asleep. Another patient was admitted with diverticulitis.

I felt sorriest of all for Julie Grogan. She was shivering from the burns. They were all over her.

'I feel like such an idiot,' she said. I told her not to, that we'd all done clumsy things and not suffered as a result. She was the unlucky one. How many times had I dodged a falling pot and got out of the way just in time?

I applied some ointment to her arm. She winced.

'Sorry,' I said.

'No problem. It's not your fault.'

Even the bedclothes hurt her. I managed to find a steel cage to keep them away from her body. It took me a while but it was worth it. She was more than happy with that.

At eleven o'clock another nurse came in on relief. Irene said, 'Would you like a break for a cup of tea?'

'Just what the doctor ordered,' I said, 'Or should I say the nurse.'

'I can see we're going to have a lot of fun with you,' she said laughing.

She paused for a second. Then she said, 'By the way, I wouldn't make too many jokes if Aggie is around. She'll make your life hell if you do.'

'You don't need to tell me.'

Another nurse arrived on the ward when our break came. Irene suggested we go down to the canteen. We had a half hour to play around with.

When we got there, a few of her friends were sitting over coffee. We ordered two cups for ourselves. They all seemed to be very friendly. One of them was called Deirdre. I was sitting beside her so we started chatting.

'How are you finding the lectures?' she asked me.

'A bit of a strain, to be honest,' I said.

'You wouldn't be alone in that. Sitting there listening to those boneheads droning on and on makes you lose the will to live.'

It helped so much to know someone else felt the same as me. She told me she'd just finished them. She was doing a case study now. She'd been assigned to the patient with diverticulitis. She was asked to write a report on him and then give a full diagnosis to two inspectors of what to do with him.

My blood froze at the prospect of this.

'Don't worry,' she said, no doubt seeing the fear on my face, 'The closest you'll come to a challenge at your stage is being asked how to make a bed - and even that will only have a dummy in it.'

'Thanks for the reassurance.'

'Just make sure you have the right attitude. And keep your hair off the collar of your uniform. It drives the ward sister mad if you don't.'

I left the canteen feeling very important in myself. Being with qualified nurses made me feel qualified myself. I'd been at 'the big girl's table' for the first time.

'Thanks for introducing me to your friends,' I said to Irene on the way back to the ward, 'Deirdre seems very nice.'

'She's my best friend,' she said, 'a real diamond.'

When we got to the ward the first thing we saw was Oisín in the medicine trolley. He was sailing up and down the floor in it, using it as a go-kart.

'Do you have to have a licence for this?' he asked me when I removed him from it, 'It gets a bit dodgy at the turns.'

The nurse who relieved us said he'd been a nightmare since we left. The first thing he did was sellotape 'Elvis Presley' onto his name tag, putting up the collar of his pyjamas and going 'Uh-huh.'

After that he'd hidden his pills under the mattress. She only discovered them when she was making the bed.

'I'm saving them up for an overdose,' he explained.

I sympathised with her. She was a rookie like myself and totally unequipped to deal with a situation like that.

Irene went off after thanking her for looking after the ward. She felt sorry for her too.

She brought me over to the desk.

'I think you know by now that Oisín is going to be a fulltime job,' she said. 'If you're giving him any more pills,' she said, 'Make sure he opens his mouth wide to show you he's swallowed them. He likes to hide them under his tongue so watch out for that.'

I wondered what was in store for me.

'He's not a bad lad,' she said, 'He just suffers from an excess of energy.'

'If only we could give him some Valium,' I said.

'I know. It would be the answer to everything. Except we'd end up across the road.' She put her hands together and made a clicking noise to indicate handcuffs. She meant in Mountjoy Jail. You could see it from the window of our room.

When I went down to look at his chart later in the day I saw he'd drawn cartoon faces all over his reports.

I had a bottle of Dettol on a trolley with me. I'd brought it with me to clean the wound on his head. He tried to trip me up as I went to apply it.

I ended up spilling the Dettol.

I had to draw on all my resources not to let a roar at him. A few minutes later he put his hand around my waist. I was bending over him to put a bandage on him at the time. He was spurting blood but he still wouldn't take it away. I gave him a slap for that. I thought it might put manners on him but it made him worse.

The next time I saw him he was prancing up and down the ward in a surgical gown. It was bare at the back. I grabbed a towel to protect his modesty but it didn't need protecting.

'Where did you get that?' I asked him.

'A kind old man gave it to me on his way back from the operating theatre. If you go next door you'll see him in all his glory.'

'Don't push your luck,' I said, 'I have a breaking point.'

'The patients were enjoying the display. Consider yourself lucky I wasn't wearing it the other way around.'

When Irene came back I told her what he'd been up to. She wasn't surprised. I had to pretend to be cross with him but in actual fact I wasn't.

The next time I went down to him I said, 'Did your bowels move today?' It was something we had to ask everyone.

'How dare you be so inquisitive,' he said, letting out a yelp, 'It's none of your bloody business.'

'Oisín,' I said, 'I like you. You're a funny young man, but what happened to you isn't too funny. It could have been a lot worse. You can make your stay here either pleasant or unpleasant, both for yourself and us. So far you've done your best to beat the system. That's not going to work. If the ward sister hears about your antics I wouldn't like to think what she'd do to you.'

He was chewing gum all through my little speech.

'Is that it?' he said.

I gave him a hard look.

'Obviously you haven't been taking in a thing I've been saying. Do you want us to cure you or laugh at you?'

'Both if possible,' he said, 'though not necessarily in that order.'

'It isn't Fossett's Circus in here. If you think it is you're sadly mistaken. It's a hospital. You fell down a stairs. That must have hurt.'

He took out the chewing gum. He stuck it onto the top of his locker.

'No, nurse,' he said, 'It wasn't the stairs that hurt. It was the floor.'

'Very funny. You can resume your comedy career when you get out of here but until then you're under me. Okay?'

He stuck his tongue out. He started panting like a dog.

'Under you? That sounds exciting.'

He reminded me of the boys in Midleton who tried to cover up their shyness with smart jokes.

'I don't find those kind of comments funny,' I said, 'Are you suffering from some kind of insecurity?'

'Maybe. Would that bother you?'

'Not necessarily but I can think of some other people it might.'

'Like who?'

'Like the other 99% of the staff.'

He laughed.

'I can see you're a bit of a comedian yourself.'

He took the chewing gum back from his locker and started chewing it again. I could see him trying to think up some other piece of mischief.

'I'm thirsty,' he said, 'Any chance you could get me a can of Fanta from the locker?'

I bent down. When I opened the door I saw a little bottle of vodka behind the Fanta.

'Aha,' I said, taking it out, 'So this is what's causing the excitement. Very clever. Alcohol that doesn't smell.'

He looked taken aback for the first time.

'Keep your hands off that,' he snapped, 'It's private property.'

'Not in here it isn't,' I said, 'I'm confiscating it.'

He scowled.

'No you're not.'

'Oisín,' I said firmly, 'There's a limit. If I don't take this away from you I'll get into trouble myself.'

He looked glum.

'You'll probably put it aside for yourself. I know what you nurses get up to in your spare time.'

'Whatever I do with it, one thing is sure. You won't be seeing it again until you're in your day clothes.'

I put it in my pocket. He sat up in the bed.

'Okay. Go off with it. Finish it off for all I care.'

I handed him the Fanta. He looked me up and down admiringly as he drank it.

'You're quite pretty you know,' he said, 'Maybe you'd like to come to the pictures with me some night.'

My face went scarlet. My first day on the job and already I was being asked out.

'I beg your pardon?

'I said maybe you'd like to come to the pictures with me some night. I mean when I get out of this mad house.'

'You really have the cheek of the devil,' I said.

'Is that a yes or a no?'

'It's a no. And don't ask me again or I'll report everything about you – including the vodka.'

He put on one of his childish grins.

'You don't know what you're missing,' he grinned, giving me a wink.

I can't remember much about the rest of the day. I have vague memories of seeing Irene give injections to people, of her advising me some more about pills, of having a woman tell me she was facing a gall bladder operation the following day.

I couldn't get my mind off Oisín's idiotic behaviour. His invitation to take me out was half way between embarrassing and flattering.

The clock on the wall seemed to go from 9 a.m. to 3.30 in about five minutes. I'd survived the first day.

Before going back to Room 19 I went for a walk to clear my head. So much had happened I needed to get rid of some of the clutter inside it.

After walking around the same streets for ages I went into a shop and bought a newspaper. Then I went into the café I'd been in with Bridget and Cáit. I read it over a strong cup of black coffee.

When I got back to the room the two of them were already there. They looked distressed.

'Where have you been, stranger?' Cáit said, 'We were about to put out a Missing Persons Report.'

'I went for a walk to clear my head.'

'A walk? Do you realise what time it is?

I looked at the clock. It was coming up to six.

'Oh my God, I had no idea it was anything like that. I went for a cup of tea. I was lost in my thoughts.'

'What was your day like?' Bridget asked me.

'A bit mad. One thing kept happening after another. Every time I thought I was finished something, I got called to something else. What about you two?'

'The same,' Bridget said. 'We were together. That helped.'

A part of me envied them. Another part was glad to have been in a different environment.

'One of my patients went into a diabetic coma,' Cáit said, 'How about that for a first day?'

'Jeepers. And I thought I was bad. How are they?'

'They came out of it but it was worrying for a while. Bridget had it easier. She spent most of the day in the X-ray department learning how to do a barium meal.'

'Is that right, Bridget?'

She nodded.

'The best part of the day was when a child wandered in holding his Mammy's hand. He'd swallowed a needle and there was no time to get him to the children's hospital. He had to be fed a cotton wool bud so it could be passed safely. He was very brave about it.' I couldn't imagine having to 'eat' cotton wool.

'How did you get on with Oisín?' she said. I wondered how she'd heard about him.

I decided to reveal all.

'He asked me out,' I said. Their eyes nearly jumped out of their sockets.

'I don't believe you,' Cáit said.

'What did you say?' Bridget asked.

Both of them sidled up to me. After diabetic comas and needle-swallowing, I didn't think this would get so much interest.

'I put him off.'

'Jesus,' Cáit said, 'He's a fast mover so he is.'

I told them the whole story. They lapped it up. Then they started on about their own day.

We talked until our jaws were sore. All three of us felt like we'd run a marathon. And yet we welcomed that after all the months of study. We were part of something now, all the moreso for having shared it with one another.

'I'm going to turn in early,' I said to them after all our talking was done.

'You're good at that,' Cáit jeered.

'Already the professional,' Bridget said.

Their attitudes didn't bother me.

I felt I wouldn't be able to function for a month if I didn't get some shut-eye.

I was wrecked.

# Working and Playing Hard

I woke up the next morning thinking: 'I'll be all right, I know I can do this now.' It was as if I'd been baptised. It was a study day so I didn't have to go into the hospital. I should have had my head in my books but I didn't feel like it after all the excitement of the day before.

I spent most of it just hanging around. I went down to the canteen at about eleven for some porridge. That turned out to be not such a good idea. It tasted like roofing material.

Afterwards I wandered into the sitting-room. I chatted to some of the other nurses who were there. I was dressed in a pair of slacks and a polo neck jumper I had. It was good to know Granny's woolly one would never be taking up space in my wardrobe again.

There was an old film on the television. I watched it in a half-daze. It was a war one with John Mills. I preferred Hayley, his daughter. I remembered Daddy saying these sort of films always had John mills in them. 'Is he the only actor in the country?' he'd say, 'I wouldn't mind if he was any good.'

I watched all Hayley Mills' films with Maureen. She was our favourite child actress. When she was kissed by Peter McEnery in *The Moonspinners* in 1964 it was like the end of an era. She'd suddenly become a woman. After that she seemed to lose something for us. The magic was gone.

I got sad remembering about all our trips to Cork to watch the 'golden oldies.' Anytime I thought of the past I felt my eyes welling up. I wanted to ring home a hundred times a day but I resisted it. If I gave in once I knew I'd keep doing it.

For the next few days I was a floater. That meant I went from ward to ward doing routine chores any unqualified person could do. On the Monday I was told to wash out the medicine trolleys with carbolic. Afterwards I had to prepare sterile ones for theatre. It was hardly a brain test. I knew they were trying to break me in gradually. After the chaos of the day before I welcomed that.

The first trolley I was asked to wash seemed to have a mind of its own. I couldn't get the wheels to move properly despite tugging it fiercely this way and that. What chance had I to master the finer points of cardiac massage, I thought, when I couldn't even wash a trolley?

At visiting time they had me arranging flowers in vases on the window-sill. Later on I was told to put on a hot water bottle for a patient. Sister Agnes nearly had a seizure when she felt it.

'Tepid, my dear girl,' she droned, 'Tepid, not hot.' She insisted on spilling some of the water out and adding colder water from the tap. 'Always make sure you tilt it like this to get the air bubbles out,' she said. I'd probably filled a hundred hot water bottles for Mammy and Daddy since I was a child. Now I was being treated like a child again. Would she be telling me how to tie my shoelaces next?

When I went back to my room that evening I threw my uniform into a corner. I felt like stamping on it. A few glasses of wine with Cáit and Bridget didn't even help my mood. I was so angry I think they were half-afraid of me.

'Don't set such high standards for yourself,' Bridget said. My feet were aching me so I put some books under the legs of the bed to keep it raised as I slept. Sister Agnes was right about the importance of strong shoes.

On the Tuesday I was sent from the orthopaedic ward to ENT. That stood for Ear, Nose and Throat. They gave me a supply of prescription sheets to get signed. I spent half the day running up and down to the pharmacy for a patient who was about to be sent home. On Wednesday I got to dole out pills to patients. I felt chuffed with myself being in charge of the drug cupboard even if it was only for the day.

By the end of the week I was back in St. Ignatius Ward again. I was delighted with that. I finally had some kind of permanent role. The first thing I was asked to do was give a bath to a patient. It was tricky because he was unsteady on his feet. He refused to hold onto the grab rail. I kept thinking he was going to fall and injure himself. It would have been a nice how-do-you-do if he sued the hospital on account of me.

Most of the following day I spent at the linen cupboard sorting out sheets and blankets. That made me feel demeaned again. Was this what I spent all the months  studying for, I asked myself - to be a glorified version of the home help? Afterwards I was asked to wheel the medicine trolley around. I watched the staff nurse dispensing pills from it.

You had to record what she was giving out. I took notes on everything I saw, even the way the nurse talked to the patients. I felt like a walking tape recorder. Before I went home she asked me to watch her doing a dressing. Then she asked me to do one while she watched. That became the pattern of the following days, watching and then doing like a performing seal.

The uniform I was wearing as a floater didn't fit at first. I had to have it adjusted. Bridget had a sewing machine so she took the hem up. She was really natty at things like that.

'You'll have to get rid of the bangle on your wrist,' Sister Agnes said to me on the Friday. I wasn't even aware I was wearing one. We weren't allowed anything feminine in case they interfered with our work. That ruled out bracelets and necklaces as well. 'The whole idea is to make us sexless,' Cáit declared, 'I wonder if they'll hack off our breasts next.'

On my second week I was assigned to a patient with a collapsed lung. Sister Agnes thought it would be a good idea to write down the details of his condition on a folder and update it each day. She said that would prepare me for further assignments. It was good advice. It set the tone of how I dealt with all the other patients.

In the evenings I went to the library to get information on people with similar conditions. I compared the man with the collapsed lung with other patients I had. I took notes on how he was responding to treatment and how fast his recovery was progressing. I liked the discipline of that. I found myself jotting down little changes that were taking place in him every time I saw him.

I was more myself the second week. Once I started moving on the ward I felt as if I was in my own kitchen. Irene came in on the Monday. She'd been on a week's leave. She'd gone up to Donegal to check out houses up there in case they had to leave.

'Did you see any interesting places?' I asked her.

'My heart wasn't in it,' she said. 'They were all very nice but I didn't give them a chance. I think I was trying to talk myself out of not liking them.'

I asked her what happened to Oisín.

'We got rid of him in super-quick time,' she laughed, 'before he pulled the walls down. The poor lad was packed off before he knew what hit him.'

'He wasn't the worst,' I said.

'He was a lovely guy outside the hospital but a nightmare inside it. That was the problem. He said to give you a big kiss for him.'

I found myself blushing.

'Did he really ask you out?' she said then.

'No way!' I lied, 'Who told you that?'

'Can't say. A little bird.'

Every little titbit of news obviously went all over the place. It was an early lesson to me not to divulge too much of my life to anyone. I wondered if he'd been serious about our date. I'd never know now.

Irene admired my uniform.

'You certainly look the part,' she said.

'That's half the battle, isn't it?'

'Three quarters, I'd say. How are you getting on at the lectures?'

'They're not my favourite parts of nursing.'

'Are they anyone's?'

'At least some of them are over.'

'The time will fly from now on,' she said, 'Believe me.'

I told her I was settling into the whole business much quicker than I expected.

'I knew you would,' she said, 'Once you're interested, that's the main thing.'

A lot of the work you could do in your sleep. We had to clean the lockers for the whole ward some days. That was boring unless you broke it up by chatting with the patients. Bridget used to say I'd talk to a lamp-post to pass the time. She was probably right. It got me into trouble if patients told me personal details about their lives. If I repeated them to the wrong person and it got back to them I knew I'd be in big trouble. As time went on I learned to keep things like that to myself too. It wasn't in my nature so I had to work extra hard at it.

The work grew on me but the food continued to be terrible. I generally avoided the canteen, either eating out in fast food places or bringing things back to my room. I became very close to Cáit and

Bridget but Sister Agnes put on a face like thunder anytime I made even the slightest mistake.

I phoned home every now and then but I didn't go into too much detail about anything that was happening to me. I knew Daddy would be up like as shot to bring me home if he thought anyone was mistreating me. Mammy would probably have advised me to stick it out, telling me things would improve with time. I tried to adopt her attitude.

Bridget and Cáit were in different groups to me for some of the lectures. In a sense that was good for us. It gave us more to gossip about in the evenings. I met a lot of new people because of that and so did they. Cáit was always making fun in the classes I went to with her. She drew funny pictures on the text books, adding limbs onto the bodies that were being displayed. Sometimes she'd even give them two or more heads. A lot of the time I had to pinch myself to stop myself laughing out loud.

Irene had to go to Donegal much sooner than she thought so she wasn't on the ward with me after the first few weeks. We threw a little party for her before she went but it wasn't much good to her. She cried through most of it, her mind more on the past than the future. 'There's nobody like the Mater nurses,' she told us.

After a month on Ignatius I was moved to a surgical ward. It was more intensive. There was more fear among the patients too. Things also went wrong more often, despite our best efforts.

I was on the same shift times as Cáit and Bridget now. We usually left Room 19 together. They were never ready as quickly as me. That was because they spent so much time doing themselves up. I was different, being one of these people who applied their make-up 'on the run.' That meant I was almost out the door as soon as I woke up.

A lot of the time we didn't bother with breakfast. If we had time we might have a quick cup of tea in the canteen to get the day going. It was a long way from life at home where Daddy used to say, 'Breakfast like a queen, lunch like a princess and dine like a pauper.' We breakfasted like paupers but I always felt like I had a hole in my stomach until we got to 'elevenses.' If a patient needed care at that time we often had to do without our break.

There were some things I really enjoyed about nursing and some things I despised. I was good at preparing patients for operations but I hated wheeling them down to theatre, especially if they were in pain. I was better at getting to know them as people than medical cases.

I enjoyed nursing them back to health after their surgeries, at least if they didn't pester me with questions about side-effects they could have. And of course I hated emptying out bedpans, but then we all hated that. The sluice was my least favourite part of the hospital.

I dreaded answering the phone too, even if it was from relatives of the patients enquiring about their condition. We were ordered not to give out information as Juniors but I couldn't see why, especially if the person identified themselves as being a husband or wife of the patient.

If the person was a next of kin we had to make sure a patient was 'up' to a call. I was inclined to let them speak even if they were woozy but other nurses felt differently. As a student I was rarely consulted about my views on who should speak to who; I just took their details down and brought them over to the ward sister. Left to myself I'd probably have had half the ward gabbing away to their relatives all day long. My judgment was terrible about things like that.

Some patients never stopped complaining but most of them were fine. My favourites were the young lads like Oisín who were full of life – as long as they didn't use the medicine trolleys as go-karts. Many of them came in with sports injuries. They were often spouting blood. They tended to want to talk about anything but what happened to them.

That was good for me. It made me less nervous dealing with them if they looked to be seriously ill. I could take their temperature and blood pressure without spending too much time worrying about giving anything away about how seriously injured they looked to me. Ignorance was surely bliss at such times.

A brazen young fellow said to me one day, 'My blood pressure was fine till I saw you. You shot it right off the scale with your pretty face.' Oisín sprang into my mind immediately but this guy was ten times worse. He wanted my phone number at any cost but I refused to give it to him.

I couldn't pass his bed after that but he made some smart comment about me. If I had to take blood from him he made out as if I was Dracula. He'd pretend to be fending me off, barely stopping short of ripping my uniform. When I told Bridget about him she said he was 'hormonally charged.' I enjoyed his carry-on most of the time but I had to be careful not to be too familiar for fear he'd corner me some day when there was nobody around.

Towards the end of the year we had two written exams as well as an oral and a practical. I did okay on the writtens and surprisingly well at my practical but I made a mess of the oral. I was asked what about the symptoms of glandular fever and I went blank. I couldn't believe this because it was something I'd studied in some detail.

Thankfully the examiner was sympathetic. She told me to come back the following day. I think she knew it was nerves rather than lack of knowledge that struck me dumb. When I went in the next day I felt a lot better. She asked me a different question this time and I responded. I managed to put a few sentences together without coming across like a total idiot.

My life at this point seemed to be taken over with symptoms and diagnoses. I felt like a walking encyclopaedia. A blizzard of terms swirled round in my head like crossword puzzles to be solved. Would I ever qualify? Would they stay in my head long enough for me to get them down on paper? I longed for a time I could be just a simple person again.

The days became shorter. Before we knew where we were, winter was in with a vengeance. I lost interest in going out at night because it was so cold. The weather didn't bother Cáit or Bridget in the least. When I kept refusing invitations to join them they started to think I might be suffering from depression. The plain fact of the matter was that I had no energy. I flopped into bed most nights after work when they were rearing to go out on the town. I felt every germ in the air was making for me as if I was a magnet.

'Maybe I have that SAD thing,' I said, 'Don't people get it when they're tired all the time?'

'It was well named anyway,' Cáit said, 'Anyone I've seen with it is bloody miserable.'

The letters stand for Seasonal Affective Disorder,' Bridget piped up.

'Know-all,' Cáit sniffed.

The long evenings should have given me more interest in studying but I couldn't rouse myself to it. Instead I read books that had nothing to do with medicine to get my mind off it, huge big escapist novels to get away from my world of pain and suffering. I read Danielle Steele and loads of other authors like her, turning the pages with a mixture of relief and boredom. I soaked myself in them with large mugs of tea and endless Club Milks. They often fell out of my hand if I was reading in bed. I'd trip over them on the floor the next morning.

When I went home for Christmas I felt as if I'd been away for years rather than months. The first thing I saw at the train station was *The Midleton Echo*. There were dozens of papers stacked in a pile on the platform ready for dispatch. The top one was raggedy from the wind but I could still read the headline. A local businessman had been given an award. I'd have something to tell Mammy and Daddy when I saw them. They always liked to keep up with what was going on.

They rushed towards me just as I was thinking of them. Both of them looked great. Daddy lifted me off my feet. Mammy scrutinised me to see if I lost any weight. They quizzed me non-stop about everything on the way home in the car. I tried to squeeze in all the important things in the short journey.

Maureen and May were at the door of the house when we got there. They were delighted to see me. They wanted to hear all my news but I was too tired to go through it all again.

'Ask Mammy and Daddy,' I said, 'I've told them everything I can think of. I'm hoarse talking.'

I went inside and slumped into a chair. Mammy went off to make tea. Daddy's back was bothering him so he went upstairs to lie down for a while. Maureen and May sat on the floor at my feet.

'Tell us everything,' May said. She reminded me of Grandad asking me to tell him everything that happened in my life since I was born. I promised myself I'd go down and see him the next day.

Maureen wanted to know all about my training. She said she was half thinking of going in for nursing herself. She pumped me for

93

information about what it entailed. May was more interested in the night life.

Aunt Bernie dropped in after a while. She told me I looked better than ever.

'Work must be agreeing with you,' she said.

'I don't know about that,' I said, 'Sometimes I wonder what I've got myself into.' For the rest of the day she sat in the corner of the sitting-room listening to all of us. She reminded me of a sphinx. She quietly took in everything that was discussed with a little smile on her face.

I totally unwound for the rest of the week. The days flew by. Everyone spoiled me with presents. I only had basic ones for them. They put a huge tree up with lots of decorations on it. We ate ourselves silly. We pulled crackers and played all the games we played as children. By the time Christmas Day arrived we'd practically worn out the record player playing Bing Crosby songs.

I had to face the long journey back to Dublin on St. Stephen's Day. Daddy was shocked I was going back so soon.

'You're hardly here,' he said.

'You never listen, Daddy,' I said, 'I told you a hundred times I was on tomorrow.'

'That's not a hospital,' he said, 'It's a workhouse.'

'People don't stop getting sick just because it's Christmas.'

'Then let someone else look after them. We rarely see you.'

'If you don't let me go,' I said, 'You'll stop me wanting to come down the next time.'

I slipped out quietly the next morning before he was awake, having a brief word with Mammy before I got a taxi to the train. I felt both sad and happy on the journey to Dublin, sad that I was leaving but happy that everyone seemed so well.

I was no sooner back in Room 19 than I felt I'd never been away. Cáit and Bridget were full of yarns about their week off. We had a great chinwag in a pub in Phibsboro but the next morning it was back to porridge.

Everyone on the ward felt flat. It always seemed to be the way with people when Christmas was over. Some of the patients who weren't seriously ill had gone home so a lot of the beds were empty.

That made things seem even flatter still but it gave me a chance to get to know the ones who were there better.

There was a hospital dance on New Year's Eve. We were allowed to bring men if we wanted but there was nobody I could think of so I just went with Bridget and Cáit. Bridget didn't have anyone either. Cáit was 'half-seeing' a rugby player she'd nursed with a groin injury. Bridget taunted her about examining him much more closely than she needed to in his nether regions.

The dance was a tame affair. It was held in the main hall of the building we were staying in. The night sister positioned herself at the foot of the stairs for most of the evening just in case we got any ideas about bringing a man up to our room. That was unlikely. The music played at the dance was like something from a Church Social. One man I danced with said dryly, 'I suppose they're going to play "Mother Machree" next.'

The only drinks on offer were minerals. We spent most of the night talking shop with each other and stifling yawns. I'd probably have had more fun tucked up in bed with my Danielle Steele. By the end of the night most of the men had departed the scene, including Cáit's rugby friend. We were left singing 'Should Old Acquaintance Be Forgot' to one another and trying to look more emotional than we actually were.

When the new year came in I wasn't as tense going to the lectures or even to work. It was as if I'd settled into a groove. At times I almost felt I was qualified. People got to know me better in the wards and that helped too. I joked with them and felt more generally at home, at least when Aggie's eagle eyes weren't peering down on me.

In the evenings the three of us went out to clear our heads. We often cycled to Dollymount beach. I had a basket in the front of my bike so I could put flasks of tea in it. We usually brought sandwiches as well. I loved the feeling of the wind in my face when we hit the sea road, or looking at the sun on the waves when we walked the pier.

Bridget liked to swim. She used to peel her clothes off in all weathers. She was a very strong swimmer. I envied her because I swam like a stone myself. Afterwards we'd run madly along the beach for fun. I enjoyed that but I got tired quickly Cáit and Bridget were much faster than me. They were like greyhounds let off the leash.

If we were off at the weekend we usually went dancing. We had to apply for extra passes to stay out late. Some of the nurses chanced going out without them by leaving a window slightly open. They usually got away with it but one night two of them were collared by Sister Agnes. She'd spotted the open window and copped on to what was going on. She caught them trying to break the lock of the front door. There was hell to pay about that. I heard she wanted them dismissed on the spot.

That would probably have happened if she hadn't been over-ruled at a board meeting. Between the jigs and the reels they ended up with nothing more than a rap on the knuckles. Even so, it was a warning to all of us. I knew Cáit tried it once or twice and got away with it. She didn't give a hoot about being caught. She hatched a plan of getting a locksmith she was friendly with to copy the key of the gate. If she was found at that it would have landed her in a nice pickle.

'Let them throw me out if they want,' she crowed, 'I'll find something better than nursing. It's a crap job anyway.'

'I believe bar work pays more,' Bridget suggested.

'I prefer being on the other side of the counter,' Cáit assured her.

Cáit was the most popular of the three of us at the dances. Bridget didn't get asked up too much. She was good-looking but you had to look twice to see it. Like me she never bothered too much with make-up or fancy clothes. She had a natural beauty but most of the men at the dances we went to  seemed too blind to see that.

Not being asked up gave her a complex about herself.

'I'm just a wallflower,' she'd say. It made her night to get even one dance.

I hated waiting to be asked up. I was a bit taller than Cáit or Bridget so I stood out. That made me uncomfortable. I'd have preferred to sink into the woodwork.

There were many nights when I didn't care one way or the other. I preferred listening to the music and having the crack.

By the end of the night the men you met tended to have more drink on them. Some of them were paralytic. They just wanted to maul you.

They'd stampede across the floor and all but demand you danced with them. They had a way of looking you up and down as if you were a cow at a mart. All you were missing was a rosette pinned to your ear. As soon as one of them gave you a gamey eye you knew what he was after.

Most of them didn't even try to hide it. They were cheeky with drink but without it I felt a lot of them would have been terrified to go within a mile of a woman. Alcohol turned them from being mammy's boys into predatory animals. It made them push up against you. You felt the stench of the drink so strong it was as if you'd drunk it yourself.

Neither myself nor Bridget drank much but Cáit made up for us. After a few vodkas in her she was a riot. She didn't know what she was doing under the influence half the time but boy could she party. She'd start doing herself up at about four o'clock on the nights she'd be going out.

She'd be still at it four hours later, putting on her 'war paint', as she called it, in big blobs. She wore her skirts up to her bum and showed a bit too much 'upstairs' as well. She had Bridget and me in stitches but we had to protect her from herself sometimes. She was capable of going off with anything in trousers.

Apart from everything else we were worried she might become a victim of violence. At the beginning of that year a young girl called Hazel Mullen was strangled by a medical student she was dating and afterwards dismembered by him. His name was Shan Mohangi. Some people believed he was trying to perform an abortion on her after getting her pregnant and that it went wrong.

Other people believed he went into a rage when she tried to end their relationship. He only served a few months in prison after being found guilty of killing her. When he got out he was deported to Africa. I thought he'd be disgraced out there but instead of that he became a politician. It all seemed so weird. For months afterwards nobody could talk about anything else.

At the end of our time on 'surgical' we had a few days off so we decided to go down to Courtown for a long weekend.

'I'm just about ready for some debauchery,' Cáit informed us.

'Me too,' Bridget echoed.

'Me three,' I added tentatively.

I wasn't used to going on holidays so I didn't know what to bring with me. I packed, as Bridget put it, 'for a nuclear winter.' The other two didn't bring much more than the clothes they were wearing. We spent the whole journey down exchanging yarns about the month just gone. When you were away from something it seemed like a distant part of your life. It did me good to get out of my routines, to see myself as others might have seen me.

The pair of them told me I needed to relax more, that I was too focussed on the job. I tried my best to.

There were discos at night. You'd see all sorts of men with mischief in their eyes at them. Bridget and I had to keep a close eye on Cáit for fear someone unsavoury would take advantage of her. More often than not she was 'flying,' as Bridget put it, which made me wonder if she was sneaking a few extra shorts on the side at the bar counter.

She kept a mysterious bottle in her handbag as well, telling us it was 'medicinal.' No matter where you were with Cáit there'd be something going on. I learned to watch her out of the side of my eye for her own protection. It was hard to keep a straight face with her antics. We used to have to physically prise her away from men a lot of the time. Otherwise we were convinced she'd end up pregnant. Anytime I ever went to a dance in Midleton, Mammy used to say to me, 'Don't come home with anything you didn't go out with.' I found myself saying the same thing to Cáit.

Back in Dublin she continued her wild ways. If we were out for a night she'd hit the bottle almost as soon as we got in the door of the pub.

'Do you never worry about the state of your liver?' I'd say to her to give her a fright. She'd shoot me a glance and rasp back something like 'Shut your trap. You're not in the hospital now.'

She continued to shovel the liquor into herself until things reached a stage where she wasn't even enjoying herself anymore. She was drinking simply because she couldn't think of anything else to do. I worried that it was becoming a real problem with her.

At the end of a night we'd find ourselves tearing her away from some man she was slobbering over. We'd drop her into a taxi and pray to God she wouldn't throw up all over the seat. The men didn't seem to mind whether she did or not. I remember one of them reproaching me.

'Leave her alone,' he snarled, She's a grown woman.' I felt like telling him she was more like a catatonic one.

If she met anyone she was attracted to, all the way home she'd be saying things like, 'You bitches, I really liked him, I want to have his babies.' It would usually be some gombeen who looked like he'd been dragged through a bush backwards. One night she took to this guy so much she went to the lengths of writing her phone number on his arm because she couldn't find a piece of paper. The next morning she told me if she ever saw him again she'd throw up.

I often wondered why she drank so much. Maybe she didn't know herself. It was as if she felt she owed it to herself to be outrageous even on the nights when she might have been more content to be sitting at home by the fire. It was as if she'd created an identity for herself in the dance-halls and she had to live up – or rather down – to it more and more the longer time went on.

Bridget and myself were more the fools to go along with it. We designated ourselves as her protectors. Once we'd slotted ourselves into that role we became victims of it as well, playing it over and over until we started to believe there was no other way to deal with her. Maybe we got some kind of fulfilment out of 'saving her from herself,' as Bridget put it.

We knew it couldn't go on forever but we didn't think about things like that then. We just lived in the moment. When Cáit was 'flying' you couldn't pay for the type of entertainment she gave us. One night after coming home she proceeded to pull all the religious pictures from the walls of the corridor and deposit them in the bin. 'These bloody things are putting years on me,' she wailed before Bridget got her into bed.

I managed to fish them out of the bin and get them back on the wall before Aggie saw them. If she had she'd probably have ended up in the cardiac unit getting mouth-to-mouth resuscitation.

I don't know how Cáit did her work on the mornings after these nights. Sometimes she didn't. I remember her having to go to the sick bay once when she fell ill on duty. It was obvious she was running on empty. There were other times I'd ring in for her. I usually told matron she had a throat infection. That was everyone's favourite excuse. It covered a multitude. Or maybe I'd say it was 'a woman's problem.' But she was an excellent nurse when she was sober. The patients loved her. The two parts of her life were totally separate. She was very sensitive behind all the bluster. If any of the other nurses got wind of her drinking she'd probably have broken down crying.

Maybe the two sides of her life had that root – sensitivity. It could well have been such sensitivity that made her drink so much. I've noticed mood swings in most alcoholics I've run into. Cáit had her quiet phases on the wards just like the rest of us. What made her ones so noticeable was the fact that they were in such contrast to the party animal that came to life at the dances.

We met every kind of men at these. Most of them came up with the same tired lines and we gave the same tired answers.

'Do you come here often?'

'Only when there's a dance.'

'Do you mind if I smoke?'

'I don't mind if you catch fire.'

When they heard my accent they often started talking about Christy Ring. It was as if he was the only person that had ever been born in Cork.

I hated being asked what I did for a living. You were often pigeonholed when you said you were a nurse. When I told one man I worked in the Mater he said, 'What's the Mater?' I thought that sounded funny.

A lot of men presumed that if you agreed to dance with them it gave them a kind of ownership over you. They'd say things like, 'How do you like your eggs in the mornin', love?' a supposed chat-up line that totally turned me off. I had a good answer for them: Unfertilised, if you don't mind.'

One night this tulip came up to me and said, 'How is your love life?' I replied, 'A bit better without the likes of you.' As I walked away from him I could hear him muttering 'Lesbian,' under his breath. There were some men who had such egos they thought the only reason a woman mightn't be interested in them was if they were that way inclined. Some of them looked like the back of a bus. It made their sense of ego seem even more amazing.

A man was dancing with me one night when he said suddenly, 'Are you on the pill?' I almost collapsed on the spot. He was so young I felt like asking him if his mother knew he was out. 'If you don't make yourself scarce mighty quick, sonny boy,' I said to him, '*you'll* be on something – a stretcher.'

I hated refusing men dances, at least if I saw they were low on confidence. There's nothing worse than crossing the floor to ask a girl to dance and having to crawl back again with your tail between your legs. I always gave those kinds of men one dance at least. They were generally happy with that. If they weren't I'd discreetly excuse myself to go to the Ladies. If Cáit or Bridget were in there we'd have a pow-wow about who we'd like to give our phone numbers to and who we'd do our best to avoid. We had codes that served as warnings for who might be trouble, little expressions we made to one another, or hand gestures to make a hasty exit.

I made a point of staying in the Ladies for the last dance of the night. This was often a slow one and therefore a temptation for someone you mightn't like to get too close. If he succeeded in that he might expect 'something extra' afterwards, like a quick fumble in the back seat of his Volkswagen so he'd have something to boast about to his friends the next morning. Bridget had a great line for fellows who asked her if they could have the last dance with her: 'You've already had it, buster.'

If someone was pushy I didn't tell them where I worked. I also gave false names. Once or twice I got calls to the hospital. I often wondered how they found out where I worked. These ones I absolutely refused to answer.

One time a troubled young man from Carlow bent my ear for a whole evening telling me about a previous girlfriend who'd dropped him. She caused him to have a breakdown. He said he was on medication now and it was helping him a bit.

I tried to be as sympathetic to him as I could. Obviously I overdid it because the next day he arrived into the ward as if he knew me all my life. He informed me he'd now decided it was me he loved, not the other woman. It was a pretty brisk exchange of affection. After listening to his *ólagóning* for a half hour – Deirdre was good enough to cover for me on the ward – I said to him, 'I don't know who you're in love with and I'm not sure I care but I can tell you one thing for nothing – it's not me.'

With that I turned on my heel and walked away. I thought that would be the end of it but it wasn't. He followed me all the way back to the ward. When I told him to get lost he pulled me towards him and tried to kiss me. I had to call a security guard to have him removed in the end. There were some strange phone calls in the following days. I suspected were from him but he didn't speak. Thank God they stopped after a while. I was always terrified he'd turn into a stalker.

Cáit was my sentry at the hospital if someone I wasn't interested in was pestering me. I'd tell her to say I was out sick. She was great at that. If she took a turn against someone she'd come up with more elaborate excuses. She'd say things like, 'I'm afraid she was bitten by a piranha fish. She's in hospital in Zimbabwe at the moment getting treated for it.' Or, 'I can't contact her at the moment. She said she wanted to go to Jupiter so she's in NASA getting her shots.'

Bridget and myself would be at the door of the ward trying to hold our stomachs in at times like this. Often we'd be so bad we'd have to pinch ourselves so we wouldn't burst out laughing.

The men usually walked off in a temper. Now and again I thought she went too far. One bozo put his foot in the door of a waiting-room on a day when she'd been particularly vicious. He looked over to a cubicle Bridget and myself were standing behind. I felt he sensed us being there. I was afraid he'd break a window on his way out.

Sometimes Cáit even slammed the swing doors on them. 'Men are users,' she'd say, 'This is one way of getting back at them, letting them know we can tell them to get lost when we want to.'

She had a great command of English when she got going. She could wipe the floor with them in ways that left them unable to squeak in reply. I had to laugh one day when I heard her saying to a particularly persistent suitor, 'What part of "No" do you not understand?' I think she got that from all the time we spent watching American television programmes.

It was tough getting up the morning after the dances with our limbs aching. We rarely went out during the week. Monday mornings were the worst if we'd been somewhere on the Sunday. Cáit said she could go on living that kind of life indefinitely but Bridget and myself felt we were burning ourselves out. We were almost glad when Lent came and there were no dances on.

Towards the end of the year she dragged us out to Dublin Airport to see The Beatles. Everyone was going mad about them at the time. It seemed they could do no wrong. Almost every record they brought out went to the top of the hit parade. Women were fainting at their concerts.

They were appearing in the Adelphi the next night. I wasn't as interested in them as she was but if Cáit wanted to do something you didn't dare say no. We piled into a Ford Escort owned by a student she was seeing at the time. He was from the Royal College of Surgeons. The space was so cramped I had to sit on Cáit's lap in the passenger seat.

She was fluthered. She sang 'Can't Buy Me Love' all the way into town. That was the only line of the song she knew. She was even more out of tune than Daddy at his worst.

When we got there everyone was screaming so loud I couldn't hear myself thinking. I said to Bridget, 'I wish I brought my ear plugs.' You'd think a head of state had arrived. I tried to pretend I was as excited as Cáit was but I didn't make a very good job of it. Maureen wasn't much better.

Cáit honoured us with the occasional glance in between screams. 'Jesus,' she said, 'You two. I don't know why you bothered. You'd think you were at a Knock tea party.'

The next night she made us go in with her to see them at the Adelphi. They arrived in a limousine. The crowds were about five deep. We hadn't a chance of getting anywhere near them.

There were police cordons all over the place. The only thing I managed to see was the back of Ringo Starr's head disappearing through a door. Everyone was pulling at him, at them all. It was a miracle nobody was trampled to death.

Cáit was still singing 'Can't Buy Me Love,' on the way home in the car, this time with a bottle of vodka in her hand. I often wondered where she put it all. She must have had the constitution of an ox.

I think that was the last date she went on with the College of Surgeons student. I dreaded to think how he must have felt the next morning. My own hangover felt like World War III. It was made worse by the fact that I hadn't enjoyed a minute of the night.

None of us knew the Beatles would become one of the most famous bands in the world in later years. If we did we might have tried harder to get some of their autographs.

The patients couldn't stop asking me about them. 'What was John like?' 'Did you get to talk to Paul?' That sort of thing. Cáit made up a selection of spicy stories to entertain them. I don't know how we did any work that day.

When I got back to Room 19 that evening I sank into a chair. I was proud of myself that I'd managed to make it through the day. I promptly fell asleep. By now I was almost able to sleep in a vertical position like the horses. I woke up after a few hours and tried to do a bit of study. We still had all these bulky books to wade through. A lot of them were still unfathomable to me.

I made a decision coming up to the exams: No more dancing and no more nights out. That was going to be the case even if John, Paul, George and Ringo asked me out on four separate dates. I needed to study hard, and to have enough of myself left over afterwards to give to the patients.

They were so appreciative of everything you did it made you want to walk the extra mile for them. A lot of the work was drudgery but the human aspect made up for it. I wouldn't have had the brains to be a doctor. Instead I tried to give them what the nursing handbook called 'TLC'- Tender Loving Care.

Bridget told me that was my best quality. Maybe she was right but I didn't see it as a quality. It just came natural to me. I was good at getting patients' minds off what was wrong with them by asking them questions about themselves.

One day a child was brought in with diphtheria. He was screaming so hard we were all nearly deafened. I decided the only way to get him to stop was to divert his attention. I started talking to him about his hobbies and he stopped. It was such a simple thing I didn't think anything of it but everyone was amazed.

Another thing I tried to do was speak plain English to the patients. When some of the doctors stood around the beds they often used big words that were like Greek to them. I never knew if they did that to show off or because they didn't have a bedside manner. When they were gone I'd try my best to translate what they said into English.

The month after we saw the Beatles, John F Kennedy was assassinated in Texas. Daddy got to love him after the Bay of Pigs incident. He felt bad about what he'd said about his womanising in the past. I remember one day he said to me, 'When John F. Kennedy came into the world, he changed it from black and white to colour.' It was a lovely way to think about him but now that colour was the colour of blood.

It was like a death in the family. I was home for a long weekend at the time it happened. We were all sitting around the television when Charles Mitchel came on. He was the news reader. He was as overwrought as the rest of us when he said what happened. We just sat there speechless. He always smiled when he read the news but this time his face looked frozen in stone.

Daddy cried as he spoke. It was the first time I ever saw him crying. How could you cry about someone you never met? We still had his photograph on the wall standing beside the Pope.

Mammy was very upset as well. So was Maureen. May was too young to know what was happening. Within a few hours Lee Harvey Oswald was arrested for the assassination but then he was shot too, by a nightclub owner called Jack Ruby.

Some people said he did it to stop Oswald talking, that it was some kind of conspiracy. Everyone started coming up with theories about why all these things happened but I wasn't really interested. As far as I was concerned, all that mattered was the fact that the most important man in the world, an Irish Catholic, had been mown down in cold blood. I couldn't stop thinking about Jackie Kennedy in her pink dress and her pillbox hat with blood all over her.

The next day we watched little John-John saluting the coffin of his dead father with the American flag draped over it. In some ways it was as emotional for us as it was for him. We felt like John-John ourselves.

It was as if the innocent world of our childhood had been snatched away from all of us in the blink of an eye.

# The Height of Ignorance

The main problem I had in my training, strangely enough, didn't come from the lectures or the inspecting team. It came from a matron called Joanne Wylie.

She was so tough she made Sister Agnes look like a pussycat. She ran the ward like a prison garrison, insisting on everything being in apple pie order at all times. She took an instant dislike to me for reasons I could never figure out. She was always mooching around me and that made me feel distinctly uncomfortable. Sometimes I felt she was hoping I'd muck things up so she'd have a chance to give out to me. I made a special effort to do more than my best when she was around but it didn't work.

She made mountains out of molehills. If a syringe went missing there'd be a Grand Inquisition to see where it was. At times like that I felt the finger of blame being pointed at me. She had a way of making you feel guilty even if you hadn't done anything.

I wasn't the only one she intimidated. Conversations in the ward were almost non-existent when she was on duty. You could sense her presence even when you couldn't see her. She was like a ghost hovering around the place, looking for something to find wrong. If visitors stayed a minute over visiting time her insistent little coughs at the bedside let them know in no uncertain terms they were meant to go.

It was torture having to face her every morning, standing there in front of me like a jailer jangling her keys. The beds had to be made over and over. Bedside lockers kept like new pins. Not only had we to scrub the outside and inside of them but even the wheels. If she saw a speck of dust you were made to feel you were the lowest form of animal life.

At times I felt I was expected to read her mind. 'Why has this patient not been washed?' she'd say, picking one at random as she flapped her arms around the place. If I said I didn't think they needed to be she'd come up with some obscure reason about body odour or ward hygiene to justify her outburst.

If a patient was any way noisy or if they were enjoying themselves watching a TV programme, she'd clap her hands and say 'Silence!' Irene believed her ideal ward would be one where there were no patients. 'That way,' she claimed, 'everything would be perfectly ordered. There'd be no noise at all.'

She had red hair and a mean little mouth. She was six feet tall if she was an inch. We called her 'The Height of Ignorance,' though not in her presence of course. If anyone said boo to her she flew off the handle. Bridget put it down to her having an exaggerated sense of her own importance. 'She thinks the hospital would fall down if she isn't there to run it,' she believed.

The world had to stop if she wanted something done. Every time I approached a patient she stood over me chanting 'TPR, TPR' like a mantra. That meant 'Temperature, pulse, respiration.' It was drummed into us so much at the lectures I almost found myself saying it in my sleep. The last thing I needed was to hear it repeated by her. If it had an air she could have sung it.

My first run-in with her took place after the weekend in Courtown. I'd asked for her permission to take the Monday out of our holidays before we went. I'd been working three weekends in a row before that, mainly because of her insisting I do that. Two was usually as much as we were asked to do but she always laid things on with a trowel for me.

She played dumb when I told her the roster was wrong, making out she had nothing to do with it. On my first morning at work after the break she greeted me with the words, 'I believe you were on a dirty weekend.' She said it loud enough for all the patients to hear. I blushed to high heaven.

'I don't know what you're talking about,' I said.

'Oh come on,' she said, 'You must have left your timetable in your other uniform.'

'No I didn't,' I said.

'Three nurses absent on the same day isn't on,' she snorted, her nostrils flaring. I wanted to say, 'I checked it with you and you told me it was okay,' but the words wouldn't come out. She had a way of striking me dumb when she fastened her gimlet eyes on me. Instead of having it out with her I apologized.

The following day she was civil to me. I thought I might have passed some kind of test by not taking her on but later in the day, just when I'd started to relax, she was on the warpath again. She saw me chatting to a man who'd had his appendix out. I was sitting on the edge of his bed. She strode towards me in a manner that let me know trouble was brewing.

'Don't become too personal with the patients,' she barked, 'You're here to do a job,' she said, 'not make lifelong friends. And no sitting on the beds. It isn't Butlin's Holiday Camp here.'

I could have kicked myself for doing that. I knew it wasn't allowed. I only sat down for a few seconds when the patient tugged my arm to make sure I heard the end of a story he was telling me. I should have realised even a second could spell disaster as far as this virago was concerned.

She was one of those people who expected you to come in to work with a long face every morning. It was as if you were there to suffer – probably because she was such a miserable creature herself.

That was Bridget's view. She thought she suffered from depression, that she needed to unload some of it onto the rest of us.

I saw the situation more simply.

'I think she has a screw loose,' I suggested.

Her voice seemed to be permanently turned up to ten. When she shouted, which was most of the time, you could almost hear her in the next ward. I played ball with her as much as I could because I knew it would keep her off my back but the more I crawled the more she stepped on me.

Sometimes she put me doing menial chores like cleaning stains off the floor. She didn't ask any of the other students to do that. It brought me back to my first day with Sister Agnes.

Was it something in me that brought out the bullish side in these people? Was I too meek and mild? Cáit told me bullies always backed down when you took them on but I was hardly in a position to here. My livelihood was at stake.

Strictly speaking I could have refused but I didn't. She also insisted I make the beds in the morning before doing my rounds. That knocked me back a half hour in my other work.

'We all have to muck in when the cleaners aren't here,' was her excuse. Another day she stopped me in the middle of dressing the leg of an ulcer patient to scrub all the bedpans in the sluice room. I could never figure out the logic of that. It was totally against the rules of the hospital to leave a job that was half done. Maybe she was hoping one of the consultants would come in and see the wound exposed. If I was hauled over the coals about something like that I certainly didn't expect her to stand up and say it was her fault.

Cáit was fit to be tied when I told her everything that happened.

'She's treating you like dirt,' she rasped, 'I'd go to the union if I was you.'

A few days later she jabbed my chest with her finger when I hadn't swabbed a wound to her satisfaction. When Cáit heard about it she freaked out completely. 'That's assault,' she said, 'You need to bring her before the Labour Court.'

'Assault?' I said, 'You must be joking. Maybe if she sliced one of my arms off I'd have a case. Even then I wouldn't be sure I'd win.'

I knew if Daddy heard about any of this he'd have been dug out of her. Mammy would probably have said, 'You get one in every hospital.' Anytime I was on the phone to them I watered down whatever happened so they wouldn't over-react. They were aware she was a bit of a demon from various things I'd said other nurses they talked to but I never told them the full story.

I talked more about her to Maureen. I knew I could trust her not to breathe a word to either of them. She had the same attitude as Bridget.

'Try your best to stay out of the line of fire,' she advised me, 'One day she'll move on, or you will. If you act like you're not bothered by her you've won.'

That was easier said than done. My body language always told a tale. I quivered when she was beside me, becoming a total butterfingers if I had anything in my hand like a needle or a forceps. I imagined myself standing beside her if she was a surgeon performing an operation. The patient would have wanted their life insurance paid up if she asked me to hand her something.

Anytime I gave someone a bedpan without warming it first it was like World War III had just been declared. 'If you don't heat it up,' she said, 'theoretically you could give someone a heart attack. That would be some price to pay for answering the call of nature, wouldn't it?'

She even got a bee in her bonnet about how I conducted myself in the kitchen. One day I had to give tea and toast to a patient. His name was Paddy Coonihan. He'd just come from theatre. She pounced on me as I walked over to his bed. I was about to hand the cup to him when she said, 'Where's the tray?'

'He likes it in the hand,' I said.

'Oh he does, does he? So what happens if it spills on him when he's drinking it and we have to take him down to theatre again with third degree burns?'

'I don't think that's likely to happen,' I muttered. Mr Coonihan looked on, wondering when he was going to be allowed drink his tea.

'He's recovering from an operation,' she roared, 'He's hardly out of the anaesthetic yet.'

'He seems to be back to himself as far as I can see,' I said, my face flushed with anger.

'Well obviously you can't see very far because to me this gentleman looks half asleep.' She looked across at him. 'No offence, Mr Coonihan.'

With that she stormed off. Mr Coonihan looked at me as if you say, 'Don't let the old bag get to you.' After a while he slurped back his tea – without suffering third degree burns.

She picked on anything to make me feel small, even the way I dressed. If there was a crease on my uniform she went into a tizzy.

'You're making a disgrace of yourself,' she'd say, 'Did your mother never teach you how to iron?' I used to have to run into the toilet sometimes after she had a go at me. I'd light up a cigarette to try and calm myself. By now I wasn't just pretending to like them. They were a necessity.

At her worst she told me I didn't know how to make a bed. 'It's not rocket science,' she rasped. She gave me a long-winded demonstration which made it look exactly like that.

My confidence descended to an all-time low as her reign of terror progressed. I knew she sensed that. To drive me further into the ground, one day she 'taught' me how to make a bed, something you'd

111

only do to someone who was in the hospital a week. She went through the rigmarole of turning the folds down over and over again in front of a patient sitting in a wheelchair waiting to get into it.

'They have to be as tight as tuppence,' she insisted, 'Wrinkles on the sheets cause bedsores.'

Things got even more horrendous after that. One day she found a strand of my hair in a glass of water. She screamed so much you'd have thought the hospital was on fire. Another time I was trying to take blood from a patient and couldn't find a vein. She started tut-tutting at the top of her voice. Then she grabbed the syringe from me. I couldn't relax with that patient afterwards.

She appeared at the most unexpected of moments, sometimes when I had the screen pulled around a bed and was treating a patient. She thought nothing of dressing me down in front of them. She was always telling me I forgot to take sputum mugs to the sluice when she hadn't even asked me to.

'I'll sort her out if you want me to,' Cáit offered when I told her about the series of events, 'Let me drop a large laxative in her tea. That should keep her out of your hair for a while.'

I wouldn't let her do that. I felt she'd have ferreted out who it was. If she did I'd be out the door. In a strange way, both of them were alike. They were equally volatile. It must have been something to do with the red hair.

'No, Cáit,' I said, 'Let sleeping matrons lie.'

'You can't be a doormat,' she said, 'Remember what happened about Courtown?'

'I know,' I said, 'She has a selective memory.'

'More like selective bitchiness,' she said.

Did Joanne Wylie spend her nights trying to think up ways to make my life hell? It didn't seem to matter if the hospital was run well, only that I was seen to falter. She had an obsession with showing me up in my worst colours no matter what I was doing. That was why I thought she was sick inside herself.

If I was taking a patient's blood pressure she'd stand over me like a policewoman, monitoring me. If I was doing something trivial like washing a dish I'd see her evil eye hoping I'd drop it or something.

She excelled herself even by her own standards the day she brought me over to a patient who'd just been admitted. In front of a group of doctors she asked me, 'What do you think is wrong with this gentleman?' I tried to put on an intelligent expression as I scanned him for symptoms but nothing struck me. I wanted the ground to swallow me up.

She stood there glowering in front of me, enjoying my misery. To get away from her I ran to the toilet – my familiar sanctuary – and bawled my eyes out. I later learned he had an obscure condition that the head specialist in the country would probably have had trouble identifying. She knew that herself too. For her it was a case of Mission Accomplished.

The next time she saw me she said, 'Maybe you should stay in the odd night and study your text books instead of tripping the light fantastic with your buddies.' I don't know where she got the idea I was out all the time. That was more Cáit than me. She wanted me to be that person but I wasn't. It would have made her dream of destroying me easier if I was.

She once accused me of trying to sneak a man into the grounds after a party without being caught. Her contention was that I had a copy of the front door key made so I could get back to my room without waking up anyone in charge in the middle of the night. I tried not to waste energy telling her she should have been writing dramas for the BBC to come up with such theories. At times like that she became tormented, a person I might have pitied if I didn't hate her so much. On the ordinary days it was just trivial accusations she got off on.

If I was a minute late into the ward she was there scrutinizing her watch. I made a point of setting the alarm for dawn so that wouldn't happen. I went to bed thinking about her and I woke up thinking about her. I stopped enjoying the patients because I knew she resented it, being jealous of any bond I had with them.

'She's jealous of your good looks,' Bridget claimed. I doubted that. I wasn't exactly Helen of Troy. But she wasn't good-looking. She could have been, but ugliness often comes from inside us. So it was with her. Even the way she turned her mouth or focussed her eyes took away whatever beauty she might have been born with.

There was talk about a failed love affair in her past. Maybe that was more likely as a reason for her vindictiveness.

Whatever her problem, my life became no good to me under her watch. In the end I stopped talking to Bridget and Cáit about her. They would both have told me I was insane not to take some action against her.

It was like heaven when she went to another ward for some reason or other. I could feel the tension disappearing out of my head as her footsteps receded down the corridor.

'I know what she needs,' Cáit said one day, making a sexual gesture. (She'd heard about the failed romance story). Sometimes when I was on night duty she'd say things like, 'No parties tonight, girleen.' She thought I had lots of boyfriends even though she'd never seen any evidence of that. Occasionally I got whistles from young men who were patients. That was enough for her to put two and two together and get five.

I stood up to her once, at least in a kind of way. It was when I was dressing a wound behind a screen. She barged in on me in her usual way, summoning me to the desk to give a patient an injection.

'I only have one pair of hands,' I said, 'It'll have to wait.' I don't know how I plucked up the courage to say that. I was so immersed in what I was doing I don't think I was even aware I was saying it. The words came out before I knew it. She must have stood there for a full twenty seconds before she moved away. I could almost see her thinking: 'You'll suffer for that.' I felt it was only a matter of time before she pounced on me again. I'd be all thumbs trying to please her as she hovered menacingly around me.

What got me most of all was when she was nice to the other nurses and like a demon with me. That let me know she was gunning for me, that she wasn't just in bad form. Then I heard she'd been asking the other nurses how I spent my nights. (I had spies who tipped me off about her interrogations). She thought I was having the life of Reilly in Phibsboro. I didn't say whether I was or wasn't. I wouldn't give her the soot of telling her I was tucked up with a book on Saturday nights when I was too jaded to hit the town. Why should I? She didn't own me.

After a while I started to enjoy riling her. I'd tell Cáit and Bridget to say things like, 'I saw her out last night not just with one man but two,' or other things that were even more spicy. They drove her mad altogether.

When I was supposed to be having these mad orgies, more usually I was cramming for my exams. I wanted to get good grades in them just to spite her. I probably worked harder than I might otherwise have for that reason so in a strange way she helped me.

I made a special effort to outgrow my hatred of academic things during those times. I even went as far as studying at home when the mood hit me, tying in holidays with endless memorisations of data on nutrition, physiology, the warning signals of sinister diseases.

'You're not still at that nonsense, are you?' Daddy would say as he saw me buried in books as big as the telephone directory. Would I be able to retain the material that was in them for my exams? I wasn't sure. The more I read, the more I was capable of forgetting. My brain was on overload.

Most of the stuff I was reading had no relation to life on the ward but on the odd occasion it did. One day when the doctors came in on their rounds I got into my stride with a theory I had about a patient nobody seemed able to diagnose. I suspected he was suffering from a perforated ulcer and I said so. They all stood there listening to me with their mouths open. I can't remember what kind of gobbledygook I was coming out with but it certainly silenced them. I was amazed at myself because I nearly always crumbled into a heap of mush in company.

My mouth usually went dry if there was a big shot in the room. Some of these people probably had half the alphabet after their names and here was this rookie telling them their business. When I think about it now I almost have to laugh. I wouldn't do it again in a blue fit, though the man in question did turn out to have an ulcer. He was the only one to thank me for my 'diagnosis.' The doctors didn't want to give me a big head. (There are no prizes for guessing that Isabel Wylie went very quiet any time his name came up in conversation after that).

A lot of the top dogs had big egos. There was one consultant I heard of who said to a woman he was treating, 'There are only two

115

people who can help you, madam - myself and God. And God is on holidays.' People queued up to be seen by this man because he was so good at what he did but he had a terrible manner. I wasn't surprised at that. What good was being operated on by someone who was nice but useless?

If you were lucky you were under someone who knew what he was doing. I heard of one man who said to a patient on the night before her operation, 'I don't think you have anything to worry about tomorrow. It all depends on how many pints I have before I cut you open. If I have too many, my hand tends to shake.'

He had a great sense of humour but some people took it the wrong way. One of his patients was a hypochondriac. He wilted in terror when he found a lump on his arm one day. He asked the surgeon if it was anything to worry about. The surgeon put on his glasses. He scrutinised it with a solemn expression. 'Probably early cancer,' was his diagnosis. It was another joke but he had the poor man reduced to shreds.

Other patients like Oisín were as casual as bedamned. I remember one young man running out of the ward one day after dislodging two drips I had him on. He put one in each pocket of his overcoat and legged it across the road to the pub. He was due to have an operation the following day but he wasn't too keen on his surgeon. (He was the man who said the thing about God being on holidays).

He said his ambition was to throw up on him in the middle of the operation. That was why he went to the pub. Luckily enough we managed to get him back to his bed and prepped for his operation before Wylie heard what he'd done. If she did, no doubt he'd have got his walking papers.

Mammy and Daddy loved it when I told them stories like this anytime I was home. I had to keep a lot of things from them, though, in case they'd be worried about me – and I don't just mean about Joanne Wylie. One time we had a criminal in the ward who'd been shot. He was recovering from his 'op.' He had a string of drug offences as long as your arm. He'd spent most of his life in prison.

Bridget told me he was hardly out of the cradle before he started shooting up. Afterwards he became a dealer to feed his habit. There was a guard stationed in the corridor all day long while he was in the hospital in case he tried to make a run for it. It turned out that's what he planned to do. When he got stronger he hatched a plan. He knew about the guard so he didn't go near the door he was at. Instead he jumped out the window. His bed was right beside it. I didn't think it made much sense putting him there but it's easy to be wise in hindsight.

The ward was on the second floor and he broke his leg in the fall. The police caught him easily enough but there was high drama around the ward for a while. He had to have a second operation for the broken leg. He wasn't put anywhere near a window this time. After he came back from surgery they watched him like a hawk to prevent any other daring leaps.

Another patient we had raided a pill cabinet one night and made off with the contents in a pillow-case. We even had a nurse who was pilfering pills. It turned out she was addicted to tranquillisers. I felt really sorry for her. She was brilliant at her work but after she was caught it spelled the end of her career. I heard she went back home afterwards and tried to wean herself off them. She grew up in Watergrasshill. That wasn't too far from Midleton. She was a great loss to the profession but the authorities had no choice but to let her go.

I didn't tell Mammy and Daddy about these people. Instead I kept them entertained with funny stories. There was one man I heard of whose doctor said to him, 'That cheque you gave me came back.' The man replied, 'So did the pain.' Another man went to his GP suffering from constipation. He prescribed an enema for him. He told him what to do with it but the man was hard of hearing. He thought he was meant to swallow it. Obviously it didn't do him any good and his symptoms persisted. He went back to the doctor the following week. He said, 'That pill you gave me wasn't a damn bit of use to me. I might as well have shoved it up my arse.'

I went home as often as I could. It made life with Wylie bearable to have these times to look forward to. Even if it was only for a weekend it was enough. My heart leaped when the train pulled into the station. But the time flew. I seemed to be only off it when it was time to go back.

Mammy presumed I was going to apply for a job in Cork when I qualified but I wasn't sure I would, much as I loved Midleton. The longer I was away from it the more independent of it I became. I knew it was there to fall back on if I got too homesick but I was aware of how possessive Mammy and Daddy were. They'd probably have wanted me to live at home if I was working anywhere in Cork and I didn't want that. There was no chance I'd ever become a Dub but I liked my life with Bridget and Cáit. I wasn't ready to give up on it just yet.

That didn't mean we had to be living the high life all the time. We actually stayed in most nights as the months went on. A lot of the time we did nothing more exciting than put our feet up and watch TV.

There were a lot of programmes we loved. My favourites were *The Fugitive* and *The Virginian*. We watched Irish soap operas like *The Riordans* and *Tolka Row* but not as much as the American ones. I loved *The Man from U.N.C.L.E.* with Robert Vaughn and David McCallum. McCallum played a character called Ilya Kuryakin. I loved saying his name. I thought it sounded so exotic. There was another show called *Rowan and Martin's Laugh-In*. It was a bit stupid. Goldie Hawn was in it. She was always giggling. David Rowan and Dick Martin were the two hosts. At the end of the show every night Rowan would say to Martin, 'Say goodnight, Dick,' and Martin would say, 'Goodnight, Dick.' That was about the level of the humour.

Bridget was a great fan of *Arrest and Trial*. We all had crushes on different men in these programmes. Cáit fancied James Drury in *The Virginian*. Bridget had a thing for Ben Gazzara in *Arrest and Trial*. I had a big crush on David Janssen. He was the doctor wrongly convicted of his wife's murder in *The Fugitive*.

The thing I liked most about him was his shyness. He was always hunched over. He had a shy smile. I suppose he brought out the mother in me. I wanted him to be cleared and the real killer caught. It was a one-armed man who committed the murder. He was like the devil to us. So was Lieutenant Gerard, the policeman chasing Janssen. Bridget tried to convince me one night that Lieutenant Gerard was the real killer. It would have been a great twist.

When all else failed there was always *The Late Late Show*. A lot of the time it was rubbish but Gay Byrne was capable of making something out of nothing. Whether it was good or bad you had to watch it. The first question anyone asked you on Monday morning was always, 'Did you see yer man on *The Late Late*?

In my final year we had to stop watching television because the exams were coming up. Life was hectic on the ward. I worked right through Christmas that year on account of us being so short-staffed. I was on with a girl called Veronica Mulligan. She'd been in my set but I hadn't seen much of her. Most of the time we were working on different wards.

She was in desperate circumstances. She was married to an alcoholic. He'd never done a stroke of work in his life and didn't look likely to now. Her salary was keeping the three of them. I felt really sorry for her, especially since she didn't complain about her lot in life. She was in the process of getting separated from him when I got to know her first. A while before that he'd beaten her up viciously. She took out a barring order against him but he still wasn't out of her life.

'I don't think he's ever going to be,' she said, 'I don't let him see me in person but he phones me when he's drinking. It's usually very late at night. Sometimes he just breathes into the phone. Then he hangs up. It's very upsetting. Other times he uses different voices to disguise himself. Some of them sound very threatening.'

That Christmas turned out to be one of the most fulfilling times of my life. I was disappointed when I was given the bad news that I wouldn't be able to go home but like a lot of things in life it turned out to be a blessing in disguise.

If somebody told me earlier on in the year that I'd be spending Christmas Day dancing with a man who had a hiatus hernia I'd have said they were mad but that's what I ended up doing. Myself and Veronica decorated the ward with a huge tree. We had turkey sandwiches for dinner and pudding for dessert. Afterwards we had some fun with the patients. We ate enough chocolates to last us a month. The people who were leaving the ward kept giving them to us and we hadn't the willpower to resist them. I probably used up my calorie quota for the entire year that week.

We had streamers from one end of the ward to the other. They started at a bed with a patient who'd just had a kidney removed. After that they wound all over the place. They went all the way to a kindly old lady who had rheumatoid arthritis.

There was a lovely atmosphere there despite so many people being in pain. The ones who couldn't get home opened up to us about their private lives. We told them a lot about ours too. It was easy to get close to people when we were all in the same boat, away from our loved ones. Veronica carved the turkey and we all sang carols with silly hats on our heads.

One of the patients had no teeth so I chopped her meat up for her. She appreciated that so much she gave me a kiss. She looked so forlorn my heart went out to her. She'd had an operation for cataracts and could hardly see anything. I'd given her drops earlier in the day for dry eyes. I never understood why they called it that because dry eyes are actually wet. I didn't know if hers were that way from crying or from her condition.

Maybe it was a combination of both. I knew she was feeling very lonely. She hadn't got a single Christmas card. I wanted to forge one and send it to her secretly but Veronica didn't think that was a good idea. She thought she might have copped on. When I thought about it I found myself agreeing with her. It would have hurt her pride to think we were pitying her. Instead we just tried to take her out of herself. We even did a twirl on the floor with her at one stage, dressed up as Santa's elves. That got a laugh out of her.

After tea our head cardiologist came in dressed as Santa. He had a big bag of gifts with him which he distributed to all and sundry. When he asked Veronica what she wanted from Santa, she said, 'A new heart, please.' I wasn't sure why she said that. Maybe it was her way of telling him she liked him. Irene told me she said she was mad about him one night when they were having a few drinks. She probably wouldn't have said it if she was sober. More often than not she was very reserved.

I wish I could have talked to her about him but we didn't have that kind of relationship. She looked really crestfallen when he left. He was very handsome – the George Clooney of his day, you might say. I think he might have liked Veronica but he was probably too shy to do anything about it. We used to call him Shaky Fingers because his hands shook so much when he was talking to you. It was from nerves but they disappeared as soon as he went into the operating theatre. In there he was as solid as a rock.

I phoned home on St. Stephen's Day. Mammy said she felt sorry for me. I told her there was nothing to feel sorry about.

'Did you not feel hard done by?' she said.

'No,' I said, 'I felt privileged.'

It was true. So many people opened up to me about themselves I was touched. I heard stories I never would have heard otherwise. I felt I was taken into their lives unconditionally.

'You gave me room at the inn,' one woman said to me as I danced around the ward with her.

'On the contrary,' I replied, 'You gave me room at yours.'

# Qualification

I did my final exams early in the new year. I was terrified I'd forget everything I'd worked so hard to memorise. I felt my head bursting with a mountain of facts. If I was lucky they'd all come gushing out but there was also the danger I'd get the nursing equivalent of writer's block and clam up. I think that was what Joanne Wylie was hoping for. She watched me in various stages of meltdown in the days leading up to the exams.

One day when I was in the Study Hall poring over an article she passed me by with Sister Immaculata, one of the older nuns. She was a kindly soul who'd always been helpful to me from the beginning of my training.

'Not there yet, are we?' she chirped.

'Afraid not,' I said, 'I'm still cramming.'.

'Deathbed repentances never work,' she said.

Sister Immaculata smiled.

'I'm sure you'll be fine,' she said to me.

Joanne said, 'Sister Immaculata will say a prayer for you, won't you, Sister?'

She nodded benignly.

'Sister Immaculata's prayers are worth their weight in gold,' she said. 'They go straight up. She has a hotline to the Pearly Gates.'

I fumbled my way through the preliminary exams not knowing if I'd done well or not. When there was someone standing in front of you firing questions at you it was easy to tell if you were pleasing them or not but a sheet of foolscap paper didn't speak. You couldn't tell for sure if you'd answered the questions on the paper until you got your grades.

I woke up on the day of the final exam with a 'going to the gallows' lump in my stomach. It was due to begin at ten o'clock. The supervisor was an officious-looking woman with a spindly figure. She had a big brass bell on her desk. She put all the papers face down on our own desks. I wanted to sneak a peek at them but she told us we weren't allowed turn them around until the dot of ten. When I looked up at the clock on the wall I saw the second hand crawling towards that. She waited until the precise moment and then said, 'Okay!' in a booming voice. She dropped her hand like someone signalling the start of a race.

'All right, girls,' she announced as she rattled her bell, 'You can turn your pages now.'

When I saw the questions my heart missed a beat. I didn't recognise any of the things I'd prepared for. I tried to take deep breaths but it didn't work.

I looked across at Bridget. She must have seen the terror on my face. She whispered over to me, 'Relax, you mad thing you.' Then she gave me a V for Victory sign.

I decided to do nothing for a few minutes. I put my head in my hands and tried to forget everything that was in the room. I heard the sound of pens scratching on paper all around me and I thought: 'Everyone is going to pass except me.' It was as if I was a ten year old again and Sister Serafina was standing over me like an avenging angel.

Before I knew what was happening I felt a hand on my shoulder. I heard a voice saying, 'Are you all right, young lady? Would you like a drink of water?'

It was the supervisor. I must have looked the colour of death because she was eyeing me with great concern. I nodded my head frantically. As she left the room I found myself trembling. A few moments later she came back with the water. I swallowed it almost in a gulp.

I now felt emboldened to look at the dreaded paper again. This time it made more sense. At least I could read the questions. I started to write, slowly at first and then with a bit more speed. With each sentence I put down I gained more confidence. One word borrowed another.

Before I knew it I was cascading down a river that led all the way to the sea. I wasn't sure if what I was writing was balderdash or not but I couldn't stop myself. Some obscure part of my brain had registered the data and I was regurgitating it like a maniac. It was as if I had a circuit inside my head that photocopied the texts. Why had it been so slow to show itself? Panic, probably. The information was locked somewhere in my subconscious and I'd just found the master key.

I was writing very fast. Cáit looked across at me at one stage as if to say, 'Are you *on* something?' I gave her a watery smile. I was on a roll and I didn't want my concentration disrupted. Whether I passed or failed I was determined that whoever corrected my paper was going to remember me. Maybe I'd give them a nervous breakdown by writing about diseases that didn't exist.

I even started doing drawings of body parts with felt markers at one point. Sketches of organs that used to turn my stomach into jelly a few years ago were now my best friends. It was amazing what the carrot of qualification could do.

When the bell finally went for 'Time Up' I was still scribbling away frantically. In the end the supervisor had to prise the paper from my grip. I refused to let go of it. There was a big streak of biro at the end of it. It probably seemed to the examiner like the last scrawl of a drowning person. Maybe that's what I was, someone rescued from the deep in the nick of time.

The supervisor was amused by me.

'There must have been something in that water,' she said.

'Maybe it came from Lourdes,' I suggested.

I walked outside in a half-dream. The air never tasted sweeter. A wind was blowing. I inhaled big gusts of it into my chest. Whatever happened from now on was out of my hands. I'd given the best of myself. What more could anyone do?

Bridget came out a minute later.

'How did you do?' she asked me.

'I don't know,' I said. I wasn't being coy. I'd filled a lot of pages but for the life of me I couldn't remember what was in them. For all I knew I could have been writing Little Red Riding Hood rather than the History of District and Psychiatric Nursing in the 20th Century. (That was one of the questions).

'You looked like a woman possessed,' she said.

'If I was, I'm not sure if it was God inside me or the devil.'

Cáit trudged out then. She didn't look too happy.

'What a shit paper,' she said, 'Nothing I crammed for came up and everything I didn't did.'

'I felt that way too,' I said to console her.

'I don't know what you're moaning about,' she said, 'You were going like the clappers every time I looked across at you. What in the name of Jesus were you writing?'

'Probably nonsense for the most part,' I said.

'Go on out of that,' Bridget said, 'Modesty will get you nowhere.'

'She's probably just fishing for compliments,' Cáit said.

'Did you do the one on risk assessment for TB?' Bridget asked me.

'No,' I said shakily. I'd hardly even remembered it being one of the questions.

'What about the one on coronary care?'

'No, not that either.'

'The History of Diabetes, Type 2?

'No, I said, 'I avoided that like the plague.'

'I didn't know there was one on the plague,' Cáit remarked. She didn't realise what she'd said for a second. Then we all burst out laughing.

'Anyway,' she said, 'That's enough of the post mortems. I think it's time for a drink.'

'Is that not a bit premature?' I asked.

'Don't be so bloody sensible,' she said.

She was right. I always had to fight that side of myself.

We went off to the nearest pub. Cáit was at the counter almost as soon as we got in the door. She ordered shorts for the three of us. We swigged them back without a thought. When our glasses were empty I ordered another round.

'Same again,' I said. I got another round after that, and then another.

'Why are you being so generous?' Bridget asked me.

'As a small thank-you to the two of you for being such great buddies to me. And to thank you especially, Bridget, for giving me all the notes to the lectures I missed over the years.'

'What about mine?' Cáit interrupted. I had to laugh at that. She'd rifled Bridget's notes too, as well as most of her hand-outs.

We polished off a bottle of champagne within a half hour. We also emptied the best part of a packet of cigarettes (or should I say the worst part of a packet of cigarettes) into our already poisoned lungs. The fact that I'd just written a thousand word essay on the perils of smoking a few hours before didn't seem to enter my mind.

Cáit was on her way to the counter for another bottle of bubbly when I decided I'd had enough depravity for one day. I didn't feel I could handle it.

'Come on,' she said, 'One more won't kill you.' Bridget was on for it too.

'I can't,' I pleaded, 'Please let me go before I fall onto the floor.'

Eventually they relented. I hugged both of them as I stumbled towards the door. I told them again how much I appreciated their friendship and kindness to me.

When I got out onto the street the effect of the drink started to kick in. It was always the way with me. I could stay in a pub half the day feeling I was stone sober but once I took a step outside it was as if a jet opened up in my head. My throat felt terrible from the cigarettes. Some nurse, I thought. I was more like an advertisement for How To Kill Yourself Before You're Thirty.

I hobbled my way back to Room 19 on decidedly unsteady feet. On the way I called home from a phone box on Dorset Street. The traffic was noisy so I had to shout into the receiver. Daddy took the call. By the end of it, I don't think he was any the wiser about whether I did well or badly. 'You sound like you're speaking from the inside of a cement mixer,' he told me.

When I got into the room I felt ravenously hungry for some reason. I demolished half a box of Milk Tray that had been given to me by a patient. If I kept all the ones I'd been given over the years I could have given Charlie from the Chocolate Factory a run for his money. Occasionally I'd had the discipline to offload them on Maureen or anyone else who was around when I was home but I was glad of them now.

Alcohol usually made me hungry. Maybe I was eating from relief as well. When I had them finished I said a prayer that I hadn't written gobbledygook in the exam. The last thing I wanted was to have to do the repeats. I knew if I never saw a text book again it would be too soon.

The results weren't due to come out till the following month so I went home to get my mind off them. From what I told Mammy she thought I'd done very well. I thanked her for her vote of confidence but being a natural pessimist I didn't let myself get too smug. I always felt that if you didn't worry about something it would come out wrong whereas if you did you had a better chance of succeeding. It was just another one of my superstitions.

When I said that to May she said, 'You're weird.' She was as bold as ever, spending most of her time doing precisely the opposite of whatever Mammy and Daddy asked her to.

Maureen was working in a travel agency in Cobh now. She'd given up on the idea of nursing but she wasn't content where she was either. There wasn't enough happening there. 'I get up and I go into work,' she said, 'and then I come home eight hours later feeling I've aged twenty years.' She did a typing course in the evenings just for something to do. After a few weeks she reached a standard of up to sixty words a minute. I thought that was fantastic. I knew she'd make a go of it.

'Sixty words a minute?' I said, 'That's a word a second! I can't believe it. You're so adaptable. You can turn your hand to anything.'

'After all that I don't know if I want to be a secretary,' she said. 'They spend too much time sitting around doing their nails.' She had no threshold for boredom at all.

The results came out the week after I got back to Dublin. I went down to the noticeboard in the main hall with my nerves in knots. A moment later I saw to my shock that my name was top of the list. It had a special citation beside it. I'd got the highest marks in my set.

Bridget almost broke my back with a thump.

'Clever clogs,' she chirped. I couldn't believe I had higher marks than her. She was always a mine of information for me over the years. She knew all the stuff backwards but maybe she wasn't as good as me at putting it down on paper.

'You mean clever *liar*,' Cáit corrected. 'There she was, trying to pretend she wasn't working all those times when the truth of the matter was that she was probably burning the midnight oil every night.'

'Honest to God I wasn't,' I said. I started to blush.

127

'Tell the truth and shame the devil,' she said, 'You might as well. It's written all over your face.'

The reason I was blushing wasn't because it was true. I always did that when someone accused me of something.

'I might have opened a book the odd night when yourself and Bridget were out but that was it. It would only have been when I couldn't think of anything else to do.'

'How did you get such high marks then?'

'I don't know. I admit I crammed over the last few months but you did too.'

'I'm not talking about that.'

'Please believe me. I always hated people who did well at exams.'

'And now you're one of them.'

'I know.'

'Why do you think that is?'

'Probably because I had something to gain. It's not like at school where you were asked to remember something like when the Siege of Derry took place. Writing about passing a gallstone is a bit more interesting.'

'Do you think so?' she said.

She put on a witchy expression as she spoke. In that moment I saw a different side to her than I'd ever seen before. It was almost malicious. How could you spend three years with someone and not know them? Maybe she felt the same about me, the sneaky swot.

Her name was half way down the list but at least she'd passed. Bridget's name was a few places up from hers. The three of us had got through. That was all that mattered.

Only one girl from our set failed. Her name was Vera Doyle. I saw her crying at the side of the notice board. I knew she'd studied hard, maybe too hard. She was probably the only person in the examination hall who was shivering more than me. Maybe she could have done with a glass of water too.

Bridget said she had a very strict supervisor for one of her practicals. Apparently he was someone who delighted in preying on vulnerable souls. Vera was even more of a butterfingers than me in situations like that. I could imagine her wilting under him. He gave most of the girls he dealt with bad grades. According to Bridget, 'He wouldn't pass water.'

'What am I going to do?' she said to me after she dried up her tears, 'I'd pinned all my hopes on this.'

'Don't worry,' I said, putting my arms around her, 'You can repeat the year.'

'We don't have the money,' she said, 'My parents are already in debt from all my expenses.'

She took a handkerchief out of her pocket. She blew into it.

'My father is out of work,' she said, 'I'll have to go home.'

'Something will turn up,' I said. I couldn't think of anything else to say. She was one of the kindest girls I'd ever met and now she had nothing. I was almost on the point of tears myself.

'Thanks so much for comforting me,' she said before walking slowly away.

I rang home that night to tell Mammy and Daddy about my good fortune. They were thrilled for me. Maureen was screeching so much in the background Mammy had to tell her to step away from the phone.

'I'm so proud of my little girl,' Mammy said, 'Now you can tell that Wylie bitch what to do with herself.'

'Not quite yet, I'm afraid,' I said, 'I'll probably be working with her for a while more yet.'

The following week I got a big 'Congratulations' card from them all with loads of Xs on it. Under my name it said, 'Also known as Florence Nightingale.' Everyone signed it. Aunt Bernie even slipped in a little note on a fancy blue Basildon Bond notepad she had. Mammy wrote 'S.A.G.' on the envelope. She always did that. It stood for 'St. Anthony, Guide.' Inside she'd done a drawing of a nurse with loads of stars around her head.

I went puce when I saw it. If my head got any bigger it would have exploded. So would Daddy's. He enclosed an article about me that was in the local paper with a photo of me beside it.

When I rang to thank them, Mammy said, 'Your Daddy photocopied it about a hundred times.' She said he kept one of the copies in his wallet. He displayed it to anyone and everyone he knew when he saw them in the pub. That was the last thing I wanted. It was like the way he was with my First Communion photo.

'Daddy,' I said when I got onto him, 'Destroy it this second. I won't be able to put my nose outside the door when I go down there now. People will be looking at me thinking I have notions about myself.'

'Don't be stupid,' he said, 'Win your spurs and wear them. I know anyone else would.' There was no point arguing with him. It only made him more determined.

Joanne Wylie's face fell a mile when Cáit showed her the article. She'd already been in a decline about my coming top of the class but this put the tin hat on it. Cáit had a great time watching her reaction. She said she looked like she'd just got a bad smell.

'I wanted to rub her nose in it,' she told me afterwards. Apparently she'd given out to her earlier in the day for something so she was in fighting form.

Joanne didn't think I had it in me to do so well. Or maybe she did and wouldn't admit it to herself. Sometimes people came down heavy on you not because they thought you weren't good enough but because they were afraid you were too good. She knew I was popular with the patients as well. That was another box she hadn't wanted me to tick.

'I suppose you think you're the bee's knees now,' she snorted as she handed the article back to me. I was shocked. She'd practically hissed the words out of her mouth. Little did she know I'd prefer to have hot coals put under my fingers than have someone flash a camera bulb in my face. I knew there was no point in telling her that. When someone had their mind made up about you they rarely changed it. If I told her I was going off to live on a desert island she'd still have accused me of being a glory hunter.

'Wouldn't you think they'd have more to write about in Midleton than that,' she huffed. 'I suppose a paper won't refuse ink.'

Mammy and Daddy came up to Dublin for the qualification ceremony. They were both dressed to the nines. Mammy bought a lovely cream dress for the occasion. Daddy was in his one good suit. They were beside themselves with pride. I was given a medal because

I came first. It had my name on it. The girls who came second and third got medals too.

There was a round of applause for the class and a special one for me. It made me a bit self-conscious because Bridget and Cáit were standing beside me at the time. I hoped all the attention I was getting wasn't going to cause a rift between us. You never knew how people might react in situations like that, especially with Cáit thinking I was such a swot.

Daddy said I looked very efficient in my uniform.

'I suppose you'll be Nurse of the Year next,' he said. That was a laugh. I felt I still didn't have a clue about nursing despite all my book knowledge. I hadn't started the real part of it yet. All that happened was I didn't have to wear an invisible set of L-plates on my forehead anymore.

Needless to say, The Height of Ignorance totally changed her tune with me for the day. Her face could have stopped a clock but she was as nice as pie to my face.

She made a big effort to ring my praises to Mammy. The words must have been strangling themselves to come out. I knew she'd have preferred to have a stake put through her heart than to congratulate me. Mammy thanked her without being familiar with her. She was all over Daddy too but he couldn't hide his anger. I knew he wanted to have it out with her but Mammy wouldn't let him.

'If you say anything to that woman,' she warned him when she got him on his own, 'I'll never speak to you again.'

'I can't be as charitable as you,' he muttered.

'The Bible says to forgive and forget,' Mammy told him.

'Forgive, maybe,' he said, 'but not forget.'

I was asked to give a speech but I refused. I'd have preferred to have crossed Niagara Falls in a barrel. In my absence, Joanne stepped into the breach. She said she was as proud as punch of my achievements. Despite my teething pains in the early days, she said, she always knew I had it in me to rise to 'the top of the tree.'

She finished by saying she was confident I'd conduct myself in exemplary fashion in the challenges I faced in the life ahead of me.

'What does "exemplary" mean?' Daddy asked Mammy.

'It means "Good".'

'Then why didn't she say that?'

She ended by telling them she was looking forward to having me work 'with' her rather than 'under' her in the future. As she spoke I thought to myself: Tell me the one about the three bears.

Everyone started to relax more once the speeches were over. Mammy and Daddy were staying in a hotel nearby so Daddy was able to drink as much as he wanted. Cáit was on the bottle as well. The pair of them got on like a house on fire.

'Your father is great crack,' she told me, slurring her words as she sidled up against me with a glass of plonk in her hand.

Mammy talked more to Bridget. I introduced her to a few of the other girls I was friendly with as well. The only blemish on the night was the fact that Vera Doyle wasn't there. She'd gone down to Lahinch, her home town, after the results came out. I heard she was trying to get work in a chemist shop down there so she could save for the repeats. I really hoped she'd be able to afford to do them. I knew she'd make a brilliant nurse given the chance.

I had to formally apply for a job in the Mater now. I felt confident I'd be accepted because of my showing in the exams and I was.

It should have been a great moment for me but in some ways it was an anti-climax. For the next few weeks I found it hard to settle into my ordinary chores. It was always like that after an exciting event: the calm after the storm.

I did a lot of my work on auto-pilot. In the evenings I felt strangely awkward with Bridget and Cáit. I knew they were pleased with me getting all the attention but I felt something changed between us since the results came out. I couldn't put my finger on what it was. Cáit's comment about me being a secret studier stayed at the back of my mind.

The best thing that happened to me at this time was that Joanne Wylie was transferred to the Rotunda. 'There must be a God after all,' Cáit said. Maureen heard through the grapevine that she'd actually applied for the transfer. I wouldn't have been surprised if that was the case. She'd hardly exchanged two words to me since the qualification party.

'I believe you're be leaving us,' I said to her the next time I saw her.

'Indeed,' she said in a bored voice, 'I've been feeling a bit stale for a while now. I think I need a challenge.' I wondered if my exam results had anything to do with her 'challenging' spirit.

As a going-away gift I gave her a tin of biscuits. It stuck in my craw to do it but I felt I'd only have attracted more attention to myself if I didn't.

'I hope you laced them with arsenic,' Cáit said when I told her. Neither she nor Bridget gave her anything. I don't think they even said goodbye to her. The atmosphere between the three of them had always been more neutral than hostile so maybe it was easier for them to do nothing. I'd spent so much time working with her it would have been too obvious if I ignored her now.

I was able to relax for the first time in years after she left. I could do my job without having to worry about her eagle eyes peering down on me. More than once in the past I'd had to take a Valium on the way to work because of the tension she brought into my life. Cáit had a stash of them in her bedside locker – she used them for hangover cures – and I often found myself asking her for them.

Everything changed over the next few months. With Wylie gone I thought I was going to be mightily relieved but instead of that I just felt flat. Trying so hard to survive her torture tactics took so much out of me that now I started to experience some of the staleness she said she was suffering from herself. Maybe I needed a new challenge as well. The fact that something was gone from my relationship with Bridget and Cáit was affecting me too. I didn't feel depressed as such, just empty.

They left Room 19 soon afterwards. I was so sad it was almost like someone died. We went out for a drink-up the night before but it wasn't the same. I couldn't help feeling they were 'off' with me. When something like happens you can't do much about it. If you say anything it only makes it worse. I thought back to the night we had the group hug. We'd told one another that we'd be friends forever that night. I wondered what had gone wrong since.

Bridget applied to do midwifery in the Coombe and Cáit went back to Birr. Her brother was in hospital down there. He'd fallen from a tractor on their farm and she went down to take care of him. He had a ruptured spleen.

When he started to improve got better she got a job in a clinic down there. I phoned her to ask her how she was doing.

'I'm bored silly,' she said, 'All I do is weigh people and take urine samples from them,' she complained. Despite her protestations I felt she'd stay. I knew she was a homebird at heart. We wrote to each other for a while afterwards but then stopped.

I hated when that happened. It seemed to be the way it was with a lot of people I got to know over the years. You became really close to someone and then it stopped for no better reason than the fact you weren't living under the same roof any more. Other girls I knew were better at dealing with situations like that than I was. I tended to get too involved with people.

I wanted to know how Bridget was doing at the midwifery but she only called me once in a blue moon. I kept phoning Cáit to ask how her brother was but she rarely returned the calls. Both of them were never anything but friendly to me but they always seemed to be rushing somewhere when we met up. I found that hard to deal with. I wasn't able to turn myself on and off like a clock.

Were you better off not to care what your friends did when your path diverted from theirs? Sometimes I thought you were for your own protection. It was like pulling a plaster off a wound. The quicker you did it, the less it hurt.

To take my mind off them, and maybe to get a flavour of the new challenge Joanne Wylie talked about, I now decided to learn how to drive. I felt if I did it would give me more independence. It would also mean I'd be able to get home more. The trains were okay but I usually travelled on them at peak times when you'd be lucky to get a seat. If you did it was often opposite someone you didn't want to make conversation with. I tended to end up beside people who wanted to moan about the rough hand life dealt them.

'It's your eyes that does it,' Mammy said, 'They're very kind.' I usually found myself beside someone who bored me to tears talking about when the tea trolley was going to arrive.

After getting my first cheque I had money in my pocket for the first time in my life. It was such a novelty. Sometimes I took it out and just looked at it. I'd been pulling the devil by the tail for so long it was like winning the lottery not to have to think about cutting corners.

I knew if I saved hard I'd probably be able to put a down payment on a car but I also knew I'd be leaving Room 19 soon. That meant I'd have to think about the cost of renting somewhere. A lot of the other nurses were moving into houses together. That halved their expenses. Anyone could see the attraction of that but I thought I'd look for a little place of my own to see how I'd get on. If I was too clingy, as I feared I was, it might help me to rid myself of some of that.

I scanned the papers for second-hand cars. A few of them appealed to me. One was an Austin. It was going for a cheap price. The ad said it only had one owner. I rang Daddy to ask him for his advice.

'Don't believe a word of it,' he said, 'That probably means 21 owners.'

After a lot of soul-searching I decided to have a look at it. It was at the right price even if it was falling apart. When I explained that to Daddy he understood. He said if I had my heart set on it he'd help me pay for it. Otherwise I'd have had to get it on the good old Never Never. There was a boom in the building trade while I'd been training and he'd been putting a bit aside for me while it was going on.

It was a banger but I still bought it. The driver was a retired schoolteacher. That suggested to me that she'd been careful. She drove me to the nurse's home in it after I paid her. I thought that was nice of her. Over the next few weeks I took as many driving lessons as I could. I'd already had a few on Ardnahinch beach. I knew my way around a gearbox even if I didn't trust myself to go on the open road unaccompanied.

I'm sure I gave the driving instructor apoplexy more than once when I got behind the wheel, especially when I was doing three point turns in busy streets as the other motorists tore their hair out. One day after a lesson he said, Congratulations. You're the first driver I ever met who managed to drive ten miles with the handbrake on.'

'I was wondering why we were going so slow,' I said, 'Why didn't you tell me?'

'I was too shocked to speak,' he said.

Eventually I mastered the mechanics of it. It was such a relief not to have to ask people to collect you when you were going out. There weren't as many women driving cars in those days as there are now. Men stared at me sometimes. I'm sure Rosemary Smith got that too. She was Ireland's most famous woman driver. I always revved the engine when they did that. I stared back at them as if to say, 'What's your problem?'

After a few months driving around Dublin I chanced going to Midleton in it. Miraculously it didn't break down, despite making various threatening noises round Tipperary that suggested the chassis was about to wave goodbye to the rest of it.

Soon afterwards I moved out of Room 19. I rented a flat in Drumcondra. It was near enough to the Mater. I was able to walk into work if I got up early enough. It was basically just one big room with a bed in the corner and a little kitchen off it. There was a sofa that turned into a double bed if I had visitors.

Mammy came up to see it as soon as I moved in. She was more interested in looking at me than the flat at first.

'You've lost weight,' she said accusingly. I knew it was from all the cigarettes I was smoking but I couldn't tell her that.

'I've been run off my feet in the ward,' I said, 'Things are hectic in there at the moment.'

She didn't look too impressed by my new living conditions.

'It's a bit on the small side, isn't it?' she said. I told her Dublin wasn't Midleton, that I'd have to put up with less space than I was used to. Besides, it was a lot roomier than where I'd just come from. She made a lot of grunting noises as she walked around. They got worse when she saw the cooker.

'This looks as if it hasn't been cleaned since about 1958,' she said.

'Daddy was as complimentary about the car,' I said, 'How lucky I am to have such supportive parents.'

'And how lucky we are to have such an independent daughter.'

I was being sarcastic and so was she.

She thought I'd be lonely on my own after all the people I'd been with up to now.

'That's the best part,' I said, 'Being able to savour the silence in the evenings. And not having to talk to anyone if I don't feel like it.'

As if to contradict that, after I moved in I got calls from Bridget and Cáit. Both of them said they were anxious to find out how I was doing on my own. I suspected Mammy gave them a nudge to ring me. I'd mentioned to her I'd been a bit put out about the way they seemed to have cut themselves off from me since we qualified.

Maureen and May came up to stay with me one weekend after I got settled in. Mammy would have liked to be with them but she didn't like to leave Daddy on his own. There wouldn't have been anywhere for them to sleep anyway.

May never stopped talking for the whole weekend. She told me she thought I was the luckiest person in the world to have my own place at such a young age. As soon as she got out of school, she assured me, she was going to do exactly the same thing. 'Why can't I drop out?' she said, 'and have a decent life for a change?'

Maureen didn't get a wink of sleep the first night on account of her moving around so much on the sofa. There was a loose spring on it which didn't help. On the Saturday morning over breakfast she told me her back was crippled.

We went into town in the afternoon. May enjoyed sashaying around the shops. 'I could get used to this kind of life,' she informed us as she paraded around them trying on the latest fashions. She begged me to bring her up Nelson's Pillar when we got back out onto the street. She was in seventh heaven looking down on Dublin from the top of it.

She wanted to go to the Gresham Hotel for tea. I told her I couldn't afford it.

'I have to see it,' she said.

'Tea in the Gresham would cost me a month's wages,' I told her.

'Then let me go to the toilet there anyway.'

'Whatever turns you on,' I said.

Maureen went in with her. They were ages in there. I stayed on the street. Eventually they arrived out. Maureen looked apologetically at me.

'Was it a penny you were spending,' I said, 'or £10,000?'

'I couldn't stop looking round,' she said, 'I have to be able to describe it to my friends.'

'I had to drag her out,' Maureen said, 'or we'd still have been there at midnight.'

We went to a film after tea. It wasn't anything to write home about but we enjoyed it. Maureen and May were thrilled to be sitting in the plush Pullman seats of the Carlton cinema after the more basic Midleton ones.

It had John Wayne in it. He was an actor I could take or leave but he was very popular at the time so the cinema was full.

Afterwards we had fish and chips in a café beside the GPO.

'You've got your wings now,' Maureen said to me as we ate, 'You can fly anywhere you want.'

It made me feel good to hear her speak like that, though the day cost me more than I'd expected when everything was put together. I even had to tip a man on a side street where I'd parked the car so that he'd 'look after it' for me. He said it was a notorious place for robberies. I gave him what he asked for despite the fact that he looked more like a robber himself than anything else. From the smell of whiskey off his breath it didn't take a genius to figure out where my tip was going to be spent.

Maureen seemed to be in pain all day. When I asked her about it she confessed that it was probably from the sofa.

'What do you recommend, nurse?' she asked me when we got home. I told her I thought it might be an idea to change places with me the next night. If I was working she probably wouldn't have let me but I had that weekend off so we swapped places and she got a great sleep. So did I. I was usually in the land of nod as soon as my head hit the pillow – at least since Joanne Wylie left the hospital – so it didn't matter to me if May was doing ju-jitsu into the small hours.

They went home on the Sunday. They said they'd love to come up sometime again soon and I said I'd love to have them. Seeing them was like having a little bit of Midleton in Dublin.

After they were gone I felt lonely but I was able to deal with it better now that I knew I could have them up again. I could also go down to them when I felt like it, even if the Austin sounded as if it was going to take off for outer space every time I revved it up. I had my 'wings', as Maureen put it. I wasn't answerable to anyone about going out at night or getting pass keys that had to be signed for.

I often drove to Dollymount to get a bit of exercise if I had a pressurising day at work. It was sad thinking of the times I'd cycled there with Bridget and Cáit but in another way it helped me to deal better with their disappearance from my life. Sometimes I went out to Howth Head and sat looking down at the Old Baily lighthouse. It was relaxing sitting there feeling the wind in your face and the salt of the sea in your nostrils. In the old days I'd have walked along the cliff. Now I was just content to sit there with my memories.

Working as a fully-fledged professional did wonders for my confidence. I got a fright the first time I heard someone calling out 'Nurse!' from their bed. Even though it was only for a glass of water I felt I'd 'arrived.' I was finally able to put all the study to the back of my mind and connect with what was in front of me. People had jaws now, not mandibles. They had noses rather than oesophaguses.

In another way I still felt like a novice. I was awkward doing routine tasks like giving people injections. One day when my mind was on something else I thought I must have almost broken a poor woman's arm by the way she winced when I put the needle into it. She was too polite to say anything. It was a lot harder than it had been on the dummies, as I predicted. I was a bit better at taking out stitches and doing dressings.

It took me a long time to familiarise myself with the routines of the ward. A lot of it was boring but at least I didn't have to clean out lockers now except when I felt like it. I tried my best to get to know the patients as people. I made a point of chatting to them while I was giving them their meds. Apart from everything else, it made the time pass quicker. There were some things I still hated doing, like emptying out the bedpans, but you just had to grin and bear it. It came with the job.

Other things were less bearable, like the first time a patient died on the ward. We'd been prepped for this on many of the lectures, and even in the practicals, but nothing prepared you for a death, especially if it was someone you knew, as I did. He was a farmer with heart disease.

He seemed to be making a great recovery from his surgery when he had a relapse. Days like that were best forgotten – if you could. I cried so much Sister Agnes came over to console me. 'Don't ever be

139

afraid to show your emotion in this hospital,' she said, 'Tears are the irrigation of the soul.' I could never forget that expression afterwards: 'the irrigation of the soul.' She went up a lot in my estimation that day. Maybe I always knew her toughness was only a shell, as Deirdre said.

No matter what happened it was a continuous relief to be free of Joanne Wylie. Our new matron, Tanya Cuniffe, was a totally different kettle of fish. She was a real darling. At least now I could make cups of tea without being informed they were too watery or be told how to stir the milk or how much sugar to put in or how to serve it to a patient without being afraid they were going to scald themselves and sue the hospital.

I was tempted to make a bonfire of all my lecture notes but Tanya advised me not to. She said a nurse never stopped learning, that I'd be surprised how often I might have to refer to things I'd written in the days to come. She was right. I stuffed them into the little attic that was in the flat. In future years there was more than one occasion when I found myself rummaging around in the crawlspace looking for advice on everything from fractured femurs to varicose veins.

Instead of pining for Bridget and Cáit I tried to make new friends with the nurses who shared my shifts. I became very close to one called Catherine O'Herlihy. She was from Glanmire. Being fellow county women was enough to start us gabbing together. Shortly after I got to know her she went on maternity leave. When she came back she was transferred from the ward she was working on to my one. As a result we became great friends.

She was engaged to be married to a teacher, Billy, who lived in Glasnevin. They doted on one another. I spent a lot of time at her place and she came over to me the odd night as well. We knew a lot of the same people in Cork. It was enjoyable sharing stories with her, especially when we were on night duty together. You could chat away to your heart's content when the patients were asleep. We also had the odd snack on the job when we were doing night shifts. These were the only times you could eat on the ward without being told off, at least if you were quiet about it. There was nothing like a salad sandwich at midnight to revive your flagging spirits.

About half way through the year the restless feelings I'd felt after Bridget and Cáit left Room 19 came back again. It was hard to know why. I had job security and a happy home life and money in my pocket but I couldn't relax.

I became moody with people. I started picking up things they said that they didn't mean. Was it because I was in the wrong job? The wrong hospital? Was it because of the pressure of thinking I always had to be in good form for the patients seeing as they were so worse off than me? I was at a total loss as to the reason.

My poor spirits meant I had difficulty keeping my mind on my work. One day I knocked a trolley of pills over on a patient. He wasn't injured but I was shocked.

When I mentioned it to Daddy on the phone, all he could do was laugh.

'You'll be fine once you get a boyfriend,' he said, 'That's all that's wrong with you. You're lonely.'

I told him to stop being so narrow-minded. I didn't know if he was saying it to wind me up.

'Boyfriends,' I said, 'are the last thing on my mind at the moment.'

Mammy put it down to the fact that I'd been so stressed during the years of training it was probably catching up on me. Maybe that was closer to the truth.

I did a few months in Casualty later that year but it didn't do much to lift my mood. I didn't get a chance to get to know the patients because there were so many of them. The injuries I saw there were pretty gross as well. We often got people with their heads split open after motorbike accidents. It turned my stomach looking at them all in such pain. Sometimes the doctors had to cut their clothes off them to treat them. I almost had to close my eyes with some of them. It's a wonder I didn't bump into the walls as I wheeled them down to theatre for emergency surgery.

A lot of them had been driving without their crash helmets. How could anyone do that? We called them Brain Donors. That sounded cruel but it was the only way we could think of them. One lad ended up being paralysed from the waist down after colliding with a truck on the Naas dual carriageway.

Drink was involved in a lot of the cases. Occasionally I got abused by drunk men. A stocious individual actually hit me one night when I tried to bandage his wound. I don't think he knew what he was doing. He seemed to have self-destructiveness written all over him.

I couldn't understand how someone could throw their lives away for a night out when so many others who'd never touched a drop were desperately clinging on to fragile health situations. I promised myself that if I ever had children I'd forbid them to ride motorbikes. I regarded them as lethal weapons. If a car hit you while you were on one of them you stood little chance even with a helmet on.

After my stint in Casualty I tinkered around with the idea of doing psychiatric nursing. Veronica didn't think that would be a good idea for me on account of the way I was feeling. (I'd told her I was a bit down).

'You can do something for someone with a physical injury,' she said, 'but not always with a psychological problem. It's ten times harder when you don't know what's wrong with someone - or they don't know what's wrong with themselves.' She could have been talking about me.

I also thought of midwifery. Bridget told me she loved it on the odd times we talked. She wasn't the only one I knew who went into it. In some ways it seemed like a natural extension of our training. Some people believed you weren't a 'proper' nurse until you'd done it. Maybe that was why I went out to the Coombe one day and filled in the forms for it.

I saw so many babies there it made me pine for one of my own. There were a lot of single mothers. I remember one woman who had her baby taken from her before she even saw it. The adoption was organised long before the birth. How terrible it must have been for her.

The attitude to unmarried mothers, as we referred to them then, was so different to today. A lot of the time they were seen as fallen women and treated (or rather mistreated) accordingly. Most of them took it but one or two hit back.

One day I heard a nun saying to a girl from a well-heeled background, 'How in the name of God did you get yourself into this position, lass?' Quick as a wink she shot back, 'By lying on my back,

Sister.' The nun stormed out of the room in a rage. She wouldn't have got away with a comment like that a few years before. (A few years later, neither would the nun have got away with what she said).

After much thought I decided not to do midwifery. Instead I stayed where I was. Maybe it was cowardly of me but the devil you knew was better than the devil you didn't. By this stage I was confident enough to be able to deal with most situations I came up against in the Mater. I was run of my feet most days and I liked that. I couldn't walk down the ward without someone asking me for a painkiller or a glass of water or to have their pulse checked.

Some of the patients just wanted to talk. I enjoyed chatting to them but I had to be careful not to spend too long at that, especially when I moved to a semi-private ward later on. There was no matron fastening her gimlet eye on me there but it wasn't good to become too involved with any one person for any number of reasons.

In the summer I had two weeks off. I spent them cycling around the ring of Kerry with two girls I'd got to know in Casualty, Hilary and Mary. We brought the bikes down on the train. Hilary was older than most of the nurses I was friendly with. She'd spent a few years working in a bank before realising that it was the last thing in the world she wanted to spend her life at. Mary was a year behind me in the Mater but I knew her to see. We really lived the bohemian life for that fortnight, sightseeing by day and staying in camp sites at night. There was no pattern to it and that's what I liked most about it. The scenery was stupendous and the air invigorating as you freewheeled down the hills.

After I came back I was transferred to a surgical ward. I wasn't looking forward to it because of my timidness in A&E but it turned out to be not too bad. I met all types there. When someone was facing an operation I always tried to give them extra attention. I knew how I'd be myself in the same situation.

Some of them didn't pull through. It took me a long time to learn to deal with that. A young girl came was admitted one night after taking an overdose. I heard afterwards that a relationship with a man she was crazy about had just broken up.

It was one of those 'cry for help' scenarios but she was gone too far to be pumped out. I'll never forget the look on her parent's faces when they came in. She wasn't much more than a child. There's nothing you can say in a situation like that. There isn't much you can do either except maybe sit with them. Or leave them alone if that was what they wanted. They were utterly devastated.

Another man I nursed died on the operating table during routine surgery. He was being operated on for gall bladder when a blood vessel broke. That devastated me. I'd had lots of chats with him over the previous few weeks and became quite friendly with him. I used to look forward to going into work every day to see his bright face beaming up at me. I couldn't believe it when I heard he'd died.

Nobody in a million years could have predicted anything going wrong. I phoned home that night and cried non-stop. I was almost at the point of leaving the job. Sister Agnes' words about 'the irrigation of the soul' were no good to me now.

Daddy wanted me to chuck it in there and then but Mammy was more factual. 'People die outside hospitals and inside hospitals,' she said, 'You won't get away from that by leaving nursing.' She was right, of course, but I knew I'd see more tragedies there than in any other job. What I had to learn was to form an attitude to it. You couldn't afford to be too close to the patients and it wasn't good to be too distant from them either. It was a delicate  balance to get.

I enjoyed my time in the Mater but after two years there I felt I needed some kind of change. I started to think about taking a year's leave of absence to travel. There was another nurse I knew who was doing that. She was about to go to Africa to teach English in a little village in the middle of nowhere.

It all sounded very exciting to me. Canada was somewhere else I thought about. I'd heard nurses worked shorter shifts there and got much better paid than we did in Ireland. Some of them were talking about 'telephone number' salaries. Money was never a priority for me but sometimes when I talked to people in offices who were getting more than I was for half the work I did it made me angry.

One night when I was leaving work I saw a stack of nursing magazines on a table in the staff-room. I grabbed the lot of them. They had names and addresses of opportunities you could avail of in various countries. A lot of them gave the phone numbers to contact. I got out my felt marker – the one I'd used to illustrate the body parts in my exam – and put rings around the ones that interested me.

Over the next few nights I went forward and back with one location and another. Some of them promised the earth but that wasn't much good if you were away from the people you loved. But would I regret it in years to come if I didn't try them out? I tortured myself looking at all the various advantages and disadvantages. Either way I won and either way I lost. At one point I was almost at the stage of flipping a coin. I couldn't come to a decision.

In a state of frustration I rang Maureen to ask her what she thought I should do. I knew she'd be a good person to have a chat with considering she was so unfulfilled in her own job.

'Why don't I come up to you,' she suggested, 'Then we can talk about it in more detail.'

'That sounds like a great idea,' I said, 'but don't tell May.'

She giggled. We both knew what she was like. She'd take over if she came up and we'd never get anything sorted.

'Don't worry about that,' she said, 'I'll say I have to go away for a day or two for work. I know she'll be dying of curiosity.'

'Let her.'

She said she wasn't even going to tell Mammy or Daddy. May had a way of wangling things out of them.

She came up the following weekend and we talked the hind legs off one another. We were so much on the same wavelength, at times I felt like she could read my mind. And me hers. If she ever came to Dublin to work I knew I'd be more than happy to have her share the flat.

As we sat sipping coffee in a café off Grafton Street she gave me lots of solid advice. She pointed out things I hadn't thought of from both sides of the situation. Even though she was a year younger than me I regarded her as being more mature than I was. She was always able to see things more clearly.

I told her about all the options I was weighing up. She listened to each of them intently. Then I showed her pictures of some of the places.

'Aren't they lovely?' I said.

'Pictures are always lovely,' she said, 'Then you get there and you realise you're in the seventh circle of hell.'

After talking for what seemed like hours I felt no surer of what I wanted than before we started.

'Over to you,' I said, closing the last magazine firmly shut.

I propped my elbows on the table. She took a deep breath as she swallowed the dregs of her coffee.

'I'll give you one thing,' she said, 'You're not jumping without thinking.'

'Maybe I think too much. Didn't someone say that was dangerous?'

'Shakespeare. But then what would he know?'

'Oh Maureen,' I said, 'What in the name of God am I going to do? Daddy spent all his money on me to go to the Mater. I got the best marks in my class and now I'm thinking of throwing my hat at it all. Sometimes I think I'm losing the plot.'

'Don't be ridiculous. You're one of the most well-adjusted people on the planet.'

'Next to Charles Manson maybe.'

'Shut up, you idiot, or I'll hit you.'

'Don't hit me. Just tell me what you think I should do.'

'Okay,' she said giving me an intense look, 'Here goes.'

She spoke lowly and slowly.

'Life is long,' she said, 'I wouldn't do anything in a hurry if I was you. Obviously you're conflicted. You think you're in a rut. Half of you wants adventure and the other half is afraid of it. Just be patient. Keep putting rings around those things in the magazines but give yourself at least another month before you leave what you're doing. You're very good at it and it would be a pity to throw it all away for something worse.'

I asked her what she thought about the financial side of things.

'The money some of these places are offering is very tempting but, let's face it, you don't really care about money. If you did you wouldn't have become a nurse in the first place. And if you went half way around the world and hated it you'd hate yourself as well. Besides, you'd die of loneliness. And we'd die of loneliness having to live without you.'

I was so touched by her words I felt like crying.

'You've always been a rock of sense,' I said, 'I envy you your clear mind.'

'You must be joking. I'm a total wreck when it comes to my own life. We're all great at solving other people's problems.'

'Maybe, but you're making a lot of good points.'

'I don't know about that. I'm probably talking balderdash. There's an outside chance you could be deliriously happy in one of those places. If you are I'll have egg all over my face.'

'That's not true. You're not saying they wouldn't suit me. You're just telling me to wait a bit. Maybe that's what I wanted to hear.'

'Sometimes when we ask people for advice we want them to say what we've already decided.'

For the next few weeks I went to work in a daze. I wasn't sure whether I was going to be in the ward for the rest of my career or if I'd be leaving it in a few months. I hated the idea of having to make a choice but in the end I didn't have to.

Before I made up my mind either way I went to a dance one night and met a man. He was someone who, it turned out, I was about to spend the rest of my life with.

# Kevin

The funny thing about the night I met Kevin was that it wasn't him who asked me to dance, it was me who asked him. It was a Ladies Choice at the Ierne Ballroom on Parnell Square. I used to go there a lot with Bridget and Cáit but that night I was on my own. It was a well-known haunt for culchies.

I can't remember who was on stage the night I met Kevin. Paddy Cole I think. You could always be sure of a good night with 'Old King Cole.' He told jokes between the songs.

Asking a man to dance was something I normally wouldn't do in a month of Sundays but I'd been watching Kevin out of the side of my eye for most of the night and I thought he looked really handsome. I could see he was looking at me too. I tried to ignore him, imagining that would make him interested in me. That's the first lesson women learn about how to behave at dances. Unfortunately it didn't work for me. I wondered if he was too shy to ask me onto the floor. Was I too shy to ask him? Usually I would have been but something pushed me to that night.

I don't know what it was about him that made him stand out for me. He hadn't made any effort to do himself up for starters. The jacket he was wearing wasn't exactly new. And his hair was a bit tousled.

When I think about it, maybe the fact that he hadn't bothered too much about how he looked was what drew me to him. I was nervous of men who looked too elaborate at dances. I always felt they were expecting something – like a visit to your bedroom. Kevin struck me as someone who was respectable but who wouldn't do much more than spit on his shoes to look good  before going out.

It took a lot of courage to go over to him but once I took the plunge it got easier. He said 'Yes' immediately. Before you knew it we were whizzing around the floor like nobody's business. When the dance ended he asked me if I'd like a mineral. We sat down at one of the tables and started chatting. I couldn't believe I was so comfortable with him. Normally it took me ages to get to know someone. Mammy used to say if you were comfortable with someone it was more important than anything else in a relationship. As I chatted with him I felt I'd known him all my life.

He asked me what I did for a living and I told him. He said he was living in a flat in Kilmainham. He was an only child. His mother had died when he was a boy. His father still lived in Athlone. That was where he'd grown up but he was in Dublin all his adult life.

When I said I was from Cork he said 'Ah, the rebel county. I'd never have guessed from your accent.' It was good to know he had a sense of humour. (Thankfully he didn't mention Christy Ring.)

When I asked him what he did for a living he said he worked in Clery's. I told him I was in there every other day getting bits and bobs for the flat.

'I probably crossed your path a few times,' I said.

'Maybe,' he said, 'but it's not too likely. They have me up on the top floor. It's so far away from everywhere else I feel like I'm in a lighthouse or something.' He was in the carpet department. It wasn't exactly the most exciting job in the world, he said, but you met all kinds there.

We were still talking when the lights went up for the National Anthem. He asked me if I'd like to go to the pictures with him the following week. I was more than delighted to say yes.

'Where will we meet?' he asked me

'Did you ever hear of Clery's?' I said, 'There's a clock there.'

We arranged a time for the following Friday. He said he'd be coming on his motorbike. I didn't mention that I had a car. I thought it might have sounded like I was a controlling type of woman. That was the last impression I wanted to give.

For the next few days I was in very good form at work. I wondered if I was falling for him already. I didn't think that was advisable considering I knew so little about him. I didn't mention him to anyone because of my superstitious nature.

On the night of the date I couldn't make up my mind what to wear. After going through my wardrobe about a dozen times I decided everything clashed with everything else. After much hand-wringing I decided to go for simplicity: a cardigan and knee-length skirt.

I got my hair done the day before. There was a fringe in it now. I was wondering if he'd notice. I wasn't mad about it. It was never a good idea to change your appearance just because you were meeting someone.

When I examined myself in the mirror I thought I looked wretched. I put on some eyeliner to take the attention away from it. People always told me my eyes were my best feature.

Next up was the foundation and the moisturiser. I thought a bit of lipstick would brighten me up but I should have known better. My lips were too small for it. It usually came out all smudgy because of that. Mammy used to say lipstick was the only type of make-up that meant anything to men. You could be doing yourself up for hours and it was all they'd notice. If that was true I was well down the field in the attraction stakes.

I arrived first. I knew that might have sounded too eager but I was afraid I'd get delayed on the bus and miss him. I was wearing a leopardskin coat. I'd just bought it the week before. It had a fur collar on it. I was usually economical with coats but I'd splurged out on this one.

A few minutes after I got there he whizzed around the corner on a Honda 50. It was red with a gap between the saddle and the handlebars to make getting onto it easier.

'I like the coat,' he said.

'Thank you.'

'What have you done to your hair?'

'Do you mean the fringe? What do you think of it?'

'It's lovely.'

'I thought you gave me a funny look.'

'Not at all. Do you like it yourself?'

'I hate it.'

'You'll get used to it.'

I asked him if he had a film picked out. He said there was one on in the Corinthian that all the people at work were raving about. I said that sounded great. I told him I'd been at a John Wayne one not too long ago with Maureen and May. He said he loved John Wayne. He put on a drawly accent and said, 'Get off your horse and drink your milk.' I thought he sounded hilarious.

'Is that from one of his films?' I said. He said he didn't know, that it was just something people said when they were imitating him.

It was a windy night. The hat I was wearing kept blowing off.

'Why don't you put it in your handbag?' he said, 'It's not doing you any favours.'

He gave me his crash helmet to wear. It was an old-fashioned one.

'It's made of cork,' he said, 'It should suit you.'

When I put it on I felt like a pilot from the war. It kept blowing all over the place even though I had it buckled under my chin. My head was obviously too small for it.

'How do you like my trusty steed?' he asked me, pointing to the Honda.

'It's very nice,' I said, 'How much did it cost you?'

'A few hundred. It's second hand but it's in good nick.'

I sat on.

'One of the wheels is a bit wonky,' he said, 'If you tilt your body to the side you won't fall off.'

'Great,' I said. I thought to myself: It would be nice to have a first date where I didn't end up in A&E.

He sat in front of me. I was too shy to put my hands around him at first but the bike was shaking so much I had to.

I felt almost high with the wind blowing through me. He was a good driver but when he tilted the bike sideways I screamed. I thought we were going to keel over.

'It's the only way to get around the corners,' he explained.

He weaved in and out through the traffic. We got to the cinema in a matter of minutes.

'We'd probably have been as quick to walk,' he said, 'but I wanted to show off my bike.'

'I felt I was travelling with Steve McQueen,' I said.

'I think he's great. What about you?'

'I like him too.'

He parked on the footpath outside the cinema. There was a man standing there. He looked like he'd seen better days. Kevin winked at him. He put a few coins into his hand. I thought of the guy I had to tip the night I brought Maureen and May to the pictures. They seemed to be everywhere.

'Do you really need to do that?' I said, 'I mean when it's not a car.'

'If you don't, it'll probably be gone when you come out. It's a racket.'

We queued up for the film. It was a James Bond one. He was very popular at the time. The queues went right around the corner. There was a scalper flogging tickets for double the price but we ignored him. 'It's a big cinema,' Kevin said, 'I don't think we'll have any trouble getting in.'

After about twenty minutes we reached the top of the queue. When we got the tickets he went over to the shop. He bought me a Coca-Cola and a bag of Perri crisps.

As we went down the corridor towards our seats I caught my coat on a nail that was sticking out of the wall. It started to rip as I tugged at it.

'Careful,' he said. He released it for me.

'I can't believe I'm so clumsy,' I said.

'It's not your fault. You could have got a nasty cut from that nail. I'm going to have a word with the manager.'

'My new coat,' I said.

'It's only a slight tear. You won't have any trouble sewing it.'

I thought to myself: That's a laugh. I was probably the world's worst stitcher. Mammy used to laugh at me anytime I tried to darn a sock. I often stuck the needle into myself instead of the sock. Thankfully I wasn't quite as accident prone with hospital needles. Otherwise there'd have been blood on the floor of every ward I ever worked in.

An usher came along waving a big torch. The row our tickets were for was full. Our sets were in the middle of it so we had to ask a lot of people to stand up to get to them. I stood on a woman's toe on the way in. She let out a roar.

'Sorry,' I said, 'It was an accident.'

'I hardly think you did it on purpose,' she said gruffly.

We sat down. Kevin put his crash helmet on the floor.

'Would you like me to take off your coat?' he said.

'Good idea. Especially with the tear on view.'

He took it off. Then he took off his own one. We had to put them on our laps because there was no empty seat near us.

The Pathé News came on. It showed the Olympic Games. A man was talking about a rowing competition from some English university. I loved the Pathé News. It used to come on after the small picture in Midleton.

There was no small picture here, just a few ads. The film started when they were over. Sean Connery was in it. He was playing James Bond. He was busily involved saving the world in between making love to a lot of beautiful women. One of them was bad. She tried to poison him so he had to kill her. 'Sorry it didn't work out, darling,' he said before choking her.

Kevin was transfixed watching it all. I pretended to be more interested than I was. I didn't like Sean Connery as much as Steve McQueen. I would have preferred a romantic film.

I wondered if he was going to kiss me. There were couples doing that all around us. They mainly did it during the boring scenes when there weren't explosions or car chases.

He tried to put his arm around me at one stage but he ended up hitting me in the eye with his elbow.

'Sorry,' he said, 'Did I hurt you?'

'Not at all. You hardly touched me.'

I crunched on my crisps. The woman whose toe I stood on gave me a dirty look. When she turned away I stuck my tongue out at her. Kevin saw me. He giggled. I don't know why I did something so childish. I was feeling giddy.

'We'll be thrown out yet,' he said.

We behaved ourselves for the rest of the film. Then it ended. Sean Connery had saved the world once again and cracked a few jokes in the process.

The lights came on. People stretched themselves. They put on their coats. When I put my one on I tried to hide the torn bit.

'Don't worry about it,' he said, 'You'd hardly notice it.'

He picked his helmet off the floor. We joined a big stream of people going down the corridor.

'Will I ask for the manager?' he said.

'It's hardly worth it. What can he do?'

'Okay. Did you like the film?'

'It was great. How about you?'

'I thought it was all right. It wasn't as good as the last one. Personally I think they're making too many James Bond films. The bubble is going to burst one of these days.'

We walked out onto the street. It was a balmy night. The bike was still there but the scalper was gone.

'Some protection,' Kevin said. 'He's probably footless up in Madigan's by now.' That was a bar around the corner.

The wind was still blowing. I couldn't stop thinking about my coat. I wondered if I'd be able to get it to look good again, or get someone else to. Veronica's sister was a seamstress. Maybe she could do something with it.

'How about a bite to eat?' he said.

'That would be lovely.'

He put the helmet on me. I sat onto the bike.

'Ready?' he said.

I sat behind him. We zoomed off. This time I put my arms around him without being asked. I wondered where he was going to bring me. He turned right. We drove up O'Connell Street. He parked on an island.

'There's a nice place around the corner, he said 'Some of the people from work go to it.'

We walked up to Parnell Street. That was where the café was. It was no time until we got to it. It looked nice and cosy. A radio was playing. It was very bright. It might have been the middle of the day with all the lights.

As we walked in, one of the waitresses nodded at Kevin as if she knew him. She led us to our seats and brought the menu over to us. We both decided we'd have fish and chips.

He gestured to the waitress. She came back over to us.

'Tea for two, please,' he said, 'and fish and chips for two.'

She took the menus.

'Nice night, isn't it?' she said.

'A bit blowy,' he said.

She went off.

'You seem to know her,' I said.

'Only slightly.'

I tried to think of something to say to him but I couldn't. Suddenly I felt self-conscious. I found myself wishing they'd turn down the lights.

An Adam Faith song came on the radio.

'He's one of my favourite singers,' I said.

'Mine too. Do you like Cliff Richard?'

'Not as much.'

'Pat Boone?'

'I love Pat Boone.'

It sounded like you were a square to say you liked him but I didn't care. I felt Kevin was old-fashioned too.

The waitress came over with the meal.

'That was quick, Shelley,' Kevin said to her, 'You haven't lost your touch.'

She clucked her tongue. The way she did it made me think he knew her better than he was letting on. I found myself becoming jealous. That was crazy for a first date. Shelley was very good-looking. She had lovely fair hair but it was obviously dyed. I was delighted to discover something I had over her.

We sat listening to the music. The chips were nice but undercooked. I watched Kevin smear ketchup all over his ones. I hated ketchup. He put lots of salt on them as well. The salt cellar was shaped like a little black corgi dog. The pepper one was shaped like a white one.

'That stuff will kill you,' I said, pointing to the ketchup.

'No sooner than the chips,' he said.

Out of the corner of my eye I saw a nurse I knew from the Mater. She was a wild one from Ardee, almost as bad as Cáit. Her name was Miranda Cawley.

She gave a whistle when she saw me.

'What's this?' she said, putting on a face, 'Nobody told me you were going out with anyone.'

'He's just a friend,' I muttered.

'The quiet ones are always the worst,' she grinned. She winked at Kevin.

'What are you doing here?' I asked her.

155

'I came in for a takeaway. We had a bit of a hooley back at the hospital. Nora had a baby. She got married a few months ago.'

She was talking about Nora Hanley, another girl from our set. I didn't know her that well.

'My God,' I said, 'She must have moved fast.'

'Maybe too fast,' she said. I wasn't sure what she meant by that. Was she referring to a shotgun wedding?

She got her takeaway and started to go out.

'What about yourself?' she said at the door, 'Do I hear wedding bells? Should I buy a hat?'

'Shut up, Miranda,' I said.

She cackled as she breezed off.

'Who was that?' Kevin said.

'Someone I know from training.'

'She looks good fun.'

'She's all right.'

I started thinking he might have liked her more than me. Was I too dull for him? Then I thought: This is ridiculous. You're on a first date. Relax.

We finished our meal. He called for Shelley again. She trotted over. He paid her, adding a generous tip.

'The last of the big spenders,' she said.

We stood up. I put on my coat. The tear looked worse. I tried to hide it.

Kevin waved to Shelley.

'Thanks again, Kev,' she said as she came over to our table to clear it..

We went outside.

'It's got colder,' Kevin said, 'I'd advise you to button your coat tight.'

'As long as I don't tear it again.'

He laughed. We walked back to O'Connell Street. When we got to the bike I put the helmet on. He got on the saddle. I sat in behind him.

'I'm getting used to this,' I said.

'You'll have to give me directions to where you live,' he said as he got on.

We drove towards Drumcondra in the biting wind. I kept shouting 'Left' or 'Right' to him over the sound of it. He nodded to let me know he knew what I meant.

By now I was getting good at tilting my body at the corners.

'You'll be as good as good as Steve McQueen yet,' he said.

We reached the flat. He turned off the ignition. The wind was dying down.

'It's good to be able to hear your voice again,' I said, 'Thanks so much for everything. I had a great time apart from the coat problem.'

'Me too, apart from half-blinding you when I tried to put my arm around you.'

'It was nothing.'

We stood there awkwardly.

'Maybe we'll go out again sometime,' he said.

'That would be lovely,' I said. I was never much good at playing hard to get. How could I anyway? I'd asked him to dance after all. When you do that, any game-playing goes out the window.

'Brilliant. Maybe I should ask you for your phone number.'

'That might help!'

I took a piece of paper out of my pocket. It was a discarded prescription sheet. I handed it to him. He looked at it bemusedly.

'Can I get the tablets too?' he said.

'Very funny. The phone is in the hall so if you ring it might take me a minute or two to get down to it.'

'Take all the time in the world,' he said.

I turned towards the door.

'Goodnight so,' I said.

'Do I qualify for a goodnight kiss?' he said.

I gave him was a quick one before running inside. Luckily for him I wasn't wearing lipstick or it would have been all over him.

As I went upstairs I heard him turning on the ignition of his bike. When I got to my room it was already just a faint hum.

I stayed awake thinking about the night for a long time. How much did I like him? How much did he like me? Would we become steady daters?

I told myself to stop being ahead of myself. I hadn't been out with enough men to know which of them I really liked. I'd gone out with a

157

few once or twice and then called it quits. There was a man from Carlow that I thought I liked but he turned out to be as dull as ditchwater. I dated another guy who was working in a shop in Drumcondra. He two-timed me so that was the end of him. A few others passed like ships in the night.

Cáit protected me from some of them. Bridget advised me against some others. I hated most things about meeting men. The way you had to stand at dances, the false conversations you had when you were jigging around the floor, the leading questions, the pretence that you were enjoying yourself when you weren't. I hated the image of yourself that you had to project that wasn't the real you and the image men often projected to get off with you. I didn't like leading them on. If I didn't think I was going to make a go of a relationship I preferred to end it sooner rather than later.

Maybe I was exaggerating Kevin's importance because my focus had been on my work for so long. Maybe Daddy was right, I thought, maybe that was why I'd spilled the pill trolley on the patient that day. I'd been lonely without realising it.

I was like a sixteen year old with her first crush. I woke up every morning with a smile on my face. When I walked around the hospital I felt as if my feet were on roller skates. I knew I was getting in too deep too fast but I couldn't help it. I kept wondering if he'd ring me or not. Did he find me boring? Was Shelley more attractive to him?

I got the answer to those questions when he rang me a few nights later. I nearly broke my neck running down the stairs to answer the phone. He said he'd love to meet me that weekend if I was interested. I didn't need to be asked twice.

On our second date he brought me for a meal in The Luna, a Chinese restaurant in the middle of O'Connell Street. I wasn't feeling confident because I'd had a bad hair day. In those days I regarded my hair as one of my best features. It came out scraggly whatever way I washed it. I put some rollers in it but they didn't help. When I saw myself in the mirror I thought I looked a sight.

I'd never been in a Chinese restaurant before but I didn't say that in case I came across as a hick. The staff were friendly. They fussed over us as if we were royalty. They wore little napkins on their arms and stood erect like soldiers. Everything was laid on as if we were the cheese. There was even a man standing at the door of the Ladies with a towel in his hand. I wasn't sure whether he expected me to tip him or not when I went in.

I had chicken curry with rice. Me being my clumsy self, most of the rice ended up on the tablecloth before I was finished with it.

Kevin was polite to the waiters. I was glad of that. Some women liked their men to act important and even be rude in restaurants. That kind of behaviour totally turned me off. I felt you could trust quiet men more than the ones who acted like know-alls. I was glad Shelley wasn't serving us.

Veronica's sister did a great job on my coat but as we were getting near the end of the meal I realised to my horror that I had a ladder in my nylons. I kept crossing my legs so he wouldn't see it.

'What are you doing?' he said, 'Don't hide your legs. They're very nice. Is it because of the ladder in your nylons?'

For some reason I started laughing.

'After I get home I'm going to throw them in the bin.' I said. How had he noticed? First the coat and now this. What would he say if he found out I hadn't a clue about anything domestic? I couldn't cook, I couldn't darn and I couldn't knit. I remembered Mammy trying to teach me when I was young. 'Plain and purl,' she'd say, 'plain and purl.' I never had a clue what she was on about.

For the rest of the evening I tried to keep still in case I ripped anything else but I overdid it because my foot went to sleep. When we were leaving I nearly fell over a table trying to stand up.

'Have you been drinking?' Kevin asked me.

'I have pins and needles,' I explained.

'That's what they all say.'

As we walked down O'Connell Street a photographer snapped us. I've always treasured that photograph. I went in to a little studio the following day and picked it out of a ledger. There were dozens of similar ones in it. When I showed it to Kevin he just laughed.

We went out three times that week By the third time I was so relaxed with him I didn't even bother putting on make-up. He told me he didn't care about things like that. This was music to my ears. Anytime I put it on (which wasn't too often) it looked like it was applied with a sweeping brush.

159

It was only now I felt confident enough to tell Maureen about him. 'Don't breathe a word to Mammy,' I said. Miranda Cawley had it all over St. Ignatius Ward already. I was furious with her. Some nurses I knew had you married to someone if they heard you'd been out with someone more than once.

Every time I saw him I got more keen on him. I liked the fact that he didn't drink. By now I'd served my time with men slobbering alcohol all over me in the Ierne any other time I'd gone there. A lot of them were hardly able to stand up at the end of the night.

He was three years older than me. When I asked him had he been out with many other girls he said, 'Just a few.' I knew by the way he said it that he didn't want to go into any details. He was private like that. I was private myself too. He tried to get information out of me about my previous boyfriends but I clammed up at his questions, so much so that he said, 'You should have been in the IRA.'

I compensated by telling him all about the hospital and my life in Cork. He was a good listener. That was more important to me than him being a good talker. Daddy used to say we were given two ears but only one mouth so we should listen twice as much as we talked.

Most of the girls I knew said they went for men with 'personality.' I never knew what that meant. All too often it suggested someone who got lots of women because they had charm. From my experience these types of men didn't stay with any one woman too long. They played the field and rarely made good husbands when they finally went up the aisle. It was too difficult for them to leave their carousing ways behind them.

I knew a lot of women whose husbands were married to Arthur Guinness. Kevin told me he used to drink a lot when he was younger but he put 'the plug in the jug' when he realised he was getting too fond of it. He was now teetotal. He said it wasn't easy for him going to get-togethers in Clery's for that reason. Most of them involved alcohol. He had to stay sober while everyone around him was getting footless. This being Ireland, people who didn't imbibe were looked on as Holy Joes. He didn't like to declare the real reason for his abstinence.

'If I did,' he said, 'it'd be all over the place that I was a raving alcoholic. There seems to be no middle ground in this country.' I felt

160

sorry for him when he said that. A lot of people didn't get to know him as a result. He said he was afraid to open up to them about his problem. The upshot was that he spent most of his time at these functions nursing a glass of Coca-Cola. He had his work cut out for him trying not to look odd without something 'interesting' in his hand.

He didn't like pubs for obvious reasons. I wasn't mad about them either so we usually met in cafes. We'd have a light meal and then go to a film. He mainly liked 'men's pictures.' Because I wasn't too mad about these (at least if they had Sean Connery in them) he brought me to some romantic ones as well. I told him Daddy used to do that when we were growing up.

One night we went to *The Nun's Story*. It had Audrey Hepburn in it. People said I looked like her sometimes, especially with my uniform on. I wondered if Sister Serafina ever thought that. Peter Finch was the male lead. I had a crush on him for a while, at least when I wasn't drooling over David Janssen.

Kevin kissed me for the first time that night. It was in a little laneway outside the cinema. I was surprised. I don't think he even knew he was going to do it himself. It was almost like something he had to get out of the way. My heart was beating really fast as he put his arms around me.

The kiss seemed to cement what we already had. Afterwards we started going steady. Was I falling in love? I didn't like to think in big terms like that. It sounded too much like Hollywood. Just like I didn't know what a vocation was, neither could I define being in love. I told myself to just take each day as it came in case something went wrong between us. I always felt smugness put the mockers on things.

If we weren't at the pictures or in a restaurant we went dancing in the Town and Country Club. It was located down by the old *Evening Press* office. They had fluorescent lights there that made you look like you had a tan when you went out on the floor.

They played great music and often got live acts as well. One night we went to see Dickie Rock. He was one of my favourite Irish singers at the time. He'd just been in the Eurovision Song Contest with a song called 'Come Back to Stay.' I was hoping he'd win but he only came fourth. I used to love it when he twirled his microphone, or when he threw it up in the air in the middle of a song and caught it on the way down without missing a beat.

The night he came back to Ireland I went out to the airport to see him. Kevin didn't like him as much as I did so he didn't go. I went with some other nurses instead. We all shouted 'Spit on me, Dickie' as he came down the ramp. For me that meant more than seeing The Beatles a few years before, probably because he was Irish.

Nelson's Pillar had been blown up the night before by the IRA. Kevin was much more worked up about that. It happened shortly after midnight. People heard the explosion for miles around. It was so close to Clery's, he said he could have been killed if he'd been doing overtime that night. The next morning he went up to the bomb site and took away a piece of rock that had blown clear. He kept it as a memento.

Daddy rang me about it later that day. He certainly wasn't shedding any tears for Nelson. 'It was long overdue,' he said. It was on that phone call that I told him about Kevin. I didn't go into any details. I just said I was seeing someone who worked in Clery's. I said we'd been around The Pillar to see the damage. 'Don't go too near it,' he said, 'What's left could fall down on you.'

If I wasn't meeting Kevin under Clery's clock we used to meet at The Pillar sometimes as well. Obviously we never would again now. It was nothing more than a stump. A part of me felt nostalgic for it. I'd only been up to the top of it once, the time when Maureen and May came up to see me. Dickie Rock claimed the explosion stole his thunder, taking him off the front pages of the papers. 'I don't think he'd have been on the front page anyway,' was Kevin's view. I told him jealousy would get him nowhere.

The stump was demolished by the Irish army a few days later. I was off work that day so Kevin brought me up to his 'crow's nest' in Clery's to see all the activity close up. We were looking out a back window behind the carpet department when the demolition took place. Even though it was a controlled one, it still shattered a few of the windows downstairs. There were pieces of glass all over O'Connell Street. Daddy would have been in his element watching the end of Horatio Nelson.

Kevin brought me to see Butch Moore in the CIE Hall a few weeks later. He'd been in the Eurovision the year before. That was Ireland's first year in the contest. He didn't win it either but he came sixth with his song 'Walking the Streets in the Rain.' I couldn't stop singing it for weeks afterwards. There was something about him that intrigued me. People said he made love to the microphone. 'What is it with you and the Eurovision?' Kevin said to me, 'Maybe if I went into it you'd like me more.'

Not all of our dates were on my terms. When we weren't at the CIE Hall or dancing in the Town and Country Club he used to bring me to soccer matches in Dalymount Park. He'd get hoarse shouting at the players to do this and that. Meanwhile I'd be looking at my watch wondering when I was going to be released from my torture.

He was a talented footballer himself. I often watched him playing five-a-sides in Kilmainham when I visited him in his flat. He never performed as well when I watched him as when I wasn't there so after a while I stopped going. He said he used to try too hard to impress me and ended up making stupid mistakes. It reminded me of how I'd been with Joanne Wylie.

Sometimes after the matches we went down to Athlone together and stayed with his father. He was always very nice to me. He tried his best to be in good form but Kevin told me he never got over losing his wife. For that reason, and because I liked him, I tried to do as much as I could for him. I made him tea and things like that.

He cut himself with a bread knife once and I cleaned the wound for him. He was so grateful you'd think I was just after performing heart surgery on him. He said to me afterwards, 'Nursing is the most dedicated profession in the world.' The kindness of that remark always stuck with me. It made me realise where Kevin got his character from. I was sorry we didn't get down there more because I felt he was lonely. He didn't talk about personal things. That was something else he shared with Kevin – and I suppose with me.

They also had the soccer in common. The three of us went to a few matches together at the weekends when Athlone were playing. I saw a different side of him emerging at these. He knew most of the players by name. I was amazed at the way he came out of himself when he was talking to them.

He introduced me to a few of them after the games. He laughed and joked with them as if he on the team himself, talking animatedly about disallowed goals and saved penalties and whatnot. It was almost like a different person. He'd been so quiet up to this. Now you couldn't shut him up.

After one of the games he brought me into the locker-room of the Athlone team. There were all these men running around the place in various stages of undress.

'I don't think this place is for women,' I said.

'I'm sure there's nothing new to you seeing men without their clothes on. You're a nurse, aren't you?'

'It's not me I'm worried about, it's them.'

They started scrambling madly for towels to put over themselves. I made a hasty retreat. He followed me out a few seconds later.

'Sorry about that,' he said, 'Sometimes I get carried away and forget what I'm doing.'

'No problem. I think I just got out in time.'

'I saw a few red faces all right.'

He was like a child at a party, an innocence lighting up his eyes.

'What would you say to a drink?' he said then.

I didn't have the heart to refuse him. He led me into a bar beside the ground. It was strange being with him without Kevin being there. I always stayed in the background when the three of us went anywhere.

He nodded to the barman. He was obviously a regular because he didn't even need to say what he wanted. Before long a pint of Guinness arrived. I said I'd have a martini.

He carried on talking where he left off at the pitch. After asking me about how the nursing was going for me he said, 'You have no idea how happy you make Kevin. He thinks the world of you.'

That made my day. It was all I could think of as I drank my martini. I was as relaxed as anything talking to him. He started talking about his wife and how I reminded him so much of her. They'd had a really happy marriage together. He had no bitterness at all about the fact that she'd died young. His only thoughts were for Kevin growing up without a mother, how devastating that must have been for him.

164

Before we left the bar he explained the offside rule to me. It was an unwritten law that women weren't supposed to understand this so I pretended I didn't even though I thought I got it eventually. I don't know why women's inability to grasp this seemed almost enshrined in law. It wasn't exactly like Einstein's Theory of Relativity.

After a few months going out with Kevin I started to think of getting serious with him. I talked a lot to Mammy about him. She seemed to think he'd be right for me. Maureen thought that too. When I showed May a photo of him she said he was a 'dreamboat.' Daddy was more cautious about having someone take their darling daughter away from him.

'You're the one who told me to get a boyfriend in the first place,' I taunted.

'That was a joke. Don't fall for him just because he's good-looking. They're always the worst.'

'He's nice on the inside as well. Don't pass judgment on him when you haven't even met him.'

'Okay, but do me a favour. Take things slowly. It's your first serious relationship and you're far too young.'

I could never see things like that. If you really liked someone, what did it matter if it was your first relationship or your twenty first one?

They were all dying to meet him in Midleton but he was fearful of that.

'Maybe I won't make a good impression on them,' he said, 'and you'll turn off me.'

'You'll make a brilliant impression,' I told him, 'Just like you did the first time I met you.'

One weekend after much gentle persuasion (and a few threats to break it off) I managed to get him to come down with me. He let me drive him in the Austin but he persisted in giving directions the whole way. On most of our dates we were still using his Honda but there was no way I was going to go down to Midleton on it. If nothing else I knew I'd have had the head blown off me with the wind. I'd have looked like The Wild Woman of the Hills after we disembarked.

As I predicted, everyone fell in love with him after about five minutes. Maureen told me I should marry him that very day. Aunt

165

Bernie said he was a total gentleman. May couldn't stop staring at him. Even Daddy was impressed. Mammy fussed over him so much I had to tell her to stop.

'He'll think I never had a boyfriend before,' I said to her.

We had roast beef for dinner. Mammy gave us all monster helpings.

'I won't be able to walk after this,' Kevin said.

'Eat up and shut up,' she told him. She could be sharp at times but he took the comment in the spirit in which it was intended.

At one stage he reached out to get the gravy and spilled it all over his trousers. Everyone was afraid to look but I got a fit of the giggles. Then everyone started laughing. He had to change into a pair of Daddy's. They were far too big for him. He wasn't too pleased about that but there was nothing else he could do. Mammy put his pair in the washing machine. When they were dry he was able to change back into them.

He said he was never as embarrassed in his life but in a strange way it made me feel he was more a part of the family.

'I hope you realise I wear the trousers in this family,' Daddy said.

'Yes,' Mammy cut in, 'but I have to wash them.'

After they got to know each other better, Daddy started talking to Kevin about soccer. I smiled to myself as I heard him calling out the names of players I didn't even think he knew. It was funny how new people in your life showed up the old ones in a different light.

'Now do you see?' I said to Kevin when we were on our own, 'We're not too bad, are we?'

'You come from a lovely family. I should have come down months ago.'

There was only one blemish on the visit. At one stage I got so elated I lit up a fag without thinking. Mammy looked at me with her mouth open. My secret was out.

'So that's why you haven't been putting on the weight,' she said, snapping her fingers. She often wondered where my appetite had gone in recent months. Now she knew.

'Have you any sense in your head at all?' she said to me, 'Did they not tell you about the dangers of these cancer rods in your training? Do you know they're behind half of your father's breathing problems?'

'I do, Mammy,' I said, 'Everything you've said is true. I'm going to give them up as soon as I get back to Dublin.'

'Never mind telling me about going off them,' she said, 'Tell me how you got *on* them.'

I put the blame on Cáit and Bridget from way back. It was handy to have an excuse. Or was it that? Was there anyone of my age who didn't think they looked 'cool' with a cigarette in their mouth? Or who started smoking to keep their weight down? Or to avoid stress? (At least if they were working with someone called Joanne Wylie).

I felt Mammy suspected I was smoking all along. Her so-called 'shock' at seeing me lighting up seemed a bit staged. I was old enough to know that daughters had few secrets from their mothers, especially a mother like mine. When I thought about it, Daddy probably suspected something too. The pair of them talked about everything together.

Back in Dublin I relaxed more with Kevin. He'd passed the Tuohy Family Approval Test. That was only slightly more arduous than rounding the Cape of Good Hope or climbing Everest. There should have been some kind of medal given out for it.

We decided to spend more time at his flat in Kilmainham. Up to now we'd mostly been in my one. I'd only been in his a few times. It was nothing special but I liked going over there. If nothing else it broke my routine. He was more relaxed in it than he was in mine. I suppose that was to be expected.

He was also more romantic there. Sometimes after coming home from a film or a meal he'd put on some soft music and low lights. Every girl in Ireland knew what that meant.

The first time he put his hand on my thigh I slapped him.

'I'm not that kind of girl,' I said. We were after being in a bar, change from our usual film routine.

'I'm not that kind of man either,' he said.

If he got too amorous I'd have to fend him off. Having said that, I knew him well enough now not be worried about the fact that he might be after 'the one thing.' Many of the men I went out in the past spent most of their time trying to find out if I'd go to bed with them without too much of a struggle. You could usually spot these a mile off. If the first thing a man asked you at a dance was if you were living alone it was a dead giveaway. I used to say I wasn't even when after I moved into the flat.

Kevin was like someone out of the last generation. He often brought me flowers if we had a tiff. Some women I knew didn't like the door being opened for them or a chair pulled out at a table but I appreciated Kevin doing things like that. If he was leaving me to the bus after a date instead of bringing me home on the Honda he always waved at me after I got on. He kept doing so until it went out of sight.

One night he told me he thought I was too good for him. That was nonsense. If anything the opposite was true. How was it that the people who had most to offer in life seemed to be the least aware of it? I met many men who thought they were the cheese. More often than not, these were the ones you'd jump under a bus to avoid.

Sometimes he had 'lads' nights out with his friends from the five-a-side soccer games. They were much louder than him and much more obnoxious. They bored me with their adolescent tales of female conquests and mad boozing. I warned him to behave himself on these nights but I was really just joking. I didn't worry about the fact that he'd go off with anyone else. Maybe that was smug on my part but I never saw him as having a wandering eye. He was the exact opposite of Reg in that way. How could two people who liked each other so much be like polar opposites of one another? It didn't make sense.

# Tying the Knot

After we'd been going out for two years, Kevin told me he'd booked a few days away for us in Paris. I couldn't believe what I was hearing. It would have been more expectable for him to say we were going somewhere like Killarney.

'Why Paris?' I said when I managed to get my breath back.

'When I met you first you told me you wanted to get out of Ireland. Well here's your chance.'

'That was when I was thinking of nursing abroad.'

'Are you telling me you don't want to go?'

'No. It sounds very exciting but how are you going to pay for it? Places like that cost a fortune.'

'Don't worry about that side of it,' he said, winking at me, 'I've been putting a few bob away for a while.'

I was bursting to tell my news to the girls at work. They were agog when I did. In those days going to France was like going to the moon.

'You've landed on your feet with that guy,' Veronica said, 'He sounds like the answer to a maiden's prayer. He hasn't any brothers by any chance, has he?'

'Unfortunately not.'

'Damn.'

I could hardly keep my mind on my work over the next few days. I was so elated I dropped nearly everything I picked up. The icing on the cake was the fact that Joanne Wylie had departed the scene. She'd have made a field day out of my clumsiness.

Mammy wasn't too happy about my Paris plans.

'You only know him a little over a year,' she said.

'We'll be in separate rooms, Mammy.'

'Can you swear to that?'

'On a stack of Bibles.'

I stretched my over-stretched budget by buying an outfit I thought would be chic enough to wear on the Champs Elysses. I got it in Switzer's.

'Is Clery's not good enough for you anymore?' Kevin said when he saw it.

'Not for Paris,' I said, 'Sorry.' If I may say so myself, I thought I looked very sophisticated in it.

That was my one extravagance. After splurging out on it I promised myself to watch every penny. So did Kevin. One evening when I was in his flat in Kilmainham he showed me a tea caddy jammed to the gills with notes and coins.

'Our spending money,' he pronounced.

'That's not fair,' I protested, 'You've paid for the flight and the accommodation. Let me contribute to one part of it at least.'

'You can bring us on our next holiday. You have enough on your plate with your rent and car payments.'

I'd actually missed a few of them but I hadn't told him. I was afraid the car would be re-possessed at one stage but Daddy helped me out once again. In my ignorance I hadn't realised all the extra costs a car entailed. It wasn't just the petrol but the tax and insurance as well. I hoped to God it wouldn't break down on me anytime I went home. That would been the last straw.

The rent on the flat was a burden too, especially considering there was nobody to share it with, but by now I'd got very fond of my independence, at least when I wasn't with Kevin.

All my worries went into abeyance thinking of my forthcoming trip. It was going to be my first time outside Ireland. What a place to start.

It was also the first time I was ever on a plane. I was so excited I could hardly talk. I was nervous too.

'Are you afraid of flying?' Kevin asked me.

'No, only crashing,' I said.

I took a tranquilliser to calm me. We had a drink in the airport lounge. I knew it wasn't recommended to mix the two but I didn't care. The combination took all my nerves away.

The take-off was the most exciting part. My stomach fluttered as we rose into the air. Ireland became a tiny dot behind us. The jigsaw of its fields disappeared. They were replaced by a bundle of clouds that felt close enough to touch.

The sky got bluer as we crossed the ocean. For a while there was only sea but then different kinds of countryside appeared below us, more well-kept fields and farms, a patchwork quilt that looked like so many paintings come to life.

'We're now over France,' the air hostess informed us. Then Paris came into view, its closely-packed streets threaded below us in a beautiful mosaic.

Kevin was very quiet on the journey. That made me suspicious. Why wasn't he as impressed as I was when we were looking out at such spectacular views? Had he something else on his mind?

'I still don't know what this trip is about,' I kept saying, half to myself and half to him. I got no reaction from him.

'Shut up and enjoy the scenery,' he said.

If being up in the sky above Paris took my breath away, the city itself did so in a different way. Even before we landed I was awed by it.

We were ages waiting for our luggage. Some of the officials looked a bit haughty to me.

'They keep looking at me as if I've done something wrong,' I said to Kevin.

'That's what they're paid for,' he said.

My eyes were out on sticks looking at the people queueing up at the conveyor belt. They looked so stylish.

'You're just as good as any of them with your new bolero,' Kevin assured me but I severely doubted that.

I got a kick out of having my passport stamped. It would be something to show off to the girls at work.

Finally we got out of the airport. A delegation of us were whisked into a bus for the hotel. We sped down a motorway. Everything looked strange to me – the buildings, the cars, even the way people walked. It was a long way from Midleton.

Paris was the most beautiful place I'd ever seen in my life. All the landmarks I'd only glimpsed on television programmes previously I was now seeing for real. Admittedly I was only looking at them from a bus but I knew I was going to be walking beside them in a day or two: The Eiffel Tower and the Arc of Triomphe and all the rest of them. .

Everywhere I looked there seemed to be a designer shop. I wondered if I'd be able to afford to buy even the cheapest blouse to go with my bolero. I was looking forward to getting a shopping bag with a fancy label on it to show off with my passport.

The hotel looked like something out of the sixteenth century. The furnishings were so ornate I could hardly find words to describe them.

We had trouble asking the simplest questions to the staff. For a while I wondered if we were going to be admitted to our room. There was confusion over the booking and they weren't very helpful trying to fix it. Kevin had to get assertive in the end, He threatened to walk straight up to our room if the manager wasn't called for. Eventually it was sorted out. It was worth it because it was such a gorgeous room. I felt like royalty walking across the carpet. I looked out the window at the lights of Paris twinkling beneath us like a Christmas tree.

Kevin's room was equally nice. There was only a wall between us.

'We can tap on it in Morse Code if we want to say anything to one another,' I suggested.

We didn't need to do that. After a glass of the most beautiful wine I ever tasted in my life I found my familiar exhaustion coming over me.

We decided to have an early night. Kevin kissed me at the door of my room. When I got inside I saw a heart-shaped chocolate on the pillow of the bed. I knocked on the wall.

'Did you get a chocolate?' I called out.

'Yes,' he said, 'I was just about to ask you the same thing.'

Breakfast the next morning was a bit disappointing. There wasn't much more than a croissant on the plate. The coffee tasted like tar. Talk about strong. After downing two cups of it I felt as if I was going to be able to levitate. Mammy would have been disgusted. Daddy would have probably walked out on the spot, missing his beloved fry-up. But I couldn't complain. There was too much luxury on view for that.

After freshening up in our rooms we walked down by the Seine arm in arm. There were loads of people all around us. I tried to make out what they were saying to one another with my Leaving Cert

French but couldn't make any headway. It sounded very important until Kevin said, 'They're probably just yapping about what they'll have for their tea.'

We wondered what we'd do for the rest of the day. I wanted to see art galleries and museums but Kevin said he'd be just as happy stravaging the boulevards.

'What about the Louvre and the Notre Dame Cathedral?' I said, 'you can't go to Paris and not see these.'

'Oh yes you can,' he said. 'Why don't we just drop into a few coffee houses and contemplate the meaning of life. Isn't that what the French spend their time at?'

We went into the coffee houses all right but I was more interested in contemplating the menu than the meaning of life. Most of it I couldn't understand. All I had was a few cups of espresso. They were stronger than whiskey. I felt like I was about to take off for outer space after drinking them.

'Those espressos sure pack a punch,' Kevin agreed, 'considering how tiny the cups are.'

We had a meal that night with so many courses I felt we'd be there for the night trying to get through it. The menu was about the size of a novel. The waiter fawned over us, probably expecting a huge tip. All he was short of was bringing out a violin.

The food was out of this world. We ate until we could hardly move.

'One meal would have done the two of us,' I said.

'You couldn't do that in a place like this. You'd be thrown out.'

We finished it off with another glass of wine each.

'I feel I'm dining with royalty,' I said.

'You *are* royalty,' he said. He could be very romantic at times like that.

On our second morning he told me he was taking me to the Eiffel Tower for the day. I wasn't too surprised  because most tourists did that but on the bus to it he was quiet again. I wondered if he had something up his sleeve.

When we got there we were ferried up the tower in a lift. When we reached the top we swooned at the splendour of the panorama around us.

Kevin went down on one knee. He was shaking. He reached into his pocket. I thought, 'Uh-oh.'

Then the penny dropped – or should I say the franc.

He took a ring out. In a trembling voice he said, 'Would you do me the honour of being my wife?'

It wouldn't be an exaggeration to say my heart skipped a beat. In another way, maybe my subconscious was half expecting it. It was such a lovely gesture from a lovely man – the fulfilment of all my dreams.

'It so happens I would,' I replied, 'Now get up on your feet you big mutt.'

Even though I sounded relaxed you could have knocked me over with a feather. Was this really Kevin Mulvey, the soccer player from Athlone who worked in Clery's? Was I the nurse from Midleton trying to find her feet in her new career? Was I standing at the top of the Eiffel Tower being proposed to?

You bet your boots I was.

The ring was gorgeous but I was too shocked to appreciate it.

'You chancer,' I said, 'So this was what you were planning all the time. Did the tea caddy money go towards the ring?'

'I couldn't wait to get it round your finger.'

I started crying when he said that. Then I fell into his arms.

'Is that what the chocolates on the pillows were all about?' I said, 'Di the people at the hotel know this was going to happen?'

He grinned.

'I might have said something to them. I forget.'

'Liar.'

We went into a café that was right beside us on the top of the tower. I can't remember what we talked about. I was too busy looking at the ring. Maybe we didn't say anything at all. I would have been happy to sit there forever but after a while an officious-looking waiter came over to us.

'Fermé!' he said as if he was a gendarme.

'We better go,' Kevin said.

My stomach quivered all the way down in the lift. I was excited and afraid and happy and nervous. When we got back onto the street I was hardly able to walk. Kevin hailed a taxi. I felt really sophisticated as I sat into it. I was an engaged woman being transported from the Eiffel Tower to a hotel. Who could beat that?

I told Mammy everything that happened on a crackly phone call later that night. She wasn't too surprised.

'We all knew you two were crazy about each other,' she said. I could hear Daddy in the background saying, 'What?' Maureen and May cheered into the phone.

After I hung up I told Kevin what everyone said. He was worried Daddy might have thought he was cheeky to propose to me without squaring it with him first. It was the old Irish thing of 'questioning the pop before you pop the question.' I assured him our family wasn't like that but he wasn't convinced.

We went out for a meal that night to celebrate. Kevin didn't spare any expense. I felt like royalty as I tucked in.

'All I'm missing is the lorgnette and the elbow length gloves,' I said to Kevin, 'Then I'd really be able to give Audrey Hepburn a run for her money.' I was thinking of the way she looked in *Breakfast at Tiffany's*.

We ordered a bottle of champagne after it. Kevin didn't take any so I had most of it to myself. It knocked me on my ear.

The waiter was amused at me when I started slurring my words. 'Maybe your French will improve now,' Kevin suggested, 'Frogs always sound better when they're drunk.'

I didn't want the night to end. At one point I launched into a rendition of the Marseillaise. When I finished it I remember telling Kevin I wanted to take out French citizenship. (For some strange reason I didn't follow up on this).

We went back to Dublin the following day. I had a hangover at breakfast but it was one of the most pleasant ones I ever had. I thought I was going to be sick on the flight home. Alcohol and turbulence don't mix so once or twice I felt I was going to throw my breakfast over my new fiancé.

Somehow I managed to hold out until we touched down.

'It's good to be back on *terra firma*,' Kevin said.

'Agreed,' I said, 'but I'm afraid I don't feel too firm.' My mind was still in the clouds of Paris.

As soon as we were through Customs I made straight for the loo. I knelt on the floor beside the toilet bowl and threw up. I felt sorry for the woman who was in the cubicle beside me. She heard everything.

The great thing about throwing up is how well you feel afterwards. When we got into a taxi I was back to myself again. When we reached the flat I thanked Kevin for giving me the most fantastic holiday of my life. I never claimed to be anything but old-fashioned. What he gave me was my 'movie star' idea of a proposal. I couldn't have asked for more.

I slept like a baby that night. The next morning I phoned home. I went through everything in more detail. I told Daddy Kevin was sorry for not asking him first but he said there was no need to.

The only thing that saddened him, he said, was having to part with his 'little treasure.' Mammy was happy for me but sad for herself. She thought of marriage as a final break from home for me. She said Aunt Bernie told her to congratulate me for her.

I asked Maureen and May to be my bridesmaids. It was an offer they jumped at. I rang Mary and Veronica as well. They were as happy for me as everyone else.

I was back on ward duty a few days later. There was great excitement when I showed off the ring.

'You're a dark horse,' Veronica said, 'You never told us you were getting serious with this guy.'

'The quiet ones are always the worst,' Hilary said.

The inevitable cake was produced at my break. It had a statue of a bride and groom on the top of it. 'A Paris proposal,' Irene said, 'That's what I call class.'

Aunt Bernie rang me that evening. She said, 'I bet you'll make the best wife in the world.' I was going to say, 'no, you would,' but I didn't. I thought it might have made her sensitive.

Kevin's father even rang to congratulate me. 'Thanks for taking that fellow off my hands,' he said, 'I thought I'd never get rid of him.'

We set the date for the following June. The next few months were all about practicalities – buying the dress, getting the letters of freedom, working out where we were going to live. And, most importantly, choosing the ring in The Happy Ring House on O'Connell Street.

I spent ages going through the various options. I went for one with a solitaire diamond in the end. It wasn't too ostentatious but it looked really classy. When I heard the price I thought Kevin was going to have a seizure but he was fine about it.

I invited practically everyone I knew to the hen party and got wildly drunk at it. That means I have absolutely no recollection of anything I said or did at it, including insulting the registrar of the Mater, though both Irene and Veronica insisted I did. (I don't even remember inviting her). My emotions were in tatters by the end of the night. That was because I knew I wouldn't be seeing everyone for a long time.

I had to give up work because I was getting married. The law of the land demanded that. It was very unfair but what could you do?

I felt miserable giving in my notice.

'Try to focus on the positives,' Maureen said, 'you're marrying the man you love.' She was so right.

Kevin didn't bother with a stag party. Too many of his friends had bad experiences at them. One of them found himself tied to a tree in Phoenix Park the next morning with his trousers round his ankles. There was no way he was going to risk that kind of humiliation.

We were married in the Holy Rosary Church on St. Mary's Road. I wanted a small wedding but as soon as we started preparing a guest list that became impossible. If you invited A you had to invite B and then you realised B knew C so you had to ask them as well. After a while the list became more about not offending people than actually wanting them there.

I even invited people I hadn't seen for years, like Cáit and Bridget. Then there was Imelda Garvey. I could hardly leave her out after all the laughs we'd had at school. Things got a bit ridiculous when I started thinking about grand-uncles I hadn't seen since my convent days or second aunts once removed.

'If you don't stop,' Kevin told me, 'You'll have the whole county there.' We made a sort of a compromise by just the distant people to the 'afters' instead of the wedding proper but the list was still twice as long as we originally envisaged. I always used to laugh at people who made a big splash of their wedding. Now I realised it was a trap you got into. If you left somebody out it could cause all sorts of trouble.

Kevin asked his friend Reg Keegan to be the groom. He worked in the shoe department in Clery's – or rather pretended to work there. I'd only met him a few times. Any time I did he was looking at his watch as if he couldn't wait to get out of the place. He was one of those people who wore it upside down. I never knew why people did that. It meant you had to turn your hand upside down to see the time. What was the point of that?

I always thought there was something seedy about him. He was the type of man I'd have given short shrift to if I ran into him in the Ierne in my dancing days. He was more sophisticated than the general type of man you got in the Ierne but that only made him seem more dangerous. He got away with doing the little he did in Clery's because he was well in with Mark O'Loughlin, Kevin's boss.

He was a heavy drinker. As soon as it got to half five he was across the road in the Cosmo snooker club with all the local drunks. It was a dingy place located in a basement. I was only in it once. It was to collect Kevin for something we were going to. You had to go in a gate and down a tiny stairs.

The smell nearly knocked me out. Kevin and Reg were playing a game of doubles with two men who looked like hobos. A lot of journalists went in there too. Most of them were from the *Irish Independent* and the *Irish Press*. Both offices were nearby. Flann O'Brien used to say he never trusted an article by a journalist if it didn't have the smell of Guinness off it. I'm sure a lot of them smelt of snooker chalk as well. I knew Reg turned night into day in there. A lot of the people he met in the Cosmo lived upside down lives, working red eye shifts like me on night duty. If snooker was the sign of a mis-spent youth, in Reg's case it was the sign of a mis-spent adulthood as well.

He drank in the Palace Bar too. That was another haven for alcoholic journalists. They discussed the art of literature and then passed out on the floor, Brendan Behan style. More than once, I gathered, Reg staggered out of there that way too. Somehow he'd make his way up to his flat on Merrion Square to get himself ready for another day of drudgery in Clery's. When Kevin asked him how he liked his job he said, 'It means spending eight hours a day trying to wrap a suitable amount of leather around some old dears' bunions.'

He was a good bit younger than Kevin. I let him know I didn't like him early on despite the fact that he was one of his best friends. Kevin usually had good judgment with people but with Reg it was way off. We didn't have much to say to each other any time we met and we didn't talk much at the wedding either.

The ceremony was brief but dignified. There were a lot of tears and some laughter too. My main worry was that I'd trip on my wedding dress going up the aisle. I almost had a fixation about it.

'If I manage to get up to the altar without falling,' I told Kevin, 'any challenge I have to face in the next forty years or so will be minute by comparison.'

I think I put the fear of God into him. He was entitled to think: 'What kind of nutter am I marrying?'

I said a prayer I wouldn't trip and I didn't. Hurdle One was negotiated. The next worry was that the ceremony itself would go without a hitch – except the obvious one of *getting* hitched.

When Kevin said 'I do,' I felt a shiver of excitement down my spine. A new chapter of my life was about to begin. I was now officially Mrs Mulvey.

Reg really annoyed me as we were getting ready to exchange our vows. He made a big performance out of producing the ring, drawing oohs and aahs from the congregation. It should have been our moment but he turned it into his. That was Reg to a T.

Maureen and May were the two bridesmaids. They looked lovely in their matching dresses. They put floral wreaths in their hair as an extra touch. I expected them to come out lovely in the photographs.

May made no secret about the fact that she was looking for some excitement on the day. The fact that I was getting married was almost irrelevant to her. She'd just done the Leaving Cert and was blossoming into her life. I knew the nuns were glad to see the back of her. Every time I went home, Mammy told me she'd been down to the school over some new incident. She'd worn a path down to it apologising for her disruptiveness in class. Things had changed even in the few years since I'd been there. If it was me I'd probably have been expelled.

We stood like performing bears for photographs outside the church. The photographer was just starting out so I was a bit nervous about him. Irene had recommended him from the hospital. I didn't like to refuse her. He was a friend of her sister's. It was always dangerous to employ someone you knew because you couldn't really complain if they didn't do a good job.

We had the reception in the same hotel where Mammy and Daddy had theirs so many years before. It set us back a month's wages but we didn't mind. We knew we'd spend our life living on the memory of the day.

The meal was delicious. Reg read out a few telegrams, putting on a funny face at the ones with double meanings in them. Reg loved double meanings. I found them childish but Kevin seemed to enjoy them.

Daddy gave an emotional speech. He drew on so many memories of my youth I found my eyes filling up. I was sorry someone couldn't have recorded it. If they did I'd have worn the tape out playing it. .

Reg came over to me with a big grin on his face when all the formalities were finished.

'You must be very happy,' he said, 'Kevin has made an honest woman of you.'

There was no sincerity in his voice. He said it with a leer. I knew I couldn't trust him as far as I could throw him but I was determined not to let him spoil my day. To do that I had to avoid him as much as I could. Thankfully there were enough people there to help me do that. Some 'Best Man.' Worst Man would have been more like it.

I moved away from him to where all the guests were gathered. They were listening to music. We'd hired a country and western band for the day. They played all the old faithfuls. Everyone tapped their feet and sang along. May had just taken up the guitar. She played a few songs with them. Even though she was out of tune we gave her a big round of applause.

In no time at all everyone was on the floor, the solemnity of the church replaced by a party atmosphere. May danced the feet off herself. I never saw her looking better. She got a lot of attention from the younger male guests. There was no better woman to capitalise on that.

Out of the corner of my eye I saw Reg looking at her with devilment in his eyes. He was eyeing up all the other 'talent' but nobody seemed interested in him. He was drowned in after-shave. Unfortunately, it couldn't conceal the smell of the whiskey. I was going to warn May away from him but I knew that would only make her want him more.

Kevin's father wasn't in good health but he did his best to enter into the spirit of things. He gave me a few dances and proved to be quite adept on his feet. Daddy danced with me afterwards and then Grandad. Despite claiming to have two left feet he pirhouetted me around the floor like nobody's business.

'When am I going to get a look in?' Kevin asked me.

'You'll be sick looking at me all through the honeymoon,' I told him.

My main worry about the day was that Imelda would disgrace herself. I was relieved to see she'd become much more sensible with the years. She was running a garden centre in Douglas now. Her husband was very friendly. He reminded me of a cowboy.

I reminisced with Cáit and Bridget about the good old days and the bad old days. After some initial awkwardness we picked up the pieces from where we'd left off in Room 19. It was good to see that they hadn't changed since I saw them last.

Cáit's brother was much better. He still wasn't the full shilling but he was getting there. She didn't have to nurse him anymore but she'd got so used to Birr that she decided to stay there. She was married to a kinesiologist and living out the country. Bridget had left midwifery. She'd gone from hospital to hospital afterwards and was now a staff nurse in Maynooth.

'Whatever happened to Joanne Wylie?' I asked her.

'Hold on to your hat,' she said, 'She got the bullet.'

I couldn't believe it.

'Liar,' I said.

'It's as true as God. She got into trouble for bullying in the Rotunda. I heard through the grapevine that she was suspended after an inquiry. It was all done very quietly but that's definitely what happened.'

I couldn't resist a feeling of sadistic delight. Wow. So someone had finally caught up on her.

'How the mighty fall,' Bridget said, 'What goes around comes around.'

'If the top dogs didn't get her,' Cáit added, 'I would have.'

We huddled into a corner. Stories were traded about her if we were still back in that time. I tried to imagine myself sitting on the bed eating Kit-Kats in Room 19. We said we'd keep in touch but I wondered if we would. Once you separated the first time in life it seemed to be a pattern that continued. It was always much harder to get back to where you used to be.

Mammy's parents behaved as grimly as I'd expected throughout the day. The photographer kept snapping them, probably because they sat in the same place for most of the day. The rest of us were moving targets.

I'd only seen them a handful of times since I left Midleton. I felt they disapproved of Kevin for the same reason they'd disapproved of Daddy, seeing him as little more than a shop boy. They hardly exchanged two words with him the whole day long. They gave us a food mixer as a present – to go with the other 78 of them we'd been given by the other guests. 'Maybe we'll open a shop,' Kevin suggested. We had enough of them to stock the parish.

My 'country' Grandad and Granny gave us money. That's what most people getting married want even if they're too shy to say it. Mark O'Loughlin presented us with a token to carpet our house for free – when we got one. 'I don't know what century that's going to be,' Kevin told him.

Reg gave us a canteen of cutlery. I suspected he got a reduction on it from Clery's.

'He broke his heart,' I said to Kevin.

'He's very short of money at the moment,' he said. He was always covering for him. If it was true, I thought, it was probably from spending more time in snug of The Palace Bar than he should have – or the Cosmo.

'When are we going to use it?' I said, 'unless we're having the Queen to tea.'

'Maybe we will,' he said.

'You can entertain her if we do. She does nothing for me. '

'Maybe we can send her down to your Dad afterwards. He could tell her the history of the IRA. I'm sure she'd be enchanted hearing all the details.'

Everyone kept asking us where we were going to live. Kevin wanted us to move into his flat. I was more interested in going into my one. There was no way I could get to work on time from Kilmainham. I'd tried it once or twice but it was a nightmare in the traffic. In the end we decided to rent one in Phibsboro that was close to the Mater. We were going to be moving into it straight after our honeymoon.

Mammy looked worried throughout most of the day. She said to me at one stage, 'I hope this doesn't mean you'll disappear out of our lives.'

'I'm not that easy to get rid of,' I told her. I said I'd be down every chance I got. I made her promise to come up and see us in Dublin too. 'Try and keep me away,' she said.

Aunt Bernie looked like she was about to cry a few times during the day. Was she thinking of her own lost love, I wondered, her old 'mistake'? Dan Toibin and Una Conroy had a barrel-load of children by now. It was a subject we never talked about and never would. Even Mammy wouldn't break her silence on it.

She left the reception early with our Midleton Granny and Grandad. I felt she'd have stayed longer if they weren't there. They were probably afraid she'd start to enjoy herself too much. Or, God forbid, fall for a shop boy.

Granny and Grandad on Daddy's side were just warming up by this stage. They could have put the young crowd to shame with their energy.

Kevin took me round the floor on a slow waltz after we'd all eaten and drank our fill. Everyone applauded before joining us. As the music struck up he got all romantic, telling me he'd fallen in love with me the first time he saw me. That was why he couldn't ask me out onto the floor.

'When you took the initiative,' he said, 'I felt I'd died and gone to heaven.' He couldn't have picked a better day to say something like that to me. If my happiness threshold was 99% before, it was now 100%. Or maybe more.

As the reception was thinning out I thought Mammy looked very sad. I remembered her saying to Daddy after I went off nursing, 'Maureen will be next.' Maybe she felt May would follow me to the altar too, regardless of her age. It was the domino principle.

I gave her a hug before going upstairs to get into my trousseau. I told Kevin I was worried about her. She looked so distraught. She had a photo of the two of us in her hands. They were shaking as she held it. On the surface she looked to be more in control of her emotions than Daddy but I knew that was an act. Beneath the surface she was totally devastated.

'Don't worry about her,' he said, 'She'll be back to herself as soon as we're gone.'

'Kevin,' I said, 'You don't get it. She's in bits.'

'She seems all right to me.'

'That's because she doesn't know you well enough.'

'Okay. Sorry for being superficial.'

Everyone applauded when we came down the stairs with our bags but she wasn't there. Maureen told me she couldn't face it.

'Take care of her, won't you?' I said to her. She nodded.

'Daddy will too,' she said.

We honeymooned in a hostel in the Aran Islands. Amazingly enough, Kevin let me drive down to Doolin to get the boat. We didn't talk much on the journey. I couldn't help feeling down. I wondered if that was the way with many women on their wedding day when the noise of the reception was replaced by the quietness of being with one person – even if that person was the one you loved.

I felt a hole in my stomach all the way to Doolin. Kevin kept saying, 'Are you all right?' 'I'm just a bit shellshocked,' I told him.

Aran was a comedown from Paris but it had its charms. I loved the primitiveness of it. Everyone made a big fuss over us because we were newlyweds. It felt funny saying the word 'Wife.' Or even thinking of myself as one. It made me feel important - but also older.

The *bean an tí* preferred the term *bean chéile.* She had very little English. I tried to talk to her in my rusty Irish but I didn't get far. I was able to say *mí na meala* but that was about it. That meant 'honeymoon.'

The hostel doubled as a post office. Our room was just above it. Every morning when we woke up we'd hear the customers doing their transactions in Irish. My own grasp of the *blas* hadn't survived from the convent but I was able to throw a few words together at a push, even if it was only something along the lines of 'Tá sé mahogany gaspipe.'

There were a lot of foreigners staying there. We were entranced by them. They had such strange accents and clothing. The German ones got up at dawn and went off climbing. They were probably half way up a mountain when Kevin and myself would be turning over for the second time. We usen't see them again until late at night. They'd have red faces and look as healthy as trouts. They never went near the bars, preferring to eat sensible foods and drink non-alcoholic beer.

'If this is how they behave on their holidays,' Kevin said, 'I'd love to know what they're like in their work lives.'

He had a thing about Germans. He thought they lacked a sense of humour. He said Reg was on holiday in Cologne once and he went for a drink with a man who sold washing machines. The man asked Reg what kind of one he had. Reg said, 'We don't have washing machines in Ireland. There are robots who do all that kind of thing for us. You buy them in shops. They walk around the place doing your cleaning and washing for you. They even talk.' He said the man believed him. I found that hard to swallow. From the little I knew of Reg he seemed like a spoofer. Kevin couldn't imagine someone would make something like that up.

One day we went up Dun Aengus with the Germans. They were expert climbers. It was heaven looking down from the top with the wind going through you for a shortcut. Another day we spent at Kilmurvey beach. The sun was splitting the stones. Kevin couldn't wait to get into the water. He was like a two-year-old as he sprang into it. He went out so far he put the heart crossways in me. I preferred to do my duck paddle closer to the shore.

At night time we usually went to the local pub, a 'spit on the floor' place that was a hive of activity. There was often a *seisiún* where everyone joined in even if they hadn't a note - like the pair of us. Daddy would have been in his element. On our last night we went to a céilí.

We spent the whole night doing sets with the locals. Neither of us had a clue how to move but they didn't seem to mind. It was just good fun. We could hardly walk the next morning. The couple who ran the hostel were laughing at us. They thought we'd been up to high jinks in bed the night before.

I asked Kevin if we could take a detour to Midleton on the way home.

'Detour?' he said, 'It's totally in the opposite direction.' But he gave in after a bit of persuasion. I was letting him know early on who was going to be the boss in the marriage.

It meant a lot to Mammy and Daddy because there were no phones in the hostel. That meant we hadn't talked to them since the wedding.

They wanted to know everything about Aran and we filled them in with all the news. I'd sent them a postcard but it hadn't arrived yet. Kevin predicted we'd see them before it got there. 'We should have brought it with us and saved the price of the stamp,' he joked.

It was strange talking to everyone as a married woman. 'I suppose you'll be all sensible now,' Maureen said to me. May was still high from all the attention she got from the men at the reception. She asked me how things went on 'the big night.' I gave her a slap for being cheeky. Thank God Kevin was out of the room at the time. He'd have gone all the colours of the rainbow.

'Why did you have to marry a Dubliner?' she said. I almost developed laryngitis telling her that he only lived in Dublin, that he was originally from Athlone. When she persisted in the barbs I got fed up and just said, 'You're right, I married a Dub.'

We left Midleton in a happy state of mind. There were no tears this time. We'd had a fun-filled time and everyone was in powerful form. It was like a second honeymoon for us. Mammy and Daddy knew they had a great son-in-law in Kevin and I knew I had a great husband in him. It was all good.

'I wonder if the wedding photos will be there when we get to the flat,' I said to him on the way back. We'd asked the photographer to send them straight there. I kept my fingers crossed that he knew his stuff. He seemed to know what he was doing but you could never tell with photos.

Kevin insisted on carrying me over the threshold when we got there. It was a bit of a struggle for him because of the weight I'd put on over the past few weeks.

'I'll have to take my Weetabix from now on,' he said, 'or maybe go to the gym.'

'Don't worry,' I said, 'It's all my fault. I've been eating like a savage over the past few weeks. I dread the thought of weighing myself.'

We looked around the room. It looked very empty even though we'd moved our furniture into it. There wasn't a thing in the fridge or in any of the kitchen cabinets.

'It will be lean rations for a while,' Kevin said.

'Don't worry,' I said, 'We'll manage.' Daddy used to say, 'Two can live as cheaply as one.'

It was only after we sat down that we noticed an envelope on the floor inside the door. I saw the photographer's name on the top of it.

'Oops,' I said to Kevin, 'The dreaded foties.'

'We don't have to look at them now,' he said, 'Maybe a stiff whiskey would help.'

'No. We have to face the music.'

I was always bored looking at other people's wedding pictures but that was only because of my natural selfishness. I gobbled up these ones. For the next hour or so we laughed ourselves sick at the expressions people put on, the way they contorted their features to try and look their best and ended up just looking stupid.

Mammy and Daddy came out really well. So did Maureen and May, as I expected. The contrast between Mammy and Daddy's parents said it all. One couple had faces as long as wet weeks while the other one beamed with delight.

Reg seemed to be at the front of most of the shots. He had the knack of positioning himself just where it mattered.

'At least he didn't break the camera,' I said to Kevin.

'You can never resist a dig at him, can you?' he scolded.

'Sorry. I don't know why he gets on my goat so much.'

'How do you think you came out yourself?'

187

Any time I saw myself in a photo all I could think of was the old Phyllis Diller joke: 'My photographs don't do me justice. They look just like me.'

'Not too bad I suppose.'

'Don't say things like that. You look beautiful.'

'I bet you say that to all the girls. What about you?'

'I suppose I could pass in a crowd.'

'You could do much more than that,' I told him.

'This is turning into a Mutual Congratulation Society,' he said, 'We better stop before our heads burst open with all the swelling.'

When we were finished analysing ourselves we decided to look around the flat and see if there was any way we could put our stamp on it without Hanratty giving out to us for changing it too much.

You couldn't swing a cat in it but we knew it would have to do for now. It was on the top floor of the building. It had a sloped ceiling that we kept bumping our heads off. There was a big main room in it as well as two bedrooms. It had a little kitchen off the main room and a toilet off the bigger bedroom. It wasn't quite an en-suite but it was as close to one as you'd get in those days. The walls were so thin if you tapped on them you could hear an echo.

The rent was cheap. The main reason we took it was to save for a deposit on a house. We already had some money put aside from the wedding gift Grandad and Granny gave us.

The landlady, Mrs Hanratty, was a right tarter. I heard she owned houses all over Dublin. She was so tight she was rumoured to still have her First Communion money. She grudged us anything we asked for from the moment we moved in, including painting the flat. We thought this would have been to her advantage.

'Let's do it anyway,' Kevin said, 'She can't throw us out for that.'

'From what I can see,' I replied, 'She'd throw us out for looking sideways at her.'

The hoover she gave us broke down the first time we used it. When Kevin told her about it she argued tooth and nail that there was nothing wrong with it. At the heel of the hunt we had to pay for a new one ourselves.

She lived on the floor under us. She kept so many tabs on us she might have been in the same room. If we were any way noisy there

188

was murder. She'd either knock at the door or pound on the floor with a broom. With the thin walls we had to be extra careful. Each night we went to sleep listening to the drone of trucks outside – or rather stayed awake listening to them.

We had a 'flat-warming party' as soon as we were settled in. We decided to invite everyone we could think of. Maureen and May even came up for it. Bridget wasn't able to make it. I got no answer from Cáit when I rang her. When I asked Bridget how she was she just said, 'Same old same old.' The two of them disappointed me. I tried to accept the fact that with each phase of your life your friends changed. It was like musical chairs.

I asked May if she'd bring her guitar up with her.

'On the train?' she rasped, 'You must be joking.'

You could take 'flat-warming' literally because there was little or no heat in the building. The only way to keep warm was by having lots of people around you. All Hanratty gave us was a little heater that sparked when you plugged it in.

'It wouldn't be a good idea to get electrocuted in your first year of marriage,' Kevin observed with his typical dry wit.

On the cold nights it was like living in an igloo. We decided to light candles instead of turning on the lights. They created a bit of heat but the main reason was for the atmosphere.

Ken invited Reg, which didn't exactly thrill me. I asked a good few people from work – Hilary and Mary for starters and then Veronica and Deirdre. Irene came as well. She was down from Donegal for a break. I'd told her she was welcome to bring her husband if she wanted.

'I'm afraid he lost his job in the bank,' she said as soon as she came in the door, 'We might be coming back here yet.'

I was shocked to hear that.

'Wasn't his job the whole reason you upped sticks?' I said.

'It was, but it didn't work out. We were misinformed about the situation.'

'How come?'

'Apparently there were cutbacks in the bank when we got there. It was a case of, "Last in, first out."'

'That's terrible. What's he doing now?'

'Minding Junior,' she said. I'd heard she'd had a baby all right.

'I hope you're listening, Kevin,' I called across the room, but he wasn't. He was too busy talking to Reg.

I hadn't seen Reg since the wedding. He burst in the door with his usual bluster.

'How is married life treating you?' he said, 'Have you Kevin house-trained yet?'

'Of course,' I said, 'He doesn't leave the toilet seat up anymore.'

'You're lucky he doesn't pee on it,' he said.

He waved over at him.

'Where's the beer, Kevin me boy?' he said, 'We're dying of thirst here.'

I found that hard to believe. He looked like he had a rake of pints inside him.

He had a woman on his arm, a foreign one. She was very glamorous but in a manufactured kind of way. I didn't really like her. She had so much make-up on I thought she must have got up at 5 a.m. to apply it. Or maybe that was just me being jealous of her good looks. She was wearing a backless dress and practically bursting out of it. Kevin said she looked like she was poured into it and they forgot to say 'When.'

I asked him how he thought someone like Reg, who wasn't exactly Elvis Presley in the looks department, managed to get a woman like her.

'Confidence,' he said, 'Confidence always attracts women.'

'Not this woman,' I assured him.

'I'd say Reg has had more dates than the rest of us have had hot dinners.'

'Please don't use crude expressions like that. I don't want to be thinking of that fellow the next time I'm having a hot meal.'

'Sorry. I'm just repeating what people say to me. Apparently all he had to do is flick his fingers and women flock to him.'

'Well he better not flick them in this direction. If he does he'll get his answer.'

I felt he had a poor opinion of women from comments he made to me at the wedding. Even the way he read the double-meaning telegrams seemed to transmit that message to me. Sometimes you can see through a person from the moment you meet them. He reminded of some of the boys I knew in Midleton growing up, the types that would be telling dirty jokes to one another behind the bicycle shed in school.

There was a great atmosphere at the party despite the fact that we were all clustered so closely together - or maybe even because of that. It made everyone more intimate. We were like wall-to-wall carpeting. People were literally falling over each other.

Reg spent a lot of his time in the arms of his girlfriend. That annoyed me about him too. I didn't care what people did behind closed doors but I felt he was showing off, especially when there were no other couples at the party. It was as if he was saying, 'Look what I can get.' Maybe he was entitled to considering he had a face only a mother could love.

When the night got on the road, he stood up in the middle of the floor and said, 'I want to tell yis all a story so listen up.'

We were all chatting but we stopped suddenly, not knowing what was coming. I suspected it was going to involve some more showing off. He was well aware he was the only man at the party apart from Kevin. The presence of a mostly-female audience was too big a temptation for the showman in him to resist.

The story concerned a customer in Clery's he encountered one day. Apparently he wasn't the sharpest knife in the drawer. He'd come in to buy a pair of shoes and Reg was showing him a selection of them. He put his eye on a pair but didn't notice there was a label in one of them. It made it much tighter than the other one so when he walked up and down the floor it made him look like he had a limp. Reg mimicked him, exaggerating his walk so much he made him look almost disabled. I wasn't very amused and I don't think the other nurses were either but May laughed her head off. She was practically on the floor. The more she laughed, the more Reg exaggerated the walk.

I felt he was going to go on forever so I went into the kitchen. Kevin followed me in.

'What's wrong?' he said, 'Are you not enjoying Reg's story?

'It was all right for a few minutes,' I said, 'but he's really milking it.'

191

He put on a stern face.

'You should lighten up,' he said, 'It's a harmless anecdote.'

'Sorry for being such a bore,' I said.

It seemed that every time I brought up Reg's name it created a division between us.

'I think I'll have a drink,' he said then.

I didn't like the sound of that but I didn't want to say anything. The last thing I wanted was to put a damper on the party – or let anyone see we were arguing.

'Why not?' I said.

He opened a bottle and took a sip from it, savouring it as it went down his throat.

'That hits the spot,' he said.

'Good,' I said, trying to smile.

He went out to the main room. I looked at myself in the mirror, wondering how I could hide my worried face. I followed him out a few minutes later. Everyone seemed very relaxed. Some people were sitting on the carpet, the first sign a party is, as they say, 'moving.'

'Anyone fancy some music?' Kevin said as he rummaged through a set of records on a rack.

'Yes!' May gushed.

The night wasn't going the way I planned. I began worrying about Mrs Hanratty. I knew she'd hear it.

He put on 'I Can't Get No Satisfaction' by the Rolling Stones, turning up the volume as far as it would go. A few minutes later the inevitable pounding started.

'Kevin,' I said, but he ignored me.

I heard her tramping up the stairs. She rapped on the door. When I opened it she waved her finger at me. The words flooded out of her.

'There are people who have to sleep in this house,' she said, 'Do you know what time it is?'

'We didn't think you'd mind,' I said, 'It's a weekend.'

She looked over my shoulder. I was conscious of her looking at everyone sitting on the carpet. Most of them had drinks in their hands. I knew she wouldn't have been too impressed with Reg either. He was wrapped around his girlfriend.

192

'What's with the candles?' she said, 'Is there something wrong with the power?'

'No, I said, 'They're for the atmosphere.'

'Atmosphere,' she snorted. 'Atmosphere won't count for much if the place goes up in smoke.'

'We'll blow them all out before going to bed.'

'That might be a good idea,' she said.

She looked around at everyone. Hilary and Veronica were smoking.

'I've always had respectable tenants here,' she said. 'If anyone drops ash or alcohol on the carpet it'll be up to you to replace it.'

I said that wouldn't be a problem. She took another look over my shoulder. Then she stomped off.

Kevin gave me a clap on the back when I closed the door.

'Well handled,' he said. I could see he was getting squiffy. He started slurring his words.

'If she comes back again I'll take over,' he said, 'She'll be lucky if I don't turf her out the window.'

Reg was loving this. He disentangled himself from his girlfriend and came over.

'Fair play to you, Kev,' he said, 'You tell the old battleaxe what to do with herself.'

I was disgusted.

'It's all right for you,' I said, 'You don't have to live here. If you did you'd have to face the music.'

'That's a good one,' Kevin said, 'Face the music. Get it? Music?'

He went over to the stereo and turned it up.

'All I want is loving you and music, music, music,' he sang, mouthing Ruby Murray's lyrics as he did a little dance around the floor.

'Did you know that song was banned for suggestiveness?' he said to me.

'It's banned again tonight,' I said, 'Sit down before she hears you.'

I ran over to the stereo.

'Where are you going?' he said.

I turned it down.

'What did you do that for?' he said, frowning at me.

'Are you mad?' I said, 'She'll have us out the door if she hears any more noise.'

He was tottering on his feet. He had a glass of wine in his hand that was full to the brim. It was dripping onto the carpet.

'And be careful how you handle that glass of wine,' I added, 'I don't feel like paying for a new carpet on our budget.'

He tilted the glass further sideways, threatening to pour more wine on the carpet. My eyes widened in disbelief. I snatched the glass from him.

'What's up with you?' I said, 'You're going to land us in all sorts of trouble.'

'Sensible Sue,' he said.

Reg went into hysterics at that. May was engrossed watching him. He was never like this any other time she'd seen him.

'I'm not as think as you drunk I am,' he said.

Reg's eyes grew wider in fascination. I could imagine him going into Clery's the following Monday with a full-blown account of The Secret Life of Kevin Mulvey.

I led him into the kitchen.

'I don't know what's in that wine,' I said, 'but this has to stop. Now.'

He looked up at me with a half-smile on his face. His eyes seemed to be unable to focus.

I got a wet facecloth and put it over his face.

'Ow,' he said, 'That's cold.'

'Don't let yourself down any more,' I said, 'I beg you. Reg is taking it all in. Just imagine what would happen if he goes back to Clery's with it.'

'Clery's?' he said, 'Where's that? Is it a shop or something?'

May appeared at the door. She had a glass of wine in her hand. Behind her Mick Jagger blared away about not being able to get any satisfaction.

'Where did you get that?' I said, 'You're not supposed to be drinking.'

'Don't get your knickers in a knot. It's a party, isn't it?'

194

'I'm having a private conversation, May. Now please go out to the other room and turn down the radio before Mrs Hanratty comes back.'

Why didn't you tell the old bag to put cotton wool in her ears if the music was too loud for her?'

I couldn't believe she was siding with Reg. My own sister.

'The old bag, as you call her, happens to hold our future in her hands. Do you fancy sleeping on the street?'

'It might be nice actually,' she said, 'I mean for a novelty.'

Kevin opened his eyes.

'Why not,' he said, smiling at her.

She took a slug of the wine.

'Give me that this second,' I said.

'No,' she said, 'I'm at a party and I'm going to enjoy myself.'

She went out to the main room. I followed her.

'Are you going to give me the glass,' I said, 'or do I have to take it from you?'

She wouldn't part with it so we started wrestling. More wine fell on the carpet. As I looked at it I thought: That's it. I'd reached breaking point.

I looked around me at everyone. Hilary and Irene had shock on their faces. Maureen just stared at the floor. Reg had an expression of what I could only call sadistic delight. You could almost taste the tension.

I turned all the lights on and blew out the candles. Then I plugged out the stereo. I crossed my arms. Everyone was as still as statues. I stood looking at them as if it was their fault instead of Kevin's. It was as if I was using attack as a means of defence.

'The party is over,' I said, 'It's time for you all to go home.'

It was a few seconds before anyone moved. It probably took that time for it to register with them that I was serious. Then they all started to reach for their coats. I felt terrible but I couldn't see any other option. If I didn't do what I did I knew things were only going to get worse.

Veronica and Mary understood but I thought Hilary and Irene were disappointed in me. I was surprised because I didn't think they were like that.

The next few minutes seemed like as many hours. I wanted to apologise but I couldn't. I was embarrassed and ashamed and angry.

Kevin appeared at the door of the kitchen.

'What's going on?' he said, 'Who turned Mick Jagger off?'

Deirdre came over to me.

'Don't worry,' she said, 'Everything will blow over. You're doing the right thing.'

I needed to hear that. I told her I'd see her soon.

Everyone shuffled out. Veronica gave me a nervous wave. Hilary and Irene looked disappointed. I wasn't sure if it was for me or themselves.

Reg was the last to go.

'Well done Mrs Mulvey,' he said sarcastically, 'Handled like a true professional.'

I didn't bother saying anything to him. I just closed the door behind him. I listened to the footsteps shuffling down the stairs and out the door. I didn't move until it shut. Afterwards there was the vague muffle of voices on the street.

There was a new type of silence now, one of calmness rather than tension. I went in to Kevin. He'd gone back into the kitchen. He was half asleep so I left him there.

'I feel so sorry for you,' Maureen said, 'after all your preparation.'

I washed some glasses to try and keep my mind off what had happened. Maureen went down on all fours pouring salt on the carpet to try and get the stains out of it.

'Leave that till tomorrow,' I told her, 'Let's all go to bed now. If I stay up I'll start bawling.'

I went into the bedroom. Suddenly I felt peaceful.

I undressed. Maureen and May went into the spare room. I lay on the bed with my head pounding. Kevin came in after a while. He seemed to have sobered up a bit. As he was taking off his trousers he fell. I didn't help him up. He got into bed. He tried to put his arms around me but I turned my back on him.

I couldn't believe what just happened. I tried to tell myself it wasn't important but it was. It was important in the way all the small events of our lives are important because they're not small when they're happening, they're everything.

I'd made a mistake. We all made mistakes. I thought the big challenge of my life was going to be my career but now I realised that was the easy part. You had control over that but not your private life. That was where everything went wrong.

I thought I was going to be awake all night but eventually I drifted off to sleep. I had bad dreams. They seemed more real than anything that happened at the party.

It was morning when I woke up. Kevin was snoring beside me. His clothes were all over the floor. I dragged myself out of bed and tidied them.

I went out to the living-room. The carpet still looked stained. I put some water in the kettle. When it boiled I threw it over it.

May was asleep in the spare room but Maureen was up. She came to the door.

'I think cold water is better for something like that,' she said.

'Just let me at it,' I said.

She went back to her room. I heard her dressing herself. She came back out again.

'Can I help you?' she asked me. I shook my head.

Kevin appeared after a while. He was in his pyjamas.

'Would anyone like a cup of tea?' he said. I didn't answer him.

'Yes please,' Maureen said.

'Is it okay if I take the kettle?' he asked me. I grunted a yes. He brought it into the kitchen.

When it boiled he made tea. He put some toast in the toaster. I heard it popping up. Maureen was annoying me watching me scrubbing without getting anywhere. I told her to go in to Kevin.

When I thought the carpet looked a bit better I joined them in the kitchen. They were both just sitting there.

'Sorry for spoiling the party,' Kevin said.

'Don't worry about it.'

'Now you know why I gave that stuff up,' he said, 'I can't handle it.'

Maureen looked embarrassed.

'I'm going to freshen up,' she said.

She went out.

'I blame myself for letting you drink,' I said.

197

'To be honest with you I've felt the craving for a while,' he said, 'It just took this to trigger it.'

'Why didn't you tell me?'

'I didn't want to. The first time I felt it was at the wedding but I didn't want to put a damper on things by saying anything. It's only on big occasions I feel it. I thought I was strong enough to resist it. I know now I'm not. Anyway, that's it for me.'

Maureen came back in. This time she had May with her. She seemed to think Kevin was still going to be merry. She clapped him on the back but he didn't react. She looked disappointed to see him back to himself.

'Good morning, May,' he said to her, 'What would you like for breakfast?'

'Champagne' she said.

I told her to act her age. I pointed to a packet of cornflakes on the worktop. She pouted as she walked over to it.

Maureen nibbled at her toast.

'What's the carpet like?' she asked me.

'Not too bad. We'll live to fight another day with Hanratty.'

I'd scrubbed it so much the colour was almost gone from it.

'I moved the sofa around to cover it but she's so eagle-eyed she'll probably cop on to that the next time she calls.'

'If she does, give her her answer. I don't think it was in great condition anyway.'

'It wasn't, but she's so cute she'll avoid that topic and concentrate on the wine.'

May looked bored.

'Maybe we should make for the train,' she said.

I was glad she brought the subject up. I wanted to be alone with Kevin.

'I'll drive you,' I said.

They got their things from the spare room. May had a face on her. Maureen said to me, 'Don't dwell on last night. Hopefully there'll be another party soon.'

'Not for a while,' I said.

They said goodbye to Kevin. We went out to the car. The last thing I felt like doing was bringing them into town but I knew it wouldn't have been fair to make them get the bus.

We sat in. On the way to town I tried to talk about other things besides the party to lighten the atmosphere. May complained about school. Maureen talked about how fed up she was in the travel agency.

I dropped them off at Amiens Street. As they were getting out of the car I said, 'Not a word to Mammy or Daddy about last night, right?'

'Scout's honour,' Maureen promised.

'And you too May,' I said, giving her a stern stare. She nodded grudgingly.

On the way back to the flat I dropped into the Mater. I wanted to have a word with Veronica about everything. It took me a long time to find her. When did, to my relief, she put her arms around me.

'Sorry about what happened,' I said.

'Don't be,' she said, 'It wasn't your fault.'

I tried to play it down by saying Kevin wasn't used to drink, that it went straight to his head because of that. In a way it was true. If there were other rumours about him I couldn't do anything about them. I knew I'd be self-conscious the next time I met Hilary and the other girls for coffee.

Kevin was back to himself again when I got back to the flat. He apologised to me again. I apologised to him too for being so hard on him.

Over the next hour he told me all about his drinking. He said he'd started as a young boy when someone from his class introduced him to it and took an immediate grip on him. I never heard him talk so much at a go. I knew it was doing him good. Now that his problem was out in the open it freed him from it to some extent.

'How bad were you with it at your worst?' I asked him.

'As bad as anyone can be. I was like the devil incarnate some nights. I was even on poteen for a while.' I remembered Daddy having a drink of that one night when I was young. He dropped straight onto the floor after it – and he was a much bigger man than Kevin.

199

'Drink made me into a different person,' he said. 'I was shy growing up. It gave me Dutch courage, especially where women were concerned.'

I told him most of the men I danced with in the Ierne seemed to have come straight from the pub.

'I could well have been one of them. It was lucky I didn't meet you on one of those nights or I wouldn't have stood a chance with you.'

'I wouldn't say that. You can always see the man behind the drink.'

'Maybe, but I remember going down a row of girls one night asking them to dance and getting ten straight rejections in a row.'

'You should be in the Guinness Book of Records.'

'I don't blame them. I was hardly able to stand.'

'That's so hard for me to square with the person I'm married to.'

'I was in with a bad crowd. I wasn't even the worst of them. One of our group went to his doctor to try and cut down on his drinking. The doctor said he'd be all right if he could limit himself to eleven units. The man said, "It'll be a struggle, doc, but I'll try it." The doctor was talking about eleven units a week but he thought he meant eleven a night. It could only have happened in Ireland.'

It was a funny story but the last thing I felt like doing was laughing.

'Anyway you're sorted now,' I said, 'That's the main thing.'

He knocked on the wood of the table.

'One day at a time, sweet Jesus.'

'Do you miss it?'

'Not if I can stay out of pubs. The worst time for me used to be from nine till eleven at night. Once I got to bedtime I was all right.'

'So you weren't one of those people who woke up craving a drink.'

'No. I usually just woke up hating myself and saying "Never again." But that night there'd be another "again." As the man said, "Every morning I was a pioneer and every night an alcoholic." It wasn't so much the drink as trying to fill in those hours.'

'From now on you can fill them in with your wife.'

'Good idea. Why didn't I think of that?'

'The first thing we have to do is not to have any more parties.'

'Agreed.'

'Apart from everything else, Hanratty would have us out on our ear for bad behaviour in a heartbeat. She knows she can click her fingers and get new tenants in two minutes.'

We'd signed a lease with her but she was the kind of woman who'd find some small print in it to get rid of us if she wanted.

Kevin didn't drink again after the party but there were times I felt he was tempted to. He had a lot of stress at the job. Maybe that made the craving worse.

I remember one night when it got to him really badly. As soon as he walked in the door I felt he was ready to scream. I asked him if he'd like to talk about it but he wasn't up to that.

He went off to the pub and I followed him. I looked in the window and saw him sitting there. He wasn't drinking. He was looking into space. Maybe he was remembering the person he used to be. I went in after a few minutes. For a second he was so lost in his thoughts he hardly knew who I was. I wanted to sit with him but he asked me to leave him alone.

I knew by the way he spoke how much he was suffering. The worst thing for me was the feeling that I could do nothing for him.

I walked round the block a few times. Each time I got back to the pub I looked in the window to see if he'd moved but he hadn't. He was just sitting there like a statue.

There was a phone box across the road. On a whim I decided to phone home. Mammy immediately sussed there was something wrong because of the tone of my voice.

'Is it Kevin?' she said. There was a time she would have said, 'Is it the job?' but there was no job to talk of now.

'I'm afraid so,' I said.

'Is he drinking?'

I knew then that May must have told her about the party. One thing about May was that she never surprised you about things like that. She could always be trusted to tell a secret.

'No, but I think he'd like to be.'

She went quiet for a while. Then she said, 'Don't fret yourself. It'll pass. I went through a bit of that with your Daddy.'

201

After I put down the phone I went into the pub. He was still sitting there like a statue but this time he looked up at me.

'Will we go home?' I asked him. I thought he looked ready now.

'Okay,' he said.

We walked back to the flat in silence. We went to bed almost as soon as we got in. I was expecting him to talk about how he was feeling but he said nothing. The next day everything was back to normal, or as normal as could be expected under the circumstances.

I had more time to keep an eye on him in the following weeks because of not working. That was one good thing about having to leave the job. I didn't want to become a nag but I needed to be sure he wouldn't break out again.

I tried to give him as many treats as I could in the meals I prepared. I wanted him to look forward to coming home and not be tempted towards the pubs again. I knew Reg went drinking most nights. I asked Kevin to promise me he wouldn't join him and he didn't. I said I had no problem with him seeing him if I was with them.

One day shortly after that I was in town doing some shopping when who should I see striding towards me but the bold Reg. He was with one of his pseudo-intellectual friends from an Arts club he went to.

'How is my favourite nurse?' he said, doing a little curtsey before me, 'Did Kev give you the day off?'

I told him I was in a hurry but he kept prattling on. He insisted on introducing me to his friend.

'This is Eoghan,' he said.

Eoghan looked like he was just after getting out of bed. His hair was like a cross between that of Ken Dodd and Albert Einstein. He was dressed in a white polo neck jumper and a black leather jacket. He had drainpipe trousers on him.

'Hello,' I said. He gave me a fishy handshake.

'Eoghan dropped out of Trinity,' he said.

Eoghan nodded vaguely. He looked like he wanted to be somewhere else. Reg explained that he'd got tired of studying Restoration poetry. He decided he'd prefer to live on lentils up the Dublin mountains.

'I hope it works out for you,' I said, 'but I really have to go.'

'Don't rush off when we're just getting acquainted,' Reg said, 'Wouldn't it be nice if the four of us could go out for dinner some night – me, you, Kev and Eoghan.'

'Yes,' I said, 'It would be lovely.' I was hoping my face registered the fact that I'd have preferred to dine with Dracula.

'How have you been since the party?' he said then.

'All right,' I said, 'I'm afraid it was a bit of a disaster.'

'Don't say that. It ended suddenly but I had the time of my life. It was good to see Kevin having some fun.'

'Yes,' I said, 'He enjoyed himself immensely.'

I gave him a fake grin.

'So how have *you* been since the party?' I said. I was determined not to let him know he was getting to me.

'Me? Oh, strictly non-event. I'm always in a vacuum for a while after a night out with Kevin. I mosey from day to day hoping we can hang out again pronto.'

I was wondering if he was using the hippie slang because he thought I was a square.

'How is your girlfriend?' I asked him.

'Which one?' he said.

I was rarely amused at his attempts to be funny.

'The foreign one.'

'Oh, Eloise. I'm giving her some time off at the moment.'

I couldn't imagine a worse fate in life than to be Eloise. She wouldn't have wanted to be waiting for him to put a ring around her finger. I felt she was lucky to have 'time off.'

I wished Eoghan the best of luck with the lentils as the pair of them 'moseyed' off. I didn't know which of them looked incongruous. Eoghan was definitely on another planet, whatever about Reg.

He invited himself round to the flat a few days later. He said he wanted us to go to a film with him. He had a big thing about European ones. He fancied himself as being something of an authority on them. He   loved dropping names of famous film directors into his conversations. These were usually people with unpronounceable names. I suspected he did that to make me feel small. I knew nothing about foreign films and he was well aware of that. Kevin used to humour him even though he didn't know too much about them either.

How could a man who worked in Clery's be such a super-intellectual?

'One of these days I'm going to break free from my shackles,' he told us, 'The world will be hearing from Reg Keegan yet.' He said he was writing a novel as well, a 'surreal' one. I didn't dare ask what that meant.

The film was showing in one of those backstreet cinemas he thought were arty. It was a French one. I don't remember what it was called and I don't want to. It took an eternity to get to the point and when it got to it you weren't even sure what it was. I remembered Kevin's comment about the French contemplating the meaning of life in coffee houses.

We went more out of politeness than anything else. Reg said everyone he knew was raving about it. That should have been enough for me. If Reg's friends were anything like him, I imagined myself staying a mile away from them – though I had a sneaking affection for Eoghan.

It was only on for about five minutes before I thought: What am I doing here? I'd prefer to be at the dentist. You could hardly make out the faces of the cast. They were all blurred. Maybe the director was trying to win some kind of art award. The camera even seemed crooked. It was as if he was operating it from a wobbly supermarket trolley or something.

I couldn't make head nor tail of the story. This guy was in love with two women, a blonde and a brunette, and couldn't make up his mind between them. As far as I was concerned he was welcome to both of them. And they were welcome to him.

There was a lot of sex in it. That didn't surprise me – it was French after all. I knew they were big into that stuff over there. The problem was, it didn't have anything to do with the story. What did? It was like double Dutch to me – or double French. There were all these bodies jumping around the place as if they were in a gym – except they were naked. I was only glad Mammy or Daddy weren't there. I wouldn't have known where to look.

I put my hand over Kevin's eyes at one stage. I didn't want him getting any ideas. Reg's ones were glued to the screen. Maybe that's why he wanted to go to it – under the pretence of being an intellectual.

After about three hours the man decided he was going to stay with the blonde. Halleluah, I thought, he's reached a decision at last. But then, just as you thought everything was sorted out, he went back to the brunette. At that stage I felt like walking out of the cinema. Actually I'd felt like that from the start. I would have except we'd paid a fortune for the tickets. Why is it that the most useless things in life nearly always cost the most money?

The worst thing of all was that it wasn't dubbed. You had to read all the dialogue from the bottom of the screen to know what they were talking about. It was written in the tiniest writing you could imagine so you had to squint your eyes up to make it out – if you cared.

It went on so long I was worried we were all going to miss the last bus home. Then out of nowhere the word 'Fin' came up on the screen. That meant 'The End.' I was no genius at French but I knew that much from our trip there. We were going to be released at last.

When we got out onto the street Reg looked like he was getting ready for a big speech.

'What performances,' he said. Kevin nodded his head. I felt he was afraid of disagreeing with Reg.

'Do either of you have the foggiest what that was all about?' I said.

'I can't believe you're saying that,' Reg scoffed. He said it was about something called *angst.* I never heard that word before. It sounded to me like a kind of stomach ache. .

'Why does *angst* mean?' I said.

'It means pain.'

'Then why didn't you say that?'

He threw his eyes to heaven.

'Because it's a particular *kind* of pain.'

'What kind?'

'Abstract.'

'How can you have abstract pain?'

He looked despairingly at me.

'Maybe in the Mater you can't. People suffer at all kinds of levels.'

'You're not making much sense, Reg,' I said to him. At that he started to laugh.

'Sorry for spoiling your night,' he said, 'I suppose you'd have preferred to be at home watching *Corrie*.' (He knew I liked *Coronation Street*). I felt like hitting him. If Kevin wasn't with me I probably would have.

'I wish he'd stayed with the blonde,' I said, 'She was nicer.'

'She was a dummy,' Reg said. I felt if I said 'White' he'd have said 'Black.' He was always trying to put me down, to make me look bad in front of Kevin.

'As far as I could see,' I said, 'both of them were dummies. But we were the biggest dummies of all to give up our night watching them.'

The two of them nattered on about 'angst' all the way home on the bus. Kevin kept saying to Reg, 'You're on the ball there, man, you're on the ball there.' I didn't think Reg knew what the 'ball' was - and I was pretty certain Kevin didn't.

When we got to the flat I could see Reg was mad to come in for a nightcap – presumably to talk about some more 'angst.' I was in no form for that after what I'd been through. I said I had a splitting headache and was going straight to bed. It wasn't too far from the truth.

Reg looked distressed.

'What about you, Kev?' he said. I stood on Kevin's toe to stop him saying yes.

'I think I'll turn in early as well, Reg,' he said, getting the message, 'I have a bit of a headache as well.' I could have kissed him for that. Reg wasn't a happy bunny going off.

When we got inside I thanked Kevin for sparing me from 'Mouth Almighty', as I called him.

'Be honest,' I said, 'You were bored out of your tree at it too, weren't you?'

'There was some good camerawork,' he said hesitantly.

'Camerawork?' I said, 'Is that all you can come up with? Do you realise I sacrificed three hours of my ironing for some eejit's camerawork?' I knew that made me seem like the most boring person in the world but I didn't care. If I never saw another French film in my life it would be too soon.

## Maureen Follows Suit

Neil Armstrong landed on the moon in 1969. I was transfixed watching it with Kevin. It was almost impossible to believe a man was up there. The idea of someone being all those millions of miles away was incomprehensible to me. So was the fact that we were travelling around the sun at such speed and that the moon was travelling around us and that we didn't bump into each other - or even know we were moving.

I read somewhere that Armstrong had to make his will before he went on the mission. What a trauma that must have been for his wife and children. How must he have been feeling as he zoomed into space? I got claustrophobia if I was longer than a minute in an enclosed space. How did people have the strength to be cooped up in space capsules for so long? He must have had nerves of steel. He looked so relaxed as he came down the little ladder.

'The next generation will be taking day trips to the moon,' Kevin said, 'just like we do to Butlin's.' I could hardly imagine that happening. I certainly wouldn't be going on one of them. I had my work cut out making it into work without a catastrophe.

I rang Daddy the next morning.

'Did you watch the moon landing?' I said.

'I saw a bit of it but it didn't mean much to me. At the end of the day it was only a bunch of rocks.'

'Don't be so cynical, Daddy.'

'I'm not being cynical. Can you imagine the kind of money that cost? We should sort out the problems on our own planet before going to other ones. I can see rocks across the road from McSweeney Terrace any day of the week if I want.'

I knew what was eating him. The Troubles in the North had just erupted. He was fuming about all the injustices Catholics suffered up there.

Bernadette Devlin was his idol. He said she was just the person to sort out the Brits. He hoped she'd be able to stand up to Reginald Maudling. He was the Home Secretary. Daddy had no time for him. Maudling said he hated Belfast. The first time he went there he said,

'For God's sake someone bring me a large scotch. What a bloody awful country.' He was hardly the kind of man was that to try and create harmony between Belfast and London.

Charlie Haughey lost his cabinet post when he was arrested for gun running in 1970. He was another idol of Daddy's. He thought the spirit of Terence McSwiney was alive and well in him. Mammy couldn't agree. She thought he was just a scoundrel. She was glad Jack Lynch got rid of him. He was the Taoiseach then. Jack Lynch was too much of a smoothie for Daddy. He didn't think he understood anything about The Troubles. Most Cork people were proud to have one of their own as Taoiseach but for Daddy it was all about the armed struggle.

Every other night I saw people on the News with blood streaming all over their faces. It was hard to believe this was happening in our own country. Belfast was so close to us and yet so far away too. In some ways it was like another country.

I was down in Midleton on Bloody Sunday when thirteen Catholics were shot in cold blood by British soldiers. They'd been protesting peacefully. Daddy was almost catatonic about it. He called it murder, pure and simple. Maudling was trying to blame the Catholics for it. He said the soldiers only fired in self-defence. Bernadette Devlin was there. She knew that was a downright lie. She scratched Maudling's face in a rage one day in the House of Commons. Daddy loved her for that. He said the British army was like a recruitment centre for the IRA, that they'd wakened a sleeping beast by their actions on Bloody Sunday.

The night afterwards we watched the British Embassy being burned down in Merrion Square. It wasn't too far away from Reg's flat. I wondered if he was there. He wasn't very political. Daddy was almost on a high as he watched the embassy being torched. Mammy was worried about his blood pressure. She had to leave the room.

She went out for a Valium for him. She always kept some in the house. It was a yellow one with five milogrammes in it. Normally he only took a white one. They were less than half as strong.

'I'm afraid he'll get a heart attack,' Maureen said to me. It was hours before he cooled down.

By now Maureen was thinking of moving to Dublin. She said she'd had enough of Cobh. There wasn't enough happening there. It was no picnic sitting in an office for eight hours every day waiting for the phone to ring.

She was on the phone to me every other night. She kept asking me how Kevin was since the party. She was always worried he'd go back on the bottle. I didn't like it when she kept harping on that subject, especially if there was a danger Hanratty was listenining. The phone was at the bottom of the stairs. I knew she was dying of curiosity to know about every aspect of my life. That meant I couldn't say very much on the calls. I imagined her ears practically falling off trying to eavesdrop on me.

Kevin didn't drink again after the party but I couldn't stop thinking about the fact that he might. The night I followed him to the pub kept coming into my mind. I remember Mammy telling me once that an alcoholic was never cured. She said someone could be an alcoholic even if they were a pioneer. I couldn't understand the comment at the time but I did now. 'Alcohol is like a match to a flame,' she believed.

I told Maureen Kevin was finished with the drink now. I kept my worries about him to myself.

'I'm so relieved to hear that,' she said.

She came up to visit me a lot. More often than not May insisted on tagging along too. It was easier for me to have them now that I wasn't working. They loved coming up. We sat around the place yapping or else went into town. I couldn't afford to bring them out for meals or to the pictures but we had a good time going round the shops. It didn't cost anything to window-shop.

'Why do you and Kevin never go out?' May asked me one night.

'Because we can't afford to,' I told her.

'Do Clery's not pay him much?' she said.

She hadn't a clue about the practicalities of life. She'd been protected from them by Mammy and Daddy as a child  and later on by Maureen and me. But now it was time to talk turkey. I told her the rent was crippling us on one salary. In fact I'd even stopped driving the car because I couldn't afford the insurance.

Maureen started going out with a man called Edward Baldwin around this time. He was a nondescript kind of man from Chester with sandy hair. She introduced me to him on one of my trips home. He was a company director. She told me his family were filthy rich. That didn't mean anything to me, or to her either, but it meant he had buckets of confidence. He was always throwing money around, buying drinks for every Tom, Dick and Harry in the pubs. He had a posh accent but I thought he talked a lot of nonsense. I didn't say that to him of course, or to Maureen. She wouldn't have listened anyway. She was besotted with him but I turned off him pretty soon. I knew he thought he was the greatest thing since fried bread and was determined to make everyone else think that as well.

She met him through the travel agency after he booked a holiday to Ireland. A girl called Kate was with him. He broke it off with her shortly after meeting Maureen. He'd called into the office to get the keys of a car he was renting to tour the country. She was flattered by his attentions but I didn't think it boded well for her that he dropped Kate like he did. Was he one of those men who thought he could fool an Irish girl easier than an English one with his charm?

'If he can drop one girl so quickly, he can drop another one too,' I said. Maureen saw my point but I knew she was too besotted with him to take it on board.

There was nothing I liked about Edward. I even hated the way he dressed. He had a Crombie overcoat that he never buttoned. It swung widely around him on both sides when he walked, making him take up much more space than anyone else.

He wore two-toned shirts. The collars had different colours to the rest of them. I remember Daddy telling me once not to trust anyone who had two toned shirts. He said it probably meant they had two faces as well. I didn't know if he was joking or not.

I always thought Edward looked down on me. Maybe he was 'off' with me because I saw through him the same way I saw through Reg He was all show.

He spent some time in London when he was in his teens and came back spouting cockney rhyming slang. It was a habit he never shook off. He couldn't say 'stairs,' for instance. It had to be 'apple and pears.' A sneeze was a 'bread and cheese.' And so on.

211

Another thing that annoyed me about him was that he kept putting 'innit' at the end of his sentences. Kevin told me that meant 'Isn't it' but Edward even said things like, 'Maureen is really looking forward to coming to Chester, innit?' That really used to get on my goat. He also pronounced 'think' as 'fink.' It seemed so much at odds with his poshness. Daddy's view was, 'He's probably new money. That's the worst kind of snob.'

He gave Maureen a present of a clock that had a map of England on the face. I wasn't impressed by the idea. How could he have thought it was an appropriate gift for her considering Daddy's Republican past? Was that why he gave it to her, as a signal that she'd be leaving such things behind to become part of 'the other side'? After a few weeks it stopped working. The second hand stopped almost beside Chester. I thought that was strange. Was it prophetic?

Maureen and Edward had a whirlwind romance. Before anyone knew what was happening she told us she was engaged to be married to him. They were going to be living in Chester.

She handed in her notice in her job soon afterwards. That part didn't surprise me but I couldn't believe she was giving up everything to go to another country with a man she hardly knew. From a selfish point of view I wasn't looking forward to the prospect of not having her with me in Midleton. Or Dublin. As for Mammy, her prediction about Maureen following me to the altar were coming true for her in the worst possible way.

Daddy was dead against the marriage. He tried his best to talk her out of it but he didn't get anywhere. When one of the Tuohy girls makes up her mind about a man it's very difficult to get her to change it. I include myself in that. But we were all shocked. She'd been so sensible up to this. I couldn't see her as the same Maureen who gave me such solid advice when I told her I was thinking of emigrating. Maybe we're all better with other people's situations than our own ones.

'Are you sure you're not pregnant?' Mammy said when she heard the news. I have to admit I suspected that as well. I'd been thinking about the similar circumstances of Aunt Bernie and her 'mistake' so many years ago.

'How could you think that, Mammy?' she said, 'I'd never do that to you after the upbringing you gave us. We've hardly kissed.'

'I'm sorry, love,' she said, 'It's just that it's all happening so fast.'

It broke Mammy's heart the day she left Midleton. She wasn't able to say goodbye to her. Daddy had to bring her to the train. She stayed with Kevin and me the night before she got the ferry. The first thing she did was ring Mammy.

'It's only across the pond,' she said, 'I'll be back every chance I get.' But Mammy was inconsolable.

She was so excited the next morning I didn't want to deflate her by saying anything negative.

'This is like a miracle,' she said to me as I kissed her goodbye, 'The man I'm going to marry got me out of a job I hate by booking a holiday through it.'

I felt like saying, 'I hope that's not why you're marrying him.'

He was meeting her at Holyhead. That was where the ferry docked. He was going to drive her to Chester. He'd bought a house there that was going to be their home. Mammy didn't like the sound of that. She thought it was a ploy to get her into bed with him. 'Don't worry,' Maureen told her, 'We won't be living in sin. We'll be in separate rooms until the Big Day.'

Despite being Protestant, Edward agreed to a Catholic wedding. I didn't want to go to it because of my feelings about him but Maureen wouldn't hear of me not being at it.

'You have to come,' she kept saying to me on call after call, 'There's no two ways about it.' In the end I gave in. May was going to be the bridesmaid again. 'I'm thinking of making a career out of this,' she said, 'It's much more fun than being a bride. You wake up the next day and you're still as free as a breeze.'

Like a lot of May's pronouncements, this one was a cover for the fact that she was on the look-out for a man.

'It'll give her a lift,' Maureen said. She'd been down in herself since the party. She needed something to be happening all the time. Since leaving school she'd drifted from job to job without much interest in any of them.

Mammy and Daddy were as reluctant as me to go to it. I was hoping Aunt Bernie would come as well but she'd heard enough about Edward's shenanigans to put her off the idea. She thought Maureen was throwing herself away on him.

For the next few weeks it was panic stations all the way. A fortnight before it was due to take place, Mammy phoned me.

'May has me driven daft about what to wear. All she cares about is impressing that English crowd. As mother of the bride, she says, I have to look the business. I was planning to wear my blue suit but she says it wouldn't be right. I don't know why she's saying that. It's only three years old and I paid through the nose for it.'

I could see May's point. I thought a brighter one might be more suitable. I told her to come up to Dublin and we'd go into Clery's together and pick out something nice. She could buy her shoes there as well. I thought Kevin might be able to get her a few pounds off.

She came up the following Sunday on the train. She was all nerves talking about the shopping but we gave her a whiskey to cool her down. I took the Monday off work from my holidays and we got the bus into Clery's. Kevin wasn't with us because he had to go in early.

As soon as we reached the shop I picked a few suits from the rack. I went into the fitting room with her. It was a bit pokey for the two of us so I said I'd go outside. A few minutes later she stuck her head out from behind the curtain.

'I'm too fat for this one.' She said, 'The zip won't even go up.'

I went in. She looked trapped into the garment. I tried to help her get out of it.

'It's not the zip, Mammy,' I said, 'The suit is too small.'

'Then let's go for another one.'

I searched the rack for a bigger one in the same colour. I liked it because the blue matched her eyes. Mercifully, the second one I picked fitted her. After that we went hunting for a hat. We eventually found a navy one that went with the blue. I could see she was worn out so I suggested a bite to eat before looking for the shoes. We had a slap-up meal and even treated ourselves to some rhubarb crumble for dessert. Then it was all stations go for the shoes. I was hoping Reg wouldn't be on duty. I knew he'd be making smart comments. Thankfully he was off that day.

She got a nice pair of navy blue ones in the end. They were made of a soft leather that didn't pinch her bunions. Before we paid for them we went up to Kevin to see about the reduction.

'Reg is the man to sort that kind of stuff out for you,' he said.

'He's not in today,' I said, 'He rang in sick.'

'What?'

'He rang in sick. Probably a hangover,' I added.

Kevin didn't like when I said anything like that, especially with Mammy there. She only knew the 'nice' side of Reg. Apparently he was able to scrub up for her like he did for May. I was different, of course. I'd 'stolen' his buddy from him by marrying him.

He had a word with the cashier before we paid. She winked at him and he winked back. That was what he called 'the language of bargains.'

'Now you're all togged out,' I said to Mammy.

She was reasonably content going home on the train. I breathed a big sigh of relief when I sat down with Kevin that night.

Such relief, alas, was short-lived. She rang me in a state the next day.

'I don't know how to say this after all you've done,' she said, 'but I've gone right off the suit.'

I couldn't believe it. I had visions of us going in and out exchanging things right up to the day of the wedding. I tried to tell her it was lovely on her but she wouldn't listen.

She came up to Dublin again the following week. To make the trip worthwhile, and to stop myself going a little bit more insane than I already was, I said I'd get my own suit as well when I was with her.

'That's a great idea,' she said, 'Now I don't feel so guilty putting you out.'

I chose a simple maroon dress. I had it selected and paid for within the hour. There was no way Mammy could be like that. She never stopped dithering the whole day long. She picked something she thought she liked coming up to closing time but that night the inevitable second thoughts started to haunt her. Would it go with her hat? With her shoes? Was it too dark looking?

'Mammy,' I said, 'It's not the president's wedding. Nobody will be looking at you. It'll all be forgotten about the next day.'

I might as well have been talking to the wall. She brought it back and got a credit note for it. By now Kevin was tearing his hair out.

'This is getting embarrassing with the Returns Department,' he said, 'and it's a bit time-consuming as well, to be honest.'

I knew how he felt. He was up and down the stairs like a jack-in-the-box changing the receipts and working out how much credit she had.

'You're on your own from now on,' he said after the third exchange. I said that was totally understandable.

I advised her to pick the first thing she saw that looked half decent on her but there was no chance of that. Asking Mammy to get something on impulse was like asking her to slice her hand off. No matter how long it took, she was determined to 'do right by Maureen.'

I knew Maureen cared as little about these kind of things as I did but that didn't seem to matter to her. The dress she finally chose – a taffeta one - was over-the-top but I was so glad to get out of the shop I kept my mouth firmly shut. I'd have let her buy a potato sack if she put her eye on one.

Daddy had a much more casual attitude. He said he was going to rent out a tuxedo in Chester itself. The fact that he was so against the wedding made him not care how he looked at it. For him it was no more than a day to be got over. He'd been hoping Maureen would marry a local Midleton man, a cost accountant with an easy manner. He'd had his eye on her for a few years. His name was Gerry Heffernan. They went out a few times but she wasn't interested in him so she broke it off. He appeared in the travel office every other day trying to get her to change her mind. That was another reason she wanted to get as far away from it as she could.

Kevin couldn't go to the wedding because he wasn't able to get off work. He wasn't too keen on the idea anyway. Like the rest of us he wasn't over the moon about Edward. In a way I was relieved. I was nervous about the whole business. I felt I'd be able to deal with it better on my own, especially if Daddy came out with some of his IRA tirades. I knew he was well capable of doing if he had a few drinks on him. He could stay off it for months just like Kevin could but if he went on a binge on a public occasion he became like a different person. I was never able to understand how two such shy men could get so carried away in company. I suppose the experts would say that's exactly why they did it. Didn't people say most actors were shy at heart?

Mammy and Daddy came up to us on the train the night before we were due to get the ferry to Holyhead. May arrived a few hours later. She'd got a lift up with a friend of hers. We had to put them all in the spare room. We took a mattress down from the attic for May. Once the sleeping arrangements were made we got our stuff ready for England.

'It's well for you all,' Kevin said. He smirked as he watched us going around the place like headless chickens trying to pack.

'That's what you think,' I said, 'I'd give my eyeteeth not to have to go.'

'That's a fine way to talk about your sister.'

'I have nothing against Maureen. You know how much we love each other. It's just the stress of it all.'

Daddy and Mammy felt like me but May was looking forward to it. She'd fallen for Edward's charm in the same way as Maureen did. I was hardly surprised by that. I felt May would have made a more suitable wife for Edward than Maureen.

I slept unsteadily. Kevin had to get up at the crack of dawn for work. Mammy was up before me. We had a quick chat in the kitchen before waking Daddy and May. May was the only one of us to have a big breakfast. She fairly wolfed it down. The rest of us just picked at our food.

We got a taxi to the ferry. The taxi man let us out too early so we had a bit to walk before we reached it. Mammy's legs were killing her. She'd squeezed herself into a new pair of shoes for the occasion and they were pinching the life out of her.

'My toes are screaming for help,' she said, 'I probably won't recognise them when I get these blasted things off.' She had her Midleton pair with her as well, I advised her to wear them instead but she refused to even take them out of her case.

She was a ball of nerves as we got on to the ferry.

'Won't you stay near me when we're at the wedding?' she said to me, 'I won't know what to say to anyone.' I assured her I would.

She was sick for most of the journey across. The sea was choppy and the weather rainy so we weren't able to go up on the deck. Daddy tried to put his disapproval of Edward to the back of his mind so the day wouldn't be a total disaster for him. I made a massive effort to console both of them – and to console myself too.

May didn't need consoling. She ate and drank her fill all the way across. She even ogled the young lads on deck when the rain stopped and the water stilled. I wanted to join her to get some air into my lungs but I felt too miserable for that.

I spent most of the journey nursing a glass of lemonade in a cubicle I found for myself and Mammy. Daddy stood at the bar talking to some farmer about the economy. Mammy was down in her boots as she contemplated what the future held.

Maureen, I thought, what have you done to us all – and to yourself?

After we reached Holyhead we had to get a train to Chester. When we got off the ferry we found there was a big delay before it came. Daddy was livid.

'Why don't they synchronise these things?' he said.

'There are more people in the world than you,' Mammy said, 'Not everyone is going to Chester.'

When it pulled in at last we were fit to drop. Daddy got return tickets as we searched for seats. It was jam-packed so we couldn't get them for love or money. After lugging our stuff through various corridors we finally found two seats for ourselves. Mammy collapsed into the first one. Daddy offered the second one to May. I felt he needed it more than her but she was into it like a shot when he said, 'Ladies first.' I didn't think she was behaving very much like a lady.

Daddy stood squashed against a window. I was squashed against one opposite him. We both kept our eyes firmly peeled on our luggage in case someone ran off with it. Thankfully there were handrails because every time the train went round a corner we were almost knocked off our feet. It reminded me of the bus driver all the years ago when I arrived in Dublin first.

There were two sergeant major types with walrus moustaches sitting in front of us. They were discussing the old days at Eton. I could see Daddy was fit to scream as he listened to them. I thought he was going to have a go at them. I was terrified he would and that we'd be kicked off the train. I looked at him pleadingly at one stage when he seemed to be on the point of pulling one of them out of his seat.

'Don't, Daddy,' I whispered across the carriage. He nodded reluctantly at me.

'Ignoramuses,' was all he said.

It seemed like an eternity before we got to Chester. We'd booked into a B&B a few hundred yards from the church where the wedding was going to take place but we had no idea where it was. We asked a few people after getting off the train but they weren't that helpful. Daddy thought it was something to do with our accents. I didn't agree. I thought the English were that way, period. In the end we had to buy a street map in a little shop adjoining the station.

We trudged our way to the B&B. I was carrying Mammy's case as well as my own. They both seemed to weigh a ton. I didn't know why because I hadn't packed much. Daddy carried his one and May's. It was no trouble to him with his strength. He strode ahead of us.

It was a scorcher of a day. That made the journey even harder for me. It wasn't much fun for Mammy either. She was inching along in her crippling heels. I felt so sorry for her. She looked like she was going up the shoulder of the Matterhorn. She was half walking and half running as she tried to keep up with Daddy.

'Slow down, Daddy,' I said, 'There's no rush. Mammy's legs are at her.'

He was always impatient about things like that.

'It would be nice to get there before it's closed for the night,' he said, stopping up and sitting on one of the cases.

Eventually we got there. It was basic but it did us. 'Cheap and cheerful,' as the landlady put it. She was cheerful herself but her husband didn't look over-enamoured at the prospect of 'the green army' descending on him. After we checked in we went down to a dress hire shop to rent out the tuxedo for Daddy. His mood had picked up a bit by now. He seemed to have a fatalistic attitude to what Maureen was doing. Mammy kept harping on about the fact that the marriage was going to be a disaster until he had to tell her to stop.

'Maureen is a grown woman,' Daddy said, 'Whatever is going to happen to her is going to happen. There isn't a thing we can do about it.'

He only tried on one tuxedo. He looked at himself in the mirror and said, 'I'll take it.' The man who ran the shop was amazed. He was probably more used to fussy English customers. It wasn't a great fit for him but I thought he'd probably get away with it if people didn't look too hard. He'd never been in one before.

'Look at him,' Mammy said, 'the prize turkey.'

'Now that I've got the clobber I'm anyone's fancy.'

'Are you going to spend the day admiring yourself?'

'Are you going to spend it moaning?'

Mammy went over to him. She knelt on the ground and tugged at the cuffs of the trousers.

'They're too long,' she said. She was right but Daddy didn't care. If we were in Ireland she wouldn't have let him take them but she was too stressed.

'My legs are going to give out if we don't get out of this place in the next few minutes,' she whispered to me.

May was in another corner of the shop trying on her bridesmaid's dress. It was cherry blossom pink with lovely flower designs on it. Edward's parents had it waiting for her. It was meant to match the other bridesmaid's one. May gave him all her measurements over the phone. She was in such ecstacies about it she hardly noticed Daddy's tux. 'I don't think I ever want to take it off,' she said.

The two of them changed back into their ordinary clothes a few minutes later. After paying the money to the man behind the counter we went back out to the searing heat. We spoiled ourselves by getting a taxi back to the B&B.

When we got there the landlady told us there was a message for us from Edward. He wanted us all to meet his parents for 'Michael Winner.' Apparently that meant dinner. I knew there was no way Daddy would agree to it. Mammy rang him to say we really appreciated the offer but that we were all exhausted after the journey. 'We're going to have a quiet night,' she said. She thought he sounded relieved.

'It was a duty offer,' Daddy said. I agreed with him. Maureen probably put the idea into Edward's head. She was always thinking of others. I was glad we didn't have to go. Tomorrow was going to be bad enough. Tonight I just wanted to put my feet up. We knew they'd be hard going, especially on a night like this when we had so much on our minds getting ready for the next day.

Mammy would love to have seen Maureen but the house Edward bought was on the far side of the city so it wasn't possible. He was staying in his parent's place for the night.

When she rang Maureen she found her in a state of high anxiety. She said Edward was obsessed about how she was going to look at the wedding. He wanted his 'Duchess of Fife' (i.e. that meant his wife) to look like a Hollywood film star. He'd made her have a facial a few days before.

'It nearly caused us to break up,' she told Mammy, 'I told him if he didn't like the face I was born with why was he marrying me?'

'Good on you,' Mammy said.

'Not really because I gave in eventually. I thought he was about to have a heart attack. He said it was for "Mum and Dad." That kind of remark generally gets him what he wants.'

For the next fifteen minutes she talked non-stop. How did the trip go? How were we feeling? What time would we be at the church?' She kept shooting questions at Mammy and not giving her time to answer. She had to leave down the phone in the end and let me talk to her instead. She was so hyped-up it was like talking to a machine.

Every few minutes May snatched the phone from me with some query about the bridesmaid's duties. You'd swear it was herself that was getting married instead of Maureen.

Mammy took the phone from me when I was finished talking.

'It's still not too late to change your mind,' she said.

I felt that was the wrong thing to say. It was like a vote of no confidence in Edward. I knew she was doing it so Maureen wouldn't feel under pressure but it gave her a different kind of pressure. She got all flustered. Mammy handed the phone back to me. I could sense Maureen's tension on the other end of the line.

'See you tomorrow,' I said before hanging up.

I looked at Mammy.

'You shouldn't have said that,' I said to her.

'Don't give out to me. I'm not able for it.'

She took Daddy's tuxedo out of its bag and looked at the trousers.

'If we were at home I could turn them up for you,' she said to him.

'Don't worry about it,' Daddy said, 'It's only for a day.'

Mammy never gave in on something like that. She asked the landlady for some pins and put them into the trouser legs. Each time she put one in she'd have another in her mouth waiting. Daddy was intrigued watching her.

'Why don't you swallow them while you're at it,' he said. 'Then we could spend the day at the hospital instead of at the wedding.'

'If you don't shut your mouth I'll hit you with them,' she said. 'I'm going to bed in a few minutes. You can take them out if you want. I don't care.'

I told Daddy to follow her in. It was only now he was starting to realise how much the day was taking out of her.

I slept in a room with May, or rather stayed awake with her. She prattled on about nothing into the small hours. Mammy and Daddy had an adjoining room. I heard them whispering to one another. After a while Mammy started crying. I could hear Daddy trying to console her.

We set the alarm for dawn. We knew we wouldn't have too much time to get ready and we wanted to look our best. I always found it difficult to wind down when I had something to think about the next day and that night was no exception. I couldn't get to sleep for the life of me.

When the alarm went off I felt I'd been asleep for about five minutes. My eyes were falling out of my head but May was all go. She pulled the covers off me and told me to act lively.

By some miracle I crawled downstairs to breakfast. Mammy and Daddy were already there. They hadn't slept much either. Apart from May we all had long faces. The landlady must have thought we were a strange bunch to be going to a wedding.

I couldn't get the breakfast down. Neither could Mammy or Daddy but May ate enough for the four of us. Mammy wanted to phone Maureen to wish her well but Daddy said there was no time.

I looked out at the day. There were clouds in the sky. Was that a bad omen? We had a taxi pre-booked so we sat around waiting for it. After a while it pulled up outside the door. We bundled ourselves into it. Daddy sat in the front and the rest of us in the back. I kept checking my face in the rear view mirror as I tried to put on a bit of make-up.

'You always leave everything till the last minute,' May said.

The taxi driver seemed to go around the world for sport on the way to the church. When we got there he quoted us an astronomical price for the journey. Daddy said he wasn't going to pay it. The driver said he wouldn't let us out of the car until he was paid in full. Daddy was getting ready for a big argument but then Mammy started crying. Reluctantly he reached into his wallet. He threw some notes at the taxi man. He said, 'Keep the change, you robber.'

Edward's parents were waiting for us as we got out. His father was a big man. His name was Jonathan. He looked like he'd consumed one too many sirloin steaks. His wife, Kitty, was petite and fluttery. She was dressed to the nines. Her make-up seemed to have been put on with a trowel. She had an expression on her face that suggested she would have dearly preferred to be somewhere else. (I knew the feeling). Her hat looked like it could contain a good section of the Botanical Gardens.

We'd spoken to them a few times on the phone but it was our first time meeting them. They gave us all hugs but I felt they were forced. Jonathan started prattling on about nothing. He had a voice that sounded like Stanley Holloway. As I listened to him I was reminded of those Ealing Studio films Daddy brought us to as children.

'I've heard so much about you,' he said to Daddy.

'Don't believe a word of it,' Daddy said, 'That girl your son is about to marry is a ferocious liar.'

Mammy died a death when he said that. Jonathan gave a nervous laugh.

'We'll get to know you all better at the reception,' he said.

Mammy whispered to me, 'Is that a threat or a promise?'

A man waved at him.

'There's Harry,' he said, 'He'll get cross with me if I don't have a word with him. I'll leave you and love you.'

'Come on, Kitty,' he said. She didn't seem to be able to make up her mind to follow him or not. Looking at the pair of them worried me. I felt Edward was cut out of him. Did that mean Maureen would be expected to be like Kitty?

I knew she wasn't my type from the few conversations I'd had with her on the phone. Mammy said she thought she was rough trade behind the façade. She always said the 'New Rich' were the most snobbish of all.

She put on a worried expression, the expression of a woman who'd just been told she was going to be stuck with the 'Paddy Brigade' for a long time.

'See you all later,' she chirped before scurrying off.

Maureen arrived in a limousine. When she stepped out of it I didn't recognise her at first. She looked really glamorous. I couldn't get over her wedding dress. It was old-fashioned but very graceful. It was a strapless chiffon one. I never saw her looking so beautiful. It had a sweetheart neckline.

As she approached the church there was a round of applause from the people gathered outside it. She ran over to us when she spotted us. Daddy put his arms out to greet her.

'Limos, begod,' he crowed as he hugged her, 'It's far from limos you were reared.'

'Not too loud, Daddy,' she said, 'If anyone hears you they'll think we're bog trotters.'

'You look lovely,' I told her, 'I'm mad jealous of you.'

'Me too,' May said, 'You're like a film star.'

'This isn't my face,' she said, 'Some very talented people put it on for me.'

'They had good stuff to work with,' Daddy said.

'When Edward wakes up tomorrow morning and sees the real me, he'll probably divorce me.'

'Stop running yourself down,' Mammy said.

'You're all out in your taffeta,' Maureen said to her.

'As you know,' she said, 'I'd prefer to be in my old Midleton duds if I could.'

'Don't you know I would too,' Maureen said.

We started to move towards the church.

224

'He's in there waiting for you,' Daddy said.

'It's the bride's prerogative to be late,' Maureen said.

'As long as your periods aren't late,' May giggled.

Mammy was shocked.

'The tongue of that one,' she said to me, 'Where did she get it?'

When we got into the church we saw Edward in the front pew having a word with his parents. He was dressed in a tall hat and tails. May walked up the aisle towards him. He waved at Maureen when she came in. She was linking Daddy.

He grinned at some men at the back of the church. They looked like rugby types. I knew Edward had a big thing about rugby. I don't think he knew too much about it but it was the sport to be interested in if you wanted to mix with the high society people.

Daddy walked Maureen up the aisle as the organ struck up 'Here Comes the Bride.' When they passed our pew I wanted to tell her she was insane to be marrying a man who was only capable of loving himself. Instead I just whispered, 'Have a wonderful day.' She turned her head towards me and smiled. Maybe I was wrong about him, I thought. For all of our sakes I hoped I was.

Edward was beaming as they got to the altar. So was May. A girl called Erica was the maid of honour. She was extremely beautiful in that 'English rose' way. Edward's brother Nick was the best man. I didn't get the name of the groomsman. He looked like someone out of a Jane Austen book, handsome in a kind of boring way.

Mammy and Daddy both cried as the ceremony began. May had her mind elsewhere. I could see Erica trying to talk to her but she didn't seem to be listening to her. She had her eyes glued on Nick. I wondered if she was going to make a play for him.

Mammy became emotional when the priest said, 'Do you take this man to be your lawfully wedded husband?' I held her hand tight. She looked at me as if to say, 'What has she landed herself with?' I tried to give her a reassuring look. Maureen had love in her eyes when she said 'Yes.' Edward seemed to have too. He handed her a long-stemmed rose as he also said yes. Maybe we were wrong about him. I hoped so with everything in myself.

The priest gave a nice sermon. He obviously knew Edward's family well. He spoke mainly of him, hardly mentioning Maureen at all. I hoped this wasn't the shape of things to come. Everything so far was on the Baldwin's terms.

When the ceremony finished we all trooped down the aisle after the married couple. The photographer made a big drama out of trying to position everyone in the best pose to snap them. He was so different to the man we'd employed for our own wedding. I imagined him costing about ten times as much to do roughly the same thing as our fellow.

Daddy put his arm around Mammy.

'It seems like only yesterday I had her on my knee,' he said.

The Baldwins stuck together outside the church. Maureen and Edward posed for some photographs beside a tree. May still couldn't take her eyes off Nick but he seemed to be more interested in Erica. Edward seemed to be fascinated by her too. I thought I saw him peering down her cleavage at one stage.

Before we knew what was happening we were all whisked off to the hotel. It was in a luxury coach. You could see some of the historical beauty of Chester from it but I was too tired to appreciate it. I tried to talk to Mammy but she was in another world. I saw a tear in Daddy's eye.

'Well it's done now,' he sighed, 'for good or ill.'

When we reached the hotel he got stuck in the revolving door. He went round and round in it until we thought he'd be there all day. May was clutching her sides laughing at him. I doubted he'd ever been in one of them before.

'I think we'll leave you there,' Mammy said as he tried to find his way out.

'It's like a maze in here,' he said, 'What ever happened to doors that just opened and closed? Would that be too straightforward for the Brits?' When he got out he was in a daze.

We went into the foyer. The smell of perfume from the other guests nearly knocked me out. You could cut most of their accents with a knife. Daddy was all on to talk to them. He thought they were looking at him admiringly but I wondered. No doubt they were used to looking at people trussed up like him every day of the week. I knew Edward moved in these kinds of circles.

Everything around us looked like a fairytale but I was still having negative thoughts about Edward. I tried to put them out of my mind. I was never a fan of showy weddings. In my experience they often resulted in bad marriages.

We moved into the reception room. I nearly died when I saw it. It was like Buckingham Palace with its gilt furnishings and oak-panelled walls. Obviously no expense was being spared by Edward's parents. I felt as if we were the poor relations – which of course we were. The photographer snapped us as we walked in. It was like being in one of those BBC period dramas you saw on television.

'Did you ever see anything like the style?' Daddy said as he looked down the rows of tables. There was a big chandelier in the centre of the room.

'You'd know all about it if that fell on top of you,' he said.

A waiter led us down to our table. Our names were written on carved pieces of wood to let us know where to sit. It was draped in Kelly green. There were shamrock designs all over the tablecloth.

'Weren't they good to do that?' May said, but I didn't like it. It made me feel self-conscious.

'I suppose we should count ourselves lucky they didn't trot out some leprechauns as well,' Mammy said.

We sat down. I felt everyone was looking at us. I couldn't imagine there being even one other Irish person besides us the whole room. Maureen wanted to invite some of her friends from Midleton but Edward talked her out of it. 'They won't thank you,' he said, 'They'll have to get you a present and then there'll be flight costs and the price of a hotel on top of that.' He was always able to get his own way with that impeccable Baldwin logic.

She came over to us. She said she was disappointed she wasn't able to spend the previous night with us. Like me she'd hardly closed an eye.

'The worst part is over,' I said, 'You can sleep all you like on the honeymoon.'

'She'll be doing other things on the honeymoon,' May piped up.

'That's enough of that,' Mammy said.

'You're Mrs Baldwin now,' I said to her, 'It sounds quite posh.'

'Thank you, Mrs Mulvey,' she returned.

She looked at Mammy.

'What do you think of the spread?' she asked her.

'It's beautiful,' Mammy said, embracing her, 'But not as beautiful as you.'

'How is my little girl?' Daddy said.

'Not so little any more,' she replied.

There was a bottle of sherry on the table. As soon as Daddy spotted it he wired into it, helping himself to a large glass.

'For God's sake don't make a show of yourself,' Mammy reprimanded.

'It's only a glass of sherry,' he said, 'Why are you getting so worked up about it?'

'Edward's parents mightn't appreciate you starting on it so early.'

'What have we to lose? I know the way these kind of people look on us. They think our idea of a seven course meal is a six-pack and a potato.'

'Maybe, but don't give them more of a reason to believe it. At least the six-pack part.'

'Feck this sherry lark,' Daddy said, 'I'd murder a pint of Guinness at the minute.'

Mammy made a face at him.

'Just do what everyone else is doing for the moment,' she said, 'We don't want to stand out. You can have all the drink you want after the meal.'

'From my experience of weddings,' Daddy said, 'It's usually about teatime before that arrives. I'll have lost my thirst by then.'

'With a bit of luck,' Mammy said.

Edward glided over to us. He was all friendship in that shallow way he had.

'At least the boat didn't sink,' he said.

'Thankfully no,' Mammy said.

'How do you like the Cain and Abel?'

'The what?' Mammy said.

'The table.'

'It's very nice. You went to a lot of trouble with it to make us feel welcome.'

Edward beamed.

'You've met Mum and Dad, I believe.'

Jonathan stepped forward.

'We're like old friends at this stage,' he said.

Kitty didn't say anything. She seemed to be as cold as ice. She looked us up and down as if we were some foreign species. (Maybe to her we were).

I took a closer look at the two of them. Kitty looked a lot younger than Jonathan but I suspected some of that could have come from the surgeon's knife. Or was I being bitchy? Jonathan had the air of a self-made man about him, all bluff and swagger.

'You haven't lost a daughter,' he said to Mammy, 'You've gained a son. And some new friends in us, I hope.'

'And you in us we hope too,' Mammy said.

'Indeed,' Kitty said, giving a kind of sickly smile.

I tried to be polite to her but every time I opened my mouth she looked through me so I stopped trying. I was glad when she moved away from us. Jonathan started yammering on about an engineering firm he worked in. He seemed to have been a big shot in it once. He said he was winding down at the moment. He was just a consultant. As far as we could tell from what Maureen told us, he'd made his fortune from 'the sport of kings.' He was more or less retired from that as well now but still trained the occasional horse.

He clicked his fingers at a waiter who was standing at a counter some distance away. He jumped to attention. A moment later he was standing beside us. He asked us what we wanted to drink.

'More sherry,' Daddy said.

'You've had enough,' Mammy put in.

'No I haven't,' said Daddy, 'People only get married once.'

'Don't be too sure about that,' said May.

'Watch your mouth, young lady,' Daddy chastised.

When the sherry came around he made a grab for the bottle but Mammy intercepted him, putting it behind her back. Jonathan gave a loud guffaw.

'Your wife seems to know you better than you think,' he said, 'Maybe the two of us should go somewhere quiet and wet our whistles.'

'With respect, Mr Baldwin,' Mammy said, 'I don't think that would be a very good idea,'

He gave a little bow.

'In that case, I'll capitulate to your superior wisdom. And please, less of the "Mr Baldwin" malarkey. It's Jonathan.'

'Okay...Jonathan,' she said uncertainly.

I wondered where he got a words like 'malarkey.' Was it to make the 'leprechauns' feel at home?

Kitty beckoned him over to her. She seemed to be discombobulated to see him fraternising with us so much. She still had that harassed expression on her.

'My lady wife is in distress,' he said, 'I better see what the problem is. Once again I must away. It's been a pleasure to speak to you all. No doubt we'll do more of that later. We're well aware how good the Irish are at that particular activity.' (He pronounced 'Irish' as 'Oirish.')

He gave a little smirk and went off. Mammy looked relieved. I watched him going over to Kitty. She started giving out to him about something.

When a waiter passed by he stopped him. He made a gesture in our direction. A few seconds later, like clockwork, the waiter appeared with another bottle of sherry. Daddy's eyes lit up.

'No more until you finish the one you're on,' Mammy ordered.

'Good thinking, Mammy,' I said.

Daddy looked crestfallen.

'What do you think of them?' May asked Mammy.

'As soon as I took one look at them,' she said, 'I knew what to expect – Edward multiplied by two. The apple didn't fall far from the tree.'

'Did it stick in your throat to have to call him by his first name?'

'You can be sure it did. It was even worse to hear him talking about the "Oirish." Who are they?'

I saw him walking towards us.

'Don't talk too loud,' I warned her, 'He's coming back.'

He appeared beside us again. I was hoping he hadn't heard Mammy.

'It's time for us all to sit down,' he said formally, 'Everyone is waiting at the top table.'

Mammy looked as if she was going to drop. The thought of having to meet any more of Edward's family was a scourge for her. Daddy couldn't have cared less. His attitude surprised me. Had he forgotten the kind of man Maureen was marrying? It had to be the drink that was doing it. It was filling him with the kind of bravado we feared.

Maureen and Edward sat at the centre of the bridal table. Nick was beside Maureen. May was beside him on the other side. It should really have been Erica, the maid of honour, but May inveigled her way into that spot. Erica was sitting beside Edward. The groomsman was on the other side of him.

Jonathan and Kitty were at either end of the table. Mammy and Daddy should have been up there too but that would have left me on my own. We decided to stay at the table with the green tablecloth.

'At least we'll be patriotic,' Daddy said consolingly.

Mammy was still going through a bout of nerves, most of it due to fear of how Daddy might behave – or misbehave.

'Try not to talk too much,' she said, 'I beg you.'

'What do you mean?'

'You seem high. I thought you'd be sad about Maureen.'

'If I appear happy it's an act. I'm only doing it to block out my worries about that fellow she just got herself hitched to. We can't do anything about it so we might as well put up with it.'

'If Kevin was English,' I said, 'he'd have had to go down on all fours to get your permission to marry me.'

'That's because you're the favourite,' Mammy said.

I couldn't believe she said that. Did she do it to annoy Daddy? It wasn't a bit like her, especially on Maureen's wedding day. I could only put it down to the horrible way she was feeling about everything.

The menu was presented to us. It was embossed in gold. Daddy held his one up. He waved it around as if it was a Rembrandt painting.

'We'll have to bring one of these home and frame it,' he said.

'I know what I'd like to do to it,' Mammy said.

231

I wish they wouldn't put all that foreign stuff on it,' he complained, 'Bacon and cabbage would have suited me fine.'

Mammy was dying a death as he spoke. Was he doing it to spite the Baldwins? I hoped Maureen hadn't heard him. She had to live with them after all.

He was right about the menu. It mostly had unpronounceable dishes on it. I played it safe and went for the roast beef.

He was right about the time factor. The food was an eternity arriving. To fill the gap I found myself digging into the sherry too. By the time the meal arrived, both of us were 'well on.'

The soup came first. It was like a meal in itself.

'The trouble about soup at weddings,' Daddy said, 'is that you fill yourself up with it. Then you have no room left for the main course.'

'There's no law that says you have to eat it,' Mammy said.

'I don't believe in wasting good food. We had to go hungry often enough in the bad old days. Do you forget that?'

The beef was delicious but I ate too much. Maybe it was out of nerves. Daddy gobbled it up too but Mammy only nibbled. She kept looking across at Maureen to see how she was doing. She chatted to Jonathan and Kitty as much as she could. When but when she wasn't talking I thought she looked very sad. I wondered what her life would be like from now on. It was going to be hard to see her. I couldn't imagine going over to Chester much, or her coming back. There would be so much inconvenience between boats and trains and whatnot.

The dessert was called 'Death By Chocolate.' It was very rich.

Mammy said, 'I think they mean it literally.'

We washed it down with cups of black coffee. That sobered me up a bit but I felt my stomach churning from all the mixtures.

Jonathan tapped on a glass with a spoon after we finished eating. Everyone shouted, 'Speech! Speech!'

He cleared his throat. He said, 'Okay, my dear guests, a few words.' Knowing him for even the brief time I did, I couldn't imagine it being just a few.

He began by saying he was delighted to see such a large gathering, especially 'the Irish contingent.' He welcomed Maureen into the family and thanked us for making the journey over. He said he was enthralled to have met Mammy and Daddy.

'I now know where Maureen got her loveliness from,' he said, 'and her beauty.' As he spoke I thought: And I now know where Edward got his charm from.

That was the end of his mention of us. After that it was Edward, Edward, Edward.

'He didn't delay too long on the Tuohys,' I said to Mammy.

'What would you expect?' she replied, 'He isn't one of us.'

'I don't care. We've crossed the ocean for this. And Maureen is a Tuohy too.'

'Not anymore,' Mammy said, 'She's a Baldwin now.' I wished she hadn't said that. The words 'Maureen Baldwin' stuck in my throat.

Nick stood up to give his speech then.

'A man is incomplete until he's married,' he began, 'Then he's finished.'

Daddy groaned.

'Is he trying to be clever or something?' he said. I had a vague memory of hearing that joke at some other wedding. Maybe he got it from a handbook: 'Suggestions for the Best Man's Speech.'

He went on to talk about nights on the town, details of which were too shocking to relate. The rugby contingent started howling at this, They slapped their thighs and stamped their feet on the floor.

One of them demanded details.

'Later in the bar,' he said, to more howls.

At the end of his speech he came out with another one of those jokes he probably got in a wedding handbook: 'A wife is someone who turns an old rake into a lawn-mower.' I felt Maureen was expected to laugh at this by the way Edward looked at her. She managed a half-smile. He started to mime the act of mowing a lawn. Everyone guffawed.

Mammy didn't want Daddy to make a speech but he insisted. He rose to his feet a bit unsteadily after Nick finished. I was glad he didn't go up to the bridal table to give it. He just stood up at our one. That made it more natural.

He went into rhapsodies about his 'Pearl beyond compare.' I was glad Maureen was getting her moment at last. It reminded me of the speech he gave about me at my wedding. He never needed notes. He had all the memories inside his head.

Maureen glowed as he spoke. Edward did too but Kitty had her nose in the air. She probably thought his accent was common. I found myself wishing the wedding had been in Cork. We'd all have been more comfortable there.

He finished after a few minutes. He would have gone on longer but Mammy tugged at his tuxedo for him to sit down. After much tugging he did, but not before toasting the whole room with a cry of 'Sláinte!' I doubted anyone knew what that meant.

Nick read out some telegrams then. Most of them were standard ones like, 'May more than railings run around your front lawn.' At the end he read one from someone with a double-barrelled name. Judging by the reaction of everyone he was famous but I'd never heard of him before. I think he was a Lord or something. His message had some kind of sophisticated joke that I couldn't make head or tail of. We were all expected to laugh like hyenas at his wit but I saw nothing funny about it.

Finally the telegrams were finished. We all clinked our glasses together to wish the newlyweds every happiness. Maureen tried her best to smile. She seemed swamped by all the Baldwins. I wished I could have cut through them all and gone up to her.

'And now for something completely different,' Edward said.

The room descended into silence. The kitchen door opened up and an army of waiters poured through it. They had the wedding cake on a huge tray with flames all around it.

'Be the hokey,' Daddy said, 'Did you ever see the likes of that?'

It was presented to Maureen and Edward. Maureen blew out the flames. Edward cut a slice of it. He gave it to Maureen. As she started to eat it there was a burst of applause. She fed some to Edward. They intertwined their arms and that led to more applause. Then they kissed.

Edward took out a handkerchief. He wiped his brow as if he was overcome with passion. The rugby crowd laughed again.

'Now, my friends,' he said, 'It's time for everyone to get drunk.'

The waiters moved like robots. They removed all the dishes from the tables. Some of them came around to us with more wine. When Daddy was asked if he'd have red or white he said, 'Both!'

'No way,' Mammy said, keeping one of the glasses for herself. I didn't want to mix it with the sherry but there didn't seem to be any alternative.

'You'll know all about that in the morning,' Mammy said to me.

A band came out after all the dishes were cleared away. They stood on a stage at the back of the room. All the instruments were already on it. The tables we were eating at were pushed back. We carried our chairs to the other end. I suddenly felt as if we were in a huge ballroom.

The lights dimmed. Edward and Maureen stood up. They did a waltz around the floor to more applause. Maureen was a wonderful dancer. Daddy and Mammy beamed with pride as they watched her. At the end they kissed again. The way Edward looked at her made me think they might have a chance of making it after all.

Other couples started to appear on the floor now, in dribs and drabs at first and then nearly everyone. The rugby players got into a scrum position. One of them grabbed Edward and threaded him through it. He was in his element. They wanted to do the same to Maureen but she wouldn't let them. They screeched like wild animals doing some kind of weird mating call.

We were all given party hats to wear. I no more felt like putting my one on than the cat but I didn't want to be a spoilsport.

Maureen came over to us.

'There was no way I was getting into that scrum,' she said.

'They'd all have had their wicked way with you in there,' Daddy said. Mammy told him to stop that kind of talk. She put her arms around Maureen.

'I'm proud of you,' she said, 'You're making such an effort.'

'It's not an effort, Mammy. I'm in love.'

Daddy said, 'I thought you were going to go on fire there for a minute.'

'It's all the go at weddings now.'

After Edward emerged from the scrum he came over to us. Daddy asked him how he was feeling.

235

'Like a rugby ball that's been dropkicked to heaven,' he said.

'Were you worried about what might happen to you in there?'

'Not really,' he said looking at me, 'I knew we had a talented nurse in attendance.' Once again he was trying to work that Baldwin charm on me.

'Sorry,' I said, 'You're on your own if anything happens to you like that. I'm off duty.'

He asked us how we were enjoying ourselves.

'It's a great day,' Mammy said.

'You look a bit tense, Mrs Tuohy,' he said, 'Can I get you a drink?'

'She doesn't drink,' Daddy told him.

'Well she'll have to have something. Mrs Tuohy, if I may say so, you look as if you've lost everyone belonging to you.'

'Not everyone,' she said stiffly, 'Just a daughter.'

'Oh Mrs Tuohy, please! It's a wedding, not a funeral.'

'Irish mothers don't know the difference,' Daddy chortled. Edward gave a hearty laugh at this.

'Stop letting Mammy down, I said.

'It's only a joke,' he protested.

'Thanks for defending me,' Mammy said to me.

A couple that knew Edward came over to him. The woman embraced him. She was dripping with jewellery. Her dress was cut very low. It didn't leave much to the imagination.

'Her breasts are more out than in,' Mammy said.

'There's certainly enough of them there anyway,' Daddy said. He couldn't stop looking at them. Mammy put her hand over his eyes.

'I don't want you getting any bad thoughts,' she explained.

'Just because I'm on a diet,' he said, 'doesn't mean I can't look at the menu.'

'I'm confining you to ones with roast beef on them for today,' she informed him.

Edward started talking about some race or other. A few other couples joined them after a minute.

'The horsey set,' Daddy sighed.

'Come on, Mo,' Edward said to Maureen, 'We're going into the VIP suite for a kitchen sink.' She was no wiser than Daddy about the rhyming slang until he explained that he meant for a drink.

She didn't want to but she felt she couldn't refuse. She disengaged herself from us reluctantly. A moment later she was swallowed up in the crowd. I couldn't help feeling she was totally out of her depth, that high society was going to be a nightmare for her.

Mammy gave Daddy a stern look when everyone was gone.

'Why did you let me down like that?' she said to him.

'Like what?'

'Your comment about funerals.'

'As I told you, it was only a joke.'

'I didn't find it very funny.'

She looked at me.

'What in the name of God is going to happen to Maureen?' she asked me.

'Stop worrying,' I said. But I knew she couldn't.

Daddy finished a glass of sherry and started on the wine.

'I wish you'd go easy on that stuff,' Mammy scolded.

'I have to do something.'

I could see it going to his head. He had the same glassy expression in his eyes I saw in Kevin the night of the party. I knew he was drinking to drown his sorrows and I was afraid of how it was going to change his personality. I didn't want him to give the Baldwins any more reasons to make fun of us. They had enough of them already.

Despite Mammy's protests, he announced to the room, 'I'm going to sing a song.'

Everyone stopped talking. Edward smiled and so did his father. His mother's expression grew more painful. So did Mammy's.

It was a republican one. He had only a few lines sung before he forgot the words. We were all relieved about that. Mammy went up to him and gave out to him. He wanted to sing 'The Men Behind the Wire' afterwards but she told him she'd walk out if he did that. Instead he started singing a song about the Famine. This was ironic considering we'd just spent the last few hours stuffing our faces with food.

It reduced the room to a standstill. It wasn't so much a song as a history of Ireland under John Bull. I knew he was taunting the Baldwins. It wasn't very subtle.

Mammy waved her arms at him begging him to stop but he wouldn't. I expected that. The more you pleaded with Daddy not to do something, the more likely he was to do it.

He went right the way to the end. It was a catalogue of disaster from start to finish. There was death, starvation, emigration, genocide. He was still fighting The Old Enemy.

There was silence when he finished. I wanted the ground to swallow me up. Then I heard a trickle of applause coming from somewhere. Was it from Maureen?

May cosied up to Nick but he didn't look happy. He still seemed to have eyes only for Erica.

'Well,' Mammy said to Daddy, 'Are you proud of yourself?'

'I am, actually,' he said.

'You've made everyone very uncomfortable,' she said to him.

'So what if I have?' he said, 'Don't these people deserve to feel uncomfortable after what they did to us?'

'The famine was over a hundred years ago.'

'I don't care if it was a thousand.'

Edward came over to them. He slapped Daddy on the back.

'Well,' Daddy said, 'Did you enjoy my song?'

'The first 37 verses were the best,' Edward said.

Daddy laughed dryly.

'Sorry I didn't get to finish it,' he said, 'You only heard the first half.'

Edward went off. Daddy sat down beside me. I saw that there was still some mischief in his eyes. I hoped he had nothing else up his sleeve to make the guests 'uncomfortable.' I wasn't sure Mammy could take it. Or me.

'Do you think I should sing another song?' he said.

'If you do I'm walking out,' Mammy said.

He stretched out on his chair. As he did so, I noticed that his trousers were held up by a safety pin. Mammy pulled the tuxedo down to cover it.

'What happened?' she said, 'They weren't like that this morning.'

238

'A button popped. They're too long and too narrow. They must have been designed for a seven foot beanpole.'

'You're going from bad to worse,' she said, 'The Baldwins are just waiting to get something on us. You're giving it to them gift-wrapped.'

'Everyone is walking around like ghosts. They look like they have pokers stuck up their rear ends. It bothers me.'

'Don't mind your bother. It's Maureen's day, not ours.'

'I don't care what these people think of me,' he said.

'Well we do,' I said.

He always listened to me more than Mammy.

'Okay,' he said, 'I'll behave myself from now on. But don't expect me to start singing "God Save the Queen."'

'I don't want you to sing anything at all,' Mammy said, 'How many more times do I have to tell you that?'

'All right, all right, all right. Just lay off me.'

Mammy stood up. She asked me to go to the Ladies with her. As we walked towards it she kept shaking her head.

'That man will be the death of me yet,' she said.

When we got inside she went into one of the cubicles. She put down the lid of the toilet seat.

'Sit there for a minute,' she said. She squeezed her feet out of her shoes.

'I have to keep taking them off,' she said, 'They have the feet torn off me.'

'Let me massage them for you,' I said.

'That would be great. Have we room?'

'Let's try anyway.'

She put her foot on my lap. I eased the tension out of it.

'That feels like heaven,' she said.

I did the other one afterwards. She closed her eyes. I put her sitting on the toilet seat then.

'Breathe deeply,' I said.

Her chest went in and out. I let her take about twenty breaths. She seemed at peace for the first time in the day.

'Will we go back in?' she said to me then.

'If you want to stay her for a while more I don't mind.'

'Maybe we will. It's so relaxing to get away from everyone.'

'I'm not looking forward to the rest of the day.'

'As long as Daddy doesn't lose the run of himself again,'

'Or as long as we don't get ambushed by "Jonathan."'

She put on Stanley Holloway's voice as she said his name. I had to laugh. It was so good to have the old Mammy back.

'I think I'm ready to face them again now,' she said. 'Are you?'

'What choice have we?'

'Okay. Here goes.'

We braced ourselves for a return to a room we now hated. Into the valley of death rode the Tuohys.

Nobody even noticed we'd been away. Everyone was immersed in conversation. I waved at Maureen but she didn't see me. Nick seemed to be telling Erica the story of his life. All I could see of May was the side of her head beside a pillar.

Daddy had a contrite look on his face as we got to our table.

'Sorry if I'm spoiling your day,' he said to Mammy.

'You're not. I know why you're doing it. I just think you've made your point.'

'Agreed.'

She looked at me intently.

'I'd kill for a cup of tea,' she said, 'It would be such a break from all this alcohol.'

'That's easily enough arranged,' I said. 'You can't beat the old cup of tea.'

As soon as I saw a waiter I nabbed him. Within minutes he came over to us with a pot of it.

Daddy didn't know what was going on.

'What's that you're after ordering?' he said.

'You can have all the sherry in the world,' she said, 'I'll stick with my Barry's tea.'

I poured her a cup.

'Drink up,' I said, 'It'll relax you.'

She sipped at it. There were biscuits as well. She nibbled at one.

'What's to become of Maureen?' she said.

'None of us knows that,' Daddy said, 'We can't live her life for her.'

We sat at our table watching all the dramas unfold around us – Maureen and Edward getting feted by Edward's friends, his parents engaging in what sounded like intense discussions with over-dressed people, the rugby crowd getting more obstreperous, May trying her damnedest to get Nick interested in her.

Some of the guests were friendly to me, the quieter ones that represented the best kind of English people, the salt-of-the-earth types who didn't have the boorishness of the rugby players or the pretentiousness of the Baldwins. I'd like to have spent more time talking to them but Edward's father or mother barged in every time I was on the verge of a conversation with them. It soon became obvious to me that from their point of view we were there for one reason and one reason only – to 'donate' Maureen to their son.

I went over to May.

'How are you enjoying the day?' I said.

'Like you wouldn't believe,' she said, 'And you?'

'Not quite that much, I'm afraid.'

'Why is that?'

'I don't know. I just can't get into it for some reason.'

'You should let your hair down,' she said. It was the same advice Maureen gave me when we were at school. Somehow it was harder to take from May.

'In what way?'

'You're sticking to Mammy and Daddy like glue. Don't be such a wet blanket. Just because you're married doesn't mean you can't have a good time.'

'You'd know all about having a good time.'

'What's that supposed to mean?' she said. Her eyes were blazing at me. I decided I might as well be hung for a sheep as a lamb.

'Maybe you're getting in over your head with Nick,' I said.

'Why do you think that?'

'Maybe you're showing him too much interest.'

'How would you know? Have you been spying on me? I thought you'd have something better to do with your time.'

'I just gazed across at you now and then.'

'We're having a bit of fun. Is that a crime?'

'No, but I'm not sure if he's right for you.'

'Where do you get off telling me how to live my life? What makes you such an expert on human relationships, bossyboots?'

I didn't know how to put it.

'He's more like Edward than you might think,' I said.

'Like Edward? Duh. Why wouldn't he be? He's his brother. What's wrong with that? Should he be like someone else? Someone else's brother?'

She was speaking so fast she was almost running the words into each other. When she did that she made me do it too.

'I just don't want you to have your head turned by him and then be disappointed.'

'Oh you don't, do you? That's very nice of you. Well guess what? I don't give a rat's ass either way. So put that in your pipe and smoke it.'

'They're not as classy as they look, May. Daddy says they're New Money.'

'So what? I don't care if money is old or new as long as it's money. You really need to get something going in your life instead of looking at other people's. It's time for you to butt out.'

'The Baldwins are rough trade behind all the gloss.'

'Jesus!' she said, 'I can't believe you're saying that. Are you jealous of Maureen? Is that what's behind all this?'

'Don't be crazy.'

'I heard Mammy going on about that rough trade stuff as well. The two of you need to move with the times. If you go back far enough we were all swinging from the trees.'

I gave up. When she was in that kind of mood there was no talking to her.

She walked back to Nick shaking her head. A moment later she was dancing round the floor with him. Probably to spite me.

The more the day went on the more everyone dropped their defences. I even noticed the accents of Edward's parents slipping a bit, their true colours coming out under the influence of one too many cocktails.

After the band played their last song, people gathered in a circle in the centre of the room. A man who seemed to be the captain of the rugby team said, 'Everyone has to do a partypiece now. If they don't, they'll be sent home on the spot.'

'In that case I'm out of here,' Mammy said.

Edward's father sang a marching song. He had a strong voice. It was a bit out of tune but nobody seemed to notice. His mother played a tune on the piano when he was finished. She hit every note perfectly. It was a classical number I remembered hearing somewhere but I couldn't put a name to it. The applause was generous for both of them.

Then it came to Edward's turn.

'Okay,' he said, 'You've asked for it.'

He said he was going to enthral everyone with his skills as a magician.

He took off his tall hat and tapped it. It sounded hollow. He asked a young woman to examine the inside of it. When she did that he put it back on his head.

'Did you find anything in it?' he asked her. She said she hadn't. He took it off his head again. This time a trail of knotted scarves fell out of it. There was a big round of applause but Daddy wasn't impressed.

'He's hardly Houdini,' he sneered, 'I've seen these things on sale in the shops for a few quid. Your ten year old could do it.'

'Don't keep knocking Edward,' I said, 'Whether we like him or not we're stuck with him.'

'Maureen may be but I'm not.'

When Edward finished his trickery we were all led outside for more photographs. The photographer snapped him with Maureen in what seemed like a hundred different poses. Afterwards there were group shots with both sets of parents. He rounded things off with a few snaps of Nick and Erica. May was disgusted to be put next to the groomsman for these. I was relieved to be spared. I always hated having my photograph taken. He was very fussy about the light for everything. 'You'd think he was a film director the way he's going on,' Daddy said.

Finally he finished. We trooped back inside. May made her way over to Nick again. This drew some hostile expressions from Erica. They both glared at one another. Nick didn't seem to notice.

243

I couldn't figure out if May was really falling for him or if she was just having the 'good time' she talked about. Maybe I was all wrong about her setting herself up for a fall.

I started thinking about her comments on the 'New Money' thing. Nick worked as a reserve PE teacher in a posh school in Chester. I imagined it carried a large salary. I knew things like that mattered to her.

The longer she spent dancing with him the more worried about her I became. Was I going to have two sisters whose hearts were broken by the same family? I knew she'd keep muscling in on Erica's territory until he either went for her or told her to get lost. If she got him he'd be a trophy for her in the same way Maureen was for Edward.

Daddy seemed to read my thoughts. He looked at her gazing adoringly into Nick's eyes.

'Maybe we'll have a double wedding with the Baldwins yet,' he said to Mammy, 'You know what they say. Going to a wedding is the makings of another.' He hummed the lines of the well-known song.

'God forbid,' Mammy said, clutching her breast.

Erica went onto the floor after the dance ended. She stood in front of Nick.

'Am I next?' she said.

He looked at May to see her reaction. She tried to act as if she didn't care but she was obviously seething.

'Of course,' she said, looking daggers at her.

A new song started. Nick did a slow waltz with Erica.

May came over to us. She tried to hide the way she was feeling but she was never much good at that.

Daddy was amused by her.

'No wedding is complete,' he said, 'until the bridesmaid runs off with the best man.'

She gave him a steely look.

'Maybe,' she said, 'or until the father of the bride gets kicked out for singing IRA songs.'

Daddy laughed but I could see he was shocked at her remark. Sometimes she had a tongue like a knife. She never knew how deep her jibes cut.

I thought an argument might be brewing so I decided to get out of the line of fire.

'I have to go to the Ladies,' I said.

'Don't get lost,' Daddy said, 'If you do, send us a telegram.'

He always tried to crack a joke when he was upset but if you knew him you could see through it.

My head was throbbing from the noise. It was a relief to get away from it. I soaked my face in water. There was nothing better when you were feeling tense.

I went into one of the cubicles to go to the toilet. As soon as I was in there I heard Kitty coming in. She was with one of her horsey friends.

They started talking. Kitty said, 'What do you think of that vile man from Eire?' Whenever I heard anyone referring to Ireland as 'Eire' I deduced they were anti-Irish.

'I'm surprised he didn't come with a balaclava on him,' her friend replied. It was all I could do not to rush out of the cubicle and clock her on the head.

They jabbered on for a few minutes talking about this and that. I waited until they were well gone before opening the door of the cubicle. The day was going downhill for me very fast.

After I got back to the main room I went up to the bar and ordered a coffee for myself. Edward and Nick were having a drink at the other end of the counter.

They were behind a pillar so they couldn't see me.

'What do you think of May?' Nick said.

'She wouldn't be too bad,' Edward said, ' if she lost that dreadful accent.'

I thought to myself: You bastard, Maureen has it too.

He held up his glass.

'Beauty is in the eye of the beer-holder,' he chortled.

Nick laughed along with him. I was shocked. How could I ever look either of them in the face again?

When I got back to the table I decided not to tell Mammy what I'd heard. I knew it would have been the last straw for her. But my face must have said it all.

'Are you all right?' she said.

'Of course. Why wouldn't I be?'

'I saw you at the bar. Did you not get yourself a drink?'

'I was going to get a coffee but  the barman kept me waiting so long I didn't bother.'

She didn't seem convinced. My lies never fooled Mammy. I decided on a different strategy.

'Mammy, I'm exhausted,' I said, 'Would you mind if we left soon?'

'I've wanted that all along. Did you not?'

'I did, but I didn't want to let Maureen down.'

'You wouldn't be. We've been here a long time. Maybe we'd even be doing her a favour by going now.'

'What about May?'

'She won't want to leave that Nick fellow.'

'Surely she can see him anytime. What about Daddy?'

'He's getting a bit droopy-eyed. I don't think you'll have any trouble there.'

'Are you okay if I tell Maureen?'

'I think it would be the best thing for all of us.'

Edward had left Nick by now. He was back chatting to Maureen. I went up to them.

'Could I steal your wife for a moment,' I asked Edward. He smiled at me.

'As long as you don't ask for a ransom,' he grinned.

I signalled her to come over to our table. When we were out of earshot of Edward I sat her down. She looked at me with her eyes wide in bewilderment.

'What's all this about?' she said, 'Is everything okay?'

'Everything is fine. We're just exhausted from all the excitement.'

'Do you want to go? Is that all?'

'Yes.'

'Why didn't you just say it?'

'I didn't want to spoil your day.'

'How could you do that? You've made it by being here. You all have.'

'You're so understanding, Maureen.'

'Don't be ridiculous. Look, this thing is getting ready to end soon anyway. We'll be heading off in no time. Why don't you wait for me to get into my trousseau? Then we can all leave around the same time.'

'I feel we're rushing you.'

'Absolutely not.'

'How are you feeling yourself? You must be exhausted.'

'I don't know where I'm getting my energy from. I feel I could fly to the moon. It's been a great day. Edward has been the perfect groom.'

'Um.' I muttered.

'It'll probably hit me tomorrow and I'll sleep for a week.'

'Surely not on your honeymoon,' I said.

She smiled.

'Maybe I'll make an exception for that. Anyway, we're going upstairs now to change into our honeymoon gear. Don't go anywhere till we come down.' I promised we wouldn't. They were going to be honeymooning in Jersey. She'd showed me all the pictures of the hotel. It looked gorgeous.

I went back to Mammy. I told her Maureen didn't mind us wanting to go at all. She was relieved.

'Now our only problem is May,' she said. 'Who's going to prise her away from her latest flame?'

After Maureen and Edward went upstairs to get their things ready, Mammy got the attention of a waitress. We ordered some tea and sandwiches.

'I'm hoping they'll wake Daddy up,' she explained. She poked him.

'Where am I?' he said. His eyes opened slowly. Only gradually did it seem to register with him what was happening.

He asked where Maureen and Edward were.

'Getting ready to go away,' Mammy said.

'What – already?'

'You've been out of commission for a while. Look at your watch.' He checked it.

'Holy mother of God, why didn't you wake me earlier?'

'Why did you go to sleep in the first place?'

I looked across the room at May. She seemed to be on the edge of a group of people. She was making the odd comment but nobody seemed to be listening to her. The rugby players were in a circle around Erica and Nick.

A hush descended on the room in the absence of Maureen and Edward. For some reason it didn't feel as if we were at a wedding any more. It could have been a picnic or any other kind of day out. None of us seemed to have anything else to say to one another. We were talked out, eaten out and drunk out. I wondered how we might avoid being snared into conversation by any of Edward's relatives. They were all gathered together at the bottom of the stairs waiting for Maureen and Edward to come down.

They finally appeared at the top of the stairs. Behind them two waiters stood holding their bags.

They walked down the stairs arm in arm. There was another big round of applause. Maureen glowed. She was wearing a beautiful pinafore dress. Edward was dressed in a tweed jacket and jeans. He was carrying a camel coat in his hand. Daddy poked me in the ribs.

'That must have cost a pretty penny,' he said to me.

I could see Mammy starting to get emotional. I put my arm around her.

'It's only hitting me now,' she said.

Maureen drew herself away from Edward when they got to the last step of the stairs. She winked at me to come over to her.

'I have something for you,' she said, 'Don't look at it until you get outside.'

She rummaged in her handbag. I wondered what was coming. She took out a small package.

'What is it?' I asked.

'Nothing,' she said, 'Just a keepsake.' She slipped it into my pocket.

The photographer appeared again. He asked Maureen and Edward to pose for yet another photograph. Edward put on a big grin. Maureen looked sadly at Mammy.

'Smile, Maureen,' he told her. She tried her best to put on a happy face but I could see it was a strain. The camera clicked.

'Now another one,' the photographer commanded.

He went over to her.

'Tilt you head a little to the right, love,' he said, sounding a bit like a dentist.

She tilted it.

'Be still, please,' he said. The camera clicked again.

He looked at the rest of us.

'I want a group shot,' he said. I felt like I was back at school.

Everybody inched forward. We stood in a circle around Maureen and Edward.

'Backwards,' the photographer said, waving us away from him frantically, 'Backwards, not forwards. Otherwise you'll be decapitated.'

He took a photograph of Edward with his parents. I was wondering if the Tuohys were going to be frozen out again. Maybe he saw me giving him a frosty look because he said, 'Now let's have one of the bride with her parents.'

Daddy strode forward. Mammy followed him. He put his arms around Maureen, beaming with pride. Mammy seemed shrunken on the other side.

'And now,' the photographer said, 'The best man, the groomsman and the bridesmaids.'

I knew there was going to be more competition for Nick from Erica and May. Despite his good looks, neither of them were interested in the groomsman. I felt sorry for him.

May moved closer to Nick. Erica stood on his other side. He looked uncomfortable in the middle of them, as if he didn't know which of them to look at.

'Everyone say "Chester,"' the photographer said.

Daddy said, 'Are you not supposed to say "Cheese".'

'Chester!' we all called out. The camera clicked.

'Now say "Chester" again,' the photographer said.

'Chester again,' a man said. Everyone laughed.

'What are they laughing at?' Mammy asked. She was too stressed to get the joke.

'Okay,' said the photographer, clicking for the last time, 'That's it. You can all relax.'

We split apart as if he was a general who'd just said, 'At ease' to his soldiers. May looked longingly at Nick. He was laughing about something with Erica.

A few seconds later I heard a horn honking outside. Maureen went over to the window. She looked out.

'It's the limousine,' she said.

It was parked on the tarmac. It was the same one that brought Maureen to the church.

'Goody gumdrops,' Edward hooted, clapping his hands. The driver came in. Edward asked him to get all the bags. They seemed to be very heavy.

'What do you have in there,' Daddy said to Maureen, 'the Crown Jewels?'

He had to make a few trips. Everything was put into the boot.

May walked over towards me.

'What did Maureen give you?' she asked me. I told her I didn't know.

'Are you not curious?'

I took the package out of my handbag. I didn't want to look at it until we got back to the B&B but with May staring at me I felt I had no option.

When I opened it I found a silver locket. I opened it. Inside it was a photograph of Maureen and me from years ago. It was taken beside a tree house that Daddy made for us once when we were children. It brought tears to my eyes.

'What is it?' May asked crossly. She was in a foul mood after what happened with Nick.

'A locket,' I said. 'Maureen gave it to me. It has a photograph inside it.'

'Of who?'

'Maureen and me.'

'Am I in it?'

'No.'

Maureen looked nervous. I knew she hadn't wanted May to see it. But May always sussed out things like this. It was as if she had an instinct for secrets.

'I have something else in mind for you, May,' Maureen said, 'I'll send it to you from Chester.'

'Don't put yourself to that kind of trouble,' May said, putting on a false smile.

She looked around.

'Where's Nick?' she said to Edward. He shrugged his shoulders.

'Search me.'

Maureen and Edward went out. We all followed them. Nick was standing beside the limousine with Erica. He had his arm around her. Maureen kissed Mammy and Daddy goodbye. Mammy kept a rein on her emotions but Daddy started to blubber.

'The locket is beautiful,' I said to Maureen, 'I'll treasure it forever.'

She blew me a kiss.

I handed her my own little gift for her then: a key ring with a rabbit's foot on it.

'For luck,' I told her. There were tears in her eyes too as she looked at it.

'Do you think I'll need it?'

'We all do.'

She kissed May.

'I won't forget the present,' she said. May didn't look too interested.

Edward gave goodbye hugs to his parents and Erica. He did some kind of a rugby move with Nick and the groomsman.

He sat into the limousine. Nick gave him a fist pump. Maureen sat in beside him. She rolled down the window. Mammy waved to her. I could see her getting ready to cry. It was good that she was finally letting her emotions out. She sank into Daddy's arms.

The limousine started to move.

'Mind yourself with all those foreigners,' Daddy called after it.

'I will,' Maureen said.

'And don't lose your accent!'

'In a few months,' Edward shouted back, 'She'll be speaking like the Queen.'

Nick laughed. May put on a face.

251

The limousine picked up speed. There was a 'Just Married' sticker on the back of it. Someone had tied some tin cans to the number plate. They rattled across the tarmac. The driver got out. He pulled them off and threw them onto a footpath.

Everyone cheered as he sat back in. He revved up. The limousine screeched off around a corner.

Suddenly everything was quiet again. Mammy stayed buried in Daddy's arms.

'Don't fret yourself,' he said to her, 'You'll be seeing her in jig time if I know Maureen.'

'If only,' she said.

I went back into the hotel. May followed me in.

'Sorry if I upset you about Nick,' I said to clear the air.

'You didn't upset me. There's no need to apologise.'

Mammy and Daddy came back into the hotel. I smiled at them. Jonathan came over to us. He started putting pressure on us to stay on for another drink, the legendary 'one for the road' he thought every Irish person had to have by law. Daddy was on for it but Mammy told him we were too tired.

'You're always tired,' he said, 'That was your excuse last night too when we invited you for a meal.' (At least he didn't say 'a Michael Winner.')

'It must be something in the Irish Sea that does it,' Daddy said, 'Maybe all the snakes Saint Patrick banished are still under there.'

Jonathan screwed up his face. He obviously he hadn't a clue what Daddy was talking about.

'I can't believe you're going off,' he said, 'We hear all these stories about the Irish partying like there was no tomorrow.'

'Unfortunately,' Mammy said, 'Our tomorrow means getting up at dawn in case we miss the boat.'

'Oh come on, Mrs Mulvey,' he said, 'Surely you've heard of alarm clocks. A few more tiddleys won't kill you.'

'Maybe some other time,' she said, 'Do you ever come to Ireland?'

'I've always harboured a great wish to get to The Emerald Isle,' he said, 'The whole 32 counties.'

No more than 'Eire,' I felt anyone who used expressions like 'The Emerald Isle' would do a hundred yard dash in the opposite direction if the prospect of setting foot on Irish soil ever presented itself.

'We'll hold you to that,' Mammy said without too much conviction.

We bade him a hurried goodbye. May was biting her nails. She looked lost. Nick came over to her. He whispered something in her ear. It seemed to prop up her spirits. Then he went back to Erica.

We walked to the cloakroom to get our coats. It was cool in there. Mammy was glad to be out of the heat of the main room. Daddy's eyes were still a bit droopy from the drink. May was in her own brown study. It was on the tip of my tongue to ask her what Nick whispered to her but I thought better of it. The way she was looking I felt she'd eat the face off me.

We got a taxi back to Chester. The driver was cheery but we were too drained to talk to him or even to each other. We just looked out the window at the beauty of the city. I was sorry I hadn't a chance to appreciate its historical riches. It was like going to Paris and not seeing the Louvre. I'd been guilty of that too.

The night was starting to darken. Everything looked lovely because of all the neon. A few buskers were singing on the street. I spotted a soldier on a horse wearing an ancient coat of arms.

'I feel like I'm in a time machine,' Daddy said as he looked around at us but nobody agreed or disagreed. If he started doing cartwheels on the roof we'd hardly have reacted.

It seemed ages before we reached the B&B. Daddy wanted to give the taxi driver a tip but Mammy stopped him.

'We'll need every penny we have if we're to have a meal on the ferry.'

'Practical Mammy,' he huffed. 'We've come from a bash run by millionaires and we can't afford a quid or two of a tip for a hard-working driver. It's just as well the Baldwins aren't with us.'

'Since when have you become sucked into their values?' Mammy said.

'That's not the point,' he said, 'It's the done thing even if we're on our uppers.' He gave something to the driver on the quiet as we got out.

I breathed a sigh of relief as soon as I opened the door of the B&B. At last we were back in our own space.

'We got through it,' Mammy said.

'Did you not enjoy it?' May asked her.

'How could I enjoy losing my daughter?'

For a moment I felt sorry for May. I think she felt Mammy wouldn't have been as emotional if it was her on the altar.

Daddy's legs went from under him as he came in behind us. He fell down like a sack of potatoes.

'Jesus, Mary and Joseph,' Mammy said, 'What are you after doing now? That's what you get for drinking so much.'

'It wasn't the drink,' Daddy said, 'There's a crack in the cement.'

'Of course. The world is always out of step with you.'

He was lucky not to hit his head off the wall.

'Did you hurt yourself?' I asked him.

'I'll live.'

I asked May to help me pick him up. He weighed a ton. Drunk people usually seemed to. I remembered that much from my days in A&E. It was almost as if they didn't want to be picked up.

'I think I'll sleep here,' he told us.

At that the landlady came out. Her husband was behind her. He didn't look best pleased but she was smiling.

'Is everything all right?' she said.

'Sorry about the noise,' Mammy said, 'We had a little accident.'

When she saw Daddy she let out a shriek.

'Oh my God,' she said. 'Nothing damaged, I hope.'

Daddy looked up at her out of one eye.

'Only my pride,' he muttered.

We lifted him up. I put him sitting on the window-sill. His breathing was very laboured. Mammy was afraid he'd get an asthma attack.

The landlady was nicer than her husband. She asked us if we'd like her to get him a brandy.

'That would be like bringing coals to Newcastle,' Mammy said, 'He's had enough drink to last him till Christmas.'

'Never mind. You were at a wedding, weren't you? If we can't have a few beverages at a wedding, when can we?'

She tottered off with her frosty husband behind her. Between us we managed to get him in the door and up the stairs and into the room.

'Get onto the bed, you big tub of guts,' Mammy said to him as she heaved him onto the mattress. It bounced up and down as he landed on it.

'As long as he doesn't go through the ceiling,' May said.

A few seconds later he started snoring. We took off his coat and shoes.

'Thank God for that,' Mammy said, 'With a bit of luck he won't wake up till morning.'

He was splayed across the bed, taking up two-thirds of it.

'How are you going to get in?' I asked her.

'Don't worry,' she said, 'I'll find a way. It won't be the first time.'

I wished her luck. May and myself went into the room next door. She jumped on the bed.

'The mattress is nice and springy,' she said, 'I wonder what Maureen's will be like.'

'Don't be so childish, May.'

There were some miniature bottles of wine on the coffee table.

'Look at this,' she said, 'Nice touch.' She opened one of them.

'Like some?' she asked me.

'Are you joking? I've had enough drink for a month.'

She guzzled away.

'What did Nick whisper to you?' I asked her.

She put her finger over her lip.

'Not telling.'

I went into the bathroom. Everything was floating before me. I examined myself in the mirror. There were lines all over my face. The mirror must have been harsher than the hotel ones. Or was that wishful thinking on my part? I thought I looked about ten years older than I did a few hours ago. That was what weddings did to you – especially ones like we'd just been to.

When I came out I saw May had almost finished the bottle. She was watching television with her feet up. She seemed content but it could have been an act. I wanted to ask her about Nick again but I couldn't bring myself to broach the subject. What was the point?

Maybe she was reconciled to the fact that that particular bird had already flown.

'Here's to Maureen and Edward,' she said, holding her glass up in the air.

'To Maureen and Edward,' I said. I clinked her glass with an empty one I picked up from the coffee table. It was the one I was using to hold my toothbrush.

I lay down on the bed. I tried to process everything that had happened in the day – meeting Edward's parents, seeing Mammy go through all her ups and downs, watching Maureen trying to put a brave face on things, wondering what went on between May and Nick.

I felt my head getting light. Suddenly I was gone from the room. Weird images started coming into my head. As my consciousness drifted away from me I saw visions of Edward in the scrum, of his mother coming into the Ladies, of Nick whizzing Erica around the floor.

I was above everything on a cloud, looking down on all the people. Then I was under water, struggling to get to the surface. I clambered up a wall. At the other side of it there horses. Edward and his father were riding two of them. Maureen was chasing after them on foot. She was screaming at the top of her voice. Daddy was asleep on the grass beside her. May was singing a song on the grandstand.

I jumped up in the bed. I heard a voice saying 'Where am I?' Then I realised it was mine.

I looked around me. It was morning. Sun streamed in through the windows.

May was sitting on the edge of the bed with a towel on her head. She had some ice cubes inside it. It took me a few seconds to realise where I was. She started laughing at me.

'You're an awful snorer,' she said, 'It's just as well the wine acted as a sleeping pill for me.'

'Where did you get the ice?' I said.

'The landlady gave it to me. I have the worst hangover of my life. Never again.'

'It's always the last one that does the damage,' I said, looking at the empty bottle of wine.

'Why did they put it there?'

'To tempt you.'

We went downstairs. Mammy already had her breakfast eaten. Daddy was sitting beside her looking terrible. I suspected he'd have a bad hangover too.

I asked Mammy if she slept well.

'Never worse in my life,' she said.

I looked out the window. Already I could tell it was going to be a beautiful day. I'd like to have gone for a walk to see what Chester looked like in the daylight but Mammy said there was no time. If we missed the ferry we'd have to spend another night in the B&B and we didn't have enough money for that.

I had a quick breakfast. May nibbled at a biscuit with some black coffee.

We went upstairs to pack our things. Then Mammy rang for a taxi. I was hoping it wasn't going to be the man from the previous night. Thankfully it wasn't.

We thanked the landlady for her hospitality. She said she was glad to have had us. Her husband was nowhere to be seen. She said she'd give back Daddy's tuxedo and May's bridesmaid dress to the rental shop later in the day.

A light rain was falling as we drove to the train station. We were all in our own worlds.

Daddy seemed to have forgotten most of his antics from the wedding. Maybe he was better off.

He asked Mammy if he'd misbehaved at it.

'No more than usual,' she said dryly. He gave a half-laugh.

We got to the train station quicker than we expected. I reckoned it took the driver about half the time of the one we had on the outward journey, the one who'd brought us on the 'scenic route.' Daddy slipped him a tip when Mammy wasn't looking, just like he'd done the night before.

We walked to the train. Mammy had her old shoes on so she was able to move faster.

I imagined the high and mighty Baldwins waking up in all their finery, imagined them telling one another how wonderful Edward was and engaging in refined chatter over breakfast.

257

Or would they be trading jokes about the impoverished Tuohy clan trundling wearily back to the old sod?

Who cared anyway. All that mattered now was Maureen. What did her future hold?

It wasn't long until we found out. She was hardly back from her honeymoon when all hell broke loose.

# Crisis in Chester

I was bursting to hear about Maureen's honeymmon when she got back from Jersey. When she rang me I expected to hear tales of high passion and visits to exciting places but the conversation couldn't have been more different than that. In fact she was so upset she could hardly speak. My worst suspicions of Edward were confirmed when she finally found her voice.

'I've just been on to Mammy,' she said, 'The week was a disaster. We fought like cats and dogs almost non-stop from the minute we left the hotel.'

She didn't tell Mammy everything because she didn't want to upset her but she poured her heart out to me. I was so shocked I could hardly speak. She was delighted with the few words I managed to get out. It was so lovely, she said, to hear an Irish accent once again.

'There was turbulence on the aeroplane going over,' she said. Her voice sounded like it was going to crack any minute. 'That got things off to a great start. After we landed we were told one of our cases had gone missing. He went bananas about that. It was the shape of things to come.'

Edward showed a different side of himself to her than she'd seen when she was dating him. At that time, as she put it, he was all over her like a cheap suit. 'It's the old story,' she said, 'If you want to know me, come and live with me.'

'But you were living with him in Chester, weren't you?'

'It wasn't the same. He was out most of the time there and when he wasn't, I was. We were so busy planning the wedding it wasn't like we were a couple. There were always other people around. And of course we were in separate rooms at night.' At least he'd honoured that promise.

Things really only started to go wrong on the honeymoon.

'I had no confidence from Day One. Most of my good clothes were in the case that went missing - along with my make-up. I thought I looked desperate. Judging by his attitude to me he seemed to think so as well.'

'What kind of reaction?'

'He didn't say anything but his face spoke volumes. He looked at me like something the cat dragged in.'

'Did things get better when you got your luggage back?'

'Not really. The damage was done then.'

'You'd seen the real Edward.'

'Exactly.'

'Tell me more.' I was lapping it up with a perverse curiosity.

'We had a roaring row on the third day. I had a beach novel with me, one of those trashy ones you bring with you just to pass the time. He almost fell off his deck chair laughing when he saw it. He was reading Evelyn Waugh himself. If I had to plough through something like that I'd lose the will to live but he expected me to. He told me to throw away my beach novel and read something decent.'

'I hope you didn't.'

'I know I shouldn't have but I did. Not because I thought Evelyn Waugh was any better but for the sake of peace. At that stage I didn't realise how horrible he was.'

'Who? Evelyn Waugh or Edward?'

'Both of them!' she laughed. 'He intimidates me so much he almost strikes me mute.'

She told me story upon story of how the honeymoon went. Each day seemed worse than the one before. I couldn't believe my ears as she related the events.

'The sun beamed down every day,' she said, 'and you know me and my skin. I kept breaking out in blotches. I couldn't match Edward. He was practically bronze.'

She got sunstroke on the third day. After that she was in bed for a lot of the time. Edward wasn't the type of man to play doctor so he did his own thing.

'Far from the charming groom he presented at the wedding, he practically froze me out. He spent most of his time on the phone.'

'To darling Daddy, no doubt.'

'And to darling Mummy, and Nick, and Erica, and all the rugby buffoons you saw at the reception. He'd sooner have talked to the dogs on the street than me by the end of the week.'

'What excuse did he give?'

'He said we were in each other's face too much.'

'On your honeymoon? Who are you supposed to be on a honeymoon with – the gardener?'

'Edward needs lots of people around him to keep him stimulated. He missed the horsey set with their intellectual conversations.'

'Stop running yourself down. You're as good as any of them.'

'Not in his book.'

'There hasn't been any other woman, has there?'

'Not that I know of. I noticed him ogling a few beauties in bikinis when we went to the beach but I didn't think anything of it. Most men probably do that.'

I couldn't imagine Kevin doing it but I didn't like to say that to her. I thought back to the way I saw him looking down Erica's cleavage outside the church at the wedding.

'He didn't seem to be aware of what he was doing,' she went on, 'I don't know if that made it worse or not.' She brought it to his attention a few times but he just shrugged his shoulders.

'Did you go out at night?' I asked her.

'Of course, but even then I felt his mind was somewhere else.'

'Were there any good times at all?'

'For the first day or two he did all the gentlemanly things like ordering me fancy meals and drinks. That was fine but when they arrived and we started eating I felt like I was talking to a ghost. It was as if he felt flat being alone with me after all the crowds at the wedding. He has a huge loyalty to his friends. It's almost like I'm a threat to them.'

I wanted her to go into more detail but she was too upset to do that.

'I'll ring you soon again,' she said as she finished up, 'I really appreciate you listening to me. You have no idea what's it's like here with nobody to talk to.'

I was shaking when I hung up – both with anger and nerves. I'd seen the writing on the wall from Day One but what good was it thinking about that now?

'What was that all about?' Kevin said. He'd just heard snatches of the conversation coming in and out of the room.

'Maureen has just discovered her Prince Charming has feet of clay.'

261

'I don't think she'd have needed a crystal ball for that.'

He felt very sad for her when I told him all the details. He had great time for Maureen. On the subject of Edward all he said was, 'What would you expect from a pig but a grunt?' Like me he felt it was only going to be a matter of time before he showed himself up in his true colours.

Maureen rang me every other day after that. She could say what she liked now because Edward was out most of the time. I felt helpless listening to her. In some ways it was worse than having a problem of your own. At least you could do something about that.

I grew to be as dependent on her phone calls as she was on mine. If her life changed since she got married, mine had in a different way. I wasn't good at being out of work and I didn't know how to fill the time when Kevin was out. You could only clean a flat so many times. I missed the routine of the wards and the people I met there. Whenever I met the other nurses for a drink I didn't have anything interesting to say. I became like blotting paper soaking up all their experiences and wishing I was back with them.

'Are you sorry you married me?' Kevin said when he saw me sinking despondently into a chair one night.

'No,' I said, 'I'm just sorry I live in such a backward country.'

I wanted to be in trendy Sweden or liberated America, somewhere that you weren't treated as your husband's chattel.

I went up and down to Midleton more than ever now. Mammy and Daddy were delighted to see me and we had some great chats. There were invasions of visitors every day, most of them wanting to hear the latest gossip from Dublin. They wanted to know what I had for breakfast.

I didn't feel like answering their questions. After a while I stopped doing so. I'd forgotten how curious Midleton could be after the relative anonymity of Dublin. I only visited my 'town' grandparents once or twice but I was up and down to my 'country' Grandad and Granny all the time. They were as friendly as ever but the years were gaining on them now. They didn't have the energy they used to have.

'I'm still recovering from all the dancing I did at the wedding,' Grandad informed me on one visit. He had bad arthritis but rarely complained about it.

When he asked me how Maureen was getting on in Chester I just said, 'Smashing.' I couldn't let him know the truth for the world. He'd have been too upset.

Aunt Bernie dropped in now and again. She was cut up about Maureen. Maureen told me she sent her money when she heard she was struggling financially. It was so like her to do that. I knew she didn't have much to spare. Even though she hadn't been at the wedding she didn't like the sound of Edward from what she'd heard of him. Once again her judgment was spot-on.

I knew the fact of me being home would take away some of Mammy's loneliness for Maureen. I let her spoil me with some of her lovely meals but I didn't really like doing that. It meant I was sitting around the place far too much. As a result I started to pile on the pounds. It made me hate myself.

Junk food gave me a quick lift but then made me exhausted and sick. I had no motivation to exercise so I just mooched around the house most of the time. When I stood on the weighing scales I put my hands over my eyes for fear of what I might see. Why was it that you could spend ten years dieting and if you broke out even one day you looked like Miss Piggy? Why weren't we made the other way? Why couldn't we eat for ten years and then lose the weight in a day?

She kept plugging me for information about Maureen but I didn't want to get into that. I kept switching the conversation for fear of letting anything out. Daddy was easier to handle. He had a great way of living in the moment. I envied him that.

We talked a lot about May as well. Both of them were having a hard time with her because of the Nick thing. She couldn't get over him and was short-tempered as a result.

Mammy said to her one day, 'Has it fizzled out?' and she went berserk. 'It never fizzled in,' she snapped.

She wasn't working now. She'd taken on a few part-time jobs but without any conviction. She was fired from one of them for ringing in sick too often. She walked out of two others.

263

Mammy put all her attention onto me to stop herself having to think about Maureen or May. She hung on to me every time she saw me.

'When are you going back?' she'd say almost as soon as I got in the door. Questions like that took a lot of the good out of my visits. They put pressure on me, the kind of pressure she'd put on Maureen after I got married. It made them seem more like duty than fun.

If I told her I was only staying for a few days she'd say, 'What are you going back to?' It was as if I had no need to be in Dublin now that I wasn't working. This was a comment I obviously never repeated back to Kevin. I know she didn't mean it against him. If I went back soon I knew I was letting her down but if I stayed on I felt I was being unfair to him.

I never wanted to stay out of Dublin too long. I felt there was a danger Kevin would go on the tear with Reg if I did. He often asked him to go for a coffee with him after work. If he did that I felt it would only be a matter of time before the coffee turned into beer - and the beer into whiskey. If he made that transition, who knows where he'd have ended up? Reg certainly wouldn't have lost any sleep over him if he slipped back to his old ways. He might even have tempted him into looking for 'talent' in one of the ballrooms he went to. It wouldn't have bothered him that Kevin was married. He seemed to have an elastic conscience about things like that.

Money was an issue too. Though I wasn't allowed go back to fulltime nursing I kept trying to think of ways I could earn something to help towards our general expenses. I did some temporary work in an old folk's home in Kilbarrack to help out.

They didn't put me on the books so I saved a few pounds on tax. A friend of mine from the Mater ran it. She'd left general nursing to go into this line of business and was making a great go of it. She paid me with 'a nudge and a wink.'

It gave me a good feeling to be able to help Kevin even in a small way. His salary in Clery's wasn't great. I'd saved a bit from my nursing days but it ran out in record time after I left the Mater.

I found myself wishing I could get pregnant to give myself some kind of role. People kept asking me if there was anything happening in that department with looks of great concern on their faces. I had to keep shaking my head as if I was the lowest form of animal life.

No matter how bad I was feeling for myself I felt worse for Maureen. It was torture not being able to see her. We'd always talked through any problems we'd had in the past. Even though she was only a few hundred miles away it seemed like the other side of the world to me. I wanted to go over to her to thrash things out with her. There had to be some solution.

I rang her.

'Remember how you helped me so much that time I was thinking of going abroad?' I said.

'I don't know if I did. I just got you to realise what you probably knew anyway.'

'Don't under-estimate yourself. You're great at figuring things out.'

'I wish I was. I haven't a clue what to do at the moment. This is a more complicated situation than anything I've ever been in.'

'You'll think of something. You always do.'

'I wouldn't be too sure about that.'

'How has he been lately?'

'He's up to his eyes in the office at the moment so we have a bit of breathing space from each other.'

It didn't exactly sound like the formula for a life of married bliss but I knew what she meant. At least he was out of her hair. Her problem was the same as mine in many ways - trying to find things to do to fill the day.

'If there was even someone local to talk to it would help but the English are so reserved. If you say anything personal to them they get half afraid of you.'

She wanted to get a job but Edward wasn't in favour of that. He said there was enough for her to be doing around the house. He sounded like one of those men who wanted their wives barefoot, pregnant and in the kitchen.

He was ridiculously house proud, she said. He wanted the house like a new pin in case his delightful Mummy called around. He gave Maureen a list of chores to perform each day. When he came home from work he checked them out as if she was the home help.

'No matter how many times I hoover the floor,' she said, 'I can't seem to get it right for him.'

He was tight with money. That shocked her more than anything. It was in such contrast to the image he put out in the pubs in Midleton when she got to know him first. He'd been buying drinks for everyone right left and centre when he was there. She now saw that as nothing more than a pose - like most other things about him.

'He's driving me mad talking about the cost of things and yet he won't let me get a job.'

'Why?'

'He's a control freak. There's no other explanation for it.'

'Does he give you housekeeping money?'

'Just enough to get by. You can be sure there's nothing left over for clothes or anything like that. He goes through everything I buy with a fine toothcomb.'

'What about your savings?' I asked. Maureen had been the thriftiest of all of us growing up.

'They went on doing up the house.'

'You did up his house with *your* money and he's close to being a millionaire?'

'I'm afraid so. That's probably how the Baldwins got to be millionaires.'

'I can't believe you let that happen.'

'Me either. I don't even know how it did. We clubbed in together for household stuff when we came back from the honeymoon but things went a bit haywire after that. He said I'd get it back.'

'Get it back? Why should he have had it in the first place?'

'It was supposed to be a short term loan.'

I realised things had now gone beyond normal.

'Maureen,' I said, 'You need to sit him down and have a serious chat with him.'

'That sounds like the logical thing to do but it's different when you're in the situation. He's impossible to pin down for that kind of thing.'

'Is he ever nice to you?' I asked in desperation.

'When he comes home from the pub sometimes he's in okay form. He's vaguely human to me then. Maybe that's to sweeten me up for the bedroom.'

'I don't like the sound of that. I wouldn't sleep with him if I was being treated like you are.'

'I'd be afraid not to. I've seen his temper a few times. It isn't pleasant.'

'That's no attitude to go into the bedroom with.'

'Believe me, he's no Casanova. He just gets down to business and then he's off to sleep afterwards.'

'It sounds delightful.'

'How did you ever get yourself in this, Maureen?'

'I don't know. I suppose I was infatuated with him. You've seen how good-looking he is. Women fall at his feet. I hate to say it but I was one of them'

'It's so unlike you.'

'I know. I can usually see through men a mile away. He was cleverer than most of them.'

'In what way?'

'In every way. He sold himself to all of us.'

'Not to me he didn't. Or to Mammy or Daddy.'

'Did he not?'

'We didn't like to say anything to you. You were so happy.'

'May said she'd disown me if I didn't marry him.'

'May is a law unto herself. Look at the way she went on with Nick.'

'That's another thing. I've told her a bit about Edward but she doesn't want to hear it. She thinks he's a way to get to Nick.'

'She won't get far there.'

'Why not?' I didn't like to tell her about the conversation I'd overheard between him and Edward.

'It's just a feeling I get. Anyway, that's trivial in comparison to what you're going through.'

'I made a mistake. That's all you can say. How many millions of women have been hoodwinked by men?'

'You're great the way you're taking it.'

267

'That's what you think. I might sound strong when I'm talking to you but when I'm on my own sometimes I crumble. It's a rollercoaster.'

'Are you angry with him?'

'Sometimes I want to kill him. Other times I blame myself.'

'How could you do that?'

'Maybe I'm not what he expected either.'

'That's ridiculous. He wanted a robot. Someone who could idolise him the way he idolises himself.'

'I suppose so. You're so wise about the situation.'

'It's easy to be when you're outside the situation. It must be very hard for you to keep it from Mammy and Daddy.'

'It is.'

'Did Edward talk about how Daddy behaved at the wedding?'

'He didn't say much but I gathered he wasn't too impressed.'

I took the bull by the horns then, telling her what his mother said about him in the Ladies. She was hardly surprised.

'There's a family of them in it,' she said. 'Imagine her calling Ireland "Eire." I thought that went out with the Indians.'

'The English love doing to pull us down. I've met some of them. It isn't only her who talks like that.'

'Do you see her much?'

'Hardly at all. Apart from Edward, Nick is the only one who seems to be aware of the fact that I exist. He drops in any time he can. It's a bit awkward for me because of the way May feels about him.'

'Does she ask you about him?'

'Almost every time I'm on to her. I can never think what to say. Obviously she knows Nick really likes Erica. They've been going steady since the wedding but I can't say that to her. She'd go off her trolley.'

'Why doesn't Nick tell her the way things are?'

'He doesn't want to hurt her feelings.'

'That's unusual for a Baldwin.'

'He's not as bad as the rest of them.'

'I always felt that too.'

'She's been on the phone to him a few times. I know he wants me to say something to her. I'm not sure if I should step in or not.'

'I'd leave it to the two of them if I was you. You know May. If you get caught in the middle of anything you'll end up being the one that gets it in the neck. She has to learn the hard way herself.'

'That's good advice. I'll stay out of it.'

'Has she asked you about what's going on between you and Edward?'

'Not really. She's too wrapped up in her own stuff. I don't go into it much with her.'

'Does Nick ask you how you're getting on with Edward?'

'Every once in a while.'

'Is he aware of how bad things are?'

'He realises it's not sunshine and roses but he doesn't get involved. If there's a row brewing between us he's out the door. I think he feels sorry for me but he's Edward's brother at the end of the day. Blood is thicker than water.'

'Does he know how badly Edward is treating you?'

'Maybe. Or maybe not. Edward probably gives him a different version of events to what I'm saying to you. He's cute enough to be nice to me when we're in Nick's company so he doesn't really see the full extent of the problem.'

'I don't know how you can resist telling him.'

'It would only make things worse. Edward would take it out on me.'

The more she talked, the more horrible the situation seemed to be.

'You need your independence,' I told her, 'The first thing you have to do is get a job. Otherwise you'll die a death in that big house on your own.'

'That's easier said than done. I went for two interviews against Edward's wishes but I didn't do any good at them.'

'Why was that?'

'I don't know.'

'Do you think it has something to do with your accent?'

'It could be but I don't think so. There are a lot of Irish here. I even met a girl from Midleton in the supermarket one day. She said some people refer to Chester as Ireland's fifth province.'

'I thought that was Liverpool.'

'Maybe it is. Maybe Chester is the sixth one.'

'A lot of Irish people come over here and fall in love with the place. I can see why. It's such a beautiful city with the Roman walls and all.'

'I know. I saw a bit of that when we were over there. It's a pity you can't enjoy it.'

'Now and again I do, believe it or not. At least when I'm able to turn my mind off all the stuff that's going on between Edward and me. What else have I to do but go traipsing round it? I'd go bonkers if I stayed in the house all day.'

'Have you ever thought of asking him to give you a job in his office?' I suggested.

'I put it to him one day but he didn't go for it. He likes to keep that side of his life to himself.'

'It looks to me as if he likes to keep every side of his life to himself.'

'I can see how you would think that.'

'Is his work going well? I hardly know what he does.'

'Neither do I. He makes out like he's keeping the country going but I think he's on a real cushy number in there. I gathered from one of the secretaries that he spends most of the day on the phone.'

'To who?'

'Bookies usually. He keeps putting bets on horses - which he invariably loses.'

'Who picks up the tab?'

'Good old Daddio most of the time. He was born with a silver spoon in his mouth.'

'It's a pity someone doesn't shove it down his throat.'

She let out a big guffaw.

'I love to hear you talking like that. Things are so tense around here it's just what I need. I never really knew what people meant when they said "You could cut the atmosphere with a knife" but I do now. I wish I had that knife.'

'Why don't you tell him what to do with himself?'

'I'm afraid of him. I'm a cowardy custard when it comes to taking people on.'

'No, Maureen, you're not a cowardy custard. What you are is a lady.'

'You're nice to put it like that. I'm sure Edward thinks I'm more like a doormat.'

'What do you care what he thinks?'

'I've never been in a situation I couldn't handle before. I don't know how to deal with it.'

'We've got to get you back to Dublin. Why don't you simply walk out?'

'I'll stick it out a while more yet.'

'Why put yourself through that? You need to get him out of your life.'

'At the moment I'm staying away from him as much as I can. That sounds crazy considering I just signed up for a lifetime with him.'

'Don't think you're unusual. It's happening every day of the week somewhere. I really admire you for the way you're coping.'

'If I could only get some of my dignity back I'd be all right.'

'He can't rob you of that.'

'He already has. If I had some money I might get it back.'

'That's why you need a job. You'd be better off working as a kitchen maid than the way things are.'

I didn't breathe a word of what she said to anyone but Kevin. He thought she was insane to stay where she was. At first I agreed with him but the more I talked to her the more I realised why she was staying put. Apart from everything else, her pride was at stake.

Mammy suspected there were more problems than she was admitting to. Daddy was easier to fool. I spoke to both of them on the phone almost every day. When they asked me about her I just said I thought she was lonely.

'She'll probably settle more as time goes on,' I said, trying to convince myself as much as them.

It worked the opposite way instead. Edward got more aggressive and Maureen became more vulnerable. Some nights when I rang her she'd be crying so much she could hardly talk. In the background I'd hear Edward roaring at her. Eventually the calls stopped. When I rang her she didn't pick up. I ended up writing to her to try and find out what was wrong.

She answered the letter with a phone call a few weeks later. Her first sentence told me everything I needed to know: 'Edward is gone back to his old girlfriend.'

'I don't believe you,' I said. She was talking about Kate, the girl he'd been on the holiday with when she met him in Midleton.

'Don't worry,' she said, 'I was almost expecting it. In some ways he's done me a favour. I was stupid to think things would improve. The writing was on the wall from the moment we stepped off the plane. That was the first time he mentioned her. You were right when you said if he could ditch her he could do it to me. A leopard doesn't change his spots.'

'When did he start seeing her again?'

'Maybe he never stopped. As far as I know she was never out of his life even when he was walking up the aisle. I saw hints of it in expressions he'd put on when he was talking about her. Any time I asked him about her he said she was letting my imagination run away with me, that she was just a friend. Then one night I was getting ready to bring one of his jackets to the cleaners. It was the day after he'd been in London at a conference. When I emptied the pockets out I found a hotel receipt for two people in one of them.'

'Jesus.'

'He was probably having it off with her every time my back was turned.'

'It sounds like something out of a novel.'

'I know. One of those beach ones he stopped me reading.'

'Did you confront him about it?'

'When he came home from work that day I showed him the receipt. He said it was for someone he worked with but I said I didn't believe him. After a while I got the truth out of him.'

'Did he try to get out of it?'

'Of course. They always do. He said it was just a one-off, that it meant nothing to him.'

'What did you say?'

'I said it meant a lot to me.'

'Good on you. You should have thrown him out then.'

'Out of his own house? Hardly. I just asked him why he married me when he obviously didn't love me.'

'What did he say to that?'

'He said he always loved me and he always would. Then he broke down crying. He threw himself at me like a baby, telling me it never should have happened and that it would never happen again.'

'I hope you didn't fall for that one.'

'I'm afraid I did, like the big eejit I am. I said I'd give him another chance.'

'I think I know where this story is going to end.'

'We were good for a few weeks afterwards, so good I could hardly think straight. He started to bring me out with him when he was going to the pub. I got presents for no reason, which made me think: This is the real honeymoon, not the one in Jersey. He even put my name on one of his credit cards so I could buy things for myself. I thought we were out of the woods. Until...'

She started to cry. I wasn't sure I wanted to hear the next bit.

'Don't go on if you don't want to.'

I could hear her blowing her nose at the other end of the line. After a few moments she composed herself.

'It was an ordinary day. I didn't expect to be going into town but I did, just for a ramble. I was walking down the main street when who should I see coming towards me but the pair of them. I couldn't believe my eyes. He was as cool as a breeze and so was she. They made out as if they'd met by accident. I was expected to believe they were after having a coffee together for old time's sake. I didn't swallow that for a second. The next time he went out at night I followed him. Sure enough, he was going to her place. By this stage I'd found out where she lived.'

'Don't tell me you caught them together.'

'Wait'll you hear.'

'I don't know if I want to.'

'It was Kate who answered the door. I brushed by her and went into the main room. When I opened the door, lo and behold, there was His Majesty on the bed, as naked as God made him. His clothes were all over the floor. I tried to act as if I wasn't surprised. He pulled a sheet over him. I said, "I suppose you just met for another coffee. It must have been a good one."'

273

'You're amazing, Maureen. I'd have been too shocked to say anything.'

'Sometimes you get so beaten down you don't care.'

'Did she say anything?'

'The two of them were stunned into silence. At least I achieved that much.'

'Did you walk out then?'

'I started to but Kate stopped me. She said she was really sorry for the way things worked out. I told her she was welcome to him, that I felt as sorry for her as she did for me.'

'I take my hat off to you for being so dignified about it all. I'd have throttled him.'

'I don't think you would. You're more like me than you realise.'

'Do you think so? It's hard to know what you'd do unless you're in the situation.'

'I thought I'd have cracked up. I don't know where I'm getting my strength from. Maybe it's the relief of knowing he's gone out of my life. It's time for Kate to start worrying now.'

'Little does she know what she has in store for her. If she has a brain in her head she'll get rid of him.'

'I don't know. Maybe they'll make a go of it. She's English after all. I was a kind of novelty to him, the lassie from across the pond. Now he's with one of his own. The savage loves his native shore.'

'I don't know. He saw her behind your back and he saw you behind hers. God only knows who he'll be sleeping with next. Or how many of them.'

'To be honest with you I don't particularly care. I'm finished with him now. It's done and dusted.'

'I don't know how he can look at himself in the face.'

'That doesn't give him any problems. It's probably his favourite hobby.'

I couldn't believe she was being so upbeat about it all.

'Has it made you bitter about men?' I asked her.

'No,' she said, 'just men like Edward.'

'I'm glad to hear you saying that. I know you're going to find someone who appreciates you for who you are some day.'

'Maybe. I can't think of things like that at the moment. I'm just working out the best way to get out of here.'

'What does his father think about it all?'

'He called around once to see if there was anything he could do to clear the air, as he put it. He wants us to give it another go. I told him there was never even a first go, that it was over before it began.'

'I didn't think he'd be like that.'

'He doesn't want the scandal of a separation. It's all tied up with the noble Baldwin name. Himself and his wife are often in the daily rag.'

'I can just imagine them parading around the place at the Chester race course.'

'That's exactly it. Mammy had them well taped when she was talking about the New Rich.'

'Speaking of which, how are you for money?'

'Not great. He cut off my credit card.'

'I'm not surprised. It's a laugh thinking about him buying drinks for everyone in Midleton when he was there.'

'That was all a pose. He's tight as tuppence really.'

The more she talked, the worse things seemed to be.

'Have you told Mammy and Daddy?' I asked her.

'How can I? They wouldn't be able to take it. I have to laugh when I think of Daddy telling me not to lose my accent. I hardly had time to lose my virginity.'

She let out a sigh.

'I should have listened to you when you were trying to warn me about him. You were on to him from the start.'

'I didn't like to say too much in case I burst your bubble.'

'It's well and truly burst now anyway.'

'You're well rid of him. Maybe I could have spared you some pain if I said something.'

'I wouldn't have listened. What do they say - love is blind?'

'But you didn't love him, did you?'

'Okay. Infatuation is blind. Is that better?'

'Much better.'

'Anyway I don't want to bore you anymore with my whingeing.'

'If you ever say anything like that again I'll hit you. You know I live for your phone calls.'

'You're too good. I wish I was back in Ireland so I could put my arms around you.'

'You will be soon enough.'

Kevin was as upset as me when I told him about the call. He really liked Maureen. He couldn't understand why she was staying in the house considering the marriage was over. I told him she was probably still in shock. That made him feel even worse for her.

'She can come here from Chester,' he said, 'if she isn't ready to go back down to Cork.'

I was so thankful to him for that offer I rang Maureen straight back. She said it was very kind of him, that she'd think about it.

For the next few days I could think of nothing but what she was going through. I always thought she'd get her ideal man when she eventually decided to settle down. She'd had so many of them after her in school. We never know how life is going to go. Sometimes the most beautiful people have the most horrific marriages.

The next time I talked to her she was more philosophical about everything. She started to look on the bright side of things, at the fact that she'd escaped a bad situation.

'I feel like Mrs Havisham,' she said, 'I'm living in glorious isolation while he's down the road with his new love.'

'Are you any closer to moving out?'

'I've packed most of my stuff but I need a few more days here to sort myself out.'

'How are you feeding yourself without any money?'

'Nick helped me out. He said he's going to pay for my ticket home as well. He's been quite good about everything really.'

'I suspected he mightn't be as bad as Edward.'

'He's a far cry from him. He knows what he's like but obviously he can't say too much, being his brother. I'd say they've had a few words together but I didn't want to get into that with him. He's not the worst. If Edward had his way I'd probably be on the street by now. He said I can stay as long as I like as far as he's concerned.'

'I don't know if that's a good idea. What's keeping you there?'

'Delayed shock probably. I want to make sure I've got everything about this place out of my system before I go back.'

'I can't wait to see you.'

'And me you. How will Mrs Hanratty feel about me being there?'

'To hell with her. I'm fed up thinking of other people. You're the priority now.'

'I don't want you to get into trouble with her.'

'You won't. We'll smuggle you into the spare room. It's only a cubbyhole. Kevin will do it up a bit.'

'The two of you are like angels. I don't know what I'd do without you.'

'It's you that'll be doing us a favour. We need a new face around the place. From a selfish point of view I'm glad Edward Baldwin is a thing of the past. I wasn't looking forward to spending the next thirty years going forwards and backwards on the ferry to see you.'

'Thirty years? We hardly lasted thirty days. There's probably still some wedding cake left.'

'Great. Bring it with you. We'll polish it off quick enough. I've developed an even sweeter tooth than I used to have since I left work.'

Before she hung up she said she had another big favour to ask me. She wasn't ready to talk everything out with Mammy and Daddy yet. She wanted me to tell them she was still with Edward, that they were trying to work out their problems.

'Don't tell them I'm coming home on your life,' she said, 'I wouldn't be able to cope with their distress on top of my own.'

'My lips are sealed,' I said.

The next time I was on to Mammy I thought she suspected something even though I did my best to sound casual. She was good at reading my mind, too good maybe. I had to use all my lying skills to convince her Edward was still in Maureen's life.

'I haven't had a good thought about that man since the day I met him,' she said.

She told me she hadn't been sleeping since the wedding. She cried almost every day. Daddy was doing his best to keep her together but it wasn't easy for him either.

On one phone call he said the thing he feared most in life was Maureen telling him she was pregnant with Edward's child. I hoped against hope she wasn't. It would have been the last straw to be carrying a Baldwin inside her as she got the ferry home.

# An Extra Lodger

Maureen arrived on our doorstep the following week. I was shocked when I saw her. She looked as if she hadn't slept for a month. Maybe she hadn't.

'Where's the tan?' I asked her, 'You posh people who honeymoon in places like Jersey are supposed to have tans, aren't you?'

'The tears probably washed it all away.'

I pulled her into the hallway.

'Come in quick,' I blustered, 'If Hanratty sees your bags there'll be wigs on the green.'

Kevin took them from her. He stacked them in a cabinet.

'I hope you have that wedding cake you promised us,' he said.

'I'm afraid I dumped it in the bin. I heard a few alleycats squawking over it. I'm sure they enjoyed it more than I did.'

'That's disappointing. I was looking forward to having some of it.'

'Believe me, it tasted just about as bad as everything else that day.'

'I'll take your word for it. Now give me your coat and make yourself at home.'

She did that. When she sat down I could almost feel the pressure lifting off her shoulders.

'The house rules are as follows,' I said, 'No wild parties or anti-social behaviour. Don't leave dirty clothes hanging around the place and don't leave the hot press on. Don't speak until you're spoken to and don't have any visitors without informing the landlord and the landlady. Above all don't have any visitors from Chester. Under any circumstances.'

'You don't have to worry about the last one anyway, whatever about the rest.'

'I'll keep a frying pan behind the door to hit Edward a bang with if he shows his face.'

'It would be long overdue.'

As soon as she was settled she went into the whole saga about Kate again. A lot of it was new to Kevin. It was good to hear her talking about him without having to face him.

'Of all the people in the world,' she said, 'Why did I have to pick him?'

'Marriage is a lottery,' Kevin said.

'I really feel I'm really putting you out,' she said. 'What will you do if Hanratty arrives on your doorstep about something?'

'We'll put you in one of the wardrobes. I'll get an oxygen mask from the Mater. You can stay there for days - provided you can sleep standing up.'

'You mean like horses do?'

'Exactly. Better still, we'll put you up in the attic like Anne Frank.'

She didn't talk much for the first few days but when she started it gushed out of her. She knew so much about Edward she could have written a thesis on him. It was a pity it was all too late.

'I should have listened to you,' she said, 'You have an intuition about people.'

'I don't know about that. I'd never have predicted what he was capable of.'

When she said he'd actually hit her one day I almost went through the floor.

'He was out of his mind with drink,' she said. 'He just pushed me out of his way really. He was trying to get at something in the fridge and I was in his way. I was off balance at the time and I went flying. I was lucky I didn't crack my head off the floor. It was a tiled one.'

'I'd have been out the door after that,' I said, 'When they do it once they'll do it again.'

'Don't ever tell Daddy that, by the way. He'd be over there on the next plane to sort him out.'

'I know. He'd swing for him.'

'Were you badly hurt?'

'Not physically but my nerves went to pieces afterwards – at least if they weren't in pieces already. I used to dread the sound of him turning the key in the door. I was permanently wired up.'

She'd lost a lot of weight with all the stress so I tried to fatten her up. She wasn't able to eat much food so I plied her with vitamin pills instead. I'd heard Veronica talking about them. They were new on the market. She said they worked wonders for you if you were run down.

The stronger she got, the more she talked. It was like a release for her. She babbled on about all the things that had gone on between them. Our eyes grew wider with every anecdote about the man she was now referring to as 'Lord Edward.'

'He told me he wanted an open marriage one day,' she said. 'It was as if he was one of those hippies from California. I know what was behind that now. He wanted an alibi for his philandering. I don't think he'd have been too happy with me being "open" but he knew there was no chance of that.'

'He sounds like the original caveman,' Kevin said.

'If you can imagine a caveman in a camel coat.'

'So what happens next?'

'I'll probably go for an annulment. I want him out of my life totally so I can move on.'

'You're right. Anyway, Maureen Tuohy sounds much nicer than Maureen Baldwin.'

'Do you think he'll fight it?'

'Hardly. Another woman might have tried to get into his millions. I told him I don't want a penny of his dirty money.'

'Do you think even 1% of him wanted the marriage to be a success?'

'Maybe. He's a bundle of contradictions that way. He'd probably have stayed with me for forty years if I let him play around. I don't think he has a conscience about it. It's just the way he is.'

'What about Nick? Is he still on his side?'

'Yes and no.'

'It was a pity he didn't follow up with May,' I said.

'I was very disappointed about that. They seemed so good together at the wedding.' No matter how many problems she had of her own she was still able to think about other people's situations.

'Did she ring him much after the wedding?'

'She was onto him every other day. When he stopped answering she rang me to try and contact him for her. It got embarrassing. I asked him to ring her back. I think he did once but according to Edward the call didn't go well. He was probably just doing it out of duty.'

'You were good to ask him.'

'I had to. She wouldn't stop pestering me about him. No matter how bad things were with Edward and me it was all she wanted to talk about. She really had a big thing for him.'

'I think she still has.'

'Well it won't go anywhere. I can tell you that for nothing. He's living with Erica now.'

'Don't tell her that.'

'Do you think I'm mad?'

'It sounds like Nick is more like Edward than we thought.'

'There's a pair of them in it. On the surface they're like polar opposites but in my opinion Nick is a bit of a ladykiller in his own way. He comes across as meek and mild but he's far from it. Some girls go for that Little Boy Lost approach.'

'Do you think he's putting it on?'

'No. He's just quieter than Edward by nature. The pair of them remind me of John and Robert Kennedy.'

'With Nick being Robert, obviously.'

'Yes. I was always more attracted to Robert than John. He looked more vulnerable somehow. '

'That's probably what appealed to May about him.'

'It's a pity it didn't cut both ways.'

'Unfortunately it didn't. May was a novelty to him in the same way as I was to Edward. I don't think he meant to give her any ideas about a boyfriend-girlfriend thing. He probably flirted a bit with her because he'd had a few drinks but that was as far as it went. It might have gone further if she hadn't come on so strong. He was only platonic with Erica at that stage. I think May drove him into her arms. She didn't give him a chance to breathe with her persistence.'

'We've all been there, I suppose. When you care a lot about a person you can't play hard to get.'

'I'm not blaming her. I'm just saying Nick didn't lead her on. I could tell he wasn't into her without exchanging two words with him.'

'I smelt trouble from the second she clapped eyes on him. I feel so sorry for her. She isn't used to people saying no to her.'

'Well she better *get* used to it. That's life.'

'Maybe he'll get back with her after he's had his fill of Erica.'

'I wouldn't hold my breath.'

Maureen stayed with us for two weeks. She kept out as much as she could so we wouldn't feel crowded. She tried to give me money for her keep but I didn't let her. She knew we were having a hard time financially since I gave up work but she was much worse off herself. I told her she should have taken some of the furniture from the house in Chester and hocked it.

'If I did that,' she said, 'I'd probably be dining at Her Majesty's pleasure tonight.'

Most evenings she came home with food for us or some knick-knacks she'd picked up in charity shops.

'They're all I could afford,' she'd say. I was always annoyed with her for spending money she hadn't got in some mistaken idea that she had to pay us back for putting her up. The more I did it, the more she bought. That was Maureen. She had to be doing something for you.

She did a lot of cleaning as well. 'You should go into this kind of thing full time,' Kevin said when he saw her work. Before we knew where we were she had the place looking like a new pin. Even the cutlery was gleaming. Kevin was used to me doing the knives and forks on a lick and a promise but with Maureen you could almost see your reflection in them. No matter how many times I washed something I could never get it as clean as she did. She had the same knack Mammy did that way. She even did some wallpapering for us. She was able (unlike yours truly) to get it done without having my inevitable bubbles peeping through.

'Your DIY talents amaze me,' I told her.

'I'm doing this as much for myself as you,' she said, 'It helps me get my mind off Chester.'

After a few weeks the worry lines disappeared from her face. She was able to talk about Edward now without grimacing.

The stories about him became comical at times.

'He'd put on this mood music from time to time,' she told us one day, 'It was usually played by weird groups I never heard of. I say

283

"music" but to me it sounded more like someone drilling on the street. I think he did it to avoid talking to me.'

'Or maybe to avoid you talking to him,' I suggested.

'Maybe that was it. Men aren't very good at listening, are they?'

I told her the old joke about the man who said, 'My wife says I don't listen to her. At least I *think* that's what she says.' Maureen laughed.

'Watch it,' Kevin said.

'Sorry, Kevin,' she said, 'I should have said "some" men weren't good at listening.'

'That's better,' he grunted.

'He was probably used to getting his own way all his life,' I said. The sun shines out of his you-know-where as far as his father is concerned.'

'His mother is worse,' she said, 'I'm sure she cooled his porridge for him as a child.'

'It's a pity she didn't stuff it down his throat,' Kevin said.

Maureen threw her head back at that. It was lovely to hear her laughing after all she'd been through.

'Coming to you two,' she said, 'has been better than a visit to ten doctors for me.'

'The pleasure is all ours,' I said.

I meant it but as the weeks went on I could see Kevin was getting stressed. No matter how much he liked Maureen, it was hard on him having her there when he came home exhausted from work and just wanted to put his feet up. When he was on his own with me he liked to kick his shoes off as soon as he came in the door but he didn't know Maureen well enough to do that. He also felt he had to be in good form for her. That wasn't always possible, especially if he'd had pressure at the job with an awkward customer or a sale that went wrong.

At the end of the day I had a special bond with Maureen because she was my sister. He was outside that even if he was the love of my life.

'I'm overstaying my welcome,' she said after she'd been with us a month. I tried to assure her that she wasn't but she wouldn't listen.

She insisted she was going to try and get somewhere of her own to stay.

She scanned the papers every night after that. Kevin felt awkward watching her.

'We're not pushing you out,' he kept saying. Maureen felt as bad for him as he did for her. After a while she started going out to cafes to read the papers. She thought it was making him feel guilty to see her scanning the ads.

I looked at some too. I also made some enquiries from Cora and Hilary to see if they knew of any places. They said they'd keep an eye out.

After a few days she saw an ad for a flat in Harold's Cross. It looked promising. She asked me if I'd check it out with her. I was delighted to.

'It's at the right price,' she said.

When we got to it we realised why. It was located in a tumbledown building. The walls were practically caving in and the presses were hanging off the walls.

'What do you think?' she said.

'I wouldn't put a dog in it.'

'Me either, but this dog can't afford anything else.'

'I don't know, Maureen,' I said, 'You could have more problems down the line with condensation and things like that.'

'It's all I can afford,' she said. 'Beggars can't be choosers. Anyway, I'm not going to be here forever. It's just a stopgap.'

The landlord was delighted she was interested in it. I wasn't surprised. I couldn't imagine anyone else giving it a thought.

'It's probably been on the market for years,' I said to her, 'Ask him for a cut.'

'I will. He was grinning like a Cheshire cat when I said I might take it.'

She got him down a few pounds but nothing significant. She was never good at bargaining.

'Thankfully I hadn't my wedding ring on me,' she said, 'When landlords see a woman on their own with a ring they up the price.'

'Why is that?'

'I don't know. I just heard it. Maybe they smell vulnerability.'

'I hope you didn't tell him anything about Edward or Chester.'

'What kind of a fool do you think I am? No, I just kept it to business. I knew he wanted me to take it more than he was willing to pretend. Renting is all about who needs who the most. If you have a kip in a crowded market you won't have any trouble letting it.'

He was all over her when she gave him the money. It was a month's rent in advance plus the same amount for a deposit. She came around to us that evening to give us the news. She was dangling the keys like a two-year-old.

'A roof over my head at last,' she said, 'and no Edward. I never knew how happy I could be to be on my own.'

'You've done great for yourself to get away from that torture,' Kevin said. He gave her a glass of wine to celebrate.

'You must be broke,' I said, 'If you need anything to tide you over don't be shy to ask.'

'Thanks but I think I'll be all right. Just about. I'll have to get some kind of a job to tide me over.'

'I'm thinking the same way myself. We're all in the same boat.'

'At least you have Kevin.'

'I know, but I don't like being dependent on him.'

'Sometimes I think back to how simple life was in Midleton. You take your house for granted when you're growing up. I remember being embarrassed about living in McSweeney Terrace any time I walked home from school with some of the girls from the fancy houses around the corner.'

'Me too, I'm ashamed to say.'

'It was a mansion in comparison to where I am now. I'm in seventh heaven to be in a place that's in rag order.'

'It's a bit of a comedown from Chester, isn't it?' Kevin said, 'Talk about going from riches to rags.'

'Things like that don't bother me. I'd prefer to be there without Edward than in the Taj Mahal with him.'

'That's what it's all about. Peace of mind.'

She'd brought some things from England that she placed in storage. I went with her to collect them the following day.

'I don't know what I'd do without you,' she said after we'd unpacked them in the flat. 'If only I could have this kind of support from May. I asked her if she'd come up to help me settle in but she said she was too busy.'

'Too busy doing what?'

'Nothing, as far as I could see.'

'She's good at that.'

'May is permanently on Planet May. I got a few phone calls from her when I was in Chester, mostly asking about Nick. But at least we're not arguing. That's a big development.'

Maureen caught a mouse shortly after she was ensconced in the flat. That would have been enough to drive me out of the place but she didn't mind at all. She even took him out of the trap to re-set it.

I assisted at an operation one time that involved open heart surgery operation. I got through it without any major panic but taking a mouse out of a trap would have driven me bananas altogether.

She caught a few more after that. She told the landlord about them but he wasn't interested. He was less smiley now than when she'd given him her deposit.

'It's the cold that's causing it,' he said, 'I've never had them before.'

Maureen doubted that. I told her one of Daddy's old jokes about a tenant who complained to his landlord about the number of mice in his house. The landlord said, 'There isn't a single mouse on these premises.' The tenant replied, 'No, they're all married with large families.'

Her own sense of humour was just as good. 'I was looking forward to the pitter-patter of little feet in Edward's house,' she said, 'but all I got was my furry friends in Harold's Cross. If I could sub-let the place to them I'd be well away. It'd make the rent a bit more affordable.'

She went on a mouse-hunting campaign with the resolve of a missionary.

'I've bought more cheese than I'd eat in a month,' she said one night on the phone, 'Every night I go to sleep to the sound of traps snapping. It's like music to me.'

Then one night it stopped. Were they gone? She didn't know. 'Maybe they're just on holiday somewhere,' she said. She took nothing for granted until her last set of traps lay unsnapped for a week.

Kevin and myself went around to her one night for a meal to celebrate the departure of her furry friends.

'You are now entering a mouse-free zone,' she informed us as we were going in the door, 'They've all moved out. They're currently staying with relatives. Permanently, I hope.'

'I have to compliment you on the way you handled the situation,' I said, 'I'd have been in John of Gods - or Grangegorman.'

'When you've spent a few months with Edward Baldwin, everything is trivial by comparison.'

She brought us into the spare room. There was a basin in the middle of the floor. Water was dripping from the ceiling into it.

'Another delightful surprise I received on Day Two,' she said, 'A leaky roof.'

She didn't make anything of it, laughing it off like a minor problem. No doubt she'd sort that out too. I imagined her going down to the local DIY shop and renting out a stepladder to tackle it. She'd buy sand and cement and have it fixed while you'd be looking around you.

She made a lovely lasagne for us. We swallowed every last morsel. Afterwards we shared a bottle of wine. With soft lights and a few chairs she'd got from charity shops she had the flat looking really spruce. She'd painted the walls and had the floors tiled.

'Where do you find the time to turn a dump into a palace?' I asked her.

'What else do I have to do?'

We got talking about Edward – inevitably. She said she was trying to work up the courage to tell Mammy and Daddy about the situation. When she was in England she'd written letters to them saying she was having some problems with Edward but that they were working them out. She hadn't posted them. Instead she left them with Nick. She asked him to post one of them each week or so to make them think she was still in Chester. He was happy to do that for her in view of everything that had happened with Edward. Maybe it was his small way of trying to make up to her.

Mammy was glad to get the letters but obviously they weren't as good to her as phone calls. Whenever she rang Chester she just got Edward's answering machine. She was on the phone to me all the time wondering why Maureen wasn't picking up. I had to keep giving different excuses.

Then the letters from Nick stopped.

'What's up with Maureen?' she kept asking me, 'I know there's something wrong.' I had to pretend she was busy, that she'd got some kind of a job working with Edward.

'She said she'll be on to you as soon as she can,' I said, trying to fend off her questions.

One day May was up in Dublin with a few of her friends when she ran into Maureen on Henry Street.

'Jesus!' she said, 'What are you doing here? Where's Edward?'

She tried to pass it off by saying she was over for a few days on business with Edward but May kept firing questions at her. She was like a dog with a bone.

'So where is he?'

'Back at the hotel.'

'Why didn't you tell us you were coming over?'

'It was all organised very quickly.'

'So you're not going down to Midleton.'

'We don't have time.'

There was no way May was going to fall for that. She folded her arms and put on her Columbo face.

'Things have got worse between you and Edward, haven't they?' she said.

Maureen knew she'd have to come clean. They went for coffee and she spilled it all out to her.

'I could have told you she was a bastard from the first second I saw him,' she declared. That was hilarious because she'd fallen for his lies just as much as the rest of us had.

Maureen gave her an edited version of events, watering it down a bit as May's eyes widened in curiosity.

'Promise me you won't breathe a word to Mammy or Daddy about seeing me,' she said as they were parting, 'Mammy would kill me if she knew I was here and didn't go down to her.'

'My middle name is discretion,' she assured her. Maureen took that comment with a grain of salt. She doubted she'd be able to resist the temptation to blurt it out with her big mouth.

'I've decided to take the train home,' she said to me on the phone that night after she'd told me of the day's events, 'I can't trust May not to let the cat out of the bag. I'd prefer to tell Mammy myself rather than having her hear it from that one.'

'Maybe she's told her already,' I said, 'She was only up for the day, wasn't she?'

'I can't do anything about it if she has. She said her middle name was discretion. That's a laugh. I felt like saying, 'What's your first one – 'In'?''

Mammy and Daddy were delighted to see her but they sussed something was up when Edward wasn't with her. She said she had something to tell them but wasn't sure where to start.

'I think we know what you're going to say,' Mammy said before she could begin, 'It's a problem with Edward, isn't it?'

The fact that Mammy said that made things easier for Maureen so maybe we should have been grateful to May after all. She hung on every word she said and had a good cry together afterwards. Daddy got all the news later that night. Maureen left out some of the more horrible aspects of her situation but assured them she was going to go for an annulment. Mammy asked her if she had an eye in her head at all to fall for that no-good. Daddy said now that the family was together again everything would be fine.

Maureen didn't tell them anything about her time with Kevin and me or about her flat in Harold's Cross. She said she'd prefer to leave that for another trip.

'When I'm telling them some of the stories,' she said to me, 'I get the feeling they know what's coming next.' At one point Mammy said, 'I had a feeling all along that you were back in Ireland. It was like a kind of sixth sense I had. There seemed to be something fishy about those letters.'

'Mothers tend to know these things,' Maureen said to me afterwards but I always suspected May told her. Whatever way it happened, it was a relief to all of us that it was out in the open now. The upshot of it was that Mammy was glad Maureen left Edward.

'Better now than later,' she said, echoing Daddy's words, 'Just think what things might have been like if she had a child by him.'

Daddy spent a lot of time talking about the wedding. The memory of it came back to him only hazily because of all the drink he took at it. 'It's always the same with these big splashes,' he said, 'They never last. We had about ten people at our one. It's not about love or commitment anymore as far as I can see. It's just a day out for people, an excuse for them to get themselves dolled up.'

He was full of anger at Edward. Maureen knew he would be. 'I know what I'd like to do to him,' he threatened, 'A man like that needs to be put out of commission full time.'

After Maureen came back to Dublin she heard from Nick that Edward had broken up with Kate. 'The lucky girl,' Kevin said to me, 'She got the same escape Maureen did.'

It was a messy divorce.

'Knowing Edward,' Maureen said, 'She'll be doing well if she gets out of it with her own clothes. I can see him hiring the best lawyer in Cheshire to make her out to be the guilty party.'

'He won't get far with that,' I said, 'Kate is a tough cookie - unlike someone else I could mention.'

Nick stayed with Erica. In fact they even set a wedding date. I thought May would blow a fuse when she heard that but she didn't. Time had been a healer for her.

She started dating a boy called Padraig now. He was from Mallow. He was going steady with a local girl called Gina when she met him. From what I heard, she broke up their relationship. She spent so much time talking to Padraig about Nick I don't know how he put up with her.

She went on a lot about Edward - or, to be more precise, about his cheating. After a while Padraig thought May was hinting that he was capable of cheating too, or that all men were. Her endless ranting on about Edward seemed to take her over. It also made her distrust Padraig. I thought that was unfair because she was the one who caused him to break with Gina.

She broke it off with him out of the blue. He tried to get back with Gina but she wouldn't have him. Both May and Padraig ended up alone at the heel of the hunt.

291

May went on a 'boy binge' after that, trading one in for another willy-nilly as she met them. It was painful for Mammy and Daddy to have to watch it. She seemed to be dating them all on the rebound from Nick, replacing one with another like a female version of Edward.

I tried to make allowances for her. No matter what age she was I saw her as the baby of the family. When I was 30 she was 24 but it might as well have been 14, or even 4. I found myself vetting her boyfriends after Padraig, telling myself she wasn't mature enough to make a considered choice. 'Don't try to run her life for her,' Maureen warned me, but I could never stop doing that.

May didn't appreciate any advice I gave her. Maureen told me once that she claimed I was 'worse than Mammy.' I never claimed to be right all the time. Like everyone else I had blind spots. I thought some men would have been ideal for her and they turned out to be nightmares. Sometimes it worked the other way. No matter what I said she fought with me. Did I steer her on the wrong course sometimes? I'm sure I did. I spent a lot of sleepless nights guilt-tripping myself about that.

I was more on the ball with my advice to Maureen, probably because we thought more or less the same way about things. From that point of view, talking to her was almost like talking to myself. Often I'd start a sentence and she'd say, 'We must be psychic. I was just going to say that.' It was like that between us right the way from childhood.

May threw herself into her work to get her mind off her problems with men. After doing a correspondence course in Business Studies she got a job working with a computer company in an industrial estate on the outskirts of Midleton. In no time at all she climbed the corporate ladder. I never doubted she would. She had a very quick mind even in childhood. She was usually just too lazy to use it. Now she had a motivation. Money.

I was glad for her. Whenever I was down in Midleton I used to call in to see her if I wasn't doing anything else. Her office was on the top floor. She felt quite important about that. She had her name laminated on the door.

I didn't succeed in seeing her the first few times I rang. I only got her answering machine. It had a message saying, 'Sorry, I'm in a meeting at the moment.' It reminded me of something you'd see on a television programme. That drove me mad. Why couldn't she say 'at' a meeting. That was the expression she grew up with. It was the American influence. I wondered if the day would ever come when she started putting 'period' at the end of every sentence.

I always found it intimidating meeting her in her office. Even going in the door was tense. She used to go ballistic if I pressed the wrong buzzer. I often pressed the one just above hers, the one for the tradesmen. After I got inside my name would be read out over the intercom. She seemed to enjoy keeping me waiting to see her. It was a bit of a shock to find myself sitting in Reception having a secretary ask me if I'd made an appointment to talk to someone I'd seen throwing her toys out of the pram not too many years before. According to Maureen she was still doing it.

She'd often be kitted out in a trouser suit. She looked every inch the smart executive. Her heels were so high you'd almost have needed a ladder to get into them. Some of the time she didn't even stand up when I entered her room. If she was on the phone there was never any hurry on her to get off it. She probably thought I'd be impressed but I was only laughing inside myself at the childishness of it all.

There was rarely any evidence of the so-called meetings. There were no ash-filled ashtrays or half-drunk cups of tea or sheaves of papers to indicate anyone else had been in the room. In fact the place usually looked about as lifeless as a crypt. Would she have gone this far to deceive me into thinking she was a woman of importance? If she had she didn't know the way I thought. I'd have had more time for someone working in a dead end job in the back of beyonds.

One day when I walked in she even more elaborately dresse than usual. When I complimented her on her ensemble she said, 'I'm afraid it's too Vivienne Westwood.' I hadn't a clue who Vivienne Westwood was so I just nodded dumbly. She might as well have been talking about Clint Eastwood.

When I went into her another day she went one better – or worse. As soon as I sat down she took up the phone. She started jabbering to somebody called Sabrina. She put her hand up to acknowledge me and then gestured me to sit in a chair. I was amused at the whole performance.

'You wouldn't be a dear, would you Sabrina,' she said in this put-on voice, 'and bring in some coffee for myself and my sister.' Then she put down the phone.

Sabrina was what she called her PA. Apparently that stood for Personal Assistant. I couldn't wait to see her. I was expecting this exotic creature but she turned out to be a rough country girl on work experience for the summer. She was falling apart with nerves as she brought in the coffee. The cups were wobbling all over the saucers. My heart went out to her. When she was gone out, May said, 'These young ones. They haven't a clue.' I felt like saying, 'May, there's probably about two years between the pair of you.'

She started clacking away at an electronic typewriter. Her guitar was propped up against the desk. It looked incongruous beside all the company reports. Was it her last nod to the past, a past she'd deserted? Where was the May I grew up with?

She gave me a big lecture about her company's sales. She brought some kind of screen over to where I was sitting and started explaining the images on it to me – unsuccessfully. Afterwards she showed me a graph of the sales statistics, or the 'stats' as she called them. I tried to look intelligent as I scanned it. It reminded me the graphs we had in geometry as a child.

'If the figures aren't up to scratch I'll be on the chopping block,' she said.

'Oops. That sounds ominous.'

'It is.'

'What can you do to stop it happening?'

'This,' she said. She fiddled around with something that looked like a pencil. She ran it up and down her screen. It showed an image of a big tree. It had the words 'Banque Nationale de Paris' written on it. 'The tree has branches,' she said, 'Get it? Bank? Branches?' I was normally slow at puns but you'd have wanted to be a right eejit not to get that one.

'We're adopting a roots and branches approach,' she explained.

I decided not to pursue the point. She opened a drawer. Inside it was a packet of cigarettes.

'Like one?' she asked.

'I wish I could but I can't. I'm going straight. Doctor's orders.'

'Or Kevin's maybe?'

She gave a little titter.

'You've done really well for yourself, May,' I said, 'You'll be running the country yet.'

'Oh for God's sake,' she said, 'I'm only small fry.'

In the following months she got further promotions. Her 'stats' were obviously doing well. Mammy and Daddy were delighted for her. She told Maureen she could get her a position in her firm if she wanted but she didn't. Maureen wasn't really interested in a career but she had to live.

After a series of dead-end jobs to pay the rent she got a phone call from her old boss in the travel agency. He said they were opening a branch in College Green in Dublin and they'd like to have her in it. It was the last thing she wanted to do. She'd vowed never to work in that line of business again but the money was good. She said she'd give it a whirl. As things worked out she got on really well there. It was a much bigger office than the one in Cobh so there was a lot more happening.

She moved from her flat in Harold's Cross now to a slightly bigger one in Rathmines. I fell in love with it as soon as I saw it. It was really trendy-looking. She got herself in with a student set there. That involved going to lots of parties. I was glad for her. She'd missed out on that kind of life by marrying early. 'Rathmines is like the Phibsboro of the south side,' she said to me.' I knew what she meant. There was a buzz around both places. I experienced some of that in the years with Bridget and Cáit.

Maureen, of course, was a freer agent than us. Having been married made her want to live a more active social life. She'd got it out of the way as it were. It seemed to make her more relaxed with men. 'She wouldn't die wondering,' as the expression went. And she certainly wouldn't fall for another Edward Baldwin. Once bitten, twice shy.

It was great to see her coming out of herself in Rathmines. I went to party once with her and I hardly saw her for the duration of the night. All the men in the room were queueing up to get close to her. She took them in her stride with hardly a care in the world. It was the old story: the less you wanted them the more they came after you. Of course she wouldn't let herself become involved romantically with any of them, at least until her annulment came through.

She knocked out a good time for herself going to plays in the Abbey and any good film that was on. She took up a lot of hobbies as well. She was into yoga in a big way and was also considering T.M. I don't know where she got the time for it all.

She spent a lot of time in Rathmines library as well. She'd always had a great appetite for information. She could discuss pottery one minute and ancient Greek civilisation the next. I often thought it was a pity she didn't go to university. She'd have made a great solicitor or accountant if she put her mind to it.

She always played down that side of herself.

'I'm a magpie,' she said, 'always darting from subject to subject. I couldn't handle the discipline of doing one thing all the time.'

I saw a lot of her around this time. Either I met her for lunch in College Green or she came out to us for visits in the evenings. We never ran out of things to talk about. Kevin often said he thought I had more to say to Maureen than to him.

We couldn't tell May about the number of times we were meeting because we knew she'd be jealous. 'Should I come in disguise?' Maureen used to say, 'in case she spots me like that time on Henry Street.'

Mammy would have loved it if Maureen moved back to Midleton. She was always harbouring ideas that we could be a united family again if she did. She even hinted at me moving back with Kevin. I always tried to nip that kind of talk in the bud.

'Maybe we could re-build Clery's down here,' I said to her one day for a joke, 'and Maureen's travel office as well.'

'Don't be sarcastic,' she said, 'It's not nice.'

By now May thought I was a total jackeen. That was absolutely ridiculous. If Cork were playing Dublin in a football match, there was no question who I'd be cheering for. I was a Midleton girl to my fingertips no matter where I lived.

I loved seeing Cork get one up on Dublin whenever there were discussions about which city was the 'real' capital of Ireland. I always enjoyed people like Matt Doolin on *The Late Late Show* during discussions like that. He was from Bishopstown. I remember one time the bin men went on strike and Gay Byrne said to Matt, 'I was down in Cork recently and the streets looked very dirty.' Like a shot he replied, 'We'd do anything to make you feel at home, Gay.'

Daddy used to slag me about being a city slicker as well. He loved jibing me about what he called my 'fancy fashions' if I wore anything half formal. 'Aren't we lucky she's giving us the time of day with her style,' he'd say. I used to poke him in the ribs when he talked like that. He knew I was the last person in the world for style.

Mammy thought he was just tipping me off about the way local people might feel.

'If you're five minutes out of this place,' she said, 'they think you're getting airs and graces about yourself.'

## Endings and Beginnings

My visits back to Midleton became less and less frequent over the next few months. I don't know why. Mammy pleaded with me to get back more but I couldn't make any guarantees on that score. She used to wring her hands and say, 'Why is everything so complicated with you?' It really guilt-tripped me when she put it like that.

Maureen went through something similar. Mammy got clingy to her now that she was split from Edward. She felt her life would be taken over by her if she spent too much time in Midleton. It would have been done with the best possible will in the world but it would have made her feel more and more like an object of pity for Mammy.

She was busy trying to get her annulment pushed through to open the way for her to meet someone else. Her religion wouldn't have allowed her to see anyone without that. My own reasons for not going down more were different. I hated people coming up to me in the street with that 'Anything stirring?' look on their faces. But I hated myself for not making more of an effort to get back. As well as being lonely for Mammy and Daddy I missed the visits to Aunt Bernie. She wasn't in good health now, battling rheumatism and osteoporosis.

The year after Maureen's marriage broke up, Grandad and Granny both died. I don't know how Mammy found the strength to come through that time but somehow she did. If it wasn't for Daddy she'd have crumbled. He was there for her every time she needed to talk – or not talk. He knew how much they meant to her even if she thought differently to them about life.

Granny was a good age when she died so it wasn't a huge surprise to me. I visited her in hospital whenever I was home. She used to say she was sorry she wasn't nicer to me when I was a child. I told her I never thought that. My only problem with her was that she was too much under Grandad's thumb. She always knew I liked my other Granny more and I felt bad about that. I shouldn't have blamed her for the way she went on about class. It wasn't her fault that she thought Daddy wasn't good enough for Mammy. Neither was it her fault that she disapproved of me becoming a nurse, or even when she said Kevin was only a shop boy. Ideas like that were engrained in her. She couldn't help them.

Grandad was totally lost without her. Mammy did her best to comfort him and so did Aunt Bernie. She even went on compassionate leave from the Post Office to be with him more. That helped a bit but nobody could fill Granny's shoes for him.

Mammy called in as much as she could but he hardly acknowledged her. He just kept looking into space all the time. His legs were bad with varicose veins now, so bad that he could hardly walk. He had emphysema too. Listening to him cough was like listening to pipes rattling. He made Daddy's asthma sound mild by comparison.

He spent a lot of time in a wheelchair. No matter how many times Aunt Bernie tried to get him to go out he refused. The days were long for him sitting around with nothing but his memories. It wasn't easy for Aunt Bernie either. She found his moods dragging her down.

After a month with him all the time she went back to work. Grandad hadn't realised how much he needed her around him. Mammy stepped in but she couldn't give him as much time as Aunt Bernie did. It was then he went downhill. We wanted him to go into an old folk's home but he wouldn't. He'd always been fiercely independent and he wasn't going to change now. A carer came in twice a week but she only did the practical things. She wasn't much company for him.

He looked distraught any time I went to visit him. If I asked him questions he didn't even seem to know what I was saying. He kept looking at photographs of Granny from an old album. One of the photos had the two of them in it. They were just after playing a game of tennis. Their arms were wrapped around each another. They were beaming at the camera and looked really happy, their whole lives stretching before them. I couldn't stop looking at it. It was so different from the severe couple I knew growing up. He kept her old letters to him in the album too.

Many of them were from that time. Now and again he asked me to read them to him. His eyes were bad. He couldn't make some of the words out. I was glad to be able to do that for him. Aunt Bernie couldn't because it made her too emotional. They were lovely letters.

It meant so much to him. As I read them to him his eyes would fill up with tears. But they were warm tears. I knew he was back in the time they were written as he listened to the words.

He only lived for six months after Granny. He hardly ate at all in that time. I tried to get him to take Complan and other food supplements but he wasn't interested. I felt he was starving himself to death There was nothing I could do about it. He wasn't much more than skin and bone.

The only thing that seemed to give him any comfort was drinking Bailey's. It was his favourite potion all his life at the social clubs he went to. It was almost like drinking tea to him now. He just kept filling one glass after another. God only knows what his liver must have been like. I tried to think of some way to water it down but I couldn't. In the end it was the Bailey's that did him in, that and the grief.

Aunt Bernie found it hard being on her own after he died. Losing one parent is bad but being without any at all changed her whole life. She'd had her problems with Grandad and Granny over the years but they were her world. She was lost without them.

'I took them for granted,' she said to me at Grandad's funeral, 'I thought they'd live forever.' She loved them to bits even though they'd stopped her having a full life. Every man she ever looked at after Dan Toibin was treated as a potential ne'er-do-well, someone who'd use and abuse her. What chance had she got to ever become close to any of them? She might as well have been in a nunnery as far as I was concerned. After a certain length of time she seemed to stop wanting a man, becoming old before her time.

Whenever we called to her now she was quieter than usual. After Grandad died I felt she needed her job more than ever. I hoped it would take her out of herself  but instead of that she said it was getting her down. She decided to take early retirement. When she did she had too much time to grieve. That was the worst thing in the world for her.

Mammy told me one day that the  retirement wasn't totally her idea. Some of the customers had started complaining about her being confused at her work, about her giving them the wrong change and things like that. Sometimes, apparently, she'd even addressed packages incorrectly. She only got a modest pension. That made us wonder how she was going to be able to make ends meet. Mammy thought she should sell the house and move into a smaller one. 'It'll get you away from your memories,' she said. But she couldn't make that leap. Like Grandad she was too tied to them.

I could never figure out how she filled her evenings. She didn't have any hobbies apart from these jigsaws she used to do. Some of them were the size of the living-room table. When they were finished they looked like paintings. I thought it was a shame to break them up but as soon as the last piece was in she was already on to the next one.

Because she didn't take care of her appearance, a lot of people in the town started making fun of her. She became this strange woman who emerged from her house at unusual hours to walk down by the river in her dark clothes. Some people thought she wasn't the full shilling. They'd nudge each other as she approached. I'm sure she noticed that. It must have been terrible for her to be living in a place where everyone was so cruel.

May, sadly, fed into that kind of bad-mindedness. She joked about 'batty Bernie' with her friends. She was embarrassed to be seen with her, regarding her as little more than a pathetic spinster who was bringing down the family name. There was also talk of her having a drink problem. People tended to say that about anyone who was eccentric. It was a total lie she was practically a Pioneer.

I wished I could have been there to make her feel better about herself when all this was going on. I tried to be with her as much as I could after Grandad's funeral but I didn't want to make Mammy feel neglected either. He was her father too.

Any time I went down to her she changed the subject away from herself, asking me how Kevin was, or Maureen, or if I missed the nursing. I kept jabbering on about this and that but I couldn't stop thinking about the way her life had been cut off before it even started. She never looked for sympathy and that made you want to give it to her all the more. I don't think I ever saw anyone with more passion in her than Aunt Bernie but she always kept it under wraps.

On a whim one day I phoned her to ask her if she'd like to stay with us for a few days. To my amazement she agreed. She looked stick-thin when I collected her at the train station and I wasn't slow to tell her so. As soon as I got her to the flat I sat her down with a big dinner in front of her, telling her I was packing her off on the next train to Midleton unless she ate every bite of it.

'You're making me feel like a child,' she said. I had to stand over her to make sure she ate it. 'Now I can see how much of a bully you must have been in the Mater,' she said.

By the end of that week she looked a bit better. Her rheumatism was bothering her but she didn't go on about it. She told me how low she'd been after losing Granny and Grandad. She felt she had to leave her job even though it broke her heart to do so. She had so much time on her hands without it. I told her she needed to get some hobbies so she said she'd work on that.

We had great chats in the evenings. They brought her out of herself more. I persuaded her to take a few glasses of wine one night. Mammy couldn't believe that she'd come out of herself as she'd been unable to get through to her at all since she left her job. 'What kind of magic did you use?' she asked me. I said there was no magic at all. I simply talked to her like a normal person.

She was a different woman when she went back to Midleton after the few days. When she rang to thank us for having her she sounded bright and breezy, just like the old Aunt Bernie.

'I've taken your advice,' she said. It turned out she'd applied to teach reading to dyslexic adults. She was also visiting people in old folk's homes. 'They're not hobbies, Aunt Bernie,' I said, 'They're good deeds.'

After that she started to come up to us every few months. Maureen came over as well. Sometimes we drove her to Bray for the day. We liked walking along the promenade. Kevin was the fittest of us. Whenever he got the chance he climbed Bray Head. We preferred to sit in a café like layabouts and watch the ships passing by.

'Isn't this like the old days in Ballynamona?' I said to her one day.

'Yes,' she said, 'except you're not on my knee anymore in the back seat of your father's car.'

Maureen and myself went swimming if it was a fine day. Aunt Bernie usually did her own thing when we were in the water. I'd see her walking along the prom with her hands clasped in front of her.

Sometimes she stopped and looked out at the ocean. It was hard to tell what thoughts were going on in her head. Was she thinking about Granny and Grandad? About Dan Toibin? About the way her life might have gone if she'd married him?

One day when Maureen was talking about Edward she said to her, 'Aren't you the lucky one that didn't get married.' I was wondering if she'd be sensitive about a comment like that but she didn't seem to mind. I envied Maureen her ability to talk about things I couldn't. I was never be able to mention the subject of marriage with Aunt Bernie without feeling awkward.

By now Maureen's annulment had come through. She was relieved as she knew these things often dragged on for years. It meant she was free to date other men if she wanted. There was no rush on her to do that after what she'd been through. It also meant Edward could do the same. Not that he'd have been too bothered about such technicalities. He was still with Kate according to Maureen. They were planning to go to the altar.

'It will give "Jonathan" another opportunity to ring his praises at the speeches,' she said. I was wondering if Kitty would come out of her shell more at this wedding. She probably would. She now had a respectable Protestant girl to welcome into the family instead of a peasant from 'Eire.'

Maureen felt bad that she didn't go back to Midleton more. It was difficult for her to arrange it now. She was as caught up in her life as I was. After establishing herself in the travel agency in College Green she went on to become the manageress of it. 'Can you imagine me as a manageress?' she said, 'I feel a total fraud. One of these days they're probably going to find out I haven't the faintest idea what I'm doing.'

Her job involved overseeing other branches that were opening up in different towns. Being Maureen she totally played down her responsibilities.

I often asked her if she ever thought of going back to Midleton to live. She said she was afraid if she did that she'd turn into another Aunt Bernie. Any time she was down there Mammy smothered her with attention. At the end of her visits she'd say the thing that used to annoy me so much when I was down there,

303

'What are you going back to Dublin for?' Occasionally she added, 'It's not as if you have a husband waiting for you.' She didn't realise how hurt Maureen was by that line of thinking. May would have given her her answer if she talked like that to her. Mammy failed to realise there was more to life than getting a man. It applied to Maureen more than anyone after her experience in Chester.

'Edward cured me of marriage,' she said to me one day.

May had a more relaxed attitude to men. She dated them when she felt like it and dropped them at will. They were like light relief from her work to her. I thought her behaviour was a result of what happened with Nick. It was as if she was getting her revenge on him by treating other men like she believed he treated her. Whenever I asked her about him, all she'd say was that he was 'as thick as Edward.' Far from being the Sir Lancelot he appeared at the wedding, he was now mud. That was usually the way it was with May. There was no middle ground in any discourse. People were either gods or devils.

Kevin was one of the gods, thankfully. Maureen felt that way about him too. The pair of them were always killed praising him. He could do no wrong in their eyes. 'You really hit gold with that guy,' Maureen used to say to me. May put it more bluntly: 'Why couldn't he have met me first?'

They loved watching him play-acting with me when they visited us. If he was cutting meat for the dinner sometimes he'd put on a mask and pretend to be a surgeon. I'd have to stand beside him with the carving knife. He'd go, 'Nurse! Scalpel!' Then he'd say 'Scissors!' or some such nonsense. When he was finished his instructions he'd attack the leg of lamb like a madman.

Other times he'd do childish things like crawl up behind them when they were sitting on the sofa and let out a big shout. They'd chase him around the room and start punching him. A few moments later they'd all be in a heap on the floor. He used to tickle them until they screamed.

'Why don't you play with me like that?' I'd ask him.

'Because you're too serious,' he'd say. Maybe I was. Maybe he'd have had more fun with them.

'Ah, you'll do for the moment,' he'd say, ruffling my hair.

They used to go into hysterics when they heard him singing in the bath. He had a voice like a crow but that only made it funnier. One day May poked her head in the door just as he was getting out. He was in the nip. She looked him up and down. Then she said, 'Not bad, I wouldn't throw you out of the bed for eating peanuts.' He whipped a towel around himself like lightning to preserve his modesty.

'As for the singing,' she added, 'Don't give up the day job.'

When Maureen and May were around I tended to slip into the background with Kevin. I didn't mind doing that. They seemed to find fun in everything he did, even the way he used to whistle as he spread the papers all over the floor for a read after Mass on Sunday. He always went to the sports supplements first, leaving the news items for afterwards.

If there was an earthquake in South America it was less important to him than a soccer player from Athlone letting in an own goal in some match nobody would ever hear of. Anything even vaguely newsy about soccer meant a call to his father. Listening to him chatting to him in his excited voice you'd think the town had caught fire.

After finishing the sports section he'd go to the main paper.

'Now,' he'd say as he opened it up, 'Let's see what's happening in the big bad world.' He'd let out a guffaw if he came across something funny. If he was feeling mischievous he might act it out like a child. That used to drive me crazy. If I gave out to him May would tell me I was being a spoilsport.

'What's wrong with a bit of fun?' she'd say.

I knew I could be a pain in the neck at times. One night we had a ferocious row when he came in from a football game. There was muck from his boots all over the carpet. I hated arguing in front of the girls but May seemed to enjoy it. If either of us raised our voices I'd see her widening with a kind of perverse fascination. Once or twice she'd go to him to comfort him. I took that as a dig at me. I often felt like telling her to mind her own business but I usually bit my tongue. Mammy used to say, 'Better be sorry for what you didn't say than what you did.' It was good advice but I felt May overstepped the mark at times.

305

One night I asked Kevin if he'd like to have married someone like May. All he could do was laugh. 'We'd be at each other's throats in five minutes,' he said. That was a relief to me. He told me he went down to the pub with her one night when I was in the Mater and she wore him out. He wasn't able to do a stroke of work the next day in Clery's. She loved being out. She thought I lived a boring life sitting in most nights. There was no point telling her we had to do that if we were ever to get away from Hanratty and buy a place of our own.

By now we were thinking in those terms. Even though I was only getting part time work and Kevin was hardly earning a king's ransom we'd been careful with our earnings and had a decent amount put aside. We knew it was money down the drain paying rent so we started thinking seriously about applying for a mortgage. Some weekends were devoted to little but looking in auctioneers' windows to see if something suitable appeared. Most of the houses pictured had no prices displayed.

When we went into an auctioneer's one day to check out what they cost we found most of them were way out of our reach.

'What kind of house are you looking for?' said an officious-looking man behind the desk.

'Hopefully one that won't fall down,' I said. He thought I was being sarcastic but I wasn't. I just wanted some place to call my own.

We spent the next few weeks searching. Kevin said it was almost like having another job. Each evening after tea we drove around looking at anything vaguely habitable. We finally found a place in Coolock that had everything we wanted.

It was semi-detached. It had two bedrooms and a little garden in the back with a glasshouse in it. It was nothing special but the second we saw it we both knew it was what we wanted. It was small but we felt we could get around that even if we had children - which, needless to say, we hoped to have. People raised up to a dozen children in some of the houses on McSweeney Terrace when I was growing up but of course the world had changed a lot since then, of course. People had become much more demanding about the size of their rooms, especially their kitchens. I knew some women who wanted kitchens big enough to raise cattle in.

'Are you thinking what I think you're thinking?' Kevin asked me as the estate agent led us around.

'Are you thinking what I think *you're* thinking?' I replied.

We both started laughing. It was like the way we felt about each other when we were going out first. A ton of weight fell from our shoulders as we realised we were both in love with it.

Things got less funny when we decided to go down to the bank manager to apply for a mortgage. Kevin was nervous about it. He wanted me to do the dirty work.

'Just bat your eyelashes at him and he'll give us the green light,' he advised.

'What planet are you living on?' I said, 'It doesn't work like that anymore. We're living in a world of hard business. I don't even have a job.'

'The marriage bar won't be there forever. You have a skill. That's the important thing. People are always going to be sick.'

'I know, but are they always going to be buying carpets in Clery's?'

'Don't be so negative.'

'I'm only playing devil's advocate. These are the kind of things he's going to be asking us. We might as well be prepared.'

We went in together. The bank manager was called Mr Gageby. (Or as we later christened him, Mr Mortgage-by). He was a fat little man with a bald head. His forehead was so slanted it looked like the back window of a Ford Anglia. He also had a terrible case of BO. It seemed to be coming out from under his arms. But we weren't there to like him. We were there to try to get him to like us.

I tried not to look as if I was in pain as he came out of his office but I could have done with some clothes pegs to put over my nose. He told us that he'd be with us in a few moments.

My knees were rattling together with the nerves.

'Relax,' Kevin said as he saw me quivering, 'He's not the Pope. He's just another wage slave like the rest of us. He's probably got the IQ of a bunch of parsnips.'

'I don't care. No matter how stupid he is he has power.'

He came out a few minutes later.

'I'm ready for you now,' he said.

307

'Thank you,' I said meekly. My tongue was so dry I could hardly get the words out.

When we got into his room he motioned us to sit down. He perched himself in his chair like the petty dictator he was. The odour coming from him was horrendous. With all his money, I thought, could he not have bought something to treat it?

He rummaged through our file with an expression of deep concern. He had a double chin that was doing its best to conceal itself behind a shirt that was buttoned to within an inch of its life around his adam's apple.

'So we're looking for a mortgage,' he said. I hated people who used the royal plural. Some of the doctors in the Mater did it and it really got on my nerves. It was so condescending. 'And I see we're going for a fixed mortgage,' he continued, 'Good thinking.'

He ushered us to our seats like a head waiter in a hotel. 'Let's dispense with the preliminaries and get down to business,' he said, 'You want the money for a house from us.'

I felt like saying, 'No, fattie, we want the money for an all-expenses paid trip to Disneyland.' Unfortunately, that would have been the end of our mortgage. Instead I just gave him the sweetest smile I could muster up.

'We're all trying to get on the property ladder these days, aren't we?' he said.

'Indeed,' I assured him.

He opened our file. The questions on it were endless. We seemed to have told him everything about ourselves except Kevin's inside leg measurement.

'So you're not working at the minute,' he said to me.

'No,' I said apologetically, 'but that could change.'

He grunted. One point lost.

'But you, Kevin – can I call you Kevin? – have a relatively steady job. Or at least as steady as anyone can say in these uncertain times.'

Kevin gave an uneasy laugh. We found ourselves slavishly licking up to this smelly little man. I kept trying to think of him like a wardrobe as Kevin suggested. He would have been a very oversized one.

'There are a lot of couples applying for mortgages at the moment,' he said in an ominous voice. 'There's a long list and a short list. To get on the short list requires something quite special in the way of earnings. You two don't have that, I'm sad to say. However, because of the sizeable deposit you've saved, there might be some wriggle room.'

He paused there. That made me feel even more uncomfortable than I was already.

'The other thing,' he said, 'is that property prices are now going through the roof.'

'no pun intended,' Kevin said.

Mr Gageby looked up at him.

'I beg your pardon?' he said.

I kicked Kevin under the table. I knew he wasn't exactly going to be the comedian of the year.

Nnothing,' Kevin said.

He went silent for ages, tapping his index finger on his lower lip as he surveyed our file. The expression on his face suggested he was about to reveal the Third Secret of Fatima.

I was proud of Kevin for what he said next.

'If you can't help us, just let us know now and we'll try some other bank. We don't want to waste your time and I'm sure you don't want to waste ours.'

That took the wind out of his sails. Now he knew he wasn't the only game in town for us. He looked at Kevin with an expression of disdain. He paused for another few seconds as he chewed on his finger. Then he said, 'Look, taking everything into account you seem like a good bet. I think we can do business with you.' Result!

I felt like letting out a scream of joy but I kept my emotions in check. He put a few forms in front of us and asked us to sign them. There were Xs all over the place. Every time we saw one we had to put our signatures beside it. 'This is like Spot the Ball,' Kevin said. We could have been signing our lives away for all we knew. You'd have needed a microscope to make out the small print.

He scrutinised them all and then stuffed them into a drawer. He stood up and we did likewise. He shook hands with Kevin but just nodded to me. After all, I was 'only' the (non-working) wife.

'If there's any change in your circumstances,' he said, 'Obviously we'd need to know post haste. And I don't need to tell you that failure to meet the payments will result in the immediate cancellation of our agreement.'

We nodded again. He gave a sickly smile as he said, 'But I'm confident that won't happen.'

We were very business-like as we said goodbye to him but when we got out onto the street I jumped for joy.

'Easy on, there,' Kevin cautioned, 'Do you realise we're going to be in hock to that sad little man in there behind the desk for God knows how many years?'

'Who cares. We'll have a house soon and he won't be able to do a damn thing about that. We won't even let him in the door if he calls.'

Kevin still had a hard face on him.

'It really sticks in my craw,' he said, 'to see nobodies like him acting like gods. Sometimes I think I'd prefer to give Hanratty her twelve pieces of silver than sell my soul to the people who work in banks. These idiots make so much of a compliment out of the loan you'd think they were paying for the house themselves. Did you hear him trying to pull the wool over our eyes about the sad state of the economy? The bottom line is that he'd be out of a job if it wasn't for people like us.'

'Don't be such a grouch. You should be delighted we got this far. What side of the bed did you get out of this morning?'

'I didn't like him, end of story.'

'Do you think I did?'

'People like him try to make you feel small. They have a little bit of power and it goes to their heads. I see it all the time in Clery's. The smaller the job, the bigger the ego. Put a beggar on horseback and he'll ride to the devil.'

'Maybe you're right. I don't care if you are or not. He's just the middleman. We got what we wanted out of him. That's all I care about. And you took him off his high horse when you threatened to go somewhere else.'

'I was glad about that. I didn't want to let him know I was sweating inside. I was bluffing if he only knew it.'

'I never realised you were so complicated. Is that how you sell your carpets – by pretending you don't care?'

'I wouldn't give him the soot of putting him on a pedestal. He was bad enough as it was, a total game-player.'

'And you were another one. The pair of you were like two farmers at a mart, bargaining over a sick cow.'

'I knew from the cut of his jib that he was going to try and make us beg for something we should have been given right off the bat.'

'You're always analysing people, aren't you? I hope you don't analyse me like that.'

'You're unanalysable,' he said. I didn't know whether he meant it as an insult or a compliment.

We put in an offer for the house we liked that very day. Afterwards it was more tension waiting to see if someone topped it. At 5.37 on the following Friday we got a call to say our offer was accepted.

We had the house. I remember the time exactly. I kept my eyes glued on the clock all through the day.

'I've managed to seal the deal,' the estate agent told Kevin, 'You're very lucky. The prices are about to skyrocket soon.' All Kevin said was 'Thank you.' Then he put down the phone.

'You sound very casual,' I said.

'I hate these people who use expressions like "seal the deal." It's so American.'

'There you go again. All I care about is the fact that we got it.'

I ran to the fridge and took out a bottle of champagne. I'd bought it earlier in the day in case our bid succeeded. I hadn't showed it to Kevin. I knew he was superstitious. He'd have seen it as putting the mockers on the situation by being presumptuous.

'None for me,' he said, 'Not after my antics at the flat-warming party. But I'll enjoy watching you empty the bottle.'

I almost did that. I got so squiffy I jumped up and down on Hanratty's couch. Kevin was amused at me.

'If you break the springs she'll kick us out.'

'Who cares. We have our own place now. We can tell her what to do with her stupid couch.'

The next week it was back to brass tacks. We sank ourselves in the insanity of bridging loans and all the other nonsense that went with house-buying.

'We won't be able to spend a penny for about a year,' Kevin said as he worked out our budget. 'For the first twenty years of a mortgage you're really just paying off the interest,' he joked. Or was it a joke? Whatever we paid, though, at least it was going towards our future now and not into Mrs Hanratty's pocket.

He asked for a rise in his salary the following Monday and they gave it to him. To earn it he had to do buckets of overtime. I couldn't do anything except try to rein in my spending.

'No more clothes purchases,' he said, 'I know what women are like when they go into shops.'

'That's not fair. I've been wearing the same old things ever since I gave up work.'

'You'll have to cut down on the fags too,' he added.

That was going to be harder. I'd been threatening to do it for years. This was my opportunity. I dreaded the thought of it but I knew they were burning a hole in my lungs as well as my pocket. Ever since meeting Cáit and Bridget I'd reached for one whenever I had a problem. Could I survive without them now?

After breakfast was the worst time. I always loved one to wash down a cup of tea. It got the day on the road for me after Kevin went off to work. I could savour the sudden silence, sitting with my feet up or maybe ringing Mammy or Maureen for a chat.

'Mortgages are God's way of telling you to go cold turkey,' Kevin told me.

I couldn't argue with that. He'd been going through the same thing with the drink so he knew all about it. The least I could do was try to give him some good example with my own indulgence.

Drinkers were lucky, I thought, because there was no such thing as a 'passive drinker' problem. You couldn't inhale cirrhosis of the liver. Maybe that's why the government seemed to go easier on alcohol than nicotine when it came to health broadcasts. I never thought of myself as poisoning Kevin's lungs as well as my own over the years. Had Daddy poisoned Mammy's? Nobody ever thought like that back then.

312

We lived like paupers for the next few weeks, grudging ourselves even the tiniest luxury. Mammy and Daddy were ecstatic about our mortgage being approved. Daddy sent us a very generous cheque to tide us over the first few payments. I knew he couldn't afford it but nothing made him prouder than to send it.

We were presented with the keys to the house one rainy Monday soon after that. The estate agent came with us. He said he had some paperwork to give us. That took a bit of the fun out of walking up the driveway for the first time. So did the fact that it was lashing rain.

Then the door wouldn't open. The rain made the wood contract. Kevin nearly had to take it off the hinges to get it to budge. He practically had to barge in eventually.

'Wow,' the estate agent said, 'You really want to get in to this house.'

'We paid enough for it anyway,' he shot back. That shut him up.

As soon as we got in we looked at him as if to say, 'You can go now.' I think he was expecting a cup of tea but we didn't like him so we didn't offer him one. He stood there with a clipboard in his hand looking self-important, which amused us. We were the important ones now. We owned the house.

He took the paperwork out of the clipboard and left it on the table. Then he went off with his tail between his legs. When he got to the front gate, Kevin took great delight in telling him to pull down the sign saying 'For Sale.'

It took a while to sink in that we really were householders. Our own shack at last. How long we'd waited. And how sweet it felt. I actually kissed one of the walls.

'We can break up the furniture now if the mood hits us,' I said, 'There's no Mrs Hanratty to say anything to us. We could get an axe and chop every chair to smithereens if we want.'

We went out to the garden to have a look at it. There was a lovely smell of cut grass. The moon shone down on us as if it was smiling. We started dancing around the place like two children. The neighbours must have thought we were nuts. It was still lashing rain but we didn't mind. Every stitch I had on me was soaked to the skin. My nose was running like a tap. We were lucky we didn't get pneumonia. It was like that film *Singing in the Rain* where Gene Kelly went splashing round the puddles in his suit.

Thankfully the back door didn't stick like the front one when we were finished. Otherwise we might have been out there for the night. We'd have looked nice standing out in the downpour, asking the man next door if he could ring the estate agent to rescue us.

'I'd love to know what the stuff in the clipboard was for,' Kevin said, 'To tell us that the house had four walls and a door into each of the rooms?' I don't know where it ended up but we certainly never read it.

We spent the next few days moving our furniture in. This basically consisted of a half dozen chipped cups, two unmatching chairs with the insides coming out and a rusty saucepan. Everything else was Mrs Hanratty's. We didn't dare bring any of it with us. If she found a spoon missing she'd probably have had the guards after us. We certainly didn't need a furniture removal van like some people got. Kevin could probably have brought a lot of stuff on his Honda if he still had it. He'd sold it for a song to give us a few much-needed pounds. I was sad to see it go, associating it with my first date with him.

I was nostalgic leaving the flat. It served us well for the time we were in it even if Hanratty was a bit of a tartar. We had a laugh looking at the carpet where the wine stain was after the flat-warming party. God love Maureen. She'd tried so hard to get it out. Hanratty never spotted it after our re-arrangement of the furniture. It was too late for her to do anything about it now. She'd given us back our deposit.

Kevin said he'd send her packing if she came over to Coolock complaining about anything. We both knew she charged us far more than it was worth, especially in view of the fact that we nearly froze to death in the cold months. Thankfully the days were gone when we'd spend evenings huddled up against her one-bar heater.

The new house had radiators in every room. I couldn't stop admiring them. As soon as Kevin saw them he put on a fancy English voice. 'Now,' he proclaimed, 'is the winter of our discontent made glorious summer by central heating.'

'What's got into you?' I said, 'Is that a poem?'

'I don't know. I heard it somewhere.'

The luxury of the heating gave us the motivation to do the house up. We found we could make a lot of improvements without spending too much. It was amazing what you could do with a little touch here and there. We never bothered in the flat because we didn't own it.

Here it was different. This was our little palace. We wanted to show it off to people looking its best. I was no great shakes in the DIY department but I rolled up my sleeves and mucked in wherever I could.

The icing on the cake was the fact that Kevin still had his carpet token. Now it was time to use it for the whole house. We didn't want to rush into anything so we said we'd get everything else sorted before that.

Some of the plaster was falling off the wall in the spare room so that was the first priority. The wallpaper in the kitchen was enough to put you off food for life so that was the second one. What idiot thought it was a good idea to wallpaper a kitchen?

We had to get a new bed next. The springs were broken on the one we had. It was like being stabbed in the back every night as you laid on it. Then we had to buy curtains. The ones that came with the house had stains on them that looked like they went back to the Stone Age. No matter how many times I washed them I couldn't get them out.

The toilet was a problem too. You had to jiggle the handle to get it to flush. We rang a plumber in but he quoted us such a big figure to fix it we told him to get lost. Kevin did a temporary job on the ballcock by twirling a coat hanger around it. He was nearly as good as Daddy with things like that. I'd have eaten it first.

We painted all the walls magnolia. As Mammy said, 'Magnolia goes with everything.' Kevin got a roller with the can of paint. That helped us get the work done fast. After that it was magnolia for breakfast, dinner and tea.

When we had all the walls nice we decided to put some pictures on them. We went to charity shops and picked up as many paintings as we could. It was Leonardo da Vinci for a pound and Vincent van Gogh for two pounds. (No wonder the poor man cut off his ear).

When we had all the basic things done we embarked on our carpet-buying spree. First off it was hall, stairs and landing, then the two bedrooms and finally the living-room. We went for a moss green colour with a pink motif shot through it.

The floors looked great now but the problem with having something that good was that it showed everything else up by comparison.

That was the thing about renovating a house. Once you started you couldn't stop.

## Back on the Wards

The marriage bar was lifted for nurses in 1973, sanity prevailing in the Irish Constitution at last. It had gone a few years earlier for female teachers, making me wish at times that I'd gone in for that instead. I'd had my fill of hanging around the house trying to fill in the time. I was aching to get back in harness in the Mater. As soon as the law of the land allowed me to do that I was first in the queue.

I re-applied for my old position. I thought I was going to be able to waltz into it but it wasn't as easy as that. There was no day roster available so they told me I'd have to settle for night duty. I wasn't overly enamoured of the idea of that but there was no way I was going to turn down any offer at this point, for the money apart from everything else. Kevin had been taking care of the mortgage payments on his own for so long I couldn't wait to help shoulder the burden with him.

I was almost as nervous going back to the hospital as I'd been on my first day. I met Hilary and Veronica in the canteen the day before I was due to start. I had some vain hope that they might be able to give me some tips.

'I'm so rusty,' I said to Hilary, 'I'll probably drop everything I pick up. I'll be the shivering wreck I was under Joanne Wylie.'

'Don't be stupid,' she said, 'Nursing is like riding a bike. You'll be back in the swing of things in no time.'

She was right. No sooner was I at my desk on the first day than it all came back to me – the routines of checking the patients, taking their pulses and blood pressure, everything that had gone out of my mind during the years of being a housewife to Kevin.

For the next few months we had a kind of 'Hi, bye' relationship with one another. I'd be coming home at dawn just as he was getting up.

'I kept the bed warm for you,' he'd say.

We might have fifteen minutes lying down together before he'd have to get up. I used to sleep till the middle of the day and put on his dinner for him around five. He'd like to have had it at one o'clock but

317

his lunch break was too short for that. I used to make some sandwiches for him as a stopgap.

When he came in from work he'd want to tell me about what happened during the day but by then my focus would be on getting ready for my own shift. The only 'quality time' we had together now was at the weekends. These weren't exactly ideal. By the time I'd adjusted my body clock to daylight hours it was back to the red eye shift again.

Sometimes my shifts lasted up to twelve hours. If there were three of us on we were allowed break it up by grabbing an hour or so of shut-eye under a blanket in the sick bay in the middle of the night. The silence used to get to me. You had to speak in a hush all the time. I tried to walk softly without creaking too many floorboards in case I woke the patients up.

I was usually on for nine nights in a row and off for three. One time I was trying to save up time for a week in Midleton so I worked eighteen nights straight. That was almost the death of me. I remember reading once about some prisoners in Germany during World War II who were kept awake for over forty hours at a go. That was to try and get information out of them. Some of them ended up going mad. I wasn't quite that bad but after twelve hours non-stop I felt my insides erupting. It wasn't tiredness as much as nausea. You'd gone beyond tiredness at that point.

Split shifts were worse. That was when you worked for four hours in the morning and then four again that night, or maybe six. It was 8 to 12 and then 4 to 8, or maybe even 4 to 10. The time you had off in the middle of the day was no good to you. I found I couldn't get myself interested in doing anything because I knew I'd be working again later that night.

I hated going to work in the dark and coming home when the sun was hardly up. It was worse in winter after the clocks went back. There was hardly any light at all then, either going in or coming home.

'I feel like we're living in Norway,' I said to Kevin one day when I it was so dark I almost found it hard to see my hand in front of my face.

'Stop moaning,' he said, 'You're lucky to be in a job at all.'

'It's all right for you,' I told him, 'At least you can see where you're going when you leave the house. One of these days I can see myself walking into a bus.'

'Or not see yourself walking into a bus,' he said. He didn't feel like giving me too much sympathy after all my years living the life of a 'lady of leisure' as he put it.

We were never as busy during the night as in the daytime. There were usually two of us on. Some nights I felt tense writing my reports in the deathly silence of the ward. If the nurse I was with got called away I started to wonder what would happen if there was an emergency and I had to deal with it on my own. One night we had a man with convulsions. I ended up giving him a sedative to deal with the situation. I knew that wasn't recommended but I couldn't think of anything else to do. My old lack of confidence came back to me at times like that.

I wouldn't have minded some more activity on these nights. There was very little to do after you gave the patients their sleeping tablets and settled them down for the night.

I looked back with nostalgia on the happy times I'd spent with Catherine O'Herlihy on night duty. When I thought about it I realised I hadn't found anyone I clicked as well with since. Catherine was long gone from nursing now. She had another two children to bring up by this stage so I only saw her rarely.

If you didn't have much in common with the nurse who was on with you there was nobody to talk to except the patients. I had to curb my instinct to do too much of that for fear of losing my 'professional' status. I remembered the way Joanne Wylie used to have a go at me for that, particularly on the day I had the misfortune to be caught sitting on the bed with one of them.

I tried to drag out tasks like loading the trolley with pills or bringing round tea to people who asked for a refill before nodding off but a few hours into my shift I'd hear the first snores and think: This is going to be another endless night.

Occasionally we got patients who liked to read into the night. This was generally frowned on because the light kept everyone else awake. One time we had a student from UCD who broke his leg playing soccer. He was studying for his B.A. so I didn't like to refuse him. He

319

had a torch in his locker and I told him he was welcome to use it if he put his books under the bedclothes. He was so happy to hear that he practically kissed me. I remembered reading a novel that way once myself when I was growing up.

I never minded patients asking me things in the middle of the night. Some nurses got cranky if they did that but I found it broke the monotony. I was always glad if someone called for a glass of water or a sleeping pill. It gave me a chance to get away from the desk. The more things you had to do, even trivial things, the faster the clock moved towards dawn. It gladdened my heart to hear the breakfast trolley clanking along the floor around 6 a.m. It meant I'd be getting off soon.

I was always looking for ways to get off the night shifts. If I was lucky I got one of the other nurses to swap a day shift with me but you couldn't bank on that. I usually felt bad asking them, especially if they'd recently come off nights themselves, or if I didn't know them well. If they agreed without really wanting to it created an atmosphere between us.

Sometimes they fell over themselves apologising if they couldn't do it. That almost made me feel worse. I hated having to change shifts myself. Just when I'd be settled down for the evening with Kevin I might get a call from someone who had an emergency or a sudden sickness. It was hard to refuse these requests, especially if the person had obliged me on another occasion, but I never gave the best of myself on nights like this.

I did them with a bad grace, which is the worst possible situation for a nurse to be in. I spent a lot of my time hoping the patients wouldn't see my long face. I was bad-tempered with Kevin a lot of the time as well. I was lucky he wasn't affected by it. Either he didn't mind or he didn't notice it. If he did I'd have pleaded 'night-itis.'

When I was back on the 'earlies' again, everything returned to its old stability. I got rid of the bags under my eyes – some of the time they were more like suitcases – and relished doing nothing on my time off. Looking out at the daylight was like a treat in itself. Things I'd been bored with over the past few years now became luxuries. When you were run off your feet at work, doing nothing became something to be aspired to but if you were idle all the time it was unbearable. The people who got the mix right were very lucky.

We became a boring married couple. We were too exhausted to do anything in the evenings except unwind. I often went to bed after tea, falling asleep with a book in my hands. Other times we plonked ourselves on the couch and watched any old drivel that was on the television to pass the time. Some nights we were so tired I think we'd have been happy looking at the test card. We watched shows like *Columbo* and *Kojak* and *Hawaii Five O*. Phrases like Kojak's 'Who loves ya, baby?' and Jack Lord's 'Book him, Dano,' from *Hawaii Five O* became part of our language. I felt I knew these people as well as some of the nurses I worked with. Coming home to them in the evening was like going home to Mammy and Daddy in Midleton. Columbo dressed in an old mackintosh coat that was so crumpled it looked like he slept in it. I felt like doing that in my nursing uniform sometimes. I'd be so tired coming off shifts it was almost an effort to take it off.

It took me ages to re-tune my body clock from nights to days. I yawned my way through a lot of the shifts at this time. For a while I got to wondering if there was something wrong with me. Kevin thought it was a delayed reaction to all the nights. He said I'd probably been working on my reserve a lot of the time and it was catching up on me now.

I thought that could be true but being my usual hypochondriac self I thought there might be more to it so I had myself checked out. When the report on my bloods came back from my GP it turned out I had an underactive thyroid, something I'd suspected for a while. He put me on medication for it and gave me a few tips about changes I should make in my diet and lifestyle. These helped in a lot of ways but the symptoms didn't go away completely. He told me I wasn't helping things by my hyperactive mind. 'It's on permanent fast forward,' he said.

Kevin agreed. He often tried to tell me some story about his day at work knowing full well I'd be a million miles away in my head. One day he said to me after finishing a story, 'Do you think he was right to do what he did?' I said, 'Definitely.' Then he said, 'That's funny, because the story was about a woman.' I hadn't heard a word of it.

321

Worse still, I wasn't even aware I hadn't. I apologised but he said he didn't mind. If it was May she'd have gone through me for a shortcut for something like that.

Mammy thought I was anaemic. I blamed my lethargy on the sudden change in our circumstances. I'd been lazing around for years and now I was expected to be at everyone's beck and call in the ward. I was thrilled to be back at work but it came at a price.

My tiredness got worse when I did overtime. I never expected to have to do this but once again the question of money came into it. I thought my work status would mean all our financial problems would be over but we were being taxed to the hilt now that both of us were working.

Sometimes I thought I'd have been better off not to go back at all. I hated to think of so much of my hard-earned money going to the government. Some people we knew thought we were rolling in it but that wasn't the case at all. May informed me people like us were known as 'Dinkies.' Apparently that stood for 'Double Income, No Kids.' It sounded great in theory - at least until the taxman came into the equation.

We were classed as 'Dulchies' – Culchies Living in Dublin. In both of our cases I think I could say we were reluctant Dulchies. I went to Athlone with Kevin as much as I could. He came down to Midleton with me more often than he used to as well. Now and again we stopped in both places for a few days. It was great to see everyone but I found myself less able for work after these trips.

We argued a good bit about how long we should stay in either place. Kevin wanted to spend more time with his father and me with Mammy and Daddy. That led to plans being changed and changed again, sometimes even when we were in transit. I probably did better than him on the overall number of visits to Cork but then I had more people to see. Anyway, women were generally supposed to be more sentimental about things like that, weren't they?

I hated when we started arguing about where we were last and how long we spent there. Sometimes it suited us best to just go our separate ways, him to Athlone and me to Midleton. The disadvantage of that was that we spent a lot of time working out where we'd meet up. The problems got worse if we were travelling on separate trains instead of in the car.

Tongues wagged if we arrived anywhere separately. May would usually be first to say, 'Another flare-up with Kevin?' if she saw me arriving in Midleton on my own. I could have crowned her when she made comments like that. It put ideas in Mammy's head that weren't anywhere near the truth. I often exhausted myself trying to explain a situation that wasn't even a problem in the first case, leading May to tell me I was protesting too much, that we weren't the ideal couple everyone thought we were after all.

The plain fact of the matter was that Kevin and I had different ways of looking at things. It took us a while to understand that, and to understand how important these differences were. He forgot our first anniversary, for instance, and that drove me into a sulk. It was years before I realised it didn't mean he loved me any the less.

He was well aware of the fact that I wasn't domesticated but it didn't bother him. Ironing was my special nightmare. I could only suffer it when I was watching one of my favourite soaps on the television. I blame some of the more exciting episodes of *Coronation Street* for most of his scorched shirts.

Unlike a lot of men these days he wasn't in the kitchen all the time. I always thought there was something cissyish about a man foostering around pots and pans. Or maybe I was so insecure about my cooking that I didn't like him looking over my shoulder.

He never minded the fact that I wasn't another Monica Sheridan. She was the most well-known cook in Ireland at that time. She was always on the television. Sometimes I found myself wondering if she did anything but eat.

When I got married I could hardly boil an egg. I wasn't interested in fancy dishes or garnishes or any of those things people went to courses to learn. As far as I was concerned you ate to live. I told Kevin the kitchen was a hard hat area for me. If I had a penny for everything I burned I'd probably have had enough money to buy a house.

Things like that didn't matter to him. When I told him beans on toast was about the limit of my culinary expertise he said, 'Beans on toast is my favourite thing to eat. They should have it on Page One of every cook book. Not enough women know how to do it properly. '

'Here's the way I'd write that page,' I said. 'Place bread in toaster. Wait until crispy enough to remove. Fill saucepan with beans. Heat to requirements. Remove from saucepan when sizzling commences. Serves two or more.'

He ate anything I put in front of him, even what we called 'tea dinners.' Daddy would have caused consternation if he was presented with something like that. He lived for his meat. On a good day I got him some pre-cooked shepherd's pie from the shop down the road.

The kitchen almost had to be quarantined if I tried anything ambitious. Before coming into it you had to check for Unidentified Flying Vegetables. If I was feeling in form for it I used to make what I called 'Sunday peas.' They were the mushy ones we used to have as children. Mammy steeped them every Saturday night for the next day. That was why we grew up calling them that. Today, of course, thanks to our brave new world of labour-saving devices, there's no need to do that. Now we can have Sunday peas any day we like. (But the modern ones don't taste half as good)

Much to my surprise, I managed to learn some recipes from a book he gave me for a birthday present one year. 'Is this some kind of a hint?' I asked him as I unwrapped it. He said it wasn't but I had my suspicions. I threw it into a drawer when he gave it to me but a few months later for the lack of something better to do I took it out and started reading it.

I tried doing the dishes featured in it. By some miracle they didn't poison him. I'd watch his face to see if I'd made a hames of them. 'Yummy,' he'd say if he liked them, 'I might keep you around here for a while more yet.' They gave him a break from the fish fingers and got my confidence going.

That's not to say the old me wasn't lurking around somewhere. She made her appearance the day the cooker went on fire. It happened after I put too much grease on a saucepan and it went up in flames. I poured cold water over it but that only made it worse. It set off the smoke alarm. Kevin waved a towel at it to try and stop it but it was too late for that. Eventually he had to take the batteries out. The neighbours were knocking frantically at the door thinking we were being burnt to death.

Another day he nearly had his eye taken out when the top of the pressure cooker came off. It only missed him by inches. By now it wasn't only Unidentified Flying Vegetables but Unidentified Flying Pressure Cooker Lids as well.

My culinary experiments ended when the night duty started to get the better of me. The energy it took out of me meant I had neither the time nor the inclination for cooking. Afterwards it was either back to basics or ordering something in. I was sorry that had to be the case but I couldn't see any alternative. The recipe book was returned to the drawer as Kevin went on what came to be called 'The Night Duty Nurse Famine.' I gave the underactive thyroid as the excuse but it was more of a general exhaustion I was suffering from. He knew all about that from his own work. It had become more pressurising as the years went on.

'We're becoming old before our time,' he said to me one night.

'That's not true,' I said, 'We've just been working very hard at the same time lately. We didn't realise how much it would take out of us.'

Now and again we made a supreme effort to rouse ourselves from our boring domestic routines. I dragged him along to an INO function one night after initially deciding not to go. I was glad I did because we met two people there that we became great friends with.

Cora Furlong and her husband Owen were both from Kerry. We fell into chat with them over a cup of tea after a lecture that was given by a visiting English nun about poverty in Eastern Asia. Cora expressed a wish to go out there some day. She was always thinking about other people.

She obviously had a heart of gold. She'd spent two years home-nursing her father down in Killorglin after she qualified. He had multiple sclerosis so he was a 24 hour responsibility. Cora would never mention anything like that in case someone might think she was looking for praise. It was Owen who brought it up.

He was quieter than she was. He taught Maths in a school in Ballymun. I gathered from some of his comments that it was rough.

One of his pupils was in the habit of bringing knives to school with him.

'Are they not confiscated?' I asked him.

'If we find them they are,' he said, 'but you wouldn't want to look too hard. You might find yourself on the receiving end of one.'

'In Midleton we even had our dolls confiscated,' I told him. He got a laugh out of that.

We used to meet Cora and Owen off and on in pubs, or else go out to their place for a night. They lived in Walkinstown. Cora was a ball of energy. She was always entertaining us with stories. One I remember particularly. It concerned a time she spent in Birmingham. That was where she trained. She told us the most unusual patient she ever had was a soldier who came in one day with a bomb up his rectum. 'It was an artillery shell he used to push up a haemorrhoid,' she informed us. The mind boggled. 'That was bad enough,' she added, 'but it was live. We had to get the bomb squad in to defuse it.'

She had another story about a fellow who tried to shoot himself one night because he'd lost all his money gambling on horses. My own tale of the young lad walking out of the ward with the two drip bags in his pockets was tame by comparison.

I never knew half the time if she was making her stories up or not. She loved being the centre of attention. Maybe she was trying to compensate for the years with her father when she didn't have any social life to speak of.

Kevin nearly fell off his seat laughing at her bomb story. 'My main worry,' Cora said, 'was that it would go off when he was under the anaesthetic. We'd have been in a nice condition with the operating theatre blown to smithereens.'

Owen just smoked his pipe as Cora went on with her yarns. In some ways his life was wilder than hers but he played it down. 'You have to get on with things,' he kept saying as our eyes grew wider and wider over his tales of delinquent youths. Some of them were the children of prostitute mothers and drug-addicted fathers. I dreaded to think how they'd end up.

'I'd say a few cells are already being reserved for them in The Joy,' he said. He meant Mountjoy Jail. He reminded me of Aunt Bernie with his philosophical attitude. He was so different from Cora.

Maybe that's why they got on so well together. If people are too alike, Mammy often said to me, life can get boring.

They only had one child. His name was Alan. They usually brought him with them when they were coming over to us. He was a right little terrier. He was always going around the house fiddling with things. This resulted in more than one object being broken. Cora went into a state any time that happened. I didn't mind unless it was something very valuable. He'd had pneumonia as a baby and they almost lost him. Maybe they spoiled him afterwards because of that.

Kevin and myself wanted children desperately but I couldn't get pregnant for ages. For a while I started worrying it might never happen. I hated going home because I knew the 'Anything stirring?' question would keep getting asked. A few girls I knew in the town had got married recently and were reproducing to beat the band. One woman said to me, 'If it's not for you it'll go by you.' That was an expression I was to hear often. I wasn't sure what it meant. It seemed to be a fancy way of saying, 'you better put up with it.'

Mammy and Daddy told me I was time enough to start a family but they knew I was desperate to have a child. We considered adoption at one stage but it involved too much red tape. I knew couples who'd have given their eyeteeth to adopt but who weren't able to for one reason or another. I thought the rules were far too strict. At the other end of the scale you had all these women who had children naturally but who were terrible mothers. It upset me to see the imbalance.

'There's no justice in the world,' I'd say to Kevin sometimes. 'What's your answer?' he'd reply, 'Make people have to fill in forms to allow them to get pregnant and then interview them to see how capable they'd be as parents?'

He always made little of me whenever I expressed feelings like that and it really annoyed me. 'I'd love to know how you'd take it if you couldn't get pregnant,' I said to him one day. He replied, 'If I could I'd be on The News.'

Behind all the jokes I thought he was more worried than I was about the situation. Down in Midleton Mammy was saying novenas night noon and morning and Daddy wasn't far behind her. Maybe Kevin said a few too. A lot of men didn't want a child too soon after they get married for fear their wife's attention will divert to the baby but he wasn't like that. He couldn't wait to be a father.

After five years of marriage I discovered I was expecting. I'd been missing my periods for a while but I didn't want to get my hopes up in case there was something else going on. Then one day my GP confirmed it. I couldn't wait to tell Kevin. I brought him out for a meal in a candle-lit restaurant and said I had some news for him. I expected him to jump with joy when I told him what it was but I should have known that wasn't his style. All he said was, 'About time.' He tried to act casual but I could see he was very excited behind it all.

Over the next few weeks I started looking in shops for baby clothes, both pink and blue because I didn't know what I was going to have. I read anything I was able to find about what to do and not to in the lead-up to the birth. I bought a book called *What to Expect When You're Expecting*. It told you everything you needed to know – and some things you didn't. I even stopped drinking coffee. To me that was like stopping breathing. I wanted to give myself every chance of having a healthy baby.

Kevin thought I was going too far into the ins and outs of things.

'Just have it,' he said. I told him it wasn't that simple. 'How did our mothers give birth to us without all that stuff?' he wondered.

No matter how careful we are, none of us have control over nature. I wasn't long into the pregnancy before I thought something might be wrong. I started feeling cramps and it stopped kicking. I kept going down to the gynaecologist asking him if there was something wrong. He didn't think there was at first but one day when I was down with him he spent longer than usual examining me, and longer than usual looking at his notes.

'I'm going to have someone else look at you,' he said then, the words I most feared to hear. And yet in another part of me I almost expected to hear them. I knew. You always know.

I miscarried the baby after four months. The reason wasn't fully explained to me. Kevin thought I should have given up work as soon as I got pregnant. Maybe he was right. I didn't think I could afford to but maybe I couldn't afford not to either.

I went into a kind of trauma the day it happened. Kevin took it nearly as badly as me. He was very kind to me at that time. I couldn't stop feeling I was in some way to blame. He kept saying, 'Don't worry, we'll have a dozen of them.' I couldn't be as hopeful as him because it took me so long to get pregnant the first time.

That was the year Daddy's father died. I was down with my GP when I heard the news. I'd been asking him what were my chances of having a healthy baby when Kevin arrived at the door. I knew there was something wrong because he never left work unless it was something important. He couldn't find the words to say it at first. The doctor didn't know what was happening. His secretary came in while he was talking to me. Kevin was behind her.

'I need to tell you something,' he said.

I went out to the reception area with him.

'You better sit down,' he said.

He stuttered and stammered for a few minutes. I had to shake him to finally get it out of him.

I broke down completely when he told me. I probably over-reacted because it was so soon after losing the baby. It was as if everything was catching up on me.

I can't remember leaving the doctor's surgery. When we got back to the house I phoned home. Daddy was so distraught he could hardly talk.

I said we'd be down on the next train. I had to get a babysitter for Cillian. Afterwards I phoned Maureen. She said Mammy told her already, that she'd been trying to get through to me all day but that the phone just kept ringing out. She came over to us within the hour. We all got the train to Midleton together. We were crying most of the way down.

'Poor Granny,' Maureen kept saying, 'How is she going to be without him?'

I kept thinking about my last few visits with Grandad, how I'd seen him tiring during them but not admitting it. He always pushed himself to be at his best for us. I used to see him going up the stairs to bed sometimes and he'd hardly be able to make it up without clutching the banister rail. Even after taking a few steps he'd get winded. He was always too proud to ask for help. If he caught me looking at him he'd try to smile but it was really a grimace.

When we got to the house the door was open. Daddy was sitting in the kitchen with Mammy and Granny. The three of them had their arms wrapped around each another. Aunt Bernie was sitting beside them looking at the ground. Maureen and May were a bit further down.

All the memories of my childhood came flooding back to me as I looked at Granny. I thought of the love she gave me, how I looked forward to seeing herself and Grandad so much, how Grandad would ask us what we were going to be when we grew up. I'd never forget Mutty and the roaring fires and the smell of cooking everywhere.

'What are you doing here, Granny?' I found myself saying, 'Why are you not in your own house?' It was only after I said it that I realised how stupid a question it was. What was there in her house for her now that he wasn't there anymore?

'Where else would I be?' she said.

'I can't believe Grandad is gone from us,' I said.

She shook her head.

'It was his time,' was all she said, 'It was his time.'

The removal was in the Holy Rosary Church. That was where I'd been married. I'd also made my First Communion there. It was spilling out the doors with people. I never knew he was so popular but how could it have been any other way? He was larger than life but now he was gone from life. 'A great man has left us,' Fr O'Kane said at the beginning of his eulogy to him. He went on for a while talking about him but for me that one sentence would have been enough. A great man had left us.

How would Granny survive without him? Or Daddy? Mammy told me he hadn't been up to visiting him much in recent years because of his asthma. Would he visit Granny now? Would she move in with us?

Many of the people from the church came back to the house after the funeral. They all said lovely things about Grandad. That helped Granny get through the day. I kept making cups of tea for them. I had so many myself I thought I'd turn into one. There was laughter as well as tears. How could there not have been? His life had been all about laughter. We'd remember his jovial nature forever.

Daddy had a headstone carved for him the following week. He visited the grave almost every day with Mammy and Granny. Granny came to live in our house afterwards, as I predicted. We all knew it would be the best thing for her.

It gave her the chance to have some quality of life. She was inconsolable for a few weeks but then she came out of herself. In time she learned to live with Grandad's absence but she never stopped talking about him. She was lucky to have been blessed with such an accepting nature.

In some ways Daddy took it worse. He started to guilt-trip himself about not having gone down to see Grandad more when he was feeling poorly. Mammy tried to console him by telling him Grandad understood about his own health not being the best but that didn't do any good. Once Daddy began to blame himself about anything it was nearly impossible to get his mind off it.

Kevin suggested bringing him up to Dublin to see if it would lift his spirits. I appreciated him doing that. We waited for a month after the funeral before making the offer. When we did, surprisingly, he took us up on it. 'Aunt Bernie must have told him how good a time she had with us,' Kevin said, 'Maybe we should put up a hotel sign and start charging.'

The visit, unfortunately, didn't do him much good. He was like a fish out of water in Dublin. He hated all the concrete on our street after spending so many years surrounded by nature. 'Are there no trees or rivers around here?' he kept saying as he walked around Coolock. All he could see were rows of houses that looked exactly the same. 'The ones in Midleton mightn't be much,' he said, 'but at least they're not like carbon copies of each other.' We told them that was the way it was in all the estates but he just kept shaking his head in disbelief.

We brought him for a spin in the car at the weekend. The Austin was living on its reputation by now. The back door was falling off. I had to tie it to the headrest of the passenger seat in the front to keep it steady. The engine sounded like Daddy when he was wheezing with his asthma. Fourth gear hardly existed. I thought back to the days when he'd be driving us to the beach and we'd all have to get out and push the car when it broke down. We seemed to be destined to have nothing but bad cars in the family.

Kevin and I both had to work on the Monday. That meant Daddy was on his own in the house. He didn't know how to spend the day. He went for a walk in Coolock to stretch his legs and then into the bookie's office. After he came back he sat watching television.

When I got home from work he was standing at the front gate watching the people passing by.

'In Midleton at least they say hello,' he said to me, 'Here they just rush by. I'd love to know where they're in such a hurry to.'

I offered to drive him down to Dollymount after tea but he wasn't interested. 'What would I do down there?' he said, 'My legs are banjaxed.' I knew I was getting nowhere with him so I gave up. Sometimes it seemed as if he enjoyed complaining merely for the sake of it.

We drove him home on the Tuesday. Mammy thanked us for having him but it was obvious he was happier in his own backyard as he might have put it himself.

Granny got dementia at the end of that year. She had to go into a nursing home. Daddy took out a loan to pay for her care. It was devastating for all of us to watch her losing touch with a life she loved so much. Her hearing started to get bad at this time as well. She shouted everything at you because she thought you were hearing her in the same way she heard herself. When she got hearing aids she whispered for the same reason. It made being with her very difficult. Sometimes her hearing aids malfunctioned. When that happened she alternated bouts of shouting with whispering.

Sometimes she didn't know us when we went in to see her. That was the hardest part of all for me. It was hard for Daddy too but Mammy thought she was happy in her own world. She always had a smile on her face. Maybe she was better off not having Grandad to think of all the time.

She had periods when she thought he was still alive. She'd ask about him and we'd have to pretend he was back in the house waiting for her to come home. She died the following April, wandering out onto the road one night in her dressing-gown when someone left a door open. It was lashing rain. She was nearly knocked down by a car. The driver realised she didn't know who she was and brought her to a hospital. She died of pneumonia later that night, slipping away quietly in her sleep. We all knew it was better for her.

'They're together now,' Daddy said, 'He'll be keeping a seat warm for her in heaven.'

Daddy inherited the house but he found it hard to go into it. There were too many memories. He put it up for sale almost immediately. I went down to it a few times to try and make it presentable. If he was with me he got emotional. 'I wish you wouldn't bother,' he kept saying, 'Everything you touch brings her back.'

One day when we went down we could hardly open the door for the amount of post that was scattered all over the floor.

'Put it in the bin,' Daddy said.

I knew I couldn't do that. A lot of it looked like official correspondence. When he wasn't looking I put it in a cabinet to look at later. A lot of it was about Granny's probate.

Another day when I was tidying up I found Grandad's 'Tara' mug in a drawer. I thought Daddy might want to keep it as a memento but he didn't. When he saw it, tears coursed down his cheeks. 'Dump it,' he said. I wished I hadn't shown it to him. He was too devastated with his memories. I slipped it into my handbag when he wasn't looking. I wanted it for myself.

The house sold fairly quickly. Daddy probably didn't get enough for it but he couldn't concentrate on things like that now. A fair chunk of the money went to the bank, paying off the loan he took out to pay for Granny's care in the nursing home. Even so, it made him financially comfortable for probably the only time in his life. He gave us all generous cheques from the proceeds of the sale, keeping only a small nest egg for himself and Mammy. 'What do we need it for?' he said, 'We're hardly going to be heading for Las Vegas at our age.'

I didn't grieve for Grandad or Granny as much as I should have. There was too much happening in my life at that time. It was only months afterwards when I was home that it really hit me. I was passing by their door one day and my mind went totally blank. I was going to knock on it when I realised it had been sold ages before and new people were living there now. My feet led me to the door without my head being aware of what they were doing.

It upset me to realise how much I took the two of them for granted.

'Don't blame yourself,' Daddy said when I told him what happened, 'We all do things like that every day of the week.'

God never closes one door but he opens another. A few months after Granny's funeral I discovered I was pregnant again. It must have been all the prayers we were saying.

'No books this time,' he said, 'We'll just let nature take its course.' I agreed. There would be no looking at baby clothes either. Instead of that I decided to take leave from work very soon into the pregnancy. I knew it would be a stretch financially but I didn't want to take any chances this time.

I did very little around the house. Kevin wouldn't let me lift a finger. He did all the cooking while I sat around like a slob.

'Remember you're eating for two now,' he said as he served my meals up to me.

'I always did that anyway,' I told him. It was true. I had a healthy appetite but when I was pregnant I went to town altogether. Some days I could have eaten the leg off the table.

I developed a passion for chocolate at this time. Kevin had a joke: 'Hand over the chocolate and no one gets hurt.' It applied to me. I devoured truckloads of it at every opportunity.

It almost got to the stage where we had to put locks on the fridge. I told Kevin I'd have to change my career description from nurse to 'Eater of Chocolate.'

I watched television almost non-stop for these nine months. There was nothing else to do. It was either that or count the flower patterns on the wallpaper. I got to know the names of all the characters in the soaps. That wasn't just the Irish ones but everything that came in from England and America too and even Australia. I was able to tell you if Rachel was going to drop Rodney when Rodney came back into her life. I watched talk shows with themes like 'My life fell apart when I fell in love with a pekingese' and 'The day I talked to the wall of my apartment in Chattanooga and it talked back to me.'

I read a lot too. Not books on pregnancy (Kevin banned me from these) but the kind of novels that seemed to have been written for people who had a mental age of five. My emotions were so jumbled up I felt that was all my concentration would allow.

It didn't suit me to be idle so I was in bad form a lot of the time. I envied Kevin going out to work every morning. As I got bigger and bigger I thought I looked terrible. I felt I'd gained about five dress sizes. I asked Kevin if he found me disgusting. 'You look beautiful,' he said. He was always a bad liar but I let him away with it.

Maureen called me a lot and so did Aunt Bernie. I was surprised at how much she knew about motherhood. Mammy was on all the time as well. I tried not to ask her too many questions about her own pregnancies.

That was the mistake I'd made with my first one. I knew too much and that wasn't a good thing. It meant you worried unnecessarily about rare possibilities. Sometimes you were better to just let nature take its course.

Was the birth going to be painful? I didn't know. I remembered Cáit saying once that her sister told her it was like having your upper lip pulled over your head, a charming thought.

I was already experiencing some pain in my back. I felt part of the reason for  that was the bulge in my front. It was putting extra pressure on it. There was nothing I could do about that except grin and bear it. It made me want to move as little as possible. I despaired of ever getting my figure back.

Kevin kept asking me if I wanted a boy or a girl. This was long before ultrasound. In some ways we were better off then. Nobody gets any surprise today. I said to him, 'I don't care what sex it is as long as it has two arms and two legs and everything else in the right place.' That was his attitude too.

I had a great gynaecologist but I was afraid of coming across as a know-all to him. It was Irene who recommended him to me. She told me he didn't like treating nurses for that reason so I tried to play myself down. I even went so far as to ask him stupid questions occasionally to give him a chance to hold forth.

He must have thought I was the dimmest nurse in existence. I often wondered how he'd have reacted if he heard I came first in the class at my finals. I said  to him one day, 'I wouldn't know a uterus from a unicorn,' and he gave a big laugh. After that he was super-nice to me.

Sometimes it did you a big favour to play the fool in life.

## Becoming a Mother

As the clock ticked closer and closer towards the birth I found myself becoming increasingly more agitated. When the nine months were up and nothing was happening I was close to panic. I had visions of having to be induced but just as I was getting ready for that I started to get labour pains. I wanted to go into Holles Street immediately but they told me to wat until the contractions got closer. I was livid about that.

Kevin was my mainstay now. I was on tenterhooks right up until the day of the delivery because of the miscarriage. He was brilliant all the time, never losing his cool. When the contractions started he had me in a taxi to the hospital 'before you could say Jack Robinson,' to use an expression of Mammy's.

I felt like someone out of a film as we sped to Holles Street. I was reminded of those ones where the woman was bent double in the middle of a New York street and the man got a police escort for her to the hospital with all the sirens blazing. We weren't quite that elaborate but Kevin told the taxi-man to break every red light as long as he could do it without killing the two of us. 'You mean the three of you,' he said.

When we got there he screeched to a halt at the door. Kevin threw the fare at him through the window and led me into the reception area. I felt I was going to deliver the baby at any moment. I could hardly walk. A nurse found a wheelchair for me and brought me down to the operating theatre.

How often had I walked through corridors like these trying to put patients at their ease? Now I was the one in the hot seat. What was in store for me? I kept trying to remember the things I read in the books I'd read when I got pregnant the first time but it was all gone, my brain turned to putty. I was placed on a trolley and prepared for the birth. Nurse or no nurse, I was a novice as a patient.

The birth was painful but nothing like Cáit made me fear with her lower lip analogy. My main worry, like that of most mothers, was that I might haemorrhage or the head would be turned the right way round. As I felt it coming out I scanned the faces of the medical team for signs that things were going to plan. They kept shouting 'Push! Push!' at me. I felt like saying, 'What do you think I'm doing? Trying to hold it back?' I pushed for everything I was worth until I had nothing left in me. At that moment it eased itself out.

It was a boy. Because of the way he looked at me I felt he knew me already. It was one of the most beautiful sights I ever saw. I'll never forget holding him for the first time. I saw my features in him, and Kevin's too. How could something so small have so many expressions? He had the same playful look in his eyes as Kevin, and the same shyness as well. It was a unique combination. I thought to myself: If he grows up to be half the man his father is I'll be doing all right.

'You had a problem-free delivery,' the midwife said. She might have been talking about a flight that came in on time. I felt like saying, 'How can you say that when I'm after getting 35 nervous breakdowns?'

I was worn out from all the pushing and fell asleep shortly afterwards. When I woke up my baby wasn't beside me. For a few seconds I thought I'd dreamed the whole thing.

Panic started to set in. I rang the bell for a nurse.

'Did I have a baby?' I asked her, 'or just imagine I had one?'

'No, you didn't imagine it,' she laughed, 'Let me get him for you.' A few minutes later she re-appeared with the baby in her arms, all seven pounds of him. All my emotions turned to putty when I looked at him. The tears flooded out of me. He gave me the biggest smile you could ever imagine as he wriggled in front of me. His eyes were like little slits. His fingers looked so small they were hardly there at all.

Athlone were playing in a soccer match that day. Normally this would have been an almost sacred event for Kevin. I suppose I should have been honoured that he sacrificed it to come in to see me. 'I had to leave at half time,' he said. I told him that should qualify him for a gold medal. Was he seriously complaining about leaving a football match? Was he like those men who got so drunk on the night their wives were having babies they missed seeing them until the next day?

I didn't have to wait long to find out. As soon as he saw the baby he melted.

'Everyone says he's like you,' I said.

'I see you in him,' he shot back, 'especially the eyes.'

We called him Cillian. Maureen came in to see him that night. Veronica and Cora dropped in the following day. They both thought he was gorgeous. Cora said he was the spit of me.

Kevin could hardly catch his breath from all the phone calls that were coming from home. Mammy and Daddy were beside themselves. Mammy was a bigger worrier than me but she hid it better. Now she could relax. Aunt Bernie sent me a Congratulations card saying, 'You did it!' May even turned up trumps with a bouquet of flowers.

We brought him home two days later. It was only when I had him on my own that I felt he was really mine. I thought I was going to be a Nervous Nellie with him but I coped pretty well. It's true what they say: You might think you're not 'mother material' but when you hold your little bundle of joy in your arms it's a different kettle of fish altogether. I felt powerful and humble at the same time.

Kevin brought me breakfast in bed the next morning. That was about as big a surprise to me as the fact that the baby had been born without complications. He rang in sick that day to be with me.

He was awkward with Cillian and that amused me. For starters he was clumsy holding him. When he tried to play with him he made noises that made him cry.

'I'm afraid I'm going to be a useless father,' he said in frustration, 'God knows what I'll be like if you ask me to change a nappy.' I told him he'd get the hang of it. In time he did. He also helped me with bottle feeds and burping. What else could I have asked for from him? He was a New Man before anyone ever thought of the term. He drew the line at wheeling a pram though. A man would have been laughed out of it if he was seen doing that in the seventies.

Maureen was over to us all the time helping out. She gave Kevin a lot of tips on how to get Cillian to go to sleep and how to play with him without giving him a fright. I was usually too tired to. I still had pains all over me from the pushing.

It was a miracle I got my figure back after the birth because of all I'd eaten in the nine months. I don't know how I managed it. I didn't even go on a diet. It just fell off.

For a while I thought there might have been something wrong with me. Kevin said it was probably caused by my personality. He knew I had to be on the move all the time. He might have been right. Or else I worried it off. I was always expecting something to go wrong with Cillian since my miscarriage. The memory of that made me treat him like glass.

We had the christening two weeks after he was born. Mammy and Daddy came up for it. They couldn't wait to see him. They were really excited as they held him.

'I hope this is the first of many,' Daddy said.

'Give me a chance,' I pleaded, 'I've hardly got used to having one yet.'

Mammy was subdued. I knew she was worried about my sudden weight loss. 'The labour took it out of me,' I said.

I asked Maureen to be the godmother. Kevin wanted Reg to be the godfather but I knocked that idea on the head. 'Reg is bad news,' I said, 'No matter how much you think of him you'll never win me round.'

Instead we chose a cousin of his from Athlone. He was in Dublin doing a course in computers at the time. We went to a hotel for sandwiches afterwards. Everyone said they were gorgeous but I couldn't eat a thing. Even the look of them made me feel sick.

I went through some post-natal depression in the next few months. I didn't know what was wrong with me because people didn't talk about things like that then. I'd just wake up feeling down in the dumps. I couldn't understand it and neither could Kevin. He was so supportive during the miscarriage I expected him to be the same now but he didn't know what to make of me.

If it was a practical problem he could have helped me, being so practical himself, but this was different. He kept asking me what was wrong with me but I wasn't sure myself so there was no way to tell him. I couldn't explain it to him except to say that I felt empty inside.

'But you have Cillian,' he said.

'You're right. It doesn't make sense.'

Eventually I went to a doctor. I didn't say I was depressed because I didn't know I was. All I knew was I had no energy. He said it wasn't unusual for me to feel drained.

'A lot of women are like that after their first baby,' he said, 'A lot of them feel low too.'

The fact that he wasn't surprised reassured me. He put me on some anti-depressants to stabilise my moods.

'Don't expect any miracles,' he said, 'At the end of the day a pill is just a pill. You have to help it along.'

Sometimes I took them and sometimes I didn't. I was never a great fan of pills. I got momentary relief from Valium sometimes but that was all. Like everything else they lost their effect over time. I was always afraid of getting hooked on anything so I tended to go to the other extreme.

I decided I'd fight this one cold turkey. Ever so gradually, thanks to the love of Kevin and the almost constant presence of Maureen every time I sought her help, I began to return to my normal life. After a few weeks I woke up one morning and thought: This is strange, I feel back to myself again. There was no reason for it, it just happened.

From now on I decided to give all of myself to be the best mother I could be. You won't be surprised to hear that resulted in me spoiling Cillian rotten. I never denied I did that. It's what every mother does with her first child, isn't it? You can't help it. You're so happy being a mother you want to wallow in it.

I knew part of the reason was because of the miscarriage. I hadn't relaxed for the whole nine months of the pregnancy. I kept thinking history would repeat itself. When it didn't he became much more precious to me than the average baby. He got everything he wanted. Enough presents to start a toy shop.

Aunt Bernie sent gifts up to him too. I was touched by her kindness, especially since she didn't have any children of her own. Now and then she came up to babysit for us. She was cracked about him. It was lovely to see her playing with him. She was endlessly amused by the contortions he made when he was trying to walk. There were times when we'd be doubled up watching him.

'He looks like he's drunk,' she said to me one night. It was so true. Most mothers remember when their child took his first step but for me it wasn't that straightforward. He seemed to throw himself into the walking stage in fits and starts.

Maureen and Aunt Bernie reassured me anytime he looked pasty or off-colour. I'd heard so many stories about bugs children could pick up I was a walking worry machine for a lot of the time. I often wished I had their temperaments. They looked as if they could sit on the edge of a volcano and not let it bother them.

I fretted a lot about the possibility of a cot death. Hilary had a sister whose baby died that way. She got depression from it. She spent three months in John of Gods. They did everything they could for her but she was never the same afterwards. It later transpired that the baby's lungs were undeveloped. She still blamed herself for lying him on his stomach instead of his back.

There was no point telling her about the lungs. She had her mind made up she was responsible. Herself and her husband adopted another child some years later but it didn't really help.

They'd been very happy together until the death but their relationship suffered a lot afterwards. Her guilt rubbed off on him. They had money problems as well because she wasn't on a good health plan. Her insurance ran out after a while. She couldn't go back to work so there was very little money coming in. He found it hard to support the two of them and after a few months it all got to him.

He took to the bottle and started seeing other women. He left her in the end, which caused her depression to become worse. The following year she electrocuted herself in the bath with a hair dryer. It was a horrible end to a horrible situation.

Hearing these kind of stories didn't do me any good. I was bad enough without them. Kevin said I shouldn't listen to them but how could you stop people talking? None of us lived in glass cubicles.

To try and ease my worries I bought one of those monitors that let you hear when your baby is crying if you're not in the room. It helped me a good lot.

Maureen came over to us a lot around this time. She was more than happy to babysit any time we wanted a night out. Then Aunt Bernie started to. She was brilliant with Cillian.

'You put me to shame,' I'd say to her and she'd blush to high heaven. One day she found him trying to crawl out the front door when my back was turned. I hadn't even known it was open. 'You could have saved his life,' I told her. Again she blushed.

'You make far too much of me,' she said. She wasn't used to getting compliments so they meant a lot to her.

She was like Maureen in her efficiency around the house. She said it did her good to be active. I marvelled at her ability to move around the place with such quiet efficiency. It was like the way she was in the Post Office. She had jobs finished almost before you knew she'd started them.

I always thought she'd have made a great nurse. 'You must be joking,' she said when I put the idea to her, 'I'd conk out at the sight of blood.' I told her I thought I was that way too when I started but after a while I got so used to it I was hardly even aware of it.

The way she dealt with Cillian made me think she'd have made a wonderful mother. She obviously adored children. If a film came on the television with a child in it she'd almost go into a trance. If it was a sad one about a child that died or was separated from its parents I'd see her eyes welling up. Did she have a child that died? I often wondered what happened to her when she was supposed to have become pregnant by Dan Toibin in her youth.

She never talked about it and I wouldn't have dreamt of asking her. Even though I was dying of curiosity about that time of her life I knew it was strictly off limits. She was great at asking you questions about yourself but she clammed up totally when you asked her one.

Sometimes she was so quiet she reminded me of a nun.

'Reg said you'd know she wasn't married,' Kevin said to me one night.

'That's a bit cruel,' I said, 'What gives him that idea?'

'He said you'd know by the way she carries herself, how closed up she is.'

I hated when he got his opinions of people from Reg. He'd only met her once. It was on a night when he called around for Kevin to bring him out. They were off to the greyhound track together.

'We're going to the dogs,' Reg said to me.

'In all senses,' I said.

He didn't like it when I gave him a smart answer like that. Wit was his department.

Aunt Bernie was nice to him but it wasn't mutual. She just wasn't his type of person. I could accept that. You couldn't get everyone to like you. The problem was that his attitude rubbed off on Kevin. When he came home later that night he started making fun of her.

'How is the crack down in Midleton?' he said to her, 'I suppose you're out on the town every night.'

Bernie didn't know what to say. She wasn't used to him talking to her like that. She clammed up even more than usual when people were sarcastic with her. It put a distance between Kevin and her. Reg was the culprit once again.

Kevin got cheekier with her a few nights after that. It was a Friday and I was looking forward to the weekend. I started drinking wine. I was laughing about something with Aunt Bernie. Kevin wandered into the room. I could see he was amused by us.

'What's so funny?' he said.

'None of your business,' I said, 'It's just women's talk.'

He stared at Aunt Bernie the way Reg might have, as if he was looking down on her.

'We'll have to get you drunk to hear all your secrets,' he said. He knew that was the most unlikely thing in the world.

He started needling her with questions then, stupid questions that had nothing to do with anything. If I didn't know him better I'd have thought he was back on the bottle. I actually smelled his breath to make sure. Aunt Bernie looked at me as if to say, 'Why is he going on like that?' I didn't know what to do about it.

'What do you think of Dublin?' he asked her.

'I don't know,' she said, 'Like everywhere else it has its good points and its bad points.' He was waiting for her to elaborate but she didn't say anything else.

He stroked his chin as if he was thinking deeply about what she said.

'It has its good points and its bad points,' he said, mimicking her voice, 'That's very profound.'

I could have hit him. I gave him a nudge to come out to the kitchen with me. When we got in there I gave out yards to him. I had to keep my voice low in case Aunt Bernie heard me.

'Don't ever speak to her like that again,' I said.

'Does that woman ever express an idea?' he said, 'You'd get more out of a stone.'

'She's had a tough life,' I said, 'Don't be so hard on her.'

He just shrugged.

'I wish you wouldn't go out with Reg,' I said, 'He makes you too giddy.'

'Don't blame him for everything. Can you not give me the credit of having a mind of my own?'

'You have a great mind. He just pollutes it.'

'What's up with you? We had a good night out, end of story. I don't know what your problem is.'

'Was Reg drinking?'

'He had a few. What's that to do with anything? We spent most of the night watching the races.'

'I don't think Reg has the remotest interest in greyhound racing. It's just somewhere for him to get drunk.'

'Now you're being ridiculous. You really have it in for him, don't you?'

'I don't care what he does on his own time. It's when he starts changing you I get worried.'

He went off to bed in a huff. I'd usually have tried to pacify him but I was too mad that night. Instead I stayed downstairs with Aunt Bernie.

'I'm sure Kevin thinks I'm very anti-social,' she said after he fell asleep.

'Not at all,' I said, trying to make little of it.

'I just can't think of things to say when people put me on the spot.'

'He's terrible. I won't let him do that to you again.'

'No, he was fine. I'm the problem. My mind just goes blank when I feel I'm expected to say something.'

She started to open up to me because I didn't put any pressure on her. She told me stories about the Post Office, about how she'd started there against her wishes and then got into a rut there, the way most of us do in our jobs.

Afterwards she talked about how things were for her growing up with Granny and Grandad in that severe house they had. She said she was never allowed give vent to her emotions and maybe she stifled them because of that.

'I was rarely allowed out as a child,' she said, 'When I got to be an adult it was even disapproved of.' Granny and Grandad's control over her meant she was alone a lot. She became too fond of her own company as a result.

I kept wanting to ask her about Dan Toibin. Was that why he meant so much to her? Was he her first boyfriend? Her only one?

I asked her if there was anything she'd change if she could live her life over again. After thinking about it for a few seconds she said, 'Only one thing,' She didn't follow up on it and neither did I but even to say that much was big from her.

The next morning she was back to reserved self, speaking of me again rather than anything else.

'You have so much going on,' she said. It pained me to think she could have had too if life had gone differently for her. Thinking about her made me appreciate the things I had that she didn't, things I mostly took for granted.

'How do you manage to be a mother and a nurse at the same time?' she said, 'I'd be a basket case juggling the two things.'

'No you wouldn't. You'd be the ultimate multi-tasker if you put your mind to it.

'That's a laugh, but thanks for being such a *plámáser*.'

Her words had an influence on me even though she was only making a casual comment. I started to think I might have been spreading myself too thin. I know she didn't mean it that way but it was the way I took it up. The next time I was on the phone to her I told her I was thinking of taking a break from the hospital.

'Is that wise?' she said, 'especially after me just saying you were so good at the two things?'

'I'm not as good as you think. Cillian gets short shrift when you're not here.'

'How will you survive financially if you give up the job?'

'We'll work it out somehow.'

'I'd think about it carefully if I were you.'

'I feel bad you having to mind Cillian so much.'

'Don't let that form part of your decision, not even 1% of it. You know I love coming up to you.'

'I do, but it's not fair on you.'

Despite her protests I gave in my notice to the Mater for the second time when my maternity leave ran out. I didn't fear boredom so much this time because of having Cillian to mind. It made all the difference. Kevin encouraged me because he knew it was what I wanted. It was going to be a stretch financially but we'd managed the last time. I was confident we would again. We'd become used to cutting our cloth by now.

When I thought about it I'd never really enjoyed nursing too much since I left my fulltime job. Shorter shifts didn't give you a chance to really get into them. It was a struggle to get motivated.

I tried my best to give everything to the patients but there was something missing inside me, some of the old drive I used to have. I lacked the kind of commitment I used to pride myself on. I always promised myself I'd get out if that ever happened.

'It's a pity you're such a perfectionist,' Kevin said to me when I told him how I was feeling, 'You place too many demands on yourself. You're a person, not a machine. Most days when I go to work I have to pretend I care more about it than I do just to get through the day.'

'It's different for you. You're dealing with products. I deal with people.'

He didn't like me saying that.

'I'm dealing with people, darling,' he said, 'You better believe it. Carpets don't sell themselves.' I apologised to him for trying to sound superior.

Another reason I didn't mind leaving was because I was getting frustrated at the way the hospital was being run. Some whizzkid doctors from prestigious colleges overseas had been inducted onto the staff. They looked like they were just out of Primary School but they acted like eminences. They strutted around the wards with their beepers flashing as if they owned the world. The older ones, meanwhile, continued to make life-and-death decisions on 20-hour shifts with their eyes falling out of their heads. Where was the logic?

A lot of the nurses were doing degrees now. I was glad to see that because it gave us more respect. It took away the overtones of skivviness about the profession but I felt some of them ran the risk of turning into secretaries more than nurses. They were in danger of forgetting why they went into the job in the first place – to take care of people. Writing reports about what you did was being seen as more important than doing it.

Cora and Hilary hated the way things had changed since they qualified. They made me realise I wasn't missing too much. I met them a lot for coffee and we talked about everything till the cows came home. Bewley's was our favourite place to meet. Nobody bothered you there. You could loll for the day over a cup and you wouldn't be moved on. At home I always drank tea but when I was out I preferred coffee. It gave me more adrenalin.

Each time I talked to them, things seemed to have got worse in the hospitals. The latest problem was one I'd never have thought of – litigation. The increase in claims against doctors for malpractice was making them nervous about making decisions that could save people's lives. Everyone was in the soup if they went wrong. You couldn't gamble even if the potential rewards were great. It was financially safer to go by the book, though not necessarily safer for the patient.

They told me there were a lot of cuts coming in. Services were being drawn back. Patients being discharged before they should have been.

I'd experienced some of that myself during my brief stint back at work. One day I saw a woman hiding in the Ladies beside St. Ignatius Ward for fear she'd be sent home. She'd had a hysterectomy and the wound became infected. A number of dressings were applied to it but they hadn't cured the problem. Her bed was needed for a more urgent case so she was told she might have to be discharged.

When she was asked what was going to happen to her wound, all they said was that she should report in to A&E for dressings. It was no way to treat someone who'd just come through a serious operation. I tried to reassure her but I couldn't give her a guarantee

348

about how long she'd be kept in. I wasn't privy to that kind of information. Decisions seemed to be made on the spot. No wonder there was a brain drain of nurses out of the country. The profession was in danger of being taken over by red tape.

One day a man told me he was being sent home because his health plan wasn't high enough. He said he was in shock since he got the news. 'It's all about money these days,' he said, 'They should put the Cash Desk beside the Intensive Care Unit.' He was joking, of course, but it wasn't too funny.

A man Hilary knew was waiting on a liver transplant. Because he had no health cover he was told he could be years on a waiting list. He got into a state of high anxiety about it. 'I'm not waiting any longer,' he said at the out-patient clinic, flailing his arms at anyone in sight.

He created such a commotion a security guard had to be called for. The man started to scuffle with him when he tried to remove him from the hospital. He said he wasn't going until he saw someone. After ages a doctor appeared. He listened to the man telling him his tale of woe but when he was finished he wrung his hands Pontius Pilate style and said there was nothing he could do.

Hearing stories like that made me feel almost glad to be out of the place. You couldn't put the blame on any one person. It was the system that was wrong. Every night on The News I heard some TD or other rabbiting on about how committed they were to treating each patient in the most caring way they could but it all seemed like so much hot air to me. When push came to shove they were still sitting there with nothing being done.

Kevin listened to me moaning about the situation every other night. Some nights I felt like throwing my shoes at the TV screen. All he could do was shake his head in disbelief. One night we watched a programme that featured a man who'd died of heart failure because an ambulance that was on its way to him hadn't got there in time. He was living in the middle of the country. The coronary care unit of the local hospital had just closed down. He died in the ambulance on the way to Dublin. His wife had been performing CPR frantically on him in between her 999 calls before it reached their house. Apparently it got a puncture on the way to him and there was no other one available.

'It seems to me,' Kevin said, 'that you'd get a pizza to your house quicker than you would an ambulance.' He added, 'It would probably do you as much good too.' I didn't find that funny. 'Don't be so cynical,' I said to him. 'Look who's talking,' he replied.

Hilary's stories weren't as dramatic as that one but they still made my blood boil when I heard them. She said there were a lot of patients coming back to the hospital with recurrences of their original complaint a day or two after being discharged due to some overworked doctor not giving them the proper attention. To her way of thinking, it seemed to be only a matter of time before one of them made a decision with tragic consequences.

The system was shooting itself in the foot due to the lack of joined-up thinking. Too many people were left malingering in A&E until beds became available. Some wards were made open plan to create more bed space. Hilary said this might have solved one problem but it created another one. It meant people hadn't the same degree of privacy anymore. A lot of them were being herded into cubicles. They ended up whispering their symptoms to doctors for fear of being heard by the people in the next cubicle.

Kevin listened to me telling him these horror stories with a mixture of shock and amusement.

'Now,' he'd say, 'Aren't you glad you got out?' I told him I was. The only problem was the financial one. I racked my brains to think of some way I could help with the mortgage but I couldn't think of any.

'Don't worry,' he kept saying, 'We'll manage it some way. We did before.'

'Not with an extra mouth to feed,' I said, 'Santa Claus isn't going to pay it.'

Cillian didn't get many toys at this time. Most of his clothes came from Mammy. Every penny we had that didn't go into paying for food or electricity was earmarked for our BO friend at the bank.

When he started school I had a few extra hours to play with so I decided to look around for some temporary work. I contacted all the usual suspects but it was Cora who turned up trumps in the end. She found me a job helping out at an old folk's home. I didn't have to use much of my nursing experience here. I was really just helping out. There were times I felt the job had been created for me. The important thing about it was that it got me out of the house. It gave me a bit of pride in the fact that I was a money earner again, even if I was only getting a pittance.

One of my neighbours collected Cillian from school. I gave her a few pounds to mind him until my shift was finished. There was the usual dashing to and fro. It was difficult trying to link up with Kevin so he didn't come home to yet another cold dinner but somehow it worked. We kept the wolf from the door but he was always hovering very near it.

I did some part-time work in a hospital for Alzheimer patients around this time. It was one of my biggest challenges. Many of them were incontinent. You can imagine how many problems that caused. I won't go into the details. You can imagine how unpleasant it was.

The money was good but you earned it. The worst part of it was seeing the patients in distressed states of mind. It was much worse on their families but it upset me too. I found myself getting depressed seeing so many people feeling confused about who they were. It brought Granny back to me. I found it very upsetting dealing with one man in particular. He'd been a university lecturer. Now he was reduced to fiddling with his pyjama buttons as if his life depended on it.

Another patient used to stare at the television screen for hours without moving. Then suddenly he'd put his hands in front of his mouth and shout, 'Up Mayo!' for no reason. He'd been a player for that county in his youth, I heard. Another one used to do these funny jumps when he'd walk down the corridor, carefully skipping every second tile. I suppose it was a version of Obsessive Compulsive Disorder. And then there was the man who had an obsession with breaking my syringes.

My most mysterious patient of all was the man who kept examining the soles of his shoes as if some eternal secret lurked inside them. One day he accused me of hurting him when I gave him an injection. I wasn't sure if I had or not but he shouted so much about it he embarrassed me all over the ward. I knew he was capable of 'going off on one', as we said, every now and then. Had I actually hurt him or was he making it up? I was never sure, but the thought that I might be, or the fear that he might try to get revenge on me, caused me a few sleepless nights.

I tried not to let thoughts like that get to me but it wasn't easy. Nobody was predictable in their behaviour. That meant you were almost permanently tense as you tried to deal with them. I hated looking at men wandering up and down the corridors in their dressing-gowns without a clue as to who I was, or even who they themselves were.

Why did some people have to suffer such horrible afflictions year upon year while others lived to a ripe old age without a care in the world?

Mammy used to say, 'Life is a lottery.' Daddy had a different opinion. 'These people are happier than any of us,' he said, 'They're in their own private paradise.' He had a point, I suppose, at least until you tried to draw them out of that world. Or hurt them with injections.

Daddy told me about a man he heard of once who thought he was Napoleon. He'd go up and down the streets of Midleton with his hand inside his tunic having these grand thoughts. Most people were afraid to approach him but he was harmless. Some of my patients veered between reality and fantasy. I found that much more worrying.

They had what we called 'lucid intervals.' They became upset when they were in the state between being in touch with reality and off in their own worlds. On certain days they were able to communicate totally normally with us, or with the people who were visiting them, but on others they didn't recognise anyone at all.

This was very upsetting for all of us. As well as the psychological problems they posed, many of them were hard to manage. Even getting them out of their beds to keep them mobile was like a day's work. We had to do this over and over again to stop them getting bedsores.

It was hard trying to make them sit still if you were putting a dressing on them or changing a poultice. I know it wasn't their fault but I couldn't stop myself getting annoyed about it sometimes. One day I let a roar at a patient in my frustration. Cillian was teething at the time. My nerves were on edge from lack of sleep. The nurse I was with at the time was shocked, but nowhere near as shocked as I was. It was the first time I'd ever done anything like that before in my life. And, thank God, the last.

Cora rang me one night to tell me she'd heard of an opening in A&E. I applied for it and got it. I was thrilled. I'd built up a kind of bond with some of the patients suffering from Alzheimer's Disease so I was sad to be leaving them but I knew deep down I wasn't cut out for that kind of work.

Having said that, Casualty was no picnic either. The world had become more violent in the few years since I'd been there before. A lot of people came in with stab wounds, some of them life-threatening. Once or twice we had a person who'd been shot. I watched one man being wheeled down to surgery after being stabbed. I knew even before he got to theatre that he wouldn't make it.

Others were touch and go. I spent many nights chewing my fingernails as emergency surgery was performed at little or no notice. I can't say enough for the dedication of the staff at times like that. A surgeon might be going off a shift after working flat out for nine or ten hours when his beeper would go off.

Many of the injuries were drink-induced but some were cold-blooded thuggery. People who'd been perfectly healthy five minutes before were now just minutes away from having their lives ended. It used to break my heart watching surgeons perform the most delicate surgery on patients who'd been waiting years for their operations and then having someone who'd never been sick a day in their life coming in with the most appalling injuries due to a row over a girl outside a chipper.

Where was the logic? How casually some people treated life when others hung so dearly to it, saying novenas that a transplant or a bypass would work.

I was reminded more than once of the time when we were all talking about Shan Mohangi, the medical student who'd performed the botched abortion on his girlfriend that led to her death. A violent death in Ireland was a rare thing then. Now it was more like a commonplace event.

Moving from the Alzheimer hospital to Casualty was a bit like going from the frying pan into the fire. I tried to turn my mind off to the more grisly aspects of it but I couldn't do that forever.

After a few months I told Kevin I wasn't able for it. He couldn't have been more supportive. When I gave in my notice it was back to the drawing board again. I kept making enquiries about jobs for staff nurses in the regular hospitals but they were at a premium.

Once you got off the treadmill it was very hard to get back on again. Kevin thought I was spreading myself too thin with all my chopping and changing but I didn't see it like that. I just did what felt right at the time.

Being a mother complicated everything. Why wasn't the marriage bar lifted when I couldn't get pregnant? Life seemed to make the right things happen at the wrong time, or the wrong things happen at the right time. Rarely, if ever, did all the parts of the jigsaw come together.

But no matter how bad you were, there was always worse. In the week before I left Casualty, Deirdre met me for coffee and told me a very sad story about Irene. Apparently her husband went through a kind of breakdown after being so long out of work in Donegal.

When he recovered they decided the only chance he had of a good job was abroad. Because of that they emigrated, moving to Montreal with their child. He got work in a bank for a while but then that job folded too. By this time Irene was doing part time work in a clinic but she was only earning buttons. Her husband had to pump gas to make a few dollars.

They were staying in a run-down apartment. Then he took to drink. One night Irene came home and found him in bed with the landlady of the apartment. She couldn't believe her eyes. He'd never looked at another woman in Ireland. He told her he didn't know how it happened, that he was out of his mind with drink at the time. Apparently he'd poured his heart out to her about all his problems and without realising it had ended up in her bed. It might have been true but Irene couldn't forgive him. She came home with the child the following week.

Her husband stayed in America. He kept begging her to go back to him but she refused. He said it was a drunken accident, that he couldn't even remember how it happened. She was as pure as the driven snow herself and didn't care about the details. The next thing she heard, he was dead. He'd shot himself in the head. It was the landlady who found him. He had a gun in one hand and a bottle of whiskey in the other.

It was her own gun he'd used. She kept it under the desk for protection. The apartment was in a rough area and she'd had a few run-ins with tenants. It was a horrible end to a tragic life. Deirdre didn't think Irene would ever get over it. She saw them both as victims. Irene never married again. She couldn't look at another man afterwards. People told her she should try again but there was no way she could do that. All she cared about was the child. She guarded it with her life

After hearing stories like that I clung even more tightly to Kevin. I didn't want to take him for granted. I knew he had a lot of problems at work and that, like the rest of us, he was less able for them as the years went on.

Some of the younger members of staff were starting to threaten his position now. I knew we'd be in the soup if he lost his job. That was always a  worry. We were still struggling with our finances and just barely managing to meet the mortgage.

Maureen, meanwhile, was going ahead in leaps and bounds in the travel agency. May also got promotion upon promotion in her job in Midleton. Mammy and Daddy were delighted to see them doing so well.

I went home as often as I could, especially now that I had Cillian in tow. Sometimes I brought Aunt Bernie back up with me for a few days.  She babysat Cillian. That meant we could get out for the odd night.

Kevin continued to see Reg. They went for games of snooker or maybe to art exhibitions or anything else that was going on. Reg had to be out all the time. It was part of his nature. Kevin said, 'That fellow would go to the opening of an envelope.'

When Aunt Bernie was babysitting I used to meet Veronica for a drink. If she wasn't able to make it I dropped into the Mater to have coffee with Hilary. It was good catching up on all the news. Sometimes I preferred having people around than going out. Cora and

Owen visited us a lot. If they managed to organise a babysitter we might go somewhere on a foursome. They enjoyed babysitting Cillian for us if Aunt Bernie wasn't there. We tried to return the compliment with Alan. It was unusual having couples babysit but it worked for us. They always left lots of food in the fridge for us and Alan was a little angel. Cora said the same about Cillian. I hoped she wasn't saying it just to be polite.

Her life wasn't without its problems. One night she opened up to me about something she'd been slow to talk about before. It transpired that she had a sister whose child became severely handicapped after a freak event. When she was pregnant she came in contact with a cat that had an infection. Her daughter was born without sight or hearing as a result. Nobody knew how it happened. It was one of those rare conditions that terrified me to hear about.

'She must be going out of her mind,' I said.

'She has her down days but she loves the child to bits. I babysit for her any time I can.'

'I really think you should leave us to our own devices anymore,' I said.

'That's not why I'm telling you. I love coming over to you.'

Despite what she said, I made her cut down on her visits to us after hearing her story. That meant our babysitting options were curtailed.

We didn't need to go out much but if we hadn't one night out a week I found my nerves getting to me. Kevin felt that way too. We promised ourselves we'd get out for that one night by hook or by crook, even if it was only to go for a drive down to Dollymount to walk the pier.

If we looked for a babysitter out of the book it tended to run into money. You didn't know what you were getting either, especially with the younger ones. One night we came home from the pictures to find Cillian crying his eyes out in the cot. The babysitter was downstairs on the sofa chewing the mouth off her boyfriend. That was the last time we employed her, I can tell you.

Afterwards I could never really relax when we were out. I'd spend the night worrying about what might be happening at home. That can't have been much fun for Kevin. I tried to hide my concern from him but my face always told a tale. That put a damper on things.

The worst nights of all were the ones where we went out with couples we didn't know as well as Cora and Owen, or people who were single. Since Cillian arrived I'd got into the habit of yammering on about child-related subjects. That bored some people to tears, especially if they didn't have any children of their own. I'd become out of touch with things that were going on in the world and didn't feel equipped to hold any kind of conversation about politics or current affairs.

I hadn't a clue what was going on in the outside world apart from snippets I'd pick up from newspaper headlines or bulletins from the radio. Reg made me feel about six inches tall about that. So did some of Kevin's other friends.

As far as politics was concerned I hardly knew what party was in power half the time. I was doing well if I happened to remember the Taoiseach's name. I envied nurses who could discuss heart surgery one minute and the trade situation in Bosnia the next. I had a total inferiority complex as far as that went. I wanted to crawl under the carpet anytime these sorts of discussions started. I knew I'd make an utter fool of myself if I opened my gob. Not that there was any danger of that. Most of the time I couldn't get a word in edgeways.

'Just be yourself,' Kevin said to me when I told him I didn't want to meet his friends. 'If you feel like talking,' he said, 'talk. If you don't, don't. It's as simple as that. Even if you put your foot in it, who cares?'

If only I could have been as relaxed as him. The problem with me was that I'd put my foot in it, take it out and then put it straight back in again, this time stirring it about until everyone else in the group was wondering what kind of a dunderhead he'd married.

'Don't give yourself the impression they know any more than you because they use big words,' he said, 'A lot of them don't have two brain cells to rub together.'

If they didn't, they certainly didn't act like it. Most of them were bubbling over with confidence. If you had confidence you could say something stupid and make it sound profound. The other side of the coin was being unsure of yourself. That made you look stupid even if you said something intelligent.

'Where did you get her?' Reg said to Kevin one night when I tried to pass a clever comment about a book I was reading. It came out all wrong. Everyone fell around the place laughing.

After a few embarrassing experiences like that I told Kevin, 'That's it.' I realised I was much happier at home. I didn't have to make any effort there. I could be a mother pure and simple.

I left the phone off the hook after teatime. There was nothing more annoying than having someone ring just after I'd got Cillian to sleep after his fourth bedtime story only to have him woken up again and erupt into screams. I couldn't leave it off during the day in case someone was trying to contact me with a job offer.

I liked going out with Kevin on his own but that was rarely possible. We were too tired most nights after playing 'cuddle ping pong' with Cillian. It was like, 'Will you take him?' 'Will you?' Then the next thing you'd hear would be the dawn chorus.

Finding babysitters got harder and harder. After getting a string of bad ones we decided it was Aunt Bernie or nothing. She was better with him than anyone we knew. As he grew up he became more demanding with her but she never seemed to mind.

'How do you do it?' I'd ask her if she got him to go to bed when neither of us could. Sometimes you'd see her sitting in the middle of the carpet on all fours having her hair torn out by him.

'I have the easy part,' she'd say, 'I don't have to deal with him all day long.'

But I felt she could have if she had to. Not just all day long but all life long.

I don't think we'd have been able to survive financially without Aunt Bernie. Whenever I was temping I knew she was ready to come up to us at a moment's notice and stay for as long as we needed her.

Childminding costs went through the roof as the years went on. The general cost of living wasn't far behind it. Every year at budget time Kevin used to throw up his hands in horror. He thought the government was targeting people in what he called 'the squeezed middle.' (I could never figure out what that expression meant).

'Why do they always hit us the hardest?' he'd say, 'The rich get richer and the poor get poorer but everyone forgets the people like us.' He changed Daddy's saying 'Two can live as cheaply as one' to 'Two can starve as cheaply as one.' By now he'd stopped voting at any election. 'As soon as they get into the Dáil they lose the fire in their belly,' he said. 'From then on it's just finding a nice big Mercedes to plant their rear ends on.'

## Additions to Our Brood

We had another child the year after Cillian. This time it was a girl. Siobhan wasn't planned but that didn't mean we loved her any the less. It was an easier birth than Cillian. She was a gorgeous baby but just as much of a handful as he was. She had an incredible amount of energy. As soon as she came out of the womb she wanted to attack life.

In another way she was more relaxed than he was. Cillian got hysterical when there was thunder, for instance, but Siobhan almost seemed to enjoy it.

She struck me as the type of baby that would sleep through an earthquake. Maybe that was because I was more relaxed when I was pregnant with her. They say these things matter. I didn't question it too deeply. You'd go demented trying to work out the finer points of all the theories people have about children.

She could wind me around her little finger when she asked me for something in her tiny little voice. I spoiled her just as much as I did Cillian.

She was a little daredevil. Kevin liked that about her but the trouble about daredevils is that they're a danger to themselves. She was always crawling into places she shouldn't have been. The stairs was the main worry. In the end we had to put gates at the top and bottom so we knew she wasn't up to some mischief on the steps.

I loved watching her as she grew up. She used to walk around the place in high heels pretending to be me. Her feet disappeared into the tops of them as she tottered around the place.

She liked to put a biro in her mouth as well, pretending it was a cigarette. She mimicked me tipping the ash into an ash tray. Kevin wasn't too pleased at that.

'I'd prefer if she mimicked some of your healthier habits,' he said.

He spoiled her even more than I did. Men tend to do that to daughters. Maybe they're afraid of making the boys too soft. But Siobhan didn't like to be picked up as much as Cillian did. Kevin would have preferred if it was the other way round.

Siobhan was everyone's friend. You only had to look at her to fall in love with her. She had the hugest blue eyes you ever saw. They were like pools. She'd stare at you forever without moving. How could you refuse her anything when she looked at you like that? She was also very kind-hearted – to the world of nature as well as people. If there was a spider or a Daddy Long Legs in the house she'd carry it outside instead of killing it. She was so peaceful, Kevin said once, 'She must have been a Buddhist monk in a previous life.'

She was skilled at finger-painting before that activity became widespread in school. We were glad to see her engrossing herself in it but it meant the washing machine was on half the day. She destroyed every stitch of clothing we put on her when she was in her Picasso mood. She was a major a messer when she was eating as well. Whenever Kevin saw her dribbling food he'd say, 'Are you going to eat that or wear it?'

We could never get angry with her no matter what she did. One day when she was old enough to go to the bathroom she took a roll of pound notes in with her and flushed them all down the toilet. All we could do was laugh – despite the fact that the money was like gold dust to us. I'd been saving it up for the ESB bill at the time. Afterwards I thought it was going to be candles instead of lights for us for a while. Then there was the time she wanted a pet tarantula for Christmas. (That's enough about that).

When she was two she caught her finger in the partition separating the sitting-room from the dining-room and nearly gave us both a breakdown. Her hand was badly injured.

I blamed myself for that. I'd just come in before her so I had my back to her. I didn't know she was behind me as I closed the doors. I never heard her screaming so loud as that day because she wasn't the type of child to scream.

We rushed her down to Temple Street in a state of panic. They were brilliant with her. She got eight stitches in all and didn't cry once. She was lucky not to lose her finger but she had a lot of pain afterwards. In fact she never fully recovered. For years afterwards I'd see her wincing when she did the smallest thing with it. The doctor who was treating her told me her nerve ends were frayed.

'Sometimes they come back and sometimes they don't,' he said. She was one of the unlucky ones.

People say having your first child changes your marriage completely but with me it was Siobhan who did that. With one you don't have to be in two places at once. With two you do. Anytime Cillian and Siobhan were in different rooms my imagination went into overdrive wondering what they might be up to.

It was worse when you couldn't hear them.

'If a child is quiet,' Kevin used to say, 'It means they're doing something they shouldn't be doing. The only time you can relax is when they're noisy.' I agreed with him. Maybe that's why I got to like noise. I suffered them crawling over me like baby elephants every morning to wake me up. They used to do that to Aunt Bernie too. Being a good mother meant falling a bit in love with chaos.

The only real time we had to ourselves now was when the pair of them were asleep. Kevin was always at me to put them to bed before they were ready to go. I thought that was a bad idea. It meant they'd probably wake up in the middle of the night.

He had a way of saying it that I didn't like. 'Have you put them down yet?' he'd say, reminding me of a vet putting a litter of cats to sleep. After months I managed to get him to change it to, 'Have you put them to bed yet?' Result!

I got pregnant with our third child two years after Siobhan. I wasn't sure if Kevin would be angry or overjoyed to have another one on the way. It was like the 'steps of the stairs' that happened often in Irish families at that time. Was he going to feel pressurised? How would it be having more sleepless nights, more screaming and teething and all the other things that went with it.

I kept the news from him for a while. We were still pulling the devil by the tail with our finances. I thought the prospect of another mouth to feed might tip him over the edge. Thankfully my fears were unfounded on that score. His eyes lit up when I plucked up the courage to tell him.

'It's great news,' he said.

My third pregnancy proved to be my most difficult one. After having such an easy time with Siobhan, maybe I got too smug. That was often a pattern in my life. As soon as I relaxed about something a different problem appeared.

I had so little pain with Siobhan I expected this one to be the same but it turned out to be a nightmare. I was as sick as a dog from day one and I kept getting infections afterwards.

At my worst I convinced myself I was going to miscarry again. I was still saying prayers to beat the band. Mammy was on the phone all the time asking me for updates. After a while I had to tell her to stop ringing. She was doing my head in. No matter how well intentioned a person is, when they keep asking you the same questions it stops you being able to think of anything else.

The nine months of my third pregnancy felt like as many years.

'You'd think I'd be getting good at it by now,' I said to Kevin, 'What's going on?'

'How do I know? I'm only a man. Ask your gynaecologist.'

He didn't know either.

He just said every pregnancy was different. All I could do was get as much rest as possible and hope for the best.

Cillian and Siobhan were fascinated by my bump. They kept patting it. 'Stop doing that,' I'd say to them, 'I'm superstitious.' I went back to the person I'd been when I was carrying Cillian, permanently in terror of something going wrong.

Eventually I was called in to the Rotunda to be induced. It was such a relief. By now I didn't care how much pain I was going to have. Waiting was worse than anything.

I had to give up pushing at a certain point because I was so exhausted. That happened with Cillian too. When the baby finally popped out without anything wrong with it I was more amazed than anything else. It was another girl. We called her Eileen after Daddy's mother.

'It was a tough one but we got there,' the midwife said to me, 'You were great.'

'Never again,' I told her.

'Women say that and go on to have families of seven.'

'You can rule me out of that one unless they develop some technology where I can give birth by proxy.'

I always felt I should have had a Caesarean section for Eileen. Maybe if I screamed louder they'd have given me one. They wanted to give me an epidural but I refused it. I heard about a woman who became paralysed after having one of these. I could never get her out of my mind even if it was only a thousand to one possibility.

Epidural or no epidural, there was no way I was going to expose myself to that kind of worry again. I said the same thing to Kevin as I'd said to the midwife, 'No more babies, no more pregnancies. I told him if he wanted to get near me in the bed from now on he'd have to have a vasectomy.

'Maybe I'll buy a chastity belt,' I said, 'or else you can sleep on the sofa.'

When I got married first I fully intended to have a big family. Three is big today but Mammy always thought she had a small family with the three of us. That was the thinking then.

Kevin was as relieved as me that we wouldn't be having any more. After Eileen was born he used to get depressed sometimes looking at all the nappies around the place. Then she got colic and it was back to sleepless nights again.

We took turns walking her when she woke up crying. He had great patience but even that was tested after Eileen. I don't know how either of us did a day's work after these nights. She was almost impossible to shush or rock to sleep.

For a while I was afraid he might go back on the bottle. Reg called round to us a fair bit around this time. I felt by doing that he was trying to draw Kevin away from me. Maybe now he sensed a new opportunity.

One night he said to Kevin, 'It's all downhill from here, buddy. Three bambinos is three too many.' If he got a chance, I thought, he'd have had him back in the pubs with him in a heartbeat.

Later in the night he said to me, 'You've caught up with your parents, haven't you? Didn't they have three too?'

'Yes,' I said. I didn't like the way he was smirking. I felt something nasty was coming.

'I'd love to have three children,' he said then, 'One of each.'

That made about as much sense as most of Reg's other pronouncements.

'Are you thinking of creating a new sex?' I asked him.

At that he jumped up on the floor and started jigging around the place. Kevin was in kinks laughing at him. He twisted his index finger into the side of his head to indicate he thought he was screwy but I knew he was enjoying it no end.

'You're a gas man,' he said.

'What are you doing, Reg?' I said.

'You said I should create a third sex. Maybe this is how hermaphrodites dance.'

He kept it up for ages. I let him at it for a while but then I flipped.

'I'm off to bed,' I said, banging the door so hard I almost took it off the hinges. As I went up the stairs I heard Reg whooping. He was delighted he'd got to me. It meant he had Kevin more in his grasp.

He stayed until after midnight that night. He made so much noise I knew there was no way I was going to be able to get to sleep. When Kevin finally came up to bed I couldn't resist having a go at him.

'Reg is really starting to get under my skin,' I told him.

'He's just being childish,' he said, 'Don't let it bother you.'

'Well it does bother me. Sometimes I think he's like the devil.'

'That's a terrible thing to say.' Maybe it was but it was how I felt.

I begged him not to have him round anymore. The visits lessened after that but then I started to feel afraid. What if he started meeting Reg without telling me? I developed a paranoia about that. It made me change my battle plan. It was like the old thing of keeping your friends close and your enemies closer. If Reg was in the house at least least Kevin wouldn't be tempted to drink with him there. Or would he?

One night Kevin was drinking a cup of tea when Reg whipped a hip flask of whiskey out of his back pocket. He offered to add a drop to it to 'cheer it up.' I told him to leave the house that night. I had to. I could see Kevin's resistance wilting.

I dreaded the thought of him seeing Reg after work even if it was only for a cup of coffee or a game of snooker. Anytime he saw him it seemed to change Kevin's attitude to me afterwards. He'd give me smart answers or refuse to answer my questions.

If I asked him where they went he'd always give the same answer, 'Nowhere.' When a man tells you he went 'Nowhere' he usually means 'Everywhere.' It usually took me a few days after the nights out with Reg to get the Kevin I knew back. He was like a different person, the person from the flat-warming party.

One night he came round to us after being in The Stag's Head. Whenever he went there he always had 'one over the eight.' He started cracking stupid jokes. At one stage of the evening he said to me, 'Did you hear about the fellow who stayed up all night studying for a urine test?' I felt I was supposed to go into kinks laughing at his excuse for wit. Instead I just put on a frozen face. Most of his jokes were much cruder than that. Almost invariably they had double meanings. He was still behind that boy's school bicycle shed.

I knew what his attitude to women was: They were the people who stopped men having fun. In fact they stopped them even wanting to have fun. They sucked the life out of them and turned them into doormats. From that point of view I was The Enemy. I felt men who had these sorts of ideas about women had some deep insecurities in themselves.

For some reason – probably his boorishness – I got the impression Reg preferred dating women who weren't very bright to intelligent ones. I never saw myself as Einstein but I always had common sense. I threatened him because I saw through him.

'When are you going to give us a day out?' I said to him once to annoy him.

'Not for a while,' he replied, 'I'm too busy fighting them off.'

'Good for you,' I said sarcastically.

'Would you like to be in the queue?' he asked me.

I thought: Not if you were the last man in creation.

He reminded me of an Irish Edward. Sometimes I'd see his eyes narrowing as he looked at me. I could almost see him thinking: If I could get her out of the way I'd have Kevin back to myself. Then the two of them could trip the light fantastic on the town.

Far from apologising for Reg's behaviour towards me, Kevin often accused me of being rude to him.

'You're too hard on him,' he said to me one night, 'I know he rubs you up the wrong way but he's a decent skin at the back of it all.' I couldn't help thinking that a part of him still hankered after the kind of life Reg was living.

'He has a terrible opinion of women,' I said to him.

'I don't agree. He has loads of women friends.'

'Maybe that's the problem. Maybe he'd be better if he just had one.'

'You mean you think he should get married?'

'It might quieten him down a bit. Or at least put manners on him.'

'Reg isn't the marrying kind. That doesn't mean he uses women.'

'I think he does.'

'That's just because the two of you don't get on. I know him a lot longer than you do and I don't see anything wrong with him.'

I waited a minute. Then I said, 'I think if he got you on his own for any length of time you could go back to the way you were before you met me.'

He came over to me and put his arms around me.

'Don't ever think that,' he said.' 'You're everything I want in life. I like Reg but he belongs to a world I'm not a part of anymore. Don't be afraid of him. He won't lead me astray. People who go astray are missing something in their lives. I'm not.'

I wasn't convinced. It was as if he was trying to make himself believe it. Kevin never denied being an alcoholic. I knew enough about the condition to realise there were no 'cured' alcoholics, just reformed ones. Or 'dry drunks' as Daddy called them.

I didn't really believe Kevin would go back on the bottle but I pleaded with him to stay away from Reg as much as he could. It was painfully obvious he had little or no interest in our family life or the children. Any time I talked to him about them he left me in little doubt about that.

I don't think I ever saw him playing with any of them no matter how many times they went over to him showing him their toys. He might pull the occasional funny face if Kevin was looking at him but that was it. If he was out of the room, on the other hand, he'd give the most enormous yawns if I was talking about them. It was hardly a subtle hint for me to move on to another subject.

Cillian came first in his class one year. When I showed Reg the certificate he won he hardly looked at it. 'Wow, what a clever clogs,' he said in a half-sarcastic way. If I was sensitive that might have upset me but when you don't care about someone, rude comments

367

don't get to you. If I respected him they might have given me an inferiority complex. Because I didn't, they didn't.

One day around this time Cillian had an accident. He fell on the street on the way home from school. There was a bad gash on his knee. I was worried about blood poisoning so I took him to Temple Street. When a doctor examined him he said there was no chance of that. He did a great job cleaning up the wound. I was looking forward to telling Kevin but when I got home he wasn't there.

Instead of that, Reg was. He'd sprawled himself all over a little two-seater we had in the kitchen. I couldn't stop staring at him. He had a big grin on his face like the cat that got the cream.

He hadn't been due to come around that evening. Instead he'd just 'swung by.' He looked mischievous in his duffel coat. There was a scarf wrapped loosely around his neck. He was drinking a glass of whiskey.

'Kev is doing a bit of overtime,' he chirped, 'He told me to let myself in.' He'd come in the back door. He knew we always left it unlocked. It really annoyed me that he was making himself that free with us but I tried to contain my anger.

'I have to put the children to bed,' I said.

'Am I in the way?'

'No.'

'What's up with Cillian? Why has he a bandage on him?'

'I'll tell you later.'

I brought the three of them upstairs. They didn't want to go to bed but I made them. My patience was low.

When I came back down I decided to take him on.

'Where did you get the whiskey?' I asked him.

He grinned at me.

'I'm sorry,' he said 'I shouldn't have been so cheeky. I know where you keep it in that cabinet over there. I thought I'd help myself.'

'I'd prefer if you asked.'

'My humblest apologies. I won't do it again. Maybe I'm doing Kevin a favour by taking temptation out of his way. Or does he bother with the booze at all now?'

368

'You know he hasn't had a drink since the party,' I said, 'Don't pretend to be even more stupid than you are.'

He started laughing at that. You couldn't insult him. He worked me up so much I ended up taking a glass myself. Then I started talking about Cillian. I don't know why. I told him the whole story from start to finish.

It was probably out of nerves. He had a way of making me say more than I wanted because of the way he looked at me. He just sat there listening to me. He didn't even bother to ask any questions. When I was finished he finally deigned to speak.

'You did the right thing,' he said, giving one of his familiar yawns, 'A nurse to the last.'

'I can see you're bored with all off this,' I said, getting fed up with him now.

All he did was laugh. He didn't deny it. Most people would have. I suppose it was a kind of honesty – the only kind he possessed in my view.

He left soon after that. When Kevin came home I told him what happened. He wanted to go up and see Cillian but I said there was no need to, that he was asleep.

It's a testament to how much Reg got to me that I started talking about him then instead of going into more detail about Cillian's injury.

'I don't like him traipsing in here any time he feels like it,' I said to him.

'That's my fault. I told him to make himself at home.'

'He certainly did that. He was drinking whiskey when I came in.'

'Whiskey? Where did he get it?'

'In the cabinet.'

'Crikey, what a nerve. I'll have to have a word with him about that.'

'Don't. I'd hate him to think I was talking about him. It's better to let it drop. I'll try to give him the benefit of the doubt. You don't have many people here.'

'I'll tell him to knock the next time.'

'Don't bother. Sorry for going on about it.'

'You're very tense tonight, aren't you?'

369

'I'm just upset about everything.'

'You're entitled to be. The main thing is that Cillian is all right. Did you tell Reg about him?'

'Against my better judgment. He didn't show the slightest bit of interest.'

'That doesn't surprise me. He isn't into children.'

'You can say that again.'

Cillian made a full recovery. Kevin bought him a pedal cycle for his bravery and our life returned to some kind of normality.

He went ahead in leaps and bounds at school. The second he came home he buried his head in some book or other. When I asked his teacher what kinds of things he should be reading he said, 'Anything is good, even the cornflakes packet.' Cillian took this literally when I said it to him. The next morning I saw him scrutinising the side of the cornflakes container to see what was written on it.

Nothing was outside his reach. He especially liked books on animals. When he was reading them, nothing else existed. He reminded me of the way Daddy used to be when he was fixing things around the house. They had the same kind of concentration  that blocked everything else out.

When he was seven he appeared as Jesus in his school's nativity play. This was around the time he wrote in an essay on the same subject: 'Mary raped Jesus in swaddling clothes.' To our immense relief, the teacher saw the funny side of his bad spelling.

Kevin thought it might get him away from the books. I thought he was great in it. We clapped like mad at the end. We hoped it would give him the confidence to be more outgoing but after it was over he was back to his bookworm self again.

He often came first in school projects, be they about poverty in Africa or monsoons or prehistoric animals. I told Kevin I thought he'd end up as President of Ireland if we were lucky. He replied, 'I'd prefer if he played for Athlone.'

He thought his bookish nature might lead to him being picked on at school. He was worried he might become a cissy. There was another reason he feared this too: Cillian wanted to sleep between Kevin and me in bed even after he started going to school. I was inclined to let him but Kevin said it was a bad habit for him to get into. I saw his point but if he had a nightmare you couldn't leave him in the cot. It would have been heartless. We argued a lot about that and didn't come to any long term conclusions about what to do.

I told Kevin he'd probably grow out of his clingy nature. He said it was important we didn't feed into it by indulging him. He thought I bought him too many books. I didn't agree. How could anyone have too many books?

'He treats them almost like human beings,' he said to me once.

'Maybe books are nicer than human beings,' I said.

Sometimes he took them out of his hand, or at least tried to. You'd have needed to be Arnold Schwarzenegger to get some of them off him when he didn't want to let go.

One year I got him the *Children's Brittanica* encyclopaedia for a Christmas present. It had information on everything under the sun. He became so enveloped in it he almost forgot to eat. He was forever reading us out titbits from it on this and that.

'I'm learning more from you,' I told him, 'than I ever learned at school.' Not that that was saying much.

Kevin tried to get him away from it by bringing him up to the local amusement arcade. When he was there he played the kind of games most children of his age were playing but they meant nothing to him. He wanted to get home to his books. Kevin said to him, 'All work and no play makes Jack a dull boy.' That had no effect on him at all. He didn't see reading as work. For him, play was more of a chore.

One night when Cillian was reading a book about Niagara Falls, Kevin said to him, 'Did you know they turn off the water there every night after all the tourists are gone home?' Cillian believed him for a second. The pair of them started laughing when he realised he was only codding. That was the side of Cillian Kevin liked best, the side that could let himself go.

He was doing a geography exercise another time. He said to Kevin, 'Where are the Alps?' Kevin replied, 'Ask your mother. She puts everything away.'

He didn't have to try as hard to get a laugh out of Siobhan. She was more slapdash by far. How is it that the first child always seems to be more serious than the ones that come afterwards? I've seen it

371

time and again. Maybe it's because the parents put so much effort into their firstborn that it makes them nervous.

There's an old joke that when your first child drops their soother you sterilize it before giving it back to them whereas if the second drops it you let the dog pick it up. We were a lot more casual with Siobhan than we were with Cillian, even if we didn't go so far as letting the dog pick up her soother. That would have been hard since we didn't have one.

Eileen's personality was more like Cillian's in the sense that she was serious. In contrast to that she had Siobhan's skittishness. In many ways she reminded me of May growing up. She demanded almost as much attention as May.

She had a curious mind. There were the usual questions. Why can't you tickle yourself? Where does the dark go when you turn the light on? Why is grass green? Thankfully we were spared Miranda Cawley's favourite, 'Who made God?'

She was resentful of the amount of time Cillian spent with Siobhan. It was almost like a carbon copy of the way May felt about Maureen and me. I wondered if these patterns ran through all families.

She screamed the house down to get what she wanted when she was in a strop. For the sake of peace we usually gave in to her. The child psychologists would have had no time for that. It wasn't good for her because she kept getting worse. The next time she'd want more. And so it went on, right through her childhood.

In time we all became afraid of her rages. She went so red in the face we'd almost feel it was going to explode. If she didn't get her way she'd stamp out of the room. She banged the door so hard you'd be afraid the walls were going to start shaking. When she was out of the house the peace was unbelievable. We'd be sitting there and someone would say, 'Why is it so quiet tonight?' Then it would dawn on us. We'd all go, 'Eileen is out!'

I didn't blame her for her behaviour. I knew she was troubled inside. Every night when I watched her sleeping I'd see her twisted up like a pretzel in the bed. Her arms would be all over the place. She was often frowning. Sometimes she had bad dreams and came running into us in a state, terrified that 'the boogie man' was following her.

A child like Eileen needed more love than the other two but it wasn't easy to give it when she was behaving so badly. If Siobhan got a treat she had to have one too, or even more than one. Mammy always thought Cillian was my favourite child and Siobhan Kevin's. Eileen played the two of them against one another to get the best deals for herself. That applied to toys as well as other things. She had to be the centre of attention if visitors called. She loved performing because of the attention. Kevin thought she had all the attributes to be an actress. I felt she lacked one of those: discipline.

Some people say mothers love the troubled child the most. I don't know if that was true for me. Usually troubled children cling to their mothers but Eileen clung more to Kevin than me, I hope I gave her as much affection as the other two even if there were times when she acted as if it was the last thing she wanted. She wasn't a child you could pick up for love or money. Neither did she take well to hugs and kisses.

Her agitation about little things brought agitation into my own head too. She made me tense in a way I hadn't been since before Cillian's birth. I was terrified my post-natal depression would come back. I didn't want to go to the doctor again so I threw myself into housework instead. It became like therapy to me. I hunted dust out of corners with frantic sweeping. Workshops were scrubbed until they were like mirrors. I hoovered carpets until Kevin thought I'd secretly bought new ones in Clery's without telling him. Most of the work didn't need to be done but I needed to do it.

I became a part of the hygiene blitz myself as well. When I showered I put my head up to the faucet until my breath almost went. I washed myself non-stop like Lady Macbeth. A line from my Inter Cert came back to me: 'All the perfumes of Arabia would not sweeten this little hand.' It was as if I was suffering from some subconscious guilt about being a bad mother.

I practically ate cigarettes at this time of my life, lighting them off one another and inhaling down to my toes. Nicotine always relaxed me, at least as long as each cigarette lasted. Then I was back to being Nervous Nellie again.

I was like a raw nerve most of the time. All sorts of crazy thoughts came into my head. I kept thinking the children would come to harm if I couldn't see them in front of me. I imagined them being knocked down on the road or being kidnapped. 'You've seen too many films,' Kevin told me. He hadn't an idea how bad I was feeling because I didn't tell him. I didn't think he'd have understood so I played it down whenever I talked to him about it.

Our plan of getting out a night a week went by the board after Eileen arrived. It was too complicated to organise babysitters on any sort of regular basis with three children to contend with. When Eileen was in the 'terrible twos' it was more difficult again. We managed the occasional weekend down to Midleton but these things took so much preparation we were often burned out by the time we got there.

I couldn't get my mind off Eileen no matter how hard I tried. Mammy took her from me when she saw me not being able to cope with her but I couldn't let that happen too much. She had enough on her plate trying to take care of Daddy. His asthma had gotten much worse over the years. It had also got much more frequent.

Eileen made strange with her too. It was as if she resented me having any time away from her. She still craved attention. I could understand it if she had colic or was teething but she was like that all the time. 'The creaky gate gets the oil,' was the way Kevin put it.

I thought things would get easier when she started going to school but they didn't. She made me pay for each hour I was away from her on the double. By now mothering was taking more out of me than nursing ever did, even under Joanne Wylie.

I continued to get part time work in old folk's homes. A nursing agency employed me on a contractual basis but these jobs were irregular. They often came at short notice as well. If you weren't able to commit on the spot, you lost them. Sometimes they involved working after the children came home from school. Having the three of them in the one school simplified things but if my shift went past 3 o'clock I needed someone to be there to collect them for me. I couldn't go to my usual 'rescuers' of Maureen or Aunt Bernie for that. It wouldn't have been fair to them.

One of our neighbours, Mrs Delahunt, stepped into the breach as often as she could but it was an awkward situation for her. Whenever

I got a part time job working in theatre in the Mater I had absolutely no idea when I'd get off. After 6 o'clock Kevin was able to mind the children but all our plans went out the window if he was stuck in traffic or delayed at work.

One day we had an emergency when a patient took a bad reaction to an anaesthetic during an operation. He'd been on diet pills but he hadn't informed the surgeon. It was very worrying for a while. Nobody knew what was wrong with him until his wife was contacted and she told us. If she hadn't come on the line he could have died. Normally you ask patients questions like that a hundred times but for some reason he slipped through the net. It was a very tense few hours for us all wondering if he'd pull through.

At times like that I was so worked up I almost forgot my own name, never mind remembering to collect the children. Kevin was ringing me to tell me he had to do overtime as we watched over a man who was hovering between life and death. When he got no answer he rang Mrs Delahunt to find out what was happening but she said she hadn't heard from me either. After that he rang the hospital but nobody picked up. He even tried the registrar at one point. When he couldn't get on to anyone his mind started to dredge up all sorts of scenarios.

Eventually he decided to drive to the hospital. By now he was in a state of panic, breaking every light he came to, even bumping the car off a bollard at one stage. The patient was out of danger when he got to the operating theatre. I was chatting to the surgeon when I saw him. I could see he was in a high state of tension by the way he walked towards me.

'What happened?' he said, 'I nearly wrote off the car getting here.' I told him an operation had gone wrong, that all our timetables went crazy as a result.

'I should have rung you,' I said, 'I wasn't thinking straight. I'm sorry.'

His face was blood red as he came up to me.

'I was worried to death about you.'

'What do you mean? I was here all the time.'

'How was I to know that? I thought I'd find you lying in a ditch somewhere.'

375

'What are you talking about?' I said, 'We had an emergency. A patient took a bad reaction to a GA.'

'What's a GA? Don't use jargon to try to get out of it.'

'I'm not trying to get out of anything. Stop giving me the third degree. We had an emergency. Surely you understand that.'

'I would have if you told me at the right time.'

'How could I tell you when I've been here all the time?'

'I've been ringing you off the hook. I couldn't get an answer from anywhere.'

'Kevin,' I said, 'A man almost died. We've all been at our wit's end.'

'You looked fairly relaxed to me when I came in.'

With that he turned on his heel and walked out. The colour was drained from his face. I'd never seen him so angry in my life. I was embarrassed about the fact that the surgeon heard him. He must have thought we had a terrible marriage. I should have been relieved about the patient but sometimes your mind can't help focusing on other things even in a crisis.

I followed him out to the car. He was still trembling with rage. I tried to explain what happened in more detail but he didn't seem to want to know. He didn't speak to me all the way home. He was still speeding and breaking lights. I thought we were going to be pulled over.

When we got home he went upstairs to the bedroom and locked himself in. Mrs Delahunt was sitting there with the three children. I gave her some money and thanked her for looking after them. She must have known by my face that something was wrong. Cillian said, 'What's up with Daddy?' Siobhan was playing with a doll on the floor. Eileen was crying.

I went up to the bedroom door and knocked on it. He didn't answer.

'Can I come in?' I said but he still didn't answer. As if things weren't bad enough, it was his birthday that day. We'd planned to go out for a meal with the children. Obviously that was all off now. I thought the night was going to be a disaster because of the way he'd reacted. I'd bought him a tape of Glen Campbell for a present. He was one of his favourite singers.

I couldn't give that to him either. I put the children to bed and went downstairs. I made myself a sandwich but I was too upset to eat it. I was sobbing to myself when he came down at around ten o'clock.

When I looked at him I suspected he'd been crying as well as me. I knew it was worry over me that caused his anger. When I handed him the Glen Campbell tape he put his arms around me.

'Sorry for over-reacting,' he said, 'Thanks for the record. You were good to remember I liked this guy.'

'How could I forget?' I said, 'You never shut up about him.'

He smiled at me.

'I wanted to treat you to a meal as well.'

'It doesn't matter. We can't afford it anyway.'

I'd got him a card from the hospital shop. 'Mater' was written on it.

'You can never leave the hospital behind, can you?' he said.

'That sounds like the beginning of another argument,' I said.

'No thanks. One of the ones we just had is enough for me.'

I was relieved we'd sorted things out. Maybe if it wasn't his birthday we mightn't have. Life is funny like that.

After that night we promised each other we'd do everything in our power not to get our wires crossed again. This wasn't easy at a time before mobile phones came in. It was all right if one of us was at home but if there was nobody in the house we had to use the public phone boxes. Sometimes there'd be a queue of people waiting to make calls. More often than not they were vandalised. You could go into one on a Monday and see shattered glass all over the place.

A few days later it would be fixed up but by the following weekend it might be in bits again. After a while it seemed like the Corporation stopped repairing them. What was the point? It was only a temptation for the vandals to wreck them again. Things got to a stage where I thought I was having an optical illusion if I found one that was working.

Mrs Delahunt deserved a gold medal for her patience when we failed to show up when we said we would. We offered her extra money for all she did but right or left she wouldn't take it so we tried to make it up to her in other ways. She loved bingo. We brought her to it once or twice and she really enjoyed herself. Another time she came to a bowling alley with us. It was Cillian's birthday. That wasn't such a good idea. The first time she tried to throw the ball she fell over. I think her body travelled further than the ball.

She was a deserted wife. I felt she was lonely anytime I saw her looking at us playing with the children. She reminded me of Aunt Bernie in a lot of ways. I often told her she was like my second mother – or should I say my third one. Some people on the estate said she'd been beaten by her husband when he was with her. We all knew she was better off without him but she struck me as being one of those women who'd have stayed in that kind of relationship indefinitely.

Women like that flummoxed me. If Kevin ever laid a finger on me I'd have been out the door like nobody's business. Everyone is different. It's a pity she didn't talk more about her life. I'd like to have known about it. We didn't get close in that way but she was great with the children. Cillian was the apple of her eye. When she talked about him she could talk for Ireland.

Sometimes we asked the teachers to hold on to the children for a while after school. That would be if either of us got delayed or if Mrs Delahunt wasn't available. It was helpful to have that as an option but we didn't use it often. I didn't think it was fair to the teachers so I only asked them if I was badly stuck.

Another problem we had at this time was a neighbour on the other side of us to Mrs Delahunt. Her name was Breege Gilmartin. She was permanently coming in to us saying things like, 'Your Cillian hit our Seanie,' or 'Stop bullyin' my child, would ya?'

I knew Cillian wouldn't hit a fly on a holy picture but I had to listen to her guff. If I turned my back on her she'd bang on the window or even follow me into the house. She seemed to have little to keep her going in life besides making up things to create trouble.

Her husband was just as bad but thankfully he was out most of the time. He was a truck driver. They both drank a lot and they threw wild parties as well. Many of these resulted in violence. It was hard to get to sleep some nights listening to the roaring. I was glad our bedroom was facing them instead of the children's one or they wouldn't have got a wink of sleep. Often we didn't either but at least the parties were at the weekends when it didn't matter too much.

I felt like telling her where to get off more than once but Kevin said that would only make her worse. Whenever she got a bee in her bonnet about something I'd ring him at work and tell him about it. That evening the pair of us would go into her and have it out. We tried to keep our voices down. If we raised them at all she started using language. Things became worse if her husband came in when we were there. We always tried to make ourselves scarce before he arrived. The sound of his truck was our signal to get out.

We rarely sorted anything out on these visits. Some people seemed to feed off fights. You had to give them a very wide berth if they tried to work you up. I found it was easier to give in even if I knew I was in the right. I was glad I only had one son. If Siobhan or Eileen were boys she'd have been giving out about them too. Or maybe the delightful Seanie would have picked physical fights with them.

Cillian was no match for him. He preferred playing with Siobhan and Eileen instead. They were liked peas in a pod when they were in a room together. Kevin didn't like that. He wanted him to play with other boys instead of being all together.

One Christmas all three of them came down with chicken pox. I was run off my feet trying to take care of them. Calamine lotion became my best friend at that time. They saw nothing else. The blisters weren't too pretty, especially when they cracked. Eileen's were the worst.

Kevin bought her toys to try and take her mind off herself. He was able to get them at cut prices in Clery's. That was a great help to our money situation. He got her a rag doll that she adored but every time she held it close to her she winced. Anything that touched her skin at all was agony to her, the creature.

He was great at entertaining her. He made funny faces at her and acted the eejit. 'You'll be better before you're married,' he told her. That brought a smile to her lips. He got her a Christmas stocking and stuffed it with all sorts of nic-nacs.

I knew he was trying to make up to her for the fact that he thought I was giving most of my attention to Cillian. I didn't think I was but there was no point arguing about it with him. He was like Daddy when he had his mind made up about something.

'A mother loves her first child the most,' he pronounced in one of his know-all moods, 'especially if it's a boy.'

'Thanks for telling me,' I said, 'I hadn't noticed.'

Siobhan was the hardest of the three to get to go to school. She used to get upset even thinking about it. I was forever writing sick notes for her. She had a cross teacher in First Class. He seemed to enjoy picking on her. I went down to him at one stage to ask him to go easier on her. She told me he hit her on the knuckles one day with a ruler when she couldn't grasp something. I hated aggressive parents but sometimes you had to take action. Kevin was useless at things like that so it was usually left to me.

I felt close to Siobhan because I'd been so bad at school myself. Eileen was brainy but she couldn't be bothered most of the time. She'd lose concentration at the drop of a hat. We were depending on Cillian to stop the teachers thinking we were all anti-school in the family. With the other two I rarely relished the prospect of going to parent-teacher meetings. I generally tended to slip away early, expecting to hear bad stuff about Siobhan and Eileen if I hung around too long.

Cillian, in contrast, had always come through with flying colours in any test he took, even from High Babies. He was particularly talented at Maths. When he hadn't his head dug in *Children's Brittanica* he was able to demonstrate his skill at mental arithmetic. That's something people don't seem to bother with nowadays because of calculators just like they don't bother with spelling because of all the texting. I hate to think what the next generation will be like. Illiterate and not able to count, probably.

I was over the moon at his progress. So were the teachers, but Kevin continued to think he was too much into the books. When I'd be encouraging him to study he'd start dribbling a ball in front of him.

'If you just leave the ball there he might play with it,' I'd say, 'Stuffing it in his face is going to turn him off it.' He didn't think much of my psychology. He kept doing his best with the dribbling but I felt he was on a losing ticket with that one.

He brought him out to the back garden some days after school for games of backs and forwards but I couldn't really see the point of these. The girls seemed to be even more interested in these games than Cillian, pulling off their jerseys excitedly to use as goalposts on the fine days.

He brought him to a few soccer matches in Dalymount Park when he got older but he was bored silly at these. 'Everyone looks as if they're trying to be the new George Best,' he used to say. Kevin's father came up if Athlone was playing. Cillian used to beg me not to have to go to these matches. I knew how he felt. I'd felt the same way when I started going out with Kevin first. When I said that to him he said, 'This is different. You're a woman.'

No matter how much I pleaded with him he kept pushing Cillian. After a while it became a big issue between us. It's one of the few things I can remember us arguing about on a regular basis. He thought soccer would make a man of him but I believed in letting children develop in their own way. I even wrote a note to his PR teacher once asking him to be excused from football practice. I never told Kevin about that. He'd have gone through the roof.

He dragged him away from his homework any chance he got so they could play football in the back garden. I could see Cillian aching for it to rain or get dark so he wouldn't have to go.

One day he came in with a black eye after they'd had a game. Kevin had been taking penalties on him. He'd hit him straight in the face with one of them. 'It was a bulltop,' Cillian said. I didn't know what that meant. He said Kevin hit the ball with the tip of his boot instead of the side of it. I couldn't imagine why he'd done that unless he wanted to knock Cillian's head off.

'He has to improve his reflexes,' he said.

I took a packet of peas from the freezer and put it over his eye. He was wincing in pain.

'Why did you hit the ball so hard?' I said.

'It wasn't that hard. He had all the time in the world to put his hands up.'

'Don't ever do that again,' I said, 'He isn't an adult.'

'He isn't a girl either,' he shot back. 'I don't want him to grow up to be a nancy boy.'

I slept on the sofa that night. It was the only night of my married life I ever went that far. I wanted to send out a message to him that his behaviour was unacceptable. He probably knew it himself but wouldn't admit it.

He stopped bringing him to Dalymount after that but he kept up the kickabouts in the back garden. It was a kind of compromise. It broke his heart the day he finally agreed to throw Cillian's football boots into the bin. I was mightily relieved. They'd hardly ever been used.

If Cillian was Kevin's problem, Eileen was mine. From the day she was born I felt there was friction between us. I wondered if it was something to do with how I'd been when I was pregnant with her. My emotions were all over the place during those months. Psychologists tell us the mood of the mother affects the unborn child. Maybe the next generation will throw more light on that subject.

When she was teething she almost broke the sound barrier. I don't know if Kevin or myself ever got a full night's sleep during these years. When she got older she developed a destructive instinct. We had to watch her like a hawk to make sure she didn't pull the house down. She was capable of knocking over everything she looked at. She started with books that were on shelves and graduated to items of furniture.

We used to look at her with a mixture of shock and awe, Cillian and Siobhan included. Kevin was more amused than anything else but then it was easy for him. He didn't have to do the tidying up.

She'd get extremely difficult if you tried to stop her. I remember watching her one day knocking over a house of cards Cillian built. It took him ages but she swept it aside in a half second. He was so upset that day I felt totally distraught. I don't believe in smacking children but I came close to it then. I gave her a stern talking to even though I knew she wasn't listening to a word of it. Her eyes were going all around the room, probably wondering what other mischief she could get up to.

If you told her it was time to go to bed and she didn't want to go it was sending her to the gallows. If she didn't want a bath and you put her into it there'd be war. She'd jump out of it and start roaring at you as she splashed the water all over the floor in a rage. She also refused to sit in her carrycot in the car, insisting on being on my lap instead.

She refused to obey me no matter what I asked her. She seemed to enjoy defying me almost for the sake of it. If I asked her to do something she'd stamp her feet so hard you'd think she was going to dislodge a floorboard. She'd fight you as soon as look at you. I tried to turn a blind eye to this as much as I could.

I knew she was troubled inside. All you had to do was look at her bed after she slept in it to see that. The sheets would be so crumpled she was probably tossing and turning all night. I could never figure out the reason why. Maybe she was just made like that. 'It can't be easy being Eileen,' Kevin said, 'She's her own worst enemy.'

She seemed to have been sizing the pair of us up from very early childhood. Whenever I read a fairytale to her she'd look at my face instead of listening to what I was saying. 'You look tired,' she'd say, or 'Why are you wearing that blouse?'

Other times she'd get bored. 'I heard that one before,' she'd say, 'Read me something else.' I didn't think that was normal. Cillian and Siobhan both liked hearing the same stories over and over when they were her age.

I had such an easy time raising those two, a troublesome child was the last thing I expected. For that reason maybe I didn't react to Eileen too well. Or maybe I was subconsciously taking my nine months of pain out on her. When people said she was a lovely child I'd whisper to Kevin, 'Yes, when she's asleep.'

Whenever I got firm with her it only made her worse. She'd screw up her eyes and say, 'Why are you nicer to Cillian and Siobhan than me?' Comments like that made me draw in my horns. We bought bunk beds for herself and Siobhan one year to try and make them closer but it didn't work. If Siobhan asked for the top one, Eileen would want it too. If Siobhan gave in, which she generally did, she'd change her mind again. Then she'd keep her awake half the night poking her.

As she got older she kept wanting more and more toys. It was so different to my own childhood where I thought I was doing well if I got a doll for Christmas. I knew a lot of it was fuelled by the monster of television blaring out ads all day.

We indulged her more than the other two put together. We spent most of our time walking on eggshells around her. Even when I was doing ordinary things like ironing her gymfrock I never seemed to be able to satisfy her. She'd find a crease in it somewhere and make me do it again. For a while Kevin thought she might have Obsessive Compulsive Disorder. He'd heard me talking about that condition from my experiences in some of the old folks' homes. 'It's not OCD,' I told him, 'She's just being a nuisance.'

Anytime she was hyper I didn't know what to do with her. 'She'll come back to herself in her own time,' Aunt Bernie said to me one night when she was practically tearing the walls down, 'She's just extrovert.' I said, 'I can think of another word for it.

She was as good with her as she'd been with the other two any time she came up to us. Whenever we were under pressure she'd offer to take them all out for a walk. Kevin would say sometimes as she was going out the door, 'you don't need to bother bringing them back.' That always brought a smile to her face.

I could never understand her ability to make them go quiet when they were acting up. It was almost as if an angel entered the room.

'What's your secret?' I asked her but she just laughed. 'Children tend to be nicer to people they don't see much,' she said. That was nonsense. I knew she'd have made a great mother. It made it all the more tragic to think of what happened between herself and Dan Toibin.

I only saw her with him once. It was on one of my trips down to Midleton. I was shopping with her for a pair of trainers for Cillian. We were looking at some pairs in the window of a sports shop when we saw him inside. From the look on his face I thought he would have preferred not to see us but once he did he had to wave to us. He came out to us a few seconds later. The way Aunt Bernie looked at him I felt she still had feelings for him. He started jabbering on a mile a minute about Una and the children. I felt he was talking fast out of nerves. Aunt Bernie had a sad smile on her face. I couldn't find it in myself to be friendly to him because of what he did to her but she was always a lady.

'How is Una?' she asked him.

'Not too bad,' he said, 'She's in the car waiting for me so I better not keep her too long. It's lovely to see you. You look great.' Before he went away he said, 'You'll have to come down and see us sometime. I'm in the book if you want to ring me.' She said she would. He gave her an awkward hug before going off.

'How can you be so nice to him after all that happened between the two of you?' I said to her as he disappeared into his car.

'It wasn't his fault,' she said, 'We weren't right for one another.'

We didn't bother about the trainers after that. We just got the bus home. She was quiet on the journey, looking out the window all the way. Her eyes were glazed. I didn't want to look too hard at her in case she was crying. After we reached the house she said she wouldn't come in. I tried to persuade her but she said she was expecting visitors in her own house.

'Mammy has a meal prepared for you,' I said, 'She'll be disappointed.'

'I'll come up soon again,' she said. When I went in I didn't say anything to Mammy about us running into Dan. It would have upset her too much. Later that night  rang Aunt Bernie to ask her how she was.

'I'm as good as ever,' she said, 'You don't have to keep looking out for me. I'm fairly tough, believe it or not.'

She put on a good performance of being so but I knew she was a sheep in wolf's clothing. It would have been lovely for her to have had someone else in her life after Dan but she never considered it. There was a man in the post office who had his eye on her for a while but she either pretended not to notice or didn't. The expression 'one man woman' could have been invented with her in mind.

She became less energetic as she aged. She was still wonderful with the children but she didn't play with them as much now. One time she came up to babysit for us to give us a break from them. We decided to go to a film. It was *One Flew Over the Cuckoo's Nest*. Nurse Ratched brought back Joanne Wylie to me with a bang

After we got home we found her flaked out on the couch with the television blaring in front of her. The children were running around her like mad things. They were having the time of their lives since there was nobody to supervise them.

'Stop it!' I shouted at them, 'You'll waken Aunt Bernie.'

'We have to waken her,' Cillian said, 'It's time for her to go to bed.'

He didn't realise what he'd for a minute. When he did, we all started laughing. When Aunt Bernie woke up she got embarrassed.

'What's going on?' she said. We were laughing so much we couldn't tell her. Cillian was so doubled up he actually fell on the floor. He was rolling around the place with tomato ketchup all over his face. That made it even funnier.

'Did you all have a good night?' I asked him when he got his breath back.

'We spent the night Auntie-sitting,' he informed me.

# The Long Hot Summer

As the children grew older they became less inclined to want to go to Midleton for the summer holidays. Up until now we couldn't afford to go anywhere else but when Kevin's salary increased and the mortgage payments came down, we decided to do something adventurous, at least by our standards.

Instead of going down to Midleton one summer, our usual practice when the schools closed, we decided to rent out a caravan in Skerries. They were being widely advertised at the time for people who couldn't afford to go abroad. They had all the mod cons and were ideal for children too. Kevin and myself had our own bedroom. There was a kitchen-cum-living room beside it with a breakfast bar in it.

It also had a toilet and a shower. The children slept in a second bedroom. Cillian had a tiny bed. It was just about long enough for him. Siobhan and Eileen were in in bunk beds across from him. To look at it from outside you'd never have thought it could have fitted all that. The man who designed it obviously knew how to make the most of his space.

By this time Kevin had learned to drive. He'd put in enough years getting nervous breakdowns as I tried to negotiate the twisting roads to Cork in my demented way. It was either that or he got fed up of people telling him it didn't look good being a passenger to a 'mere' woman. Reg, surprise surprise, was one of them.

'Good to see you have the wheels now, Kev,' he'd say, looking disparagingly at me. He couldn't say 'car.' He always had to have these trendy expressions like 'wheels.' It was like the way he called our kids 'bambinos.' (People who called children 'bambinos,' I noticed, usually didn't have any).

He used to drive us down in mid-June. Then he'd join us for the last week in July and the first one in August. That was when he got his annual leave.

The original plan was just to go for one summer but we had such a good time that first year we made it into a habit. It became our home from home, the place we returned to each year like migrating birds. It was different enough from Dublin to make you feel you'd been on an actual holiday and near enough to it to make the travelling not too much of a burden. It was the ideal place for us to recharge our batteries for the year ahead.

The children liked it best when the tourists were around. There was a lot of activity then but I preferred the quietness. I loved walking the beach when it was deserted. It became my special place at times like that. When I was the only person on it I was able to delude myself into thinking I was the only person in the world who knew about it, despite the fact that it had been thronged with holiday-makers 24 hours before.

Every year the same sights greeted us as we got to our destination: the scruffy dunes, the pale sky over the silent sea, the little shop with the beach balls hanging from a ball of twine outside the window. I did things like making sandcastles with the children and joining them on the swing boats and in the amusement parlours. It's true what they say about being a parent: The more time you spend with children the more you become a child yourself.

One year I won a teddy bear for Eileen by throwing a rubber ring onto a hook. Afterwards I felt like dancing a jig of delight. It reminded me of the teddy bear Aunt Bernie gave me when I was a child, the one that played 'Tulips from Amsterdam.' I probably got more excited than she did. Cillian had to tell me to tone it down a bit. There were too many people watching me.

When it rained we watched television on a little portable set we had. Because the caravan was small, the television didn't seem to be. Everything was relative. We were reduced to the dimensions of our little world.

We lived in each other's pockets for two months. We thought we'd argue more than we did but it actually worked the other way, bringing us closer together. We made do on little. There was a cooker in the caravan. I put fish fingers on the grill every other day. The kids loved them. I also cooked a lot of junk food which they happily demolished – or should I say 'we' happily demolished. Despite my promises not to 'let myself go' any time I was on holidays, I always piled on the pounds in Skerries.

This entailed many trips to dressmakers to have my clothes let out after we got back to Dublin. At times it seemed I only had to look at a box of After-Eights for my weight to increase. When I started to dig in for real, that increase was multiplied by a hundred. In time I learned the truth of the old saying, 'A minute on the lips, an eternity on the hips.'

During our last summer there, the hottest on record, I met a man. He owned one of the other caravans in the park. He usually looked troubled whenever I saw him.

He was in his mid-forties. There was a car outside his caravan that seemed to have the bonnet permanently up. His head was often buried in it as he revved it up and down checking things. Sometimes he'd look over at me and I'd wave at him. I didn't know whether I was supposed to say hello to him or not. Was it rude to ignore him? Or too familiar to wave?

There was something about him that made me want to talk to him. He had a way of looking at you that made you think you knew him. He didn't have to say anything. It was just there. He used to nod at me when I was walking the beach with the children. We never talked but I felt we still had some kind of connection with one another. It was a nice feeling but in some ways I was afraid of it.

I was walking along the prom one day when he appeared beside me and we fell into conversation. The children weren't with me. They'd been getting on my nerves with the noise they were making and I'd had to get out.

He said his name was Tom, that he was a car dealer from Kildare.

We sat on a bench looking out at the sea. After a while we started talking. I can't remember what we talked about. It was probably something ordinary like the weather. I was glad to get a break from the children. No matter how much I loved them it did me good to speak to an adult now and again. I knew it would be ages before Kevin got down to us. He was having an especially difficult time at work with orders coming in from Europe.

He had a packet of sweets in his hand and he offered me one. As I sat eating it he said, 'Do you mind if I say something personal to you?' I didn't know what was coming.

'Go on,' I said.

He put his head back and looked up at the sky. He was on the point of tears.

'My marriage is just after ending,' he said, 'My wife left me.'

'That's terrible,' I said.

'She's taking me for every penny. I've lost my business as well. Lock, stock and barrel. All I have is the shirt on my back. Sometimes I think she's going to be looking for that too. She cleaned me out.'

A part of me wanted to make some excuse about having to be back with the children but a part of me was curious too.

'Do you have children?' I asked.

'Thankfully no.'

'Is she with someone else now?'

'Yes.'

He told me about how they met, how they started going out together, how everything was rosy in the garden for the first few years. Then she began to get bored with him, telling him she was frustrated about the fact that they never went anywhere.

'She was right,' he admitted, 'I was too busy trying to make a living to think about bringing her out.'

His business got bigger as the years went on. That meant he was out even more. Then she started to go out. One night when he came in from the garage unexpectedly he heard her talking to someone on the phone. She hung up in a hurry. When he asked her who it was she said, 'My mother.'

Something about the way she said it made him doubt her. After that he began to wonder if she was seeing other men. Then one night he found her in bed with one of his customers. He was someone he'd just sold a car to. He was devastated but he forgave her. She said it had never happened before and never would again.

'From that moment,' he said, 'the marriage was over.'

They rumbled on but something was gone from the relationship for him, something he couldn't get back. His business continued to grow and she continued to be out more. After a while he stopped caring if she was seeing other men or not. There was nothing between them even when they were together. What depressed him most of all was the fact that he didn't care. They started to live separate lives despite being under the one roof. It was a horrible situation.

The more he talked, the more I found myself getting wrapped up in his story.

'How long did you go on like that?' I asked him.

'Too long for her but not long enough for me. One day I came home from work and she was gone. There was a note pinned to the fridge. It said, "Your dinner is in someone else's oven." I never saw her again.'

I asked him if he qualified for anything from the government but he said he couldn't because he was self-employed. He had some savings but the solicitors got whatever was left of them when she put in her oar.

He started to cry then. I always felt uncomfortable when people cried in my presence. If I knew him better I could have put my arms around him. I should have told him I had to go but I didn't. I hung on, feeling more and more involved in his predicament.

Why? I wasn't sure. A lot of things were getting in on me. Eileen had been getting on my nerves for the usual reasons, acting up half the day without any reason. I was also missing Kevin. He was supposed to have come down to be with us the previous week but something came up at work that he had to deal with. It was to do with the union. He was getting involved in that side of things now to protect his position. I was feeling sorry for myself sleeping alone every night. Was Tom a kind of replacement for him? I wasn't sure.

'Would you have a drink with me?' he said then. Normally I'd have run a mile from any man who asked me that but instead I just went blank. The question stunned me.

'Please,' he said.

I thought the children would be safe for a while at least so I said okay. When I did, his face lit up. He said it meant a lot to him to have someone to listen to him. He'd been keeping his problems to himself for so long.

We went to one of the local pubs. It was dark and run down. There was a lot of grease on the counter. At almost every table there were unwashed glasses and bottles. The ashtrays were overflowing with cigarette butts. It wasn't the kind of place I'd have gone to with Kevin in a million years.

391

We sat at a table and he ordered the drinks. He was having a pint of Guinness. I said I'd have wine. After it arrived he carried on talking where he left off on the promenade. Even from the first sip I could feel it going to my head. I felt I was listening to the script of a film. He filled in the details of how he'd been married to this demon from hell who'd fleeced him for every penny he'd ever earned, a woman who was evil personified in his eyes.

'Wasn't I lucky she left me the caravan?' he said, 'If it wasn't for that I'd be living in my car. I had to for a while. I got quite used to it. The only problem was the absence of indoor plumbing.' I wasn't sure if I was meant to laugh or cry when he said that. I gave a kind of nervous giggle.

They'd bought it not long after they were married. Things were going well with them then. It was meant to be somewhere for them away from the tar and cement, somewhere they could go to escape the impersonality of the city. Now it was all he had.

'Those were the good old days,' he said, 'We were like yourself and your husband.'

It made me uncomfortable to hear him talking about me. Had he been watching us? I asked him how he knew about Kevin. He said he'd seen him the day he drove us down.

'I know you have children as well,' he said, 'I see you playing with them.'

'Have you been stalking me?' I said half-jokingly.

'No,' he said, 'Just envying you.'

I started wondering if he was laying on his misery to try and get off with me. I knew a lot of women would have seen him as one of those 'My wife doesn't understand me' Lotharios trying to seduce them.

They may have been right but I decided to give him the benefit of the doubt. My normal instinct was to take people at face value. His story seemed to be too fantastic for him to have made it up.

'She was a total nutter,' he said, 'If she didn't divorce me I had visions of her throwing me out a window.'

When I looked at my wine glass it was empty. I couldn't believe it. Normally I'd get a night out of a glass but we'd only been in the bar for what seemed like about ten minutes.

'Will you have another one?' he said.

'I don't know if I should.'

'Go on,' he said, 'You only live once.'

'All right, but this will definitely be the last. I have to get back to the children.'

He went up to the counter. As he was standing there a woman at the next table started staring at me. She was staying in one of the caravans near us. She knew I was married because she'd seen me with Kevin. Was she thinking I was having an affair? I didn't look back at her but I could feel her eyes burrowing through me.

When he came back to the table he started talking about his wife again, this time more intensely. The faster he talked, the more questions I threw at him. I was drinking really fast. It was only my second glass but already I felt drunk.

Even though he was talking about a tragic situation I felt myself getting almost high.

'I hate her,' he said, 'If it wasn't for her I wouldn't be reduced to living in this kip – no offence.'

He went into all the details of going to solicitors to plead his case. He said she told so many lies about him they must have thought he was some kind of psychopath. When she went to court for a separation they made mincemeat of him. She was so good at it, he said, she could almost have been a solicitor herself. She'd obviously been planning it for a long time.

'It's easier for a woman to pull the wool over a judge's eyes than a man,' he said. When I thought about it I probably agreed with him despite the fact that it sounded like an anti-woman comment.

She lied about him having other women, he said, and everything else she could think of.

'You never know a woman until you meet her in court. Even the way she dressed was different. I hardly recognised her.'

The more he went on the more my eyes were opened to what some people would do from greed. Most of the stories I'd heard about marriage break-ups concerned men who were alcoholics or beating their wives up or cheating on them. I now saw men could be the victims too.

'I knew she was bad news from the beginning,' he said, 'but I loved her. Love can be a bad thing sometimes. It's where you always go wrong. It uses up all your chances.'

I sat gazing across at the woman who stared at me. She gave me another glare. Then she stomped out of the bar. She made me feel really tense

He wasn't even aware of her.

'Well, that's my sob story,' he said, 'I hope I didn't bore you too much.'

'How could you have bored me? I feel really sorry for you. It's so unfair. Everything you worked for gone down the drain like that.'

He went quiet. His eyes were sleepy.

'We better go,' I said.

He stood up unsteadily. He still had half a pint of Guinness left.

'Are you not going to finish that?' I said.

'I'd be better off if I never started it.'

We went out into the night. The wind from the sea cut through us. He walked me back to the caravan as the sun was going down.

I put my hand out to shake hands with him as we got to it but instead of shaking it he kissed it.

'You have no idea how much today meant to me,' he said.

I found my heart starting to beat fast. I wanted to run away from him but I couldn't. My feet felt like lead. I looked into his eyes, those eyes that reminded me of Daddy's. They looked at me pleadingly.

Then he kissed me.

In the normal course of events I'd have beaten him away but I found myself kissing him back. Was it the drink? Could I really have kissed a man I didn't know from Adam?

'I've never met anyone I could talk to like you,' he said.

His eyes became sad again. He reminded me of one of those wolfhound dogs that look at you as if they're going to cry. I couldn't believe I was standing outside my caravan in his arms.

He tried to kiss me again but this time I stopped him.

'I have to go,' I said, releasing myself from his grip. I was terrified someone would be looking at us. I kept thinking of the woman in the bar.

'Please don't go in yet,' he said, 'I promise I won't try and kiss you anymore.'

I looked in the window of the caravan. Cillian and Siobhan were sitting at the table playing cards. Had they heard anything? If they had, my life was over.

'Just walk with me to my caravan,' he said, 'It's only a few minutes away.'

I started walking with him without realising what I was doing. It was as if my feet were being propelled by some other being. He talked non-stop all the way. He was like someone who hadn't talked to anyone for a month and now it was all flooding out of him.

When we got to his caravan he reached into his pocket for the key to the door. When he did so everything that was in it spilled out.

'Just what I need,' he said, 'Brilliant.'

He knelt down on the ground.

'I can't see a damn thing,' he said. He looked pathetic scrambling around. I wanted to help him but I didn't. I was afraid he'd leap on top of me or something.

He found the key eventually.

'Eureka,' he said, smiling at me.

He put it in the door.

'Will you come in for a minute?' he said, 'You know you can trust me now, don't you?'

I followed him in. The stench of whiskey hit me as soon as I got inside. Everything was in a mess. The lino on the floor had a big tear on it. A few empty whiskey bottles were lined up on the window sill. There was a row of beer cans beside them, crushed the way some people crushed cigarette packets when they were finished with them. I thought to myself: This is his life.

A dirty teapot stood on the table. It had a little cap on it like one you'd wear on your head. .

'Is that meant to be a tea cosy?' I said.

He nodded.

He must have seen the look of amusement on my face. He said, 'When you're living on your own you don't care about things like that.'

I tried to look sympathetic. The nurse in me wanted to clean everything up but I knew that would have been wrong. It would have sent out some kind of signal. In any case, what would have been the point? It would probably be back like this again in a few days.

He had a little television set on top of the fridge. It was about the same size as our one. There was a car racing programme on. The sound was turned down. Beside it sat a little plant. It looked like it had been there since the last century.

'Has the TV been on all the time you were out?' I asked him.

'Probably. Looking at it drowns out my thoughts.'

'Do you mind if I turn it off?'

'Of course not.'

He had a convector heater in the corner that was on as well. It was rattling like the propeller of a helicopter.

'Has that been on all the time too?'

'I suppose so.'

'These things cost money. You should be more careful.'

'What's a few pounds when you're bankrupt? When you go that far down the ladder, you have to almost look up to see the bottom.'

'Don't be so negative. Things could turn around for you.'

'I'm sorry. I don't want to take out my problems on you. My head is in a jamjar these days. The place could go up and I'd hardly notice.'

'It certainly will go up if you play around with electricity.'

I went over to the sink. Everything looked filthy. I washed a few of the glasses.

'Don't start that or you'll be at it for the two days,' he said.

There were some potatoes on one of the plates. They looked like octopuses with the roots hanging out of them. A blue-moulded slice of bread was beside them. I threw them all into the bin.

'You'll get into bad health if you don't mind yourself,' I said.

'You're a nurse, aren't you?' he said then.

'How did you know that?' I asked him but he didn't say.

'Do you mind if I open a window?' I said.

'Be my guest. This place needs a woman's touch.'

That was the understatement of the year. It wasn't so much a woman's touch it needed as fumigation. I felt I was going to suffocate if I didn't get the window open but the catch was rusty. I cut my hand on it.

'Jesus!' he said. He ran to a drawer for a plaster.

'It's nothing.'

'Nonsense. You're a nurse. You should know the dangers of rust in a wound. Let me wash it for you.'

He took my hand and ran it under the tap. It stung for a minute. He put the plaster on.

'Do you think I'd make a doctor?' he asked me.

'Undoubtedly. You could specialize in gangrene complications.'

He asked me to take my coat off so I did. I looked out the window. There was a battered car outside. He saw me looking at it.

'It's knackered,' he laughed, 'I'm trying to get it going again but it's a bit of a job.' It looked it had been hit by a truck. 'It's like a friendly old dog to me at the moment,' he claimed.

He was hyperventilating as he spoke. He was so white I thought he was going to faint.

'If you don't mind me saying so,' I said, 'Your lifestyle doesn't seem to be too healthy.'

'It's a miracle I'm not in hospital. I've been living on a diet of fingernails and coffee.' I hadn't noticed his nails before now; they were almost bitten down to the quick.

He threw a few clothes off a chair.

'Sit down there,' he said. 'Excuse the mess. The cleaning lady ran off with the milkman.'

I didn't associate him with humour. Maybe it was black comedy – the only kind he had left.

His tablecloth was the previous day's newspaper. It was open at the racing pages.

'Can I get you a cup of tea? he said. 'Maybe you'd like another glass of wine.'

There was a bottle on the table.

'Okay,' I said for some crazy reason, 'We might as well be hanged for a sheep as a lamb.' I was turning into Kevin in his worst days.

'That's my kind of talk.'

He poured a glass for each of us. His hands were trembling. As he cleared the table to make way for the glasses I saw solicitor's letters scattered everywhere. Some of them had wine stains on them. I imagined him reading them in the small hours over other glasses on other evenings, wondering where his life had gone.

'I don't think I should be here,' I said.

'Is it because of the mess?'

'No. It's because of…everything.'

'Don't think about it. We're not doing anything wrong. This might sound dramatic but you're giving me the will to go on again. My parents are dead. I'm an only child. The people I thought were my friends have been fair weather ones. You don't know how good it feels to have someone to talk to. You don't even need to talk back.'

He gulped down the wine. Then he poured himself another glass.

'What about you?' he said.

'No,' I told him. 'Not this time. I'm way past my limit.'

I felt my bladder was about to explode but I didn't ask him if I could go to the toilet. I was afraid of what I might find in there.

Just as I was about to tell him I had to go he broke down crying. He started to re-hash the whole thing about his wife again, burbling into a handkerchief like a baby. Was it an act or was he really this devastated?

I went over to comfort him after a minute. He gave me one of those looks I was afraid of, the Daddy look. A moment later I was in his arms and we were kissing again, more passionately this time. I couldn't stop myself. I felt myself being sucked into a black hole by some invisible force.

The crazy thing was, I wasn't even attracted to him. Why was I doing it? Was it out of pity? Had another person invaded me?

Before I knew what was happening he started running his fingers through my hair. Then he put his hand up under my jumper. He tried to unhook my bra. I felt as if I was seventeen again in the back seat of a car with someone I'd met at the Ierne.

'Stop!' I shouted. I drew myself away from him. He looked startled. I went back to my chair.

My shout seemed to wake him from a trance, to wake both of us from one.

'I'm sorry,' he said, 'I've never done anything like this before.'
It was like a line from a bad film but somehow I believed it.
'Please don't kiss me again,' I said.
'Don't worry about that.'

I felt sick. Sick from the wine and from what I'd done. How could I go back to the caravan? Even if nobody was aware of what I did, how could I live with myself?

'I'm going now,' I said. This time he knew I meant it.
'Can I see you again?' he asked in a desperate voice.
'I don't think that would be a good idea.'
'Please. I need to. Not for anything romantic, just for a chat. It would mean the world to me.'
'We're only living a few doors away from one another. I'll talk to you when the children are there.'
'All right. I understand.'
'Please let me go now.'
'Okay.'

I stood up.

'Maybe you'll meet me some day for a coffee. In a public place. When people are around. People other than your children.'
'Maybe.'

I put on my coat. As I walked out the door he put his hands up in a pleading gesture to me.

'Goodbye,' I said, trying to put an air of finality into the word.
'Goodbye.'

He closed the door and went back in. He looked out the window as I started to walk away but I didn't look back.

I walked towards the caravan but when I got close to it I found myself getting tense. I knew I couldn't go back in the condition I was in even if the children were all asleep. Before I reached it I changed direction, going down towards the sea instead. I needed to clear my head.

How had I let this happen, I asked myself. Was I not happy with Kevin?

I got to the beach, a beach I'd been to so many times over the years. It looked different now. That was because I wasn't used to coming down to it so late at night. The tide was in. I'd never seen the moon so bright. Waves crashed their way towards me. I sat down beside one of the dunes. I should have been freezing but I wasn't. Was that because of the wine?

I felt my bladder was about to burst. The toilets were locked so I had to go to a Portaloo behind the lifeguard's hut.

I sat down on the sand after I got back to the beach. Shadows drifted over the dunes. A dog was chasing a seagull. It dipped towards him and then flew away as if taunting him. He barked at it with his tail wagging.

The moon glinted through the clouds. The sun was just above the horizon. It seemed to disappear below it in a matter of seconds, carrying the last light of day with it.

I was the only person on the beach. There were pebbles all around me. I took off my coat. I put it under me so they wouldn't dig into me. The wind came up and made me shiver. It blew my hair into my eyes. I listened to the seagulls screeching above me like predators.

The summer was dying. Maybe that was what was wrong with me. I always hated change. In Skerries I turned into another woman, my childhood self. I'd let myself be sucked into something because I was afraid of going back to my boring Dublin one. I was afraid of the routines of being a mother, a wife, the kind of woman May made fun of anytime she saw me. A part of me was wild, wild with the wildness of a child. But it was only a small part. I knew I needed to get back to my Dublin personality. Being here was wrong for me. It was a dangerous freedom.

I smelt rain on the wind. The sky was streaked with purple. It seemed very close to me, so close it might have fallen down on me. It was full of stars. The tide came in some more, slushing against the rocks. I watched waves running to the shore and then ebbing back, sucking the pebbles on the sand with them.

The wind whistled through me like a banshee. A weird sense of calmness descended on me. The sky breathed down on me like a balm.

I knew I should go back but I didn't want to. I wanted to swim out to sea, to travel away from all my problems on the tide.

A mad thought struck me. I could walk out into the waves now and it would all be over, all my guilt and all my shame. Then I thought: You're crazy. Nothing happened. You're blowing it out of all proportion.

I remembered a story Kevin told me once about a man he heard of who decided to drown himself on Dollymount. He walked into the water one night with a bottle of whiskey in his hand. He was hoping to get dutch courage from it to do what he intended to do. The tide was going out, though. After ten minutes walking it was still only up to his knees. He was freezing cold. He said to himself, 'Feck this for a game of cowboys. He ended up bolting back to the shore and driving home to his wife. They both had a laugh about it the next morning.

Was I as mad as that man? Who was putting these thoughts into my head? Pull yourself together, girl, I kept saying to myself, you're behaving like an adolescent.

I looked out at a ship on the sea. A line of poetry I'd learned at school came back to me: 'As idle as a painted ship upon a painted ocean.' Everything looked to be frozen in time. I felt I could have sat there for three hours and it would have seemed like as many minutes. That's what wine did to me. It made time slip away like grains of sand.

I tried to process what just happened. Was it trivial or significant? I wasn't sure. There must have been some want in me to let him come on to me like he did. If it happened once it could happen again. I had so many people who loved me and yet I'd gone into a caravan with a stranger and kissed him. I needed my head examined.

The waves licked at my feet. I watched the night growing darker. Lights went off in the houses around me. I thought of Tom settling down for the night in his chaos, thinking of all he'd lost.

Tom. I'd never once called him by his name. That said it all.

Were his intentions honourable towards me? Or mine towards him? Our meeting had come from nothing. Now I wanted it to go back to nothing.

I knew that might be easier said than done. I'd opened a door for him. Even if we just went for a coffee the next time it would be awkward.

I walked back to the caravan. I was soaked to the skin. As well as everything else my shoes were letting in. I picked my steps across the garbage containers that divided the beach from the houses. There was barbed wire beside them. As I tried to make my way through it I caught my coat on it. I had to tug it free. It was like that first night at the pictures with Kevin. What would he think of me if he saw me now?

When I got to the caravan I stood outside for a moment trying to collect my thoughts. I could hear Siobhan and Cillian talking inside. They seemed to be watching television.

I went in. I was shaking, either from the cold or my guilt. I kicked off my shoes. Cillian smiled at me. I wondered if he'd seen anything. I'd have been mortified if he did. I was supposed to be the sensible one of the family.

'Hello, stranger,' he said.

'Hello, pet. How are things?'

'Fine.'

His eyes grew wide as he looked at me.

'Hey, you're wringing wet. Where were you? You look like you went for a swim with your clothes on.'

'Maybe I did,' I said. He gave me a strange look. I'd never spoken to him like that before. He was enjoying it. Little did he know how close to the truth he was.

I looked at myself in the mirror. My mascara was smudged. I thought of the old saying: 'Don't go out with married men if you're wearing mascara.' Except in my case it was rain rather than tears that smudged it.

'How about a cup of tea?' Cillian said.

'I'd love one.'

'The milk is sour,' Siobhan said, 'Cillian forgot to put it in the fridge.'

'Liar,' Cillian said, 'It was you that left it out. I knew you'd say that to get out of it.'

Normally I'd have refereed an argument like that but I let them at it.

Cillian put the kettle on.

'Your coat is torn,' he said.

'I know. I caught it in some barbed wire beside the bins.'

'Were you at the beach?'

'Yes.'

'When?'

'About twenty minutes ago.'

'What brought you down there?'

'My legs.'

'Very funny.'

'It's not against the law, is it? It was a lovely night. I felt like a walk.'

'You're always telling us not to go down there at night in case we got attacked.'

'That's different. You're children.'

He brought the tea over to me. I started to drink it.

'Who was that you were with earlier?' he asked me.

'How do you mean?'

'We saw you talking to someone a while ago.'

'Oh you mean Tom,' I said casually, 'He's just someone I met on the prom.'

'Is that they guy who's usually sitting by himself?'

'I don't know. I've never seen him before.'

'What were you talking about?'

'Nothing much.'

He looked at me strangely as if he knew I was lying. So did Siobhan. I was glad Eileen was in bed.

'I think I'll turn in,' I said, 'I feel exhausted.'

'Have you been drinking?' Cillian said.

'Why do you say that?'

'There's a smell of wine off you.'

I thought fast.

'That's my perfume.' He shrugged as if he didn't care one way or the other.

'Goodnight,' I said. I wanted to get out of there as fast as possible.

'Goodnight,' they both said together.

I went over to the washbasin. I started to brush my teeth but the toothpaste plopped out of the tube onto the floor. It was only then I realised how much my coordination was off. I was lucky to be able to find my mouth with the brush.

I felt more relaxed when I got to the bedroom. I sat down in front of my dressing-table. Suddenly I was back to my own life.

There was a box of chocolates on the window-sill. For some reason I felt ravenous. I opened it and started eating. Once I got the taste of them inside me I couldn't stop. I wasn't sure how long they were there. I had a vague memory of getting them as a present from someone I'd nursed through a hip replacement in the year dot.

The drawer of the dressing-table was open. A photo of myself and Kevin was sticking out. It was almost as if it was taunting me. I slammed it shut. The tiredness hit me again. I crawled onto the bed in my clothes. I thought of Tom in his caravan. How would he be feeling, I wondered, in his tense, lonely world.

I felt like being nice to myself so I put on a hot water bottle. I took two Panadols and lay down. I expected to nod off immediately but I didn't. Too many thoughts were churning around in my head. Eventually I drifted off but I had bad dreams. In one of them I was drowning and nobody came to save me. I wasn't sure what the significance of that was – probably that I thought of myself as a worthless specimen of humanity by now.

I woke up at 4 a.m. with my chest heaving. I knew the last thing I should have had was a cigarette but I still smoked one. And another one. And another.

My throat felt sore so I decided I'd have a hot whiskey. I went out to the kitchen. There was half a bottle in one of the presses. I poured some into a glass. Then I added sugar and cloves. I opened the fridge to get a lemon but when I took it out I saw it was full of bluemould. It nearly made me sick to look at it.

I threw the whiskey down the sink and went back to the bedroom. Was I turning into Tom, someone whose life was going off the rails? I spent the rest of the night tossing and turning. If I got half an hour's sleep it was as much. Anytime anything went wrong in my life it made me into a total insomniac. People used to say to me, 'Try counting sheep.' That was one of the stupidest suggestions I ever heard. What was the point of counting anything? You were awake for a reason.

When I woke up the next morning I was a wreck. I had a ferocious hangover from the wine. How many glasses had I drunk? If you didn't know, it was too many. It always affected me more if I was tense.

My tongue felt as if I'd been chewing on sawdust for the evening. That was from the cigarettes. Thank God I hadn't drunk the whiskey. I had the bluemoulded lemon to thank for that.

I could hear the television from the next room. The noise was like a drill going through my head. There was a weather report on. It was a cheery meteorologist telling us it was going to be rain, rain and more rain. Why were cheery morning people so irritating? Especially when they were telling you the summer was over and you felt like something the cat dragged in.

Cillian bounced into the room.

'Ugh,' he said, snuggling up against me, 'Your breath smells like the inside of an ash tray.'

'Thanks,' I said, 'You say the nicest things.'

'You have to get up,' he said, 'The troops need breakfast.'

'The troops will have to make their own breakfast this morning,' I croaked, 'Mammy is on strike.'

I turned away from him to let him know I needed to be on my own but after he left the room a pang of guilt hit me. I was their mother. No matter how bad I felt I had to get out to them.

I stumbled out to the kitchen They were sitting at the breakfast bar looking at me. The hungry sheep looked up. Would they be fed?

'Breakfast for the troops,' I said, putting my arms in the air. They all cheered.

I opened the fridge and started taking out things. The milk jug spilled on the floor.

'I'm after spilling the stupid milk,' I said.

'It wasn't the milk that was stupid,' Eileen said, 'It was you.'

Cillian said, 'Are you all right?'

'I'm a bit wobbly,' I said, 'Can you help me?'

'Of course.'

He told me to sit down. As soon as I did I started to feel unwell. I had to make a bee-line for the toilet. When I got there I threw up. I flushed the toilet to dry and drown out the sound but I imagined they heard it.

Mammy was supposed to be in charge but the captain of this ship was its most dangerous passenger.

When I got back to the kitchen I saw a bowl of cornflakes on the breakfast bar. No sooner had I put the first bite into my mouth than the bowl fell onto the floor. Butterfingers was making a comeback even though there was no Joanne Wylie to be seen.

I felt so frustrated I let out a curse. None of them had ever heard me utter one before. They were shocked.

'Oh my God,' Siobhan said.

'I'm sorry,' I said, 'I didn't mean to say that. I'm feeling terrible at the moment. I didn't sleep a wink last night. I think I'm coming down with something.'

'Go back to bed,' Siobhan said, 'We can get our own breakfast.'

'No,' I said adamantly, 'I'm up now so I might as well stay up. Sorry for the language. And for drinking too much last night.'

I'd admitted it without realising it. So what. There was no point in hiding it anymore.

I looked into the fridge to see if I could find anything that might act as 'blotting paper.' That was what Kevin called food you took for a hangover. All I could see was some stale cheese. It reminded me of something I might have seen in Tom's caravan. My stomach lurched as I looked at it.

I had a splitting headache. I looked at myself in the mirror and got a fright. There were some dried cornflakes stuck to my dressing gown.

My hair looked like I'd had a fight with a chainsaw. It was matted to the top of my head as if it was glued down. Why were mirrors so harsh? Could they not make ones that flattered your features? If they did they'd sell out on the spot.

Kevin hated when I wore the dressing gown. At least he wasn't there to see me. A small mercy.

Cillian wiped the cornflakes up.

'Sit down and I'll make you some breakfast,' he said.

'Thank you, Sir Lancelot, but I'm afraid I couldn't face breakfast this morning.'

'Then eat it with your back to it,' he said.

I put on a forced smile.

'You're very funny, sweetheart,' I said, 'but I'm not in the mood for jokes this morning.'

The kettle boiled. He made me a cup of tea. My head was still throbbing. Everything was annoying me. I didn't want anyone to even talk to me. I put the radio on loud to try and block out my thoughts.

'What are you doing?' Cillian said, 'You'll deafen us all.'

It was usually me who told them to turn the radio down. Now things were the other way round. He couldn't understand it.

I looked out the window to see what the weather was like. It was raining. Huge drops were falling on the windows. They ran down in rivulets. So the cheery meteorologist was right. I stared out at the sand dunes, at the sea. They never looked more miserable.

I found myself getting woozy again. The cup of tea felt loose in my grip. Cillian took it off me.

'Go back to bed,' he said.

This time I did. Sometimes when you were feeling bad enough there was nothing for it but to curl up under the covers.

I was sneezing like a train from the drenching I got the previous night. I didn't have any hankies so I used toilet paper to blow my nose.

I lay down on the bed. Before long I was asleep. I dreamt of Midleton, of days on the beach in Shangarry, of Daddy buying us ice cream cones and 99s and macaroon bars.

I woke up in the middle of the afternoon. The rain had eased off. I looked out the window. Siobhan and Eileen were playing with a frisbee outside. Cillian was reading a comic beside me.

'What time is it?' I said.

'Half three,' he said. I couldn't believe it. I was disgusted with myself. Where had the day gone?

'I can't believe I slept this long,' I said.

'So what? We're on our holidays.'

'No. I have to get up.'

'Why?'

'Because I have to.'

I dressed myself finally. Maybe now the day could begin for real. Or could it?

My heart was beating like a drum. I decided to have a shower to try and calm myself. I felt any kind of activity would do me good.

I stepped into the shower. Only a trickle of water came out. The pressure was always poor in the caravan but I didn't mind. I stayed ages in there letting the water flood over me.

When I came out I wiped the steam from the mirror. I looked at myself again. People think that if you keep looking at yourself you're vain but I always thought it was a sign of insecurity. I kept asking myself, 'Who's that strange woman gazing out at me with the demented expression on her face?' Why did some mirrors flatter you and others make you look like the wreck of the Hesperus?

I wrapped a towel around me. Cillian stared at me as I dried my hair. He asked me how I was feeling.

'If I was any better,' I said, 'I'd be worried about myself.'

He didn't know if I was joking or not.

I tried to comb my hair but it was like trying to comb steel wool. It was as if there was barbed wire on my head. I made a mental note to dump whatever shampoo I was using.

I looked out the window again. The day seemed to be brightening up. I decided to go out for a walk.

'Have you had anything to eat?' I said to Cillian.

'We got some sweets at the shop,' he said.

I told him I was going out. He looked surprised.

'When will we expect you back?'

'I don't know.'

I meant what I said. I wasn't sure where I was going. I went zig-zag across the dunes to delay reaching the beach. When I got there I sat down on the sand. I listened to the lapping of the waves.

I don't know how long I sat there. I hadn't my watch on me. My only idea of the time came from the darkening of the day.

Ever so slowly my tension evaporated. When I felt ready to face the children again I got up. I took a deep breath, inhaling the air like food.

As I was on my way back to the caravan I spotted a phone box. On the spur of the moment I decided to ring Kevin. I don't know why. Maybe I wanted him to protect me from myself.

I fumbled in my pocket for change. Eventually I found a few coins. It took me ages to be connected. When I got on to him he told me he was in the middle of serving a woman who was giving him problems. He kept me on Hold for a few minutes. I started stuffing coins into the phone thinking I'd be cut off. It seemed like an eternity before he came back to me.

'I finally got rid of her,' he said, 'What's wrong?'

'I need to see you,' I said.

'Why?'

I paused.

'Because I miss you.'

I hadn't spoken to him like that in years. He was more amused than anything else.

'That's touching,' he said, 'but Mark has me down for overtime for the next two weeks.' He'd worked for Mark for over fifteen years. Sometimes he referred to him as 'JR' after the character Larry Hagman played in *Dallas*. That was the soap opera we were all hooked on at the time. JR was always up to some tricks..

'Can you not do it some other time?'

'I don't know. It's manic here.'

The excitement I felt as I went into the box disappeared. I felt flat again.

'Okay.'

'There's nothing wrong, is there?'

'Not really.'

'What does "Not really" mean?'

'Nothing.'

'Thanks. That's a great help.'

'It's lonely without you. The day are hard to fill.'

'You seem to be doing pretty good from all the stories I've been hearing. Are you still winning teddy bears?'

'Don't be childish.'

His tone became harsh.

'How do you think I feel up in Dublin? I come home to an empty house every night.'

'So do I.'

'What's that supposed to mean?'

I felt my tongue running away on me. I was afraid of saying too much.

'I don't know. I'm not saying it's easy for you either but that's not the point.'

'What is?'

'You're usually down here at this time.'

'I know, and I would be if I could. But I have a living to earn. If I wasn't up here you wouldn't be able to be down there.'

'You're right. Sorry for being selfish.'

'Don't be sarcastic. I know you're annoyed with me.'

'I'm not. You're just doing what you have to do.'

'Do you not think I'd prefer to be sunning myself on a beach than selling carpets to troublemakers?'

'Just forget I said anything.'

I heard the pips going then. I reached into my pocket but I had no more.

'I hear the pips,' I said, 'I'll have to hang up.'

'Don't go off like that. I'll see if I can arrange some kind of compromise.'

'Thanks.'

'How are the kids?'

'Fine.'

'Okay. I'll see you soon then. That's a promise.'

'See you soon.'

I tried to sound upbeat but I was sick inside. The longer he was away, the more I was afraid of running into Tom. What would I say to him if he asked me to see him again? A part of me wanted to grab the children and head for the nearest train station.

For the next few days we all pigged out on junk food. I had no discipline. It continued to lash rain but I didn't mind. It gave me an excuse not to go out.

I kept showering for something to do, rinsing my hair like there was no tomorrow. I must have used up the best part of a container of shampoo on it. Showers always propped up my spirits. So did washing my hair. I put the water pressure up so high it took my breath away as it lashed down on me. I thought of Mitzi Gaynor in *South Pacific* singing 'I Want To Wash That Man Right Out Of My Hair.' Maybe I was trying to do the same thing with Tom.

I kept looking at the calendar waiting for it to be time for Kevin to join us. The more I looked at it the more the days crawled by. I felt bad for not being able to be a better mother to the children or not to be able to enjoy my surroundings more. I woke up to beautiful views every morning when other people my age were slaving into work. I blamed myself for not being able to count my blessings. It was the first time I'd ever been in Skerries where I found myself wanting time to pass. Up until now the summers were too short and the holidays over too fast.

The children sensed my distress. They wouldn't need to have been geniuses to do that. To be fair to them they entertained one another, leaving me to my own devices. Then Eileen came down with whooping cough. She'd always been a demanding patient. This was no exception.

In a way that was good for me. It took my mind off Tom. Cillian and Siobhan stayed out most of the time. One day they went on a ghost train. In the evenings they rode on the chair-o-planes or played the donkey derby. I gave them more pocket money in those few days than I usually did in a month. They didn't know what hit them. Up until now I was in the habit of doling it out to them in very small doses.

The caravan was like a tip with damp clothes hanging off every chair and table. Normally that would have driven me bonkers but for some reason I didn't mind. I bought wine from the local off-licence and had a glass or two at night. That surprised everyone because I rarely drank at home. I left the cork off the bottle one night. It tasted like vinegar the next day but I still drank it. All my old discipline was gone. I was also smoking cigarettes like there was no tomorrow.

Somehow the time passed. I watched television like a zombie. When it got cold I put a blanket over me and tucked my knees under my chin. I did crosswords to try to focus my mind on something.

I decided I was tired of the whole business of being a mother. I was tired of getting up to face three children hanging out of me for meals, tired of telling them to brush their teeth and wash behind their ears. I was tired of being the practical one. I wanted to be the child myself for a change.

I remember watching Eileen drawing a rainbow on a copybook one day. She was concentrating so much she might have been splitting the atom. Because she thought it was important I did too.

'Is that a good rainbow, Mammy?' she asked me. It was unusual for her to take me into her confidence like that, unusual even for her to show me anything.

'It's the best rainbow I ever saw in my life,' I said.

Sometimes something small can help you turn a corner. Seeing Eileen draw a rainbow and seeing her recover from the whooping cough were worth any number of Toms.

She drew a few more rainbows. Then she said, 'I want to go for a walk.' When Eileen suggested something you didn't dare say no.

'You better muffle up,' I said. 'You've been very sick. We don't want you getting a relapse.

She put on her anorak. She zipped it up to her neck.

'Is that far enough?' she said, pretending to choke.

'Just about.'

She wanted to go by the sea, which meant passing Tom's caravan. I didn't like the thought of that but I didn't like to say no to her. What if he came out? Could I give her as an excuse for having to rush away? I couldn't face the thought of hearing any more of his pain. I was having too much of my own.

My throat felt sore as we walked by his caravan. It was one of those ones that are sore on only one side – the worst kind. Maybe my tension was contributing to it.

I quickened my step. Eileen asked me why I was walking so fast. I told her it was because I was cold. I ran as fast as I could and she ran after me. When we reached the dunes we ran down to the sea. She started laughing but then she got a stitch in her side.

'I want to go home,' she said.

That was a relief for me. On the way back we stopped at a chemist and I bought some Fisherman's Friends. Back in the caravan I placed a towel over my head. I lowered it into a basin of boiling water. I dipped some Friar's Balsam into it and inhaled. Slowly the pain subsided.

Kevin came down to us the following week. I'd been pestering him with calls almost every day since my first one. He came to some sort of arrangement with 'JR' to defer the last part of the overtime.

I was never as glad to see anyone when he pulled into the caravan park. I hugged the life out of him as soon as he got out of the car.

'Behave yourself,' he said, 'I can hardly breathe.'

'That's what happens when you play hard to get.'

Eileen was beside herself when she saw him. He whirled her round and round until she was dizzy. He did the same to Siobhan. Cillian was too grown up for that. They play-fought with each other, pretending they were boxers.

'You're all acting as if you haven't seen me in years,' he said.

It seemed like that. Time always moved slowly in Skerries but never moreso than that year.

He had presents for all of them. Siobhan got a box of sweets. He had a doll for Eileen. Cillian was presented with a Manchester United shirt. His face fell when I saw it.

I went into the caravan with Kevin.

'Will you never learn?' I said to him.

'What are you talking about? Everyone is going mad for them in Dublin. They're like hen's teeth.'

'Cillian isn't everyone. You must know that by now.'

'I thought it might help him get into the football more.'

'That's not the way to do it. It's only going to turn him off.'

'How do you make that out?'

'It'll make him self-conscious. Anyone who wears a shirt like that thinks something of themselves. If you fumble a ball in your ordinary clothes it's no big deal but it is in that.'

'It'll be a challenge for him to live up to it.'

'He doesn't want that kind of challenge.'

'All right, I'll give it back.'

'Don't do that. Sorry for going on about it. It's great to see you.'

'Thanks. For a minute I thought I should turn the car around and go home.'

'I shouldn't be giving you a hard time. I know you're always trying to do the right thing. You have no idea how much it means to have you down here.'

'Why is that?'

'I don't know. Maybe because you're the nicest man in the world.'

He embraced me. It felt good holding him close, smelling his lovely smell.

When I looked around me I saw the children had come in behind me. I found myself blushing.

'Kiss him,' Eileen said.

Everyone laughed.

'Stop it, Eileen,' I said.

She gave me one of her bold looks. I could see she was warming up for something.

'Mammy's been drinking,' she said.

Kevin put on a face.

'Really?' he said.

'She's only joking,' I said. I was furious with her.

'Are you sure?'

'What do you mean am I sure?'

'Either she is or she isn't.'

'You know Eileen.'

'Yes, but do I know you?'

'What's that supposed to mean?'

'You look different.'

'In what way?'

'You're pale. Maybe you're run down.'

'I have a sore throat.'

'People shouldn't get sore throats on their summer holidays.'

'Well I got one.'

'I hope you didn't go out with it.'

'I could hardly leave it behind me.'

'Ho ho. Seriously though, you need to mind yourself.'

'I do. I'm a nurse, remember?'

'You *used* to be a nurse. Now you're just a mother.'

'Just a mother. I object to that.'

'I didn't think I married a feminist.'

'Watch it, sexist husband, or there won't be any more hugs.'

We went into the caravan. Everything was all over the place. I hadn't even bothered to wash the dishes.

'I can see it still looks like a palace,' Kevin said.

'Try living here for a month and you'll see how hard it is to keep clean.'

'I'm only joking. Don't go down my throat.'

He took Eileen up in his arms.

'How is my little girl?' he asked.

'Hungry.'

She knew he'd have sweets. He took a Crunchie out of his pocket. She put out her finger pretending it was a gun.

'Hand over the Crunchie and no one gets hurt,' she said in a John Wayne voice he'd taught her. It was a little joke they had.

He gave it to her. Then he produced some Rolos.

'What about me?' Siobhan said. He gave her a Macaroon bar.

Cillian put on his serious face.

'Why does Eileen get more things than Siobhan?' he said.

'Because she's Daddy's little girl,' Siobhan said.

'What makes you think that?' Kevin said.

'Because you're always saying it.'

'Well if I am I'm telling porky pies. The reason she got more things is because she has the biggest stomach.'

She put out her stomach and started laughing. Then she opened the Rolos.

'What have you for me?' Cillian asked.

'Wait till you see.'

He went out to the car. A few seconds later he came back with a football. Cillian groaned. He'd have preferred the sweets. Maybe he'd have preferred a stick of gelignite to a football.

Siobhan grabbed it. She could be a real tomboy at times. She ran out the door with it. I watched her kicking it high in the air. As it came down she tried to head it. Most of the time she missed but it didn't bother her.

'Sorry for cutting you off on the phone on your first call,' Kevin said to me, 'I was with an awkward customer. I had to humour her. She drives me bananas.'

415

'Mrs Keaveny?' I said. He was in the habit of boring a hole in my ear about her.

'That's the one. She collared me just after you rang. She was in flying form this week. At one stage she threatened to close the shop down if I didn't refund her on a rug she bought. As far as I was concerned it was fine when it left the shop but she claimed it was stained.'

'So you gave her a refund.'

'Bloody sure I did. If you lose a customer it's regarded as your problem even if they're in the wrong. O'Loughlin keeps saying every customer we lose has twenty friends. If you screw up with one of them, the other twenty are gone too. That's the way he looks on it. It's like a domino effect.'

'The customer is always right, in other words.'

'Exactly. Especially if it's Mrs Keaveny. It's a bit like a referee in football. Which reminds me - why don't I have a kickaround with Cillian to break in the new ball?'

I looked at Cillian's face. It wasn't what you could call happy.

'I don't feel like one now,' he said.

'How could anyone not feel like a game of football?' Kevin said, 'When I was your age I couldn't wait to get at it.'

'Cillian is different,' I said, 'Don't push him.'

'Wait till he gets signed up with Athlone Town. He'll change his tune then.'

'Please don't keep going on about that,' I said, 'He's not interested in it.'

'Not yet maybe.'

'Never. You know it and I know it.'

'Thanks, Mammy,' Cillian said.

Kevin looked upset.

'I'm only down here and already the pair of you are ganging up on me. Maybe I should just turn the car around and go back to Dublin.'

'Don't be childish,' I said, 'We'll go in now and have some tea. We'll discuss our plans later. Something all of us might like.'

'We need to work up an appetite. Siobhan, will you have a game with me?'

'Okay,' she said.

'What about you, Eileen?'

'If you give me more sweets.'

He grinned.

'You drive a hard bargain. Come on, Cillian. We have a full team now. Me and Eileen against you and Siobhan.'

He picked a patch of ground beside the caravan. There were a few bollards lying around that he used as goalposts. I went inside to put some rashers on the grill.

They started playing a game of two-a-side. Kevin and Cillian were the goalkeepers. Siobhan and Eileen fought for the ball in centre field. Siobhan let Eileen win their tackles. She scored a few goals against Cillian. Siobhan got one against Kevin at the other end. He pretended to do his best to save it by diving frantically before it went in under his legs.

Siobhan cheered. Cillian looked bored. Eileen ate her Rolos. I knew Kevin would have played till the cows came home but I felt sorry for Cillian. I'd been that soldier myself once too often in Dalymount Park.

I tapped on the window of the caravan.

'You'll ruin your appetite for tea,' I called out.

'No we won't,' Eileen said back.

They played until they were fit to drop. Kevin put Cillian on his shoulders and carried him off the pitch. Siobhan tried to put Eileen on hers but she toppled over. The pair of them wer half laughing and half crying as they made their way to the caravan.

Kevin was out of breath as he dropped Cillian onto the floor.

'He needs to practice more,' he said.

'It's not the World Cup,' I said, 'Relax.'

'Thanks, Mammy,' Cillian said.

They sat at the table.

'I'm starving,' Siobhan said.

I hated that word.

'Don't put it like that.'

'Like what?'

'Saying you're starving.'

'But I am.'

'You're not a famine victim. You've had breakfast and dinner. It isn't like you haven't eaten for a month.'

'I don't see why it matters how I say it.'

'All right. Maybe it doesn't.'

I plonked the rashers down in front of her. Then I got the ones for the rest of them. They started eating them like mad things.

'Stop picking on her,' Kevin said.

'I'm not picking on her. I'm just stressed, okay?'

'Sorry, sweetheart, we don't appreciate you half enough.'

'That's better.'

'If you ever give up nursing full time,' he said, 'You should become a cook. This is scrumptious.'

'*Cordon bleu*,' I said, 'Skerries style.'

'That was a great game, wasn't it?' Kevin said to Cillian. Cillian nodded half-heartedly.

'You let in a goal on me,' Siobhan said to Kevin.

'No I didn't,' Kevin said, 'You were too good for me. And Eileen was too good for Cillian.'

'Stop it, Kevin,' I said. Sometimes he had the psychology of a duck.

They went on eating. Everyone gobbled up what they had except Cillian. He left half his plate behind him.

'Did you not like it?' I asked.

'It was fine. I just wasn't hungry.'

'You should eat more,' Kevin said, 'You need to get some hair on that chest of yours.'

'Kevin,' I said, giving him a harsh look.

'Sorry.'

Cillian went out. Kevin asked me what I'd been doing since we came down.

'Not much,' I told him, 'After Eileen got sick she took up most of my time.'

'How are you now, chicken?' he said, going over to her.

'Not too bad,' she said.

'Poor Eileen,' he said. He gave her a hug.

'What about the other two?' he said to me.

'They're having the time of their lives,' I said, 'Right, kids?'

'Is your throat any better?' he asked me.

'A bit. It's one of those tickly ones. I'd love to put my hand down and scratch it.'

'Why don't you?'

'Kevin, you're impossible. Sometimes when you say something I think I'm listening to one of the kids.'

'Cillian told me you were out in the rain one night without your coat. That's not like you.'

'I don't know what came over me.'

'You'd want to be careful with the weather down here. You could catch your death.'

'I'll be all right in a few days.'

He got up from the table. I started tidying away the dishes.

'How did it work out about the overtime?' I asked him.

'I did some of it. The rest can wait. As soon as I'm away from that place I forget all about it. I have you to thank for getting me away early. That Keaveny bitch was driving me up the walls.'

Eileen almost choked on one of her Rolos.

'That's a bad word,' she said.

'Oops,' Kevin said, 'Sorry.'

'You tell them not to talk like that,' I said, 'and then you do it.'

'I know.'

'Mammy said a bad word too,' Eileen said.

'Did you?' Kevin said.

I blushed. It always happens when you give out to someone about something. You end up being the bad guy.

'It just slipped out a few days ago.'

'Pot kettle black,' Kevin said.

'Two wrongs don't make a right.'

'Believe me, if you had Mrs Keaveny as a customer you'd be saying worse things about her than I did.'

'I feel sorry for you.'

'It's not too bad. That's what you get paid for, putting up with bad customers. Selling carpets is easy by comparison.'

'I know what you mean. I found the same thing in the Mater.'

'I wouldn't have thought patients could be cranky. Surely you were the one in charge when they were on the flat of their backs.'

'People can be cranky no matter what condition they're in.'

'I suppose so. The difference between you and me is the fact that I'm trying to get money out of the people I deal with.'

'Agreed. I never tried to sell carpets to patients.'

'Maybe I should try asking Mrs Keaveny about her bunions. She's always on about them. It might sweeten her up.'

'Good idea. It could boost trade. You could put a sign up: "Hall, stairs and landing for the carpets and we'll sort out your bunions as well."'

It started to bucket rain then. Kevin was fuming because he'd been hoping to play some more football. Cillian was relieved. He began to read a book. Siobhan and Eileen played with a Rubik cube on the floor.

Between the showers I went out walking with Kevin. It meant so much to have him there. I hugged him so tightly he didn't know what was coming over me. As I snuggled up to him on the prom I said, 'No matter how much you love your children, it's nice to get a bit of time alone.'

'Agreed.'

When we got back I found myself getting sleepy again.

'I thought this place was supposed to give you energy instead of taking it away,' he said to me.

'It usually does. Maybe it's all the concoctions I've been taking for my throat.'

'I'd go easy on them if I were you.'

'Is that your considered medical opinion?'

'Exactly. That will be twenty guineas please.'

I decided to head for the bed again. If I didn't I knew I'd be worthless for the rest of the day. I fell asleep as soon as my head hit the pillow. It was probably all the stress catching up on me.

# Recovery

Kevin was already dressed when I woke up the next morning. When I went out to the kitchen he was sitting there in his tracksuit.

'You were dead to the world when I got up,' he said, 'I didn't like to wake you.' He was whispering because the children were asleep.

I sat down at the breakfast bar.

'I don't know what's wrong with me,' I said, 'I don't have a puff of energy these days.'

'Go back to bed,' he ordered, 'I'll bring you in your breakfast.'

This was too good to be true.

'I might keep you around. You have all these hidden talents.'

I went into the bedroom. A few minutes later he came in. He had tea and toast on a tray.

'Breakfast for Lady Muck,' he said. He put the tray down on the quilt.

'This is the life,' I cooed, sipping at the tea. At that moment it was worth more to me than a four-course meal in the Gresham.

'Will Her Ladyship be requiring anything more?' he asked.

'No, Jeeves,' I said, 'You can take the rest of the morning off.'

I tried to get back to sleep but I couldn't. The breakfast had woken me up. I went out to the main room.

'Would you like a walk on the beach?' I asked him.

'I was going to go for a jog but I didn't think you'd be up to it.'

'Why don't you see what the weather is like?' I said.

'All right.'

He went out. I started dressing. After a few minutes he came in.

'What's the verdict?' I asked.

'Dull, I'm afraid.'

'So what? Let's try a walk anyway.'

'Are you sure it's wise with your throat?'

'Let's live dangerously. It'll kill me or cure me.'

'I never argue with a woman.'

'You jog and I'll walk.'

'Now you're starting to sound sensible.'

We left a note for the children and went out. Everywhere we looked there were clouds. They were full of rain. There seemed to be no hope of the sun coming out.

He sprinted away from me. I listened to the seagulls cawing along the pier. He moved so fast he was soon out of sight. I tried not to think of Tom - or anything else.

He reappeared a few minutes later. I thought he looked out of breath. He raced towards me.

'Was I fast?' he said, like a child looking for affirmation. I clapped my hands. He fell down on the sand, pretending to faint.

'Get up, you trickster,' I demanded.

He stood up. He was panting.

'Don't overdo it,' I said, 'Even if you're fit you could do damage to yourself.'

'Yes, nurse.'

We walked down by the prom.

'You seem back to yourself,' he said.

'Whoever she is,' I said.

I was just starting to relax when I spotted Tom sitting on a bench. Oh no, I thought.

'There's that man who always looks lost,' Kevin said.

I didn't know he'd seen him before. I was afraid to wave to him so I looked away. I felt terrible doing that but what option had I? I couldn't face having to introduce Kevin to him. My face would have told everything.

We went back to the caravan. The children were up. They were jumping around the place.

'Siobhan hit me,' Eileen said. Her lower lip was trembling.

'She kicked me first,' Siobhan said.

'Then you're even, I said. 'Now stop fighting. Seriously.'

Cillian gave me a hard stare.

'Where did you two go?' Cillian asked.

'Out for a walk.'

'Why didn't you tell us?'

'You were asleep.'

'We could have been kidnapped.'

'Don't say things like that. You know I'd die if anything happened to any of you.'

'It might give us a bit of peace if someone took them away for a while,' Kevin said.

Siobhan put her tongue out at him.

'Where's my breakfast?' Eileen said.

'What did your last servant die of?' I said.

'Laziness,' she told me.

'Don't be cheeky or you'll get a thick ear,' Kevin said. He was joking. He'd sooner have died than raise a finger to any of them.

We all went out in the car that afternoon. We had dinner in one of the local restaurants. It felt so different with him there. I wished he could have stayed longer but I knew his mind was on the overtime he was losing out on.

'If you have to go back tomorrow I'll understand,' I said to him after we'd finished our meal.

'I hate going. I was just starting to get into the slow pace of Skerries.'

'It usually takes me about a month before that happens.'

The day brightened up after we got back to the caravan, so much so that the children decided to go swimming. Kevin joined them. He had no togs with him so he went in in his underpants. I paddled at the edge.

It was a nice lazy day. In the evening we played records and had a sing-song. Eileen surprised us by joining in.

Sunday was equally overcast. As soon as I woke up I felt it was going to stay like that. We'd all be miserable if it did.

On my way to the toilet I banged my foot off the bed. I screeched in agony.

'What's up with you?' Kevin said, 'You sound like you've just given birth.'

'You'd know all about that,' I said.

'What happened you?'

'I stubbed my toe off the leg of the bed.'

'Let me look at it. Get up there on the operating table.'

I sat on the bed.

'How is it that the first thing you do in a day is always the most dangerous?' I said.

'Most accidents occur within five minutes of home.'

'Well, doctor,' I said, 'What's your prognosis?'

I could see he was starting to enjoy the game, having already asked me for my twenty guineas.

'Take three painkillers immediately and then put on a fry for your husband. That will take away the pain immediately.' Imagine if he knew Tom had been playing doctor with me too. If it wasn't so tragic it might have been funny.

Cillian was watching us.

'I wish more doctors were like Daddy,' he said.

I hobbled around the place for the rest of the morning.

'I'm miserable when I'm not mobile,' I said.

'Stop moaning,' Kevin said, 'Keep taking the tablets and you'll be fine. Your subscription is renewable every three weeks.'

I tried to read a book but the words kept swimming away from me so I had to leave it down. I always hated Sundays. I never knew how to kill them. Even when the shops were open I still felt, 'Yuck, it's Sunday.' It was probably a throwback to my childhood when nothing happened, when you almost felt guilty for smiling or playing a record.

When I looked in the mirror I let out a screech.

'What's up with you now?' Kevin said.

'I feel about ninety.'

'Stop looking at yourself.'

He took the mirror up in his hands.

'Will I break it for you?'

'No. I don't want seven years bad luck.'

'You seem to be having it anyway.'

'I need to get out, even with my bandy foot. Maybe you can drive us somewhere before you go back.'

'Maybe. I have to ring O'Loughlin first.'

'Ask him if you can stay another day anyway.

'I'll try but I doubt he'll bite.'

'What's the big deal? You're not the Chancellor of the Exchequer.'

He drove off to the phone box, the one I'd rung him from the day I was feeling bad about Tom.

I kept drinking tea to keep myself awake. When the children got up I told them they'd have to minister to themselves.

'Mammy is lame,' I said.

'You can't be lame,' Eileen said, 'You're Mammy.'

Cillian got his breakfast. Siobhan put on something for herself and Eileen.

Kevin came back after a while.

'I made the call,' he said, 'but I'm afraid there was no joy. He's putting the boot in. I have to go back.'

'Damn. They're heartless in there.'

'Maybe, but they're the people who keep the wolf from the door for us. Whose bread I eat, his song I sing.'

Mass was at twelve. I told the kids to tidy themselves up. Siobhan put on a nice dress. Cillian combed his hair. Eileen just groaned.

'Why do we have to go to Mass?' she said, 'It's boring.'

She was always the hardest to get to go. Asking her to say the rosary was like asking her to go to the Himalayas. Her idea of Lent was sacrificing cheese and onion crisps for salt and vinegar ones.

When I thought we looked reasonably presentable we trooped down to the little church round the corner from us. I always loved nipping in to it to say a quick prayer in summers gone.

This was different. I wasn't able to concentrate on my prayers because of the way I was feeling. I felt Fr O'Gorman, the priest saying Mass, was looking at me judgmentally.

Wasn't it just my luck that the gospel was Saint Matthew's one where he said, 'If thine eye offend thee, pluck it out.' Did that mean I was never to look in Tom's direction again? Saint Matthew went on to say, 'What would it profit a man if he gained the whole world and suffered the loss of his soul?' Unfortunately that applied to women too.

The sermon seemed to go on forever. I tried to look more interested in it than I was because I didn't want to give bad example to the children. Cillian prayed hard but the girls kept looking around them and talking. Kevin had a job trying to keep them quiet. I was in my own world so I let him at it.

425

I didn't go to Communion. Kevin gave me a funny look as he stepped out of the pew.

'I'm not feeling well,' I said.

It was true but not in the way he thought. The woman who'd seen me in the bar with Tom was sitting in one of the benches opposite us. At one stage I thought I saw her poking her husband in the ribs to look at me. I could just imagine what she was whispering to him. 'Look at that trollop – a Sunday morning Catholic as well.' The look on her face made me want to crawl under the seat.

The second reason I didn't go was because I hadn't been to Confession. Fr. O'Gorman would have recognised my voice. He knew us all to talk to.

How could I have said 'Bless me Father, for I have sinned. I kissed a married man. And I'm a married woman.'

It would be the last time we'd ever be able to go to Skerries for a holiday again – and the last time I'd ever be able to look him in the face.

As soon as the Communion was over I made a bee-line for the door.

'What's the big rush?' Kevin said when we got outside, 'You look like someone put a stick of gelignite under you.'

'I have to get the dinner ready,' I said, 'You wouldn't know anything about things like that.'

'How is the stomach?'

'A bit better.'

When we got back to the caravan I gave them the inevitable fish fingers. I wasn't up to anything else. They didn't look too pleased but I wasn't in the mood for complaints. I threw them onto the table with a 'Like it or lump it' look on my face.

'You should take out shares in fish fingers,' Kevin said. If he wasn't leaving soon I'd have snatched them from him for that.

Everyone helped wash the dishes. I kept looking at the clock. Each tick was a second closer to him going back. How would I be without him? There was no point torturing myself. There wasn't much of the summer left. When it ended I was determined never to put myself in the position I'd been in with Tom – or anyone else - again. I had too much to lose.

'Does anyone feel up to going out?' I said when it came up to mid-afternoon, 'If I have to hang around this place any longer I'll go spare.'

Kevin looked half afraid of me.

'Okay,' he said, 'I'll bring you for a spin to shut you up. But I can't stay out too long.'

He looked at the children.

'Are you lot interested in coming with us?'

They never needed to be asked twice. It would have been like asking a dog if he fancied a walk.

We bundled ourselves into the car. I didn't care where we were going. We drove for a few miles just enjoying the drive. I felt my head clearing with every bend of the road. Cillian was beside Kevin in the front. I was in the back with Siobhan and Eileen. At one stage Siobhan nudged me in the ribs to show me a heart she'd drawn on the condensation on the window. Little things like that always propped up my spirits.

Kevin turned off the ignition after we'd been going a few miles. He looked out the window.

'There's a nice field,' he said, 'Let's have a kick-around.'

The inevitable kick-around. Nobody wanted it but I didn't like to refuse him on his last day.

'I'll be the referee,' I said, 'I can't do anything else.'

'Like most referees,' Kevin said.

This time the boys played the girls. Kevin gave me a whistle. I kept blowing it for no reason at all. Eileen was laughing so much at me hobbling around the place she could hardly contain herself. At one stage she dropped down on the grass and covered her face with her hands. She was hysterical. I could see her stomach going up and down as if she was doing exercises. Kevin gave out to her in case she was making me feel bad.

'Don't be cruel,' he sang, mimicking Elvis as he shook his hips. I told him I didn't mind, that it was good to see her having fun, even at my expense. God knows, she didn't laugh much.

The boys let the girls win. The final score was 19-1. Cillian had managed the losing side's only goal in extra time.

427

Everyone was sleepy on the way home. Siobhan and Eileen sang a victory song. We all seemed to have the sniffles. I spent most of the journey spreading a packet of Handy Andys around.

I made a salad when we got back to the caravan. I wasn't in the humour to cook anything more elaborate. Eileen wouldn't eat it. 'I don't like lettuce,' she said, 'It's like eating grass.'

'Think of the starving people in Africa,' Kevin said to her.

'Send it to them, so,' she said.

Another father would have given out to her but she was his pet. He let her away with it.

Instead he turned the conversation on to me.

'Remember the time you burned the chips?' he said.

'What?'

'The time you burned the chips, back in the flat.'

'What's that got to do with anything?' I said.

'I just thought it was funny.'

'Mention it again,' I hissed under my breath, 'and I'll divorce you.'

After tea he got ready to go back to Dublin. He'd packed so little it all fitted into a carrier bag.

'I'm glad I came down,' he said when he was out at the car.

'Me too.'

'Will you be all right?' he asked me. He knew there was something wrong with me besides my throat. And that I didn't want to talk about it.

'I'll try to survive without your delightful company.'

He slipped some money to the children.

'Don't spend it all in the one shop,' he said as he gave it to them. He always said that.

'What about me?' I said, 'How am I going to afford next week's shopping?' That was a joke. He'd already given me enough for everything. We didn't want the children to know I was flush. If they did, the money would walk.

'Maybe you can go out singing,' he suggested, 'That should bring in a few bob.'

'No thanks. I think I'll have to rob some piggy banks.'

'Just you try it,' Eileen said.

He got into the car.

'Maybe next year I'll stay with you all the time,' he said.

'That would be great. Do you think we could afford it?'

'If Mrs Keaveny stays off my back. And if we win the lottery.'

He turned on the engine. We all waved at him.

'Take care of that bug,' he said as he started to drive.

'I will,' I said, 'And you stay away from Mrs Keaveny.'

'I'm going to buy a dartboard on the way back. I'll draw her face on a piece of paper and stick it onto it. Then I'll spend the day throwing darts at it.'

'I thought you were an adult.'

He put on a funny face.

'God forbid that would ever happen to me. It's too much fun being a child down here.'

'Then why are you going back?' Eileen said.

'Sorry, sweetheart,' he said, blowing her a kiss.

He drove off. We all waved at the departing car. Eileen said, 'I want to go with him.' That hurt me.

'Come inside with me,' Siobhan said to her, 'I'll get you a Choc Ice from the fridge.' That seemed to quieten her.

The caravan felt empty. None of us knew what to do with ourselves. We sat sprawled over the sofa. A film came on the television and we half-watched it. When it was over I cooked some hamburgers. Afterwards Cillian and Siobhan played Monopoly. Eileen joined the dots on a picture of a sheep from her colouring book as she chomped on her Choc Ice. I put on a fry for all of them. We washed it down with large glasses of Fanta. Before we knew where we were it was bedtime again. We all felt like slugs.

Over the next few days I saw Tom outside his caravan a few times. He was usually pottering around at his car. He seemed nervous about approaching me and I didn't approach him. We just waved at each other like we used to do before we got to know one another. The way he looked at me sometimes gave me to believe he still wasn't over me. I felt bad about leading him on, even with that simple kiss.

I only talked to him once. It was shortly before we went back to Dublin. I was in the shop buying a paper when she shuffled past me. He was sweating profusely

'I'm going back to Dublin to live with my aunt,' he said in a rushed voice, 'Sorry for everything that happened.'

'I'm glad for you,' I said.

'I need to get out of here. It was killing me. It's great to have someone who cares for you.'

'She'll get you back on your feet,' I said.

He put his hand on my shoulder and looked me in the eyes.

'You turned my life around,' he said. Then he was gone.

My heart lifted after that meeting, short and all as it was. I felt he was over the worst part of his life. Afterwards I played with the kids with a new animation. Contrary to what I'd feared, I felt really happy in my little world now that my momentary madness had passed.

The next time I looked over at his caravan the car was gone from outside it. New people had moved in, a husband and wife with two jolly children. They got a skip to clear out all his things. It was like a new world dawning. I thought of his car wheezing up the motorway and him wheezing behind the wheel in a different way. Somehow, I thought, he'd make it.

The following summer I told Kevin I didn't want to go to Skerries anymore. He didn't understand why.

'The children are getting too big for it,' I said by way of an excuse.

'That's the first I heard of it. They're always on about the brilliant times they have there every year.'

'They're just being polite,' I insisted.

'You must be joking. That's one virtue our lot are in no danger of ever picking up.'

I asked him to scan the travel brochures for other places nearby.

'Why not go abroad?' he said, 'even for an experiment. Everyone is doing it.'

He mentioned places like Torremelinos. I felt they weren't our style. What would have been the point of lying on beaches for hours like idiots pretending we were enjoying ourselves as the sun baked down on us?

Kevin didn't agree.

'Let's try a few of them,' he said, 'We don't want to get old without having seen the world.' To please him I gave in.

We went to the Canaries once just to try it out but the stress of the red tape exhausted me even before we left the house. I was the type of person to realise I'd forgotten to pack my passport over a martini in the Departures Lounge so I had to make an extra effort in that department.

There was a big delay checking in. Then the flight was delayed. 'Are you sure this was a good idea?' I asked Kevin as we boarded the plane, 'I'm exhausted and the holiday hasn't even started yet. I'll need another one after we come back.'

I got burnt to a frazzle on the second day. I only had to look at the sun for that to happen. A few days later I came down with food poisoning. Afterwards I told Kevin that was 'it' for me as regards foreign holidays. I don't think there was a day of it I enjoyed. I was bored at the beach and equally bored buying things at the arcades that I didn't want. What was it about arcades that made you reach into your pocket to pay for something you'd run a mile from if you saw it in a shop?

We tried to chat with the locals but they weren't interested. They looked at us as if we had two heads because of the language barrier. I was always too lazy to learn foreign languages. What was the point? You'd be home in a week anyway.

We went to France another year but I found it stifling in the heat. The people weren't very friendly either. They seemed to be looking down their noses at us all the time. They were probably like that the year I was over there with Kevin but I was too much in my own world to see it.

The year after that we went to Switzerland. The scenery was beautiful but there was something dead about it all. And about the people. Their culture was so different to ours. One day we crossed a road when the traffic lights were against us. We didn't realise how major an infringement that was. A policeman hauled us aside as if we'd just murdered someone. The way he talked to us, I thought we were going to be locked up for life.

People often recommended Ibiza to us but I had no wish to go to a place where the main ambition seemed to be to get so drunk you forget who you are and then have sex on the beach with someone you met five minutes beforehand.

'Next year it's Skerries again,' Kevin said after we had our fill of these places. It was only after we came home we admitted we'd really only gone to them to keep up with the Joneses. As we got older we realised it didn't make sense to do that. The Joneses didn't give a hoot where we went, or even if we went nowhere at all.

'If you got the tan itself it might have been something.' Kevin said to me on the way back from Switzerland. The funny thing was, I was never into tans. It took so much time to get them and then a few weeks later you were back to your milky Irish skin again. What was the point? Especially if you almost ended up in hospital with third degree burns.

Kevin was looking forward to telling Reg about the holiday when he went back to work but he wasn't at his counter when he went up to it. There was another man there that he'd never seen before. He was surprised because he hadn't been scheduled to take a break. When he asked Mark where he was he just said, 'He left.'

Kevin asked him what he meant.

'He went off to edit some magazine,' he said.

Kevin couldn't believe his ears. He wanted to prolong the discussion but Mark wasn't in any mood to. He said he was on his way to a meeting and couldn't delay.

He rang him that evening to find out what happened.

'How is the mystery man?' he said.

Reg laughed.

'I was going to tell you before you went off to Switzerland but I thought I'd surprise you instead.'

'You certainly did that. What's going on?'

'It's been on my mind for a while to leave that place. I don't want to become old in there. It's a dead end job.'

'Mark said something about a magazine.'

'*Art Attacks*. Available from all the best shops.'

'And you're the editor.'

'Editor cum owner. I've been sending stuff to it for a few years. The guy who used to run it was looking for a buyer. He's gone off to live in a boat in Amsterdam.'

'So you took over.'

'It didn't happen overnight. I was helping him with the editing for a few years but I didn't really enjoy it. I felt the focus was too limited. I wanted to branch it out to cover all the arts. Larry – he's the guy who went to Holland - was more interested in art than I was. As you know, I like films as well. I'm going to bring everything into it – theatre, music, dancing, sculpture, the lot. It'll be coming out every month.'

'How are you going to fund it?'

'I have a list of advertisers as long as your arm. They'll be paying my wages from now on instead of O'Loughlin. How does that sound?'

He came around that night to show us the first edition. It had a photograph of Salvador Dali on the cover. He was dressed in leotards and hanging from a helicopter. On the inside cover in big bold letters were the swords: 'Editor: Reg Keegan.'

'What do you think?' he said, beaming like a child.

'Fame at last,' Kevin said.

I tried to muster up some enthusiasm.

'It looks really impressive,' I said.

Kevin took out a bottle of champagne he'd bought on the way home from work. We all had a glass to toast the new literary genius.

'I'm not expecting it to be all plain sailing,' Reg said as he sipped his drink, 'Believe me, this wasn't a decision I made lightly.'

'How did Mark take it?'

'I don't think he was too impressed. He said he was grooming me for management.'

'Did you believe him?'

'Who knows? People will say anything to hold onto you. In any case it was too little too late. I've had my bellyful of that place for a long time now.'

'I'm sure it's going to be very exciting for you,' Kevin said, 'Doing what you love instead of going to work just to pay the bills.'

'That's the general idea. Fingers crossed it works.'

'I'm sure it will. There's nobody like you for the arts.'

He employed a few of his old cronies from The Palace to do features on plays that were coming up in the Abbey and the Gate. Some other people added the visuals.

The next issue had a photo of W.B. Yeats on the cover. I remembered studying a few of his poems at school. I always found him hard to understand. Like Reg I imagined him having his head in the clouds.

The issue after that had a sexy blonde on it. I didn't know who she was. Some dancer or other, I gathered, that just flew in from Yugoslavia.

'I interviewed her,' Reg said, 'She wouldn't give me her number. Drat.'

He did the film column himself. I browsed through a few of his reviews without any great interest. As I expected, he wrote it as if he swallowed the dictionary. If you were confused by a film when you were watching it, you'd be even more confused after reading Reg Keegan's review of it.

'Do you think there's a market for this in the long term?' I asked Kevin one night after yet another edition dropped through the letterbox, 'There are a lot of arts magazines out there.'

'I hope so. He seems to know what he's doing.'

The honeymoon ended after the sixth issue. It was meant to be a bumper one. Reg went to town expanding it. There were lots of new sections but when push came to shove the advertising wasn't there. Everyone ran for cover when he tried to make contact with them. Apparently the word went around that not enough people were reading it so all the backers pulled out.

Reg was left holding a very large – and expensive – baby. He tried to hold off his creditors but they got aggressive with him, demanding money upfront. Kevin told me one of them even threatened him with physical violence. The contributors were looking for their money as well. The sixth magazine hit the shelves but there it remained. Nobody seemed to want to go near it. Reg had to drive around to all the newsagents collecting the unsold copies.

He'd had taken out a large loan from the bank to set *Art Attacks* up. There was no way he could afford to pay that back now. He came round to us one night in a state. It was the first time I ever saw him shaking. We had to give him a whiskey to cool him down.

He started talking like a machine.

'You have no idea of the cut-throats in this game,' he said, 'Arts my granny. Mafia is more like it.' He asked Kevin for a loan to bail him out. He said he'd pay him back as soon as he got back on his feet. Kevin gave him as much as he could but it didn't go anywhere near what he needed to stay afloat.

In the end he went down on his knees to Mark asking for his old job back. From what Kevin told me he practically begged him for it. Mark wasn't too pleased as he'd spent the last few months training the new man in.

He gave him the job but he told him he'd be going back as a new recruit. Anything he'd built up in all the years he was there before was gone. He'd be starting at the bottom rung of the ladder again. Reg said he didn't mind. He almost fell over himself thanking him but it was the end of any managerial status he might once have held.

No longer was he the Golden Boy of the shoe department.

## Changing Fortunes

The years rolled by almost without me realising it. As I got older my social circle narrowed and so did that of most of the people I knew. A lot of my nursing friends started devoting themselves more to their families than their work. When I met them now they talked about other things than the patients. They were knee-deep in mortgages, childcare arrangements, car repayments. There were less humorous anecdotes and less drinking. We didn't chat as much and our nights ended earlier. We were all slowing down.

It happened closer to home as well. May was devoting herself almost exclusively to her job. Her social life was practically non-existent. She was out of the country every other week on some assignment or other. Now and then I'd see her face on the cover of a magazine. She was interviewed for one of them in the 'Women Who Matter' slot. She started to power-dress to beat the band. When I talked to her on the phone I felt I was talking to a stranger.

Maureen even started to get more serious. When she didn't leave the job she was in she was told she'd have to go 'up or down.' That meant taking promotions or facing demotion. It was a Catch-22. She didn't want demotion for obvious reasons. Promotion was of no interest to her either because she wasn't ambitious but she couldn't admit that. The upshot of it all was a huge increase in her work schedule. She had to travel more and take on assignments she'd have run a mile from a few years before. I was glad people were finally realising how capable she was but the work took a lot of the fun out of her.

I thought her annulment would have led to her meeting someone else but she didn't. A lot of the dates she went on were with friends of friends. She felt there was something contrived about them because of that. If she went to clubs she often met the wrong kind of men. 'Where are all the good ones gone?' she said to me one night, 'Where are all the Kevins?' It made me feel blessed to hear something like that. Every time I went out with the nurses they told me about yet another marriage that had bitten the dust. People didn't seem to be able to handle problems anymore. At the first hint of trouble it was like, 'I'm out of here.'

Kevin underwent some problems in Clery's as the new breed challenged him for tenure. He fended them off as best he could but it wasn't easy. There was one in particular, a little pipsqueak called Rory Gilsenan who was madly ambitious. He'd just married a Claims Manager from an insurance company and they were both on the up and up. They'd bought a house in Malahide and were desperate to make the repayments. According to Kevin he'd have sold his own grandmother down the river to make a pound.

I kept telling him to take things easier but he couldn't do that. If I suggested him leaving the place altogether he blew a fuse. 'I wouldn't know what to do with myself,' he said. He'd been in the job since leaving school and it was all he knew. He attended an interview for a rival chain once to shut me up but he didn't have his heart in it and he didn't get the job. It went to some little whippersnapper who knew the interviewer. As if that wasn't bad enough, news of Kevin applying for it got back to Mark O'Loughlin. Was it Gilsenan that snitched on him? I never found out but I wouldn't have put it past him. Kevin didn't think it was for a minute. When he got the rejection letter he seemed almost relieved. 'Are you happy now?' he said to me as if it was me who applied for it instead of him. After that it was back to 'the devil we knew.'

I didn't really mind going on as we were. Some people might have thought my life was in a rut but I didn't see it that way. There was nothing I wanted that I didn't have. Kevin earned enough for us to get by and I pitched in with whatever I could drum up from agency work and the odd fill-in for a friend in need. We were an average couple making do, raising our family as best we could on the resources we had.

The children seemed to become adults almost without us being aware of it. The things they came out with both stunned and shocked us. Their physical growth was dramatic as well. Cillian had been small as a baby but once he started growing he didn't stop. Siobhan was more rounded but Eileen was like a beanpole as well. I didn't want them to grow up too fast but what could you do about it? They all wanted to be older, like most children, while I secretly hoped their body clocks would stop.

When they got into their twenties I knew they'd want to be younger but what was the point of saying that to them? It was like telling them not to smoke or stay out late. Restrictions were boring. 'Mammy' was the one who tried to stop you having fun, to stop you trying to be a 'grown up.' You couldn't do anything about it so you might as well accept it. When I thought about my own past I had to accept the fact that I was like that too. One day I was a girl and the next a woman. It happened in the blink of an eye, the transition from Midleton to the Mater to motherhood. What was it about life that made the years fly by you and the days go slowly? It was as if our brains were wired back to front.

Cillian continued to read books like there was no tomorrow. Siobhan barrelled through her days without a care in the world. Eileen kept us going with her tantrums. She entertained us in between them with all the dreams she had about her future. Most of these she discarded after about five minutes but that didn't bother us. You generally knew to expect the unexpected with her.

Just when I started to feel some stability coming back into my life, another tragedy hit me. Aunt Bernie died when she was in her early sixties. The news hit me like a thunderbolt.

We hadn't been seeing her much at the time. I rang her as often as I could but she wasn't herself on the calls. She'd become more distant with the years. Maybe she thought we didn't need her as much now that the children were that much older.

I could sense her drifting farther away from me on each call I made to her. It was like seeing someone's spirit crumble. After coming off the phone I'd feel very low. She always put the best foot forward and that made it worse. There was one person talking to you and another one behind the scenes that you'd never know. You couldn't help her if you didn't know what was wrong with her.

When I got the news I felt like I'd been kicked in the head by a horse. It was Mammy who rang to tell me. Even before she spoke I seemed to sense something.

She could hardly speak.

'It's Bernie,' she said. She didn't need to say any more.

I dropped the phone. Kevin rushed over to me. He didn't know what was wrong with me. I fell into a chair in a state of disbelief. Everything about her flooded back to me – her generosity, her sadness, the fact that she spent her life thinking about everyone except herself.

Because she never talked about her problems you stopped thinking they were there. I always thought she'd go on forever. I kicked myself for not doing more for her, for not seeing the signs of her withdrawal into herself. Was she reaching out to me on the calls she made to me at that time even if she couldn't put it into words? I gave myself the excuse that she wouldn't have wanted my pity but that's what it was, an excuse. Because she never thought of her life as being important you fell into that way of thinking too. Now that she was gone it seemed more important than anyone's.

When Kevin came home from work that day I was too distraught to tell him what happened. My voice went as he came in the door. It was only when he got a glass of water for me that it came back.

That didn't make it any easier for me. He wasn't a man to show emotion much but he showed it that day, burying his head in his hands and crying his eyes out. Neither of us could imagine a world without her. She was far too young to die. And yet what was there for her to look forward to?

'How did it happen?' he asked me.

I said I didn't know, that Mammy was too upset to go into any details. I didn't even want to hear about them. What did they matter now?

He made me a cup of tea. I drank it, and then another cup. And then another. Tea was almost like whiskey at times like that. You drank it almost without being aware of it.

'I'll turn into a cup yet,' I said.

'Whatever gets you through.'

We spent the day reminiscing about her. I told him I felt I'd let her slide out of my life in the previous few months. That was the worst part.

'Don't guilt-trip yourself,' he said, 'We saw her much more than some people.'

'You don't understand. It's not just the guilt. I loved her.'

439

'Do you not think I know that?'

I kept asking myself why I didn't make a point of seeing more of her in the last few years.

'She wasn't well enough to come up,' Kevin reminded me.

'I know,' I said, 'but we could have gone down to her.'

'You didn't even have time to get down to your own house,' he said.

That may have been true but it didn't make me feel any better. Nothing could have.

'You can always make time for things if you want to,' I said to him.

We went around in circles all day without getting anywhere. At a certain point of the day I had to tell myself it wasn't about me or about my level of commitment to an aunt. Aunt Bernie had died. That was all that mattered. She was gone from us and we couldn't bring her back. I kept phoning Mammy for more details of what happened but she was too distraught to talk. She was closer to her than any of us. I phoned Maureen too. Mammy had been onto her after she told me. She was as upset as I was.

Why did we wind down on her visits to her? It was the old story: Life got in the way. Or maybe she'd started to get less out of them. I thought that was less likely. I felt they did her some good even if she hadn't the same spark as in the old days. What hit me hardest was the fact that I was too caught up in the children to see what was happening. The children she'd done so much to raise.

I finally got Mammy to tell me some details of what happened. It turned out she'd been dead two days before she was discovered. A neighbour hadn't seen her out and became worried. She went up to her house and knocked at the door. When she got no answer she looked in the window There was a light on even though it was the middle of the day. She rang the police at that stage. They had to break a window to get in. When they went upstairs they found Aunt Bernie dead in her bed. She'd had an aneurysm. There was a copy of the novel *Far from the Madding Crowd* open on her bedside locker. Thomas Hardy was her favourite author.

We drove down to Midleton the next day. There wasn't much talking in the car, just lots of memories – and tears.

Mammy was still very upset when we got there. She was so emotional she couldn't talk to us. She tried to but she kept tripping up on the words. I sat her in a chair and told her to say nothing until I brought her a cup of tea.

When she got her voice back she said Aunt Bernie hadn't been calling up to see her much recently. 'She was much more in on herself than when you saw her last,' she said, 'She wasn't looking well either. Sometimes she complained of headaches. I should have seen the signs. But you couldn't tell Bernie anything. She never bothered getting herself checked out.'

She said something then that made me feel worse than anything.

'Did you know she spent her last birthday alone? We always used to invite her up here for it but your father's asthma was bad so we weren't up to it. We didn't even send her a card.' It shamed me to think I hadn't sent one either.

I felt I was going to cry so I went out to the kitchen. After a minute Kevin came in.

'Don't torture yourself,' he said, 'There was nothing you could have done, nothing any of us could have done.'

Maybe he was right. Maybe the effort to put on a good face for the world finally got too much for her. Daddy said, 'She reminded me of a car with the battery running down.'

He was unusually quiet for him. He didn't know how to deal with situations like this. He stayed in the kitchen making tea for everyone. Cillian and Siobhan helped him. When Maureen went in to him he started talking to her about Aunt Bernie's 'mistake.' It was a constant source of curiosity to us what happened on those mysterious visits she made to England after Dan Toibin broke it off with her. Did she really give birth to a child over there? We never stopped wondering. Maybe it was just one of those rumours that grew up in small towns any time anyone got the boat to Holyhead.

There weren't many people at the funeral Mass besides the family. I thought that was because she'd kept herself to herself so much. The priest gave a eulogy. He obviously knew her well. It was full of stories about her, stories that brought her back to me just as clearly as if she was sitting there in front of me. At one stage everything became too much for me to handle. It was so bad I had to leave the church. Mammy came out after me. We fell into one another's arms. Then Maureen appeared beside us. 'There was only one of her,' she said through her tears, 'She broke the mould.'

After a few minutes we went back in. May scrunched up her eyebrows. She couldn't understand why we'd had to leave.

'Where were you?' she said, digging me in the ribs. Maureen shook her head at me to say nothing.

'We just went out for some air,' I said, 'It's a bit stuffy in here.'

She pointed to one of the other pews.

'I bet that's Dan Toibin over there,' she said.

I looked over at where she'd pointed to. I suspected it was. He looked very sheepish.

'Wouldn't you think he'd have brought his wife with him,' Daddy said.

'That's the last person he'd want with him,' Maureen said, 'She probably doesn't know a thing about what happened.'

'We don't either,' I added, 'so we shouldn't give scandal.'

'Don't be holier than thou,' May said reproachfully, 'The dogs on the street know what happened. And that's what he is – a dog.'

'Don't say things like that,' Mammy chided, 'He looks in a bad way.'

'And well he should be after what he did to her,' May snapped.

Maureen didn't agree. 'What would have been the point of marrying her if he didn't love her?' she said.

'He should have thought of that,' May said, 'before he used her for sex.'

'I wish you wouldn't talk like that, May,' Mammy put in, 'We're in a church. Anyway, it takes two people to make a baby.'

'Aunt Bernie was as pure as the driven snow,' Maureen said, 'There's no way he would have gone to bed with her unless he pushed her into it.'

Dan slipped out of the church before the end of the Mass. As he passed our pew, May said, 'I hope that man realises he ruined Aunt Bernie's life.'

'Shhh,' Maureen said, 'I think he heard you.'

'I wanted him to. He makes my flesh crawl.' She was staring him out of existence but he didn't look back.

442

The coffin was carried down through the church after the Mass ended. There were six pallbearers, Daddy and Cillian among them. After it was put into the hearse we all exchanged memories of Aunt Bernie. Nobody had a bad word to say about her. How could they have? We drove behind it at snail's pace to the grave. When we got there the priest said some prayers. After the coffin was lowered into the grave, one of the women she worked with in the post office came over to me.

'She thought the world of you,' she said. That really moved me. I knew she wasn't the type to talk confidentially with people. 'She was taken from us far too soon,' she added.

I asked her how she'd found her recently. 'God love her,' she said, 'She was always suspicious of us being curious about her. That drove her more and more into herself. If she could only have realised we didn't care about anything that happened in her past.' Nobody except Mammy knew what that had been. I respected her for not telling us about it. Aunt Bernie's secret died with her.

A few weeks later we put her house up for sale. I hadn't been in it for ages. She usually preferred coming down to us rather than having us going up to her.

May came with me. We went around to get it ready for the auctioneer to value. The first thing we did was open the shutters. Grandad and Granny always kept them shut. That was one of the reasons the house always looked so dark. I wondered why Aunt Bernie hadn't opened them after they died. Maybe she was so used to them being that way she didn't even notice it.

Everywhere looked like a new pin when the sunlight flooded in. It was so tidy it made me feel ashamed of our own place. Her dresses and overcoats hung so neatly in the wardrobes they could have been displays in a department store.

There were pictures of Granny and Grandad on the walls. I also noticed a few of Mammy and the rest of us when we were young.

We found a bunch of letters in one of her cabinet drawers. Most of them were addressed to Dan Toibin. There were no stamps on them so obviously they were never posted. Some of them had a Norwich address on them. They were written to a person whose name I didn't recognize. Obviously these weren't posted either. We all knew she'd visited Norwich a few times. Was this something to do with her 'mistake'?

May wanted to read them but I didn't let her. I insisted on burning them. That annoyed her to bits. I almost had to pull them off her. She went off in a huff. After she was gone I found an envelope tied up with twine. When I took it off I saw a photograph of a young girl in a First Communion dress. It looked like Aunt Bernie but it couldn't have been her because it was in colour. All the photos we had of her were in black and white. The similarity was in the eyes. I didn't show it to May but I didn't burn it either. I put it into my purse and brought it home with me.

The solicitor handling her estate was someone I didn't think I'd be able to trust at first. He was a little old man with thin slits of eyes. He wore crumpled trousers and a shirt that could have done with a wash. His office looked like it hadn't been cleaned in years. There were files hanging out of drawers and another stack of them on the floor. I fell over them every time I walked in the door. I thought he was going to be useless winding up her estate but once he found her file he proved himself to be a total professional. He said he was a great friend of hers. I don't think he was making it up. He seemed genuinely emotional when he talked about her.

Mammy and Daddy got some money from the sale of the house. Aunt Bernie had quite a bit saved. She left that to me. I went into shock when I heard that. I couldn't stop crying when the Will was read out. I always suspected I was her favourite but I never expected that. I blamed myself for not talking to her more, about not telling her how much I loved her. She must have saved every penny she earned from the Post Office because her salary was harmless.

She stinted on things like heat and light. I imagined her half frozen to death in front of a one-bar heater like the one we had in Hanratty's flat. She was generous with others but frugal with herself. The only time she ever spent anything on herself was on these mysterious trips to Norwich.

After she died, I hated passing by her house any time I was home. I was glad when it was sold. The auctioneer's sign was hardly down before the new owners blitzed it, removing all traces of her. I didn't mind that. What was the point of having it the way it was when she wasn't in it? I preferred to think of it when she was in her prime, when she played the piano for us in front of Granny and Grandad, when she dandled me on her knee like she did in Daddy's car and sang nursery rhymes to me. That was the Aunt Bernie I'd always have with me, the one that would never go away.

Mammy was upset for ages after she died. She felt the same as me about her not being appreciated for what she was. She clung on to me in her grief even more than she did to Daddy. I listened to her telling me the same stories over and over again until I almost knew them by heart. She could never tell them to me enough times. They brought Aunt Bernie back to me like a film I played inside my head. It helped me forget my worries, transporting me into a past where everything had a sheen of happiness around it.

Back in the real world, the kids continued to be demanding. Eileen was still a headache. She'd been that way almost since the day she was born. Now that she was a young adult, or at least trying to be one, the friction between us grew.

She was out of the house most of the time. The good thing about that was it meant we couldn't argue. The bad thing was that she rarely told me where she was going.

I wondered about what kind of company she was keeping. I heard about all these games young people were playing where they tried to outdo each other's drinking for a dare. I'd never experienced this kind of thing in my own life, not even with Cáit, the biggest drinker I thought I'd ever encounter. No matter how bad Cáit was I always felt she got drunk despite herself rather than consciously. The crowd Eileen palled around with, in contrast, went out with just that intention in mind. They wanted to get footless as soon as possible

Sometimes I wondered if the people she knocked around with were human at all. They had tattoos in parts of their bodies I didn't know existed. Their hair was often dyed in a half dozen different colours. Some of them had dreadlocks. Others were decked out like Goths, with black clothes and pale faces.

They weren't exactly communicative either. If you got a few words out of them in a night you were doing well. If they were listening to music on their headphones you might as well forget it.

Her mind was out to lunch a lot of the time. For a while I started to think she might be on drugs. She didn't seem to be connected to life like most other people.

She had a lackadaisical attitude to everything. I almost had to book an appointment to talk to her. If you asked her to load the washing machine or take something in off the line it was like asking Hannibal to cross the Alps.

She left the hot press on every other day. If you asked her why she did it she'd just mutter, 'Oh sorry, I forgot to turn it off.' She had no *meas* on money. I talked to her until I was blue in the face trying to make her aware of the value of a pound.

Kevin said to her once, 'Would you also "forget" to pay the ESB bill if I gave it to you?' She skittered laughing at him when he said that because she knew he was such a softie. No matter how many threats he made to her he never followed through on them. It doesn't take children long to cop on to things like that.

Her room was nearly always like a bombsite. Clothes were left strew over the floor for you-know-who to pick up. I said to her one day, pointing to the wardrobe, 'Eileen, that piece of furniture is called a wardrobe. It's where clothes are put. There are hangers inside it. They look much nicer on these than on the carpet.' 'That's interesting,' she said, 'I never noticed it before. Thanks for pointing it out.'

She did her best to work me up. I had to use psychology not to let her. If I called her down for her dinner she took an age to arrive. One day I said to her, 'Sometimes I think I'd be better off sending you a postcard. You might get here quicker.' 'Great idea!' she said, clapping her hands, 'I love postcards.'

She bit her nails down to the quick. I bought her some Stop 'n'Grow to try and get her out of the habit but it did no good. The next time I saw her nibbling at them I asked her why she wasn't putting it on. 'I did,' she said, 'but I got to like the taste of it.' That was nonsense because it tasted vile. She was capable of eating something that turned her stomach just to thwart me.

My main gripe with her was to do with the phone. Like many teenagers, sometimes she had to be physically dislodged from it when I needed it. At times she seemed to be surgically attached to it. It was a problem if I was waiting on a call from a medical agency about a job.

When she started getting into boyfriends it was like listening to the Mulvey version of *Romeo and Juliet* in the house every night. Pregnant silences were followed by about 87 repetitions of 'I love you' until she finally hung up. Meanwhile I'd be wondering if someone's appendix had burst in the Mater Private and I wasn't there to help. The day after some of these calls I'd ask her about the Romeo in question and she'd say something like 'That idiot. What a waste of space. I don't know what I ever saw in him.' Then a week or so later they'd be like love's young dream again. They'd be pledging undying troth to one another on the same phone line as I tore my hair out trying to get on the line.

I often delegated Cillian to keep tabs on her because of her tendency to wander off with people. She was gullible that way. Neither Kevin nor myself thought she'd ever suspect them of leading her astray. I had visions of her being kidnapped as she talked to strangers. That was something I made Cillian and Siobhan swear they'd never do under any circumstances.

I tried to have Kevin with me any time I gave out to her. I knew he tended to spoil her and that she exploited that quality in him. It was important for her to see we were 'on the same page,' with her, as the Americans said. Unfortunately that wasn't always possible. He'd often be at work when I was having an issue with her. By the time he came home I'd probably have cooled down or he'd be too tired to do anything about it.

He was having problems of his own at this time. Computers were being introduced to Clery's and they didn't suit him at all. He'd prefer to have done without them but that wasn't possible. The world was changing and if you weren't a part of it your job could be gone.

He was much happier dealing with people than machines. He was like me in that. A lot of deals were done with a shake of the hand when he started out but now everything had to be tabulated.

'They want a record of a sale more than a sale,' he said to me one day. I told him I saw some of that coming in to the Mater too before I left. Would we one day see robots running carpet stores – if not hospitals?

I wish I could have helped him more when he was undergoing these kinds of problems but I couldn't. I was often drained at the end of a day, either from one of my stand-up rows with Eileen or from the household chores I did to recover from them. I'd often be running around the place like a headless chicken when he came in. I'd be drying dishes or trying to get the washing out of the machine or ironing his shirts. Many nights we went to bed without having exchanged more than a half dozen words with one another during the day. He rarely slept on these nights.

I've always regretted not realising the full extent of this when it was going on. Kevin wasn't the type of man to say, 'I need to talk to you,' but sometimes he did. On these occasions I was more asleep than awake so I didn't really engage with him.

One night when we were getting into bed he said he'd had a coffee with a girl from the jewellery department in Clery's earlier that day. Her name was Cathy. I only knew her slightly. She was very good-looking with long shapely legs. I remembered him telling me she'd gone out with Reg a few times but it hadn't ended well. (Did it ever with Reg?) I imagined him promising her the earth and then doing a bunk when he got what he wanted out of her.

Kevin was casual about having the coffee with her but it gave me the fright of my life. I didn't think there was anything going on between them but it still sent up alarm bells for me.

No matter how much I loved the children, if anything went wrong between Kevin and me I wouldn't have been able to function. What I went through with Tom made me more than aware of that. I knew he hadn't met her to give me any kind of message about ourselves but it had that effect on me.

Afterwards I made a point of setting some time aside every day to be there for him if he needed me. It was just as well I did. The discussions we had over the next few weeks made that clear to me. All sorts of things were doing his head in, not only concerning the job but the children as well.

The noise they made was driving him batty for starters. That was something I hadn't a clue about because he never went on about it. I thought I was the only one with cloth ears in the house. His problem was that he was too easy-going. Every time they broke the sound

448

barrier with their rock music he just moved to another room. That might have been a kind thing to do but it obscured an important fact: he was going just as loopy with the din the kids made as I was.

The bigger they grew, the more they took over the house. They always seemed to be in the bathroom. I'd see Kevin hopping from one foot to the other in frustration as he waited to get in. I had the experience of being in that position too but I wasn't as patient as him. I usually battered the door down until they came out. I didn't care if they were swearing at me or dripping with water or if they had towels over their heads or even if they were only half dressed. All's fair in love, war and bathrooms.

No matter what room you went into there seemed to be one of them in there, either playing music or entertaining their friends. It wasn't like it was our house anymore once 'Minority Rule' (as Kevin called it) came in. I thought a lot of it had to do with the kind of television programmes they were watching, the ones we imported from abroad that alerted them to the importance of 'expressing themselves.' (When would the day come when parents could express themselves?)

Sometimes I had a hankering to go back to the simplicity of Midleton fulltime. I knew it would have meant the world to Mammy and Daddy. It was a pity Clery's hadn't a branch in it. I could probably have got a job doing private nursing there from all my contacts. Mammy would have been an automatic babysitter for us.

Anytime I floated the idea by Kevin he gave it the thumbs-down. Leaving Clery's would have meant forfeiting his Golden Handshake. That was the drawback. Mark O'Loughlin might have given him some kind of gratuity for his years of service but he didn't think it would be enough for us to live on. We'd have saved something by selling the house and buying a cheaper one in Cork but maybe not enough to live on until we got to pension age. In the end it came down to a question of whether we were willing to sacrifice everything we'd built up for a shot in the dark. We said we'd keep it open as a possibility but not do anything immediate.

He was a Section Manager in Clery's by now. There were a few people under him, including Rory Gilsenan, the man he always believed was after his job. I thought he'd be delighted with that but he said it was an empty title. It didn't carry much authority with it and the increase it brought to his salary was a joke.

'They gave it to me to keep me quiet when I asked them for a raise,' he said, 'It was cheaper to put a dog tag on me than pay me any more money.'

He worked like a Trojan but rarely got credit for it. Some nights he wouldn't be home until nine or ten at night and he wouldn't even have been paid overtime.

'You're out of your mind,' I'd say to him but he'd tell me he had no choice.

'If I complain, it only gives them more of a motivation to demote me.' I couldn't believe he was being treated like a menial after all his years of service. His problem was that he was too nice to everyone. Nice guys come last, as the saying goes.

'If you don't put a price on your head,' I said to him, 'No one else will.' That wasn't the way he saw it. It was natural for him to do what he was asked. His father had brought him up to believe that was the best way to get ahead. In an ideal world it might have been but from my years of listening to him I thought the opposite applied. The more you did, the less they respected you.

More young people were recruited to the staff as time went on. The upshot was that Kevin got passed over when promotions were in the air. He wouldn't have minded too much if the juicy positions were being given to talented people but they weren't.

'You wouldn't believe what they're letting in these days,' he'd say to me, 'People who can hardly spell their name are getting the top jobs.' I told him he should have listened to me years before when I was advising him to be tougher.

He was ready to be tough now but it was too late. He'd missed the boat. There were all these chinless wonders leapfrogging over him and there wasn't a thing he could do about it.

The unions were also getting very strong by this time. 'If you look sideways at anyone working for you,' he said, 'even if they're a waste of space, you could be reported. If you sacked them, not that I'd have the power to, you'd probably be taken to the Labour Court. You could end up getting done for unfair dismissal.' He often had to put up with shoddy workmanship from the new recruits because of that.

Some of them hadn't a clue about the different features of carpets. One day Rory Gilsenan was asked a question about the way the pile went and he didn't even know what it meant. 'It was laughable,' Kevin said, 'I learned about that on my first day in the job. Actually I didn't need to learn about it. I knew it already.'

He said it was hard to get anyone to do anything beyond the call of duty anymore. That was another result of the power of the unions. I'd noticed the same thing coming into nursing towards the end of my time in the Mater. One day a patient asked me to close a window on a particularly cold day. I was about to close it when I was informed I wasn't allowed to by the nurse on duty. 'Why?' I asked. 'Because you don't work on this ward,' she said. I'd just wandered in to get a syringe from Hilary.

'It's ridiculous,' he said, 'We're losing customers hand over fist because some of these geniuses aren't pulling their weight.'

I told him not to worry about it. It wasn't as if he had shares in the place. 'That's not the point,' he said. If he wasn't able to give a job his all he'd have preferred not to get up in the morning.

'Gilsenan is after my job,' he said, 'He thinks I'm over the hill. Maybe I am but he still has to climb it. He keeps telling O'Loughlin you can't teach an old dog new tricks but you can't teach a new dog old ones either. I'm able to make deals in a way he can't, the old-fashioned way. That's what annoys him most of all.'

I advised him to look for other jobs in the carpet line. If he did, I thought, his vast experience in the field would be an enormous advantage to him. He reminded me of the fact that he'd done that once before and that it got back to Mark. If he did it again it could threaten the famous Golden Handshake.

I didn't see the point of putting too much importance on that. There was nothing down on paper about it. It would be at the discretion of Mark as an *ex gratia* payment when he left. I didn't like the idea of that kind of pressure being put on him. It was like a white elephant that might never turn into anything.

'Apart from everything else,' I said, 'That place is bad for your mental health.'

He didn't like that kind of talk. It reminded him too much of my 'Health is wealth' speeches.

451

'You can't live on mental health,' he said to me one night, 'It doesn't put bread on the table.'

'Actually it does,' I said, 'You can't buy bread if you're lying on the flat of your back in a psychiatric hospital.'

'Is that where you think I'm headed?'

'It upsets me to see the humiliation they're putting you through in there. You'd be better off sweeping the streets.'

He was too practical to look at it like that. I watched him growing old before me and it broke my heart. In many ways he was like another Daddy. Why was I surrounded by men who couldn't stand up for themselves?

Every time I talked about him retiring he ran to the cabinet in the kitchen where we kept all the bills. He took them out and spread them out over the table like a deck of cards. The mortgage. The ESB. The food we ate. The clothes we wore. The house insurance. The fuel we used. The children's education. It went on like an incantation until I'd be sorry I opened my mouth.

Even the expense of running the car was trotted out. When you added tax and insurance onto things like petrol and repairs it came to a pretty penny. Most of the time it sat in the driveway because he went into work on the bus but it was nice to have it there for the trips down to Mammy and Daddy.

We were still going down to them on the odd weekend. The Austin was now on its ninth life. I got a major surprise every time I turned the ignition and it started.

He was always after me to trade it in for something 'vaguely resembling a car,' as he put it, but I was so fond of it I wouldn't let him. It was like a cuddly old pet I refused to have put down even though I knew it was ready to pack up at any minute. It shuddered if you went any way fast at all, making you feel like you had a flat tyre or were going across speed bumps. The only way the choke would work was if you put a penny under it to hold it out. The centre of gravity was on the right hand side, which meant Kevin had to sit behind me sometimes instead of opposite me. That was the only way we could hold the road. It made me feel like a taxi driver. 'Where would you like me to let you off?' I'd say to him for a joke.

Maureen came with us sometimes. She was going out with a dentist now. His name was Adrian. She'd gone to him for treatment for a tooth that had been giving her problems for years She was taken with his sympathetic approach to her. Pretty soon the relationship went way beyond the professional level.

He was a good bit older than her but after the Edward experience she didn't place too much emphasis on things like that anymore. 'The few years might give him a bit more maturity,' she said. That wasn't always the case with men but with Adrian I felt it was. He had a good head on his shoulders.

I actually met him before Maureen did. It was at a coffee morning. He was drinking tea. That was so Adrian. He'd cut himself shaving and had a little bit of toilet paper on his chin. That was very Adrian too.

I was fundraising for Cystic Fibrosis at the time. It's a wonderful charity with many great people working for it. Adrian was involved in a mini-marathon that was being organised for it. He wasn't the fittest person in the world but he gave it everything, running himself into the ground. All along the way people were selling '65 Roses.' These were little bags that folded up into the shape of a rose after you used them. This was the famous mispronunciation of the disease by a child called Richard Weiss. He suffered from it in America in the sixties.

Adrian was very sensitive. He blushed if you praised him. That reminded me of Aunt Bernie. He was very unsure of himself. I always felt people who were that way were more genuine than brash types. Maureen said he was a brilliant dentist but that he lacked a bedside manner. He was popular because of the work he did rather than his facility for small talk. That just didn't exist. If you said 'Good morning' to him, according to Maureen, he practically got a panic attack. When most people were talking about the weather he was thinking about root canals. He was capable of saying 'Nice weather we're having' to his patients even if it was lashing rain outside.

I always relaxed with him. He did a filling for me once. I didn't feel the needle going in when he anaesthetised me. He was very gentle.

I was glad he wasn't one of those dentists who went in for idle chat. Our Midleton one loved asking you questions like 'Where did you go on your holidays?' when you had about 45 things in your mouth. Any time I tried to answer him I probably sounded like a woman from the Stone Ages.

One weekend when Maureen was going down to Midleton with Adrian she asked Kevin and me if we'd like to join them. I thought it was a great idea. The four of us went down in Adrian's car. The children weren't with us. Cillian was staying with Kevin's father in Athlone. The two girls were brushing up on their Irish in a Gaeltacht in Connemara.

Adrian had a BMW. That intimidated Kevin. He only agreed to travel in it to save him the worry about the Austin breaking down.

Mammy and Daddy were delighted to see us but they were a bit dubious about Adrian after what happened with Edward. After him, every man Maureen went out with was regarded as being guilty until proven innocent. Mammy liked him but Daddy viewed him with suspicion. He was never too fond of dentists anyway.

'You guys charge you a fortune to keep filling our teeth,' he said to him, 'and then you yank them out when you can't squeeze any more money out of us.' Adrian – predictably - blushed at that. I felt sorry looking at him. He wasn't sure how to react to Daddy's dry sense of humour.

He stayed in a B&B. There wasn't enough room for him in the house even though May had gone from it now. She was living in a flat on the edge of the town. Mammy didn't push her to stay with her, as she probably would have if it was me or Maureen.

'Sure she's only a stone's throw away,' she said, 'I wouldn't be surprised if she was back next week.'

May was curious to see Adrian after hearing so much about him from Maureen. She spent a lot of the weekend for us. The five of us went out on walks together and for meals in the evenings. May was amused by Adrian. She loved embarrassing him.

She'd stayed in the same job but she was going higher all the time. Her latest promotion involved a lot more work with computers but that was hardly a problem to her. The way she worked on them was like magic. They didn't knock a feather out of her.

Daddy watched her rising up the corporate ladder with amusement.

'You're far too involved with your job,' he said to her one day, 'You'll never get a man that way.'

That kind of comment always caused her to scream in horror.

'You're back in the Stone Ages, Daddy,' she said, 'I need a man like I need a hole in the head.'

Daddy was indignant.

'You have to kiss a lot of frogs before you meet a prince.'

'I don't believe in kissing frogs. In fact I'm not even sure I want to kiss a prince.'

'Is it Women's Lip that has you thinking like that?'

He thought it was Lip instead of Lib. May burst her sides laughing at that. It seemed to take the harm out of what he was saying. He was always getting those kinds of things wrong.

Feminism passed Daddy by. I don't think he even knew what it was about. That made him more lovable to me. I preferred him that way than falling over himself trying to be a New Man.

May had a busy life in the evenings. She was in a dramatic society and she played the guitar in pubs as well. It was amazing how she found the time to crowd so much into her life. She had to be at something all the time, whether it was her job or her hobbies. I remembered how bored she used to be growing up if there was nothing happening.

She took up the guitar as a result of her fascination with Elvis. When she started it first she couldn't get the hang of it. We often laughed about her playing it at Maureen's wedding. At that time it was like listening to a bag of nails falling on the floor. Of course you didn't dare say anything like that to May. With her temper she'd have gone for you.

When Elvis died she almost had to go into therapy. She cried as if it was a member of the family who'd just been taken from her. I was sad too but I thought his life was such a waste. Who wouldn't have killed to have all the gifts he had? I was more angry at him than anything else when he died. God love him, he had so many problems at the end of his life.

455

'How could a man who had everything get so obese?' I said to May after he died. She thought that was heartless of me.

'He was the greatest singer in the world,' she insisted.

'Maybe he was,' I said, 'but shouldn't great singers know when they're killing themselves?' I thought he owed it to his audiences to live longer, especially his Irish audiences. What a pity he never came to Ireland.

'I realise it's not as bad as if something happened to Dickie Rock,' May said when she saw she wasn't getting anywhere with me, 'or Butch Moore.' She never lost her talent for being bitchy.

Mammy hated seeing us arguing. She thought it would make us less inclined to come to the house if we weren't getting on. She loved having us all together. I could see her mood darkening when our visits were coming to an end. Even when we were arguing it was better than nothing for her. 'Will we ever be a family again?' she'd say as we got ready to go, wringing her hands in frustration.

Daddy was more understanding.

'They have their own things going on,' he'd say but I could see Mammy's point. It wasn't the same for her because we weren't sitting together at night for a recollection of the day's events like we used to. She clung onto each one of us more tightly when we were with her as a result of that.

The house was very tidy now but that bored me. I missed the higgledy-piggledy way it used to be when we were growing up. Everyone was coming and going then like in a revolving door. Life was an endless party with Mammy and Daddy and the three of us and Granny and Grandad and Aunt Bernie and anyone else who happened to drop in. Mammy used to fret about the fact that she hadn't enough chairs for everyone when we sat down to eat. There were lots of chairs now but no atmosphere.

Daddy looked older. Bad health had forced him to give up work. All he did now was the odd nixer. He wasn't able for most of the things he used to do and got out of breath very quickly. We all knew he didn't take care of his health enough. I wanted him to have himself checked out from top to bottom but he said he hadn't the money for that. He wasn't in the VHI. I wished I was still in the Mater. If I was I thought I might have been able to get a consultant to see him without breaking the bank.

He kept getting bugs that proved increasingly difficult to shake off as he aged. We were always trying different antibiotics on him to fight them but as time went on he seemed to become immune to them. In the end we decided to let nature take its course.

'What do your medical text-books say about that?' he said to me one day, taunting me in a way that suggested all my years of learning were useless.

'If that's what works for you,' I replied, 'Why not?'

I knew it was going against everything I'd been told in training to say something like that but I didn't care. Sometimes you just had to ride things out of your system the natural way.

It hurt me to see him looking so frail. He'd been like Charles Atlas as a young man. Even doing something simple like taking a bale of briquettes from the car was a chore to him now.

When he went upstairs he had to stop on almost every step to get his breath. 'One of these days,' he said, 'I'll have to bring a packed lunch with me on the way to the way to the bathroom.'

For a while Mammy considered selling the house and buying a bungalow. I said I thought that was a great idea.

'So do I,' she said, 'but his nibs won't hear of it.' I understood that. It would have been too big an uprooting for him.

The other option was to get a stairlift but he wouldn't agree to that either. 'We can't afford it,' he said flatly. I made some enquiries from the health board and found he could probably have qualified for a grant. I couldn't wait to ring him with my news but when I did he poo-pooed the idea. His pride wouldn't allow me follow up on it. He preferred to suffer the pain.

He spent a lot of his time in what we called his 'good' clothes, the suits we used to only see him in at the weekends or if he was going to a wedding or funeral.

I missed the days when he'd come in from work looking as if a house fell on him, days when he'd tramp in wearing his big boots and Maureen and myself would sit him down and try to pick the cement out of his hair after removing the inevitable butt of a cigarette from behind his ear.

Sitting there with his hair neatly combed and his shirt buttoned up to the neck he wasn't like the old Daddy at all. His jackets were too small for him now. He'd gained weight from all the years sitting around and he wasn't the type to spend money on new ones.

'I'm like a lad decked out for his First Communion,' he joked if we passed a comment on him, 'It's all your mother's fault.'

'At least it's better than the way you used to be,' she'd say, 'I'd be terrified the neighbours would come in. They'd think I wasn't looking after you properly.'

They started to argue more with one another as they got older, something I'd never remembered them doing when I was young. It was probably due to them being too much in each other's company. Arguing about money in front of us was something they hadn't done before. Because Daddy wasn't earning anymore he told Mammy we'd end up on Skid Row if she didn't tighten her belt.

She wasn't extravagant by any means but he watched every penny she spent. He even asked her for copies of her receipts from the shops. 'He's turning me into a nerve case,' she'd say, throwing her hands in the air.

I knew what she was going through. She'd had her own life when he was on the buildings. She'd go off to Mass in the mornings and dilly-dally on the way home chatting with the neighbours, dropping in to them for a cup of tea every so often. That was all changed now.

She was like a prisoner in her own house. He'd be checking his watch if she wasn't home exactly when she promised to be. 'Where have you been?' he'd say to her if she got delayed even for a few minutes, 'Was there a fire somewhere?' That drove her up the walls.

'What's the point of rushing back?' she'd say, 'We never do anything anyway.' That really hurt Daddy. It brought it home to him how his life had slowed down so much.

He couldn't drive now. After he got one of his bugs the doctor told him to stay in the house until he felt better. Because he wasn't allowed drive he let the insurance on the car slip. As time passed it became rusty from lying in the garage. He tried to tune it up once but there wasn't a meg out of it.

One day he wheeled it out onto the road to see if he could get it going. He asked one of the neighbours to give him a push. It lurched into life for a second but then sputtered out again.

'It has no poke,' he complained to Mammy. The next time I saw him I told him the Austin was going that way too. Some days it just stopped in the middle of nowhere for no reason. I'd be on some back road and a cow would be looking at me from over a hedge with an expression that seemed to say, 'How in the name of God do you expect that thing to go?'

'Maybe we should sign them into the same junkyard,' Daddy said. 'And ourselves as well.'

Mammy hated it when he talked like that.

'It's his nerves,' she said, 'He has to be at something. Then he takes on too much and gets run down again. Because he hasn't any job to go to he's clutching at straws to keep himself busy.'

When he was at a loose end he picked on her, becoming fussy about things in the house. Every night before we went to bed he'd get into a tizzy about whether all the lights were off and the doors locked. He even locked the sitting-room door.

'If a burglar gets in the window,' he said, 'He'll be trapped in there.' Sometimes he got out of bed in the middle of the night if he thought he heard a noise in the back yard. Usually it would be nothing more than a cat disturbing a bin lid but he'd still have to go down and investigate.

'Go to sleep for God's sake,' Mammy would say, 'You'll have the whole road woken up mooching around the place.'

Too much inactivity had narrowed his world to the dimensions of the house. If he heard about a break-in in the area he'd go to pieces altogether. One day I found him cementing pieces of glass onto the top of our back wall.

'Is that not illegal?' I asked him.

'Who told you that?'

'I don't know. I thought I heard it somewhere.'

'It's a sad state of affairs if you aren't allowed to protect your own property.'

He was right. The world we were living in was crazy. All the rights seemed to be on the side of offenders. He said he had to stop reading papers because there were so many reports of light sentences given to criminals.

Mammy was upset by his ranting. She threw herself into the housework to get away from him, becoming as manic about that as he was about the safety.

If she wasn't cleaning she was cooking. If Daddy was in bed she'd bring him in his dinner on a tray. A few minutes later she'd have something served up to me. It was like magic. She waited on me hand and foot, not letting me lift a finger. I knew she liked spoiling me but I needed to keep moving, probably as a result of all the years whizzing around hospital wards. If I went to make a cup of tea she'd be at the kettle before me.

'Sit yourself down,' she'd say, 'You're here for a break, not to work.' As I was sitting there she'd suck every scrap of information out of me about my life in Dublin. There was usually a fight between us to wash the dishes. At night-time she insisted on filling a hot water bottle for me even if it was summer.

'I'm not a baby anymore,' I told her one day when she was running herself off her feet. I didn't know if she was doing it to get me to come home more. She probably thought spoiling me would make Midleton more attractive to me than Dublin. I remember having a nosebleed once and she treated it as if I needed open heart surgery.

She criticised Daddy for being hyperactive but she put him into the shade. If we went shopping she was always first out of the car and into the supermarket. She'd run around the aisles picking up things we didn't need half the time. Over coffee one day after she'd got her weekly order she told me how much good it did her to get out of the house.

'Daddy is rarely in good form now,' she said, 'After a while it rubs off on me.'

I wished things could have been different between them. I couldn't think of any way to bring that about. It was retirement, pure and simple. Every family had to go through it. I was going through a form of it myself. It was ten times worse when bad health came into the equation.

Daddy had a nebulizer now. It replaced the inhalers he'd used as a young man. These became useless to him when his breathing got worse. Even the nebulizer didn't work all the time. It was painful having to watch him fighting for breath. What could you do except sympathise?

He hated talking about his health. If I mentioned anything about it he clammed up. If I got anyway intrusive I was accused of playing the nurse. Anytime I took his blood he laughed me off as being a vampire.

Mammy worried about what was going to happen to him in the future.

'If he ever has to go into a wheelchair he'll die,' she said to me. I felt she was right about that. I prayed with all my heart it wouldn't happen.

His mind wandered as he got older. One day I saw him dipping his shaving brush into a cup of tea instead of into his shaving mug. Mammy laughed about that but I thought it was worrying. I was afraid he might be getting dementia. I wanted him to have an MRI but he wouldn't agree to that.

The last time he had one was when he was complaining about a pain in his chest but it showed nothing. He went for a check-up the following month. As he was leaving the surgery the doctor said to him, 'If the pain comes back we'll take another peep.' Daddy replied, 'I don't think so. The last peep cost me half a year's wages.'

'I've kept away from doctors most of my life,' he told me, 'and I'm not about to change now. Most of them know as much about medicine as a pig knows about a holiday. They keep poking at you until they find something wrong. Most of the time they've caused it themselves. If I went into hospital I'd probably come out of it in a box.' I knew I couldn't change his view so I didn't bother trying.

One of his favourite expressions was, 'Doctors differ and patients die.' He liked to tell a story about two doctors who were discussing a patient with a serious medical condition. They agreed that they couldn't save his life but didn't seem too concerned about that. What was more important to them was which of them was more knowledgeable about what was wrong with him. At the end of their conversation, one of them said to the other one, 'Wait till you see. The autopsy will prove I'm right.'

461

He went down to the pub with Kevin a good few nights. By now he'd started to take the odd drink again. He'd been off it so long I was nervous about that but he assured me he'd never go back on it in a serious way. He said he believed people mainly became alcoholics because they were lonely or had nothing else in their lives. I thought it was a bit more complicated than that but I didn't argue the point with him.

Daddy was glad to have a fellow imbiber with him.

'I never trusted people who don't take a drop,' he used to say. He always felt they were watching him.

They stayed out so long sometimes I'd get to wondering if something happened to them. Then out of the blue they'd roll in as if they'd just gone out five minutes beforehand.

'What did you talk about?' I'd ask Kevin. He'd usually say, 'To be honest with you I can't remember.' I didn't think he was making it up. Maybe that was the difference between men and women. Men forgot what they said five minutes after saying it but women remembered the slightest comment for years afterwards. I wasn't sure which of us were better off.

One night when they came in I noticed Kevin's eyes looking dazed. From experience I knew he'd had one too many. It reminded me of the night of our flat-warming party. He fell on the stairs going up to bed.

When Daddy tried to lift him up he fell too. They looked like a pair of clowns from a circus.

'The blind leading the blind,' was the way Mammy put it. For a minute we thought Daddy might be hurt but as soon as he got up he started nattering away to Kevin without a bother on him.

'At least we didn't lose the whiskey,' he said. He had a Babypower in his pocket that he'd brought home for a nightcap.

I used to go to the pub with Daddy on the nights Kevin wasn't around. He loved showing me off to all the other drinkers. I pleaded with him to stop but he wouldn't. It embarrassed me to high heaven.

'This is my beautiful daughter,' he'd say to anyone who passed by. Most of them knew who I was anyway. That made it ten times worse. But that was Daddy.

462

He wasn't inclined to talk to me much on these nights. He preferred looking around at who else was there. He'd sip at a pint of Guinness and maybe follow it with a glass of wine if he was feeling merry.

He usually got bad hangovers from mixing 'the grape and the grain.' I tried to get him to stick with Guinness. 'I thought I left the ball and chain at home,' he'd say any time I pleaded with him not to go to the counter for his chasers.

I didn't want to be a stick-in-the-mud. Anytime I played the role of the nurse with him I didn't get anywhere. If I told him drink made people depressed he'd come back with some crack like, 'I get much more depressed when I don't have it.'

Sometimes he drank hot whiskeys into the bargain.

'Purely for medicinal purposes,' he insisted one night when I told him off about all the mixtures, 'I have a bit of a sore throat.' Long after the so-called sore throat was cured he was still lashing into the hot whiskeys.

He used to be quiet after coming back from the pub. He often sat in the kitchen for hours. Sometimes I went down to get a glass of water in the middle of the night and he'd be just sitting there looking at the wall. Everything would be as still as a graveyard. All you'd hear would be the purring of the fridge. He was displaying his 'autumn colours,' as he put it. At times like that it was impossible to cheer him up. He'd start talking about his poor health, about being an 'old crock' who was on the way out.

'Do you think we go anywhere after we die?' he said to me one night as he cradled a bottle of whiskey, 'or do we just have a big sleep?' That comment amazed me. I'd always thought his faith was rock solid.

'I don't know,' was all I could think to reply, 'I believe we do but maybe that's because of the religion I was brought up with. Maybe people simply go on believing what they were told in childhood.'

'You might have something there,' he said. Daddy didn't think of faith as a gift. For him it was just something you either had or didn't have.

'I could never understand why God hides,' he said then. 'If he's there, why doesn't he show himself?'

463

'People would only be good out of fear of him if he did,' I said, 'or because they wanted their reward.'

'But isn't that the way things are anyway? Don't most people do good acts because they think it's going to be made up to them in the hereafter?'

I had no answer for that.

'My father often wondered what age he'd be in the next life,' he said, 'He used to ask me if I thought he'd be twenty or forty or sixty.'

'What did you tell him?'

'How could I tell him anything? You can't answer a question like that. What do you think?'

'In the spirit world you're no age,' I said. 'Or maybe every age.'

'But the priests tell us to think of meeting our loved ones as we remember them. How could I remember my father when he was twenty? I wasn't even born at the time.'

I saw his point but I couldn't answer that either. All I could think of was to say the quote from the Bible: 'Eye hath not seen nor ear heard what joys God has contemplated for us in heaven.'

'Is that not avoiding the issue?' he said, 'There are lots of pictures in the Bible to counteract that.'

He was talking about an illustrated copy of the Old Testament we had. Some of the paintings of hell used to terrify me as a child.

'They're just guides, Daddy,' I said, 'They're not the real thing.'

'I was brought up to believe Adam and Eve were "the real thing." Now they're telling us they weren't. I wish they'd make up their minds.'

'They were symbols, Daddy. It's the message that's important. They suffered from the sin of pride, like Lucifer. They had to be punished. That's why they were banished from the Garden of Eden.'

'I can't see God sending someone away from him forever.'

I found that hard to imagine too. I often wondered if Hitler was in hell, or Judas. Could we judge anyone without being inside their head?

I started thinking about Imelda Garvey, about the day she made fun of the catechism. Who made the world? God made the world. If there was a God.

'Someone was telling me the other day,' Daddy said, 'that he thought this world was hell, that if we serve our time in it we all deserved to go to heaven afterwards.'

'That's an interesting idea,' I said, though I thought it sounded a bit dramatic.

'This discussion is getting a bit heavy, isn't it?' he said to me then. I told him I agreed. I was wishing we had Imelda to relax us.

'When I have a few more of these in me,' he said as he took a slug of his whiskey, 'I won't care too much if anything exists in the hereafter or not!'

When the drink started to get a grip on him he cut down on it. He went on non-alcoholic beer for a while but the doctor told him it had too much sugar in it, that wasn't good for his cholesterol. He laughed when he heard that diagnosis.

'You're damned if you do and you're damned if you don't,' he said. He told me he'd prefer to die on a bender than from excess sugar in the blood.

Sometimes I thought he drank more from boredom than anything else. When he was working he hadn't had much time for it. Mammy and myself drove ourselves demented trying to think up some hobbies he could occupy himself with but we always drew blanks. In the end he usually settled on television, the old faithful.

Real life programmes did nothing for him. The films that were usually on weren't his style at all. He didn't like modern films. Nobody could measure up to the classic stars of Hollywood's Golden Age for him – people like Errol Flynn, Randolph Scott, Stewart Granger. The new crop of stars were lightweight. They lacked charisma.

Modern films were also too spicy for him.

'Why does everything have to have sex in it nowadays?' he'd say to me.

I used to be embarrassed looking at  sexual scenes with him. One night I sat frozen-faced watching a pair of lovers cavorting around a bed with pained looks on their faces. It was one of those European films Reg liked to go to.

'They don't seem to be having much fun, do they?' Daddy said. It was great when we were able to have a laugh at times like that. It took the tension away.

He kept changing the channels to keep his interest going. He wasn't able to settle on any of them for very long. I knew his nerves were on edge when he did that. The only time he'd sit still for any length of time was if Cork were playing football. The sight of the red and white mesmerised him even in the dullest of games.

Otherwise he'd be up and down out of his seat like a jack-in-the-box. 'Look,' he said to me one day as he clicked the remote, 'More rubbish no matter where you go. I've been flicking up and down the channels for the last hour and I still can't find anything half-decent. Can you explain to me why I was happier when we just had RTE 1 and RTE 2?'

'Probably because they were better,' I suggested.

'Exactly. I think I can do without knowing about the history of pottery in Eastern Russia. Not too many people talk about that in Spar when you're down there looking for a pound of butter and a sliced pan.'

He was more interested in the mechanics of the television than any of the programmes that were on it. Whenever it broke down he took great delight in fixing it. I couldn't believe how he managed it because he had no training in that line. It reminded me of the days when we had the television with the rabbit's ears on the top of it. He was great at taking things apart and seeing how they worked. Sometimes I thought he'd be secretly hoping it would break down again so he could fix it.

He was so good with his hands he had to be doing something with them instead of just sitting there. That was the problem with the modern world for him. It had so many contraptions in it he wasn't motivated to do anything creative. Everything was readymade.

I saw the same thing happening with the kids. When our generation was young we were able to entertain ourselves for hours on end banging a stick on a piece of wood. The new one had to have everything packaged.

I thought it would help Daddy if he moved with the times. One night I tried to teach him how to record a programme but I didn't get anywhere. It would have been easier to teach a monkey to fly to the moon.

'Let's just watch what's on now,' he said.

There was an old typewriter in the attic. I took it down one night and showed it to him. I thought it might help him to keep in touch with us more if he learned how to use it. That was another idea that went nowhere.

'I prefer using a pen,' he said.

'Daddy,' I said, 'you never do that either.'

At Christmas and birthdays it was usually Mammy who filled in for him. You'd be lucky if you got a smile face drawn at the end of the page from him. But in a way it was nicer. Don't they say a picture is worth a thousand words?

## Learning to Let Go

The children became more distant from me as they grew older. I suppose that happens in every family but I wasn't prepared for it. Their network of friends increased. That meant they spent less time with Kevin and me. They didn't talk to us as much as they used to about what was going on in their lives and didn't ask for our advice as much either. Half the time I hadn't a clue where they were going on a given day. In time I learned to accept that. Sometimes you just had to take a deep breath and hope for the best.

Kevin told me it was only natural that they'd want to go their own way. He was much better at dealing with the situation than me. Maybe all fathers are. Even going back to the days when they were in Primary School he'd be telling me to let them make their own way home, that it would be good for them. I preferred to be there when they got out. Maybe it was easy for me when I didn't have a job to go to. When I did I tried to work their school hours around that.

I stopped collecting Cillian and Siobhan from school when they were around nine or ten. Eileen didn't want me at the gate at any age. Having a mother waiting for you wasn't 'hip' and if Eileen wasn't hip she was nothing. Another reason she didn't want me collecting her from school was because often she wasn't there.

She mitched any chance she got. It took me ages to cop on to it. If I quizzed her about a suspicion I might have had that she went off somewhere she'd look at me with her 'Trust me' eyes and tell me the most elaborate lie possible. If she said she'd been kidnapped by extra-terrestrials I'd probably have believed her.

Her deception came to light the day the principal phoned and asked me to go up to the school. When I got there he said to me, 'Where has Eileen been?' 'What do you mean?' I said. I couldn't honestly answer him. To this day I don't know where she was. All I knew was that she wasn't where she was supposed to be. I gave out stink to her when I got home that day but she brushed it off like it was nothing.

468

I always felt there was a gap between Eileen and me that I couldn't bridge. She used to look into the middle distance when you were telling her something. She reminded me of those changeling children you read about in fairytales. 'Is she of this world at all?' I'd say to Kevin.

One day she came home from school carrying a bird with a broken wing. Another time it was a pup with a lame leg. Then there was the time she saw a programme on television asking people if they'd like to 'adopt' an elephant. It was all she could talk about for weeks afterwards. ('It wouldn't work,' Kevin told her, 'We'd have nowhere to put him.')

In her Inter Cert year she developed a fascination with Madonna. She knew the words of all her songs. She watched her videos on television and mimicked her movements, bopping around the room in various stages of undress. Kevin said, 'It's a pity she wouldn't be as interested in the other Madonna.' He didn't like to see her making fun of nuns and crucifixes.

She started smoking around that time. I had to put my foot down about that. I went into her room one day to tidy it and got the smell of tobacco. Normally she denied it when you accused her of something but there was no way out of that one. 'You told me you hid your smoking from your mother too,' she said when I confronted her about it.

She couldn't take correction. If I tried to give it to her she went into one of her screaming fits. 'Read my lips,' she'd say, 'I'm not going to do what you're asking me.' I presumed her vocabulary came from American TV programmes. Another great one of hers was 'I didn't ask to be born.' I told her I didn't either. It was just something that happened to me. Sometimes she acted as if she was doing you a favour by breathing the same air as you.

Kevin was softer on her than I was. It was like 'Good cop, bad cop.' I'd tell her she had to stop going on like she was 'Or else' and then he'd go into her room and soothe her furrowed brow, imploring her to try and understand why Mammy was being so horrible to her.

I grew to fear her rages in time. It would have been easier to fly to the moon than to get her to calm down. Her favourite bone of

469

contention was the old chestnut about me having more time for Cillian and Siobhan than her.

She thought I praised them more than her too. I was killed telling her I treated the three of them exactly the same way but she never accepted that. The wounds were buried too deep.

I thought modern parents praised their children too much anyway. I was only praised as a child when I did something that deserved it. Parenting 'experts' seemed to recommend going into ecstacies anytime their little darlings blew their noses.

I once heard of a book called *A Medal for Everyone*. It was about the importance of all children being presented with a medal on school sports days regardless of how well they'd performed. The thinking was that they needed to be endorsed early on in life. Being excluded from prize-giving ceremonies could fill them with feelings of low self-esteem. It was a nice idea but hardly a good preparation for life. What happened when you left school and performed badly at something? Would you still want a medal? (I need hardly tell you the book was written by an American).

Cillian got five Honours in the Leaving Cert. He decided he wanted to study English at UCD. 'Is that going to bankrupt you?' he asked us. Even if it was we'd have found some way around it. He'd never asked for anything growing up. We knew it would be a stretch for us but it would have been a shame to deny him since he was so good at English. Kevin often accused him of swallowing the dictionary for breakfast.

Nobody in either of our family's history had been in university before. The cost was an eye-opener to us. Apart from the fees there were lots of books to be bought and food and transport to be thought of.

Kevin was proud leaving him at the bus stop every morning on his way into work. People used to look at him if he was carrying his books. He quoted Oliver Goldsmith to him: 'And still they gazed, and still their wonder grew, that one small head could carry all he knew.' Every evening he arrived home with new ones. Most of them weighed a ton. I could hardly pronounce the names of some of them, never mind read them. They looked like they'd been written in a foreign language. It was a bit like what I had to study for my nursing exams except even more dense.

'If you use big words in the English faculty you sound impressive,' he said, 'It doesn't matter if you're talking nonsense or not.'

He came out of his shell completely in the Uni. I watched him at an L&H debate one night. The theme was, 'Has Ireland Lost the Run of Itself?' He was the main speaker. I was gobsmacked at the kind of stuff he came out with. The lecture theatre came to a standstill as he was speaking. You could have heard a pin drop. After he was finished there was a huge round of applause. On the way home in the car Kevin said to him, 'Who was that guy on the podium tonight? I certainly didn't know him.' Cillian went as red as a beetroot. 'Thst's the kind of crap we talk about every day in the refectory,' he said, 'It doesn't mean anything.'

Sometimes he brought a friend from his class home with him. His name was Donal. He was from Foxrock. He seemed nice but his accent put me off a bit. It was very posh in an artificial way. His father was an architect. Cillian said his house was one of the biggest he'd ever seen in his life. They had a penthouse on the top floor. His father kept a telescope up there for looking at the stars. It was mounted on a gigantic tripod.

Even though Donal was friendly I was self-conscious with him. One night he came over and studied with Cillian. I don't think he'd ever been over to the north side of Dublin before. He arrived in a taxi. They ordered a pizza and shared it. I brought them in tea to have with it. We had cups that came from Granny's house. We only took them out once in a blue moon.

I almost dropped the tray on top of them because of my nerves. They were discussing some author I'd never heard of. I think he was from Russia. For the rest of the evening I kept out of their way as much as I could. I was afraid I'd say something that might let Cillian down. I didn't want to display my ignorance of literature.

A few days later I was going through town in a shabby coat when I ran into the two of them coming out of Easons. I scuttled off after chatting with them for a few minutes.

'I think Cillian was ashamed of me,' I said to Kevin that night.

He hated it when I ran myself down.

'Because of that yoke from Foxrock? What's he got that we haven't? A few swanky syllables? Don't fall into the Baldwin trap again.'

'I won't, but I don't want him to lose Donal. As you say, he's only had the girls for a lot of the time growing up. A bit of male company won't go astray.'

'Agreed. Just don't put Donal on any pedastals because he's from Foxrock. Even if he lived in the Taj Mahal it doesn't make him any better than the rest of us.'

'What makes you think I would?'

'I noticed you got out the best china for him.'

'I wouldn't give it to him to say to his parents that he drank from a cracked cup.'

Cillian had a lot of poems to study for his courses. Sometimes I listened to him discussing them with Donal. They might as well have been talking about the man in the moon for all it meant to me.

I could never understand poems. Cillian showed me a sonnet once that seemed to have been written in a foreign language.

'What does it mean?' I asked him.

'It's not supposed to mean anything,' he said. I couldn't get my head around that. Why was it written if it didn't mean anything?

He joined Dramsoc one year. That was the name of UCD's dramatic society. Kevin and myself went to see him in a Shakespeare play. It was one of his history plays. I can't remember the name of it. Cillian was wearing tights for the part, or at least what looked like them. He said they were leotards. When we saw him in the dressing-room afterwards he still had them on. 'You better get out of those before you get to Coolock,' I said, 'or you'll be arrested.'

'I'd loved to go in for acting fulltime,' he told Kevin later that evening. He said it all began for him with the nativity play when he was knee high to a grasshopper.

'It's a quick way to starve,' Kevin said. He wanted him to become a teacher. I knew what he meant but selling carpets in Clery's seemed so drab in comparison.

'English isn't very practical for jobs, is it?' he said to me later that night. I felt it was far too early for thinking about things like that. I thought he might go into the Civil Service, or maybe teaching.

We had to scrimp over the next few years to pay for his education but it was worth it. He never failed an exam. He went abroad most summers to work. We didn't ask him to give us anything he earned. He had enough on his plate trying to support himself. Every time he came back he seemed more like a man to me.

The girls were all flocking around him now. Eileen couldn't get her head around that. She said, 'I don't know what they see in him.' I thought there was an element of jealousy in her attitude. She saw him as having it all ways – in the looks, the attention of young women and the academic ability. 'I can't wait to get out of that torture chamber,' she said, meaning the school, 'If it doesn't happen soon I can see myself burning the place down.'

Siobhan was more disciplined than Eileen but she was no lover of study either. After doing the Leaving Cert she started working in a beauty parlour. It wasn't wildly exciting but the conditions were pleasant and she had a very good manner with the customers. She thought she might become a therapist in time. There were lots of courses you could do in the evenings.

Kevin got Cillian some work experience in Clery's the year before his graduation. He was trying to give him a taste for what a 'real' job was like but it wasn't a good idea. Cillian found it so boring he walked out after a week. Kevin was disgusted with him. I thought I might be able to get him a job as a porter in the Mater but he wasn't interested in that either.

'A summer in Ireland isn't like a summer at all,' he said. That made me worry about the fact that he might one day emigrate for good.

At Christmas one year he got temporary work as a postman. The post office was always advertising for this on account of all the cards people sent to each other at that time. He got a great kick out of it. .His only problem was the amount of angry dogs he had to deal with in driveways. I used up a lot of plasters thatyear. He often came home with his ankles bleeding.

'They should give us danger money,' he said.

473

One of his friends got so fed up of being bitten he threw all the post in the Tolka one night. Cillian was shocked as he watched them all drifting down the river. He thought it was a horrible thing to have done.

'Imagine denying people messages from the people who loved them,' he said. There was probably a lot of money inside some of them too.

Eventually he qualified. I never doubted he would. He sailed through his exams just like he had in secondary school. The day he got his final results we were all sitting around the kitchen waiting for the postman. He jumped up in the air when he opened the envelope. They'd given him top grades in almost everything.

He went out on the town that night with some of the people in his class. He got roaring drunk. It was the only time I'd ever seen him like that. He acted very strangely when he came home. His eyes were glazed.

'I can see you twice,' he said.

'Lucky you,' I said.

He put his arms around me and told me he loved me. That was so unlike him. He was usually guarded in the expression of his emotions. Kevin didn't know what to make of him. 'I'll leave you two at it,' he said. The next morning he apologized to me for being drunk but I told him I was only amused by him.

'What did I say to you?' he asked awkwardly.

'That you loved me more than anything else in the world and wanted to marry me,' I said. He went all red.

He did the H. Dip the following year. You had to do that if you wanted to be a teacher. He enjoyed the lectures but he found some of the children cheeky during his teaching practice. A lot of them had no interest in learning.

Kevin said he was that way at school too.

'Maybe you were,' Cillian said, 'but I doubt you were disruptive.'

'Do you want to bet?' Kevin said with a glint in his eye.

Cillian sailed through the 'Dip' too. He was now qualified to teach. After sending out a load of applications he landed a job in a girl's school in Portmarnock.

474

He took to it like a duck to water. The pupils loved him. He had them for English and History. That was his second subject in UCD. He was their first male teacher. I think a few of them had crushes on him.

A lot of them had horrible home lives. From some of the stories he told me it looked like he was a shoulder for them to cry on. His favourite pupil was the daughter of the lollipop lady. She was the woman who stopped the traffic outside the school when the pupils were crossing the road. She carried a sign that looked like a huge lollipop.

Cillian was different to the pupils' other teachers. He gave them essays that related to their lives. He asked them things like 'What was your first memory in life?' Questions like that stimulated them. I often wished I had teachers like that instead of people like Sister Serafina who was more interested in rapping me on the knuckles. The only kinds of essays we ever got were boring ones like 'A Day in the Life of a Penny.'

A lot of people think teaching is a soft job because of the short days and long holidays. They don't consider all the preparation and corrections teachers have to do. Some years coming up to the summer holidays I'd see Cillian almost shaking from the stress. No wonder so many teachers retire young.

'In the old days it was just talk and chalk,' He said to Kevin one night, 'Now you have to be *in loco parentis*.'

'What's that?' Kevin said.

'It means you're a substitute for the parent.'

'*In loco parentis*. More like plain loco.'

Kevin retired from Clery's during Cillian's second year of teaching. He was young to bow out but I thought it was the right decision. I was the one who persuaded him. We'd had loads of discussions over the years about the possibility of him going. At the end of all of them he'd always say, 'Let's leave it at that for the moment.' I knew he was going to keep saying that unless I put my foot down. I could see his health failing if he stayed on.

'I could forfeit my Golden Handshake if I walk out,' he kept saying to me. I said, 'What good is a Golden Handshake if you're lying in a coffin in Glasnevin Cemetery?'

He'd had a grumbling ulcer for years. It used to become aggravated with stress. Some mornings he lay on in bed not wanting to get up. It was so different from the days he'd be jumping out to do his press-ups on the floor the second the alarm went off. I had to drag it out of him that he was miserable in there but after repeated interrogations I did. When I heard that I made my mind up.

'You told me when it was time to leave my job,' I said to him one day as I watched him crawling down the stairs to his breakfast, 'Now I'm going to tell you it's time to leave yours.' Amazingly he listened to me. Maybe he was waiting for me to say it.

In the course of a soul-searching weekend we debated the ins and outs of him leaving over innumerable cups of black coffee. I was about to pour one of them over him when he finally agreed to call it a day.

We rang Mammy and Daddy to tell them. They were thrilled. So were Maureen and May.

'Nobody deserves a break more than you do,' Maureen said. 'And so say all of us,' May chirped.

It took Eileen, who else, to put a damper on things.

'What are we going to live on now?' she asked me.

'Bread and water,' I told her.

Cillian said, 'We'll have to have a ceremonial carpet-burning to celebrate the occasion.' He cut out a little patch from the corner of the room and put it on a plate. We put a few firelighters around it and set it ablaze.

'I feel like one of the Vikings,' Kevin said, 'Didn't they do stuff like that?'

'A bit more elaborately, I think,' Siobhan told him.

Afterwards we threw a little party for him. I wanted to do something that would help him take his mind off himself. I knew he was capable of going back on his decision if even one discordant note was struck. Thankfully that didn't happen. After our little spread we had a sing-song. Everyone seemed as happy as the day was long.

Then came the hard part, the watershed moment where he had to formally announce his retirement in Clery's. He did that on the following Monday, going in to Mark O'Loughlin's office to give in his notice even before he took off his coat.

He took it quite well, which surprised Kevin. Maybe he knew it was coming. Kevin always wore his heart on his sleeve. I'm sure Mark saw him losing his zest for work more and more as the years went on.

'If anyone deserves to bow out,' he said to him, 'You do.'

He was a bag of nerves when he came home from work that day.

'What am I going to do with the rest of my life?' he asked me.

'What do any of us do?' I said, 'Breathe in and out, get up in the morning, go to bed at night, and in between try and have some fun.'

I don't think he was too impressed by my advice.

'Thanks,' he said, 'you should be a life coach. The courses would be very short.'

There was a 'do' for him in Madigan's on the following Friday. That was his last official day at work. A corner of the pub was booked for it. He dreaded going and so did I. Both of us hated formal occasions.

'Am I allowed alcohol tonight?' he asked me that morning at breakfast.

'I couldn't deny you that,' I said, 'You can drink the bar dry and I won't say a word to you.'

He looked very distressed going off to work on the Friday morning. He said it was going to be a bittersweet day for him. I told him not to come home at 5.30 but to meet me in Sherie's instead. That was a café near Clery's. We used to meet there a lot of the time when we were going out together so we knew it well.

I got there early and ordered a pot of tea. When he came in he looked very tense. He had a package under his arm.

'What's that?' I said.

'A going-away present from Reg.'

'Why didn't he wait till tonight to give it to you?'

'He thought I was going home. He wanted to get it off his hands rather than having to bring it all the way in from Rathcoole.' He'd bought a little house there recently.

'What is it?'

'A pair of shoes.'

I had to laugh.

'I'll give you three guesses who's paying for these. They're probably seconds.'

'Don't say things like that. He's broke.'

'Broke. Where have I heard that before?'

'What do you mean?'

'This is like a carbon copy of the time we got married. Remember when he gave us the cutlery set for a wedding present?'

'You have a memory like an elephant.'

'I think we used it about twice.'

'That's not his fault.'

'I don't mean that. It was a lousy present.'

'Give him a break. He's struggling with the mortgage repayments at the moment. He told me he's already in negative equity.'

'If it's not his arse it's his elbow. Maybe we should put the shoes with the cutlery.'

Kevin wasn't amused by my attitude. He never was when it came to Reg. He shook his head in frustration. That made me sorry I brought the subject up. I'd made him even tenser than he was.

'I hope I'm doing the right thing going to this pantomime tonight,' he said, 'I wouldn't have any hesitation doing a U-turn and heading home.'

He hated anything formal at the best of times. I knew it would be a hundred times worse for him with everyone gawking at him.

'Stop being dramatic,' I said, 'All you have to do is put in an appearance.'

'Put in an appearance? I'm the bloody guest of honour.'

'So what? You can drift into the background after the formalities are over.'

'There are two chances of that.'

'You said to me after we got married that we were the two most ignored people at the reception.'

'That was different. I've spent half my life with these people.'

'And you've spent half of it with me.'

'You have an answer for everything.'

'I hope I mean more to you than that place.'

'Do you really need to ask me that?'

I was teasing him to relax him. Afterwards I ranted on about a problem I was having with the washing machine to distract him. After a few minutes listening to my *ráiméis* he said, 'Okay. Enough of that. Let's head in.'

There was a soccer match on the television when we got to the pub. Everyone was cheering wildly. The Clery's crowd were cordoned off from the ordinary drinkers by a rope tied on to some steel posts. The soccer spectators seemed to be having a much better time than them. I knew which side of the cordon Kevin would prefer to have been on if things were different.

Cathy Donnelly was the first person to come over to us. She was the girl who'd gone out with Reg in the old days, the girl Kevin told me he'd met for coffee once without any strings attached. She was really nice.

'You're doing something the rest of us haven't the guts to,' she said, giving him a warm handshake, 'I really hope it works out for you.'

She gave me a hug.

'You're lucky to have him,' she said, 'He's a great guy. All the customers speak very highly of him.'

'Try living with him,' I said.

She said she'd love to retire but it wasn't on the cards for a long time. She was married now and had four mouths to feed.

'Five including *mo dhuine*,' she said. I presumed that was her husband. I felt sorry for her. Kevin told me she suffered from sciatica. A lot of tall people seemed to. I'm sure it didn't help that she spent most of the day standing.

Mark came over to us after a while. He gave Kevin a firm handshake.

'Will you miss us?' he asked him.

'The only person I'll miss is Mrs Keaveny,' he said.

That drew a laugh from Mark. He knew well what she was like.

'I'll send her a farewell card from you,' he said, 'I'll draw a picture of your face with some tears coming from it.'

He clenched Kevin's shoulder.

'We better get this show on the road,' he said.

He went over to a podium. People were huddled in little groups chatting. He tapped his finger on the microphone.

'A little bit of hush and lots of shush,' he said.

Kevin blushed. He turned towards me.

'What have I let myself in for?' he said.

'I want to say a few words about Kevin,' Mark said.

He blushed again.

The 'few' turned into many more than that. He talked at length about what a huge asset he'd been to the company and how he'd been instrumental in putting it on the international map. My chest heaved with pride as I listened to him.

The younger people were bored. I saw some of them trying to stifle yawns. All they were waiting for was a chance to get up to the bar for more gargle. Most of the people Kevin started with were long gone out to pasture.

Another man gave a speech after Mark finished. I hadn't a clue who he was. Kevin told me he was one of the new recruits, one of the people who'd been after his job for years.

'Now they can fight for it among themselves,' he said to me.

'May the best man win,' I said.

'I'm afraid the worst one will. They usually do.'

Rory Gilsenan wrapped the proceedings up. I hadn't known he was there until he spoke. As soon as he opened his mouth I knew what Kevin meant when he said he was dangerous. He was a small man but like a lot of small men he had presence. Kevin used to say he was like Marc Antony to Mark's Caesar. ('The other Mark.')

His speech was measured and perfectly worded. I could see him taking everyone in as he talked, including me. After he was finished he stood at the bar chatting to Mark. The two of them were obviously as thick as thieves. I suspected Kevin was right, that Mark was grooming him to be the new Section Manager.

Everyone swelled around us after the formalities were finished. I was hugged by a lot of people I'd never met in my life but who all seemed to know me. It was as if I was living in some kind of Big Brother society where you were being watched without realising it. I had a woeful memory for names. My Dilly Dream personality went back to the days in the convent when the nuns told me I was in a permanent daze.

I didn't want to speak to Rory but I knew he'd be over to me sooner or later. He kept skulking around us. As he strode across the floor I felt a mixture of apprehension and distaste.

'Mrs Mulvey,' he said, 'I've heard so much about you.'

I resisted the urge to say 'Likewise.' He might have taken it as a compliment. Connivers, I knew, didn't always see themselves as that. Some of them just saw themselves as ambitious.

'Thanks for a lovely evening,' I said. When I shook his hand it was as cold as I expected it to be.

'It's no less than Kevin deserves. He's kept this place going during the good years and the bad ones.'

He chatted to me for a few minutes and then went off. As I watched him going back to Mark I thought he looked like a snake even in the way he moved, slithering from side to side.

Some women from the clothing department started talking to me. They were going on about the latest fashions in their catalogues and what they planned to buy from them. Because of the night that was in it they said I could avail of some very attractive deals. Cathy gave me a wink from behind their shoulder. I wasn't sure if she was encouraging me to take up the offers or if she was mocking them. I tried to look interested but when you've spent most of your life watching people with horrible diseases it's hard to get excited listening to someone telling you about a new dress that's on the market that you can get for half price.

Reg drifted in when the night was nearly over. He was wearing the same duffel coat he had on him the night he 'swung by' after Cillian had his fall. I don't think he wanted to come. I never saw him looking more subdued. I thought he resented the fact that Kevin was getting out when he couldn't afford to. Out of the corner of my eye I saw Cathy giving him a dirty look. I felt they'd be staying well away from one another for the remainder of the night.

'Sorry I'm late,' he said, 'Bus Eireann was its usual punctual self.'

'You missed all the speeches,' Kevin said.

'Did Gilsenan give one?'

'You better believe it.'

'He was probably working on it all week.'

'I'd say so.'

'All I can say is, thanks to Bus Eireann for its tardiness.'

There was a time he could have been a Rory Gilsenan, a time when we all thought Mark was going to anoint him as the new General Manager. That was all scuppered when he left to set up his magazine.

'Thanks for the shoes,' I said.

'They weren't for you,' he said, giving a nervous laugh.

'How is the house working out?' Kevin asked him.

'Not good. I feel like I'm in Outer Mongolia.'

'You shouldn't have bothered coming in. You have enough on your plate settling in to your house.'

'I wouldn't have missed it for the world.'

'What's the story with the mortgage repayments?'

'They're crippling me.'

'You're not alone in that. We were lucky to get on the ladder early.'

'It's probably worth about half of what I bought it for now. Sometimes I think I have the inverted Midas touch. It wouldn't be so bad if I wasn't living in a shoebox.'

'That's the way it seems to be nowadays. The more the prices shoot up, the pokier the buildings become.'

'Now you've said it.'

'What kind of mortgage did you go for?' I asked him

'A 25-year one. Any shorter and I wouldn't have been able to meet the repayments. I'll probably be pushing up daisies by the time I own the dump.'

'Does that mean no more wild nights on the town.'

'I'm afraid so. Every penny is earmarked.'

I was amazed to hear him talking like that. I imagined him staying forever in Merrion Square, being visited by the trendy people who used to write for him in his magazine. It didn't suit him to be living in a one-bedroomed semi in the sticks.

There were a number of reasons why he'd done it. From the few conversations Kevin had with him he thought he was starting to panic about age creeping up on him. He'd had a heart scare the year before.

It turned out to be a false alarm but it put the wind up him. He went straight to a gym after coming out of the hospital. I was glad to hear that. Up until then, the only part of his body that got any exercise was his elbow in The Palace. By this stage most of his arty friends had settled down. Some of them had even died. The person who once said to Kevin that his job for him meant nothing more to him than spending eight hours a day trying to wrap 'a suitable amount of leather around some old dears' bunions' was now turning into something of an old dear himself.

If marriage was a trap for Kevin in his eyes, Clery's was even more of a one for him ever since the *Art Attacks* debacle.

'You have no idea how much I hate the place, he said to Kevin at one stage of the night. He was staggering on his feet as he spoke. I suspected he'd had a few jars before he came in to Madigan's. I didn't think it was Bus Eireann that was responsible for his lateness but rather Arthur Guinness.

'I'd give my right arm to be in your shoes now,' he said.

'You could be if he gave them to you,' I said, but he was in no mood for jokes.

'You tried it,' Kevin said, 'Fair play to you for that even if it didn't work out.'

'*Art Attacks* was the worst mistake I ever made in my life. It gutted any chances of promotion I might have had.'

'Don't beat yourself up. How can we know these things in advance?'

'It must have been the shortest living magazine in history.'

'How many editions did you bring out?'

'Six. I still have them. Maybe they'll be collector's items someday.'

'In that case hold onto them.'

'Don't worry. I have them in a safe place. Once the world realises how brilliant they are I'll be able to retire on them.'

'And tell O'Loughlin what to do with himself.'

'Exactly.'

'I've seen you having a few intense discussions with him lately.'

'He knows I need the job now more than ever because of the mortgage. He's using that to drag extra work out of me.'

'Like what?'

'Unpaid overtime.'

'I hadn't noticed that.'

'You're usually gone home when I'm doing it.'

'Why did you not tell me about it?'

'You had enough going on with your retirement plans.'

'Would you not go to the union?'

'You must be joking. The atmosphere is bad enough between us as it is.'

'It must make the day very long if you're working late.'

'And getting up earlier.'

'I forgot about that.'

'I have to be up at the crack to get into that kip now. I'd prefer to be going to Beirut.'

As I looked at him I thought: How could I ever have been intimidated by this man? Suddenly he wasn't my least favourite person in Clery's anymore. That honour was now held by Rory Gilsenan.

'Anyway, that's enough about me. This is your night. How are you enjoying it?'

'About as much as you are.'

'You going is like the end of an era. What are we going to do without you?'

'You'll survive. I'm only a cog in the machine.'

'A very big cog. Maybe the whole machine will collapse now.'

'I doubt that. I've felt out of my depth for a while.'

'Is that because of the computers?'

'Them and everything else. The human touch is gone.'

'I agree.'

I could never see too much of the human touch in Reg but I did that night. The only time I'd ever seen him vulnerable before was the night he came round to Kevin looking for a loan after *Art Attacks* collapsed. That was desperation. He was more subdued now. I found myself warming to him in a way I'd never done before. I started to wonder if I'd been wrong about him over the years. I asked myself why I seemed to the only person in the world who seemed impervious to his charms. Maybe I intimidated him in some way just as he

484

intimidated me. If I did, that could have been what was behind all his smart comments to me. Sometimes people behaved badly when they were threatened. It was like a safety valve.

They chatted for a while more. Kevin was enjoying it but Reg looked nervous. He kept looking over at Mark and Rory but they ignored him.

As it came up to eleven o'clock he looked at his watch. He was still wearing it upside down.

'Jesus,' he said, 'I didn't realise it was that time. I better go or I'll miss the last bus.'

'What hurry is on you?' Kevin said, 'I'll give you a few quid for a taxi if you're short.'

'Don't be mad. It's not the money. You'd be queueing up for ages at this time of the night.'

'God be with the days you could walk to your flat in Merrion Square.'

'I know. I really miss that place.'

'You were great to come in.'

'It was nothing. Enjoy the rest of the night.'

He looked like an old man to me as he closed the buttons on his coat. How time changes us, I thought. I wondered who was in his flat at the moment, what young blade starting out on life with dash and vigour. Would he too be pulling the devil by the tail when he got to Reg's age and had to think about looking for a roof over his head in the middle of nowhere?

He gave me a kiss on the cheek as he was leaving. I nearly had to pinch myself to believe it. Up until now all I'd ever got from him whenever he was leaving us for a night was a punch on the arm – or an air kiss if I was lucky. He clenched his fists at the door and smiled. He whispered 'Good luck' to Kevin.

'He's not the worst,' Kevin said after he was gone.

'I agree. Maybe I've been a bit hard on him over the years.'

'You did well to get the kiss.'

'Tell me about it. I won't wash my face for a week.'

I started to relax into the night after that. All around me there were conversations going nineteen to the dozen. I watched people I knew only from Kevin talking about them. I tried to fit them to the stories he'd been telling me about them over the years. They were all ages and sizes. Most of them I'd been vaguely aware of as I raced through the shop looking for this and that. I'd seen some of them growing from boys to men, from girls to women. They looked so different now in their casual gear. It was amazing what drink could do, how it could loosen tongues so much that people were willing to part with secrets they guarded so closely in their nine-to-five lives.

'Penny for your thoughts?' Kevin said to me.

'I'm not really thinking about anything,' I said, 'I'm just day-dreaming. Or night-dreaming.'

'Maybe you'd like to mingle more.'

'No thanks. This is your baby. Maybe you'd to, though.'

'You must be joking. This is a nightmare for me.'

'Stay put then. We can just be the boring old Mulvey couple talking shop together.'

'All right. I'll let the mountain come to Muhammad.'

'Now you're talking sense.'

Mark waved over at us a few minutes later. Kevin waved back at him.

'I think he wants me,' he said, 'I better go over to him.'

'Why doesn't he come over to us if he wants to talk to you? I thought you said the mountain should come to Muhammad.'

'Don't be funny. He's my boss.'

'Not anymore he isn't.'

'I wonder what he wants.'

'He looks merry.'

'Don't let that fool you. He pretends he's drunk to get things out of people.'

'Do you think he'll mention anything about money?'

'You never know with Mark. His mind is always working overtime.'

He went over to him. Mark put his arm around him. For a second I thought they looked like a father and son. He ordered a drink for Kevin. They started talking intently about something. I wished I could have been a fly on the wall. I was hoping I'd be asked over but I wasn't. From their body language I guessed it was business talk. I searched Kevin's face to see if I could gauge anything from it but I couldn't. He looked very serious. Then he smiled. Mark patted him on the back when they were finished. He winked conspiratorially at him before letting him go.

Kevin looked excited as he made his way back to me.

'What was that all about?' I said.

'The *ex gratia* payment, believe it or not.'

'Go away.'

'I'm serious.'

'It was the last thing on my mind.'

'I had it at the back of mine. I didn't like to mention it in case he didn't.'

'What did he say about it?'

'That he'd courier it out to me tomorrow morning.'

'That's brilliant. Did he say for how much?'

'He's too cute for that. He didn't get to be Managing Director for nothing.'

'Did you not ask him?'

'Absolutely not. You can't bring things like that up at your farewell party.'

'He did.'

'That's different.'

It was all we could think of for the remainder of the night. We chatted to people but without much concentration. Cathy was as friendly as could be. So were some of the others whose names I didn't know but it was hard to concentrate on what they were saying. Mark had lit a fuse in our heads. I looked over at him once or twice but he was busily engaged with other people. He looked so insignificant, I thought, and yet he held our future in his hands. It was like Mr Gageby all those years ago.

The party climaxed with a presentation to Kevin from the staff. It was a vase. They'd all chipped in to pay for it. You could tell it was a very expensive one. It was Waterford crystal. Kevin was touched.

'I always knew you loved me,' he said.

'It's only because you're going!' someone chirped up. Everyone laughed.

'I was expecting a clock,' he said to Mark, 'Isn't that what people usually get at retirement parties?'

'Your days of looking at clocks are over,' Mark laughed, 'Tiime shouldn't exist for you from now on.'

That was the end of the official business of the night. People started to scatter. Some of them went in to watch the end of the soccer game.

There was a cheer for Kevin before everything wrapped up. A few feet away from us the soccer followers were engaging in different kinds of cheers as the game they were watching came to an end.

'At last our ordeal is over,' Kevin said as we were released into the night.

He was clutching the vase under his arm. I was carrying the shoes. Reg had stuffed them into an old paper bag. The bottom was coming out of it. I had to hold it tightly to stop them falling out. There was a time that would have driven me mad. Now I was just amused.

Kevin let out a deep breath as we walked to the bus.

'How do you feel?' I asked him.

'Relieved. There's no need to tell you the party you threw in the house meant a million times more to me than this one.'

'It was nothing.'

'No, it was everything. What did you think of Gilsenan?'

'He looks lethal.'

'I'm glad you got that. He gives off this cuddly personality but he's as hard as nails inside. I wouldn't like to meet him on a dark night.'

'Or even a bright one.'

'Reg says his smile is like the silver plate on a coffin.'

'I can see Reg in him.'

'Really? How?'

'I mean the way he was when he was his age.'

'Mark does too.'

'Maybe that's why he arrived late – to get out of having to talk to him.'

'It's possible. He hates his guts.'

'Sometimes we hate people because we want to be them.'

'Now you're getting too intellectual for me.'

'You're the one who's being intellectual.'

'Why do you say that?'

'Talking about Rory Gilsenan's smile being like the silver plate on a coffin.'

'They used to say that about Dev, didn't they?' He meant Eamon de Valera.'

'Somehow I don't think Rory will become president of Ireland.'

'Managing Director of Clery's is all he's after, thankfully.'

'We won't deny him that. Good luck to him if he gets it. I'm just relieved you're out of that rat race forever.'

'So am I.'

'I'm glad to hear you saying that.'

'I always told you I wanted to be. My only worry is how I'm going to fill the time. I'm not quite ready for the pipe and slippers yet.'

'Don't worry, I'll keep you busy around the house.'

'That's not what I meant.'

'Relax. I'm only joking. You're one of the lucky ones. How many people have to trundle on till they're seventy because they can't afford to make ends meet?'

'I'm not complaining. I just feel a bit shellshocked. I can't stop thinking about how much Mark is going to send me tomorrow. Obviously he knows himself. It would have to have gone through Accounts today.'

'Stop thinking about it. Whatever it is, you'll have to take it. Legally he doesn't have to give you a penny.'

'I know. That's what's worrying me.'

'Well stop worrying. I'm going to take control of things from now on. I'll be the new Mark O'Loughlin in your life. You can start by bringing me breakfast in bed tomorrow morning.' He promised to do that.

I told him I was going to bed then. I was exhausted after the day. I told him he should come up with me but he said he was too worked up.

'You need to get your mind off that cheque,' I said. 'Come up to bed and take a sleeping pill. You'll be the better for it.'

'I wouldn't sleep if I took forty pills.'

I knew there was no point arguing with him so I left him sitting there. He was biting his nails as I went up the stairs.

489

I heard him pacing up and down the floor as I got into bed. His tension made me tense too. I ended up taking the sleeping pill I suggested for him. I drifted into a lovely sleep with it.

I woke up in the middle of the night when I heard a crash on the floor. For a second I didn't know where I was. I jumped up in the bed.

'What's going on?' I said.

Kevin was kneeling on the floor in his pyjamas. He was picking up loose pieces of glass.

'Sorry,' he said, 'I spilled a glass of whiskey. I was drinking it to try and wind down. It fell out of my hands.'

He brought the pieces of glass to the bathroom and threw them into a waste paper basket. He came back in with a towel and dried the floor. As I watched him down on all fours he reminded me of Maureen all those years ago trying to get the wine stains off Mrs Hanratty's floor after our flat-warming party.

'For God's sake come back to bed,' I said, 'Leave that till the morning.'

'If I don't get it dry we'll break our necks.'

There was no talking to him. It was ages before he came back to bed.

'Will you take that sleeping pill now?' I said, 'I took one myself.'

'We'll turn into a pair of junkies,' he said but he took it.

He didn't expect it to work. It didn't for a while but eventually he nodded off. He started snoring. I hated it when he did that. He only did it when he was really tense. It made it impossible for me to sleep beside him.

I decided to get up. It was nearly dawn. A chink of light came through the curtains.

I tiptoed to the door but it squeaked as soon as I opened it. He was a light sleeper and he woke up.

'Is that you?' he said. He opened his eyes slowly. 'Where are you going?'

'Go back to sleep. I'm getting up.'

'I'll do that too.'

'Don't. You were awake half the night.'

'So were you.'

'No I wasn't. I came to be long before you. I was sleeping when you were drinking your whiskey.'

'I have the rest of my life to sleep. I want to be downstairs when the courier comes.'

'Don't be mad. Get your mind off him. He won't be here for hours.'

He staggered onto the floor. I went downstairs in my dressing gown. I put the kettle on and put two slices of bread in the toaster. He came down after me a few minutes later. I had some cornflakes even though I didn't feel in the least like eating. The toast popped up and we had a slice each. Then the kettle boiled. We sat eating and drinking in the half-dark. Neither of us were up to talking. He kept biting his nails. I wished there was something I could do to relax him but I knew it was hopeless. He was like a raw nerve.

I washed the dishes and went back upstairs.

'I suppose there's no hope you'd join me,' I called down from the landing but he didn't answer me.

I drifted in and out of sleep. After a while I heard him opening the front door. He started talking to someone. I ran over to the window. There was a van outside. A man went into it. He wrote something on a jotter and then drove off. I ran down the stairs taking them three at a time.

'Was that the courier?' I said.

He nodded. He had an envelope in his hands. It had to be the cheque. He ripped the envelope open and looked inside. His eyes were bulging as he took out the cheque. Then they closed. He dropped it onto the floor.

'Feck it,' he said.

'What? What's it for?'

He picked it up.

'Read it and weep,' he said.

He handed it to me. I couldn't believe it when I looked at it. It was for 10,000 punts. That was about half of what we were expecting. I was flabbergasted. Kevin was grey in the face.

'Oh God,' I said, 'That's very disappointing.'

'Not even a letter with it. That's how much I represent to them. It makes a mockery of his speech.'

491

'I'm shocked, I really am.'

'No wonder he hadn't the guts to give it to me last night. He probably thought I'd walk out of the pub.'

We'd placed the Waterford vase on the mantelpiece the night before. He took the cheque from me and put it behind it.

'I feel like throwing it in the fire,' he said.

'It's better than nothing.'

'Is it?'

'We have to make do with it.'

'How? You're living in cloud cuckoo land if you think that's enough to live on.'

'It'll tide us over for a few years.'

'Yes, but what then?'

'Then we'll put on our thinking caps.'

I couldn't get a word out of him for the rest of the morning. I tried to talk to him but he wasn't interested. He kept walking in and out of rooms. I never saw him looking so dishevelled. His hair was all over his face. He had his pyjama tops on over his trousers. His shoelaces were untied. Every so often he'd take the cheque from behind the vase and look at it. It was as if he thought he could change the figure by looking at it often enough.

'Let's spend it on a holiday,' I said as it got towards lunchtime and he still wasn't talking to me, 'We could have a good time in a South Seas Island on that.'

He looked at me as if I was a total stranger to him.

'What are you talking about?' he said.

'I'm talking about a nice holiday for ourselves. We deserve it.'

'And what happens after we come back?'

'We'll worry about that bridge when we come to it.'

'You don't seem to realise what just happened.'

I was so frustrated with him I decided to try and shake him out of his misery with some sarcasm.

'I could take in washing,' I said, 'Or maybe we could sell the children into slavery.'

'I can't believe you're joking at a time like this.'

'Sometimes it's all you can do. Look, Kevin, at the end of the day it's only money. We'll get by. Wouldn't it be worse if one of us was sick?'

'I can't think that way now. This is treachery. O'Loughlin more or less told me I was good for twenty grand a few months ago. I bet Gilsenan talked him out of giving me what he intended to. That rat could even have some of it in his own pocket. I wouldn't put it past him.'

'Now you're being paranoid.'

'You don't know what he's like. He's probably the main reason I'm in this situation.'

'I've never heard you talking that way before.'

'Maybe I never saw the full picture till now. The cards are all falling into place. They cooked up a double deal to get me out. I wasn't pushed but they made me jump. It was so subtle it was a masterstroke. The sweetheart deal that never was.'

His mind was on fire. It was creating its own momentum. He paced up and down the floor like a man possessed.

'Remember the way your mother told your father not to have anything to do with gentleman's agreements? Now I know what she meant. They're all very well if the two people are gentlemen. I don't think O'Loughlin knows the meaning of the word.'

'Whether you're right or wrong, we are where we are. You have to make the best of it.'

'I can't think like that. You've always taken the crap that's been thrown at you in life. Men are different. We do something about it.'

'So what are you going to do? Go to the union? You're not even in one. You're not an employee of Clery's. You weren't sacked. You have no rights at all.'

'That's the killing thing. I've been such a fool. I shot myself in the foot.'

'If you did you have to learn to live with it. Take your beating. It's not the end of the world. I'll go out working if I have to.'

'No you won't. I'm drawing the line at that.'

'Then we'll survive somehow. We're not on the breadline.'

He seemed to mellow suddenly. He stopped pacing up and down the floor.

493

He sat beside me.

'Sorry for putting this on you,' he said, 'I just had to get it off my chest.'

I clutched his hand.

'I feel so bad for you. I wish there was something I could do.'

'You listen to me. That's a lot.'

It took him a week or so to get over the insulting cheque but when he did he came back to himself. We both sat down at the kitchen table one night and worked out a plan of action. It brought me back to the night years ago when we were saving for our mortgage. Do all our lives have these circular patterns – preparing for the first half and then the last one?

He had some savings and so had I. When we put them together we thought we could have a reasonable standard of living until we reached pension age if we didn't do anything crazy – like going off to a South Seas Island.

A bigger worry for me was whether he'd get depressed sitting around the house. I was afraid of him turning into Daddy, fussing about nothing as the years gained on him.

Cillian told me he didn't think there was any danger of that. For one thing he was a lot younger than Daddy when he retired. And his health was better. Being away from Clery's meant he could exercise all day if he wanted. He'd be as fit as a fiddle in no time. He felt confident he'd find something to engage him before too long.

He was right. As soon as he came to terms with our new situation he started thinking about hobbies he could take up. He went into all the different possibilities in incredible detail, even looking up classes in a college down the road to see if there was anything that might appeal to him.

He tried a few options but they didn't float his boat. As things worked out he spent most of his time doing what most retired people do – gardening. I advised him to use the shoes Reg gave him for it.

'At least we'll get some value out of them,' I said. (There was a stain on the leather so I was probably right about them being seconds).

The first thing he did was to plant a row of grisolinia bushes half way down the back garden. Beyond it he made a vegetable patch. He planted scallions and rhubarb there. Later on he added other vegetables. Before we knew where we were he had it looking like a regular little farm. If only Daddy had a hobby like that.

When I phoned him to tell him what he'd done he said, 'I didn't think he'd sit still long.' My reason for the call wasn't to look for praise for Kevin. I wanted him to copy him.

'You have another think coming if that's why you rang,' Mammy said on a later call, 'It's like pulling teeth even trying to get him out of the chair to have his dinner.'

Nothing seemed capable of stimulating him. He spent a lot of his time dozing in front of the TV set. I tried to get him up and about anytime I was home but it was a hard job. You always know when someone is bored by the look in their eyes. Most of the time I felt he was gone from me.

More worryingly, I felt I was gone from him. I wasn't his daughter anymore, I was just someone who tried to mould him to my wishes. He saw Mammy and me as a double act curbing his wishes.

He got crankier with Mammy than me, probably because she was around him all the time. He reared up at her over trivial things. If he found a hair in his soup he was capable of stomping out of the kitchen. He'd do the same thing if the potatoes on his dinner plate were too hard. He'd never have behaved like that in the old days.

I knew a lot of his mood swings were due to his bad health. The thing that bothered him most was, as he put it, his 'waterworks.' He spent ages in the toilet trying to empty his bladder without success.

'Maybe I have prostate cancer,' he said to me one day.

'Don't be ridiculous,' I said, 'Just go down to Dr Farrell. He'll sort you out.' Dr Farrell was our GP.

To my amazement he did. When he had his bloods done he was told his PSA level was up. He had a condition called prostatitis, a swelling of the prostate gland, or the 'prostrate' gland as he called it. It wasn't serious. He was able to treat it with antibiotics.

He was like a ten-year-old when he rang me a few weeks later to say he'd got the all-clear.

'I'm going ten times a day now,' he beamed.

'Too much information!' I said.

Kevin was amused by him. He told me a George Burns joke about this guy who went to his doctor and told him he couldn't pee. The doctor said, 'What age are you?' 'Eighty-five,' the man replied. The doctor said, 'Go home, you've peed enough!'

I was delighted to have Kevin home with me all the time now. It was good for the children as well. He was able to talk to them in ways he never could when he was working. He did his best to advise Eileen about what career he thought she should go into. She'd just scraped through the Leaving Cert. That was a minor miracle because she hadn't done a stroke all year. I had my mind made up she was going to crash and burn.

Cillian, meanwhile, kept us entertained about stories from the classroom in Portmarnock. The things the pupils said to him were hilarious, at least when they weren't downright embarrassing. He had his work cut out keeping control of them. From what he told us, they'd have driven Sister Serafina into a mental home.

People often said to me at this time, 'Why did Cillian go on for further studies and not Siobhan or Eileen?' They were implying it was some kind of decision we made. I had to tell them it wasn't like that. They simply weren't interested. We all knew families who sent their sons to university and didn't bother about their daughters but that wasn't the case with us. Just as I never wanted Cillian to play football when I saw he had no interest in it, I tried to get the girls to make their own minds up about what they wanted to do with their lives.

To the best of my knowledge I didn't make distinctions between them. If they wanted to play with trucks instead of dolls I wouldn't have minded. In fact Eileen did for a while. Kevin wasn't too pleased about that. He was much more old-fashioned than I was.

Eileen gave us a lot of problems in her teens. Some of them were a result of her being bullied in school. Neither Kevin nor I knew about that when it was happening. If we did we'd have done something about it. How could we have been so blind? It was only when I saw marks on her arms one night that my eyes were opened.

I let a scream out of me when I saw them. My first instinct was to ask her if she was on drugs. She broke down crying when I said that. When she recovered she told me what was going on.

496

'It's only a small section of the class that's doing it,' she simpered.

'One would be too many,' I said.

The next day I went down to the principal's office. It turned out she wasn't the only one who'd been targeted. The strange thing was that the marks on her arms weren't from the bullying. They were from self-harming. It was a coincidence but maybe one caused the other. We brought her to a psychologist afterwards and he explained what was happening. He said she blamed herself for being bullied. I found that hard to take in at first but it seemed to make sense when I thought about it.

We were so relieved it was out in the open at last. Diagnosis is half the battle in any condition as I well knew from my nursing. Once we realised how much Eileen was suffering we gave her round-the-clock attention. Her recovery didn't happen overnight but she was a different girl in the next few months.

She got eczema afterwards. Anyone who has a child with that will know how terrible it is. She kept breaking out in blisters. They were very difficult to treat, even with creams. She developed fierce itches with it. It was practically impossible to get her to stop scratching herself. When she did that it undid whatever good the creams were doing.

She had acne too. That was a doddle by comparison. With both of these conditions at least I felt I could do something to help. And they were visible. The problems you can see in your children are usually the easiest ones to cure. It's the invisible ones you have to worry about.

After she left school she developed a problem with anorexia. That became an even bigger trauma for her. Once again I was slow to cop on to it. She'd always been a fussy eater but I never expected anything like that.

I remembered her looking disgustedly at some of the lunchboxes I prepared for her as a child. For me it was just Eileen being her usual picky self. I took it to be a vote of non-confidence in my cooking skills rather than any problem she might have had. She'd say things like 'I'm not hungry' or 'I already ate,' if I suggested cooking something for her. One day I saw her twirling a pea around her plate with a fork as if it was her greatest enemy in the world. I was amused watching her. It's only in later years you look back at these things and realise what they meant.

After a while she developed a passion for Limits biscuits. That should have been a red flag for me. I knew overweight people took them to try and cut down their appetite. My suspicions were only aroused when she started bringing her meals to her room. I should have paid more attention to that at the time, and to all the hours she spent in the bathroom.

'What are you doing in there?' Kevin used to say, 'Removing the fittings?'

'Leave her alone,' I'd bark back, 'She's a teenager, they're all like that.'

Then one day he found her in there on her knees. She was wrapped around the toilet bowl trying to throw up.

When it all came out I could have kicked myself. I often wondered if it was something to do with Kevin saying she had a big stomach that time in Skerries when he brought her more treats than the other two. We never know the effect a throwaway comment can have.

One day when she was in the toilet I went into her room to tidy it. It was in its usual 'bombsite' state. When I started to make the bed I found the remains of a dinner stuffed into a plastic bag under it. Up till then I didn't think anything of the way she'd leave the table with her plate in her hand. It turned out she was dumping the food in the bin every night after we went to bed. She went spare when I told her I'd found the bag, accusing me of spying on her, but then she broke down and it all flooded out of her.

I was ignorant in those days. The first time I heard about anorexia I thought it was all a slimming sickness. ('I wish I had it,' Kevin said when he started to develop a pot belly). It was only afterwards I learned it was much more complicated than that. Eileen didn't even know why she was refusing the food. Her analyst thought it could have been connected to the self-harming. Another theory was that she'd thrown up one day as a child, which gave her a subconscious fear it might happen again if she ate too much.

'Did you ever push food on her as a child?' the analyst asked me. The things these people come up with. I wasn't long putting him right on that one.

'She got exactly the same as everyone else,' I told him, 'and if she didn't want it she left it on her plate and there was no more about it.' No matter how many theories they come up with on these conditions, I don't think anyone will ever know for sure what causes them. Sometimes I think it's just the way you're made.

It took me ages to understand how someone could starve themselves like she did. I had a sweet tooth ever since childhood. It took me all my willpower to give up sweets for Lent. I'd be counting down the days till Easter Sunday when I could stuff myself again. To think someone would deny themselves food for something other their figure was beyond me.

Eileen became a big worry over the next few years. I suspected a lot of her problems were due to a bad self-image. When she was a child she was always washing herself. I didn't think anything of that at the time either but psychologists are now telling us it can be a sign of guilt. Who'd be a parent? It's a pity it doesn't come with a book of instructions.

She was in and out of hospitals a lot around this time. It was very hard for all of us. Kevin and myself were at our wit's end trying to figure out how to come to terms with it. It was painful watching the weight literally fall off her. At her worst she looked like someone out of a concentration camp in Dachau. Her arms were like matchsticks. Her ribcage jutted out as if she'd just had an operation. And yet in her own mind she probably thought she was overweight. It was too much to get your head around.

There were a lot of rehab groups that helped her. Most of them had classes. She did her best to keep up her attendances at these but then they ended and she was left to her own devices again. Kevin said they reminded him of Alcoholics Anonymous. He'd gone to it for a while before he met me. 'Never think you're cured,' he said, 'That's the mistake most people make.' Eileen's analyst said much the same thing. He said we couldn't expect any quick fixes, that she had to deal with her problem day by day.

When she started going to discos I lost a lot of sleep worrying about what kind of men she'd meet up with. If she was in a certain mood, like Cáit, she was capable of going off with anything in trousers.

When she got over her anorexia she developed a very attractive figure. Even walking down the street with her I'd see fellows with their eyes out on sticks looking at her. Kevin wasn't sure if she was aware of it or not but I thought she was. I was a woman after all. We have peripheral vision.

After she started dating she took to wearing revealing dresses and skirts well above the knee. According to Kevin, you'd get more material in a handkerchief. If I tried to persuade her to wear longer skirts she'd put one on her to shut me up and hide a shorter one in a bag. She'd put it on as soon as she got to whatever pub or discotheque she was going to.

I noticed a few of her longer ones disappearing over the years. I wouldn't have put it past her to have dumped them in the nearest bin when she replaced them with the short ones she'd been hiding on these nights. She wasn't the type to fold them up and bring them home for 'good wear.'

'She's dressing like a slapper,' Kevin said to me one night. Like me he worried about the fact that she might be attacked some night after the pubs closed. Dublin was a much more dangerous place now than when I'd been going out on the town with Bridget and Cáit. We weren't just talking about rape anymore but murder too. One often led to the other. I worried myself sick if it got to midnight and she wasn't home.

Siobhan was a good chaperone but Eileen escaped from her whenever she got half a chance. She didn't like anyone telling her what to do, as we well knew. 'It's a free country,' was one of her favourite sentences. By now she was in her 'white lipstick and dyed hair' phase. One night she even dyed it beetroot. I think that was to annoy us. The more you tried to get her to stop doing something the more she did it. Sometimes you were better off to keep your mouth shut.

The thing that saved Eileen from herself was when she met a boy at one of her rehab groups. His name was Jack. He'd had a drug problem in his teens. A friend of his told me he'd taken an overdose one night. He didn't know if it was deliberate or not. He was lucky they caught him in time. They pumped his stomach out and he survived. I never told Eileen about that. I knew she'd say it back to him and his friend would get into trouble. Jack tended to get into a temper if he felt his privacy was being invaded.

Neither Kevin nor I thought Jack was the ideal man for her. On the other hand, because he'd suffered from some of the same kinds of problems she was going through, we thought they might be able to help one another in a way neither of us could.

Eileen liked Jack's sense of bravado. No matter how many problems he had he carried an air about him that suggested he owned the world. He reminded me of Reg in that. Neither of them were exactly blessed with good looks but they made up for it with their personalities. I've often noticed that people with a lot of things going for them in life tend to be unassuming whereas the ones with little or nothing act like they're God's gift. Maybe Kevin was right after all when he said women were attracted to confident men.

Shortly after Eileen started dating Jack she got her tongue pierced and a stud put into it. When I saw her I said, 'It's just as well you didn't go into nursing.' I tried to imagine the face of Joanne Wylie if I turned up for work with a pierced tongue. We weren't even allowed wear ear-rings.

I worried a lot about Eileen when she was out with Jack I don't think I got a full night's sleep any two nights in a row. Kevin was almost as bad. If he was Siobhan's boyfriend he might have been able to warn her against him. You could never consider that with Eileen. She was too much her own woman.

'What if he tries to do himself in again?' he said to me, 'or if some of his friends call around looking for him and he's with us? I don't want to open the door some night and find a man with a baseball bat standing in front of me.'

That was a concern for me too. One night he asked Eileen if she thought Jack would ever go back on drugs.

'Drugs to him are like what drink was to you,' she replied matter-of-factly, 'If you were growing up today you'd probably be sticking needles in your arms.' Kevin looked as if he was going to have a fit when she said that. 'One of these days,' he said to me later that night, 'one of these days…'

Eileen eventually moved out of the house to live with Jack. That was the hardest thing of all for us to take in even if a lot of my friend's children were doing it. They were staying in a pokey little flat in Donnycarney around the corner from Jack's parents. It was owned by a friend of Jack's. I think he gave it to them for half nothing. There was no way they could have afforded the rent otherwise. Eileen had a part-time job in a department store in town. Jack was scrambling whatever money he could from the dole and some nixers he did on building sites.

We wanted them to get married. Even if Jack wasn't our ideal choice for her we thought it would have given them more stability. Eileen didn't care too much about the bit of paper – her phrase for the marriage certificate – so she ruled that out

'What about your soul?' Kevin said to her, 'Do you care about that?' I wouldn't have talked to her like that. I thought it would only push her farther away from us. She hadn't much time for religious talk. It was a long time now since Eileen stopped going to Mass. Cillian and Siobhan were still going. Kevin and I both had problems with the church, especially after the scandal about Bishop Casey and Annie Murphy broke out, but we were still hanging in there.

I found it hard to think of Eileen living like a married woman at her age. It didn't seem so long to me since she came out of the cradle. The first time I saw her in a bikini was a shock for me. We were in Brittas for the day. She'd gone in for a swim. It was at the height of her anorexia so there wasn't a pick on her.

'Are you sure it's a good idea to go in swimming?' I said to her, 'It's not that hot.'

She laughed at me and ran off into the waves. When she came out I could see she was freezing but she wouldn't admit it. I wrapped her in a towel and started rubbing frantically at her. She looked lost inside it. A gust of wind could have blown her away. She put on her clothes then. She was wearing one of her micro-minis and a little denim jacket. She looked so fragile in it I wanted to put my arms around her and cradle her. Of course you couldn't do anything like that to her anymore. She'd have gone mad.

Kevin refused to visit Eileen and Jack in their flat but he helped them with some of their expenses. I went around a few times. Jack was polite with me even if he didn't exactly shower me with affection. Eileen appreciated the fact that I'd accepted the way she was living. She knew it was the last thing I'd have wanted for her. I gave them some extra money without telling Kevin.

'I'll never darken that door,' he said to me once, 'I didn't spend all those years working like a black to see her ending up with a junkie.' He held good by that promise.

They chugged along somehow. Kevin often worried that Siobhan might follow in Eileen's footsteps but I didn't think she would. At this time he gave her a lot of pep talks about getting the right foundations in life, citing Cillian as an example. I didn't like him giving those kinds of lectures to her. I thought there was always the possibility of 'the forbidden fruit' being a thrill to her.

I knew it would spell trouble if Siobhan reported details of these conversations back to Eileen. She liked visiting her for the contrast their flat offered to our own house. They had it done up in a bohemian way with lots of potted plants around the place. There were posters of people like Bob Marley and Che Guevara on the walls.

Things reached a head one night when Eileen and Jack visited us. They said they'd like to stay the night. Jack was in his customary tracksuit and runners. It pained Kevin to see him decked out like that. The boyfriend he had in mind for Eileen would have been in a neat suit with his shoes shined up like the Starship Enterprise.

His eyes were glazed. I suspected he was 'on' something but of course I couldn't say that. Kevin thought he was as high as a kite.

I told Eileen they were welcome to stay but it wasn't on for them to share a bed. Whatever they were doing in Donnycarney, I thought it would have been giving bad example to Siobhan. She blew a fuse at that.

'You're from the Ark,' she said.

'That may well be,' I said, 'but if you want to sleep in the ark you'll have to go into separate beds.'

She stamped off in a rage. It was months later when I saw her again. She was short of money at the time. She had to swallow her pride by ringing me to ask me if I could come down to them.

Kevin could never accept the fact of unmarried people 'doing a live-in,' as he called it. He used to say men started on dates these days with women at the places his generation stopped. He thought a lot of modern relationships were as transitory as disposable cameras. 'Marriage is almost as bad,' he said, 'It's almost like a casual arrangement between two people who don't have a clue what they're getting into.'

I couldn't tell Mammy and Daddy about Eileen and Jack for the life of me. They doted on Eileen, still seeing her as the baby they cooed over when she was in one of her romper suits. They'd have both got seizures if they had to contend with the fact of her sleeping with a man who wasn't her husband - especially one with Jack's history.

Much to everyone's astonishment, Eileen had a baby with Jack. It was beyond me how that tiny frame have managed to produce a child? I was a basket case during her pregnancy, convincing myself that something would go wrong at every turn because of all her health problems but miraculously it didn't. Isn't it often the case in life that the things we worry about don't happen and the things we don't worry about do?

Sam, our first grandchild, was only five pounds in weight but he was organically sound and that's all that mattered to any of us. Eileen and Jack adored him. Kevin even thawed out. He put his morals to one aside when he saw him. When I looked at him I felt a mixture of joy and depression – joy at his beauty and depression at the fact that I was now a grandmother. In other words. 'an oul wan.' Kevin tried to console me.

'We'll put you in for the Glamorous Granny competition,' he said. The last thing I felt was glamorous.

He was warmer than usual with Jack at the christening. Jack was finally showing he was committed to the relationship with Eileen. That meant Kevin slowly came to accept the circumstances of their relationship. When Sam started to grow up, Kevin got almost as close to him as he'd been to our three.

He'd been very caught up with his work when Cillian was born. The same was true with Siobhan to a lesser extent. He played with Sam almost as much as he did with Eileen.

As I watched him making faces at him I found myself wondering which of them looked the more childish. It reminded me of the way he used to tickle Maureen and May when they were younger. Eileen nearly had to pull him off him sometimes to feed him. She never had to ask Kevin to babysit. He was practically begging to be allowed to. Maybe the fact that Sam resembled him in appearance helped his enthusiasm.

Like a lot of young people, Jack didn't talk much. That was another thing Eileen liked about him. She thought there was too much nonsense talked in our house. Maybe she was right.

One night I went over to them to babysit Sam. They were going to a Pigeon Fanciers convention in Meath. Jack raced pigeons as a hobby

He was sitting in the kitchen. Eileen was doing herself up in the sitting-room, getting ready to go out. For some reason, I don't know why, I found myself saying, 'Why did you take drugs, Jack?' He looked me up and down as if it was the most ridiculous question imaginable.

'I took drugs because I took drugs,' he said.

He didn't elaborate and I didn't expect him to. Maybe it was a stupid question. It was like asking an alcoholic why he drank. (Brendan Behan gave the best answer of all to that question: 'Because I like the taste of it.')

I didn't think Jack was being disrespectful to me but when I told Kevin about it he got annoyed.

'If he talked like that to me I'd give him a thick ear,' he said.

'That would be disastrous. Anyway I know you wouldn't.'

'Don't be too sure. Why should we have to put up with the kind of thing from him?'

'It's not up to us to put up with it. He's Eileen's concern now.'

'He's our concern if he's not supporting her.'

Jack told Kevin once that his ambition was to spend his life on the dole. Kevin replied, 'I hope it keeps fine for you.'

Work was a dirty word to him. It just wasn't on his radar. He thought of it as something that was invented for other people to do, wage slaves like Kevin and me. He was like, 'Work? What's that? Who works anymore?'

505

Kevin could never understand his attitude. I thought it was ironic that he'd once said to Cillian, 'All work and no play makes Jack a dull boy.' Now he had an actual Jack in his life and he didn't work at all.

'It doesn't matter what we think of him,' I'd say, 'The important thing is that he worships the ground Eileen walks on.' I knew that was true because of the way he looked at her, especially after she became a mother.

'Only an addict can understand an addict,' Eileen said once. She was referring to her anorexia. Jack was better at helping her deal with that than any quote unquote 'healthy' person. When they were down in the dumps they seemed to be able to pull one another out of them, even if they didn't have two ha'pennies to rub together most of the time.

That was the thing that hurt Kevin most of all. He'd love to have seen Eileen dressed up in finery. It pained him to see her in Siobhan's hand-me-downs, or fragments picked up for her by Maureen in the charity shops.

One night I took my courage in my hands, showing Jack a job I'd seen advertised in the paper. It was a company looking for someone to train pigeons. I thought it would be right up his alley.

He looked at it for a moment and then handed it back to me. He was smiling.

'Sorry,' he said, 'Not interested.'

I asked him why he had such an aversion to work.

'Because the government is corrupt,' he said. 'Why would anyone want to work for a corrupt government?'

I decided to take him on.

'Would you not consider getting a job that involved exposing that corruption?' I asked.

He guffawed at that.

'Mrs Mulvey,' he said, 'I think you need to back off at this stage. For both our sakes. We can have a discussion about Trotskyism some other time.' The way he looked at me I knew he meant it. I never brought up the subject again.

Kevin joined Jack for a drink every so often but they weren't a good match. They didn't have anything in common except for the subject of addiction. Kevin told Jack what Eileen said to him about the drug culture of today being like the drink one of the past. He said he thought she was right. He told him he'd had a struggle to stay sober in his drinking days. He asked him if he went through the same problems with the drugs.

'I know you're asking me that because of Eileen,' Jack said. 'Don't worry. That's all over now.'

Kevin believed he meant what he said but it was always at the back of his mind that he could slip back into his old ways. He knew all about that.

It was all very well to compare the world of drink with that of drugs but nobody ever killed anyone over the price of a pint of beer. Every other day, we read of drug murders in the paper. Kevin got very nervous reading them. He'd say something like, 'To think Jack could have been caught up in that.' All I could say was, 'There but for the grace of God go we all.'

We eventually had to tell Mammy and Daddy about Eileen and Jack. It happened due to one of those chance circumstances that usually lead to the divulging of secrets.

May was up with us for a visit when Eileen popped in with Sam to ask us if we'd be able to babysit that night. I rushed her into the kitchen. She asked me what was going on. I whispered to her that it might be better to say she was minding Sam for a friend of hers but she grew indignant at that, accusing me of being ashamed of her.

That wasn't my intention at all. When she came back to the living-room she showed Sam off to May with pride. Her face was a picture. I could already see her rushing in the door in Midleton saying, 'You'll never guess what's happened up in Dublin.'

We could have asked her to keep it under her shirt but we knew from past experience that didn't work. Instead of that I decided to ring Mammy and tell her everything before May got to her. It felt good dialling the number. For once I'd be able to steal her thunder.

Mammy took it well after the initial shock. I made sure I emphasised how good Jack was to Eileen. I didn't mention anything about his drug addiction or about Eileen's anorexia.

May proved to be a harder nut to crack, especially when Eileen told her about Jack's drug past.

'Once that stuff gets a hold of you,' she said, 'it's only a matter of time before you go back to it.' She firmly believed Jack would turn Eileen into a junkie too – if he hadn't already done so.

'I beg you not to say any of this to Mammy,' I pleaded.

'Why is it such a big deal?' she said.

I didn't press it. There was no point. She was going to do what she was going to do anyway.

I cried on Kevin's shoulder.

'I'd give it ten minutes before they'll all have it in Midleton,' he said.

He was probably right. Mammy never went into it with me. If May told her, at least she had the courtesy to say it in confidence.

'An Irish secret,' Kevin said, 'is when you only tell one person at a time.'

'Or at least a May secret,' I said.

Now that she was filled up with so much gossip she was on the phone to me more often than usual in the next few weeks. She pumped me for information about Jack. I tried not to be rude by rebuffing her but I was determined to tell her as little as possible. If I did I knew she'd go into high drama about it. If she saw something about a drug killing on the news she was on the phone to me about it within the hour.

At times she seemed to have a sense of glee as she regaled us with the gory details. 'Don't mind her,' Maureen said to me anytime I rang her for a shoulder to cry on about her dramatic outbursts, 'She won't be happy until all the heroin addicts of Dublin congregate outside your house for a shoot-up.'

Maureen eventually married Adrian. I was thrilled for her. After all the hoo-ha with Edward she opted for a quiet wedding. Mammy and Daddy weren't even at it. They understood why she was doing it that way. May took the hump when she told her Kevin and me were going to be the only other people there.

'Are you wise risking her wrath?' I said to Maureen.

'I'm not going to lose any sleep over it,' she said, 'If she hadn't that to go on about it'd be something else.'

The wedding took place in the Stephen's Green church. I was the bridesmaid and Kevin the best man. We went for a meal afterwards in the Shelbourne. Everything was so low key it was hard to believe we'd actually been at a wedding. Maureen left her dress in Chester, not bothering to bring it back to Dublin with her. It only had bad memories.

'Maybe Edward gave it to Kate for their own nuptials,' she joked, 'He wouldn't be averse to saving a few quid on something like that. Maybe he fished the wedding cake out of the bin I put it into.' She had a wicked tongue when she wanted.

She was dressed in a simple pink suit. It looked lovely on her. We were all beginning to realise it didn't matter what you wore as long as you were with the right person. I wished her all the happiness in the world. 'You couldn't have got a nicer man,' I said.

One of the things I liked most about him was his droll sense of humour. I said to him once, 'How can you spend your whole life looking into people's mouths?' He replied with a wry smile, 'It certainly beats looking into their backsides like you medical people do.' He told me a joke about a woman who went to a dentist one time. She told him she was so nervous she'd prefer to have a baby than an extraction. He said to her, 'You better make up your mind which you want before I adjust the chair.'

Mammy and Daddy liked him almost as much as I did but May never hit it off with him. I couldn't understand why. He was always kind to her. When she was struggling with money once, he wrote her a blank cheque to get her out of trouble. I heard she put a big figure on it but barely thanked him. Maureen and myself would have been on our knees in the same situation but she took it in her stride. It was as if she expected it.

'Believe me,' she said afterwards, 'That fellow has his nest well feathered. It was just pocket money to him.' I didn't know what relevance that had to his generosity. Maybe she was still in a huff about not being invited to the wedding.

She stayed with Maureen and Adrian for a weekend once but it didn't go well. From the moment she went in the door she thought they were trying to lord it over her with their style.

'They think they're the cheese with their bay windows in every room,' she said to me.

'Do you not think Maureen deserves a bit of luxury after all she's been through?' I said. May knew she'd been in a lot of dives after the Harold's Cross place but that didn't hold any odds with her.

She couldn't resist giving out about everything she saw, even the name on the house. They'd called it *Rus in Urbe*.

'What's that about?' she said, 'Who are they trying to fool?'

'It's just a name, May,' I said, 'Get over it.'

'I beg your pardon, it isn't just a name. It's two people trying to act as if they're gentry.'

She even gave out about the fact that they had a dishwasher.

'For two people. Can you believe it? It probably takes them longer to load it than it would to wash the bloody dishes.'

When she saw a pair of 'His' and 'Hers' towels in the bathroom she almost flipped her lid.

'I felt I was in a Doris Day film,' she said.

'What's the problem with you? You're just looking for things to give out about. At least they'll be dry.'

'Oh they're dry all right,' she said.

'Don't be sarcastic.'

'And Adrian is such a wimp.'

'He's a perfect gentleman. He hasn't a bad bone in his body.'

The fact that he wore sandals was another reason for her to make fun of him. In her book any man who wore sandals was a sign to do the 100-yard dash in the other direction.

When he brought her for a game of golf on the Sunday she practically lost her reason. Now her suspicions about him being a snob were doubled.

'I know for a fact that he hates the game,' she said.

'What gives you that impression?'

'He told me so.'

That might have been true at one time but he didn't take it up to be 'high hat.' Most of the dentists he knew played it. He only joined them because he didn't want to be seen as different.

He played with May and me in Midleton once but that didn't go well either. She was bored out of her mind for the whole game, yawning her way through it. It wasn't exactly my cup of tea either but

I tried to make the best of it, even if I took about 89 shots for each hole.

We went into 'the nineteenth hole' afterwards. May got giddy there after a few drinks. When Adrian went up to the counter to order a round she started mimicking the way he stood when he was lining up a shot. Sometimes he threw a blade of grass in the air to see which way the wind was blowing. She did that too.

'Stop it, May!' I said, kicking her under the table, 'He'll die a death if he sees you.'

'I don't think Jack Nicklaus ever spent so much time over his golf,' she said, 'I hope you'll let me know if the Masters ever moves from Augusta to Glenageary. He'll be the hero of the hour.'

# The Ground Slips Away

Daddy died in 1993. He'd been in and out of hospital for years with one ailment or another, most of them emanating from his breathing difficulties. Maybe because of that we didn't pay enough heed to any particular one of them. It was like the boy who cried wolf. I used to hear him coughing in the kitchen in the middle of the night and it broke my heart.

The worst part of being a nurse is when you can't do anything to help someone. You can multiply that by a hundred when it's your father. I often used to go in to his room and ask if there was anything I could do for him. Often he tried to answer me and got a fit of coughing. 'Let's talk about something else,' he'd say, 'I'm worse when I think about it.'

He always sat in the same chair, the one under the picture of the Sacred Heart. He'd have a cup of tea to try and ease the burning sensations he felt. I loved it when he told me stories about his young life, about things that happened long before I was born. It was as if he knew his time was limited, that he wanted me to know everything about him before he died. I treasured these conversations more than anything else in all my years with him.

'If I ever get to the stage where I can't function,' he said to me one night, 'I want you to pull the plug.'

'Don't be talking like that,' I said, 'You have nothing to be worried about at the moment.'

'Nothing to be worried about? And you're supposed to be a nurse? That's a laugh.'

I told him he was better off than a lot of people who didn't know they had things wrong with them. At least his condition was treatable. I knew it was Job's consolation but it was all I could think of to console him.

'You have the heart of a twenty year old,' I told him.

'I bet that's what you say to all your patients. I'm not falling for it.'

'I wouldn't lie to you. It's in perfect working order.'

512

'What good is that when my lungs are in tatters?'

'Don't be such a pessimist.'

Two years before he died he had a bad asthma attack. Mammy played it down. She was so worried about him she didn't want to let him know it was serious. I was washing the dishes when she phoned me with the news.

'Daddy's taken a turn,' she said. She told me he'd been feeling poorly for a few days but he hadn't mentioned it to her. When he did she phoned Dr Farrell immediately. Because of his history he ordered an ambulance. By the time they got him down to A&E he was doubled up in pain.

Maureen and myself went down to see him the following day. He was sitting up in bed like someone who'd just been on a holiday - but then Daddy was always a great actor.

I asked to see the consultant and there was the usual endless wait. When he finally arrived he told me it could have been much worse. 'Your father has a good constitution,' he said, 'If it wasn't for that he mightn't have come through this.''

'So what do we do now?' I asked him.

'You need to tell him to listen to the messages his body is giving him. He's gambling with high odds at his age.'

I tried to relay the gist of this message to him but he shrugged it off.

'Something will get you eventually,' he insisted, 'The people who fret too much worry themselves into early graves.'

Before he took bad the last time I got a letter from Mammy. 'I'm worried about Daddy,' she wrote, 'Come home as soon as you can.'

Maureen got the same letter. Neither of us knew what to make of it because he'd made a good recovery from the asthma attack. Even so, we obviously agreed to go.

I decided to chance the Austin instead of taking the train. To my relief it didn't make any more strange noises than usual on the journey. When we reached the house there was a note on the kitchen table saying Daddy had been taken into hospital again. I got a fright when I saw that but she'd added a P.S. saying not to worry, that it was just precautionary. That lifted a bit of weight off my chest.

We went out to the car again and started to drive back. On the way we went in to the St. John of Baptist church. We prayed our hearts out that he'd be all right.

We didn't know what to expect at the hospital but when we got there he was full of the joys of spring. It was just like the last time.

'What are you two doing here?' he said. We told him we were down for a visit when we saw the note on the table. Obviously we weren't going to say Mammy summoned us. He seemed to accept that.

'What's going on?' I asked her when I got her on her own in the corridor, 'He looks fine from what I can see.'

'That's your Daddy. He scrubs up well when there's company but it's different when I'm on my own with him. You should hear him coughing. He's worse than ever. It's as if there's something lodged in his throat that he can't shift. I'm worried to death about him.'

'Don't let your imagination run away with you,' I said.

I went over to the nurse's station. The nurse on duty seemed nice. I asked her if I could look at his records. She said that wasn't allowed. I told her I was a nurse but it didn't make any odds with her. She said she didn't think there was any cause for alarm, that he was getting constant care.

When I went back to his bed he was chatting to Maureen. It was as if he hadn't a care in the world. Then Mammy came in.

I told her what the nurse said. That seemed to calm her down. We talked with Daddy for a while more. Then the three of us went out to the corridor.

'Sorry if I dragged you both down here on a false alarm,' Mammy said to us, 'It was just a feeling I had.'

'I'm glad you did,' I said, 'Now that we're here we'll stay.'

'I don't think you need to.'

'Whether we do or not we're staying.'

When visiting time ended we went back to the house. May was sitting there looking cool enough. She was going through some company reports she had to have in to her boss by the next morning. She said she was going in to see Daddy in the evening.

I put on the kettle to make tea. Maureen tried to relax Mammy. She talked about Adrian and how things were going with them.

514

May was already gone when I came in with the tea. Mammy asked me about Kevin and the children. To take her mind off Daddy I gave her as much news as I could.

Now and then she stopped me to ask a question. She seemed to be confused by the things I was telling her. I knew she was exhausted from all the worry.

'Sorry,' she said, 'I can't concentrate for the life of me. I feel bad about bringing the two of you down on a wild goose chase.'

'We were planning to come down anyway,' Maureen said, 'It's great to see you apart from everything else.'

We went to bed early that night. Mammy couldn't sleep. I heard her tossing and turning for hours. I wondered if there was something she wasn't telling us.

The next morning the three of us went into the hospital again. Daddy said he'd had a good night. He was full of the joys of spring but Mammy was flustered as she sat by the side of the bed. She listened to us chatting without saying much. After a while Daddy fell asleep.

'There's no point in you two staying on any longer,' Mammy said, 'Go back to Dublin now. I'll call you if there's any change. Tell Kevin and Adrian I'm sorry to have taken you away from them.'

'Never think about things like that,' Maureen said to her, 'Better to be safe than sorry.'

'I shouldn't have worried you. I feel bad about it.'

We told her we'd ring her that night. She said there was no need but I insisted. I said we'd come down again if there was any change.

All the worries of the past 24 hours lifted from me as I went in to say goodbye to Daddy.

'Sorry to be leaving so soon,' I said as I kissed him goodbye.

'It's all right,' he said, 'I know you wouldn't have bothered coming to see me if I hadn't been in this boneyard.'

'That's not true,' Maureen said, 'In fact Adrian said he'd love to have you up to see us anytime.'

'Go on out of that.'

'I'm serious.'

'Really? I'll hold you to that so.'

515

We went back to the house to get our things. After a quick cup of tea we got back on the road again. We were as casual as you please on the journey. We hardly talked about Daddy at all. Maureen asked me how Kevin was taking to retirement. She said she'd love if Adrian retired too. They were planning to go around Europe when he did. Then she asked about the children. She was a great listener and loved catching up on all the news.

It seemed like no time until we got to Dublin. I persuaded her to come in for a bite to eat. We hadn't stopped to eat on the way back so we were both starving. By now we'd almost forgotten about Daddy.

That's always the time when life hits you with a shock. As soon as we got in the door I saw the answering machine blinking on the hall table. I pressed the Play button. I was expecting it to be Kevin or one of the children saying they'd be home soon.

Instead of that it was Mammy. Her voice was shaking so much I could hardly make out the words. 'Daddy had a heart attack,' she said, 'He's stable now. You were hardly out the door when he got bad. I rang the house but you were gone.'

I fell into a chair. My body felt numb. I put my head in my hands. Maureen stood stunned before me. Guilt mixed with shock inside the two of us.

'I can't believe we left him,' Maureen said.

A coronary. After me telling him he had the heart of a twenty year old.

The door of the house was still open. We walked straight back to the car. The seats were still warm. I sped down the motorway with my head in a spin.

'Don't go too fast,' Maureen said, 'He's in good hands. The last thing we want is an accident. You don't want to end up in hospital yourself.'

'You're right,' I said but I couldn't stop myself speeding. It took my mind off the horribleness of the situation. I was nearly relieved when we ended up behind a tractor on the motorway. He was going at snail's pace and he forced me to as well.

We drove along the same roads we'd been on just a day before but they looked a lot different now. The car seemed different too. There was a pull on the steering as if it was trying to go a different way to what I wanted. My hands were shaking so much I could hardly change gears. They kept slipping on the gearstick. At one stage Maureen started hyperventilating from tension. I had to pull the car onto the hard shoulder. There was an empty bag on the back seat. I gave it to her to breathe in and out of. After a minute or so she recovered her composure.

'You're a lifesaver,' she said, 'I thought I was going to conk out there.'

'You looked it too. You're as white as a sheet. It's just as well we had a bag.'

'Did you learn that in training?'

'I thought everyone knew it.'

'I wish I had one of them the night I saw Edward with his lady friend.'

It did us good to talk of something besides Daddy. It was pointless worrying about him until we knew more. The doctors would tell us everything. I wanted to get to them before Mammy did to spare her any way I could. I didn't want her to hear anything that might work her up.

As we got near Cork we started praying. We had an ejaculation we always said when we were worried: 'Oh sacred heart of Jesus I place all my trust in thee.' My push-button religion was clicking into gear. Anytime I was afraid of something I prayed to him for help but I often forgot to thank God afterwards if the news was good.

I smoked non-stop at the wheel, lighting cigarettes off each other as if they were going out of fashion. Maureen was almost as bad as me. The ashtray was broken in the car so we had to tip the ash out the window. It was freezing with the two windows open but we didn't care. My hands shook as I smoked but it wasn't from the cold, it was from fear of what was in store for Daddy. After a while we rolled up the windows and used the floor for an ashtray.

When we got to Midleton the sky was swollen with rain. That seemed like a bad omen to me. It looked like it was going to burst open at any moment. Then it did, pounding down onto the roof of the car like a million tap-dancers.

517

We drove into the grounds of the hospital. Both of us only had light coats on us. Neither of us had umbrellas so we were getting soaked to the skin.

'Will we make a run for it?' Maureen said.

'Let's do that.'

We charged out of the car towards the door of the hospital. We were like two drowned rats when we got to it.

'It only feels like five minutes since we've been here,' Maureen said as she shook her hair dry. In another way it was like an eternity.

Before we went up to the desk she sat down on a bench for a few seconds. I knew she was trying to work up the courage to go in. Then she stood up. She was biting her lip. I asked her if she was okay.

'It's probably worse thinking about it than being there,' she said.

He was in the Intensive Care unit. We were brought down by one of the nurses. She was very friendly to us. I didn't like that. I knew from experience that the friendlier hospital staff were with you, the sicker someone usually was.

When we got to the ICU I looked through the glass on the door. Daddy in a bed with lots of tubes coming out of him. He seemed to be smiling. Mammy was sitting beside him with May, her eyes glistening with tears. You could see the worry lines etched on her face. After a few seconds a nurse came out.

'It's not as bad as it looks,' she said to me. For a second I thought her face looked familiar. 'It was a silent attack.'

Another nurse summoned us inside. We got up slowly, picking our steps as if we were going into a church. Mammy threw her eyes to heaven when she saw us. May just looked at the ground.

A shudder ran down my back as I walked across the floor. My chest felt as if it was locked in the grip of a vice. Daddy's eyes were puffy. His face looked bruised, making me wonder if he'd fallen when he got his attack.

'How are you, Daddy?' I said, sitting down on the edge of the bed. There was a curtain around it. I pushed it back to get a better look at him.

'Massive,' he said. 'What are you two doing back so soon? Is it my birthday?'

His voice was low. I had to lean in close to hear him. He gave one of his chesty coughs.

'Are you in pain?' Maureen said.

'Divil a bit,' he said. I knew that was nonsense. His face was so contorted he could hardly even form the words.

'They told me I had an *episode*,' he said. 'In my day we called it a heart attack. Why are people afraid to call a spade a spade today? An "episode" to me is part of a TV series.'

I laughed out of nerves. Maureen and May joined in. Sometimes it's all you can do. Even Mammy smiled.

He looked around the room.

'I must be bad to have the lot of you here,' he said, 'I can't remember the last time so many people were so interested in me.'

'Don't say that, Daddy,' May said, 'You make it sound like we don't care about you.'

'No, I never thought that. But I get nervous when you care too much.'

The room was silent with our tension. Nobody knew what to say. I listened to the ping of the machines he was attached to, machines I'd seen attached to so many other men over the years. They seemed different now.

Daddy sensed my nervousness. He pinned his eyes on me.

'Well, nurse,' he said, 'What's the prognosis?'

I thought hard.

'Eat lots of fruit and vitamins and you'll live to be a hundred,' I said.

He wheezed out a laugh.

'A hundred, begod. I think I'll settle for that.'

'You'll get a letter from the Taoiseach,' Mammy said.

'He can keep his letter,' Daddy said, 'unless there's money in it.'

'It's hard to kill a bad thing,' Maureen said.

'In that case I'll live forever,' he assured us.

'Good on you, Daddy,' May chipped in.

'What about the Guinness?' he said, 'Am I still allowed that?'

'We'll give you intravenous injections of it,' I told him.

A cardiologist came in then so we had to step back from the bed. He must have known I was a nurse because he said he'd talk to me later.

'We're concerned about your breathing,' he said to Daddy, looking at the chart on his bed.

Daddy replied, 'You're not half as concerned about it as I am.'

The cardiologist put his stethoscope in his ears. He listened for a few seconds. We sat watching him. I wondered if we were in the way. He jotted down some notes. Then he smiled.

'I'll talk to you later,' he said to me, 'I have to go now.'

'How is his heart?' I said.

He paused for a moment.

'He has the pulse of an athlete,' he said.

Mammy broke down crying after he went out. She held me so tight I thought I'd burst. I tried to use my training to be efficient, or at least to act as if I was.

I turned my back on him so he wouldn't see me but you couldn't hide something like that from Daddy. He'd have spotted it a mile off.

'Don't cry,' he said, 'I wouldn't have got this far if I wasn't pretty strong.'

'Agreed,' I said.

'Off ye go now and let me have a snooze.'

His eyes started to close. Mammy stood up.

'I'll wait here with him,' she said, 'Why don't you three step out for a while? He'll feel he has to talk to you if you're here.'

She told us to go down to the café . I didn't want to but Maureen and May thought it was a good idea. Mammy almost pushed us out the door.

'I'll sit here and hold his hand,' she said.

When we got out to the corridor I asked Maureen to order a coffee for me while I had another word with the nurse. They went down the stairs. I walked over to the nurse.

'How is he?' I asked her.

'I'm afraid it's worse than we thought,' she said.

I felt a shiver down my spine.

'How do you mean?'

'I didn't like to say it to you inside but there's been quite a lot of damage done.'

'I thought the cardiologist said he had the pulse of an athlete.'

'He may have, but that's not what we're worried about at the moment.'

'What are you worried about?'

'There are a few things. I don't want to go into too much detail at the moment. We're waiting on some tests to come back. Try and keep your mind off them. I'll be around all day if you need to ask me any more questions. For now it's just a waiting game.'

I went down to the café in a daze. Maureen was looking into space when I got there. May was eating a scone.

'Did you learn anything more?' Maureen asked me.

'No,' I lied. There was no point worrying her until we knew for sure.

'So what did the nurse say?' May asked me.

'She doesn't know any more than we do at the moment. He's in God's hands now.'

God took him into his hands there and then because Daddy never woke from his sleep.

He died fifteen minutes after we left him. Maybe Mammy knew he was going to. She was holding his hand when he slipped away.

We were sitting in the café drinking coffee when she tugged the arm of the ICU nurse to say his face seemed to have changed colour. A few seconds later the heart monitor showed a flat line. After the alarm went off, an emergency team ran into the ward and worked on him. They did everything they could to resuscitate him but it was hopeless.

We were on the way back from the café when we saw all the consternation. A doctor ran past me, almost bumping into me. I prayed that he wasn't running towards Daddy but he was.

When we got to the ICU this time we weren't allowed in. We paced up and down fearing the worst. Then the cardiologist came out. He didn't need to tell us what happened. We knew.

Mammy came out after him. She was remarkably calm. Maureen hugged her. May broke down.

'Daddy died,' she said.

521

I couldn't take the words in. A nurse came over to us. She tried to calm May. Then Maureen tried to.

'He went in his sleep,' she said, 'God spared him any more pain.'

May's crying got louder. It seemed to divert me from the shock.

'I knew it was serious from the moment it happened,' Mammy said, 'All day long I've been preparing for it.' Her eyes looked as clear as the sea, even through the tears.

I didn't know how I was feeling. I believed it and I didn't believe it. It was a shock and yet I expected it, I expected it almost as much as Mammy did. So why did I leave the room? Did some part of me not want to see it happening?

I felt cheated that I hadn't got a chance to say goodbye to him. I wanted to have told him he was the greatest father in the world, that I loved him more than anyone could love anyone, that he'd always given us the best of himself. I tried to think of all the happiness we had but at that moment none of it meant anything. He was gone from us without warning and we'd never have him back. If I felt cheated, it was me who'd cheated myself.

'I can't believe I went away from him,' I said.

'You didn't,' Mammy said, 'I sent you away. It was selfish of me. I wanted him for myself.'

We went inside. I looked at him. Mammy was right. He died peacefully. Maybe he was better off out of his pain. I didn't stay long. I preferred to remember him as he was, sitting up in the bed joking with us even if he was secretly afraid. I couldn't believe I'd never see him again.

'He was never right after the last asthma attack,' Mammy said, 'I knew it even if he didn't say it. The worse he got, the less he talked.'

Mammy went back out to the corridor. I didn't know whether she wanted to be on her own or not but I followed her anyway. Maureen and May came out a few minutes later. The nurse started talking to me but I didn't hear what she was saying. I didn't care. What did it matter now? The cardiologist asked me something too but I walked away from him.

I can't remember getting to the car. The next thing I knew I was standing beside it listening to the wind in the trees. I felt it was carrying his spirit with it. The sun was shining but it was a cold sun. It glistened through the trees like a knife.

People strolled up and down around me as if it was a normal day. Could someone die on a normal day? In films and in television programmes there was always drama in death. There were parting words, emotional farewells. Daddy's death wasn't like that. He didn't act like he'd never see us again. How could his last words have been something as ordinary as, 'Off ye go now and let me have a snooze?'

I blamed myself for not seeing the signs that he was sicker than he was. Was he trying to protect us in his final moments? Did he want to spend them alone with Mammy, as she did with him?

'We better go home,' Maureen said, 'Would you like me to drive?'

I nodded. She got into the driver's seat. I sat in beside May. She was still crying. Mammy was in the passenger seat looking into space.

'What are we going to do without him?' Maureen said.

'I'm going to sue the hospital,' May said, 'They killed him.'

'Let's just remember him,' Mammy said, 'Let's remember him every day of our lives for the lovely man he was and the love he gave all of us when we had him.'

Was he in heaven, I wondered, or merely having that 'big sleep' he talked about that night in the kitchen? If he was in heaven, was he twenty years of age? Was he forty or sixty? Wherever he was, I hoped he wasn't in distress.

I can't remember the rest of that day or any of the days following. Everything became mixed in with my own jumbled thoughts.

Kevin came down from Dublin with Siobhan and Eileen. Then Adrian arrived. We drank tea and told stories about Daddy. People streamed in and out of the house to pay their respects at all hours. We stayed up late into the nights, so late sometimes that it was the next morning before we lay our heads down. I drank coffee to keep me awake and took tranquillisers to help me sleep. Everyone slept in a different room to the one they were used to in the past.

Eileen took it the worst. I felt she would. Her emotions were so tightened up all the time. Even small things caused her to go off the rails so I knew a death was going to knock her sideways. It was her first experience of it.

'Where's Grandad?' she said to me one day. She was wiping the tears out of her eyes with her thumbs.

'He's gone to heaven,' I said.

'But I don't want him to be.'

'I don't either, love, but God must have a reason.'

'What kind of reason?'

'I don't know.'

'Why is God so cruel?'

'He isn't being cruel, Eileen. Everything happens for a reason. Grandad is happy in heaven. He's praying for us all now.'

'Why can't he pray for us down here?'

Once you answered one of Eileen's questions, a flood of them followed. I was relieved when she got too tire to ask any more of them and just cried into my shoulder. When she did that I felt she was like an infant again, the Eileen I loved most. Her softness helped me deal with what happened better because I was able to break down with her.

Kevin took her to a hotel that night with Cillian and Siobhan. There wouldn't have been enough room for everyone in the house. Mammy also needed time with me on my own.

She couldn't stop talking about Daddy. It was like a release of all the tensions that were building up in her since he got sick. There was no pattern to her talk. It went from the time they met to when they got married and had the three of us and all the joy and heartache that went with that.

She talked about his problems with health and money and trying to do the best for all of us in such difficult circumstances. She spoke so fast at times her words ran into one other. Then she'd stop and lose her voice altogether and break down.

When she recovered her composure she said she believed most of his problems were caused by his personality, a personality that could never wind down. 'He pushed himself too hard,' she said, 'He should have retired young.' But of course he couldn't afford to because he had no pension. He missed out on the property boom of the Celtic Tiger, dying before it took off.

'I'm late for everything,' he'd said to me once, 'I'll probably be late for my own funeral.' Sadly, that was one thing he wasn't late for. He was too early for it by about ten years.

Cora and Owen, my friends from Walkinstown, came down for the funeral. I was really touched by that. We didn't see them all that much but we liked them a lot. I didn't know how they found out about it. As soon as they paid their respects they were gone again. They wouldn't even stay for a cup of tea back in the house. 'I know how much you loved him,' Cora said to me before she left, 'and how much it broke your heart to see him going downhill.' She was right. Maybe I should have been relieved he was gone. He hadn't had much fun in his last years.

I often thought he might have had a touch of dementia during that time. I remembered him asking me one day how I was getting on with the narky matron.

'That was years ago,' I replied. He said he was only joking but I wondered. Mammy gave out to him for living in the past but he said that was where he felt most comfortable. I wasn't too keen on the modern world either with its shallow values. Everything seemed so streamlined in it. I loved the glint that came into Daddy's eyes when he talked about 'the rare oul times.'

Over the next few months Mammy went into a world of her own too. This was hardly surprising to any of us. I wondered if she'd ever come out of it. We kept asking her up to visit us but she said she wasn't ready for that yet.

People tried to console her by telling her she'd be able to do all the things that were denied to her during the years she was nursing him but she wasn't interested in that kind of talk. She just kept on doing the same things she always did.

That's the thing about life, isn't it? We make plans for ourselves and try our best to carry them out but when it comes to it something always gets in the way. It's like our feet are stuck in cement. Mammy had her freedom when Daddy died but she couldn't use it. She was too cut up in her grief.

This came out in strange ways. One day when I was out shopping with her it started to rain as we were coming out of the supermarket.

She had a carrier bag in her hand at the time, one of those paper ones. It was full of her groceries.

The bottom fell out of it because of the rain. I watched an apple roll across the street and some vegetables fall into a drain. Mammy would normally have laughed at something like that but that day she got into a state. She ended up throwing all the other things that were in the bag on the ground. She put her head in her hands and started bawling.

I found the house very different after Daddy died. Everything looked strange to me, even the furniture. When Daddy sat into his chair he almost seemed to become a part of it, to be growing out of it. Now it was just a chair.

Mammy couldn't sleep for months thinking about him. She was up and down to Dr Farrell like a yo-yo for sleeping pills. I had difficulty sleeping too. I kept asking myself how could Daddy be gone from us. It was unthinkable. He'd been as much a fixture in my life as the moon or the sun.

I did some temping in a nursing home over the next few months to try and get my mind off him. I knew I needed to get out of the house but my heart wasn't in the work. No sooner would I be in the door than I'd be running into the toilet to cry. Occasionally I went into a little church across the road and sat there thinking of him. I tried to pray but I couldn't.

I started acted strangely with Kevin at this time. He didn't know what was going on with me a lot of the time. Men grieve differently to women. They're stronger than us, at least in that way. Or is it a sign of strength not to fall apart when your father dies? Maybe they just don't feel things as much as we do.

Kevin's own father had died the year before. He was affected by it, of course, but not as much as I thought he'd be. In some ways I think I took it worse. No more than Daddy, he'd been in poor health for a few years before he died. He had Parkinson's Disease. He shook so much he could hardly talk at times. It began slowly but then got dramatically worse. He had to go into a nursing home in the end. The house was sold to pay for his care. We visited him as much as we could. It broke both of our hearts to see him lose his passion for life. I found it hard to think of him as the same man who'd got so excited talking about football in the past. Kevin often came home from these visits feeling very depressed. 'The life is gone out of him,' he said to me one day, 'I don't know who he is anymore.' 'But he knows who *you* are,' I said, 'That's the important thing.' I was thinking of Granny with her Alzheimers. Of course it was easy to say that. I knew how depressed he was.

He tried his best to comfort me in my grief just as I'd tried to comfort him in his. I was breaking down crying at all hours of the day for no reason. It was difficult for him to deal with that.

'Don't worry,' he'd say, 'These things always pass. What doesn't kill you makes you stronger.' His words were comforting but you have to come through experiences like that in your own time and in your own way. When I did my doctor told me he thought I'd had a kind of nervous breakdown without knowing it. It was a bit like what happened after my miscarriage.

Mammy never got over Daddy. She pretended she was fine any time we were with her but none of us were fooled. She used to go out to the garage sometimes and spend hours there just looking at his car. She refused to sell it even when it turned to rust. It was like her last keepsake of him.

'Everyone tells me to get rid of it,' she said. 'They say it's only bringing me down but I can't let it go.' I told her she was right, to do anything that made her feel better.

'To hell with others people's opinions,' I said. She thanked me for that.

I tried to get her to talk about Daddy as much as she could. I knew she needed to. 'He was my first boyfriend,' she kept saying, as if I didn't know. Theirs truly was a marriage made in heaven. He'd been the centre of her life since she turned from a girl into a woman.

Maureen and myself went down to her on shifts now rather than together. That would have been too hard to organize. Adrian's secretary had left to have a baby so Maureen was taking appointments for him. She managed to tie this in with her job in the travel agency. Despite all her plans to leave it over the years she'd hung on.

'My feet could nearly find their own way in now,' she said, 'I'm doing it totally on auto pilot.' She was so established she could set her own work times. Her boss let her off for a few hours every day to work for Adrian.

May only called in to Mammy occasionally. Her work took her overseas sometimes. When trips like that were on the cards they were all she could think of. It seemed to me she was never around when Mammy needed her. If I asked her to drop in more she bit the nose off me.

One day I couldn't get Mammy so I rang May instead. I asked her if she'd check in on her to see if she was all right.

'Don't try and tell me how to run my life,' she said, 'You think the world should stop because you can't get your little call.'

I said it wasn't like that at all, that I didn't need my 'little call.'

'It wouldn't kill you to look in on her,' I said, all too well aware I was taking my life in my hands by my brazenness.

'Believe it or not, she does actually go out now and again,' she said. 'If she isn't picking up it doesn't necessarily mean she's stretched out on the kitchen floor.'

'There's no need to adopt that attitude,' I said.

'What attitude?' she said. She was almost screaming into the phone now.

'You're impossible,' I said.

'You don't even live here,' she said, 'You haven't a clue what's going on.'

I came off the phone with her feeling my nerve ends were about to split open that day. I took it out on Kevin.

'We should buy a cat,' he said to me, 'Then you could kick that instead.'

May saw more of Mammy than Maureen and me for obvious reasons but I felt she'd have preferred if it was the other way round. We understood her better. A lot of the time we didn't even need to talk to her when we were with her. Just being there was enough.

I used to go to the shops with her or maybe bring her for a walk down by the river. These were the things we'd always done together, the things I wanted to continue doing. It was the only way her life could go on, the only way to stop her brooding about Daddy.

She never stopped talking about him no matter how old she got. Often she'd divert herself from whatever she was doing to dredge up some anecdote from long ago that came into her mind. It always did her good. She told me things I hadn't known about him and I pitched in with my own little stories whenever I could think of them. 'Did he really say that?' she'd say like a schoolgirl if I told her something she didn't know. Or maybe she was just pretending she didn't to make me feel important.

I always felt guilty going back to Dublin after a visit with her no matter how long I stayed. I offered to bring her up with me most times but always said no. She needed her independence. She probably thought it wouldn't have been fair to Kevin either.

'The fact that you asked me means everything,' she said to me once, 'The fact that you wanted me even if it's not on.' Maureen made the same offers to her but she refused those too.

Mammy died three years after Daddy. She had a lot of physical problems in these years. Only some of them she told us about. I think it was really heartbreak that killed her, just like with Granny after Grandad. You won't find this listed on death certificates but it's the cause of more fatalities than we'll ever know.

I don't like thinking about how it happened now. That whole time is a fog to me – the hospital visits, the doctor's appointments, the endless tests.

The GP she went to after Dr Farrell retired was useless. He missed all the warning signs of the cancer that killed her, even the recurring pain in her chest. He said these came from a virus that was going around. How he ever got a licence to practice is beyond me. What he didn't know about medicine would fill a very large book.

She died of lung cancer. That was so unfair because she'd never smoked. I knew people on thirty or forty cigarettes a day who escaped it. When she finally owned up to me about the pain I sprang into action, putting her in for all the tests under the sun.

At first we were told there was a good chance she'd recover but when they did more tests they realised it was gone too far. I kept hoping for a miracle but I knew too much about her symptoms to expect one. Maureen and May were more hopeful than me.

For their sakes I pretended I had hope too. We said the rosary for her every night but she was worse each time we went in to see her.

She declined quickly, going from the strong woman she'd always been to a shadow of herself in a matter of months.

My medical training was no good to me now. All I could do was sit with her. I asked her questions about her past to take her mind off herself. Sometimes she answered them but sometimes she was too tired to. She kept falling asleep and waking at odd hours. She was usually disoriented when she woke up. She'd say, 'Where am I?' as she looked around the ward. It took her a few minutes to get her bearings. When she did, she'd say something like, 'You've been here too long. You need to go home and have something to eat.'

Kevin had no problem with me being in Midleton all the time. He knew I needed to be. Adrian was the same with Maureen. We said prayers to my favourite saint, Therese of Lisieux, nearly every night. Mammy always called her The Little Flower.

She was transferred to a Dublin hospital shortly afterwards. It was from now on that things really started to go wrong for her.

She got the vomiting bug there and it dragged her down further, removing the last ounce of her resistance. What was going on in our hospitals? That would never have happened in my time. Whatever I may have had against the nuns, they always kept the wards spick and span.

One day when I was in the Ladies after visiting her I saw a doctor leaving a cubicle and then going out to the corridor without washing her hands. I felt like reporting her.

Another day the nurse who was treating her mixed her up with another patient whose name sounded like hers. This resulted in her being given the wrong medication.

This time I did step in. I went up to the registrar and said I wanted to lodge a formal complaint. She knew who I was. That caused a huge degree of surprise to register on her face. By now I didn't care if I got the nurse in question into trouble or not.

'Are you sure about this?' she said. I said I was more than sure. I'd never done anything like this before in my life and never thought I would. My anger had made me strong.

The other nurses were cool with me anytime I went in to see Mammy after that. They closed ranks. It was as if I'd turned against my own kind. If I asked them any questions about her they got defensive with me, telling me I'd have to talk to a doctor.

One of them had been in my set in training. I was shocked by her attitude and maybe she was shocked by mine. I tried to think how I'd have reacted if I'd been in her shoes. I suppose it would have depended on how close I was to the nurse I reported. I hope I would never have compromised my integrity no matter how close I was to her.

Some nights I waited for hours to see a doctor only to find out he was off duty.

I got so upset about all the games they were playing it made what I was going through with Mammy a million times worse.

She was having chemotherapy now. I didn't think it was a good idea because it made her so sick. Maureen felt it was just postponing the inevitable. I started thinking about what Daddy once said about 'pulling the plug' if he got bad.

My religion could never make me agree to any form of euthanasia but what was the point of putting her through chemotherapy when it had no chance of doing her any good?

One day Maureen and myself were walking up to her ward when we saw a physiotherapist tapping her on the back. I thought she seemed to be very rough with her. I went up to her and asked her what she was doing.

'We need to get the phlegm up,' she said.

Mammy had a pillow clutched to her stomach. She looked to be in a lot of pain. I couldn't understand the point of the physio. How could her lungs get any more clogged than they already were? The surgeon had said her system was like a traffic jam, that nothing was going anywhere.

'I can't watch it,' I told Maureen, 'I know I'm a coward but I don't care. Why is she getting physiotherapy when it's not doing her any good?'

I wanted to complain her just like I complained the other nurse but Maureen stopped me.

'You've already come to the hospital's attention,' she said, 'If you do it again they'll see you as a troublemaker and take it out on Mammy.'

I took her advice but Mammy went downhill very fast after that. By now my novenas to 'The Little Flower' were replaced by ones to St. Jude for Hopeless Cases.

She died a few weeks later in Midleton. This time we were all there beside her, having learned our lesson from Daddy. Neither did she have any pain. She'd always prayed for a happy death and she got that.

She had a smile on her face when she died. I knew she was ready to go. As she might have said herself, she'd packed her bags for heaven.

She might have had peace but I didn't. I got over Daddy in time but with Mammy it was different. She was like an extension of me. Losing her was like losing a part of myself.

I didn't react immediately to her being gone from us. I'd been taking a lot of tranquillisers to try and cope but after I came off them her death hit me like a ton of bricks. Maureen and May had the same reaction. She was the glue that held the three of us together even if we didn't all live in Midleton. No matter what problem you had you knew she was only a phone call away. Her advice was worth that of a thousand psychologists.

When Daddy died we still had Mammy but with both of them gone there was a yawning chasm. I felt a sense of isolation. It was like being on the edge of a cliff with the ground slipping from under me. The pair of them had always been my buffers against danger but now there was no buffer left. There was no shelter or shield to protect me from the sharp fall and the raging tides underneath.

Back in Dublin I went off my food. I couldn't get interested in anything, not even Kevin or the children. None of them knew what to make of me. They'd never seen me like this before apart from that brief time down in Skerries.

I found it very difficult to sleep at this time. When I did I had a lot of nightmares. Mammy was coming towards me on a train in one of them. I was waiting for her at the platform but the train always stopped before she got to me. I know that's the way it is in a lot of dreams. They stop before the dramatic part, like when you're falling off a cliff. It was a bit like that in my one.

In some ways I felt my dreams helped me. I always looked on them as therapy, as getting rid of all the tensions inside your head, especially the subconscious ones. It was like your mind going to the toilet.

Kevin knew I was having a different kind of breakdown than I'd had for Daddy, a much more serious one. That made it difficult for him to figure out how to deal with me.

Whenever he was talking to me my mind would be a million miles away. Sometimes he'd stop in the middle of a sentence and ask me to repeat what he'd said. I was rarely able to do that.

He tried to indulge me every way he could but nothing worked. I'd be fine for a lot of the time but then it would hit me from nowhere, when I was doing the dishes or making the beds maybe, and I'd be all over the place again.

'You had more love for your mother than you have for me,' he said to me one night. He didn't believe that but I knew why he said it. He was frustrated about the fact that he couldn't get me out of the pit I was in.

He'd lost his own mother so early in life he hadn't gone through the grieving in the same way as I was doing now. I almost felt sorry for him for his inability to grieve for me. Because of that we drifted apart from one another for a time.

How could that happen with the man I loved, the man who was my best friend as well as my husband? For a long time after Mammy died we lived separate lives. He'd be off playing football somewhere after work and I'd be crying on my own at home.

When he came back to the house he'd ask me how I was and I'd do my best to put a few sentences together. It was almost like formal conversation, like speaking to people we hardly knew. After we got married we promised ourselves that we'd never be apart if we could help it but now we seemed to almost arrange it that way.

We didn't argue but I often felt it would have been better if we did. Things always come out in the open in arguments, things you're brooding about that you mightn't even be aware of. The fact that we didn't get them out in the open meant that they festered inside us. Our conversations were reduced to talking about things like who was picking the children up from school or dropping them off at hockey or ballet or whatever they were doing at the time.

For a long time after Mammy died I had trouble praying. At times I thought I was losing my faith. I wondered how God could have let someone suffer like she did.

How could he have let Daddy suffer either? Neither of them had never done anything bad to anyone. That set me thinking about everything that went wrong for people in the world, hurricanes and tidal waves and disasters that wiped families out, innocent little children among them. How could that happen? Why didn't he do something to stop it?

The way Kevin put it was, 'It's a mystery. It tests your faith.' I knew that would have been Mammy's attitude as well, if not Daddy's. I couldn't see it that simply. I was angry with God and I wasn't sure if there even *was* a God. That seemed like a contradiction. I couldn't explain it to myself.

I kept saying, 'Oh Sacred Heart of Jesus I place all my trust in thee.' It was the prayer I'd said with Maureen when we were on the way to see Daddy that time when he got the asthma attack. I wasn't sure if I believed it or not now but the repetition of the words comforted me. I remembered Sister Serafina saying 'Don't forget your prayers,' before I left Midleton.

I also said The Memorare. Ever since childhood it had been my favourite prayer: 'Remember O most gracious Virgin Mary, never was it known, that anyone who fled to thy protection, implored thy help or sought thy intercession, was left unaided.'

Was I being unaided now? In a sense I felt I was. A kind of anger rose inside me, making me doubt everything I'd ever been taught at Mammy's knee. Was I turning against God or had he turned against me? Should I dispense with him or go back to Kevin's blind faith?

I felt I had to do that to keep my sanity. The prospect of a godless universe was too horrible to contemplate.

# May Takes Over

The house was left to May as we knew it would be. Mammy often asked Maureen and me if we'd have any problem with that and of course we didn't. We had our own places now. She became more tied to it as the years went on, going out less at night and devoting herself to doing it up in every way she could think of.

Her career continued to be another obsession. Daddy's words came back to me: 'May is married to her job.' Mammy thought she refused to put herself out for a man. I thought that was true too. After having them fall headlong for her for a brief time in her late teens she expected that to be the case forever but the offers thinned out as the years went on. She had to face the fact that no Lancelot was going to arrive at her door and whisk her off to his castle.

'Are all the boys in Midleton blind?' Kevin used to say to me. It was as if the only thing that mattered in relationships was how you looked. I thought it was more important how you related to people. May had some lovely boyfriends over the years but the nicer they were the more she seemed to turn against them. Sometimes I thought she liked them more if they mistreated her. She enjoyed the thrill of the chase. Once she'd snared her 'prey' – if that was a fair word to use – she tended to get bored with them.

I remembered her dropping a man once simply because he wasn't good at getting the attention of barmen when she went out for a drink with him. She said she found that 'unmanly.' God help her, I thought, if she met someone with a real problem. 'All my friends' marriages have broken down,' she complained to me another time, 'Most men are brutes. I don't want to be a statistic.' I thought that was something of an overstatement. She went on to say, 'I'm thinking of getting a dog. I believe they're easier to house-train.'

It was hard to know if she came out with this kind of nonsense to amuse herself or because she believed it. Maybe it was a defence mechanism. I knew women who acted as if they didn't care about getting married but if you knew them well enough you could see through that. When she went on her tirade about men being brutes I tried to point out that there were still a few marriages that worked in the world, believe it or not.

'Everyone is different,' I said to her, 'Look at me and Kevin, for example.'

'Exactly' she said, 'You and Kevin. Mr and Mrs Perfect.'

That wasn't what I meant. You couldn't say anything like that to her or she'd take it up the wrong way. Or maybe she knew what I meant and she was trying to pull me down. I was never sure if she was envious of Kevin and me or whether she looked down on us for what she saw as our smug lives in dull suburbia.

Maureen said to me once, 'May is an unusual mixture of a superiority complex and an inferiority one.' I thought that was a good way of putting it even if I didn't understand fully what she meant. Maureen was always much better at expressing things than me.

'Why don't you put yourself about more?' Mammy used to say to her, 'A man isn't going to come down the chimney.'

She'd go into convulsions at that, saying women were put on the planet for other reasons besides marriage. But deep down I think she'd have liked to be married, despite all her rantings about Woman's 'Lip' as Daddy called it.

For a time she tinkered around with the idea of getting herself pregnant by a man she was going with without telling him. 'I'd like a child more than a husband,' she said, 'At least you know a child won't dump on you.' It was just as well Mammy and Daddy weren't around to hear that kind of talk. They'd have had fits.

Life works in strange ways. I always thought Maureen would have been the one to stay in Midleton and May would have got out as soon as her legs could carry her. It was Maureen's relationship to Edward that led her out of Midleton and May's job that kept her there. Who could have predicted those two things? Often life seems to make our decisions for us rather than ourselves. We're just the people caught at the end of them.

I was never relaxed in the house with Mammy and Daddy gone. May told me to come down any time I liked but she always made strange with me when I was there. She let me know in subtle ways – and often not so subtle ones - that it was her house now. I was at her mercy if I was on my own. She didn't try it on as much if I had someone with me.

Siobhan was my best bodyguard with her. She was the only one of my children May was weary of. That was because she stood up to her. May knew she couldn't work her up the same way she could me. Her sarcasm ran off her like water off a duck's back.

She was still working in the beauty parlour. May was all ears about that. She thought Siobhan saw herself as some kind of super-model whenever she talked about the products she was selling. It bothered her if she had a top-of-the-range perfume on her. 'Doesn't she wear an awful lot of make-up?' she said to me once. I told her she had to for her job. It wasn't true strictly speaking but I didn't want her to think Siobhan was vain. You had to look the part in that line of business.

Eileen was rarely mentioned during any of my visits and May never invited her down. She was working in a health shop now. 'Isn't that strange?' May said when the subject came up. I asked her what she meant. She said, 'Eileen in a health shop? It just doesn't make sense.' Maybe she was thinking of how underweight she was. She loved throwing out these veiled insults. She always thought of Eileen as the black sheep of the family. She gave her little chance to get back on the rails.

Cillian was hardly mentioned either. May saw him as the picture of sense, 'a chip off the old block.' That probably meant he was as boring as Kevin and me to her way of thinking.

I had to be careful what I said about all of the children when I was talking to her. She was capable of twisting anything and repeating it back to them the wrong way. Mostly it was better not to talk about them at all. If it was bad news she'd rub my nose in it. If it was good, she'd see it as boasting. You couldn't win.

'Why do you put yourself in for such punishment by going down there?' Kevin used to say to me. All too often he'd witness me coming back to Dublin drained after a visit to Midleton. I saw his point but I couldn't stop going down there. It would have been wrong to let her deny me my home.

Having said that, the house became less recognisable every year because of all the changes she made to it. She extended the kitchen and had two bedrooms made into one upstairs by knocking down a wall. Afterwards she had all the carpets taken out and replaced with wooden floors. 'They're only dirt traps,' she sniffed. She got rid of all the old family chairs as well, putting in leather ones instead. These weren't my cup of tea at all. I found them cold.

When I said that to her she said, 'I don't care if they're warm or cold. All I care about is the fact that they're easy to keep clean.'

Everything was based on practicality with her. She had the lawn rotivated and artificial grass put over it. 'It cuts down on maintenance,' she said. That was a great word of hers, 'Maintenance.' Why didn't she just say 'Work'?

She had a plasma TV installed in the living-room. They were the latest things on the market. She loved to be first with everything. Maybe that was part of its appeal for her. She had it fitted above the fireplace. I used to get a crick in my neck trying to watch it. It seemed to take over the room. I never thought televisions should have that kind of importance but that wasn't the way May felt about them. If she was watching a programme you had to be as quiet as a church mouse in case she missed a line. It was almost like having another person in the room.

I gave out to Kevin and Maureen about all the changes but they didn't really bother me. One thing I asked her not to do, however, was remove the family photographs from the walls. If you ever asked May not to do anything, that was probably the first thing she'd do. So it was with the pictures. No sooner had I spoken than they were removed. They were deposited somewhere in the attic, never to be seen again.

She replaced them with modern art. I didn't appreciate that kind of thing and didn't pretend to. I don't know why someone would want to paint an arm growing out of someone's leg or a person with three heads. When I said that to her she said, 'Don't act the philistine. It doesn't suit you.'

I said if being a philistine meant not enjoying looking at people with five heads or seven arms then I was happy to be one, thank you very much. She reminded me of Reg with his European movies.

Some of the paintings looked more like platefuls of miscoloured spaghetti bolognese than art. A lot of the time I don't think she even liked them herself. She bought them because they looked well when she was 'entertaining.' Whatever her reasons, she was welcome to them. I told Kevin I'd have preferred to see a cow in the meadow drawn by Cillian when he was in Senior Infants. If I said that to May she'd have gone for me bald-headed.

I was always tense with her. She had the ability to work me up like no other person I ever knew – including Joanne Wylie.

May didn't appreciate me cleaning or tidying the house on my visits and that led to other kinds of conflicts with her. In the mornings I'd even be nervous raking out the ashes in case she'd think I was trying to take over from her in some way. It was natural for me to do jobs like that but I always got the impression she didn't want me to.

When I asked Maureen what I should do in these kinds of situations she said, 'If I were you I'd do nothing at all.' It was good advice but nothing was the hardest thing of all for me to do on these trips. I'd be breaking out in a cold sweat trying to entertain her with stories about Dublin and she'd be gazing into the middle distance and sneaking the occasional glance at her watch to let me know in no uncertain terms that it was past her bedtime – and mine.

After our initial exchange of news we never seemed to have much to talk about. If I was quiet she'd keep saying 'Is everything all right?' I hated it when people said that to me. Even if there was nothing wrong with me it started to make me feel there was.

After a few of these nightmare scenarios I made it my business to bring Maureen with me as much as I could. May was still jealous of our closeness. Because of this she tended to leave us to our own devices a lot of the time.

She always had our room prepared for us like a hotel room. The covers would be turned down on the beds and everything tidied away in the wardrobes. You almost expected her to say, 'Breakfast will be served at ten' as she led us to our quarters. She kept telling us to make ourselves at home but even the use of that expression seemed all wrong to me. It *was* our home.

The old May tempers raged if you stepped out of line with her any way at all. If I turned off the thermostat or moved a piece of furniture she was on it like lightning.

'Who was at this?' she'd say, her eyes dancing in her head. If I said it was me she'd stop for a second before saying, 'Oh, no problem.' The way May said 'No problem' generally let you know it was a very big one.

I hated the wooden floors. The carpets might have been dirt traps but at least they were cosy. The way everything was now made me feel as if I was in a hospital. I was very conscious of neatness and hygiene in the Mater but when I came home I liked a bit of untidiness. If you were too streamlined all the time you'd go off your trolley but that seemed to be what May wanted. She made me conscious of every step I took, every sound I made. Being the clumsy clod that I was I felt if I wasn't careful I'd knock over one of her fancy lampshades or something.

'What's up with you?' Maureen would say to me sometimes, 'You're like a hen on a hot griddle.'

That was exactly what I felt like.

One time when I went down on my own she wasn't in the house when I arrived. There was a Post-it sticker on the door saying, 'Key under mat.' When I got inside there was another note with 'Gone to Angela's' written on it. Angela worked with her. In a way I was glad. It meant I had some time to myself.

I sat listening to some of our old records on a gramophone we had. That was one thing she hadn't got rid of. I much preferred the old 78s to cassettes or CDs. I loved looking at the needle curling round the record, listening to the scratchy sound it made. It reminded me of the old days.

When she came back she said, 'Sorry I had to go out. I'd arranged to see Angie weeks ago.'

'Don't worry about it.' I said, 'I was having a good time here listening to the music.'

'I envy you your personality,' she said. 'You could sit for hours, couldn't you? I have to keep on the move.' The way she spoke, she made it sound like an insult.

I suggested a walk but she made some excuse. I tried to make conversation with her but she gave very little back. We moved around the rooms like two strangers. I felt I'd have had more in common with someone I met at a bus stop. After a while she went off out again, making me think she didn't want to be with me.

I got fed up sitting around so I left a note for her saying I was going out for a walk. I decided to go to the pictures. I didn't even look at the poster outside the cinema to see what was on before I went in. It turned out to be one of those Sylvester Stallone ones that was full of violence. I felt like walking out half way through but I stuck it out. When I got back to the house there was nothing to do but read. I found myself really missing Mammy and Daddy.

It was almost midnight before she got home.

'Oh you're here,' she said, swanning in. I felt like saying, 'Where else do you think I'd be?' She took up the note and read it out loud: 'Gone for Walk'

She gave a little titter. 'A walk. That sounds exciting. Did you meet anyone better-looking than yourself?' I didn't bother answering that. She was full of apologies about being so late back but I didn't really buy them. She'd known I was coming down for a week beforehand so she had loads of time to cancel any other arrangements she might have made.

I felt miserable for the whole weekend. It made me realise how much I'd have hated not to be married. That made me feel less annoyed with her. Was she trying to cover up her loneliness by her snippy comments? I didn't want to analyse it too much.

Another time I went down with Adrian when Maureen was sick. I wasn't looking forward to her reception this time because we hadn't been able to get there at the time she was expecting us. We got delayed in the rush hour traffic going down. The M50 was like a sardine can.

We were in my car because Adrian's was being serviced. It seemed to be about to break down a few times. It was all hours before we arrived. When she answered the door she was in her dressing gown. She also had her rollers in.

'Oh,' she said, 'I thought you weren't coming. I was getting ready to hit the hay.'

'We got caught in the traffic,' he explained, 'Half the country seemed to be on the motorway.'

'You should have known it'd be bad at the weekend.'

He tried to apologise but she cut him off.

'Don't worry about it,' she said, 'You're here now. We'll make the best of it.'

'We can stay in a B&B if it's inconvenient,' he offered.

'You'd be mad to do that,' she said, 'Just let me take these rollers out and I'll put on some tea for the two of you.' This was music to my ears. My tongue was hanging out for a cup.

She hardly looked at me before swanning off into the back room. When she appeared again she had a plastic smile painted onto her face.

'You'll have to excuse the dirt,' she said as she handed Adrian his tea, 'I'm not like these people who have all day to do their cleaning.' I felt that was a dig at me but I didn't say anything.

'I don't know what you're talking about,' he said, 'The place looks immaculate.'

'Immaculate,' she said, 'That's a very nice word. Do you mean like the Immaculate Conception?' He knew she was being sarcastic with him but he took it.

She went into the kitchen. A moment later she came out with some sandwiches wrapped in tinfoil.

'They're from the garage down the road,' she said, unwrapping them, 'I got them in case you decided to grace me with your presence.' Again she put on the plastic smile. I could have screamed.

'They look lovely,' Adrian said nervously.

'They're supposed to be BLT,' she said, 'but they're probably full of additives. And probably about two weeks past their sell-by date.'

I looked at the wrapping to see if I could see anything written there.

'Don't worry,' she laughed, 'I destroyed the evidence.'

She laid them out on a plate. We started to eat them. I was going to make some comment about the 'sandwiches' in the old days but thought better of it

'You're far too thin,' she said to Adrian, 'Is that sister of mine feeding you at all? She's probably starving you if I know Maureen.'

'That's unfair, May,' I said.

'It's the truth. Look at him. He's wasting away.'

Adrian blushed.

'She feeds me very well, actually,' he said, 'I probably just worry it all off.'

'Oh! Are you a worrier? I never knew that. You seem more like someone who could walk through a tornado and not get flustered.' She looked at me. 'Unlike someone else I could mention.'

'What's that supposed to mean?' I said.

'Nothing.'

We continued to eat. I could see Adrian was getting more nervous by the minute. He started gobbling the sandwiches to avoid having to talk. Then he got a fit of choking. I thumped his back.

'It's okay,' he blustered, 'I'm fine. Something just went down the wrong way.'

'Let me get you a glass of water,' May said. She ran out to the kitchen. Adrian said he was all right when she came back but she still held the glass up to his lips. She tilted it back as if he was a child.

'Well,' she said, 'After that little drama I'll be thinking you don't like my sammies.'

'They're lovely,' Adrian said again. He started eating much slower now in case he choked again.

'Well nobody died yet anyway,' said May, 'Maybe they're not so bad after all.'

'They're lovely,' Adrian repeated a third time.

'I'm sure you'd prefer a pizza or something more substantial.'

'Not at all,' he said.

He seemed terrified of her. Her eagle eye watched us digest every morsel, challenging us to be dissatisfied.

'So you thought you weren't going to be able to make it down here?' she said, putting on a kind of false concern.

'That's right,' Adrian said, 'Apart from the gridlock, the car was making funny noises.'

'Funny noises? Like what?'

He imitated the car doing a rattle. He exaggerated it so much, May burst out laughing. It was strange to see him doing anything like that. He was usually so reserved.

'You're obviously not giving it enough love,' she said, 'Cars need love, you know. Like people. Isn't that right, sissie?'

I felt like clocking her one.

'It was my car, May,' I said, 'not Adrian's.'

'Ah! Then it can't be short of love.'

'Thank you,' I said with a frozen smile.

'And now,' she said, 'You'll both have to sample my apple tart. It's a mortal sin.'

'If I have anything else I'll explode,' Adrian protested.

'Nonsense. I won't take no for an answer.'

Again she disappeared into the kitchen. I looked at Adrian but he was too worked up to look back at me. His eyes were pinned onto the floor.

She came out with the apple tart a few minutes later. She put slices of it onto three separate plates. It was dosed in sugar. As I started to eat it I thought: This is my calorie count for the entire year.

'What's wrong?' she said, 'Is it off?'

'It's beautiful,' I lied. Adrian was eating his one like a terrified pupil at a boarding school.

After we were finished she reached into a cabinet. She took out a bottle of wine.

'My God,' Adrian blubbered, 'This is turning into a banquet.'

May giggled.

'It's nice to know someone appreciates me.' I wasn't sure if this was a dig at me.

She poured a glass for each of us.

'It's a good year,' she announced, looking at the label on the bottle, as if Adrian would care about things like that. I wasn't sure if that was a joke either.

'What about some music?' she said then. Adrian shrugged. She went over to her hi-fi and turned on a CD. It was a classical music track.

'I'd say that was your style, Adrian,' she taunted.

'It's certainly very powerful,' he said. He was probably afraid to say anything else. I knew he wasn't into classical music at all. (His favourite singer was Don McLean).

The CD finished. Nobody seemed to know what to say. I wondered what else she had up her sleeve.

'So how are things going at the job?' she said to Adrian, 'Are you still poking around in people's mouths for a living?'

'Trying to!' he said, giving his nervous laugh.

'That's all any of us can do,' she said May, 'No complaints anyway?'

'Thankfully not. Business is booming. I have a few root canals on hand at the moment.'

'Or rather in mouth!' May said. Adrian gave another nervous laugh.

There was another silence then. Adrian kept looking at the floor. May glowed. She knew she was putting him through it, putting both of us through it.

It started to rain. He looked out the window.

'You wouldn't know what the weather is going to do,' he said.

'That you wouldn't,' she said dismissively, 'That you wouldn't. We get the whole four seasons in one day here. It's not like Dublin. I believe Glenageary is like Bel Air. Sunshine all the time.'

'Oh I wouldn't say that,' he said, 'We get our share of the old showers too!'

He started to choke again. May jumped up.

'Another glass of water?'

'No, I think I'm all right this time.'

I didn't know what was coming next. I tried to say something but she cut across me.

'Will you be leaving your shoes outside the door for polishing in the morning?' she said.

'Of course!' Adrian assured her.

She kept this up for the whole evening, making us sink lower and lower into our seats. Her eyes bulged wide as she ranted on about one thing and another. I tried to get a word in every now and then but she kept cutting me off. I watched Adrian getting increasingly frustrated. I kept thinking he was going to choke again. He had his hand over his mouth a lot of the time. He started to stammer when he talked. Maureen told me once that he did that when he was uptight.

She finally stood up.

'Okay,' she said, 'It's time for *hausfrau* to deal with the dishes.'

She marched out to the kitchen. This time I followed her.

'What are you trying to do to the poor man? He's in a terrible state.'

545

'I'm only having a bit of crack,' she said. 'He probably enjoys it. I don't think he has much fun with Mo.' Mo was her nickname for Maureen.

'Please lay off him,' I said, 'for all our sakes.'

'How can I?' she said, 'He's hilarious. Did you notice he was wearing odd socks?'

I hadn't but I wasn't surprised. Maureen called him 'The Absent-Minded Professor.'

'For the love of God don't say it to him. He's bad enough.'

She ignored that. For the rest of the night she continued badgering him in that passive aggressive way she had.

'I suppose you two will be hunkering down together,' she said when it got to bedtime, 'now that Kevin and Maureen aren't here to keep an eye on you.'

Adrian's face went a deep puce. Obviously it was only a joke but he wasn't the type of person you said things like that to. He skedaddled up the stairs like a greyhound coming out of the traps. May went into convulsions.

I couldn't hold my temper any longer.

'Did you invite us down here just to have fun at our expense?' I said, roaring at her at the top of my voice.

'If you don't like the heat, get out of the kitchen.'

'I will. I'll be on the first train back tomorrow.'

'Oh for God's sake don't be such a baby. There was a time I could have a joke with you.'

'There's a difference between a joke and psychological torture.'

She just shook her head at that. Then she went over to the hi-fi and turned it up. It was left at top volume for the rest of the evening, competing with the sound of the television. When I couldn't take anymore I headed up to bed. I made sure I gave the door a big bang when I got into the bedroom. I expected her to come up and apologise but then I thought: She's May, she doesn't know what the word apology means.

I woke up the next morning trying to piece together the events of the night before. I wondered what kind of twisted mind May must have had to enjoy making Adrian suffer as she did.

I kept out of her way for most of the morning. She was on the phone about her job a lot of the time. She sounded like efficiency personified. It was as if another identity took her over.

She had to meet a friend for coffee in town at eleven. Adrian stayed in his room until she was gone. He looked shook when he came down.

'I don't know what her problem with me is,' he said.

'I don't either.'

'I'm not sure what to do.'

'Just humour her. If she sees she's getting to you, she's won.'

'Maureen told me a bit about her but I didn't expect this.'

'She excelled herself last night, even by her own standards.'

When she came back from her meeting she was all smiles.

'That's another contract in the can,' she beamed, 'I get most of my clients over coffee these days. Who needs boardrooms?'

She talked about her job non-stop all through lunch. I was never so bored in my life. Then she produced her *piece de resistance,* some more company reports. I'd have preferred to watch paint dry.

'How is Kevin enjoying the easy life?' she said as she finished her lunch.

'He worked along enough to earn it,' I said.

'Relax,' she said, 'I can't say anything to you these days or you pick it up.'

'I'm not picking anything up,' I said, 'I'm just making a comment.'

She brought out some fruit cocktail for dessert.

'Isn't it great Eileen is staying off the drugs?' she said as she served it to us. She addressed the comment to Adrian. I didn't know him well enough to have shared information like that with him. I doubted Maureen had mentioned anything about it either.

'Eileen was never on drugs,' I said sharply.

'Oh that's right,' she said, 'Sorry. It was Jack, wasn't it? Unless you call drink a drug.'

Adrian jumped up from his seat at that.

'May,' he said, 'Thank you s-s-s-so much for your hospitality but I h-h-h-have to go now.'

'Go?' she said, 'but you're hardly here.'

'I…I just remembered I have an urgent phone call to make this evening.'

'Are you not going back with me?' I said.

'No,' he said, 'I'll get the…the train. I couldn't risk the car breaking down.'

I didn't know what to say. It looked like he was going to faint right in front of our eyes. He was as white as a sheet.

He went upstairs to get his things. The arrangement I'd made with Maureen was that both of us would be staying two nights. He was obviously at breaking point.

I looked daggers at May but she pretended not to notice. Adrian ran down the stairs with his bag in his hand. He hugged me nervously and then shook May's hand.

'I think there's a train at three,' he said. His face was still ashen white.

'Go-o-o-d-bye' he muttered, waving at both of us as he closed the door behind him. Then he was gone.

May sat down on the sofa. She puffed her cheeks out.

'I'll never understand people,' she said, 'An urgent phone call. Why didn't he think of that before he came down? I hate it when people only stay a night after me airing the room. I'll still have to change the sheets.

'Why do you give Adrian such a hard time?' I said to her.

'What do you mean?' she said.

'Don't play the innocent. You're well aware of what you did.'

'We just don't hit it off,' she said, 'He's too sweet to be wholesome. I wish he wouldn't keep apologizing for being alive.'

I nearly dropped when she said that.

'It's called being nice,' I said.

'Sure. You'd know all about that. You wrote the book on niceness.'

'What's that supposed to mean?'

'I don't have too much time for "nice" people. Most of them haven't lived.'

'Are you saying he hasn't?'

'He never had to struggle in life like the rest of us.'

'Come on, May. Don't act as if you were born in a manger.'

'He came from a five bedroom house. That's a bit different to McSweeney Terrace.'

'His parents may have been wealthy but he worked hard for everything he got. Anyway, it's none of your business where he came from. He's good to Maureen. That's all that matters. Are you jealous of him?'

'You always thought that, didn't you? That's probably why you're so vengeful towards me.'

'I've never done anything to you in my life. Look in the mirror if you're talking about vengefulness.'

'If you must know, Adrian gets on my goat. Everything about him makes me want to scream.'

'Is that why you packed him back to Dublin a day early?'

'Don't try that one on me. He packed himself back. He's the one who mucked up my weekend, getting down here so late and leaving so early.'

She was a dab hand at turning things back on the other person when she'd been the guilty one. I felt terrible because he'd been so good to bring me down. He'd even refused to accept petrol money from me when I tried to press it on him.

I was sick of the whole rigmarole by this stage.

'Maybe it's me you're angry with,' I said. She screwed up her eyes.

'That's bullshit,' she said, 'and you know it. How could I be angry with Miss Perfect? Someone who thinks everything out so intricately, who looks left and right before she crosses her legs?'

I felt like throttling her but I stopped myself. When she was in this kind of mood you had to flick a switch inside your head that said, 'Just let her vent.'

I quietly simmered. She'd won – again. I'd have preferred to have a stand-up fight with her to clear the air but I knew that was impossible. She'd have wiped the floor with me.

'All I ask,' I said finally, 'is that you don't tell Maureen anything that went on with Adrian.'

'Why not? Do we have to wrap her in cotton wool at her age?'

If she only realised it, she was the one that had been wrapped in cotton wool all her life. Now we were reaping the harvest.

549

I spent as much time as I could outside the house for the next few days. Sometimes I got the bus to Cork and just wandered around. I needed to do nothing to clear my head. It was a nightmare being around her. She was like someone with a permanent period. I made a promise to myself that I'd try not to argue with her any more. It wasn't worth it.

One day I went down to the graveyard where Mammy and Daddy were buried. You could hardly see their names on the headstones now. I found the graves only by knowing where they were from memory. There were weeds all over them. In a way I liked the roughness of it all. It seemed more natural. It reminded me of the untidiness of the house as we were growing up. I said a few prayers for them – and to them. What would they make of May, I wondered. Mammy had always stopped us fighting when we were young but we were different creatures now. The stakes had been upped.

When I got back to Dublin I told Kevin about her antics. He let out a large guffaw. He'd seen her in action a few times already.

'If she was my sister,' he said, 'I'd swing for her. The fact that I'm away from the situation makes it easier for me to laugh about it.'

I rang Maureen to see how much Adrian had told her. I knew she'd have been surprised to see him home a day earlier than she'd expected.

'What did he say to you about Her Majesty?' I said. (We called her that when we wanted to be bitchy).

'Nothing,' she said. 'Adrian doesn't talk. He just kept biting his lip. I know he's upset when he does that. He stayed out of work the next day though. For him to do that I thought he'd have to have suffered something like a multiple coronary because he was a total workaholic. I gathered from his grunts that May dispatched him back to Dublin prematurely.'

'Got it in one,' I said. I decided I wanted it all out in the open now even though I'd asked May not to say anything.

'She probably put the fear of God into him,' she said, 'Am I right?'

'More or less. It's terrible that he has to bear the brunt of her bad moods. We're used to it but he isn't.'

'So what did she do?'

'What *didn't* she do, you mean. Her nose was out of joint from the minute we arrived.'

'Why was that?'

'We got delayed on the journey.'

'Oops. It doesn't surprise me to hear she'd be put out about that. If you're not there on the dot for our May you're asking for it.'

'I knew that but what could we do? The traffic was septic. We didn't even stop for a bite to eat on the way down.'

'May expects people to be divinely inspired about things like traffic jams.'

'As soon as she opened the door I felt we were in for it. For a minute I wasn't sure she was going to ask us in at all. She was getting ready to go to bed.'

'Lady Muck likes her beauty sleep. At that stage I'd nearly have turned around and hightailed it back to Dublin.'

'If we did that we could kiss goodbye to any other invites to ever go down there and I don't want that. I feel sorry for Adrian though. He'd driven all that way. He looked like he was ready to drop.'

'Thanks for thinking of him.'

'I was thinking of myself too. I needed to get in somewhere to take the weight off my legs.'

'You were honoured she allowed you that luxury.'

'She looked us up and down first. I felt like a cow at a fair. Even when we got inside I felt tense. I wondered if she was going to ask us if we had a mouth on us.'

'Did she?'

'Much to my amazement she produced some sandwiches.'

'Were they nice? She's never exactly been cook-of-the-month, has she?'

'I can't say boo about that because I'm not either. She said she bought them at a garage.'

'Charming. How did they taste?'

'Not too bad, but she kept making jibes at Adrian as he was eating them.'

'Some day that girl will go one step too far. She knows everyone is afraid of her. That's why she gets away with it. Sometimes when I'm talking to her I forget I'm an adult.'

'Me too. That's because she doesn't treat us like adults.'

'You deserve a medal for putting up with her.'

'What's the point of fighting with her? It won't do your nerves any good - and you won't beat her. She loves fighting.'

'The reason she's so good at it is because she's had so much experience at it. It's probably what she does best in life.'

'At the end of the day you have Adrian and I have Kevin. She's probably just lonely. Maybe even lonelier than Aunt Bernie was. With her it came out as love. May expresses it as anger.'

'That's it in a nutshell but I'm not as nice as you are. I get tired making allowances for her. I feel like telling her to take a running jump for herself.'

'I've done that over the years, believe me, but it doesn't work. She has a way of making it rebound on you. She's obviously mad jealous of yourself and Adrian. Maybe she even fancies him. I've seen her give him a certain look sometimes. Some women express their interest in a man by taunting him.'

'You might be right. If that's the case I'm glad I wasn't with you.'

I was going to tell her what she said about Adrian and me sleeping together but thought better of it. She'd probably have gone through the phone.

'Anyway, going forward, as they say, I think it's best if we both stay out of her way as much as you can. I refuse to let her deny me my home even if she owns it.'

'That's all very well but somebody needs to put her in her box. I'm fed up toadying to her. If she wasn't my sister you'd be visiting me in Mountjoy now on a homicide charge. Life is too short for us to have to spend our time waiting for her next explosion.'

I was surprised to hear Maureen speaking so strongly. Maybe the pressure of all the years was finally catching up on her. She was quiet for a moment. Then she let out a sigh.

'Dealing with her is worse than digging ditches,' she said.

'When did you ever dig ditches?' I said.

'Seriously, though, I've had enough of her. One of these days it's going to be handbags at dawn between us.'

Thankfully that day never came. Maureen and myself continued to go down there in staggered visits. We stayed out of the house as much as we could, going  shopping or to the pictures or for walks through the town. We had to keep telling ourselves that there was more to Midleton than May, that there was more to it than our house or our past.

Most of the people I knew had left the town by now. Tim O'Neill, who lifted up my dress that day at school, was running a dance-hall in Leixlip. Sean Coughlan, who preferred me to Maureen for a date, was an orderly in a hospital in Douglas. Davina Mulcahy, my old friend from school, had married a bank manager. Peter Cronin had become fat and bald. He was living somewhere on the outskirts of Douglas with his cats.

The Dineens were scattered far and wide across the globe. All of them did well for themselves. The last I heard of the twins they were making jewellery for film stars in Sacramento, California. Some other people I grew up with either disappeared or died. That made those who stayed behind all the more precious to me.

I ran into them sometimes in the street or at the shops. They usually started conversations with the same sentence, 'I was very sorry to hear about your parents.' If I spotted an old school friend I dallied with them for ages, pestering them for news of mutual acquaintances. A few years before, when Mammy and Daddy were alive, I wouldn't have given two hoots for this kind of talk but now I was lapping it up.

Suddenly I began to understand how hungry Mammy had been for stories about my life any time I came home from Dublin. When there wasn't much happening in your life you became desperate to hear even the most trivial bit of gossip.

Had I given her enough of this, I wondered? Was I selfish not to go into more detail about things she'd wanted to hear about over the years? Probably not. Now I had the same hunger. I remembered an old saying I heard once: 'Sooner or later we all turn into our mothers.' Maybe it was true.

One day I bumped into a girl called Ann O'Sullivan in the supermarket. She'd been in my class in school. We were talking about this and that when she said, 'I was very sad to hear your parents died, especially with all the problems your mother had.' I asked her what she meant by that. She said, 'Oh, with your father's drinking and all.'

I was shocked. We all knew Daddy liked his drink but I never thought of him as having a problem with it. The thing about him, as I've said before, was that he couldn't hold his drink. He tended to get a bit stupid even after two pints. I was never sure if that was a good or a bad thing. It was probably good because it stopped him having too many. But that still didn't stop tongues wagging. If he was seen drunk once in public that was enough to have him tagged as a raving alcoholic.

When I delved further, it turned out Ann thought he'd been kicked out of 'the building game,' as she called it, as a result of his drinking. That was just a small example of the kind of lies that circulate in small towns. People often have nothing better to do with their time except make up lies. There were probably many more if I cared to investigate but I didn't. The more you got sucked into that kind of thing the more you lost yourself. The incident made me glad I didn't live in Midleton all the time.

How did May cope with it? (When I thought about it, though, people would probably have been too terrified to say anything like that to May with her temper the way it was).

I told Ann I was as insulted by the fact that she believed such a lie as by the lie itself. She got all flustered then, telling me she only mentioned it so I could knock it on the head. 'I don't believe you,' I said. I hated it when people went back on something they said out of cowardice. Be one thing or another.

The funny thing was, I always liked Ann. Her brother had been killed in a car accident when she was a child. He was crossing the road against the lights one day in Mallow when a truck hit him. I can't imagine anything worse than that happening to a person. I felt it coloured her attitude to everything afterwards. Her parents never recovered from it and both of them died young.

Ann married soon afterwards but her husband was a no-good. She also had a son who was mentally impaired. It was another cruel blow. She loved him passionately but life afterwards wasn't much fun. I always thought she had a sadness about her that she could never totally hide no matter how hard she tried.

These are just some of the people I knew – and know – in Midleton. I could write another book about the ones I haven't mentioned. Sometimes people used to say things to me like 'Where have you been? I thought you must have emigrated.' It was only at times like this I realised how little I'd mixed around when Mammy and Daddy were alive. I'd say, 'I don't know what you're talking about, I've been home every few months.' I was so immersed in my own bubble I forgot there was a world outside the house. I needed that world now. I was grateful to anyone who'd share it with me.

I don't regard myself as a Midleton person today. That's because I've spent so long out of it. They say you can take the man out of the bog but you can't take the bog out of the man. I'm not sure of that. If you've been away from a place long enough you lose something of it. That's even more true when you don't have roots there anymore. When Daddy died it was the first big parting of the way between me and the town. His death separated me from it much more than going away to be a nurse. That was only a geographical thing. His death severed me emotionally from it. When Mammy died I told myself I never wanted to see the place again.

If Maureen lived down there and May was in Dublin things might have been different. I always felt May didn't want me to be there even if she said she did. She usually seemed to be protesting too much when these sorts of discussions came up. As the years went on and she became more engrained in the house, I almost felt like an interloper. She had her own life there now and I totally appreciated that. Why shouldn't she?

I felt she was threatened by me. She saw me as a nurse trying to treat her like a patient. The fact that she often behaved like one was beside the point.

The other bone of contention between us was that she didn't think I appreciated how hard she worked at life or how much she achieved in it. I plead guilty to that. I never took her guitar-playing seriously, for instance. I thought of it as an overly self-conscious attempt to make up for her career ambitions. I have to admit I felt the same way when she took up acting. (She appeared in a few local productions of John B. Keane plays). Acting was a passion for Cillian but with May I just saw it as a hobby. You could tell that a mile away by the way each of them talked about it. It was the same with the guitar. I thought she was playing it not so much from love as because it was a trendy thing to do.

I said to her once, 'I never knew you were so big into the guitar.'

'Have you a problem with that?' she said.

'How could I have a problem with it?'

'I know pop music isn't your thing,' she said, 'You're more into ballads, aren't you?' When she said something like that she always made it sound disparaging, as if ballads were the last refuge of a scoundrel.

On one of my visits down to her I went to see her playing in the Two Mile Inn, a pub that nurtured new talent. She was wearing a buckskin blouses and a pair of Levis. Her get-up stunned me. It was such a contrast to the power-dressing her job required. I couldn't help thinking it was a pose.

She sang a lot of Joni Mitchell songs. Mitchell did nothing for me but she was one of May's idols so she gave it everything. She was great at working a crowd and the audience lapped it up. Some of them even stamped the floor. Between songs they came up to her and high-fived her. As I watched her bantering with them I could see how she would have seen me as Mrs Suburbia. I almost felt ashamed of myself. I was totally out of my depth.

'I'm thrilled for you,' I said when she came offstage, 'You had them in the palm of your hand out there.'

'Yeah, all five of them,' she said. That wasn't true. It was a big gathering. I could see a lot of them knew her. She interacted with them in a way she never did with Maureen or me. Was that our fault or hers? Maybe it was nobody's. Maybe it was just the way we were made. The important thing was that I was seeing a side of her I didn't know existed.

'Thanks for coming along,' she said. I offered to buy her a drink but she wasn't interested. Already she was gone from me. She started talking to an ageing hippie type, a man with a beard, dressed in Levis like herself but too old for them in my view. He said something to her that put her into hysterics. The pair of them were practically on the floor laughing as I left the bar.

I went straight to bed after getting back to the house. I woke up in the middle of the night and heard music downstairs. A fiddle player was striking up. I heard May's voice, or a voice that sounded like hers, among many others. The music seemed to go on for a long time. I didn't dare go down, or castigate anyone for keeping me awake.

The next morning I woke up with a headache. I didn't go downstairs until about eleven o'clock. May was already up. I couldn't believe she could burn the candle at both ends like that. She was reading one of her reports.

'That was some night last night,' I said.

'You should come down more often. We'll turn you into a bohemian yet.'

'I'm afraid it's too late for that,' I said.

I asked her if she had any Panadols. She went to a drawer and handed me one.

'Excuse me for being rude,' she said, 'but I have a report to do. If I don't get it into them they'll be sending up smoke signals.'

I got the message. It was time to make a cup of tea for myself. I drank it in the next room. Obviously she wasn't going to talk to me. I'd been relegated to the Boring Sister role.

I rang Cillian. He'd moved out of Coolock by now. He was renting a house in Malahide to be closer to work.

He'd been at a roller disco with his pupils. One of them had fallen and dislocated her shoulder. She was in Temple Street. May came in just before I hung up.

'Did I hear something about an accident?' she said.

I told her the details. Maybe she'd already got the gist of it. She said, 'If you were Mary Poppins you could fly up to her on your umbrella.'

I asked her if she had any other gigs planned.

'I don't know and I don't care. I enjoy them when they're happening but then they're over and I'm on to something else. I can never think beyond the moment.'

Maybe that was the most honest thing she ever said to me. Maybe it was the reason she didn't seem to be able to be in a permanent relationship with anyone.

I got the train back to Dublin that afternoon. 'That girl has your head all over the shop,' Kevin said to me when I told him about the night, 'I don't know why you go down there. What's in it for you?'

But I kept going down. Maybe it was the masochist in me. Another night as I sat listening to her in a dead-end pub she stopped playing suddenly. She said to the audience, 'Tonight we have a special guest – my sister. I want to dedicate this song to her.' I got the fright of my life when she said that. I felt she was doing it to embarrass me because we'd had an argument shortly beforehand. She took great delight in wrong-footing me at times like that. She'd cut you to the quick and then be as nice as pie five minutes later.

The longer I spent around her, the worse things became. She picked up on things that were nothing to do with anything. One night, for instance, I decided to make myself a cup of coffee.

'Coffee, mind you,' she sniffed, 'Is tea not good enough for you anymore? I'm just after making it.'

'Okay,' I said to keep her quiet, 'I'll have the tea so.' She was delighted at that, as she was at any little victory over me.

'I suppose you still think I have a drab married life with Kevin,' I said then.

She always rose to any possibility of an argument like a bird of prey.

'How could I think that when you're so busy saving lives?'

'Come on, May,' I said, 'You know I retired from nursing years ago. 'Why do you make comments like that?'

'It was a joke,' she said, 'You really need to sort yourself out. You're jumping on everything these days. Are you depressed or something?'

I couldn't let that go. All the frustrations I'd been building up about her came flooding out.

'Why do you spend your whole life putting me down?' I said, 'Are you jealous of me? Are you guilty about the fact that you got the house instead of Maureen or me? Are you jealous of us being in happy relationships when we aren't? Is that why you keep engaging in all your perverse little games?'

For once she was quiet but it was the quietness of tension, even hatred. She stared at me with those X-ray eyes of hers and then left

558

the room. For once I wasn't afraid of her. The tyranny was over. The mouse had roared.

. I wondered if I should follow her out but then I thought, No, that's what you've been doing all her life whenever she threw her toys out of the pram, that's half the problem.

There was a bottle of brandy on the table and I started to lash into it. I never drank brandy. I would have taken anything I saw before me. My hands were trembling.

I don't know how many glasses I had but it knocked me for six. I fell into bed in my clothes for the 769$^{th}$ time in my life.

I woke up with a hangover worse than the other 768 but it was worth it. The beast had been tamed.

I couldn't remember what I'd said to her for a few minutes. When I did, I thought: Oh no, this is the end.

I went down to the kitchen. She was sitting at the table. 'Good morning, May,' I said. She grunted in reply, looking into space as if nothing happened. I decided to bite the bullet.

'Sorry about last night,' I said, 'I shouldn't have said what I did. I didn't mean it.'

To a normal person that might have elicited some kind of a response but all she said was, 'I don't even know what you're talking about. I can't remember what you said.' For the rest of the morning we walked in and out of rooms like two strangers. There was a time this would have unnerved me too but now it didn't.

She drove me to the train. We didn't speak on the way there either. When we got to the station she gave me a kiss on the cheek, something she'd never done before. I saw it as a Judas kiss, the kiss of death.

That was my second last time in the house. For my last visit I brought a coat with me that I'd bought in Clery's. Kevin was still able to get me cuts there even though he'd left it so many years ago. Unfortunately, the day after I bought it I decided I hated it. (That wasn't unusual for me). I was going to give it to Maureen but then I started thinking it would suit May more. I thought the gesture might help heal the breach between us but I should have known better. The second I gave it to her I knew by the look on her face that it had been a crazy idea.

'It's nice,' she glowered, 'but I can do without Kevin's seconds.'

'Please take it. It looks great on you. It does nothing for me.'

'I had enough of your cast-offs as a child,' she said, 'Put it where the monkey put the nuts.' With those words she released me from her grip.

A few days later I gave it to Maureen. She was delighted with it. Why hadn't I done that in the first place? I don't know. I was always bending over backwards to please May, probably because she played so hard to get. But after the coat incident all that changed. I knew now that she'd never speak down to me again.

At 48 years of age I was finally growing up.

## Recent Times

I don't know if I've given a proper account of my life in these pages. I only put down what I remembered but maybe the things you don't remember are even more important.

Maybe I've gone into too much detail about some things and not enough about others. The reason for that is because I like talking about the things I feel strongly about rather than the ones that don't matter. I don't want to bore you so I'm going to fast forward through some of the more recent events of my life.

I'm sure you can do without me telling you about my experiences with HRT, for example, or the hot flushes I got during that dark period, or the hell I put Kevin through, or all the months I spent wondering what was wrong with me before coming to the conclusion that it was nothing at all, just life, so when I went to the doctor finally and he prescribed some anti-depression tablets for me I flushed them down the toilet.

Neither do you need to hear about my late fifties, when I did a charity walk for the Chronic Pain Foundation and ended up becoming a patient of it, or the way I continued to treat my children as if they were still in nappies – so they told me anyway – or how I continued to spar with Eileen, winning occasionally on a technical knock-out, or how things got worse and worse with May. Nor do you need me to tell you about the night of my sixtieth birthday when I entered a karaoke competition in the Sheaf of Wheat, our local pub, and succeeded in giving half the population of Coolock earache as a result my tone deaf rendition of Neil Diamond's 'Sweet Caroline.'

Nor do I need to give you all the details about how Kevin's bowling team became the champions of North Dublin one year, or how Siobhan blossomed into someone as beautiful as the women who graced the walls of her salon on life-sized posters, or how Cillian keeps plugging away at his job and getting little thanks for it, just like his father, or the fact that we finally paid off the mortgage (cue much dancing and some mild hysteria) and all the other hundreds of things that happened in that decade. They seemed so important at the time but now they're nothing more than pleasant memories to me.

Maybe the most amazing thing of all was the fact that Reg finally drew in his horns. Kevin went for a game of snooker with him in the Cosmo one night and they had a drink afterwards. He told him he went through a very dark period after the literary magazine collapsed. Then he fell in love. It was with an American girl he met at TCD during a film festival. From Kevin's description of her it sounded like she was one of those peroxide blondes that are ten a penny over there.

'She had a face that looked like it came from a magazine cover,' he said. It was unusual to hear Reg talking like that. The old Reg would have been more focussed on her breasts or her legs. He told Kevin he chased her all over Ireland. They had a brief romance but then she went back to her surfing boyfriend in California. Reg was gutted. It was probably the first time he'd been rejected in his life. A few weeks later he started dating what he called a 'sensible' girl from Tipperary. She was a laboratory technician called Breda. It seemed to me as if he was dating her on the rebound. She didn't sound like his type at all.

A few weeks later an envelope popped in the door with embossed writing on it. When Kevin opened it he said, 'You won't believe this. Reg is getting married. He's asked us to the wedding.'

My eyes were out on sticks as I looked at the invitation and read the words on it: 'Breda and Reg would like you to attend their wedding.'

'Now I've seen everything,' Kevin said.

He rang him to Clery's to say we'd be delighted to go. After a few minutes he handed the phone to me. His voice sounded very quivery as I congratulated him on the new path his life was about to take. It was almost like he was apologising for it.

'What age is she?' I asked after putting down the phone.

'I'd say mid-forties from his description of her.'

That seemed to be about twenty years older than his desired age. Every time I saw him his girlfriends seemed to be getting younger. I told Kevin he'd probably end up with an embryo.

Breda was hardly that. Being in her forties probably meant children were out of the question for them. I'd always wanted to see what Reg would be like holding a baby but now I doubted I would. Not that he'd have regretted that. I always figured children or the lack of them would have been much of a muchness for him. I don't think he'd have known what to do with them if his behaviour with our lot was anything to go by. He always seemed to regard them as these irritating little creatures who wandered in and out of rooms looking for things when they should have been engaging in deep discussions about life - or at least about Reg's life.

We invited the two of them round for dinner the following week. Breda was a tall thin woman. She was dressed in a brown woolly jumper and a pencil skirt. She had a pleasant face that seemed to be fixed in a permanent smile. Her gently greying hair was tied in a ponytail. I could see she'd probably been a stunner when she was younger.

'I hope you can put manners on him,' I said to her after we'd eaten and got acquainted.

'It's already done,' she said, 'The job is Oxo.'

'How did you manage it?' I asked, enthralled at her achievement.

'It was easy,' she said, 'Isn't that right, Reg?'

He put his hands out as if he wasn't sure whether it was or not.

'He was ready to settle down when he met me. Buying the house in Rathcoole changed him.'

I thought the Californian girl probably changed him more but obviously I didn't say anything about her. I doubted Reg told her about her. It might have made her suspect his motives in settling down with her.He wasn't the first ageing Lothario I'd seen going to the altar when he felt he'd run out of road.

Breda had been married before. Her husband was a bad egg. It was the usual story – he left her for a younger woman. But at least she got the house. She had two children by him, Ricky and Elaine. They were both in their twenties.

The wedding was a very subdued affair. It was Reg's first trip up the aisle but he'd done everything else. As Kevin said, the wedding cake was probably the only thing that was new to him that day.

He had a seen-it-all look on his face as he slipped the ring around her finger. It wasn't until that moment I felt sure he wouldn't make a bolt for the door.

'He makes the tuxedo look like a straitjacket,' I said to Kevin.

Breda was very matter-of-fact about everything. She didn't seem to care too much about his downbeat look. Maybe that was because she'd been married before. She'd probably seen more than one Reg Keegan come and go.

She put him through his paces at the reception like a misbehaving child. He'd invited a few of his 'culture vulture' friends as a gesture to his past life but he didn't seem to have much to say to them. When they got a fill of pints into them they raised enough hell to give him the illusion he still belonged to their world, even if it was going to be at a remove now. I saw them as his last nod towards a life he was leaving.

'What do you think of them?' he said to Kevin at one stage, 'Total degenerates, what?' I knew they regarded bachelordom as a kind of holy grail. He was a rat deserting a sinking ship and they slagged him something awful for it.

His hair was grey now, or at least the bit that was left. He had a pot belly too. From the look on his face I felt Breda was going to be calling the shots in their relationship from now on. It was such a contrast to all the years when he had women dancing attendance on him. Had they all deserted him after the *Art Attack* fiasco?

Kevin said most of his problems went back to his mother. He thought she ruined him. He was an only child. How many Irish mothers did that to their only children? Or all of them?

He sold his house in Rathcoole shortly after the wedding. They moved in to Breda's one in Rush. That made more sense than moving into Reg's one. He still owed quite a lot on the mortgage. Now that was all wiped out.

Ricky was still living with Breda. Elaine was married but according to Reg she called in so often she might as well not have moved out at all.

'That's daughters for you, Reg,' Breda informed him blithely when he remarked on that fact, 'They never really leave.'

Any time she called he made himself scarce after exchanging the dutiful pleasantries with her. He often grew impatient if she hung on chatting with Breda. 'Sometimes I feel like a tenant in the house,' he told Kevin.

Elaine's husband was mad into GAA. That wasn't Reg's area of interest at all. He thought he was a bit dim so he didn't bother much with him.

He didn't get on with Ricky either.

'No matter what room I go into,' he told Kevin, 'he's there. He's either sitting on the floor watching the television or playing with one of his computer games. Most of them would be more suitable for someone half his age.'

He often tripped over his legs as he crossed the floor. I'm sure his language was choice at times like that. He found it hard to say anything to Breda about any of this. If he hinted at any kind of dissatisfaction she reminded him of the fact that he went into the situation with his eyes open. He wanted her to sell the house in Rush and get a place for themselves. She'd have agreed if they could have brought Ricky with them but Reg wasn't on for that. The main reason for him wanting her to sell up was to get away from him. They couldn't afford to leave him in the house and go off themselves.

'I'm sorry I didn't move Breda into my shack in Rathcoole,' he told Kevin, 'Then I'd have been able to tell that horror she brought into the world what to do with himself.'

I watched Reg become more and more subdued as the years went on. In a strange way it made him more human. He became more civil to me than he used to be anytime I ran into him with Breda. I never quite managed to get another kiss on the cheek from him like the one he gave me at Kevin's farewell party but you can't have everything. It gladdened me to know that he'd finally come down to the place where the rest of us live. Maybe we all mellow with age – or infirmity. We give ourselves to God, as someone said, when the devil wants nothing more to do with us.

Reg is tipping sixty now. He was in his fifties when he got married. I don't think Breda is too far behind him but she doesn't look it. She could pass for forty. Why is it some people never show their age? I have to confess to being madly jealous of such people. Joan Collins once said that beauty is like being born rich and getting poorer every day. Some of us get poorer than others. Joan modelled for *Playboy* when she was fifty. That's pretty rich.

Before I knew it I was celebrating my seventieth birthday. It was both a sad and happy occasion for me. Sad for obvious reasons and happy because of the love I got when I reached such a milestone. The children pulled out all the stops for it, clubbing together to pay for a trip for Kevin and me to go to Paris. I was gobsmacked. How do people come up with ideas like that? I think Siobhan was behind it. It was the loveliest surprise you could imagine.

We re-visited all the places we went to on that first magical trip so many years before. We were more grizzled now but we did our best to forget about that. By now Kevin was on for us doing the touristy things like visiting the Louvre. I'd planned to do that on our first trip there before he swept me off my feet with his wedding proposal. I was looking forward to finally seeing it now.

In the event I have to say it was something of an anti-climax. There were some impressive exhibits but the main reason everyone goes there is to see the Mona Lisa. I thought it was over-rated. If there wasn't such a hullabaloo about it over the centuries, would any of us have really thought it was that great? I mean, who cares if she's smiling or not?

We also went up the Eiffel Tower. It was exhilarating looking out at the vast panorama around us. I asked Kevin if he'd like to go down on one knee again to recreate his romantic proposal of yore but he declined, pleading arthritis.

I let him away with it because I suffer from that condition too. Maureen even has a touch of it. We compare symptoms sometimes. 'God be with the days when we were comparing boyfriends,' she says. Amen to that.

It annoys me that I can't do half the things I used to. Part of the reason is my body and part my mind. For most of my life I had to force myself to stop doing things but now I have to try and entice myself to do them. Kevin tells me I've paid my dues in that respect. 'You deserve a rest,' he says. Maybe, but that's not the point. I've never enjoyed resting but what can you do when your body won't let you perform tasks that once came so naturally to you? Hit the remote and say, like Scarlett O'Hara in *Gone with the Wind*, 'I'll think about that tomorrow?'

Sometimes it seems to be the only option but tomorrow never really comes. If Scarlett taught us anything it was that. I still can't think of that film without Grandad coming into my mind. He loved it so much. And Clark Gable was so gorgeous in it, wasn't he? I wonder what ever happened to the 'Ara' sign that was outside the door. I don't think the new owner would have had much time for it. He was from the IT sector.

Clery's is gone now, being yet another victim of foreign infiltration. Or was it simply the unpopularity of anything smacking of the old world? Kevin was shocked at the treatment the staff got when it closed its doors for the last time.

'Thank God I got out when I did,' he said, 'Just think of those poor creatures thrown out on the street without a bean after a lifetime of service.' He knew a good few of them.

I'd never forget the day he brought me in to watch the demolition of Nelson's Pillar from one of its windows. What are they going to replace it with? Another sports shop like the one that stands where Boyers used to be? Will there come a time when everything of the old Dublin has given way to the conglomerates?

We don't go out much these days. Kevin jokes that the biggest journey he's had to make in the last few years is the one from the fridge to the dining-room. That's not true because he's still very active. He started playing golf with Adrian after Adrian retired. He's not exactly Tiger Woods but he has a gift for it.

They brought me out with them a few times but I seemed to move more grass than golf balls every time I took a shot so I didn't last long. I've never been sporty. Kevin says I couldn't hit a barn gate with a banjo. If I ever get a hole in three it'll probably be balls rather than strokes I'm talking about. I'd like to go with them for the exercise but I don't feel up to it most of the time. I wish I could say 'The spirit is willing but the flesh is weak' but the spirit is weak too. That's the worrying thing.

I try not to think of my age. 'It's only a number,' Kevin tells me. 'Yes,' I say, 'but in our case a very large number.' I think that's a Woody Allen joke. He can be so funny at times, can't he?

I don't feel 75. I don't even feel 25. They say everyone has a mental age that doesn't change no matter how old you are. I think mine is about ten. My body disagrees with me. I think it was Mark Twain who said the tragedy of old age isn't that we become old but that we don't. That makes it harder to deal with.

We don't tell our bodies to do when we get old. They tell us. So every morning I say to my one, 'What plans have you for me today?' And I carry them out. Or I don't, as the case may be.

The cigarettes haven't killed me yet. Maybe they've stopped trying. But I cut down. If I didn't I'd have been a Walking Nicotine Factory by now, like Daddy.

I joined the local Active Retirement group a few years ago. We go on bus trips to places like Donegal and Antrim. The free travel is great. People give out about Charlie Haughey but at least he got us that. Back in Dublin we arrange outings to plays and films. I'm even in the choir. I sing like a crow but nobody seems to notice. That's the thing about choirs. The good singers drown out the bad ones. At Christmas sometimes we put on our own plays. The best part is dressing up for them.

I'd like to go out to the pub with Kevin the odd night but what would we talk about? We've been living together so long we can almost predict what the other one is going to say before they say it. The night would probably cost us the earth and we'd have to add in the taxi fare home as well. Besides, people talk such nonsense in pubs, don't they? And in some of them you'd be in danger of having your eye knocked out.

It's cheaper to stay in and watch television. We find ourselves doing a lot of that lately. Kevin likes *The Late Late Show* but I haven't been able to enjoy it since Gay Byrne retired. For me he was a one-off. None of his replacements hold a candle to him in my opinion. I'd like to have seen Gerry Ryan try his hand at it but he died, the poor man. I often wondered if he got in on the drugs out of frustration at being passed over for it.

Sometimes I think back to all the nights I spent watching shows like *The Virginian* and *Arrest and Trial* with Cáit and Bridget in Room 19. Has television improved since then? I don't think so. The special effects might be better but I doubt if the acting is, or the storylines. And of course if a programme doesn't have sex in it today it won't sell. Is that our new God? I've never thought of myself as prudish there's too much of it around. When I was growing up it was brushed under the carpet but now we've gone to the other extreme. People keep waving it in our face as if they invented it. And then there's all that internet pornography. I wouldn't like Siobhan and Eileen to be growing up today and being exposed to that. If any of them were out late I'd be in a panic about them. I was bad enough as things were.

I watch a lot of medical programmes. Though I'm long retired I like to keep in touch with what's going on. For a while I got hooked on a show called *Doc Martin*. It's about a grumpy doctor in a village in Devon. He's always coming up with brilliant diagnoses of rare conditions.

Kevin doesn't think much of it. 'He's like a cross between Superman and Sherlock Holmes,' he says.

'At least it beats watching programmes about the retail trade,' I say, though to be fair he wouldn't bother much with things like that.

He's mostly hooked on soccer. I nearly need to tranquillise him when the World Cup is on. I miss all my soaps for that month. He guards the remote like an extra child. If it was hosted in Athlone he'd have to be taken into Intensive Care for anxiety. When Ireland was doing well in the 1990s he wanted to go to the finals. I'd just had a loan approved for an extension to the kitchen at the time. He was hoping to use the money for the trip.

'Don't even think about it,' I told him.

'You don't understand,' he said, 'We're in the quarter-finals. The Pope is even getting involved.'

'I don't care if the Lord himself is rooting for us,' I said, 'We're not going.'

Eventually he relented. I don't think I could have taken it thinking about the fact that every ball kicked was a brick less in our extension. How could someone get so worked up about a soccer match?

Gaelic football is different. I got more excited about Cork than I did about Ireland. Why did I ever bother learning about the stupid offside rule? All it meant was that Kevin never shut up about it.

Anytime Ireland got knocked out of the World Cup his only interest in the competition seemed to be the hope that England would get knocked out too. I found that hard to understand because he

569

always got excited watching the England players playing for their club teams on *Match of the Day*. When I told him I was confused he said, 'It's simple. I only hate the England players when they're playing for their country.' (Was that simple? I didn't think so).

I was glad I was able to talk him round. The kitchen turned out brilliant and it didn't take us too long to pay back the money. The banks did their best to get us to take out other loans after that. They kept offering us money during the boom. Once they have you on their books as a good credit customer they never let go. Of course they make their money back on the treble from the interest.

We considered taking them up on their offer for a while. We were going to buy an apartment in Bulgaria as an investment. Eileen was all on for it. She thought it would have been a nice bolthole for us. Kevin said, 'That's a laugh. She means a nice bolthole for herself and Jack.'

We didn't go for it in the end. 'If we took the money those bastards were throwing at us,' he said, 'we'd be in hock to them for the rest of our natural.' Instead we just sat tight on the little nest egg we had. It's still there for the rainy day. So many of our friends got caught up in it and lost everything. They were living in mansions without a penny to their names. One day I saw an accountant I knew begging on the street in Coolock. If you saw it in a film you wouldn't believe it. He used to live in a five-bedroomed house in Foxrock. Maybe we were better off in our little shack in Coolock. At least we knew where we stood.

I don't go back to Midleton much these days. When I do I keep more or less to myself. I find it does me better to do that, especially because of the ways things are with May. I'm still in the bad books with her all these years on. We're fine with one another for a while but then something erupts out of nowhere to bring us back to square one. She gets on better with Maureen than she does with me – probably because she doesn't have to endure any 'family talk' with her.

Maureen doesn't take her as seriously as I do. That's her secret. May is more relaxed with her than she is with me. She's long forgiven her for her carry-on that time with Adrian. They still laugh about the day she spotted her in Dublin when she was supposed to be in Chester.

The two of them are on the phone to one another quite a bit. Maureen goes down to stay with her if there's something on, like the Arts Festival or National Heritage Week. Every so often May comes up to them to stay. She stayed with Kevin and me for a few nights last year when she was up for the Theatre Festival but that was as far as it went.

Before she retired she used to stay with us when she was in Dublin for work purposes, visiting her clients on the north side of the city or whatever.

I thought that might be the start of a reconciliation but afterwards she went into her cocoon with me again. I'm not sure why. There's no point thinking about it. These things happen. I'd like to have it out with her but she wouldn't be interested in that. She prefers to act as if everything is hunky-dory. Maureen tries to get her to ring me any time she's up with her but she isn't up for that. I don't mind. It's her business.

I went down to Midleton with Maureen a few years ago. We did a tour of the Ring of Cork, starting off at the Choctaw Monument and going down along the banks of the Owenacurra estuary towards Ballinacurra Creek and Saleen village. Afterwards we walked towards Rostellan Woods to Aghada. There was a lovely view of Cobh from there. We thought about getting the ferry to Spike Island but it was a bit late in the day so we decided against it. We never told May about that trip. We knew it would only have increased tensions between us.

I rarely stay in McSweeney Terrace now even when I'm in Midleton. I prefer going to the Park Hotel. It's near enough to the town. If Kevin is with me we try to do something more ambitious than visiting old haunts. Sometimes we walk out by the Dungourney Road to the distillery. We come back by the Famine Graveyard and East Cork Oil.

One time we got a bus to Carrigtuohill. We visited the Fota Garden Centre in Coach Horse Lane. Afterwards we walked through Ballyannon Woods on the shores of the Owenacurra estuary. It was very romantic. Fota House is another place I love. When you go around the grounds you get a real feeling of what it must have been like to live there in the old days.

When I pass the family home I often feel as if it's a stranger's house to me. I still have my key but I wouldn't dare go in without telling May. I always knock at the door first. If she's not there I go away and come back later. We chat about anything and everything and then I go back to the hotel. It works out much better that way.

We don't eat much in the house. It's easier to go out. There's a place called Mad Monk on Joe's Lane where you can have a pizza. May loves pizzas. Or else we go to McDonald's on Riverside Mall, pigging out on Big Macs and large helpings of chips. May usually adds a chocolate milk shake just to complete the decadence. When we're in places like that she seems more relaxed with me. She chats more naturally when she's removed from personal things. It sounds like a contradiction but I understand it. In McDonalds she seems to revert to the young woman who came up to visit me in my flat before she did the Leaving Cert. She was ready to conquer the world then, as we all were at that age.

She never married. I feel sad about that. I think she'd have liked to even if she doesn't admit it. No more than Aunt Bernie it just didn't happen for her. I don't think she ever got over Nick despite putting a lot of men through her fingers after him. Nick stayed with Erica contrary to what I expected. I always thought he'd be another Edward. They had two children. They sent them to private schools. Why didn't it work with May? I don't know. Maybe it was simply a culture gap.

She went through a bit of depression during her 'change of life' but thankfully came out the other end. She confided a lot to Maureen during that time. I was no help to her at all. Any time I tried to advise her about anything she changed the subject.

Maureen didn't have children but she's had a happy life with Adrian. For a while I thought not having them might have caused problems in their relationship but now I think it probably helped it. So many relationships are destroyed today because of the tensions caused by a family. Then you have all these tug-of-love situations. And the 'McDonald's dads.'

My three worked out fine, thank God, but if I had a penny for every marriage I heard of that broke up due to people having children they couldn't cope with I'd be as rich as Bill Gates. I'm not saying that would have happened with Maureen and Adrian but they get on so well together it wasn't a major problem for them.

'You're lucky,' she said to me once, 'You had a happy marriage and children as well.' I suppose I am. I feel sad sometimes that they don't have cousins.

It's hard to believe Cillian and Siobhan are in their forties now. Little Cillian who came out of me after that mad dash to Holles Street in the taxi. And darling Siobhan, who was so quiet you'd hardly know she was there.

Eileen isn't far behind them. Poor troubled Eileen, who tries so hard to do the right thing all the time but keeps changing her mind about what that is.

Cillian married when he got into his thirties. His wife is from Kerry. Her name is Catriona. She's as sensible as he is. Her father is a guard and her mother a teacher. She's part of the family now. She rambles in when she feels like it, the way Aunt Bernie used to do in Midleton. From the moment I saw her I knew she was the right woman for him.

He met her when he was on holidays in Killarney one year. She was working as a receptionist in the hotel he was staying in. The fact that she had chalk in her blood, as they say, gave them an immediate connection. They have two lovely daughters, Ellen and Crona. Ellen is a horticulturist. Crona is studying politics at UCD.

I don't think either of them ever had a doubt but that they'd spend their lives together. It's great when things work out like that. She got a transfer to Jury's after they married. Like me she gave up her job after she had children. In her case, though, it was by choice. Later on she became a designer of jewellery.

Cillian is still teaching in Portmarnock. He loves his job but he had some rough years when he got classes that put him to the pin of his collar trying to get anything into their heads.

For a while he thought of leaving to teach abroad. It would have killed me if he did that. He went as far as getting a visa for Libya one year. He did a TEFL course to prepare himself for it. That stands for

573

Teaching English as a Foreign Language. He even did interviews for a school out there. He'd have made a fortune but what good is money when you're leaving everything you know? I kept saying that to him, hoping it would have an effect on him. Catriona didn't want him to go either. He hummed and hawed for ages before finally knocking the idea on the head. I was so relieved.

He's probably the one I'd have missed most if he emigrated. It would also have been a great loss to the teaching profession here. He still gives the job everything. They're lucky to have him. At present he's the Assistant Principal.

Some of the children are from broken homes. They don't have much of an interest in learning. It's hard to blame them. Cillian likes to tell a joke about a person who doesn't want to go to school. His mother wakes him up one morning and he says, 'Mammy, I'm not going to school today.' She says, 'You have to.' He says 'Why?' She says, 'Because you're the Principal.'

Maybe it's not so funny when you think about it. In our day it was the pupils who were afraid of the teachers. Now it seems to be the other way round. I heard of a school in New York recently where a six year old child brought a loaded gun into his classroom. Maybe it's only a matter of time until that happens here. Bob Geldof wrote a song once about a girl who shot her teacher because she didn't like Mondays. I was never too keen on Mondays but I never thought about going that far. Maybe Imelda Cawley did.

One of the perks of teaching, of course, is the long holidays. Cillian has been bringing Catriona and his kids to far-flung places for years now during the summer breaks. Ellen and Crona have probably forgotten more countries than I'll ever know of. He gets just as much out of them as they do. Maybe it helps to cure his itchy feet to sail off into the sky like that. It makes up for not getting to Libya.

He laughs at me when I talk of following the sun with Joe Walsh. That was what my generation did, at least if we were lucky enough to be able to afford it. Kevin and myself thought we were being exotic going to France and Switzerland. Modern transport has made it convenient for Cillian and Catriona to whizz halfway around the world without thinking twice. Most of the places they choose are hard for me to pronounce, never mind spell. They've offered to bring Kevin and me with them umpteen times but we don't take them up on it. We wouldn't have much time for hauling ourselves over to sun-kissed places like Singapore or Madagascar. What would we do there? Is a beach not a beach no matter where it's located? As Kevin said once when Cillian showed him a slide of Cyprus, 'If you closed your eyes you could be in Midleton.'

Siobhan left the beauty parlour years ago. It just wasn't for her in the long term. She promoted products for Estee Lauder for a while in Harrods before moving on.

'I don't want to spend my life at something so superficial,' she said. I saw her point but she didn't have any concrete plans. That concerned me.

'Are you eating well?' was always my first question to her any time I rang her. She used to laugh when I said that. It was the same question Mammy always used to ask me after I moved to Dublin. Maybe we all turn into our mothers.

She spent a few years in and around London, drifting from job to job without much thought. I always thought that would have been more like something Eileen would do. I worried myself sick about her during those years. She didn't tell me much about what she was doing.

The more I enquired, the more she drew herself away from me. I realise now that I was too interfering at that time. I used to ring her up at all hours of the day and night to find out if she was all right.

'either let her live her life or lose her,' Kevin said. It was good advice. She came back to me in her own time.

Of all my children she was the one I least expected to emigrate. She was so quiet growing up. I thought she'd marry a local lad and settle down to an old-fashioned job like teaching or the civil service. But life never works out like we plan.

When she told me she was going to England I almost had a fit.

'England?' I said.

She was amused at my reaction.

'You make it sound like the Hebrides,' she said.

I deserved that. It's different now to what it was like when Daddy was thinking of going over there. All I could think of then was grotty bedsits in Kilburn or Kentish Town.

'At the moment we're the Riverdance generation,' she said, 'It's all very trendy.'

She had her pick of jobs once she got installed but I still worried about the kind of life she might be living over there.

'Relax,' Kevin said to me, 'She isn't Eileen. She has a good head on her shoulders.'

'Maybe,' I said, 'but the people she gets in with mightn't have.'

It was only when she settled down to a steady job in insurance that I stopped fretting about her. She met Malcolm around that time. He was teaching dancing in Maida Vale. When they started getting serious with one another I got a new attack of nerves.

'Don't marry an Englishman whatever you do,' I said to her. But that's exactly what she did. It took me a long time to realise they weren't all like Edward Baldwin. I didn't meet Malcolm until a few days before the wedding but I could see he was mad about her.

They got married over here. I cried all the way through the wedding. That's something I've been good at over the years. I did the same at Cillian's one. 'Tears run in my family,' I like to say. (It's one of my few jokes). The icing on the cake was when they came back to live in Ireland fulltime a few years later. It made all the difference to me.

'I didn't have to twist his arm,' she said, 'After meeting the Tuohy clan he became more Irish than the Irish.' He owns his own restaurant in Kinsale now. Siobhan did the books for him for a while but then she got fed up of it. It was too time-consuming and figures always bored her. They're planning to open a second place in Temple Bar soon.

I often had a hankering she might go in for nursing. She reminded me so much of myself growing up. We bought her a nurse's kit one year but she didn't show much interest in it. She played with it for a while but then tossed it aside to go back to her dolls. I was disappointed but I had to accept it.

Children are like trees. Sometimes their branches go one way and sometimes the other. Every parent feels the urge to change their direction but they usually go back to the way they want to be whether you like it or not.

Eileen was always my big worry in the family. Maybe that'll never change, even if I live to be a hundred. Anytime I talk to her she acts as if she has her life sorted but I don't think that day will ever come. She has her nails bitten down to the quick and still struggles with weight and self-esteem issues.

She spent some years in childcare after she moved in with Jack but it was never going to be for her. She only stayed in it for the regular income. When she got into her twenties she left it. Afterwards she studied acupuncture. It was at night somewhere over in Stillorgan.

'Aren't you lucky you can do so many things at unsocial hours with Sam to take care of?' I said to her one day. She didn't see it like that. Maybe nobody in this generation can. They take creches and day centres for granted. They don't have to go cap in hand to people like Mrs Delahunt like I did after I left my fulltime job and was scrambling around for agency work to keep body and soul together.

Creches are wonderful developments but I wonder if the modern woman bonds with her children as much as the ones of my generation did. I know they give them 'quality time' in the evenings (to use yet another of those American expressions I hate) but in my opinion there's no substitute for 'quantity time' (to use an Irish one). Having said that, Eileen always devoted herself 110% to everything she turns her hand to. She never had a problem juggling jobs with motherhood. And Jack, to be fair to him, was there to look after Sam when she wasn't.

He was always a good househusband so they're well matched from that point of view. He never worked apart from a brief time in his thirties when he drove a forklift for a company that made car parts. He had an accident in his second week and got some kind of gratuity from them for his injuries. I gathered they were harmless enough from certain conversations I had with Eileen but Jack made capital of it.

It brought him from the dole queue to the disability one. To this day he says, 'The government supports me in the way I'm accustomed to.' Anytime I ever ask him about the idea of getting a

577

regular job he says the same thing to me: 'Mrs Mulvey, I'm allergic to work. It's against my religion.' How are you supposed to reply to a comment like that? 'Good man yourself'?

It would be great if Jack and Eileen shared more of their life with me but I gave up hoping for that long ago. Most of what I know about them I get from Cillian and Siobhan. I used to keep in phone contact with Eileen for years but I never got much back so I gave it up as a bad job.

The only times she rings me now is when she wants something. I occasionally hear things about her from her friends but obviously I'd prefer to get it from the horse's mouth. I'll never forget the night she fell in the door drunk when she was just sixteen. That was my first eye-opener about her. I always fear the anorexia will come back even though she's been good in that area for the past number of years, touch wood.

She went to Switzerland for her holidays last year. Jack organised it. Don't ask me where he got the money from. Sam, probably. He works in a merchant bank. Kevin didn't agree. He thought it came from a drug deal Jack was involved in. He said Jack knows some shady people, the kind who shoot up in places like Temple Bar or The Five Lamps on the other side of midnight. I didn't want to go there. Thinking these kind of thoughts did my head in.

'Switzerland is a bit different than Skerries,' I said to her when she told me she'd booked the trip, 'I'm sure you remember going there with us as a child.'

'Unfortunately I do,' she said, 'Lough Derg would have been more exciting.'

'You were happy enough when you were in it,' I said.

'I suppose so.'

'What's the big deal about Switzerland anyway?' I said, not wanting to let her away with it, 'The snow can't be any whiter there than it is in Ireland.'

'It isn't whiter,' she said, 'but there's more of it. If you hear of anywhere with ski slopes in Ireland maybe I'll stay here next year.'

In some ways Eileen is the most witty of my children. She amazes me with some of the things she comes out with. Anytime I tell her she has a quick mind she says, 'That's because yours is so slow.' (Don't ever expect your children to say nice things about you). She thinks I need to be hit over the head like a donkey sometimes to see the obvious. Maybe she's right.

She can size people up in a shot but that's not always an advantage. My first impressions of people are often wrong. At the same time I'm happy to change them if I have to. Eileen would never change her mind about anything. I worry about that.

At the end of the day I have to accept her for who she is, just like I do with the other two. They're all doing as well as can be expected in life and they all have their health. That's the main thing.

My world was more limited than theirs. I don't want to turn into the kind of parent who says things like 'Skerries was good enough for me so it should be good enough for you.' They can go wherever they like and what's wrong with that? I have to get rid of my idea that Ireland is everyone's cup of tea.

As for Midleton, if Eileen spent five nights in it in the last ten years it's as much. You could probably say the same for Cillian and Siobhan. Cillian used to bring Crona and Ellen to Trabolgan when they were younger. After they grew out of places like that they tended to want to go farther afield.

Midleton is still a lovely town but like most towns in Ireland these days it's lost something of the individuality it used to have. People don't talk to each other as much as they used to. Or maybe I think that because I don't know as many of them. Maybe I'm turning into a grouch.

In the centre there are a nest of one-way streets. They were brought in to make the traffic flow faster but in my opinion they only create more pollution. When I was growing up it was an event to see a car. Now you have to wait half the day to cross the street unless it's pedestrianised.

How do you stop traffic jams? It would be like trying to hold the tide back. And then you have all these trucks belching smoke out at you. I know that happens everywhere but are one-way streets the answer? I have this vision of a committee of town planners twiddling their thumbs as they come up with these new-fangled ideas.

Occasionally a Topaz goes up, or a Tesco, and a few more locals get employed to help us forget the bad old days when so many people were out of work. Unfortunately, such developments – if they can be called that – mean we're becoming just like every other town in Ireland. The people seem to reflect that too. A lot of them speak in terms they've picked up from TV shows and the radio. When I listen to them I feel I might as well be in Dublin.

Midleton is still a beautiful town but in many ways it's like a ghost town to me now, at least if I walk through it late at night. Even though we're told Ireland is on the up and up again, the boom hasn't trickled down there except in small doses.

There are boarded-up houses on McSweeney Terrace. There's a joke about the pub down the road that business is so bad, the bouncer was arrested for vagrancy. That's not really true because a lot of the time it's really buzzing, especially at the weekends. Early on in the week nobody seems to have any money.

The new drink-drive laws have killed off a lot of the pub trade. I know these used to be too lax in the old days but sometimes I think we've gone to the other extreme with our zero tolerance. Is one drink too many? From my experience most fatalities occur when people are way over the limit, or driving at crazy speeds, not because they've had one drink. But you can't express these kinds of opinions today in our politically correct age. You'd be shot.

Around me I see shops that had to close down because of the recession. There are 'House For Sale' signs everywhere. Sometimes I feel the town is dying before my eyes - and a little bit of me with it. Why do I keep going back there? To tidy the flowers on Mammy and Daddy's graves? To re-ignite memories of the family home?

May has been in it for so many years now I'd be better off forgetting the way it used to be instead of pretending it means any more to me than the stones that created it. Visiting its rooms can only hurt me considering the people who made them meaningful for me aren't in them anymore.

I've changed myself too. Am I really the girl who played Blind Man's Buff at the Clonmult Monument? Who climbed Mr McDermott's wall to the tree house Daddy built for us? Who brought Daddy lettuce sandwiches to broken-down tenements on fine days? Am I the girl who thought she knew it all when she graduated from the Mater, as if memorising a few facts about our bodies entitled me to think I could heal the health of the country?

Getting first in m exams was a big thrill but it came with a price. In a sense it cost me my friendship with Cáit and Bridget. I think I could count on the fingers of one hand the number of times I talked with them since I got married. I brooded about that for a long time but then I forgot about it. Cáit rang me now and again and I have to say she was always herself despite the gaps between the calls. She'd always start them the same way, 'How's tricks? Anything new?' as if we'd spoken the day before. Like a lot of people who were wild in their young days she turned out to be a paragon of sense with her kinesiologist husband.

On one of the phone calls she apologised to me for the fact that she hadn't kept in touch with me more.

'I hope you didn't think I was out with you,' she said.

'Not at all,' I said, though I had.

'I went through a bad time when I came down to Birr first,' she told me, 'It was so quiet I nearly went off my trolley.'

I told her not to worry, that I felt a bit hurt at the time but I got over it.

'Was there any other reason you didn't ring me more?' I asked her then. She paused for a few seconds before answering me.

'It would have upset me too much to think about the world I'd left behind,' she said.

When she put it like that I started to see her in a different light. I'd been so immersed in my loneliness I didn't stop to think that other people could be lonely too. In some ways she probably took leaving Room 19 worse than me. Birr was her Midleton. She loved it but it turned into a kind of trap when it became her fulltime residence.

I asked her about Bridget then. Had she her reasons for avoiding me?

'Bridget went through a bad time in Maynooth,' she said, 'She knew nobody down there. It was worse for her than Birr was for me. In fact she even suffered from depression for a while.'

Bridget was the last person in the world I could ever have imagined being depressed. She didn't stay long in Maynooth, Cáit told me. She met a farmer one night at The Hitching Post in Leixlip

581

and fell head over heels for him. She'd gone there to see Johnny McEvoy, a singer she liked. They got serious with one another quickly. Before she knew it he'd proposed to her. He was living in Stepaside at the time. They bought a house there after they married. She had three children in as many years and was very fulfilled with that.

'Why didn't she ring me now and again?' I said.

'I think she was ashamed to,' she said, 'Too many years had elapsed.'

I said that was a pity. I wouldn't have thought any less of her even if there was a twenty year gap between the calls.

'There's something else I have to tell you about Bridget,' she said then. I didn't know what was coming.

'I wasn't going to mention this but one of her daughters died from epidermolysis bullosa.'

I nearly dropped the phone when she said that. I'd come across the condition in books I read but I never met anyone who had it. I knew it as The Butterfly Disease. Some people called it that because if you had it your skin was as sensitive as a butterfly's wings.

Poor Bridget, I thought. And her poor daughter. I remembered Eileen when she had the chicken pox. Obviously it was a million times worse than that.

'Oh my God, Cáit,' I said, 'I'm in total shock. Why didn't you tell me before now? Or why didn't Bridget tell me?'

'We didn't want to upset you. We heard you were going through some tough times with Eileen.'

'That's ridiculous, Cáit. I'm insulted that you thought I'd be so wrapped up in my own problems that I wouldn't have time for anyone else's.'

'I'm sorry. I didn't mean it like that. Bridget wasn't up to talking anyway, even to me. You have no idea what it did to her.'

'I can imagine.'

'It caused some problems in her marriage as well. To be honest, I don't like talking about it. It was so many years ago.'

'I can understand that but I'm still glad you told me.'

'I was often on the point of ringing you. I picked up the phone a few times but put it down again. What was the point of burdening you with it when there was nothing you could do? There was nothing any of us could do.'

'What are friends for if you can't share your problems with them?'

'Some problems are nearly too bad to share.'

'What was the girl's name?'

'Denise.'

'How long did she live?'

'Only till she was seven, God love her. It was a blessed release really. The slightest thing made her break out in blisters, even the clothes she was wearing. She had no quality of life. That was the only consolation for Bridget when she died.'

'How is she now?'

'She says not a day passes without her thinking of her. The two others keep her going. They're girls as well.'

'How is her husband?'

'He couldn't take it after Denise died. I think he might have left Bridget for a while. But he came back. They're much better now.'

'If anything like that ever happens again,' I said, 'Please bring me in on it.'

'I will, but I hope it doesn't.'

'Needless to say I do too. To any of us.'

After that phone call I resolved never to judge anyone again. Everyone had their reasons for things. How could Bridget and Cáit have put Eileen into the same barrow as Denise? No matter how many problems I had with her at least she was still alive.

In a strange way the phone call with Cáit helped me. I bawled after I put down the receiver but in the following days I realised I'd been unfair to the two girls. How many times do we think people have turned off us only to realise something totally different is behind their actions? That's why you can never say you know it all no matter what age you are. Every day is a learning experience of some sort.

I had my 75th birthday recently. Everyone was at it – Maureen and Adrian, Cillian and Catriona, Siobhan and Malcolm, Eileen and Jack. Ellen and Crona came as well. I love both of them to bits. Their childhood was so different to mine or to my children's. It was one of

Tae Kwon Do and Netflix and Utube and satnav and zumba dancing and theme parks and bouncy castles and trips to Euro Disney.

I wouldn't like to be raising children today. We used to let ours play in the street even when it was dark. If you did that now you'd be worried about never seeing them again.

Sam was in Kuwait but he sent me a message on Eileen's phone. May couldn't make it - what else is new – but she sent a bouquet of flowers. There was no note but I appreciated the gesture. It was as close to an olive branch as I was ever going to get.

Maureen and Adrian got me a lovely Father and Son lamp. The children clubbed together for an elaborate recliner chair. It had buttons you could press for whatever angle you wanted it to be at.

'Adrian should have bought this for me,' I said as I sat into it, 'I feel like I'm in a dentist's chair.'

'We were going to get you another trip to Paris,' Cillian said, 'but you mightn't have been up to it.'

'That's for sure,' Kevin said, 'If we can make it down to the Sheaf of Wheat these days we're doing well.'

'We won't have to go anywhere now,' I said, 'I'll just spend all day reclining.'

'Who'll make the dinner?' Kevin said. I told him he was old enough now to know where the cooker was.

Crona and Ellen came over to me. Crona works in the IT sector. She spends a half hour on a treadmill every morning and then drives to work. Her job is ten minutes away. I keep telling her she should get rid of the treadmill and walk to work.

When I looked at Ellen I did a double take. She had piercings all over her face – her ears, her lips, even her tongue.

'How do you speak with those things in there?' I asked her.

She had a tattoo of a butterfly on one of her shoulders as well. All her nails were painted different colours.

'You must be going to join a circus or something,' I said.

'Everyone I know looks like me,' she said. That's the problem with the modern world, I thought, but I said nothing.

Crona was dressed in a pair of cut-off jeans. She said she paid a fortune for them. I told her I'd have chopped them up for nothing for her if she asked me. She said she had a thong on under them. I'd like

584

to see thongs outlawed. I can't understand how anyone would want to wear them. Are young people today masochists?

'You should see Crona's boyfriend,' Ellen said, 'He goes around the place with his shirt hanging out. It's all the rage nowadays.'

I'd seen a few of those boyos around Coolock. It never ceased to amaze me what people did for fashion. If you had your shirt out in Midleton when I was growing up you'd have been laughed out of the place. If you went around with holes in your trousers people would have started throwing money at you from pity.

But I suppose we wore ridiculous things too. I remember a pair of flared trousers I had in the seventies. I thought I was the cheese in them. They must have had about twenty colours on them, all sewed in together in squares like a tablecloth. When I think about them now I wonder why I wasn't locked up. I looked like Bobo the Clown.

Ellen wanted to buy me something called an Ipad for my birthday.

'What's that?' I said, 'Is it something that goes over your eye?' Everyone laughed when I said that.

'No,' she said, 'You use it to store all your things.'

I said I had a chest of drawers for storage purposes. That caused more laughter. I didn't mind. I was never technological and never would be. Kevin told me it was one of those new-fangled things that did everything but make the dinner. 'Give them time,' I said.

The presents were great but seeing everyone together was even better. Crona kept taking photographs as if I was a Hollywood star. Then the cake came out. Siobhan baked it. 'Happy Birthday to Our Wonderful Mother' was daubed on it in bright red icing. That reduced me to a blubbering wreck. Kevin started singing 'For She's a Jolly Good Fellow' and everyone joined in. They wanted me to give a speech but I couldn't. I was lost for words.

I managed to blow out all the candles. There weren't quite 75 but there were a good few. 'That's my exercise for the week,' I said afterwards,

I asked anyone if they'd like me to make them a cup of tea.

'You're under orders not to move for the evening,' Crona said.

585

She wanted something called a skinny latte for herself. I wouldn't have known what that was if it bit me on the nose. I'd heard about them but I couldn't have made one for the life of me.

She said she usually had them in a place called Insomnia. Apparently that was a restaurant. How could you call a restaurant Insomnia? Did people not want to relax in places like that? One of the things that put me off coffee was the fact that it kept me awake if I drank it late at night. Maybe today's children liked being awake all night, at least if my theory about them being masochists was right.

'What are you going to have with it?' I asked her.

'Nothing,' she said, 'I'm watching my figure.'

'Is that why you wanted a "skinny" latte?'

'Very funny.'

'There's not a pick on you,' I said.

'You must be joking,' she said, pulling up her blouse, 'Look at my inch pinch.'

It was more like a millimetre pinch. I hoped she wouldn't end up like Eileen. Of course I couldn't say that to her. Why was it that people were so extreme? In my day everyone seemed to have a normal weight. Now people seemed to be either obese or anorexic. There was no in-between. But there was no point getting worked up about it. The young would always have their way. I was probably like that when I was their age too. I decided to stop worrying about things and just enjoy the party.

We all had wine. Then we sang a few more songs. I got tired coming up to ten o'clock. God be with the days I could have gone on past midnight.

'We'll go, Granny,' Crona said.

I hated being called Granny. Grannies were what other people were. Inside myself I still felt ten. But my body didn't agree with me.

There was a time I would have hung on to them but I was no company when the tiredness hit me. I said reluctantly to Crona, 'All right, I won't hold you. The night is probably only beginning for some of you.'

After that they all started to move. 'Go out quickly, ' I said, 'or I'll get emotional.' When they were gone I had a nightcap with Kevin in my recliner in front of a blazing fire. It was the perfect end to a perfect day.

For a week afterwards it was all I could think of. I kept running it through in my mind like a film. I was 'happy out' as they say down home.

Though I made the joke about not being fit, I'm not too bad in that department. I'm a bit more spread around the middle now than I used to be but I keep moving as much as I can. Overall I enjoy good health. I get some twinges in the hinges of course but who doesn't at my age? The ears aren't the best, especially the left one, and my eyes aren't what they used to be, but everyone has something. As long as I can stay out of hospital I'm happy. (Nurses make very bad patients, as you know).

Kevin feels the same. He has a list of complaints as long as your arm but he doesn't go on about them. Who'd listen anyway? Everyone has too many problems of their own. You'd only depress them if you started talking about yourself. Maybe they'd run away from you.

I'm thankful my lungs have held out considering the battering I gave them with the fags over the years. I'm sure they feel like crying out for mercy sometimes after a half century of nicotine going into them. St. Therese must be looking after me.

I try to keep all my medical appointments. Beaumont is the hospital I go to now. I suppose it isn't any worse than the rest of them. The last time I was up there they gave me the all-clear. My examination consisted of asking me how I was, nothing else – despite the fact that my file was about as big as The Book of Kells. I felt I could have had cancer, muscular dystrophy and multiple sclerosis and they wouldn't have noticed.

'We don't need to see you again until January 23$^{rd}$, 2020,' the doctor said after my 'examination.' He was Indian. He looked about twelve.

'Thanks a lot,' I said, 'I hope I'm not inconveniencing you.'

He smiled at me as he opened the door to let me out. He didn't even realise I was being sarcastic.

'Do you realise that's eighteen months away?' I said.

'I do,' he said, 'Unfortunately that's the way things are here now. Some people have to wait much longer.'

'I'll make a note to set the alarm as soon as I go home,' I told him, 'I wouldn't want to sleep it out.'

A part of me was tempted to write a letter of complaint but thenI thought: what good would it do? It's not anyone's fault; it's just the way things are. It would be nice to be back in the sixties when we had all the time in the world to give to patients but those days will never come again and we can't do anything about that. We just have to put up with it.

I feel my life has gone by me in a flash. The years are stolen from under our noses and that's probably why we should never complain about being bored. We take them for granted and then they're gone and we feel old overnight. We pine for even a piece of them to be given back to us but that's not possible. They've drifted away from us like feathers, like congealed snow.

As I write this I'm looking at the photograph of myself and Kevin that was taken by the street photographer on that day years ago when we came out of The Luna restaurant arm in arm. It's barely held together by sellotape but we're still the same people we were then, even if we're hardly recognizable from the pair that rambled up O'Connell Street with hardly a care in the world. People don't keep photographs much nowadays because of camera phones but I'll treasure that one forever.

I don't like camera phones or any of the other developments of technology. It bothers me that people have their noses stuck in them every time I stand beside them at a bus stop or in a dentist's surgery. Crona believes civilisation as we know it would end if she had to do without her one. What ever happened to real communication?

Neither do I own a computer, nor read articles about J Lo or Bill Gates or whether Brad Pitt is going to get back with Jennifer Aniston or what the Kardashians are up to. I have enough on my plate trying to deal with an ingrown toenail, or the next ESB bill.

Crona and Ellen want me to go on Facebook. I said I don't want my face on any book. They're both on it. So are all their friends. I gather it's some kind of news service where every time you blow your nose you tell half the world about it. Utube is almost as bad.

588

Sometimes Kevin shows me some things on it. He has a laptop computer. It might be something about a child from somewhere like Oklahoma doing somersaults on his skateboard. I know I'm supposed to get highly excited but I can't. We did things like that when we were growing up but we didn't feel we had to tell the world about them.

Thanks but no thanks. What's the point? I'd prefer to send a letter to someone if I have any news. You can't beat the plop of an envelope coming in your door. That's something the modern generation miss out on. They're too busy writing emails and sending selfies.

I'm regarded as an old fossil when I say things like that. So be it. Take me out and shoot me if you want. I refuse to cave in to technology. Why should I? I've survived long enough without it. Maybe one of these days the whole system will overload itself. If it did I wouldn't be sorry. We could go back to the simple way things used to be. We could get carrier pigeons to send our communications to one another like in the old days. Wouldn't that be romantic? Maybe I'll start a campaign: 'Death to Instagram! A curse on Skype and Spotify! Ban all computers! Make them illegal!'

I don't know how I've got to be where I am. Somehow I've survived the whips and scorns of time. My children grew up without any major mishaps and made lives for themselves. I don't claim credit for that. I always tried to do my best for them but I'm not naive enough to think I didn't make many mistakes along the way.

I'm well aware of the fact that I spoiled Cillian, for instance. That was probably because I had to wait so long for him to arrive. I enjoyed doing that but it wasn't fair to him. It probably made life harder for him as an adult. I spoiled Siobhan too but I don't think it affected her as much. In many ways I think Siobhan raised herself. She would probably have turned out the same if her parents were Mother Teresa as Jack the Ripper. As for Eileen, I fought with her until neither of us could throw punches anymore and maybe that was all right too. Maybe it was what she needed and what I needed. We're friends now, having downed our weapons, though Kevin says a truce for Eileen simply means she's re-loading her rifle. (Another May? God forbid!)

589

Kevin has been my rock all through my life. Parenting has been a learning curve for him as much as me. He stayed in the background a lot of the time, just as he was a backseat driver in those early days in the Austin before he got behind the wheel himself and didn't have to suffer my kamikaze behaviour on all those roundabouts that led to Cork.

People say marriage is easy if you love the man you're married to but that isn't always the case. The more you love someone the more you have to lose if something goes wrong with that love. None of us can be our best selves all the time and I had my ups and downs with him over the years.

The thing about Kevin and me was that we could deal with the big situations well enough. We could handle the crises that split other couples apart. What dragged us down were the little things, the arguments about who forgot to put the bins out or who should have been in the house when they should have been out or out when they should have been in, all those trivial things that happen in everyone's lives. They usually blew over the next morning but sometimes they didn't. I was blessed that he put up with me when I threw wobblies over things that were going wrong in my life.

It's not as if everything worked out for him either. He was disappointed in the way they treated him in Clery's, for instance, especially in his final years. And he didn't succeed in making Cillian into the next George Best. But then neither did George Best himself succeed in that ambition with his own son so that's nothing unusual. Didn't he become a model or something? Kevin would have lost his reason if Cillian went into that line of business.

I think he still misses his father a lot. He still won't talk to me about things like that. Men never do. That's probably why they have more psychological problems than us women. We yap them all out of ourselves. Maybe we drive the men in our lives into mental homes in the process. That's beside the point.

If you asked me if I was a particularly good wife I'd have to say: I don't know. Did I overcome life's pitfalls, as Sister Serafina predicted I would the day after I did the Leaving Cert? I don't know that either.

I was in my own little world a lot of the time. After I left nursing fulltime I didn't earn much. If it wasn't for the money Kevin was earning I couldn't have done it. Did I successfully juggle the pincer-jaws of work and home? Maybe not so well. Some women are brilliant at multi-tasking but when I was nursing I always felt I was that much less of a wife when I was doing it. And that much less of a mother as well.

Alongside the photograph of Kevin and me sauntering up O'Connell Street I have ones of the children. I like to put them in a collage from their different ages, leaping through the decades like a film in fast motion. One day they were crawling around the floor as infants. The next they were teenagers doing their own thing. Then they were married or living together and I had to come to terms with that.

Did I give them the right guidance when they needed it? Did I get to know them as much as I should have? Some of their life choices alienated me from them or them from me but I don't think anything could have been done about that. We all have to play the hand we're dealt in life even if its aces and eights.

As they've got older I think they have more in common with each other than they have with me. I was always the one who told them to be careful, to be home early, to avoid so-and-so because they weren't good enough for them. I was Mrs-Don't-Do-Anything-Stupid, the fusspot May made fun of and still occasionally does. It must have been boring for them hearing me drone on with my advice. But then what mother doesn't do that?

I wouldn't like to be young again. There are too many temptations out there, too many tripwires. Every day of my life I read about people being raped or beaten or murdered. I read about people destroying their lives through drink or drugs or getting involved with the wrong people.

Why is so much modern life characterised by tragedy? Is it because of prosperity? The decline of religion? The technological revolution? Whatever the reason, there seems to be a different breed of person out there than the ones I grew up with, a breed that's stronger in some ways and more fragile in others.

591

I wonder if I'd have done anything different in my life if I had it to live over again. People say 'Don't look back,' but sometimes you have to. My childhood was magical and that's why I keep trying to recreate it in my mind, and maybe in my children. My adult years were tough, especially after leaving Midleton, but no tougher than for anyone else. I missed home too much and that came against me. It stopped me from throwing myself into things the way I should have. Kevin always noticed that.

'Only half of you is here,' he'd say to me when I was in one of my daydreams, even during our early years together. I haven't gone into too many of these recently. He's had all of me for many years now, God help him.

We're like chalk and cheese in our personalities and maybe that's why we've lasted. I get fidgety about things whereas he's so laidback he's horizontal. I have to take a sleeping pill some nights when my thoughts are racing but he wouldn't take a pill to save his life.

I envy him his relaxed personality. When I say that to him he says, 'I have my own form of nerves.' I say, 'If you have, you keep them well hidden.'

He gives out to me when I rant on about how the world has changed so much since we were young. He's had to deal with that too but he doesn't go on about it.

I say it's not as mannerly as it was when I was a child, that it's not as respectful, that it's not as caring. And he says, 'So what? Deal with it.'

I've tried my best to do that. I've stopped expecting it to be. That's probably a step in the right direction. I don't expect anyone to hold a door open for me when I'm in town, for instance, or to give me their seat on a bus.

When I go into shops these days I see the workers chatting to one another about where they were the previous night instead of stopping to serve me. I don't bother myself too much about things like that anymore. They're trivial when you consider the major problems of the world – war, poverty, disease, homelessness, lack of love.

The fact that Kevin and myself are still together is the only thing that matters. A lot of our friends aren't. I don't feel superior about that, I just feel lucky. Marriages don't break up because people are bad. They break up because the wrong couple went up the aisle together or something happened to them after they did.

I would have been against divorce as a young girl in the same way as Mammy and Daddy were, imagining it to be an import from 'pagan England,' but I've changed in that. I realise now that my thinking was naïve. I've heard too many stories of women being beaten up by their husbands or being betrayed by them and not being able to do anything about it.

I witnessed many victims of spousal abuse in my Mater days. Maybe I wasn't as sympathetic to them as I should have been. Despite what Mammy and Daddy might have thought, it was important for divorce to be introduced in Ireland. They heard stories of bad marriages in Midleton when they were young too. The thinking then was that you made your bed and you had to lie on it. That was what priests told you in Confession. It was even what some doctors told you if you came into them with scars on your face.

Roddy Doyle wrote a book once called *The Woman Who Walked Into Doors*. That was what you had to pretend happened to you in old Ireland if you were beaten up by your husband: you walked into doors. I heard of a doctor who used to beat his wife up and then put medical make-up on her so she could go to work without showing evidence of the bruising.

No matter where you go you get good people and bad people. It's as simple as that. It's a myth to say the Irish are the nicest people in the world. It takes all sorts. But I'm still glad I was born here.

Time has brought good and bad changes to our country. I've lived through the doldrum years when Daddy couldn't get work and also during the boom when everyone was flocking here from other countries and talking about Ireland as the greatest country in the world.

Afterwards we came crashing down. We're crawling out of the recession again as I write these pages but who's to say we won't fall again? Who's to say we won't go mad spending like we did the last time? Will we take off to foreign places to scout for snazzy apartments? Will we spend the last of our money in the mistaken hope that tomorrow we'll be earning even more?

What goes up has to come down. You don't have to be a genius to see that. It's just gravity. We're a wealthy economy now but it won't always be that way. We need to learn from the mistakes of the past. Two of my children managed to get mortgages because they bought their houses during the boom, but many of their friends didn't, or else they had them taken away from them by the banks when they fell into negative equity.

That's a fact of life nowadays. It's led to the problem of homeless people we see on our streets every day, a problem the government has mostly turned a blind eye to. I throw a few pennies to them to ease my conscience but what good is that going to do? Pay for their next cup of coffee? Or their next bottle of wine?

A bigger problem is our medical system. We've had a First World economy in Ireland for many years now but a Third World health service. Charlie McGreevy used to say money pumped into medicine disappeared down a black hole. That was a cop-out. Becoming Minister for Health was often a poisoned chalice for politicians. Look what happened to Mary Harney. She had some good ideas but the job proved too much for her at the end of the day.

The trolley crisis was bad in her time but it's a farce now. So are the waiting lists for life-saving operations. I saw many people coming into the Mater in agony over the years and being refused surgery simply because they didn't have the proper cover for it. I saw many people howling in pain as they waited for heart or lung operations. I knew many of them would die before they got them because they couldn't afford the cost.

Is there any answer to this state of affairs? Barack Obama tried his best to solve it in America. Donald Trump tells us he's going to throw Obama's ideas out. Don't get me going on Trump. What else would you expect from a man who made money his God?

Don't get me going on Simon Harris either. I voted No in the abortion referendum. That made me unpopular with a lot of people I knew but I couldn't bring myself to be a part of the abortion culture. I thought there had to be a better way to deal with rape and incest or fatal foetal abnormalities. Maybe that's naïve of me. People tell me I betrayed women by my vote but I didn't see it like that. In the week of the vote I wore a badge that said 'Love Both' – the mother *and* the child.

Eileen tells me I'm behind the times when I talk like that. She says abortion is 'in' in most countries. I say back to her, 'Does that make it right?'

Cillian shares my view. This makes him a focus of fun for some of his liberal friends. Siobhan doesn't know what to think. She sees both sides of the debate. She says Ireland was hypocritical to let so many women take the boat for Holyhead over the years. On the other hand, she thought it was disgraceful to see them dancing around O'Connell Street on the night the 'Yes' vote was carried.

'They're celebrating murder,' Kevin said. I thought that too. Eileen didn't. She said she'd be embarrassed if any of her friends met me because of the views I held.

So be it. Maybe I wouldn't like her friends anyway. How could you be friendly with a person who put no value on a human life?

The latest I hear is that 99% of Down Syndrome children are being aborted in some countries in Europe today. Are we approaching an era where Hitler's master race idea is making a comeback? According to an article I read recently we'll soon be able to predict any ailments our children are going to suffer from as soon as they're born.

Imagine if I said I didn't want Eileen because I knew she was going to be anorexic? Or that she was going to self-harm? I heard of a woman the other day who wanted her child aborted because she heard it was going to be a girl and she wanted a boy. Will we get to a time where someone says they want a child aborted because they have the wrong colour eyes? Or a cleft palate? Sometimes I think we're headed that way.

The nurses went on strike this year. It was high time they did. We're losing too many of them to foreign shores. A rising tide should lift all boats but that didn't happen when our economy picked up. Nurses are always the forgotten ones, aren't they? People just say they're saints and then forget about them. Well I've got news for you. Saints have to eat too.

How is a trainee nurse going to be able to survive on the exorbitant rents landlords are charging today? They've always been out of step with the rest of the world. The first time I realised that was when I was thinking of emigrating, the time Maureen stopped me. I couldn't believe the kind of money they were getting in Canada and Australia. Something has to be done. For too long we've been the Cinderellas of the medical profession. A woman typing a letter for a bureaucrat gets more today for one assisting at a life-saving operation in Intensive Care. There has to be something wrong there. How important is life? Is it more important than the next fast car? The next fast airplane? Are we going everywhere too fast in the world today but not really getting anywhere?

To be honest I don't know. Sometimes you can ask too many questions. From the way I'm going on you might think I stay awake at night worrying about things like that. In actual fact I don't. Like most people, I just fumble my way from day to day. 'Your health and enough is all you need,' was the way Mammy put it. (She meant enough money).

I see a lot of suffering around me and I think: That could be me. That's why I try to see the glass half full in life. I didn't think I'd be able to cope when Mammy and Daddy died but somehow you do. Maybe it's Saint Therese looking after me.

Where are they now? Will I ever see them again? I believe I will but many people from my generation don't. They have more hope than faith. Many of the young generation don't have either.

It's easier to think about the past than the future. At least that's factual. It happened. As I get older I find the far away days are more real to me than the ones just gone. I remember my childhood more than my teenage years and my teenage years more than my adult ones – if I ever became an adult. I remember conversations that took place decades ago more than where I left my car keys yesterday. Maybe everyone is like that. We hold onto the things that are important to us and forget the rest.

Going outside the family circle I think of Room 19. I think of being late for work on that first day in the Mater and Cáit and Bridget and Irene and Veronica and Cora and Hilary and so many others I've forgotten. I think of seeing the Beatles, of getting togged out with Mammy for Maureen's wedding, of dancing with the man who had a hernia on the hospital ward that Christmas Day when we all felt like an extended family.

Where's Oisín, the lad who used my medicine trolley as a go-kart after falling down the stairs? He wasn't much younger than me when I nursed him. Is he still playing the rascal or has he cooled down? He could be bungi-jumping in Mexico or in a nursing home in Rathfarnham. That's the richness of life, and its sadness.

Where's Edward? Or Kate and Nick? Or even Joanne Wylie? I feel only pity for her now. I wouldn't want to see her again for all the tea in China but the anger I used to feel towards her is gone. Anyone who spends as much time as she did trying to make another person unhappy must be deeply unhappy within themselves.

Whatever happened to Sister Serafina? Or Sister Agnes? I used to give out about Cáit and Bridget going on with their lives without me but I did it too with many others who might like to have been a part of mine.

I didn't look up Mr Carmody, for instance, the man who smoothed my path into my new life by giving me some very kind advice that first night in Dublin. He'd just lost his wife but I never enquired as to how he got through the following years. The fact that he lived so close to where I worked makes that fact even more unforgiveable.

'Don't beat yourself up for what you didn't do,' Kevin tells me, 'Just try to do things better tomorrow.' He's right, of course, but that's easier said than done Very few of us can forget the things we did wrong. If we do, they come back to haunt us.

As we get older our orbits narrow. We communicate more with our families and friends than anyone else. They're our 'Go to' people, the ones we can ring up in the middle of the night when nothing appears to have any meaning and we're crying out for someone to comfort us. The others, meanwhile, get lost.

Maybe I shouldn't ramble so much. That's something old people are famous for. All I want to say is that I can't believe the life I've led or the things I've done. I may not have assisted at any heart transplants with Christian Barnard or found a cure for cancer but in my own tinpot way I made my mark on life. To me that's enough.

If you told me fifty years ago I was going to have all the experiences I've had and meet all the people I've met I'd have told you to send for the men in the white coats.

Twenty minutes ago I did my Leaving Cert. Ten minutes ago I met Kevin. Five minutes ago I had my three children. That's how it seems to me, how it will always seem.

Tonight I sit in our glasshouse and look out at the night throwing shadows onto the trees in the garden. I think back to an average night in our Midleton kitchen. I see the condensation coming down the wallpaper.

Mammy is ironing May's gymslip on the drop-leaf table pulled out to its full size. She has her tongue out like she always has when she's trying to concentrate on something. Daddy is trying to scrub the cement from his fingers at the sink. Buddy Holly is singing 'That'll Be the Day' on our radio, the one with the crackle on it because we always forget to buy new batteries. May is crying because it's too loud. Maureen is tapping her feet to it. She's doing her homework at the table. One of its legs is shorter than the other three. It's shaking so much I'm worried she's going to blot her copybook

I think of the fridge with its wonky door, of the formica table with the chipped edge and the leg that didn't balance, of Mammy making toast by putting a piece of bread onto a fork and holding it in front of the fire.

I remember her ironing my gymfrock and telling me to button my coat as I walked down the road to the convent and making me wash my hair on Saturday nights when I didn't feel like it. I remember her preparing the Sunday peas and washing my clothes at the sink with Rinso and giving me Syrup of Figs and Milk of Magnesia when I was sick and how I had such a horror of such things.

I remember reading *Bunty* and *Judy* after school and playing Hide-and-Seek games on Ballynamona beach and sitting on Aunt Bernie's knee in Daddy's car and leaving Midleton for Dublin on the train and my first kiss with Kevin in the Regent Cinema and being proposed to by him in Paris and marrying him and getting pregnant by him and coming home from Holles Street that first day with Cillian and crying with joy because he was mine and nobody could take him away from me.

I want to go back to all those times now and yet I don't want to. They're not there anymore.

We're not the people we were. Some of us have died. Others have emigrated or disappeared into the wilderness

Many nights I find myself crying for no reason. Kevin asks me what's wrong and I say, 'I wish I knew.' He never presses it because he understands me.

Sometimes I think of Tom, the car dealer I had that little flirtation with in Skerries. I wonder what happened to him afterwards. Did he find someone else or is he still on his own? I know now that he meant nothing to me, that I fell into his arms for no better reason than that I was tired from all the years of mothering. I'm not proud of that but I don't regret it either. Maybe we all need to go a bit mad every now and then.

The sky is slate-grey tonight as I look out at the trees in the park across the road. Soon it will be spring. The days will be getting longer. My New Year resolution is to stop complaining about things. It does no good and it only makes you feel worse in the end. Maybe I should stop remembering too. Too much of it is unhealthy.

That's why I'm going to stop writing now. But before I do I want to share a little story with you. It concerns events that happened a long time ago but which had a big effect on me for reasons you'll see.

# An Unexpected Visitor

A couple of months ago I had a visitor to the house, a middle-aged woman with an English accent. As soon as I saw her I thought I recognised her from somewhere.

'Would you mind if I invited myself in?' she said when I answered the door. I was surprised at this but of course I agreed. She came into the living-room.

'I'm sorry if I appear rude,' she said, 'You must think I'm terrible barging in on you like this.'

'Not at all,' I muttered, feeling a bit flummoxed.

'My name is Bernadette,' she said, 'You're very good to give me your time.'

We shook hands. I took her coat and told her to sit down. She asked me a few questions about myself and listened intently as I answered them.

It turned out she'd only been in Ireland a few days. She'd come over with her husband. They were staying in a hotel in Cork. She'd got the train to Midleton. She loved Ireland, she told me. It was her first time here but she hoped it wouldn't be her last.

'Now tell me about yourself,' she said then. That made me even more perplexed. I prattled on about Kevin and the children for a few minutes. As I was talking she kept nodding her head at me and smiling. I paused after each few sentences to give her a chance to talk. When I'd told her as much as I could think of – much more than I normally would to a stranger – I said to her, 'Can I ask you why you've come here? Why is my life of such interest to you?'

At this she took a deep breath, making me wonder what was coming next.

'Though I've spent my life in England,' she said, 'I have Irish roots. I've come over to explore them.'

Now I was really confused.

'And you think I can help you?'

'Yes.'

She paused again as if she was uncertain how to continue. When she started to speak this time I saw her eyes welling up.

'I'm sorry,' she said, 'This is difficult for me.'

'Could I get you something?' I said, 'Would you like a cup of tea?'

'That would be lovely,' she said.

I went out to the kitchen and put the kettle on. All sorts of thoughts were going through my mind. Why had she chosen me to come to? Was I involved in her past in some way?

When I brought in the tray she seemed calmer.

'You'll have to forgive me for being so pushy,' she said, 'but I want to tell you about myself. I'm an adopted child. I came across your name in some letters recently. They belonged to my adoptive mother. She died recently. According to the letters my birth mother was from Midleton.'

I nearly died when she said that. I was rooted to the spot. My heart was going a mile an hour.

I dropped the tray. The cups shattered all over the floor.

'Oh my God,' she said, 'I've startled you. I'm so sorry. I should have waited until you sat down.'

'Don't worry,' I said.

I bent down to pick the cups up but the strength was gone from my hands. She stood up to help me but I told her to leave them. I sat down with my knees shaking.

'Aunt Bernie,' I said.

She came over and sat down beside me.

'I would have come sooner,' she said, 'if I knew the circumstances of my birth. I didn't find out until after Mum's funeral.'

I was still in shock. I wanted to say something to her but my tongue clung to the roof of my mouth. My heart was still heaving. I tried to stand up but I couldn't.

'Let me pick up the cups,' she said.

'No,' I said, 'I'll do it.'

I got a dustpan and scooped the broken bits of porcelain into it. I put them into the bin and came back to her.

I scanned her face for clues, clues as to what kind of a person she might be, what kind of childhood she might have had. She seemed to be reading my mind.

'Now let me tell you some more about myself,' she said. 'Your aunt gave birth to me in Norwich. She gave me to a couple she knew from Midleton who'd moved to there, Richard and Brenda Costigan. They were good friends of hers. They weren't able to have children and she couldn't keep me so she gave me to them. They brought me up.'

In those few sentences she obliterated all the decades of speculation for me. I was stunned but in another way it felt like I was hearing something I always knew in my subconscious.

'We often thought something like that happened,' I said.

'I'm sure people must have suspected. Many such babies were born like that at the time. What did they call it? An Irish solution to an Irish problem. I'm sure it must have been awful for her.'

'Do you know who your birth father was?' I asked.

'I heard a rumour about who he might be. If it was this man I believe he wasn't very supportive to her.'

'That's true,' I said.

'He's still alive, I believe.'

'Yes. He married someone else.'

She didn't seem interested in meeting him. She paused again. All sorts of thoughts were flooding through my mind.

'How often did you see Aunt Bernie? I said.

'She visited us every year for my birthday. I was told she was Mum and Dad's cousin. She was my godmother.'

'She's mine too,' I said.

She paused again.

'Then suddenly she stopped coming,' she said. 'It was after I made my First Communion. I didn't know why. I used to ask Mum and Dad if they knew but they said they didn't either.'

I tried to think what might have been going on in Aunt Bernie's mind. What year would it have been? Was it when she was going through one of her 'silent' times, one of those times when she didn't go out much, when she was making mistakes at her job?

'What age were you when you were told you were adopted?' I asked her.

'In my teens.'

'And you hadn't seen Aunt Bernie for many years by then.'

'No, and that made me very sad because she'd been so kind to me. I used to ask Mum and Dad about her for years afterwards but they said they didn't know where she was.'

'I can understand why. It wouldn't have been right for them to tell you who she was. Not right for them or for Aunt Bernie - or even for yourself.'

'I think they were protecting me.'

I tried to fill in the jigsaw, to think of the times she made all these mysterious trips to England over the years. How much did Mammy know? Or Daddy? Did they know anything at all? How terrible it must have been for her to have carried her secret for so long all on her own.

The skills she showed at mothering came back to me, how good she was with Cillian, I thought about the advice she gave me about him when she was babysitting, how she was able to quieten him when he was acting up, even the way she held him. How could I have been so stupid not to guess where that all came from?

More important than anything else, I thought of the night I'd asked her if there was anything she'd have changed in her life if she had it to live over again. 'Only one thing,' she replied. What did she mean? Was she trying to tell me she'd have kept Bernadette regardless of what her parents thought, regardless of or what the social pressure of the time would have meant?

It was too much to take in. I couldn't think what to say next. My mind whirled around like a washing machine.

'How did you get on with your parents?' I said to change the subject.

'I had a perfect childhood. Mum and Dad were so grateful for how everything worked out.'

'But they're dead now.'

'Dad has been gone for many years. He got a brain haemorrhage when I was thirteen. Mum passed away just a little over three months ago. After her funeral, as I say, I found some letters about my adoption among her effects. That's when I found out everything about your Aunt Bernie being my mother.'

It was strange hearing the words 'Aunt Bernie' and 'my mother' in the same sentence. I didn't know whether to be happy or sad. I was both.

'I found a letter from her when I was going through Mum's things,' she said then. 'It was written after I'd made my First Communion. I have it here if you'd like to see it.'

She took it out. As she unfolded it I recognised Aunt Bernie's handwriting immediately. She used the same blue Basildon Bond notepaper she always did when she was writing to people, the paper she'd used to send me the 'Congratulations' note when I qualified as a nurse.

I held it up to the light and started to read it, the words swimming before my eyes.

'Dear Richard and Brenda, Thank you so much for looking after my little darling over the years. You have no idea how much it's meant to me. I'm not very good at putting my feelings into words but that doesn't mean they're any the less strong. In bringing up my child so wonderfully you've made me happier than I could ever have believed possible. It's been almost as good as having her myself knowing that she's in such good hands, growing up as any mother would want her child to, surrounded by love.'

I turned over the page and read on. The writing seemed more indistinct here:

'I've greatly enjoyed my times with you but now I have to give you some sad news. I won't be coming over to you anymore. I say this with a heavy heart. You've been so patient with me on my visits. That must have been very intrusive on you. I'm sure a lot of other couples would have insisted I stay away.

'Only now do I feel ready to do that. I'll keep in touch with you. Please keep in touch with me too, but for the moment it's time to let goMy little girl needs to grow up in her own surroundings without her overseas 'godmother.'

With much love,

Bernie XXX'

I handed the letter back to Bernadette. I imagined the tears rolling down Aunt Bernie's eyes as she scratched her pen across the page. I was close to tears myself as I witnessed the outpouring of her thoughts. In those emotion-filled pages she became alive to me again. I heard her soft voice as she made her heart-breaking decision. She'd now given her daughter up not only once but twice. The second time would have been just as hard, maybe harder.

'I hope I haven't upset you,' Bernadette said.

'You've answered so many questions that have been nagging at me for many years,' I said, 'How could that be upsetting? It's a beautiful letter.'

'There were others as well, some of them mentioning your name. That's how I found out where you lived. She had a special fondness for you.'

'She was like my second mother.'

'And my first one,' she said, 'even though I didn't know it. We both had two mothers!'

I smiled through my tears.

'But now both of them are gone,' she said, 'That's the worst part.'

'I know.'

I sat back in my chair trying to piece together the sequence of events, wondering if there was anything I missed in Aunt Bernie around the time of Bernadette's First Communion, any sign of a change in her behaviour.

'And now I must ask you the hardest question of all,' she said.

'Go on,' I said, half afraid some other shock was coming.

She gazed at me intently and said, 'Did your Aunt Bernie have a happy life? Was that possible for her after what happened?'

She waited so long before asking me that, I wanted to give her a fair answer - at least if I knew what it was. How could you compute happiness? Were any of us truly happy or unhappy? Did we not all live in the middle of these states most of the time, including my mysterious aunt?

'In some ways,' I said. 'She had times of great joy because she was such a giving person, many of them with my own children. But she also had her down times. She went quiet for periods and we didn't know what was wrong with her. Now we probably do.'

'Thank you for that,' she said, 'I'm sure you knew her better than anyone. Maybe even better than your mother, or her own parents.'

'I can't say I did,' I said, 'She kept so much to herself.'

I didn't know how to continue the conversation. I was sitting opposite a person I'd never seen before in my life, a person I now felt I knew almost intimately because of our shared history.

'We still haven't had the cup of tea,' I said.

She laughed. When she did that I found myself laughing too. It was important for both of us to do that, to get away from all the intensity.

As memories of Aunt Bernie continued to revolve around my head I thought of the photograph I had of her First Communion, the one I found when May and I were clearing out her possessions.

'I have something to show you,' I said.

I went over to the cabinet where I'd been keeping it. It was in a drawer in an envelope. I had it bound up with the same little piece of string as when I found it. I took it out and brought it over to her. She looked at it with love in her eyes.

'I remember her taking that,' she said, 'I never saw it until this moment.'

She sat staring at it.

'She was sad that day. Now I know why.'

I hugged her, this woman who felt more like an extra sister to me suddenly than a cousin.

'I'm sorry I didn't meet you until today,' she said, 'We have a lot of ground to make up.'

I went back to my chair. There was nothing more to say, at least for now. I felt as if I was coming out of some kind of trance.

I looked out the window. The evening was fading around us. How long had we been talking? It seemed like hours but maybe it was less than an hour, maybe even less than a half hour. In another way it was a lifetime.

The sun blazed down behind the horizon. I had a sense of being outside myself, of being outside everything. My head was still spinning.

'Let's have the tea now,' I said, 'or we'll both collapse.'

She came out to the kitchen with me. I put on the kettle again.

'There won't be a tray this time,' I joked, 'thankfully.'

We sat at the kitchen table.

'Tell me about your own life,' I said. I needed something to take my mind off all I'd heard.

'It's been pretty boring, I'm afraid. I'm married to a businessman. We have two children, Rachel and Rob. Both of them are married now with children of their own. Rob is a technical engineer. Rachel is in Human Resources.'

The kettle boiled. I poured the tea.

'It's a pity Aunt Bernie didn't marry,' Bernadette said.

'I know. She would have made somebody a wonderful wife.'

'She was a very gentle woman. I remember that much even from the brief times I had with her. She was always bringing me gifts. We used to go down to a park that was near our house. She'd put me on the swings, or we might play with a ball. It was so long ago it's all very hazy to me now. I regret that.'

The night came on. She asked me about Kevin, about the children. She knew I was a nurse so I talked a bit about that. I tried to microscope my life into a few sentences the way you do when you meet someone you don't know and they ask you about yourself.

As I looked at her I saw more and more of Aunt Bernie in her. At a certain point of the evening she seemed to almost turn into her. I felt as if I was back in the past, back in our house in Midleton. Suddenly everything was the way it used to be. Aunt Bernie's presence was still there. It was in me and in her daughter.

We finished our tea. She got up to leave.

'I better go,' she said, 'My husband will think I've been kidnapped.'

I took her coat from the rack. She put it on.

'I hope you'll call again,' I said.

'I'll make a point of it the next time I'm in these parts. Or maybe I'll make a point of it even if I'm not. You've been very hospitable. I know now why your aunt  - or should I say my mother – thought so much of you.'

'She was so good to me. And to my children.'

I opened the door.

'I'll treasure the photograph,' she said, 'Maybe you'll have some more the next time I see you. Of Aunt Bernie I mean, not me.'

'I have any number of them,' I said.

I walked her to the door. She went down the driveway to her car. I waved to her and she waved back. Then she drove off. As she did so, images of Aunt Bernie came into my mind. I thought of the way she used to dandle me on her knee as she sang to me in Daddy's Ford Anglia on the way to Ardnahinch beach, of how she reached out to Dan Toibin that day we ran into him outside the sports shop, of the night she fell asleep with the children running riot around her when they were 'Auntie-sitting.' And I thought of the Madonna-like look that came into her face any time she held Cillian in her arms.

It all seemed to make sense to me then. As Bernadette drove off to her other life I realised that despite all the sadness and tears, despite the loneliness and the desolation, despite the impenetrable distance of the Irish Sea, the baby she was forced to part with all those years ago hadn't been a mistake after all.